Friends of the Yreka Library

A Fire

in the North

TOR BOOKS BY DAVID BILSBOROUGH

Annals of Lindormyn

I. *The Wanderer's Tale*
II. *A Fire in the North*

A Fire

in the North

ANNALS OF LINDORMYN: II

David Bilsborough

TOR®

A TOM DOHERTY ASSOCIATES BOOK

NEW YORK

A FIRE IN THE NORTH

Copyright © 2008 by David Bilsborough

Printed in the United States of America by special arrangement with Pan Macmillan.
Published simultaneously in the United Kingdom by Tor UK, an imprint of Pan Macmillan.

U.S. edition edited by James Frenkel

A Tor Book
Published by Tom Doherty Associates, LLC
175 Fifth Avenue
New York, NY 10010

www.tor-forge.com

Tor® is a registered trademark of Tom Doherty Associates, LLC.

Library of Congress Cataloging-in-Publication Data

Bilsborough, David
    A fire in the north / David Bilsborough.—1st ed.
        p. cm.
    "A Tom Doherty Associates book."
    ISBN-13: 978-0-7653-1893-0
    ISBN-10: 0-7653-1893-8
    I. Title
    PR6102.I47F57   2008
    823'.92—dc22

                                        2008005264

First Edition: June 2008

Printed in the United States of America

0   9   8   7   6   5   4   3   2   1

To the memory of over a hundred thousand citizens of Indonesia who were killed by the British, Dutch, and Japanese "Fasces" of 1945–46

Also,
to Wangari Maathai, and others like her

And lastly,
to A. J. (and why not?)

Acknowledgments

All those people at Pan Macmillan who have worked so hard on my book, especially as I wasn't even around at the time to thank them personally. Especially: Peter Lavery, Liz Cowen, and Rebecca Saunders, for the gargantuan editing task; Liz Johnson, Chantal Noel, and Jon Mitchell, for the foreign deals; Emma Giacon and Vivienne Nelson for the publicity; Neil Lang, Rafaela Romaya, and Clare Sivell, for the design; Amelia Douglas, for the production; and Sarah Castleton, for the freelance typing.

Special thanks again to Peter, who made it all possible in the first place, and in such a way changed my life.

Thanks also to Robert Hale of the *Malvern Gazette*, to *SFX* magazine, and to the sundry Internet sites (especially Damon's) who publicized the first volume so enormously. I owe you all.

Thanks also to everyone at E.L.T.I. Yogyakarta, for their help, support, and just for being so unfailingly *nice*.

Vaagenfjord
Maw

Wyrld's
Point

Jagt Straits

Wrythe

Eotunlandt

*Dragon
Coast*

F R O N

*Seter
Heights*

Fram Point

Ghoulem

Blue Mountains

Fram Peninsula

Herdlands
of the
Tusse

**Old
Kingdom**

*Hawdan
Valley*

Friy

*Nail
Mountains*

Goddtha

**Blighted
Heathlands**

Hrefna Forest

Tyvenborg

Bhergallia

Venna

*Crimson
Sea*

Rhelma-
Find

Moel
Bryn

P E N D O N I U M

Grendalin

*Crouagh
Forest*

Ymla-Eligiad

Q U I R A V I A

Drachrastaland

Lazhor

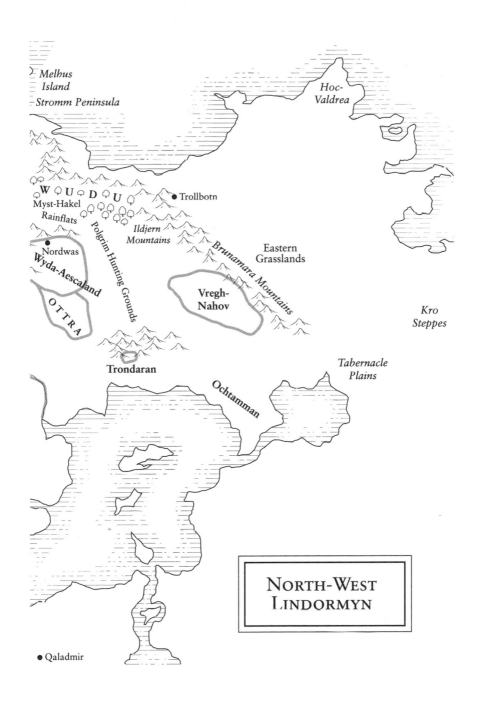

Melhus
Island
Stromm Peninsula

Hoc-
Valdrea

W U D **U**
Myst-Hakel
Rainflats

Trollbotn

Ildjern
Mountains

Polgrim Hunting Grounds

Brunamara Mountains

Eastern
Grasslands

Nordwas

Wyda-Aescaland

O T T R A

**Vregh-
Nahov**

Kro
Steppes

Trondaran

Ochtamman

Tabernacle
Plains

**NORTH-WEST
LINDORMYN**

Qaladmir

A Fire

in the North

That Hidden Threshold

Who am I?

It's silent here, and it's dark—totally, transcendentally dark. In this silence, this darkness, I could be anyone—anything. I have no story, no memory of a life, no thoughts nor impressions. Nothing.

What am I?

I am freezing, that's what I am—numbed almost senseless. This, at least, I realize now. And there's an enormous weight of pressure upon me, all about me, wrapped around and crushing the very soul from me. It presses hard and brittle fragments into my face—shards of stone, splinters of bone. Am I buried alive? Yes, I can smell it: ancient granite, grimy earth all around me—part of me. My hair is woven with tendrils and shoots, my face mingled with the cold clay. I am buried, yes, but am I dead or alive?

I am alive. Yes, I must be alive to have awareness of such things. Yes, of course, I am alive, I am a man. And with a man comes a name, but . . .

Bolldhe, that's who I was—am. Bolldhe from Moel-Bryn. Yes. The dreadful crush of earth's cold grasp seems to lessen somehow, not so oppressive now that I have a name. I embrace that appellation and sink away from this world, this dream, this nightmare, whatever it is, and my soul flies back to the warm days of youth, and those familiar scents of upland turf, walnut coppice and clovered lea. Moel-Bryn—a land mantled with woodlands of rustling, fallow gold, and braided with rillets of sparkling effulgence; yet tough-boned, a place of granite hills, stockaded walls, and robust soldiery. Who am I? I'm Bolldhe, the son of a Peladane, of a holy crusader.

But not a Peladane myself—rather a traveler. For I left that land of the war-cult, abandoned them all to their ridiculous displays of metal pomposity, their stiff necks and their strutting. Roamed the world, far and wide. But no explorer, soldier, nor merchant was I, for mine was the way of the wanderer, a free spirit, a bird of passage.

. . . A runaway, an itinerant. Eighteen years of aimless drifting, like an insect blown far from its colony, and every bit as useless. I was by trade an augur, a fortune-teller, and a fake one at that, scratching a mean living by selling lies to any idiot who would pay for reassurance. I touched nobody's life, and nobody touched mine and the strange thing is, I seemed to believe that made me better than anyone. Oh yes, I was a real Jack-the-Lad . . . one of life's meanest failures.

Then along comes Appa, the mage-priest, and from then on nothing would ever be the same again.

I found myself by then in Nordwas, a town of many cults—even my old child-hood faith—and all of them in stormy debate about the rumored "Second Com-ing of Drauglir," all of them "quest-hungry." My first day in town, a total stranger there, and this holy man simply comes up to me and tells me I'm the chosen one—the Rawgr-Slayer—the world's only hope against the wolf-demon from the north. That was Appa, the mad old priest of Cuna, the god of Truth and Light (ha!), hounding me like a fierce little terrier that would as soon bite your hand as wag its tail and probably not know the difference. Nobody else believes a word he says about me, not the Peladanes, nor his fellow priests, not even his brother-in-faith Finwald (that sibylline charlatan whose prophecy initiated this quest in the first place). Certainly not I myself. But it's money, I suppose—Peladanes' money. And, for no reason other than that I've got nothing better to do, I go along with it. Never been to the far north, anyway. Might even be fun.

So began the quest to destroy Drauglir, a rawgr already slain five hundred years ago, and which few men, other than various cultists, actually believe will rise again. And my life hasn't been my own since. Together with the two mage-priests, the warlord's son and his esquire, and three others, we journeyed north, far beyond the lands of men, upon a mad hooley of adventure, blood-shed, and fear. Two of the company it has claimed already: Methuselech Xil-vafloese the desert mercenary, fallen to his death in the Valley of Sluagh, and the Peladane's esquire, poor young Gapp Radnar, hurled down into the dark by the monstrous Afanc. . . .

The Afanc—that obscene miscreation of darkness, waxing in size and foul-ness with each hurt we dealt it. The mere thought of that warped nightmare incarnate sickens me. Would that I had never stirred it from its pit in the first place! Did it really hound us all those miles, all those days, just to retrieve the sword we stole from it? My soul shudders at the memory.

But there's more to it than that. I wasn't running just from the Afanc—not even from those terrible giants that finally crushed it underfoot. I was running from myself—from the crime I'd just committed, from what I'd now become. For, only moments before we fled from the giants, I did a terrible thing—a deed which has changed me forever. Something happened to me when I was a child, something which has haunted me ever since, like a scream that echoes down the years, its horror reverberating down the arterial, stony tunnel again and again— that sick, demented laughter as great crimson holes blossomed in human flesh . . . I'd kept my ears stopped to that memory, but now I've crossed over a threshold, a hidden threshold, and there'll be no going back now. . . .

What am I?

And then the word came to him, and he knew what he was.

"Murderer!"

1

Elfswith and Ceawlin

"They look like Bolldhe's boots."

(Pounding; dull, but mighty enough to shake the world to its foundations; unrelenting, constant; rhythmic as a heartbeat; all around him. Bombardment.)

"No, his are always covered in kack. Leave them—it's probably just another bloody thief."

(Pressure; painless, but immense enough to squeeze him out of this world; enveloping; uterine; crushing as a landslide; all around him. Entombment.)

"No, seriously. I'm sure they're his. I think I recognize the heels."

(Words from outside, words of mirth, words before birth—smell of earth—Mother Earth—mother tongue—no, another tongue; words familiar to him, but in this state, under all this weight, too wearisome for him to translate.)

"Well, pull him out anyway. If it is a thief, we can always break his neck and claim he was dead when we found him."

The words meant little to Bolldhe, and came to him muffled, as if his head were wrapped in a heavy blanket. His concern right now was only with the immense pressure all around him . . . and then the feel of hands tugging at his feet. Tugging hard.

". . . probably not such a good idea at this moment. Come what may, it looks like we'll have to put aside our differences with these thieves for now. We're not even out of Eotunlandt yet."

Bolldhe could finally feel himself being pulled out from the suffocating mass. Like an earthworm plucked from the soil.

"Come on now," another voice was saying through the din, a shaky voice, but which carried within it the hint of a smile. "You can do it—just one more push."

Then, from crushing darkness Bolldhe emerged suddenly, into the glare of orange torchlight, and all about him there were smiling faces.

"It's a boy!" came a voice in delight. "What shall we call him?"

Bolldhe sucked cold air deep into his tormented lungs, then continued with huge, bovine gasps. That hefty pounding noise still continued from outside, shaking clumps of earth and fragments of stone onto him from the tunnel roof and filling the close air with a choking dust.

Moments later, the terrible bombardment from without began to fade away. Within minutes, it had ceased altogether and, as its last echoes rolled on up the tunnel, so too died the rumor of the storm behind it.

Into the silence that followed, there rose a collective sigh of relief.

Deliverance.

Retching violently, Bolldhe opened his eyes, blinking furiously. Above, regarding him closely, were three creatures apparently made of stone, like rocks that had come to life and assumed human form. Judging from their faces, though, they had not done a very good job of it; the features were distorted, the skin no more than crude masks of clay.

But their eyes, at least, looked human, and through them the humanity of souls deep within could be detected clearly through the stoniness of those visages. Already the freshets of sweat and tears streaking their dust-plastered faces were expanding and converging to wash away the clay that would claim them, until they had made a muddy delta of each face.

Nibulus, Finwald, and Kuthy: these three, at least, had made it through. They looked weary, and several years older than Bolldhe recalled, but they were clearly *alive*.

"All right, Bolldhe?" Nibulus grunted. "You really do leave things to the last second, don't you?"

Nibulus. Of course. If there was but one member of their company who could be counted on to survive any catastrophe, weather any storm, or come through any battle, it was that solid, dependable bastion of strength and pugnacity, Nibulus Wintus. Son of the warlord Artibulus, Wintus Hall's finest Peladane, he would still be around, Bolldhe suspected, long after he himself had been snuffed out. Besides, since it was the warlord's money that had funded this entire expedition, Nibulus was not the type to let a mere herd of two-hundred-foot giants come between him and his father's investment. What would the bards have to say about that?

Still half-buried, Bolldhe spluttered and spat out gobbets of spittle-soaked soil. He then convulsed in a fit of coughing that further tortured his frame. But, in the midst of this convulsion, it occurred to him that at least no bones were broken.

Then he felt something warm nudge him gently, and immediately recognized the familiar musky odor of his horse.

"Zhang!" he croaked, and reached out to clasp the Adt-T'man's muzzle closer to him. "Zhang," he continued in a half-whisper. "Friend-horse. My only friend, you came back to save me." He held the animal's head close, stroking it fondly with a shaking hand, and within moments his face was streaked with a muddy delta all of its own.

Eventually, he let go and wiped the grime from his eyes, focusing his gaze beyond his immediate rescuers. Through the dim, dust-infused light of a few torches, he recognized that they were confined somewhere inside a long tunnel. Its rough-cut walls were only about four feet apart, but the roof was higher. With his companions' help, he gingerly pulled himself out from the mound of debris and got to his feet. He looked behind him, and saw how the cave-mouth they had entered was now in ruin, totally blocked off by rock and soil. Not even the thinnest sliver of daylight penetrated from the other side.

Entombment.

One arm draped for support over Zhang's shaggy neck, Bolldhe peered around to see who else had survived. Over there, slumped against the wall, was the aged mage-priest Appa, one hand folded limply around his precious amulet. But for once, not rapping his ring against it constantly, an irritating habit whenever he felt stressed. Was he even alive . . . ? Yes, bless him, there was a bare first hint of movement beneath that grubby, biscuit-crumb-stained woollen mantle cloaking the scrawny collection of brittle bones he called a body. Bolldhe managed a smile. So the old bugger had survived Eotunlandt after all, frayed, but unbroken, like a thin piece of hairy string that refuses to snap.

There, too, was the dark mercenary Odf "Paulus" Uglekort, standing with his back to them, but easy to recognize from his crow's-feather cowl. Now *there* was another nut not to be easily cracked. Maybe one day Paulus would succumb to the fits that occasionally racked his body, or to the creeping necrosis that already disfigured his face and made him a pariah even among his own comrades, but it was doubtful he would ever fall to an enemy's sword. Paulus, the mercurial, murderous, but elite mercenary from Vregh-Nahov, had his blade drawn even now, as he stood between their company and a separate group of shadowy figures huddled miserably just beyond the halo of torchlight. How many of those bandits had managed to reach the tunnel in time, Bolldhe as yet did not bother to guess. All he knew for sure was that, of his own companions—counting them off in his dizzy head—six had made it safely through. Out of how many? He could not think straight, but he was sure there was someone missing. . . .

He glanced back at the three men who had pulled him out of the rubble. Nibulus was already unstrapping the various pieces of his elaborate armor from the solitary horse and was trying to put them on before the thieves got a chance to recover their nerve and maybe launch an attack. Ever the soldier, ever the professional, but not so professional that Nibulus could control the trembling in his fingers. If those thieves were going to attack, Bolldhe reckoned, they would be well-advised to do it now, while the Peladane was so cumbrously distracted.

Finwald, the younger mage-priest, sat silently upon a large boulder all by himself. He cradled something long and metallic in his arms and Bolldhe peered at it, then almost cried out in disbelief as he recognized the serpentine blade that snaked out from the hilt. *Flametongue!* That bloody sword again! After all they'd just come through, after escaping being giant-crushed into oblivion by the narrowest hair's breadth imaginable, was that antique weapon all the priest could concern himself with?

Bolldhe just could not fathom how a Lightbearer, of all people, should care so much about a weapon of war. And one which was not even his own posses-sion either. Finwald already owned a sword, that little silver one he'd had forged especially for this quest. *"The only way to destroy Drauglir,"* he had pro-claimed to the council Moot before they set out, *"is to pierce its heart and brain with a magical blade. Failing that, silver plated iron will do. . . ."* So when Bolldhe had discovered this strange, spell-woven flamberge sword down in the mines, somehow in the possession of the gruesome Afanc, it had seemed like a particular stroke of fortune.

Bolldhe grimaced. Having rejected the ways of the Peladane in his youth, he loathed swords beyond all loathing, and everything they stood for. He wished now, more than ever, to have his plain old axe back. Had it not been stolen from him earlier by a sneak thief, he never would have picked up yon cursed flamberge in the first place. But now that that enchanted sword had fallen into their hands, Finwald seemed to think their quest was as good as won. He seemed to even think the weapon was more important than the lives of his companions. Bolldhe still could not believe how, in their moment of danger, the priest had just snatched up the flamberge and run off with it to the safety of the tunnel, abandoning his companions to the giants without so much as a backward glance. Finwald was a good man at heart, Bolldhe knew, and much liked by everyone, but clearly nothing—not even his friends—came before his precious quest.

Unlike Kuthy Tivor over there. That one *had* no friends, and the only quest precious to him was looking after himself. The aging soldier of fortune had started tagging along with them only a couple of weeks ago, but had proved nothing more than a pain in the backside ever since. At the moment, he was busy brushing the dust out of the writhing liripipes adorning the hat that still miraculously clung to his head. They now stood out from the cap itself like the hairs on a frightened cat, and were trembling at the tips. Kuthy was murmuring to them soothingly as he stroked them in turn, but it looked as though it would be a long while before his hat settled down to normal.

In spite of his trauma, Bolldhe could not help but grin. *Serves him right. He's got nobody to blame but himself.* After all, it was Kuthy ("the last of the liv-ing heroes") who had persuaded them to take this route in the first place, through enchanted Eotunlandt, this "fairest, most wonderful land that has ever beglammered my eyes." Some shortcut—it had damn near been the death of them! Bolldhe shuddered at the memory of it. . . .

The sky's countenance had darkened, broiled, and from the churning black mass of clouds that rolled out across this land of giants, outpoured its full fury upon their heads. Amid the deluge of the storm, and the blinding white light that scorched the earth all about them, they had run for their lives, tempest-lashed, their wits wholly departed. Summoned into being by the bloodletting between the travelers and the bandits they had encountered, the giants had come for them, and chased both venturer and thief alike over the inundated uplands, while hell's rolling barrage thundered from horizon to horizon.

But Kuthy, for once, had not failed them, but brought them as he had promised to the secret doorway leading out of this land. Keenly they had plunged beneath the clay, just before the giant's foot, like the Hammer of God, smote down upon them. Night had obliterated day with one immense detonation, and flooded its victims like ants down into their nest.

But with the two clashing groups of interlopers now safely sealed into their temporary grave, those phantom but very real-seeming giants had retreated from this land, this reality. Now, down through the rocks that were the crumpled ruin of the gate, seeped the rain and turned all to slurry. . . .

Forsooth's sake, Bolldhe reflected, *that was a close one!* He began to quake violently at the memory, having himself been the tiniest fraction of a second away from utter annihilation. Death by giant. And though he hated to dwell on it, he could not help wondering what it would have felt like. Would it have been simply too quick to register, or would there have been time for him to feel every bone in his body crunch, every muscle rupture, and his innards shoot forth from his mouth?

"Just how flattened can the human frame get?" he wondered aloud.

"About as flat as the ants we used to crush when we were little boys," came the reply from a large boulder resting atop the rubble where the portal had once stood.

It was Wodeman. As caked in dust as the others, he now looked like a permanent part of the cave. He lifted himself with difficulty from his crouching position, letting fly a fall of loose soil from his shaggy wolf pelt, and clambered down to squat next to Bolldhe.

Number seven . . . Bolldhe thought to himself with relief. There was something he had to say to the shaman, but he could not think of the word.

"By Kulhuch, did you see the size of those things, Bolldhe?" Wodeman muttered. "And I'm sure the one in the front was carrying a steaming kettle. . . ."

Bolldhe regarded his savior with concern. There was a definite look of shell shock in the shaman's eyes, and he was having difficulty keeping the hysteria from his voice.

"This is getting worse and worse by the day," Wodeman went on, "the farther north we journey. And it won't get any better, either. If you think this is
bad, wait till you get to Melhus itself. I ask you, Bolldhe, what can *insects* like
us possibly do against beings like those? Eh? If we ever get out of this, I swear
I'm heading straight back to Nordwas. And when I get there, I'll not stop either; I'm going to pick up the kids, and whichever of their mothers want to
come along, and just carry on south as far as I can go. The farther away from
these hellish northern lands, the better . . . But we'll not get back out that way
again," he pointed to the pile of rubble, "though dig we might for a week and
a day. We're trapp—"

"Thank you," Bolldhe interrupted him. That was the word he had been trying to think of.

Wodeman stopped in mid-sentence, and stared at him.

"You came back for me," Bolldhe went on. "You could've been killed—by
rights you *should have* been killed—but you came back anyway. Nobody's ever
done that for me before. Thank you."

Wodeman continued to stare into Bolldhe's eyes. He beheld the steadiness
there, something he had never noticed in the traveler before. He held onto it,
and gradually grew calmer himself. And Bolldhe, for his part, enjoyed for the
first time a brief feeling of warmth toward his unwanted mentor. Nobody had
asked Wodeman, this self-appointed "Dream-Giver," this "messenger of the
Earth-Spirit," to join them on this quest; not Bolldhe, who had always resented
the shaman's intrusions into his private thoughts, and the visions he wove into
Bolldhe's mind; not the priests, who considered Wodeman's pagan meddling
with their protégé something of a threat to their own monopoly on proselytizing; and certainly not their Peladane leader, who deemed that any association
with such "coppice-hoppers" was, to be honest, embarrassing. But Wodeman
had come anyway, ever counseling Bolldhe, weaving dream-spells into his tired
mind, essaying to enlighten him as to his divine calling.

They were, of course, all mad, the three priests: Wodeman, Appa, and
Finwald. Of that Bolldhe was sure. He no more believed that he was the
Chosen One than he believed that their gods were anything other than the
worst disaster that had ever afflicted the world. Any devotion he had was to
himself and himself alone. Nevertheless, this weird priest Wodeman had
snatched him out from under a giant's foot, and for that, at least, Bolldhe
could feel beholden.

"The giants are gone now," he assured the shaman. "They won't trouble us
anymore. We *beat* them. Whatever lies on the other side of that heap of stone,
forget it. It's none of our business now; we're headed the other way."

The sorcerer's eyes, after flitting back to the blocked portal, did appear to
regain some composure. He nodded, and clamped his hand upon Bolldhe's
shoulder.

"Forget the tunnel entrance," Bolldhe reassured him. "We've crossed that threshold, and there'll be no going back now. Just keep thinking of the other exit. And that lies up *there*. Come on, I think the others are ready to move."

What Bolldhe said was true: the giants really were gone. In the barrow-like deadness of the tunnel, no sound could be heard—save the men's unsteady voices. Not even a whisper came from outside, so that some began to wonder if the giants had ever existed. Just as the Spirit of War had summoned them, and the mortals' terror sustained them, as they now huddled in this rat's runnel they realized that those Elder Spirits had returned to wherever they had come from. Battle was done, its frenzy had departed, and this world was no longer any place for such as *they*.

The giants now banished from their thoughts, the two vying groups—both questers and thieves—now turned their attention to the tunnel ahead.

It was an odd feeling, these two parties that had only hours before been at each others' throats, now forced together into an alliance in order to survive. It was, to say the least, an uneasy truce. Though there was hardly the energy for hostility left in anyone now, there were some among the Thieves of Tyvenborg who were still openly ill disposed toward the Peladane and his party. Notably among these was Brother Oswiu Garoticca, who was not at all happy that Bolldhe's group had managed to snatch back the flamberge sword he had earlier stolen from them. Hlessi (who, let's face it, was a Grell) remained openly antagonistic, and also Khurghan (who was by his very nature a spiteful, beady-eyed, malevolent little runt at the best of times).

Wisely, however, their leader Eorcenwold kept these few malcontents well away from the Aescals, at the far end of the line.

Fortunately, the only Tyvenborger who might have caused real trouble, namely the Dhracus demi-human Dolen Catscaul, was still unconscious. Judging by the unctuous odors hovering around her, she was now in the healing care of the Hauger Flekki and her dubious salves. Once the giants had appeared in the middle of the men's conflict, all her "friends" had disappeared so rapidly one could almost have heard a sound implosion from the speed of them. As a result, none of them had been around to witness how Bolldhe, of all people, had saved the Dhracus from certain death. Almost without thinking he had thrown her unconscious form across his horse's back, then ordered Appa to get her into the shelter of the tunnel. The sight of the priest bringing her to safety may have baffled the thieves, but surely it did go some way to cooling their animosity.

For some reason Bolldhe had not been able to bring himself to leave her there, even though she had almost killed him in their duel. Not after what he had done to her swain . . . Not after he had become a murderer.

There it was again, that awful word. Once more came to him the image of Eggledawc Clagfast's lifeless eyes staring back up at him, and with it an awful sickness in the pit of Bolldhe's soul. His mind recoiled with the horror of it, yet this same horror also held for him a cold fascination. The memory of it—the slicing of the windpipe, the gristle separating, the arterial spray—Bolldhe found himself repeating the sequence in his head over and again, almost *savoring* it. But even worse was knowing that, at the time, he had *enjoyed* it— become aroused, excited, maybe addicted, lost his head in its every scarlet detail, feasted on it, could never get enough of it. . . .

Bolldhe had crossed that threshold, he knew, and there was no going back.

Now all that the members of either group wanted to do was get out of that accursed tunnel, leave this land, and never set eyes on each other again. And even though the final destination of both parties was obviously the same, nobody made any mention of it. They would cross that bridge if and when they came to it.

By tacit agreement, the thieves set off first into the darkness ahead, with Nibulus and his men trailing behind at a respectful distance. Neither party wished to stay any closer than was absolutely necessary, yet both were loath to let the other out of their sight. Certainly neither Nibulus nor Paulus had any intention of letting the thieves get far enough ahead to set some sort of trap or ambush for them.

It was a long journey, this ascent through the mountains, and—as it turned out—even more gruelling than the tunnel leading into the other side of Eotunlandt. This passage was as narrow and airless as their most claustrophobic nightmares, and, as each one of them was constantly aware, every step took them deeper and deeper into the heart of the Giant Mountains.

The tunnel itself was a mystery. Bolldhe, aiming the beam of his lantern around at its stone surfaces, continually wondered who, or what, had made it. It snaked around with no apparent design, sometimes level and sometimes sloping, yet was too regular in its width and height to be merely some kind of natural cave network.

Then came the steps. These, at least, appeared genuinely man-made. Their narrow flights might take the travelers up for a hundred yards or so, before once again leveling out, but they might equally go on ascending for an hour or more, without respite. Slick with icy water, crumbling with age, they gradually, slowly, took their charges up into the mountain heights.

"Hakkevana lepeu'ah! Ghevaccanema!"

This phrase, one that not even Bolldhe understood, his Aescal companions heard time and time again being uttered somewhere up ahead. In their haste to escape the giants, the thieves had abandoned most of their gear, and were forced to ration their torches stringently. From their lower position some way behind, the Aescals could hear the scuffing of unsure feet and frequent cursing as a thief would lose his footing on the treacherous surface and fall flat on his face. At first this was almost amusing, especially as Nibulus and his men were much better equipped for this second tunnel. But after over two hours of listening to exactly the same expletives, it did begin to whittle away their patience.

"Hakkevana lepeu'ah! Ghevaccancma!"

Frequent rest breaks were necessary on these longer flights of steps, and on such occasions Nibulus and Paulus would position themselves a little closer to the thieves, just to keep an eye on them. It was almost comical how both groups could be seen, one by the other, in the scant light, both eyeing each other suspiciously.

So it went on tediously for the rest of the day.

Before nightfall (though it seemed long after nightfall to most of them) they began to notice narrow beams of light filtering down through the ceiling above. The fissures were never wider than a keyhole, so the light that penetrated was pale and distant. But to the exhausted travelers they were like life preservers appearing suddenly to drowning men. Hearts lifted, anxiety subsided, breathing grew calmer. Gradually these pencil-thin shafts of illumination dimmed, and dimmed further, until very soon they faded altogether. But the air yet retained its new cleanness, and hope remained in the hearts of the travelers.

Then, sometime around an hour after sunset, the Peladane's men emerged unexpectedly into a wide cavern. Most of them enthusiastically reveled in the sudden sense of freedom, while the slough-horse positively whinnied in delight. But Wodeman, Appa, and Paulus felt that familiar sense of unease begin to rise again within them, and they looked around uneasily, fumbling for amulet or weapon.

"Er, Nibulus," Appa called out in a low voice, "where are they? Our friends from the Thieves' Mountain?"

All of them looked around in sudden alarm. The thieves were nowhere to be seen, and of their earlier clumsy progress, not a sound could be heard.

Without hesitation they all retreated back to the relative shelter of the passage, and readied their weapons in anticipation. They listened carefully, but all was still. Save for the tremor of their own breathing, there was no sound to be heard at all.

In that pause, Bolldhe felt the hilt of a sword being pressed into his palm. He glanced to one side, away from the light cast by his hooded lantern, and in the shadows next to him beheld a shape with eyes that burned red in the flame, eyes that regarded him with intent.

It was Finwald—and he was returning the flamberge.

"Take it, Bolldhe," the priest whispered conspiratorially. "It is yours, after all."

He sounded like an indulgent grandparent pressing a sweet into the hand of a child while its parents were not looking. Bolldhe almost expected him to fold a hand over his own and wink at him mischievously.

Bloody priest seems hell-bent on me using that damn sword! Bolldhe cursed to himself. *I wouldn't be at all surprised if it was* him *who stole it from me in the first place.*

Bolldhe's mind went back to that night, that murky, drunken, confusing night a month ago in Myst-Hakel when he had left the pub and staggered over the creaking shackleboard walkways, through the dark and empty streets, and back to the old temple where they were all billeted. . . .

. . . Just in time to see the furtive shadow stealing out of the window of their lodgings—with Bolldhe's axe in his hands. Of all the things to steal. Nothing else had been taken, not gold, amethyst, nor any other precious item, but a crappy, notched old broadaxe.

Finwald *had* been in the pub with the others when Bolldhe had left, though, hadn't he? On the other hand, it had taken the ale-addled Bolldhe some time to find his way back to their lodgings. Bolldhe now appraised Finwald carefully. For a priest of the God of Truth, he seemed to have rather a lot of secrets. Why hadn't he told them his real identity earlier, that he was originally called Nipah Glemp, an alchemist's apprentice? Why be so cagey about everything?

Well, whoever the thief was, he had seemed most determined about the axe. Didn't drop it at Bolldhe's angry shout, nor during the ensuing chase; kept a tight hold on it all the way out of town and over the marshes . . .

. . . Leading him all the way to the abandoned mine. All the way—so conveniently—to the chamber, and the flamberge, just waiting for him among the debris . . .

And to the Afanc, also just waiting for him among the debris. Bolldhe blanched, the memory of the Beast far too fresh in his mind. Especially in this fearful place, so like the mines.

He sighed loudly, and the sound echoed eerily throughout the underground spaces. They all listened intently to it. Judging by this echo, they must have arrived at the beginning of an extensive network of caves that stretched ahead through the mountain. Countless stone surfaces amplified any sound tenfold, sustained it, and sent it back to them in multi-pitched discords. Yet of their unwanted companions, the thieves, not a whisper could be heard.

This was all very unnerving, for only seconds earlier, Eorcenwold's men could be seen and heard, stumbling awkwardly twenty or thirty paces ahead of them, cursing like grumpy old dwarfs as they dragged themselves and their unconscious Dhracus onward and upward.

Or had it been longer ago? Minutes, perhaps? Maybe half an hour? Now they came to think about it, none of them could actually remember even approximately how long ago it was since they had last heard any sound of the thieves. At the beginning of their ascent, the Peladane's company had kept themselves very much aware of their enemies' presence. But now, in this new cavern, everything seemed so unsure. Trying to remember anything clearly felt like grasping at dreams. Cut off from the world above in this granite tomb, time seemed to have become every bit as distorted as the echoes that flitted back to them.

"It's just like the other tunnel," Nibulus whispered, "the one on the way in. You lose all sense of time."

"No, no, this is altogether stranger," Appa remarked. "That last tunnel was nothing more than a shaft cut straight through cold, dead stone. This one, however . . ."

"There's a presence," Wodeman stated, "something ancient. No, not ancient—timeless. Fey or human, living or . . ."

From a far place now came the sounds of fighting. Conflict: a clash of arms, iron upon iron, bronze beating against leather and wood, the shouting of men and other things, the crackle of pyrotechnics, the roar of unknown creatures that may have crawled up from the underworld.

Then that sound faded, lingering for but brief seconds on the border of hearing as the merest vestige of an echo. There was a remote, dreamlike quality to it, also, but this remoteness was one of time rather than of distance.

Bolldhe glanced at the two priests questioningly. Both, however, merely shrugged.

"Tivor," Nibulus whispered harshly, "you've been this way before—any ideas?"

There followed a pause, a long pause. Nibulus was about to jab their guide in the ribs, when the soldier-of-fortune Kuthy finally replied: "There was something like this happened last time—something I didn't understand. But I plugged my ears with oiled cloth, and pressed on as swiftly as I might." His voice was low, and held none of his customary assurance.

Bolldhe's eyes widened in awe. "You mean you heard . . . that, and still you went on? Alone?"

Kuthy's voice dropped even lower: "It is best to ignore the illusions of Fey. Those who let themselves be waylaid by the Huldre are rarely seen again."

"So at last!" Paulus hissed. Clearly, he at least was more than ready to be waylaid. Wodeman, though, wrinkled his nose and spat on the ground. Appa, possibly the most intuitive among them, was wary but surprisingly not alarmed.

Still unsure, Nibulus tarried a moment. He strained his ears and squinted further into the void beyond the lantern's beams. But, in the total absence of any clue, he resigned himself to following what Kuthy recommended, and ordered them onward.

Before them lay many different exits from the cavern, but Kuthy knew exactly which one to take. They tried to quicken their pace, eager to get free of this place, even if that did mean heading toward the source of the strange sounds they had heard earlier. But the tunnel now took on an entirely different character. Gone were the flights of steps, the half-level floors, the regularity of the tunnel's dimensions. This new passage was almost entirely natural. It

twisted and turned, rose and fell, widened unexpectedly into chambers or narrowed so tightly that their claustrophobic beast of burden had to be dragged
or pushed forward. All around them now could be seen lumps and outcrops
of grey limestone that squatted there like malignant, petrified trolls. Their
moving shadows danced in the lamplight, like witches capering in the cave of
beasts. Bolldhe glanced backward as he passed by, and saw with horror that
these shadows began sprouting long, spindly arms with cruel, claw-like hands.
He was sure he could even hear them sniggering.

"Don't look around you, Bolldhe!" came a warning voice immediately to
his rear. "Or behind." It was Kuthy. Bolldhe instantly snapped his head back to
face in front of him, from now on his eyes fixed dead ahead.

Occasionally the clash of ancient battles seemed to echo down the passage
straight ahead, or resonate from the rock all around them. Occasionally the
ringing of blades was replaced by a sound like the dull thud and crunch of
wood or stone, and the voices were altogether more grunting and animal. At
these sounds, the cave walls sprang to life with primeval dancing, shadows that
cavorted in the sanguine light of their torches, yet it was difficult to identify
their source. The company shook their heads in exasperation, and pressed on,
their weapons dangling uselessly from their belts.

A while later, Wodeman grasped the Peladane by the arm, halting the party.

"Do you hear it?" he murmured.

They listened and, after a moment, they did: a soft sobbing, as of a child,
far off but distressingly plaintive. It soon resounded all about, and filled them
with a dread that sickened every one of them. They shuddered to their very
souls.

Then came the footsteps: knok-knok-knok. Two legs. Cloven hooves.
Stealthy, purposeful. Suddenly a scream of terror and agony rang out, and
filled every crevice and bounced off every stony surface within the caves. The
travelers froze. Then, as the scream trailed off with a wail of damnation and
despair, it was followed by a sick little laugh, not quite human, laden with
malice.

"Illusions, right?" Nibulus hissed at Kuthy in barely constrained fury. The
old campaigner nodded vigorously, and fumbled in one of the little leather
pouches at his belt. He extracted two little plugs of pitch-scented cloth and
thrust them into his ears.

"Just keep looking ahead," he instructed them, "and ignore anything you
might see out of the corner of your eye. Believe me, it isn't there."

Everyone stared at him. If only half the stories about him were true they
knew that in his lifetime he had seen things that they could not imagine, and
had enough experience to gauge whether danger was genuine or not. He took
the torch from Nibulus, and for once led the way.

Paulus followed without hesitation, the only one among them still holding his weapon out ready. But Bolldhe and the three cultists would not budge an inch. Not one of them believed for a second that such phantasms as they had just witnessed had also been visited upon Kuthy the last time he had ventured this way. No one, not even he, could suffer such terror, alone, and still retain the courage to go on.

If, as he claimed, he had been *alone*.

Nibulus hesitated. This was all more than a little beyond his experience. But then he recalled Eorcenwold's commanding tone, and the fact that the thief-sergeant must surely have got his men through this ordeal already. He gritted his teeth and, like all soldiers, pushed his fear deep down inside. He had stared death in the face too many times throughout his life to fear such impish bewitchment now.

"Come on, men," he commanded levelly, "forget this bullshit. I have no intention of spending the night in this hole."

The way after that became somewhat easier. Random noises and visions flitted by them, trying hard to get their attention, but were always stoically ignored. Kuthy led the company on too swiftly to allow them the chance to falter in either speed or resolve. By degrees they felt that they were regaining control of their situation, and with that control came confidence.

About half an hour later, Kuthy halted. "If my reckoning is right," he informed them, "we should be out of this tunnel very soon."

"And where will we be then?" asked Nibulus.

"High up in the mountains. But for this last stretch, we will need to be quick. There is a place up ahead where the enchantment is . . . considerable, and I don't wish to give it a chance to do its work."

The others looked at each other doubtfully.

"Just keep on as you have been going, and we'll be out very soon, I promise you."

Various moans. That was probably the worst thing Kuthy could have said to them. Even now, in certain lands, the expression "as sure as a Tivor-promise" was popularly used to denote situations that were anything but sure. He had the reputation of being as slippery as a barrelful of jellied eels on a frozen pond. But had Kuthy heard this adage, he probably would have smiled approvingly; it took most heroes centuries after their deaths to achieve the repute that he possessed while still alive.

Sure enough, within minutes they could detect a sickly greenish-purple light glowing from the tunnel ahead. As they drew nearer they saw that it came from a series of torches set along the walls. They would puff into light as the travelers approached, and gave off a stink of burnt meat. Despite Kuthy's strict admonishment not to look upon such manifestations, all eyes were drawn, by irresistible, morbid compulsion, to behold these lych-candles as they passed.

They were bones: human bones jammed into cracks in the rock, and surrounded by a halo of light the same hue as a dying moon's reflection upon the surface of a weed-pool. Behind them, lines of garish violet pulsated in the corpse-pale stone, like the varicose veins of a marsh-drowned vagrant.

On they marched, while the lych-candles continued to sputter into huldrelight at their approach, then flutter out behind them once they had passed. After a while, a subsonic tremor could be felt in the stone all around them, and before long it waxed into a deep rumbling.

Kuthy urged them on to greater speed. "We're not far now," he called back anxiously. They followed as best they could, though the way was steeper, each one of them soaked through with sweat.

Minutes later they arrived at a crudely built archway. Of disturbingly alien design, it looked every bit as ancient as the mountains themselves, and had clearly not been fashioned by any of the mortal races. It had the air of a barrier, a boundary gate, almost as if it were the doorway to another world. Immediately beyond, the passage rose even more steeply up a narrow stairway. What lay up there, though, they could not tell, for there were no lamps along its lightless length. Even when Bolldhe directed his narrowed lantern beam up into it, the light could not penetrate the damp blackness. The rumbling sound, too, was much louder, and could now be discerned as a cascade, thundering powerfully through the stony hollows.

"Up!" Kuthy ordered, and everyone followed him.

Upward through the terrible darkness they climbed, like rats scrambling up a chimney. Within moments they began to sense that greenish light ahead of them once again. Nibulus and Paulus now took the lead, so were the first to emerge from the dark stairway into the grotto that lay beyond. They both stopped and stared at what lay therein.

One by one, the rest of the company joined them. They stood there without speaking, shivering in the clamminess of their sweat-soaked clothes and trembling with the fear that was beginning to get dangerously close to its limits.

The grotto was entirely natural. Slender pillars of fused stalactite-stalagmites honeycombed the cave, and the walls glistened green and purple with crystal and quartz. To their right a cascade roared down from a vent high above, hurtling down a slope and out through another hole. Long icicles of sapphire-blue rimed the roof immediately above it. And right in the center of the cave, a low mound of stones had been deliberately placed to form what looked like a crude cairn or barrow. The hub of all the weirdness in this cavern, the focus of all their fear, it squatted there ominously, and radiated an awful sense of wrongness.

"What the bloody hell is that supposed to be?" the Peladane breathed, summing up precisely what the rest of the company felt at that moment.

There also did not appear to be any exit.

"Well, this is a nice surprise, Kuthy," Wodeman said. He was by his very

nature unused to sarcasm, but then he had never readily relished being buried
alive either and, after all they had been through today, he felt he was fast approaching that stage where strange things happen to the mind.

That familiar edge to his voice did not go unnoticed by Nibulus either. As a
captain of thousands, it was nothing new to him. "Come," he commanded
without hesitation, and strode briskly toward the mound. The others followed
closely.

With hissing torches held aloft, they peered down at the pile of rocks. Immediately, they saw the large hole that cratered the top of the mound, and the
many loose stones that lay scattered about the cave floor.

"It's been plundered," Nibulus stated.

"Not by me," Kuthy said impatiently. "It was already like this the last time I
was here. Come on, let's go. You really don't want to tarry here of all places."

"Go where, exactly?"

"Away," Wodeman stammered, "anywhere. We need to get out of here
right now." He almost leapt after their departing guide, who was already striding toward the cascade.

The others were about to join him when Nibulus called out: "Wait! I want
to find out whose grave this is."

"Who cares? It'll be ours if we don't get a move on!" Kuthy retorted, with
increasing agitation.

But the Peladane ignored him. He reached down and picked up a thin,
slate-like piece of stone. He squinted at it hard, then read out what was carved
onto its surface.

"Gwyllch."

Kuthy tutted and rolled his eyes as he headed on out.

"Gwyllch?" Bolldhe repeated. "*The* Gwyllch?"

"The very same," Kuthy admitted. "Didn't I say earlier you might *eventually* find out what became of him? Now, can we please just get out of here?"

They all did so, swiftly, and Nibulus the swiftest of all. He caught up with
their guide in a few strides and grabbed him by the arm.

"All these years you actually knew the location of the burial place of our
greatest hero, and you never thought to tell anyone?" the Peladane snarled.

"It's a *secret* tunnel," Kuthy retorted, refusing to be detained. "A secret land,
remember? All the bards say is that he was 'intered as dhe tryumfante hoest
didde wende its way hoem,' and I am quite happy to see it remain that way; the
last thing Eotunlandt needs is a pilgrimage site to attract all *your* lot here."

He continued on his way, and the others followed him anxiously. All except
Nibulus. Bolldhe looked back at him, standing all alone in the cavern, gazing
back at the plundered grave of his venerated idol. Their leader appeared quite
at a loss.

"He'll want to do something . . . holy, I suppose," Bolldhe said. "Can't we
give him a few minutes?"

"That's exactly why I said we needed to be quick," Kuthy called back irritably. "Now the young idiot will be here for ages, trying to collect all the bones, and—I don't know, exorcise them or something."

"The bone lanterns?"

"Yes. But they're not real. They aren't even there, really—haven't been for five hundred years. Like I said, fey illusions. The huldre would've robbed that grave the instant the Peladanes left, used the bones as playthings, or worse."

"We require vengeance," Paulus announced darkly, "and we're not leaving before we get it."

"I know what you require," Kuthy muttered under his breath, then called out, "Nibulus!"

By now he had led them from the grotto by way of a steep ledge running along the side of the cascade. Stars could be seen through the fissures in the roof, and the smell of fresh, snowy mountain air began to finally ease their dread. A few minutes later, Nibulus caught up with them. He looked grim and said not a word. In his hand he still held the small slate-like headstone.

So, shattering their way through the curtain of icicles that screened a cave-mouth, the seven of them emerged at last from the tunnel. As if just reborn from the uterus of the earth, they breathed real air deep into grateful lungs, and stood blinking at this new world they had come to. Where they were, even when they were, they were not sure, so confused had both distance and time become inside the cave.

It was dark. The night sky was filled with the crepuscular sheen of a billion stars, whose light was caught up in the virgin snow that lay all about. Mountain peaks soared to celestial heights, and yet the company could also discern other peaks far below them. A living wind sang about them, spangling their outer cloaks with cobaltite brilliance, and great black oceans of forest could be heard murmuring in the night with the soft sibilance of sea foam upon a shingly shore.

"There are no tracks," Wodeman was the first to note. It was true; of the Tyvenborg thieves there was not a trace. It was as if they too had been as much an illusion as the lych-candles, as phantasmal as the giants. Perhaps they had never existed, even before entering the tunnel; were no more than chimeras evoked by the company's collective imagination on encountering the two corpses in the entry tunnel ten days earlier. For who could tell what was real or not in Eotunlandt?

Eotunlandt: it was a fey place, for sure. But had they fully left it yet? The return to snow, and a climate more realistic for this northern part of the world suggested that they had. Certainly the cold seemed no illusion. Yet at the back of their minds they could all sense still a hint of enchantment in the air.

Down a snowy slope from the cave mouth Kuthy led them. Even as they went, they could hear behind them the tiny chinking, shimmering sounds of the icicles reforming, sealing up once again the secret entrance into Eotunlandt. They did not dare turn round to observe the process, but instead resolutely followed Kuthy.

They trailed him some distance until he brought them to the shelter of a cave he himself had used before. Bolldhe noted that he kept looking about expectantly, scanning the landscape as if he were waiting for something to appear.

The cave was small, but easily large enough to accommodate them all, and it had the added advantage of being roughly L-shaped, so that tucked around its corner they were well out of the worst of the wind. The company struck up a fire there, and settled down for the night, more exhausted now than they could ever have believed possible.

There were, however, things that some among them felt needed to be said before they gave in to sleep. Nibulus was still staring at the little memorial stone in his hands, but his eyes were far away. At length he spoke, in a tone of voice they had not heard up till now.

"I know what people say about me back in Nordwas; I know I haven't exactly lived the life of a model Peladane. . . . But this," he brandished the stone, "this just isn't right. Gwyllch was one of the greatest champions of our people. He was there at the siege of Melhus. He alone stood by the High Warlord Arturus Bloodnose as he fell, slaying the firedrake that wouldst immolate his master."

Careful, Nibulus, Finwald thought. *You start using words like "wouldst," and you'll end up saying things like "unto" and "behold" too.*

But this was no fleeting effusion of an overtired mind: Nibulus needed to say his piece. He, the son of a warlord, had today backed down from a fight with a foe he could have defeated, run from a foe he couldn't fight, spent hours tormented by a foe he could not see, and finally been insulted by a foe he would never be able to reach. So much dammed-up adrenaline and no release for it whatsoever. He was simply supposed to go to sleep on top of all this? He felt as though he were being torn apart inside by an entire battalion of internal struggles, and was barely able to hold himself together. And, like a dam striving to hold back an ocean, the first part of him to break was his voice, and the first leakage, his eyes.

"I don't call many men great, but Gwyllch was a great man. And for those . . ." Nibulus searched for words sufficiently acerbic to vent his bile, "for those thieving little testi-grubs to desecrate his tomb . . ." He trailed off, unable to conclude either the sentence or his thoughts.

The fire grew higher, and the travelers tried to relax. Then, utterly out of the blue, Bolldhe suddenly spoke:

"Gwyllch was a butcher and a rapist. He was just one of hundreds who fought the drake and only then for the reward he expected."

To say that the atmosphere grew chilly would be an understatement; the air itself seemed to turn to poison, to sprout steely barbed knives, and bristle with dragon tongues of forked lightning. No one had expected words such as these ever to be uttered within at least two continents' distance from Nibulus, and especially not by one in Bolldhe's current position. What in hell's name did he think he was playing at?

But it did not stop there. . . .

"And Bloodnose was only on the ground because he was cowering," Bolldhe continued. "It was greed, not bravery, that caused Gwyllch to act so."

"Bolldhe . . ." hissed Finwald, warningly.

But Bolldhe would not be quieted. Not this late in the day.

"Like all your great champions," he went on caustically, "your venerated expurgators of evil, and all you would-be heroes right now. How many inno-cents have to die upon the altar of your holy ambition? And your Nahovian mercenaries, where do they fit into your crusades against evil, eh? How many women and children have you yourself butchered, Paulus, in the service of the Peladanes?"

"Silence!" Nibulus roared, and hurled the headstone at Bolldhe. It hit the cave wall above the wanderer's head and shattered into pieces.

"At least that's what they say in Trondaran. . . ." Bolldhe muttered an ad-dendum in a slightly more conciliatory tone.

"Then they are all mattress-hugging, knock-kneed, pox-ridden catamites in Trondaran!" Nibulus retorted.

"Actually most of them are farmers," Bolldhe corrected him, "but there are many renowned scholars amongst them too—including historians. And if you'd heard even a fraction of the histories I've heard about the siege of Mel-hus, Nib, you wouldn't be here in this cave now. You'd more likely be doing something useful, like trying to make amends for the crimes committed on be-half of your religion. Believe me, boy, you should be grateful the Olchorians exist, 'cause if they didn't, Peladanes would be the single most hated people in all Lindormyn."

There was a pounding silence in the cave. Nobody had ever spoken to Nibulus like that. *Ever.* He had crushed men's heads for less. But it was per-haps a measure of just how much had changed for all of them these past few days that the Peladane did not, in fact, do a thing. This place was unreal, their journey had been unreal, and somehow it all seemed so much easier to forget that this day had ever happened at all. It was time for sleep.

But just before Nibulus lay down, he called out: "And why are you in this cave now, Bolldhe, on a Peladane's quest, instead of doing something useful?"

Bolldhe declined to comment. He half-considered informing Nibulus that the Trondaranians' word for the pox was treponema-Peladane, but was too tired to bother.

Paulus dreams. He is back in the woods near the knoll back in Eotunlandt, and the thieves are out there, waiting for him. The air is hot, sticky, and soured with the tang of imminent bloodshed. This time though, he is all alone, and he cannot quite remember why he is here at all.

A purpose? An urgent purpose? He is here to do something crucial, he knows—but what? So little time! Think, Odf, think before it's too late!

His heart beats rapidly, and his eyes scan the jungle all around, taking in everything. He is stalking through the trees that thrust up from the bushy undergrowth extending on all sides. *He is looking for something.*

No, not looking; hunting. Not a leaf turns that his eyes miss. Each sound is magnified, conveying a message to his brain, even the slicing of a wood-ant's mandibles through a leaf. His long, wet tongue flicks out, and he finds he can taste the air.

But time is running out, and quickly, trickling through his fingers like blood. He must do something *now*.

Then he freezes, and a second later he hears it, the sound he has unwittingly been awaiting: the muted, singsong trill of a child's laughter. Its gay, musical, twisted pseudo-innocence quickens his heartbeat, and his mouth goes dry. His head swivels round to the left on stiffened cordage, and with new direction he begins to pad softly forward.

It grows ever hotter, and sweat beads his skin. Softly, softly he moves, through the hanging creepers and trailing vines. Bright red flowers open up at his approach, their petals peeling back to reveal pulsating pollen buds from which emanate the stench of rotting flesh. As he passes, they scream at him in insane laughter. A scaly lizard hisses at him from its perch, swelling to twice its size.

A voice speaks in his head. It is Kuthy's. *What d'you expect to find in here, Odf? There are no Huldres in Eotunlandt. . . . Or are there?* He glances up and notices in a detached way that the Tivor is perched upon a branch extending just above him. The soldier of fortune's eyes are wide, and he is picking the flesh off a glowing human bone. *Mm, tasty,* Kuthy sniggers, scraping the dead meat off with his rasping tongue. *Off the bone, just how I like it.*

Odf ignores him and creeps on. Again the laughter—closer now. It begins as a childish giggle, but ends in a coarse, scornful cackle, devoid of mirth. Odf's blade vibrates and whines, yearning for blood. His fingers tightly grip its rock-hard hilt. He advances.

Then his heart stops. He has caught a glimmer of white from the corner of his eye. Slowly his head turns, and finally he sees it.

The succubus. The sweet, seductive siren of the Hidden Kingdom. An icy inner light glows through her fluttering white gown like a lych-candle. Long hair that shines like the sun's reflection upon hoarfrost writhes about her in slow, serpentine undulations. Eyes beautiful and unnaturally large, black as the Pit, wink at him. The corner of her mouth twists in a knowing smile. One long, slender finger beckons him.

Blood pounds through his veins, and Odf almost chokes. He can feel his "problem" starting again.

Then she melts from his sight, disappearing through the trees.

Released from the spell that has held him, the Nahovian pounces after her, and plunges like a stampeding bull-baluchitherium through the tangle of steamy undergrowth, his blade pointed forward.

Hated Huldre! Where'd she go? Wherewherewhere—?

For a second time, he freezes. Fingers as soft as sunlight creep across his shoulder. He spins around. She is right behind him. His weapon rises. His breath comes in short gasps. The blood throbs madly in his grisly eye. And then she says it, in a voice as sweet as a fountain:

"Fancy a smoke, handsome?"

With a howl of steamed loathing, Odf plunges his weapon deep into her shimmering form. Again and again and again. Sweat pours from him, adrenalin surges through him, his hatred waxes greater with each successive thrust.

But the succubus merely throws back her head and shrieks with buzz-saw laughter at his impotence. Not the merest fleck of blood stains her pristine white gown. She wriggles and giggles, twists and whirls, then arches her back, stretches out her arms, yawns languidly . . .

. . . And turns into a troll.

Her long and lustrous, gracefully gyrating hair contracts as if shriveling under a harsh sun until it is frizzy and dry. Those previously delicate grey lips swell and pucker until they resemble a fungus growing around the foetid orifice of a mouth filled with disintegrating teeth and bleeding gums—a slobbering monstrosity fit only for bawling drunken obscenities at aged passersby. The eyes contract into piggy, bleary globes of watery lifelessness, and the whole body swells as if being filled by a hose pipe until it sags and wobbles. The Huldre stuffs the roll-up, now a filthy dog-end, into the corner of her mouth, slumps heavily onto an enormous, flaccid backside, belches wetly, then says, leering: "Ready when you are, lover boy."

He has seen women like this in the roadhouses of Venna, lumpish termagants with a staggering dearth of self-respect and possessing all the allure and social graces of a freshly picked scab. But it is too late now. He has lost any measure of self-control, and without further hesitation Odf Uglekort surrenders himself to the full madness of his ire:

"I don't care what you look like," he snarls. "I'm having you, ya filthy whore!"

He grabs the hefty face in both hands, and clamps his lips firmly to hers in a fierce, urgent, tongue-entwining kiss.

"PEL'S BELLS, PAULUS! WHAT D'YOU THINK YOU'RE DOING?" spluttered Nibulus in horror as he wrenched himself from Paulus's grasp, and backed away.

"Wha'?" Paulus replied in dazed confusion.

"I always thought you were a bloody minstrel," Nibulus spat, "and now I know!" He wiped the saliva off his mouth.

He had been trying to wake up the sleeping mercenary who had been moaning a little too loudly in the stillness of the night, disturbing their rest. Now, while Paulus was still trying to grasp what was going on, the Peladane transferred his bedroll to a part of the cave as far away as possible, and lay down, grumbling.

Both Bolldhe and Kuthy chuckled, and went back to sleep.

It was the dead of night, and absolutely nothing was moving. Appa, the last sentry on watch, had been unable to stay awake, and was now slumped against the cave wall, his head on his chest. So grey and inert he was that he appeared to have petrified and melded into the very stone around him. None of the others' breathing was to be heard either; the day had exacted a terrible toll from them all, and they slept the dreamless slumber of the dead. Even the wind of the witching hour had long since spent itself. The stars shone brightly in a cloudless sky, and the air had that hard, icy stillness that can be found only in the small hours before dawn.

Zhang, however, could get no sleep. The horse was restless. His tail kept flicking from left to right, and his ears would frequently point forward, then lie back flat. Something was not right. Stilling his anxious soul, he sent his keen animal senses out into the night, but nothing came back to him. He could hear nothing, smell nothing in the air, nor feel any movement through the ground. Yet he knew beyond doubt that there was something out there—out there in the night.

Something strange. A presence. Fey yet beast. And it was calling to him.

Zhang was not like other horses. The Adt-T'man breed, stumpy and unremarkable though they may have appeared, nevertheless could not help looking down upon other breeds. There was an intelligence in them very rarely seen in herd beasts, and a measure of self-control unknown in all but a few others of the animal kingdom. Their bond with humans was one of mutual benefit and respect, rather than obsequiousness. Yet their instincts, especially those outside the usual five senses, were at least as sharp as the sharpest herd animal's.

Zhang looked down at his devoted master. The bond between them was strong, and unique, but tonight the human's pleasantly rancid odor within the closeness of the cave did not reassure him as it normally did, and neither did the regular sound of his sleep breathing produce its usual soothing effect. Zhang leaned forward and nuzzled Bolldhe, and stamped his foot. But Bolldhe was too far under. Zhang could sense that his master was totally out of this situation; there would be no help from him. Zhang was on his own tonight.

Suddenly his ears snapped forward. There it was again. The call. It was not a sound, no, for all was dead here. More like a voice, or a single high note, the clearest, purest ringing of a tiny bell, which appeared in his brain without entering through his ears.

What was it?

With one last glance at his master, Zhang shook his mane and stepped out of the cave. Immediately he was a part of the night. No longer a steed, mount, nor any other vassal of man. He was beast. A single animal entity. The dullness of spirit and senses inherent in his normal subordination to humankind fell away, and everything sharpened into focus.

The horse was shivering, partly from the cold but mainly from the multitude of new sensations that surged through his mind and body. A wonderful or terrible experience, he could not tell, but he had never felt anything like this before.

He trotted on. His agile hooves tapped softly upon the rocky path that led upward. To one side rose a sheer wall of black cliff face. To the other a steep drop into emptiness. Zhang snorted in alarm, but picked his way carefully forward.

Eventually the path emerged onto a high, snow-covered plateau. Zhang whinnied in sudden fear, and rolled his big eyes. There were great stacks of rock standing about upon the snowfield, like silently watching giants. The slough-horse halted and would not go on. This was not a place to come to at night. Why had he allowed himself to be lured here?

But, of course, everything was strange and unnatural these days: the closeness of that tunnel, with its strange things flitting about, only hours ago now; the Land of the Young before that, with its terrifying Thunder-Spirits and the summer humidity that they had brought with them. And only hours later the blue-aired iciness of these mountains. No, nothing was ever normal when you traveled with humans—

Then he saw it. Some shape, something big, disengaged itself from the blackness of one of the rock stacks, and stepped out into full view. Zhang took a step back and tossed his head vigorously, but held his ground. The thing, whatever it was, did not come for him, but slowly unfolded two great leathery wings. On two legs it stood, and a large head, beaked yet somehow equine, bobbed up and down on a long, long neck. It swayed about, seeming to sniff the air, then turned its slitted, mazarine-blue gaze upon the horse, and whined.

The smell of rain-soaked slate and mist came back to Zhang as he recalled the Blue Mountains, and those enigmatic caves, high above any path, with their trails of smoke rising from within. There was something primordial, something mythical, something fabulous, about the beast that stood before him now. Like two rampant guardant emblems on a heraldic shield, the pair of them stood, facing each other across a sable and argent background. Yet there was no knight-versus-dragon enmity here.

Then a soft laugh resounded through the still air, somewhere off to Zhang's right, and music began to play. The horse's head swept round, but he could not locate the source. The melody was stark, intense, weird and beautiful all at once, and Zhang was held captivated—unmoving, unblinking, unbreathing—in its spell. The tone was forlorn, empty and vast as the benighted mountains, as cold as the ever-creaking snow, as icy as the stream of sparkling crystals that coruscated from the horse's flared nostrils. It held within its harmonies a depth as ancient as the world, and beneath it all there was just a hint of fear.

As abruptly as it had started, the music stopped, and a second figure stepped out onto the snowfield. It cocked its ragged head and chuckled.

". . . The night was rife with darkland life; you set my heart alight." The singer finished his song, then approached.

"My, my, what a beautiful animal, eh, Ceawlin? Come, my beauty, let's dance."

The night and the mountains belonged to Zhang and his strange new companions, as they danced in a whirlwind of scintillating ecstasy.

Back in the cave the humans were beginning to stir. After the ordeals of the previous day, sleep had come easily. But once they had recovered from the worst of their exhaustion, the frigid mountain air began to thin their slumber.

The first thing Bolldhe noticed as he awoke in the early dawn was how freezing it had become. In Eotunlandt they had grown used to a warm and sunny climate, and now the sudden change was robbing them all of the rest they still so badly needed.

Bolldhe blinked the sleep away, and the second thing he noticed was that his horse was missing.

"Zhang!" he cried, and leapt up in panic. He would not normally have been so worried, for Zhang was, after all, an independent beast and apt to wander off by himself. But some instinct told Bolldhe that his mount had not been in the cave for quite some time, and in these strange mountains that was a worrying thought indeed.

Then Bolldhe stopped dead . . . for the third thing he noticed was Zhang cantering merrily down the path toward him with what looked like a couple of new friends.

"Er . . . fellows," he called.

Zhang trotted up to him and nuzzled him affectionately. The horse was steaming with sweat, but exuberant with vitality.

"Fellows!" Bolldhe called again, a little more urgently. "I think we have guests."

Still only half-awake, Bolldhe's companions hardly registered his words, but something in the tone of his voice made them all sit up immediately. From their sheltered position around the corner they could not see out through the cave mouth to identify what he was staring at. All that they could see was Bolldhe, faintly illuminated by the bluish glow of dawn's first light, staring outside with a look of utter perplexity upon his face. They could see plainly enough that something was up, but it was only Wodeman who recognized in the way he was holding himself the same posture of a rabbit fascinated by the weasel-dance.

In the time it takes a heartbeat to quicken, they were on their feet. Weapons were snatched up, cloaks were hastily secured, and all save Appa and Kuthy advanced to stand by Bolldhe's side.

What they saw standing outside their cave caused every one of them to step back in fright and break out into a cold sweat.

"Lord P'ladan save us!"

"Jugg's Udders!"

"Euch!"

". . . !"

Behind Zhang loomed the great, stalking figure of something that none of them had ever believed they would see in their lifetime—at least, not this close up. Images of dragons, horses, reptiles, even orthopterous insects, flashed into their confused brains as they sought to make sense of this thing standing before them; and yet the mental image that overrode all the others was that of a crane. Like a great wading bird it stood, though fully three times larger than the horse.

"Retreat slowly," Nibulus ordered calmly, "around the corner."

"Why?" Kuthy asked matter-of-factly, on joining them.

"It's a bloody wyvern!" the Peladane retorted through gritted teeth. "It might breathe on us!"

Kuthy swaggered up to the cave mouth, smiling. "Well, unless you've got some extreme hypersensitivity to bad breath, I don't see why that should bother you," he mocked. "Wyverns ain't dragons, you know."

Everyone in Lindormyn knew for sure that wyverns do not breathe fire. But it was more than a little worrying to discern two thin lines of smoke (or possibly steam) drifting up from the nostrils on its beak.

Then, to the horror of all there, Kuthy sauntered up to the beast and reached out to stroke its flank.

"WHAT THE—GET BACK FROM THERE, YOU IDIOT!" Nibulus cried out, as all the company leapt away. But the wyvern did not seem at all aggressive—more like curious. That long, tapering, eagle-like head drew back on its serpentine neck, squinted at the human inquisitively, then sniffed him carefully. Satisfied, it recommenced its study of the others cowering inside the cave.

"I'm getting my armor on," the Peladane said. "Just stand still here, and don't make any sudden—"

"Oh, grow up!" Kuthy sighed, patting the wyvern on the flank as one might do to a cow. "By the time you're all strapped up it'll be sundown."

There was no denying it, Kuthy was a cool one. What had at first appeared to be incredible stupidity and bravado now just seemed incredible. Was there nothing that worried this man? Could anything in the entire world hold any surprise for him?

The tenterhooks, on which they had been, now having blunted a little, the others eased off their guard, and studied the creature, though none would venture any closer. It was a formidable beast, to be sure. Powerful, reptilian legs that ended in cruel talons gave it the look of a bird of prey, as did the sharply hooked, yellow beak. But those twitching forelegs with their raptorial claws were held before it in the manner of a praying mantis. Its hide was as hard as a lizard's, but without the scales; at a certain angle it appeared a very dark brown, almost black, but when the light caught it, broad stripes of electric blue and chromatic violet could be discerned. A tail far too long flicked menacingly about from side to side like a cat's, and ended in a bulbous yellow sac of poison adorned with a vicious barb. Those vast wings definitely possessed a bat-like quality, vibrating oddly; but the creature looked far too heavy and muscular to be capable of flight.

At that moment, nobody had any idea what it was doing here, how it came to be in company with Bolldhe's horse and, more importantly, why it seemed now to be *talking* with Kuthy. A low murmur was vibrating down from its head; not quite words, but the thought of words, or the vague impressions of meaning could be understood. It used no audible language, but deep within those sonic vibrations there was definitely communication. For a few moments the wyvern and the adventurer exchanged greetings, and then, without warning, Kuthy called out, not to the creature, but behind it.

"Hello, Elfswith." The tone was conversational.

Who he was greeting they could not see, for his glance was fixed on a point well beyond their view. But a moment later his words were answered by a tinny, scraping little voice:

"All right, Kuthy. How's it going?"

A little man appeared. His long hair was dark and ragged, and fell about a pale yet comely, fine-boned face. His eyes, a piercing yellow, flicked cursorily over the company before settling back on Kuthy.

"You took your time," he observed.

"Got held up," Kuthy replied, still stroking the wyvern's neck.

"It happens," the newcomer acknowledged, then nodded toward the others in the cave. "Who're the citizens?"

"Hireli- er, highly appreciated traveling companions," Kuthy caught himself just in time, and smiled wryly at his diminutive friend.

"What about that one?" the newcomer asked, seeing Bolldhe with his scabby face for the first time. "Nothing catching, I hope?"

Kuthy smirked semi-apologetically at Bolldhe, who merely turned away.

In a way, this little man was almost as surprising as the wyvern itself. While one might have expected a beast that fabulous to inhabit a place like the Giant Mountains, his companion—basically of human stock—looked more like the type of low-life denizen one might expect to encounter in a sleazy opium den. He wore a huge, baggy coat of many pockets that reached down to the ground, but despite the freezing cold, wore only an unbuttoned shirt and light trousers underneath, and absolutely nothing on his feet. He had the artful air of a dodger, with the casual nonchalance and cocky swagger of a backstreet bawd, and no doubt considered himself equally at home wherever he might be. Even here, up in the Giant Mountains, wandering about in the early dawn with just a wyvern for company.

"Mr. Tivor," Nibulus called out in mock politeness, "sorry to bother you, but do you think you might explain?"

The adventurer winked at the ragged little man, then took a deep breath and reentered the cave, leading his two friends inside with him.

They had all seen wyverns before, of course. At least once in a lifetime most inhabitants of the north would witness the mass migration of these great creatures, their distant silhouettes sailing gracefully across a yellowy sky beneath the low mass of dark clouds on a blustery early autumn evening. But to stand so close to one—to be actually sharing a cave with one—was an experience new to all of them but Kuthy. It was a bit like having a great white bear step into one's house and curl up in front of the hearth. They could not begin to guess what thoughts or intentions lay behind those glittering mazarine eyes; it looked, all at the same time, wild, calm, vicious, wise, or as Nibulus commented, "permanently pissed off."

But evidently this particular wyvern—a female answering to the name Ceawlin—was here along with Elfswith for some reason that would possibly be disclosed to them, if and when it suited him.

While Elfswith made himself comfortable, Appa leaned closer to Bolldhe and asked: "What is he, then? Human?"

Bolldhe knew what Appa meant. "I reckon he's closer to human than any alien race I've ever seen," Bolldhe answered. "Maybe he's got a little of the Hauger in him."

"I've never yet seen any Hauger with yellow eyes," Finwald commented doubtfully. He himself was not at all happy: this was getting completely out of hand. Ever since they had fallen in with Kuthy, nothing seemed to be under the priest's control.

Lowering his voice, he added, "And what's that papuliferous marking on his chest supposed to be, eh?"

They peered closer. What at first had appeared to be some sort of necklace they now realized was a blemish on his skin, just visible where the shirt buttons were unfastened. It could have been a line of scabs, possibly the residue of some kind of disease; then again, maybe it was something more permanent.

"Just a birthmark," the little man announced without looking up at his observers, before fastening the buttons against their prying eyes. He then reached into one of his many huge pockets and felt about inside. There came from within a surprising series of sounds, the sort one might expect to hear when someone is rooting through a kitchen drawer or an old trunk. Eventually he pulled out a packet of tobacco, made a roll-up, and flicked it into his mouth. Then he started rummaging around for a light. After checking further in several pockets he succeeded in drawing out not matches, but a blackened and battered old coffee pot. He was about to put this back, but thought better of it, and handed it to Nibulus.

"Make yourself useful, son," he said, and returned to his rummaging.

The Peladane stared at him, and handed the pot on to Kuthy. Ceawlin, meanwhile, padded around in a circle, then settled down comfortably, Kuthy moving to her side.

Soon Elfswith, searching other pockets, found a large packet of very strongly tar-smelling coffee, and a sealed earthenware jar of strange appearance. While the others watched, totally absorbed, he twisted the jar until it clicked open into two halves, revealing a kind of glass container within. From this container a soft, red glow emanated, and they could just about make out the flicker of flame. Elfswith first lit his roll-up, then handed this stove to Kuthy, who, evidently familiar with the equipment, busied himself with preparing the coffee.

From yet another pocket, Elfswith managed to extricate his mandolin. He shook his head and thrust it back. Yet more rummaging produced a ruel-bone whistle. "Nearly there," he smiled, and began to fumble about again in yet another pocket. From this one he pulled out his mandolin again, despite having put it back in a different one.

"Really need to get these pockets organized," he muttered to himself. "Spend half my bloody life searching for things. . . ."

A moment later he grinned as his groping hand alighted upon what he was seeking. He tugged hard, and hauled out a long, tightly rolled-up bedroll that immediately fluffed up into a deep and soft mattress. He wasted no time in making himself comfortable—looking as at home in this dark mountain cave as he would in any palace.

The others gaped at him in equal measures of perplexity and intrigue. "I don't suppose you've got a bathtub in there, too, have you?" Finwald finally inquired.

"Did have once," Elfswith replied, "but I think it must've slipped through a rip in the lining."

They could not be absolutely certain if he was joking or not.

"That's quite a remarkable . . . garment you have there," Appa ventured.

Elfswith regarded the elderly priest as a prince might look at a footman who has just proffered an unsolicited opinion. "Why thank you," he condescended, and left it at that.

"What's it made of?" Wodeman asked, more bluntly. "I reckoned it was ermine when you were standing outside in the snow, but here in the dark it looks more like mink. Seems to be composed of many creatures and colors all at once."

Elfswith settled back, and plugged his roll-up into the end of his whistle. He began to play a beautiful, haunting melody while simultaneously blowing smoke rings that emerged a different color depending on which note he had produced.

"Yes, it is," he eventually replied, still without looking at Wodeman. "Ermine, mink, ocelot, hyrax, flamingo, narwhal, green mamba, dragonfly—a hundred different pelts for a hundred different situations—or moods."

He settled farther back into his bedroll, and the coat's color shifted into the luxuriant warmth of fox-red.

Kuthy handed the coffee round. The first cup he presented to the Peladane.

"So," Nibulus began, "how long has this little reunion of yours been planned?"

Kuthy drained his cup in one go, closed his eyes in rapture, and exhaled loudly. "Listen, I can tell you're a bit suspicious of me—"

"You could say that," Nibulus replied flatly.

"And a bit angry, I'd guess." Kuthy grinned a mock-sheepish smile that fooled nobody. "Well, maybe I could have been a bit more candid with you. But you're not really expecting me to say 'sorry,' surely? Look at us now; we're all here safe, well fed and loaded with fresh supplies, and you are weeks ahead of your schedule. Let's be honest, I've saved you a huge distance and a lot of danger; you should be thanking me."

"What?" Bolldhe cut in, leaning forward sharply. "More danger than two-hundred-foot tall giants? You want us to thank you for that? We were nearly killed back there!"

Kuthy met the glare of Bolldhe's increasingly bulging and bloodshot eyes with a look of cold disdain, such as a parent might give to a mewling child. "You could've been killed in Fron-Wudu," he pointed out. "While the only threat in Eotunlandt was the giants, and they can be seen miles off, and easily avoided. Especially by sensible travelers who don't go lighting fires on hilltops at night, or prancing about in a daze looking at all the pretty flowers."

There was a sudden splutter of coffee from Elfswith's direction. "They didn't, did they?" he sniggered.

Kuthy nodded. "Believe one who knows," he went on. "There are far more dangers lurking in the forest; and I don't just mean the Afanc, which I drove off, I might add. If it hadn't been for me, you'd still be wandering around in those woods with a long, long way to go."

That was not the right way to talk to Bolldhe. It only made him worse. Which was probably exactly why Kuthy did so in the first place.

"You used us," Bolldhe said coolly. "The only reason you ever joined us and led us through Eotunlandt was so you could have your own personal bodyguard on your way to meet your friend here."

The only thing Bolldhe still admired about Kuthy now was his fluency in Aescalandian; he would have loved to rant ten-to-the-dozen at the old trickster in front of the Aescals, but his anger was making it more difficult to speak in this tongue, not less so. In the end, he just had to revert to his native Pendonian:

"You deliberately played down the dangers of Eotunlandt. We almost got thief-slain and giant-squashed there. And by the time we realized we were being set upon, you'd already scarpered! Not so much as a word of warning! Just abandoned us to it, to save your own hide, you lying, twisted little shit!"

Bolldhe's voice was rising, and the more it shrilled, the more he rose from his sitting position, and the closer his face got to Kuthy's. The old soldier, though, did not move at all, just sat there regarding the younger man with unconcern. By the end of the rant they were only inches apart, and might even have touched noses had the wyvern's nostrils not let out a soft whistling like a steaming kettle.

"Take a seat, Bolldhe," Kuthy replied in Bolldhe's native tongue. "Ceawlin gets upset by the sound of raised voices."

Bolldhe's gaze swiveled toward the curled-up wyvern, and caught the glint of mazarine watchfulness behind her eyelids. He did as he was told.

"We traveled together for mutual protection." Kuthy reverted to Aescalandian. "We helped each other. Where's the harm in that?"

"Just leave it, Bolldhe," Finwald interrupted, wondering why his traveling companion was getting so worked up. "No one forced us to go with him. Remember, it was agreed on the assurance of myself and Appa that there was no evil in this man."

"Speak for yourself," Paulus snapped. "I never agreed to having him along."

The Nahovian was still seething at the thought of how Kuthy had goaded him on with the false promise of Huldre-meat. No one else, however, seemed particularly interested in taking him up on this point.

"I've given you a shortcut here, and I'm not asking for anything in return," Kuthy continued magnanimously. "I have my own purposes, as do you, and I believe both have been served to satisfaction by our brief journey together. Look, I know I've kept a few things from you, but it all worked out well in the end, didn't it? I thought a bunch of—how shall we put it?—inexperienced, wet-behind-the-ears tyros like you lot (and I mean that in the nicest possible way) would've bolted if I'd told you in advance about the giants. And that stuff about me going to Myst-Hakel and all . . . Well, the fact is I was never intending to go there in the first place. I just said that because I didn't know you well enough to trust you then—"

"You, trust us?" snorted Paulus.

"—Elfswith and I have unfinished business here, matters of a somewhat confidential nature."

"What, here?" exclaimed Nibulus. "In these damn mountains?"

"This is my home, fatty," Elfswith cautioned, flipping his cup up to the cave roof and then letting it fall straight into his pocket. "So just you watch that lip."

"What is this business of yours, then?" Nibulus demanded of Kuthy, ignoring the little man's impudence.

"Our affairs are private," Elfswith stated. "They've got nothing to do with you." There was menace in his voice that carried weight, for none of the company knew anything of this little creature in the baggy coat, and, if that were not enough, there was also the matter of his gigantic raptorial friend.

Kuthy gave up on diplomacy. *Let them get hacked off, for all the good it'll do them.* "Listen, when I first met you in the woods, I just took advantage of a fortuitous situation, that's all. But if you're worried about your strings being pulled, then don't. We've traveled our course together, we've helped each other. Now we can go our separate ways. Bolldhe, rest assured I won't have the chance to manipulate you anymore. Myself and Elfswith are going on to Wrythe. If you want to join us, you're more than welcome . . . . But probably not, as you wish. If not, I've brought you almost to the Jagt Straits; from there you can carry on to Melhus on your own."

At the mention of that name, Elfswith's long ears pricked up. It was not often that mere "citizens" interested him, but for once they did.

"Melhus?" he said, "so you're going to the Maw? Rather you than me."

"If that's some kind of warning about the dearth of pickings to be found there, " Nibulus said, desperate to recover some pride, "then it may surprise you to learn that we're actually not a bunch of grubby little tomb raiders."

Both Kuthy and Elfswith inwardly raised eyebrows at the Peladane's willingness to reveal even this amount about his private business. What an idiot!

"I could tell that just by looking at you," Elfswith responded. "Tomb raiders are much more professional—not that I could give a damn what you're up to. No, I was merely referring to the Dead."

"What?"

"The Dead," Elfswith repeated, "You know: the Dead-that-walk. They've been getting a tad frisky of late, wandering about on Melhus Island and all. Oh, I'm sorry, didn't you realize even that?"

"How do you know?"

"Like I said, these mountains are my home, and the lands all about are well known to me. The air's clear, and Ceawlin's wing is swift. We see a lot from up there. I tell you, the Dead are abroad, and that means something's up. Nowt to do with *your* business, I suppose?"

There was a stunned silence. The Dead were abroad! Just as reports had claimed, the reports of those few of the Melhus expeditionaries who had actually returned. Nothing the Aescals had not heard about before, of course, but to learn it from a local . . .

"Sweet Pel above!" Nibulus breathed, his face turning chalk white. "It's true after all."

"Of course it's true!" Appa snapped irritably. "What do you think we came all the way here for? Young idiot!"

"I know," Nibulus stammered, "but . . ." He trailed off, and knocked back the gritty remainder of his coffee, swallowing hard. He began toying with the buckles on his left vambrace.

Bolldhe studied him intently, questioningly. "Mr. Wintus," he inquired, "exactly what is going on here? This is your intended quest, isn't it? We did come here to destroy Drauglir, didn't we?"

"Destroy Drauglir!" Kuthy and Elfswith cried out in unison, astonishment as evident in their eyes as in their voices. Even Ceawlin lifted her head to stare at Bolldhe.

"Perhaps if you shouted it a little louder," Nibulus rounded on the three of them, "Drauglir himself might even hear. I'm sure he'd be very interested to know our plans."

"So that is the plan, then?" Bolldhe asked for confirmation. "To destroy him?"

Nibulus shifted a little, and began scratching his stubble. "Well, yes, I suppose."

"SUPPOSE? SUPPOSE!" Bolldhe cried shrilly. "What d'you mean, 'suppose'? These past few weeks have been the hardest in my life! I've been dragged over mountain, marsh and forest, almost lost my life more times than I can count, and now you're suggesting you're not even sure why?"

"He knows exactly why," Kuthy cut in, "and you should too. By Dzugota, is it really such a mystery? Zibelines! Amethyst! MONEY—that's what it's all about, isn't it, Nib?"

Four pairs of eyes narrowed on the Peladane: the two Mage-Priests', the shaman's, and Bolldhe's. Nibulus continued scratching his stubble agitatedly. It was not in his nature to squirm, but squirm he did on this occasion.

"Well?" Appa demanded hoarsely. He of all of them had suffered the worst, and he felt sick to the pit of his leathery old stomach to think that their leader did not even believe in the quest.

"Well . . . well, put it this way," Nibulus muttered. ". . . Yes."

A strange sibilant noise ensued. They were not sure if it came from the ice-laden wind that coursed up from the deep valleys outside, or the scaly rasping of breath in Ceawlin's throat. It might even have been the sound of Nibulus's frying face. But to Bolldhe it seemed like the sound of the atmosphere crystallizing around them all.

Appa cleared his throat. "I think perhaps it's time we put our cards on the table. Where exactly does everyone stand on this rather important issue, hmm?" His voice remained calm, but some might detect a hint of hysteria there.

"Already done that, me," Kuthy said glibly, continuing to stare hard at the Peladane. "Your turn now, Nib."

Nibulus declined to comment, preferring instead to scrutinize the stubble-scrapings under his fingernails.

"My purposes have always been the same," Wodeman stated proudly. "The earth must be protected."

"And I think I speak for both myself and Appa," Finwald said, "in that as far as we're concerned nothing has changed. Like Wodeman, we're here to kill a Rawgr."

"I'm here to see that Bolldhe does whatever Lord Cuna desires him to," Appa corrected him.

"Nothing's changed with me, either," Bolldhe claimed. "I never had a bloody clue why I'm here, and I still don't. What about you, Paulus?"

"My plans are just the same as when I started out, too," Paulus agreed. "I'm in it for the money. Just like Wintus."

"You mean you knew?" Appa cried, aghast.

"Of course," Paulus replied. "He's a Peladane, isn't he? That's what they're always after. Why, what did you think?"

"Oh Lord," Appa breathed. "I think I'm going to be sick . . . ."

"Look, you idiots!" Nibulus suddenly exclaimed. "What is the big surprise? Like Paulus says: I'm a Peladane! We fight wars! That's what we do! War needs feeding, and it has an insatiable appetite. At the moment we're fighting an ongoing crusade against the Villans, and it's draining every last copper zlat from our account. Now I don't doubt any of those who say there's nothing of value left in the Maw nowadays, but if we can pull off one or two quests against Evil, everyone loves us—we're the golden boys. It doesn't matter if that Evil never existed in the first place. Try to look at the big picture. And Melhus is so remote, nobody's going to know any different."

Appa drew his grimy stick of a hand slowly down his face. "So why not just hole up for a few months in, say, Hawdan Valley, or even Myst-Hakel? Lie low, then come back home with your filthy lies? No one would be any the wiser."

"They might," Paulus said. "There's always a chance word might get back from those places, if not this year, then next, or even in ten years. And then where would their reputation be?"

They all looked at the Peladane.

"It's true," he admitted. "I can't say that my father or indeed any of my household really believe in the legends of Drauglir's rise, or the stories that have been going the rounds lately. All those adventurer types who came back from the north with their scary stories, well, they're bound to, aren't they? Sounds so much more exciting than the truth, doesn't it? Those liars!"

Bolldhe was almost too stunned at the Peladane's hypocrisy to utter a word, but he just about managed: "Perhaps they were just looking at the big picture."

"Maybe you and your father should have listened to the stories of the ones who didn't come back," Appa added morbidly.

"Quite," Bolldhe agreed. "And which type are we going to end up as, eh? The returning liars, or the ones who stayed to keep the Dead company?"

"As far as Wintus Hall is concerned," Nibulus went on, ignoring them,

"Drauglir died on that day five hundred years ago. The Peladanes burnt his corpse to a blackened husk, and built a sturdy vault around what was left of it, where it lay atop the ziggurat. But we need popular support. And the legend, and all the gossip, and—excuse me for saying this, Finwald—Finwald's visions; it was all so conveniently timed. A simple quest, no real danger, and we're back in business! The zibelines pour in from every quarter!"

"But the Dead are abroad, aren't they?" Finwald reminded his old friend pointedly.

". . . Yes," Nibulus admitted with a nervous laugh. "Hadn't really accounted for that, I must admit."

It was one of the maxims of Cunaism that disillusionment is a fine thing, in that anything which might remove a false idea, and thus bring one closer to the Truth, is to be lauded. But to see the utter despondency in the faces of Bolldhe and the three priests, one might be forgiven for doubting this. Appa looked mortified, even though it was not his religion that was being ethically disemboweled before them. Both he and Wodeman seemed to be having a great deal of difficulty in taking all this in. Finwald merely seemed disappointed. Not at his friend's religion, but at his friend. He knew now why he had been barred from all those top-level meetings at Wintus Hall earlier that year. Still, he had to hand it to the lad, it must have taken a great deal of courage for a Peladane to admit all that he had just admitted; maybe the presence of the Lightbearers was rubbing off on him after all.

Even Bolldhe, the "seen-it-all, done-it-all" master of cynicism who had ceased to believe in anything long years past, was saddened. His hand touched something hard and sharp upon the cave floor where he sat. On examination it turned out to be a shard of the slate Nibulus had hurled at him the previous night. The G for Gwyllch was still visible.

"How things change," Bolldhe said pensively, half to himself. "When I was a kid, the heroes were only heroes for how they died, not how they lived. They could be the biggest shit in the seven counties, and yet if they died a hero's death, the skalds would sing their praises for all eternity. A bit like old Gwyllch back there. But nowadays . . . well, maybe things haven't changed that much, after all; now, instead of a hero's death, it's a hero's hoard."

"What do you mean?" Appa inquired, only half-interested.

"What I mean is, the only way any of us are remembered these days is by the wealth we've amassed by the time we die. 'Look at this grave,' they say. 'That fellow may be dead, but he's got ten times more zlats than I'll ever have; what a hero!' "

Nibulus avoided any eye contact with Bolldhe thereafter. He also avoided any further mention of the banishment to which he had sentenced their "faithless coward" earlier. He still did not care for the man, and neither did he trust him; the scent of Fossegrim blood still lingered around Appa's "almost-executioner."

But the saving of the Dhracus was testament plain enough for anyone that Bolldhe was not a complete coward, and taking into account all that had been disclosed just now, well . . . the Peladane decided to simply drop the whole subject.

Bolldhe, on the other hand, was still of two minds about what to do next. He had just been invited to join, for a while at least, the Tivor and his extraordinary friends upon one of their journeys. It was a tempting offer; the chance to travel alongside one of the foremost heroes of Lindormyn, see some of the wonders he saw; the chance to be a part of the legend, no matter how small; the chance maybe to fly. And it would certainly be a way out of this whole Melhus mess, which now looked far more frightening and perilous than it had at any other time. And a clean break from the dubious company of the Peladane and his men.

Yes, it was a tempting offer, and one that a younger Bolldhe would have jumped at without hesitation. But for the older Bolldhe, there was still the matter of Kuthy, and put quite simply, Bolldhe could no longer stand the sight of the man. Just hearing his voice nowadays made his hackles rise.

Heroes? he thought to himself. *Bollocks!*

What Kuthy and Elfswith's business together was, exactly, the men from the south never did find out. There was enough despondency at that time to dull even the most inquisitive mind. In any case, the time for the parting of their ways was almost at hand, and neither group had any reason to take any further interest in the other's affairs.

In fact it was true to say that both parties were heartily looking forward to being rid of each other. As far as the Aescals were concerned, it came as no surprise whatsoever that Kuthy and Elfswith were partners; they truly did go together so well. Elfswith, in the short time that they had known him, appeared to suffer from just about every character flaw that Kuthy did, and more besides. He was aloof, contemptuous, ignorant, and even antagonistic when he could be bothered. But unlike Kuthy, he did not even show any sign of that garrulousness and relaxed humor that the soldier of fortune was apt to display now and then.

Nibulus had taken an instant dislike to him. As he would put it later, Elfswith was "one of those cocky little gits that could do with a damn good kicking." The son of the Warlord Artibulus was not accustomed to being talked to in the way Elfswith did, but if this journey had taught him one thing, it was to keep his feelings to himself while stuck up an icy mountain hundreds of miles from civilization in the company of strange little men and their massive wyverns.

Paulus agreed. He never liked anyone, but Elfswith he found to be particularly detestable.

"I've never been to Vregh-Nahov," the little man had said to him earlier. "Do they all wear great long coats like yours?"

"They do," Paulus answered dryly, "even the women and children."

Elfswith snorted derisively. "Must be difficult for the kids; don't they keep tripping up on the hem, or are they all nineteen foot tall, too?"

Paulus checked his anger, and declined to reply. There was something very fishy about their host, and it was nagging the Nahovian greatly.

Appa just thought he was rude, plain and simple. "They certainly deserve each other," he commented about Elfswith and Kuthy. Wodeman, however, was of the opinion that the wyvern deserved a lot better than her present master.

Only Finwald had nothing to say about him. From the start he had kept a low profile, and it was noticed that he avoided any eye contact with him at all. Elfswith, however, did not reciprocate this evasion, and of all the Peladane's crew, it was the young mage-priest who caught his attention. It was hard to say why, but he would often cock his head and stare at the downcast face of the Lightbearer appraisingly.

It was only Bolldhe who reserved his judgment for the time being. He was merely curious. It was not often that people held much interest for him; the more he traveled, the more people seemed the same. But Elfswith he found intriguing, and it was this curiosity that resulted in his later uncovering one of Elfswith's little secrets.

Not for nothing did he wear a big coat. . . .

But decisions had to be made. Kuthy and Elfswith were keen to get on with their affairs, whatever they were, and wanted to be off as soon as could be. Now that Kuthy had found Elfswith and Ceawlin again, he would be doing his traveling by air. Nibulus and his men too had a decision to make, and it was one that could not be put off any longer.

"Our business takes us first to Wrythe," Kuthy explained to them, "then after that we're headed southwest to the Dragon Coast, and then Ghouhlem. If you're still thinking about trying your luck with Wrythe, maybe we could put in a good word for you before you arrive, but as I said before, I don't recommend it."

"Why not?" Nibulus demanded. "You're going there, aren't you?"

Elfswith made a loud show of stifling a laugh at this. The impudence of the man!

"As you yourself said back in the forest," Kuthy explained, "word hasn't come out of that place for a long time. Well, me and Elfswith have been there, and I can tell you without a word of a lie that there's a very good reason for that. Don't be fooled by the old stories of the Fasces, Nib, or that old chronicle of yours. Times have changed, and the Oghain no longer take kindly to outsiders. Of late there've been many southerners who've sought to exploit any hospitality there might be in that town on their way to the Maw—usually to their cost. The Jarl of Wrythe is not a nice man, and not to be buggered about with. Oh, he knows us three, and he'll tolerate us for a short while, but any other strangers would do well to give him and his town as wide a berth as possible. Honestly."

" 'Honestly,' " Appa mimicked. "Are you sure you're not just trying to keep us away for your own reasons?"

"Suit yourself." Kuthy shrugged. "It's no skin off my nose either way."

"No, I've heard rumors too," said Finwald. "Back in Nordwas there was talk of one party that had to give up on the Maw and come straight back just because they couldn't get a boat across. Very strange place, Wrythe, it seems."

Nibulus had heard the rumors too. "It was always odds on we might have to steal a boat from them—"

"—Until we met friend Kuthy here," Wodeman reminded them.

"You all still thinking of that ice bridge?" asked Bolldhe.

"Indeed." Nibulus nodded. "If what Mr. Tivor tells us is true—and there's always a first time, right?—we could avoid Wrythe and save ourselves several days' travel into the bargain."

Appa was crestfallen on hearing this. He was already missing the warmth of Eotunlandt, and was prepared to take any risk that might mean he could warm himself by a big fire in a comfortable longhouse, eat real dinners, and sleep in a real bed.

Nibulus reached under his Ulleanh and brought out his chronicle. He opened it at the back where there was a crude map, and pointed to it. "You know these mountains," he said to Elfswith, swallowing his pride. "How long d'you reckon it'll take us to reach the coast?"

"We could get there in a matter of hours," Elfswith replied, nodding toward the wyvern. "But for you . . . I don't know, two days?"

"Two days, then. And you're sure the ice is strong enough?"

"It'll be thin this time of year," Kuthy admitted, "but you should be able to get across to the other side."

"To Stromm Peninsula," Nibulus said. "And what after that?"

"It is a land of fire and ice," Elfswith interrupted, "the most hostile land I have ever known . . ." He fished about in a pocket and drew forth a candle, which he lit, and held under his face for dramatic effect. "Here the four elements are at their fiercest, and wage constant war with each other. Great jagged teeth of granite do thrust up through the ice that encrusts the land the whole island over. Mountains of fire there are, that brood like sleeping behemoths in whose infernal depths dwell the terrible Jutul, the fire giants. If perchance you happen upon the great steaming, smoking fissures that reach out from their mountains across the ice field, mayhap you will hear the never ending beat of hammer upon anvil, like unto war drums in the deeps—"

"I once knew a fire giant," Bolldhe commented. "Big, friendly fellow he was. Made a great cup of ginger tea."

"—And gales there be, howling like a host of demons, screaming from the very heart of Eisholm across the flat expanses where there be no shelter; winds filled with shards of ice and the insane voices of chaos, ferocious enough to flay the very skin from your bones . . ."

He looked around at the rapt faces of his audience, and shared a barely perceptible smirk with Kuthy. "But I'm sure you'll be all right," he concluded, and snuffed out the candle.

It was difficult to tell how seriously the assembled company took him, but Appa for one did not look very well.

"Is it really so . . . terrible?" he asked.

"You can't believe it unless you've been there," Elfswith solemnly replied.

"And you have?" asked Finwald suddenly. It was not doubt in his voice, but an intense interest. Again, Elfswith gave him that long, hard stare. Then he answered: "I've never actually set foot in the place, but Ceawlin is a strong flier. Yes, we've been there."

"But do you think this map is accurate?" Nibulus pressed on.

"Hard to say, really," Elfswith replied, "but the important thing is: see that mountain there? That's Ravenscairn, the tallest peak on the north coast. Your map doesn't say so, but it's shaped like a cat's tooth. Very unique. If the weather's clear you should be able to see it from many miles away. Once you cross the frozen sea and reach Stromm Peninsula, just keep heading northwest, and within a few days you'll be in sight of it."

"Ravenscairn," Nibulus muttered, "and that's right above the Maw, right?"

"That's the one. Just use the cat's tooth to guide you in."

"And then?"

"And then you're on your own. Truly alone. Like I said, I've never been to the Maw, and I don't ever intend to. The Dead are on the move down there. If it's death you're looking for, you'll find it in abundance in that place."

"But what do you know of the Dead?" Finwald again cut in. There was a slight tremor in his voice which could have been fear, or excitement.

"Look," Kuthy took over, an uncharacteristic hint of earnestness in his voice, "we don't go near those places. We don't care for that sort of thing. But if you really are intent on going up against the Rawgr—if it's actually alive—then I can guarantee there'll be times when you'll be confronted by the Dead. And maybe I can help you."

The company leaned forward and listened intently to what he had to say.

"It is in the nature of our business that myself and Elfswith have had need to look into such matters as necromancy—no, it's no problem Elfswith, they're all right—and in the course of our search we've at times come across many mutually conflicting legends from all over the world. These may or may not be of any use to you, but the one thing that they do seem to have in common is: if you want to put the Walking Dead back to sleep, you must sever the link between brain and heart, thus destroying the life force that reanimates the body."

"So," Nibulus considered, his thoughts hovering somewhere between professionalism and relish, "decapitation?"

"That would do the trick, yes."

"Severing the spinal column," the Peladane went on quickly. "Skewering the heart or brain . . . Ripping out the heart or brain . . . Total immolation by fire or acid . . . Smashing the entire head to a pulpy mass . . ."

"Yes, yes, that sort of thing," Kuthy replied, frowning at the Peladane. "I'm sure the possibilities are endless for one as experienced and imaginative as yourself."

"Oh they are indeed," Nibulus agreed.

"Just make sure you've got the right weapons, that's all. Clubs will be useless in the hands of any but the strongest," he said, eyeing Appa and his crow's beak staff doubtfully. "And if I were you, Wodeman, I'd try to pick up something a little sturdier than that quarterstaff of yours. I don't doubt both it and you are strong enough to crush a few heads, but you could find yourself up against more than just a few. Also, stabbing weapons including arrows are only good if you're really accurate."

"Slicing weapons, then," Nibulus concluded happily, gripping his sword Unferth.

"Exactly. You, Paulus and Bolldhe here should be all right. Yours are heavy enough. But, Finwald, that sword-cane might work all right against town ruffians, but you'll need something with a lot more weight behind it in the Maw."

Finwald seemed deep in thought. Suddenly he said, "Would a silver blade do?"

"Silver?" Kuthy repeated in surprise. "That's for Rawgr-slaying. Right now we're only getting the Dead out of your way."

Finwald held the man's stare silently.

"Well, yes, I suppose it would work, indeed," Kuthy acknowledged, "if you've got one handy. What's good for the demon is good for the Dead, as they say. But if I were you I wouldn't go risking it on those stiffs. Save it for Drauglir himself. What would you do if it broke, or got snatched away from you?"

"Oh, that's all right," Bolldhe broke in. "Finwald can use his silver one against the Dead if he wants to. When it comes to putting paid to the Rawgr, I'm the one who—"

"Not another word," Finwald said darkly, and again lowered his eyes to the floor.

Elfswith regarded the pair of them for a long moment, but did not say another word.

Later that day they left the shelter of the cave, and continued on their way through the mountains, heading gradually down toward the coast. Though the Peladane and his men were keen to be rid of their eel-like guide and his strange friends as soon as they could, it was clear from even the most cursory glance that they did not have a hope of negotiating their way unaided through the terrain they found themselves in now. The Giant Mountains were wild and terrible, and only Elfswith and Kuthy knew the path through them.

It was a land encrusted in ice half a mile thick, snow that never melted, freezing fog, and vertiginous falls. The cold was quite unbelievable, and they realized that they would not survive a single night out in the open. They had to get down to lower ground as swiftly as possible, for even a short delay might be the end of them. How even their guides could find a way through this semi-vertical land, they would never know.

There came sounds, too, from high peaks above and deep valleys below, that were inexplicable to these men from the south. Occasionally a sudden tumble of snow or rocks would be followed by a forlorn hooting noise, sometimes several at once, which would cause Zhang to drop his head and utter a strange, low, hitherto unheard whinny. Whether these hootings were voices or something entirely different, neither Kuthy nor Elfswith would say. They would just wrap their outer garments more tightly about them and forge onward. At such times, Bolldhe was interested to note, even the wyvern would glance about herself nervously, her wings involuntarily raising as though she longed to take to the air and be rid of this place.

Clearly the Aescals were stuck with their present companions for a while longer, and for this, for once, they could only be grateful. They were continually aware that at any moment Kuthy could hop on board the wyvern along with his friend, and the three of them could take their leave with nothing more than a casual wave and a valedictory flick of the creature's tail. Any resentment Nibulus and his men had felt toward the oily duo was set aside for the time being.

Toward the end of the first day the fog lifted somewhat till the sun shone pale and weak in the western sky. By then they had reached a high saddle of the land strung between two peaks, and from there could see clearly for miles both to the north and south. Behind them, the way they had come, it was a land of mountains, frigid and blue. Gripped by cold, the giant peaks crowded together as if to keep out the intrusive light of the sun, resentfully guarding their over-shadowed secrets from prying eyes. Mist crawled constantly up from the depths of sheer-sided valleys that never saw daylight, its clammy breath snaking up snow-filled couloirs and spilling over the narrow cols that topped them.

But ahead of them the Giant Mountains at last tumbled down toward the sea, and the whole of the far north lay spread before them. As before in the Blue Mountains when they had first gazed upon the Rainflats extending below, the feelings of the company combined a giddy mix of excitement and dread. But this time it was magnified tenfold, for their final destination lay there before their eyes:

Melhus.

In that filtered light it was difficult to tell apart the land, the sea, or the ice that covered both, and impossible to discern exactly where the mainland ended and Melhus itself started. But for the bulk of the island, it was clear to all. Like a great oil slick it lay in a dead sea devoid of any color. Black and smoking, pocked with ice fields the hue of dried, flaking vomit, it sprawled north as far as the eye could see. The conical volcanoes that disfigured its surface would occasionally flare like ripe, angry pustules, erupting with a sound like some giant hacking phlegm in the early morning, only to discharge thin streams of glowing matter that spread sickly across the landscape.

Melhus Island, tinged with great chunks of floating ice, lay like a dead leviathan sprawling in the scum of its own putrescence, alien and forbidding.

Bolldhe turned to look at his companions. The evening light made their ruddy faces glow, and the unstill air whipped their hair about. Kuthy even allowed them to take turns with his telescope. They passed it round in trembling hands, and gazed intently at the land below. As they did so, Bolldhe studied their countenances, each one in turn. It was with these men he would be entering that land shortly, and he wished to gauge the measure of them all. Doubt, apprehension, even fear: these he knew they must be feeling. But what other thoughts were going on behind those roseate faces, he could not tell. For each of them, it was a private matter.

And what of himself? What words could possibly describe the confusion of emotions, the tide of memories, and the flashes of prescience that filled his mind? Not even he knew the whole of them. But there was, as he stared upon that dread isle, as the briny smell of the distant sea seeped into his consciousness from afar, an undercurrent of feeling that he could not deny.

Death.

A voice at his side startled him from these dark thoughts. It was Kuthy.

"There it is then, folks: Melhus. I hope you're happy now. And it's at this point that we finally leave Eotunlandt! From this pass onward, we are officially in the far north."

"Officially?" asked Nibulus.

"Well, spiritually. Once we start down this mountain you'll feel the difference. No more weirdness, you'll be glad to know, Paulus."

This last was said with a slight sneer, but the Nahovian mercenary resolutely refused to rise to the bait.

"I don't recall any weirdness in Eotunlandt," he said bluntly, and set off down the slope in long strides, his black boots sinking deep into the fresh snow as he descended.

After a minute, the others caught up with him, Ceawlin flying overhead. "That's the spirit," Kuthy called out from behind. "There's nothing weird about Eotunlandt. . . . Nothing fey."

Paulus did not respond.

"Isn't that right, Elfswith?" Kuthy went on.

"Oh absolutely," Elfswith agreed, and then, half-turning, he waved good-bye in the direction they had come. " 'Bye, girls!" he called back casually.

Paulus carried on down the slope, ignoring their taunts. His teeth were clenched, and his eye fixed straight ahead. But suddenly he stopped dead in his tracks. As if in answer to Elfswith's farewell, he had just heard a chorus of laughter behind him, with one or two voices calling back: " 'Bye, Elfswith!"

It was childlike, girlish laughter, and filled the pristine air with a spangling cadence of musical notes; falling upon Paulus's ears like the soft, chilling caress of snowflakes; burning through his blood as his heart began pounding; echoing among the mountains on the very edge of Eotunlandt; strangely, weirdly, almost like . . .

". . . HULDRES!" Paulus screamed in rage, and spun around.

There, back at the spot where the company had recently been standing, stood a line of five Huldre-girls. Their hair was long, golden and wild. Their tiny bodies were tightly clad in gossamer slips, and they stood on tiptoe waving excitedly at the departing men, and arching their backs in that way only girls can do.

With a scream of fury, the mercenary snatched out his sword and charged up the bank. Snow flew everywhere under his onslaught, but as he approached them, the Huldres began to fade. Though a white glow still emanated from within them, their outlines wavered, their forms faltered and became unsure. To the last, their bright smiles flashed, and their little eyes sparkled wickedly.

Then, just as he finally reached them, they giggled " 'Bye, Paulus" in tiny, singsong voices, and were gone. Paulus's bastard sword hissed through the air toward where they had stood, and he collapsed off-balance, his face plunging with a muffled grunt into the snow.

On the extreme edge of his hearing, as if it came from the other side of the mountains, a final flurry of laughter burst out. Then that too faded, and echoed into nothingness.

With a spluttering gasp, Paulus wrenched himself from the snowdrift and flailed madly about. His one sound eye bulged redly, and the rest of his face began pulsing horribly.

"Oh no," breathed Nibulus. "Here we go again."

There, indeed, they went again. Neither Kuthy nor Elfswith had ever witnessed one of Paulus's fits, and they gladly made the most of the visual treat.

By nightfall they were still traveling, yet were still high in the mountains. The cold had numbed nearly all feeling from their bodies, their faces were windburned raw, and they all felt exhausted by the never ending, monotonous tramp downhill. It was with immense relief, therefore, when Elfswith announced that they were now approaching somewhere they could shelter for the night ahead.

It turned out to be, in fact, another of his homes. Like the previous one, it was a cave, but unlike the previous one—merely a temporary shelter—this one was genuinely a residence of sorts.

Drawing near, however, the men from Nordwas did not even spot that there was a habitation here. When Elfswith proudly announced to them that they had arrived, they peered at the snow banks all around, and shrugged in confusion.

"Where?" Nibulus asked finally, feeling that dark presage of danger an outsider always feels when he has been led into a dead end by a local.

From the outside, Elfswith's proud abode resembled nothing more than a lattice of tree roots, thickly covered in icicles, trailing across the exposed surface of a low bank of rock. But, at a word from its host—or rather a melodic rhyme that seemed to set the air around them tingling—the roots slowly parted and transmogrified into a beaded curtain that glowed warmly with refracted light. Through this the wondering company passed, one by one, into a grotto that was filled delightfully with light, warmth, and color.

"Welcome into my home, you lucky proles," the little man chirped.

The first thought to enter Bolldhe's head was that he had just stepped into one of the cave temples of Muzhtelig-Kuchtyr, found east of the Kro Steppes. Efreet-fingers of fragrant incense coursed idly through the air and wove among the clutter of artifacts and paraphernalia heaped in every available space. Pelts as sundry and diverse as those their host currently wore on his back were strewn across the floor or hung from the walls. Myriad points of glittering light sparkled from every surface that could be seen amid this treasure trove.

Yet this place was too random, its artifacts too eclectic, to be the spoils of any one temple. There seemed to be items derived from every country, culture and cult in Lindormyn, all randomly gathered together and crammed into one place: bells, bongs, bronze gongs, vials and vestments, librams of songs; an armillary sphere, an artillery spear, an orrery, a sextant, staves and wands; amulets, anvils, augers and awls, an anemometer, ancient ciboria, censers, caducei, candlesticks and cawls; figurines and idols, mortars and pestles, chemicals, scalpels, measuring vessels; dried plants in crates, pickled invertebrates, musical instruments, prismatic seeing instruments, preserved beasts, cultures and yeasts, a long-spouted retort, a half-written report, armor, weapons, both long and short; strings of crystals, crystal balls, treasures and relics from ancient halls, and wall upon wall, shelf after shelf of literature, pictures, engraving and inscription of all and every type of description.

It was a true collector's den. There were artifacts that Nibulus and the two mage-priests recognized from their own cults but which had passed out of usage centuries ago. There were ill-favored idols from dark religions right next to silken vexilla bearing images from lighter cults. There were grotesque masks of animist design (some of which Wodeman had himself used) placed next to state-of-the-art alchemical instruments (all of which Finwald wished he had had the opportunity to use). And festooned across it all hung calligraphy-daubed banners of sendal and gauze.

"Quite a collection you have here," Nibulus remarked with an uncertain frown, and immediately realized the lameness of this understatement.

"Knowledge, belief, and magic; past, present and, more than likely, future," Finwald summed up with a touch more perspicacity. He was rapt at the sight of it.

"I wouldn't quite go that far," Elfswith responded, "but I do take an interest in such matters."

They stared at him, but he did not elaborate further, beckoning them instead to take their ease while he walked around singing the various lamps into life.

Soon everyone, Ceawlin and Zhang included, was warm, comfortable and rested. Elfswith produced food in abundance, mainly types of meat, but from where, they could not tell. Strings of tiny silver bells and wind chimes fashioned from various types of scented wood stirred to life, and a soporific ambience hung over all.

Bolldhe stared about in wonder. This to him was like a trophy room of all the lands he had ever visited, and many more besides. He was beginning to wonder again if he really ought to be passing up the opportunity of traveling further with these two, for a while at least. Finwald, too, was indulging in nostalgia, poring over various familiar alchemical tomes, and smiling at certain instruments he recognized from his youth. He was sure he even recognized the golden astrolabe that once stood in the Dome of Spheres back in Qaladmir, all those years ago. Meanwhile both Nibulus and Paulus took time to appraise a cluttered heap of strange and exotic weapons and armor assembled in one corner, while Appa was more morbidly interested in the crowded display of figurines standing upon a shelf in a wall niche.

"Every religion, every land, every material," he muttered, wondering at it all, yet disapproving. He, like the others, could not begin to guess what purposes lay in Elfswith's mind for this collection. Or in the Tivor's, come to that.

Wodeman was less enchanted than his fellows. He contented himself with examining the fantastic collection of musical instruments that were to be found in every part of the cave. He smiled shrewdly, and out of all the company, it was he who began to make guesses about their new companion.

Exactly why Elfswith was suddenly being so hospitable to them (for it was clear his only purpose earlier was to meet up with Kuthy) they did not know. But they guessed it was due to the quiet persuasions of the soldier of fortune himself. Kuthy might be manipulative and self-serving, but it did at least seem that he felt he owed his reluctant "hirelings" something in return for all the trouble he had put them through.

Elfswith even informed them—somewhat sullenly, it had to be said—that they could if they must stay to rest here for a couple of days before embarking upon the final leg of their quest. It came as an even greater surprise to find that Kuthy had further persuaded him into providing them with an assortment of warm pelts for the icy days ahead, and as many other supplies as they could carry.

In all, everything they had been hoping to purchase for themselves at Wrythe. So it seemed too good to be true.

Bolldhe, having come across such generosity from strangers many times before, was content to accept this beneficence as it stood. But Appa could not shake his earlier suspicion that Kuthy and Elfswith were trying to steer them away from Wrythe for their own purposes, especially as neither of the pair had ever disclosed just why they were going there. All they would vouchsafe was that, before going on to Wrythe, they would accompany the party down to the Last Shore.

"Trying to see us safely on our way," Appa commented suspiciously.

The more they tried to understand Elfswith, the more confused they became. Beyond what they saw, they knew nothing of him, not even his race. How could such a ragged little man live in such abundance, even luxury, all by himself in this bleak land?

The only insight they ever gleaned would arrive on the following day.

Elfswith was busy explaining to them how to use the various items of equipment he was lending them for their journey: grapnels, crampons, ice saws, whale-bone skates and skis, cooking equipment. He appeared quite animated in this task, for once almost interested in their expedition. Meanwhile, Kuthy was training Bolldhe, Wodeman, and the mage-priests in the proper use of slicing weapons, starting with a lesson in the correct method of handling a tulwar. During a break in one such session, Finwald drew Kuthy aside and asked him bluntly who and what Elfswith actually was.

"It's the religious thing, isn't it?" Kuthy replied, without answering Finwald's question. "All those idols and symbols in the cave, right?"

He stared long and hard at the young Lightbearer (still awaiting his answer), much in the way Elfswith had regarded him, too, when they had first met. But then Kuthy said: "No, that's not it, is it? You're not interested in religion. You're still an alchemist at heart. Am I right?"

Finwald remained silent, expressionlessly, patiently awaiting his answer.

"Very well," Kuthy concluded, "if you won't tell me about yourself, I won't tell you about my friend."

He waited, but still Finwald was silent.

"Oh, come come!" Kuthy prompted, smiling. "No need to be shy."

But Finwald was not to be goaded. Kuthy was about to turn away, but suddenly stopped and added: "It's a dull old world, really, isn't it, Finwald?"

"What?"

"This world? No matter what you do, how hard you try, how gifted or imaginative you are. It's so tedious. So pointless. Mind you, we're luckier than most; since we don't toil for sixteen hours a day and still live in poverty, with little hope that things will ever improve. Now, *those* folk need religion . . . need to believe in something . . ." He sought for the right words. ". . . Something 'out there.' But for those of us who don't have that need—no, that's not true, as we all need something to believe in, or hope for—well, those of us who can't believe because we've seen too much of the world—"

"What are you going on about?" Finwald interrupted. "You're starting to talk like Bolldhe."

Kuthy laughed again. He was unused to talking so candidly. Again, he searched for the words that would answer this last question from Finwald, the strange young man who was such an interesting enigma, without actually giving anything away.

"Me and Elfswith," he finally confided, "are looking for a way out. Trying to break the chains of this world—and of time."

Finwald thought about this for a second. "That's death you mean, isn't it?"

"I hardly think that takes much searching out."

"I mean, what lies beyond death."

"Religion? Blech! We believe in the promises of religion about as much as you yourself do. No, that might be all right for the peasants, but we're not going to be taken in—gods are the very last ones you'd want to trust in."

"Immortality, then?"

"Shit, no! Life's too dull to prolong forever. No, we're looking for real wild times, unfettered by the constraints of this existence. And there's got to be a way, somewhere out there. I've traveled the world, Elfswith yonder is centuries old, and civilization itself is incalculably vaster and more ancient still. Between the pair of us, if we dig deep enough, maybe some patterns will emerge, some questions might be answered."

"You really *are* starting to talk like Bolldhe."

"He's better than most people, I must admit," Kuthy remarked thoughtfully. "At least that one tries; but he limits himself by his dearth of self-esteem. In his way, he's every bit as fettered by this world as are the ordinary peasants."

"We all are, aren't we?"

Kuthy looked shrewdly at the younger man. "You almost sounded then as though you meant that," he replied. "Don't treat me like an idiot, Finwald. Me and Elfswith have clocked you, even if your mates haven't. You ain't that different to us—are you?"

So, four days after they had first met Elfswith and his wyvern, the company from Nordwas finally set foot upon the frozen causeway. Earlier that day they had left the little man's cave, and traveled, with Kuthy, Elfswith, and Ceawlin, the last stretch of the way down the mountains to the Last Shore. Fully equipped and supplied, and clad in the warmest pelts Elfswith could provide, they set off across the ice bridge to Melhus, waving good-bye to the three others, who were now on their way to the town of Wrythe.

"Freaks!" Nibulus muttered immediately they were out of earshot.

"Deviants, and cowards," Paulus agreed.

"Insolent," Appa chipped in, "but generous, at least." He, of all of them, could not get over the cozy luxury of the massive bear pelt he was buried in—which endowed him with the appearance of a two-legged sea urchin.

"Nomads," added Finwald dismissively.

"Just 'nomads'?" Bolldhe queried.

"Nothing more," Finwald confirmed. "Wandering minstrels roaming the world in search of stimulating experiences to pique, for a time, their jaded sensibilities. Losers in life."

"Hmn, perhaps," said Bolldhe uncertainly, still unsure as to whether he was traveling with the right party or not. Then as an afterthought, added, "never did find out what Kuthy looked like under that hat of his."

Turning to wave to them one final time, Bolldhe was slightly disappointed to see that their erstwhile companions were already stalking off rapidly westward, without so much as a backward glance in their direction.

Then he was amused to see Elfswith suddenly skid and fall flat on his face upon the ice.

Whereupon, he was stunned to see what lurked beneath Elfswith's baggy coat, as it flew up around his shoulders.

A tail. A little, twitching tail, almost like a cow's.

Elfswith leapt up and hurriedly brushed himself off. Simultaneously, he glanced back at the departing travelers, in case they had spotted his little secret—and realized that Bolldhe had.

With a guilty smile, the little man pointed over at Paulus and shook his head. Then he winked conspiratorially and was gone.

2

The Last Town in the World

It was the Dead Time.

He had no idea where he was, or how he came to be here. All was utter darkness. The chill vapor of night air against his skin told him he must be naked, but he could not see for sure. He could not see anything.

Gradually his eyes adjusted, and he found he could now make out shapes. He was lying outside, in some forest. The trees, bark as pale as old bones, stood all around him, hedging him in, spreading twisted boughs above him to keep out the moonlight. Whispering among themselves and creaking with laughter, they crowded round to listen to him, watch his every move. Great, serpentine fingers of old moss hung down out of their branches, and used the excuse of the stirring air to brush against his skin in playful molestation. Within their boles, night creatures lurked and cackled. Mist leaked from the damp, peaty ground, swirled queerly, stinking of decay. In the darkness it could just be seen crawling over the slug-silvered layers of dead leaves, slithering between tussocks of sedge and reed.

It was the Dead Time—and this was the Land of the Dead.

A sudden hiss of wind disturbed the canopy above, and an unwelcome moonbeam touched upon something pale, there at the base of a tree whose roots clung like grotesquely knuckled fingers to the bank on which it perched. Between them was an earthy hollow, hung with growths of moss, grey in the moonlight. He approached, dreamily curious. He brushed away thin strands of old cobweb beaded with motes of soil, which hung adorned with one spinning caddis-fly larva still in its rough case.

He peered closer at the pale thing. It was a headstone. A headstone split down the middle by the never-ending vigor of tiny roots. It was overgrown with dark ivy and cryptogamous algae, feeding on the dead.

Who ever buried their dead in the hollow of a tree?

Compelled by some sick caprice that had surely not arisen from within himself, he found himself kneeling before the stone, and then scrabbling at it, scraping away its fungal garb until his fingernails were at first filthy, then broken, and finally bleeding.

He stopped and stared at a patch of bare moonlit stone with letters engraved. He looked closer, his face just inches from the stone itself.

Two letters.

His eyes strained to see. *Shogg's breakfast, why was he doing this? Wasn't it obvious whose initials they were?* But no—not his own initials. The first looked more like an M, and the second . . .

Then the fear smote him from behind, a sickening fear, a sense of dread malice, animal yet horribly unnatural. It was right behind him. He felt a chill breath of air upon the nape of his neck. It lingered there a while, stroking softly, and then, drawn by the warmth and odor of his sharpened exhalations, fingered its way around his throat, cupped his chin in its enfolding embrace, and rose further to explore his mouth and nose. It smelled of dank, stony caves, and brought with it the hint of a sound: the soft tinkling of golden bells, the strains of weird, foreign music, and the wail of ululating voices accompanied by the rattle of bones.

Every nerve in his body told him to run, or at least turn around. Yet he continued to stare at the headstone. And as he did so he realized now that there were six letters, not two. The name on the stone was . . .

"MAUGLAD."

Who the hell is Mauglad?

Then the blackness and animal terror descended upon him in full, and he could remain there no longer. He spun around, stared about him in panic, saw nothing, then fled blindly off through the trees.

Leaves and twigs reached out for him, tore at his naked skin, grasped at his body as he sprinted away from his enemy. The forest all about him was alive with grunting and snuffling. Images of tiny eyes, bristling backs, and ripping tusks filled his mind. But *it* was coming, and nothing but flight now mattered.

RUN!

Suddenly he saw an opening ahead, a clearing or a path. New hope surged. He sprinted on.

Then stopped dead. A shape, lit by the moon, stood in that opening. Its slitted eyes venom-yellow. Black fingers, bedecked with ancient rings of gold, twitching. A long mace, slung at its side. Malign, evil, sick. Shunned even by the denizens of the Maw, disgorged from the maggot-ridden earth that could no longer contain It.

"Mauglad . . ." the boy said, and his knees gave way beneath him.

Swaggering, it approached. Those creatures of the night too loathsome to be suffered by the world of light, even they now quaked in their holes, retched with fear, begged it to pass through swiftly and be gone. A tattered grey robe hung upon it like dead skin and trailed its damp hem across the marshy ground. A half-decayed nose, upturned like a bat's, sniffed the air for blood. Mist-wraiths flew about its head, whispered murderous humors in bedlam voices. The leafy earth at its feet crawled with nature's darkest pariahs in the wake of its passing.

It stood over the gibbering boy, and drew back its cowl. The boy's eyes dilated in terror, and his mouth froze in a silent scream. The face revealed was that of an insect. With a single convulsion the chitinous mask split wide and its contents spewed forth. A slurry of steaming black leeches wriggled across the ground toward him, drawn by the warm scent of his blood. . . .

With a strangled cry, Gapp awoke, flung his blanket aside, and vomited. It was a chill morning, and the forest all about him was mantled in mist.

"Oh flip," he groaned, still quaking uncontrollably. "What a start to the day!"

Gapp had never liked mornings—or, rather, getting up in the morning. For him, as for most youths his age, that particular activity was the single most detestable aspect of life. It was that dread sense, as soon as he awoke each morning, that he hated the most, that sense of *Wuih! Not another day! Please, not another day!* It's freezing, you haven't had enough sleep, you have to get out of the womb-like warmth of your nest, get dressed in clammy clothes, eat a hateful breakfast of something hard and tasteless, then travel the half-hour or so from mother's house to the Wintus estate through darkness and freezing fog, just so you can do a twelve-hour day of grinding toil among people you can't stand, then return home to a meal and bed again. Such was the lot of Nibulus's esquire—though now sadly separated from his master.

But then a voice from the other side of the clearing reminded him he was not in Nordwas anymore. "What's the matter with you?" it mocked.

It was Methuselech Xilvafloese, his master's mercenary friend, the weird foreigner who seemed to Gapp to be becoming more weird and foreign with each passing day. Gapp groaned again, and wiped a long strand of saliva from his chin with the back of his hand. It seemed to have no end, sticking to him almost as mucilaginously as did Methuselech, and he finally acknowledged defeat.

He had been feeling weak for five or six days now, drained by the constant traveling, no doubt. But it was only in the last day or so that he began feeling sick. Yesterday morning he had thrown up too, and he realized he had been plagued by nightmares ever since being reunited with Methuselech.

At this precise moment, many miles to the east, Nibulus and his company were leaving Elfswith's cave for their final trek down to the Last Shore. Though Gapp was unaware of this, unaware that they were even alive, still his thoughts dwelt upon his master, and he would have given anything to be with the main company once more. It had been five weeks since he had last seen any of them. Gapp sighed, remembering all that had happened to him subsequently. . . .

Then the boy cursed. One misplaced step—*just one shogging step!*—was all it had taken to send him down into the pit. Maybe if he had been that little bit lighter on his feet, that fraction of a second quicker, he could have avoided the Afanc's lunge, and stayed with the company to share whatever fate had become theirs. But the earth had swallowed him up, for better or worse, embraced him in its icy, subterranean waters, borne him far along through its dark places, tormented him with its infernal horrors and, when it had grown bored with him, spat him out in a far distant land, naked and alone.

Well, at least he was not alone now. At least one other of the original company was with him again. If Methuselech could truly be called company. How they had ever managed to meet up again, to arrive at the same place, at the same time, in the middle of the forest, he would never understand even if he lived to be as old as twenty. Gapp's own injuries had been bad enough, his lonely journey long, but Methuselech had hauled himself right out of a *chasm!* He had climbed the very cliff he had fallen down, out from the Valley of Sluagh, a place of such evil it had sent the whole company packing as soon as they heard the keening from within it. Yet Methuselech had been dragging his wounded body through the wilderness for over a week before Gapp had taken his tumble. And had been doggedly following his former companions ever since. That took something more than just physical strength.

But it had paid off. For, by chance alone, the two of them had been reunited, there in the forest town of Cyne-Tregva—that strangest of places with its weirdest of races, the Vetterym. And, ever since, all Methuselech could think of, all he had been doing, was trying to get back to rejoin the main company, no matter how exhausted the pair of them were. For nine days they had been traveling, Gapp and Methuselech riding their antler-headed Paranduzes, and Schnorbitz the forest hound running alongside. Nine days of hard riding through the vast, seemingly endless reaches of Fron-Wudu, using trails known only to the Paranduzes themselves. Every day was the same: they would rise at dawn, eat a hurried breakfast, and be off as soon as they were packed. Then, each gripping onto the Parandus antlers that swept back down from the rear of the creature's head, they would ride, and ride, and ride, pausing only for the briefest of rests, and not stop until it was dark.

Their steeds, Hwald and Finan, were incredible, untiring, like creatures made of a stone as hard and resilient as the flint of their moon-spears. With their multilayered, tasseled scarves fastened firmly over nose, mouth, and neck, they fixed their eyes upon the path ahead and never once deviated from their course. But still Methuselech would urge them on to greater speed, so much so that for Gapp each passing day blurred into the next in a haze of trees eternally flashing past. At nights he could hardly sleep due to the unassuageable cramps and aches that racked his whole body, and from the sensation that he was still riding. But when he did sleep, the nightmares would return, and by morning he felt even more drained than before.

Groggily, Gapp got to his feet and breathed the damp morning air deep into his lungs. He stank of sweat, and his clothes stuck to him like flypaper. He looked around, and noticed the Paranduzes nearby. The two hulking great beasts appeared to be occupied with, of all things, plaiting each other's hair. Their big faces were furrowed with concentration, as though this task was the most important thing in the world to them.

Gapp shook his head. They were strange, those two, such a complete mystery to him that he did not even bother wondering about them anymore. Instead he just put them from his mind. Like every race that dwelt in the forest-town of Cyne-Tregva, they were so bizarre in every way that they were beyond the young Aescal's comprehension. Gapp sometimes wondered if perhaps they did not actually exist but were in fact just some hallucination of his exhausted and foggy mind, a kind of psychogenic coagulation of the creatures he had encountered on this journey and the creatures that inhabited his dreams; the body of a warhorse or a stag, a mace-like glypto-tail, the torso of an ogre or some other giant sprouting from the withers, and a face so much like that of Yulfric, the forest giant who had rescued him a month ago.

Over the past nine days both he and Methuselech had picked up some of their steeds' strange language, mostly functional words and phrases necessary for the simple tasks at hand. But as yet even limited conversation with them was impossible. For their part, the Paranduzes seemed quite happy to obey the wishes of their new master, Methuselech, which for now just meant getting him and Gapp to the town of Wrythe as fast as possible. Gapp had a feeling that, even if they could, the two of them would never have questioned Methuselech's word. When Methuselech had asked the Vetter chief Englarielle for the fastest steeds in Cyne-Tregva, Hwald and Finan were what he had been given: Cyne-Tregva's finest, both under strict orders to do whatever Methuselech wanted. As far as the Paranduzes were concerned, that was all they needed to know. They just ran as instructed, and any words they might voice were nearly always directed solely at Methuselech—never to the esquire.

Gapp felt alone, thoroughly isolated and cut off. He felt more alone now than at any time since leaving Nordwas. What with the silent Paranduzes, his hound, and the obsessed Methuselech Xilvafloese, who drove them all on like a fanatic, there was hardly any conversation. He felt like little more than excess baggage. Why had Methuselech even bothered to bring him along? Why did they always have to travel so fast? And what were they supposed to do once they got to Wrythe? None of it made any sense.

Gapp jumped as he unexpectedly felt a great lump of warm wet meat plunge into his ear, and felt a blast of hot fishy breath over his face. It was the forest hound, tonguing him awake again.

"Thanks a lot, Schnorbitz," he sighed. "That's just what I needed."

He patted the massive hound roughly, and inspected him. Clearly Schnorbitz had already breakfasted, and well, too, judging by the fresh blood on his snout. This dog, which he had known for only a month, he felt to be his only remaining friend now. Loyal, fearless, ferocious, Schnorbitz. Four feet tall at the shoulder, the largest of Yulfric's pack.

But thinking about Yulfric only made Gapp feel guilty. How did the forest giant feel about losing his number-one hound? He had taken Gapp into his home when he had found the youth lost, alone and starving in the depths of Fron-Wudu forest; given him food and shelter, taught him much about forest lore. And when they had traveled north to hunt for the great blackfruit of Perchtamma-Uinfjoetli, the stupid boy had repaid him by wandering off too far and getting caught by the Jordiske. If it hadn't been for Schnorbitz, the fastest of the pack, the only one to penetrate through to the Jordiske's underground lair, Gapp would now be dead.

Well, Schnorbitz had rescued him, but they had never had the chance to find their way back to the giant. For they had been found instead by the Vetters, and taken back to Cyne-Tregva—where Methuselech had by chance also ended up.

At least that part of it had not been Gapp's fault, he knew, but he could not help feeling guilty about effectively taking Yulfric's best hound away from him. And how did Schnorbitz feel about all this? He had never asked to come along on this mad journey to the north. Wouldn't he rather be with his master Yulfric and the rest of the pack than with a weak boy, two multi-part freaks, and— probably the oddest one of all—Methuselech?

Yes, there was trouble there, too. From the outset, Schnorbitz had shown an uncharacteristic mistrust of Methuselech. Right from day one he had refused to look Nibulus's friend in the eye, and as the days progressed, so did his antipathy grow. Only last night, Gapp had awoken in the dark to the sound of a fearful snarling, and had had to step in to prevent Schnorbitz from ripping the mercenary to shreds. Everything was subdued for the moment, as the two of them, Methuselech and Schnorbitz, kept a wary distance from each other. But what had provoked the hound's attack in the first instance, Gapp just could not begin to understand. However, the problem, he sensed, was not with the dog, but with Methuselech himself.

Gapp was becoming increasingly perplexed with his companion as the days went by. Before Methuselech had fallen into the Valley of Sluagh, they had traveled together for more than a month; endured hardship and pain, fought side by side. Men become well acquainted with each other in such times, and Gapp had learned beyond doubt that Methuselech was no zealot. It was camaraderie, not causes, quests or crusades, that had brought him along on Nibulus's campaign—not to mention the promise of cash.

So why all this commitment now? What was it that drove this mercenary on with such fanatical urgency? And where had the old blithe, jocular manner gone?

Methuselech these days kept himself apart from Gapp, and therefore, especially since the boy no longer had his spectacles, he had little chance to see his companion in much detail. But once or twice he had got close enough to look into the other man's eyes, and noticed an intensity in them that had not been evident before, a disturbing intensity more usually seen among fanatical monks.

Then there was the matter of Englarielle and the Vetters. What on earth had Methuselech been thinking when he had told them about the quest? And not only that, but fired them up so, telling them tales of high adventure, of quests, of Rawgrs, of things the poor Vetters could never have any real understanding of? Despite their bestial appearance, those hairy little imps were excellent hunters, agile and ingenious, ideally suited to their environment. But they had *no* knowledge of the world beyond their isolated forest realm. So for Methuselech to deliberately go stirring them up about the Second Coming of Drauglir, actively encouraging them to join in with the mission, launching an entire war party of them off up to the far north, to the Last Shore, where they were to rendezvous with Methuselech and Gapp later, well, it seemed like exploitation of the worst variety, and Gapp could only see disaster for the Vetterym in the very near future. Many times he had tried to ask Methuselech these questions. But Methuselech always evaded any attempt at such interrogation and, when they were not riding, kept himself very much to himself, brooding. Always at a distance.

Yes, that was it: he never allowed the boy to approach him closely. It only occurred to Gapp now, how Methuselech always ate and slept several yards away from him. Actually, Gapp was grateful for this, because Methuselech smelled. He smelled badly. Of course, they all stank, but this was worse. That rancidity that occasionally wafted across to him on warmer nights was like the smell of decay. Gapp would have loved to see beneath the tattered clothes that this once-vainglorious desert warrior kept wrapped so closely about his person. Were those wounds he still bore gangrenous? They certainly smelled it.

But Schnorbitz knew something for sure. Even now Gapp could see the hatred in his hound's eyes as he glared at the mercenary across the clearing, could feel the tenseness in him, hear that strange whine, almost beyond hearing, gathering in his throat.

He followed Schnorbitz's stare, and his heart almost stopped when he saw that Methuselech was returning that wicked gaze, with venom even worse.

That same day, their tenth of nonstop riding, was the worst for Gapp. The previous night's sleep had done him no good, and it was all he could do to stay on Finan's back. True, they were riding hard, as always, but even so, Gapp could not understand why he felt quite so utterly drained and hazy.

So it was an immense relief to him when they encountered the woodcutter, and Methuselech decided to call a halt to their day's ride a couple of hours earlier than usual. The woodcutter himself was a strange little chap, just a solitary Hauger who appeared to live by himself in a small log cabin. It lay in a little clearing at the end of a half-hidden track that wound through dense fern and conifers. They would never have realized it was there at all had not the Paranduzes smelled the smoke. Investigating, they had followed the overgrown path, and found the hut, and its little dome-shaped charcoal kiln. All around were piles of logs and tools scattered about, and from one window the little man's face peered intently out at them.

He did not seem particularly alarmed at the approach of such an outlandish and ill-assorted group. This did not surprise Gapp, however, for he sensed full well the mettle of any that would dwell alone here in Fron-Wudu. They needed to be as hard as the frozen trees they lived among, and as resourceful and cunning as Old Reynard himself. Once he had satisfied himself that they were not hostile—though he had nothing worth stealing—he offered them his hospitality for the night.

They shared some food, and once Gapp had washed the grime of ten days' travel from him with a bucket of cold water in the outhouse, he gratefully accepted the offer of a burlap and wood chip mattress, and fell immediately asleep.

Sometime during the night he awoke on being bitten painfully by an enormous beetle. He crushed the insect and scooped it into his mouth, and, just as he was about to turn over and go back to sleep, overheard Methuselech talking quietly to the woodcutter.

Gapp's ears instantly pricked up. Both Methuselech and the Hauger were conversing in a strange, droning language that Gapp had never heard before. Methuselech's voice sounded hoarse and cracked, as it had for two days now and, in speaking this language, it sounded almost entirely unrecognizable. With no idea of what they were talking about, Gapp again felt that increasing sense of loneliness and isolation.

He peered out at them from under his blanket, as they sat together within the orange halo of a single candle, talking haltingly, but earnestly.

Just listen to them! Chatting like old friends, the boy reflected. *Why am I always kept in the dark?*

He was in fact beginning to feel angry. Ever since being reunited with Methuselech, he had been told virtually nothing. Day after day their leader drove them on as if they were the Wild Hunt, spurning all attempts at questioning. It felt to Gapp as if there was a conspiracy going on, and he, for some reason, was being kept deliberately out of it.

Maybe that's it, he pondered. *Maybe it* is *a conspiracy. Maybe even Nibulus is in on it, but has chosen not to tell me. I wonder how many of the others are—or were—involved. Probably not Bolldhe, or Appa—and definitely not Wodeman— they were always outsiders. But Finwald, on the other hand . . .*

Now there's a thing: it must all have something to do with that "dead snake" of his, two years ago in the forest giant's stockade.

Yes, that had been troubling Gapp ever since the giant had told him about it. But Yulfric had been adamant: two years ago a man called Finwald, matching exactly the description of *the* Finwald, had been wandering lost and starving in the forest. Apparently on a preaching mission to Wrythe. All alone.

It seemed so incredible, so out of character. Finwald was simply not the kind of man who would attempt to travel through all those miles of wilderness on his own. And he was carrying—according to Yulfric—something long and undulating, like a dead snake, wrapped up tight in a sack that he guarded very closely. Why had Finwald never mentioned any of this earlier venture to his companions? It was not as though such an extraordinary undertaking could have just slipped his mind.

It was this subterfuge which Gapp could never quite come to terms with: that a man seemingly as decent and *open* as Finwald should have kept such secrets from his friends.

And when he had told this to Methuselech, well . . . He could still picture clearly the man's expression, that horror in his eyes when, back in Cyne-Tregva, Gapp had told him about Finwald's secret, about the snake-shaped package. His desperation to continue the quest had at that moment multiplied tenfold. That must be what this was all about. That was what had propelled the pair of them upon this mad journey he was now enduring.

And now that they were almost at Wrythe, it was all coming together. Gapp tried to think things through. But what with his exhaustion and that strange vagueness of his mind these few days past, the more he tried to organize his thoughts, the more hopelessly lost he became. Through the droning of the two men conversing and the red glow of the candle fire, his mind drifted lazily, hazily. It was as if he were trying to find his way through a labyrinth, but had already taken several wrong turnings. The deeper he went, the harder it was to retrace his steps. But all the while a writhing snake of fire danced before his tired eyes.

Then weariness took him, and he drifted off into a troubled sleep, a sleep in which he was being chased through a maze of stony passageways by a robed Hauger with an antlered head and a huge axe.

"So what did he say?" Gapp asked Methuselech as they saddled up the next morning. It was a crisp day, but they could smell rain on the wind, and wanted to be away as soon as possible.

For once, Methuselech seemed happy to talk. "Our small friend," he informed the boy, "was just telling me about Wrythe."

"He knows about the place?"

"He does indeed. And, from what he tells me, we should be there some time tomorrow."

Gapp felt a prodigious weight begin to lift from his soul, but instantly checked that before it rose too far. "You're certain he knows what he's talking about?"

"He can't be far wrong. He speaks a little of their tongue, so we must be fairly close."

Methuselech was strapping a sizeable bag of provisions onto Hwald's back.

He had paid for it with one of his golden ear chains, a sacrifice that for some reason made Gapp feel rather uncomfortable. They were especially precious to the Asyphe, one of the focal items making up his dashing image, not mere baubles to be casually used as common currency. Whatever had happened to that care and attention Xilva had previously paid to his appearance?

"I didn't know you spoke their language," Gapp probed, somewhat provocatively. But Methuselech simply smiled at him and continued packing.

Undeterred, the boy pressed on. "What can we expect to find when we get there, then?"

Methuselech paused. "From what he says, it seems the place has changed a lot since I was last—since I last heard about it."

"In what way?"

"In every way, I'd say. If I were you, I'd forget all the old stories and songs about fierce, noble warriors living there. The Fasces alliance that defeated Drauglir was five hundred years ago, and the Oghain residing there haven't had much to do with the outside world since then. They do a little trade with anyone that might pass by, and of course there's those meddling little rats always sticking their prying noses into Vaagenfjord Maw. . . ." He paused, and shook his head violently. "But from what I can gather from yon Hauger, Wrythe has darkened." He stifled an odd little chuckle. *Only what they deserve!* he whispered through gritted teeth.

"You think we'll have trouble?"

"Oh there'll be trouble all right, for some anyway."

"Beg pardon?"

Methuselech looked up suddenly. He had not meant to say this last so loudly. "The woodcutter counsels us to go by cart," he went on, ignoring Gapp's questioning look. "A heavy cart, preferably armor plated, roofed over, and with sturdy shutters. He suggests we don't stop, or slow down long enough for the locals to climb on, and if we have to wind down the shutters, not to do so within biting distance of them."

"Are you *serious?*"

"The Hauger seems so. 'Don't let the sun go down on you in Wrythe.' That's what he said."

"Sounds mighty encouraging," Gapp muttered.

"I shouldn't worry too much," Methuselech commented. "They sound like they've become so primitive now they probably don't even possess proper weapons anymore. I expect they make do with shards of old bone lashed to branches. Nothing sophisticated."

"Right, nothing to worry about then," Gapp replied sarcastically.

Methuselech ignored that. "Listen," he said, "how are you feeling?"

"What?" said Gapp, somewhat taken aback by this sudden display of concern. Then he thought about it. "Um, tired, I suppose."

Gapp had never been one to court sympathy, but even by his standards this was probably the biggest understatement he had ever made about himself. In truth he felt dizzy, disoriented, and befuddled with exhaustion, and although last night's sleep had for once refreshed him a little, he was still sapped of any real vitality.

"Hmn, that's too bad." Methuselech frowned. "Because I want to ride with the greatest haste today."

Gapp's jaw dropped. "WHAT? You mean even faster than usual?"

"We have no choice. We *have to* reach Wrythe before our friends do . . . or better still, at the same time. If what the woodcutter says about the men of Wrythe is true, I don't fancy hanging around in that place any longer than I have to."

"But what d'you really think our chances of meeting up with them are?" Gapp asked earnestly. "They might not even still be alive."

"If they are alive," Methuselech muttered, more to himself than to Gapp, "then we must be there to meet them. Even if it means waiting for them out in the woods, away from the locals."

"And if they've already passed through?"

"That," he admitted, "is my greatest fear. Why do you think I've been cracking the whip so intensely? But if they *have,* we'll have to follow on as swiftly as possible."

"Meth," Gapp tried, though he knew it would be useless, "what is this all about?"

The desert man stopped what he was doing and glared fervidly northwards: "justice," he whispered.

Justice? Gapp considered, by now utterly dumbfounded. *What in hell's name is* that *supposed to mean? Maybe he really is mad. Maybe he was even before we lost him back in the mountains . . . That would certainly explain why he gets on so well with Peladanes.*

But the exhaustion had caught up with him, and all he managed was: "What the heck are you talking about, old man?"

He did not even have time to flinch away. With the speed of a chameleon's tongue, Methuselech had grabbed Gapp by the shirt, and before he knew what was happening, he found himself dangling in front of the mercenary like a rabbit. As their eyes locked, Gapp realized for certain that there really was something wrong with his companion.

"JUSTICE!" Methuselech hissed. "Once and for all! That's what I'm talking about! And I will not have a little turd like you slowing me down, understand? No one will get in my way. Finwald's sword must *not* go to the Maw!"

He dropped the boy, and spun away. "Pox, that squeaky voice! Like angels scraping their nails on the inside of my skull!"

The Hauger emerged to see what the fuss was about, but Methuselech merely waved him a curt farewell, and mounted his Parandus Hwald. Gapp managed an apologetic smile, and followed him on Finan.

What an armhole! he thought sullenly. *I can't believe he was ever a friend of Nibulus.* Gapp did not see why he should have to put up with this sort of treatment. He had come through much worse than Methuselech had endured on this trip. He was better than him. In fact, if he had thought Finan would agree to it, he would have walked out now on the miserable old sod. Gone back to Cyne-Tregva, or Yulfric's.

But he felt, truly, so unutterably tired, and he knew with certainty that it would now take all his failing reserves just to get him as far as Wrythe.

Come what may, for the foreseeable future, he was stuck with Methuselech Xilvafloese.

It was the darkest part of the night, and Methuselech, alone with his inner ponderings, was standing alone in the darkest part of the forest.

He breathed in the cold night air deeply, and smiled. He liked this place— in as much as he could like anything in this detestable existence. Yes, breathing could be good sometimes—in the right place. Back there where he had climbed out of the darkness, he had breathed profoundly, sucked the mountain air deep into his lungs. He had smelled it, tasted it, held it there a while and essayed to experience its earthy warmth and wholesome vibrancy once more, and all the good it might do him. And for a moment he had indeed believed it to be something of worth.

But that had been a lie. For there was no sensual pleasure for him to delight in. Nevertheless he had held it in for nearly an hour—determined to enjoy it after all these years—before remembering that such was not the way with breathing; one was supposed to expel again, then repeat the whole process, again and again and again . . . In the end, he had simply stopped trying altogether. So much effort for so little gain.

Like so many other things: food, drink, the simple act of chewing or swallowing. All these things he had missed at the very beginning, yearned for them achingly. But after the first hundred years or so the desire for such corporeal delectations had faded.

But at least on this night, here, he could enjoy a breath or two, for old times' sake. This forest clearing reminded him so much of home, so unimaginably long ago now; the darkness, the closeness, that sense of something unhallowed. Trees stood like the stone columns of his subterranean temple, their bare limbs arching out above to form a fan-vaulted ceiling, dripping with the mist that hung heavy in the air like the cardamom incense from his sacred braziers. Here and there, the occasional screech of a bird or beast: lives snatched away in the night, devoured—sacrifices to the inhuman god, the Rawgr he had once served but would now defy. The black loathing and insanity distilled from eons of inconceivable torture were fueling a weapon soon to be unleashed upon a world grown sleepy. He was mere days from the Maw, and then, after all these ages, justice would be meted out, and meted out in full.

If—and only if—he could reach the Maw before those meddlers from the south.

Ah, how things changed! His old purposes, desires, loyalties. They had died years ago, as had his former life. And judging by the increasing pungency from beneath his robes, so would this new life if he did not do something about it.

He looked down at his robe. Stiff with filth, it was wrapped tightly about him like the rough sheath of a chrysalis. He opened it and was straightaway assaulted by the sickly-sweet stench of his wounded body. The voluminous shirt and trousers that had once billowed out in the wind like the crisp white sails of an ocean-striding bison, were now the hue and texture of an ulcer. Like a heap of discarded septic bandages in a derelict hospital, they were caked with dried blood and pus, and stank of infection and death.

Back then he had always feared death, feared it with an obsession, and it was this obsession that had chosen for him his trade. Yet now, in his wisdom, he knew there were things far worse than death.

Take life, for example.

"A life in death, and days that will soon be no more . . ."

Or so that bard had once sung. Maybe he should have listened more to the bards, instead of merely hooking their lungs out through their mouths. Those lyrics certainly seemed to speak true of his current situation. He peeled back the clothes further and gingerly prodded the skin beneath. It was going bad. Very bad. Methuselech frowned in consternation as his finger sank in a full inch. The decay was worsening with each day that passed and, despite his best efforts, it was spreading.

As a necromancer, of course, he should have been fascinated by this process, eager to see what happened next. But time was running out, and his exigency brooked no delay. As it was, had it not been for the timely arrival of the boy, his skin would probably have begun sloughing off him days ago. The wounds from the fall back in the mountains had been terrible, and even with the sustenance the boy provided, this body would not last him much longer.

He glanced over at his companions. They were fast asleep, of course, and how could it be otherwise? He had driven them harder that day than ever before. By the Rawgr's ichor, how those Paranduzes could run! Did they never tire? Both Hwald and Finan lay nearby, legs folded beneath them, heads upright, arms folded before their chests. Each faced in an opposite direction, out into the night, guarding the campsite like a pair of sphinxes. But they *were* asleep, or at least as asleep as a Parandus could be. There was still a subconscious vigilance behind those lidded eyes. But, Methuselech thought with a smile, it was directed outward, not to any dangers within the camp. Short of an attack by predators, nothing would wake them now.

The desert mercenary's black eyes flicked from them to Gapp, who lay inert, sprawled face down upon the ground where he had dropped as soon as they had halted for the night. Since then—hours ago now—he had not moved once. Not even twitched. It was only the faint stir of his breathing that confirmed he was alive at all.

Methuselech smiled. Would the poor fool have been able to sleep so well knowing that his friend here had once been what he was? Or the real reason why he himself had been dragged along on this journey?

No, the boy knew so little. But despite the strength being leeched out of him almost daily, he still retained enough wit to wonder. Oh yes, he never ceased wondering! Always asking questions, especially about the mage-priest's affairs. Fleetingly Methuselech wondered whether he ought to tell the boy the truth about Finwald's little adventure two years ago. It might work to his advantage.

But no—better not to open that can of worms. Not yet, anyway. Who could tell what the morrow would bring? What was Wrythe like after five hundred years? No, there were too many unknowns to consider still. Best to stick to his plan for the time being. The boy was useful, and might prove useful for a little longer yet.

And healthy! He and that great slobbering brute that slept by his side (mercifully exhausted, too) were true forest dwellers. Gapp's juices were young, hot, salty, charged with vitality, pulsing with life.

Methuselech's face curled into a grin.

"Ready when you are, Master Greyboots," he said, and crouched over him like a bat.

"Remember," Methuselech was saying, "the Oghain do not trust outsiders, and they will not tolerate anyone disturbing what they consider is best left alone. Our mission *must* be kept secret, so we'll have to go in the guise of skin traders. And if Nibulus hasn't passed through yet, we will have to stall for time, maybe a long time . . . I say, are you listening to me?"

Gapp clearly was not. The younger man rode by his side as if in a trance, his eyes port-red in a death-pale face, alternately nodding forward and jerking back upright. Methuselech, now that he had an idea of how close they were to Wrythe, was allowing an easier pace. Even so, Gapp was spent, his head fuzzy with exhaustion. Earlier that morning he had vomited until his insides were hollow and sore. Even now he could not rid himself of the taste of bile.

He had no idea of the time of day. He was not even certain if he was awake or not. Sometimes he seemed to be, for he could see the trees, a ghostly hardwood army marching silently toward him out of the mist, passing by on either side in never-ending ranks. But even when he knew his eyes were shut, still this vision continued.

At other times he did not even know where he was. And on one occasion he had struggled to remember why he was here. *Something about a mission?* Yet even in his more lucid moments when he did remember, none of it seemed all that important. Not even his family, his friends, or his own life. He felt he was losing himself bit by bit. Like a drowning man drifting off into peaceful unconsciousness.

The cold though, he could feel: it was bitter. But, like his mind, his body was numb, and he was past discomfort. Past all human feeling. Almost all vitality had been drained from him, and he was wandering in the world of the half-living, neither in this world or the next.

Methuselech regarded his companion briefly, then bade the Paranduzes slow down further. He leaned over close to Gapp, and said into his ear: "We're traders, all right, just traders. Seal pelts, whale bone, walrus ivory, elk hide, that sort of thing. Who we really are, who we were, that's in the past. Forget about it."

Gapp made an attempt to wrap his cloak about himself against the forest mist. *I know who I am,* he thought, *but I have no idea about you.*

Yet to be honest, with each day that passed in the company of the mercenary, he was even beginning to forget who he himself was. He rubbed the itchy swelling on each of his wrists, and rode on.

"Stop!"

Methuselech's hiss of command cut through the silence, and jolted Gapp from his torpor as if an icy hand had just slapped him across his red, raw face.

"Mmm?" he managed, blinking the frost out of his eyes, and gazed around at his surroundings.

It was an empty landscape, dreary and dead. The sun, which had reached its pitiful zenith only moments earlier, Gapp was sure, now sat just above the western horizon, cold and colorless in an iron-grey sky. Already the moon could be seen, a pale scimitar reaching the end of its cycle, insubstantial and ghostly. The black shapes of trees, lifeless and petrified, slick with freezing fog, stood all around, silent watchers unmoving in the still air. Gapp noted how much they had thinned out, and from that realized that they must finally be nearing the end of Fron-Wudu.

He was struck then by an overwhelming sense of isolation. They were actually now *north* of the great forest! It really did feel like the edge of the world.

"Over there! See?" Methuselech whispered, pointing off to their left. Both the Paranduzes were stamping in agitation, and growling to each other in their strange language, clearly frightened at something, and even Schnorbitz was whining.

His eyes followed Methuselech's pointing finger. He squinted hard.

"Just trees," he said optimistically. "Nothing else."

Then he too saw it. Though it appeared blurred from his shortsightedness, he could see a light moving unsurely among the trees. How far off it was, neither of them had any idea, so its size and nature was indeterminate. At first Gapp guessed it to be some form of incandescent flying insect, for it flitted

about in such a wayward manner. Then it became clearer that it was still a fair
distance away, and must therefore be considerably larger.

"A torch?" Gapp suggested. "Or a lantern? Maybe we've arrived."

Methuselech paused. "No," he decided at length. "Too pale to be naked
flame, and a lantern would need to be held much steadier. . . ."

It was getting nearer, they could sense. Dancing through the trees, it came
toward them: a white figure, blurry and diaphanous, but moving with a speed
no human would be capable of.

Instantly Gapp's brain was overwhelmed with terror. In his mind's eye he
saw again the Ganferd in the Rainflats. In rapid succession, several other images flashed through his head: the look of terror and despair in his horse's eyes
as the poor animal sank to his death; Paulus hacking at the animated trees like
an avenging black-souled harpy . . . the baby-skings fluttering in the
treetops . . .

A hand closed around his shoulder. With a cry he spun about, and beheld
the foreign mercenary; gaunt, rank, and dripping, as much a part of the forest
as the trees all about them; silent and expressionless.

Had he led him to this frightening place deliberately?

"What is it?" Gapp hissed, partly to break the spell of fear by engaging in
rational talk with his strange companion.

But Xilvafloese's reply did nothing to reassure him. "The people of Wrythe
are human, but that thing is nothing human or anything like it."

Here, as in the Rainflats, Gapp was smitten by that empty feeling of utter
remoteness from civilization. This was wilderness, chaos. Hard, cold, and brutal. He was no more than a naked candle flame in the . . .

Gapp peered back into the gloom, and gasped. The floating fire, or whatever it was, had disappeared. And, with it, the last of twilight's gleam that only
seconds ago had lit the forest. It was nighttime.

"Wh-what's happening?" he stammered. "Why's it gone dark all of a sudden?"

Then he became aware that not only was it pitch dark, but all sound, save
that of his own voice, had faded. Both Paranduzes stood stock-still, as if petrified; he could feel the stony rigidity of Finan's body beneath him.

"Methuselech," he whispered, "what is this darkness?"

No answer.

He tried again, this time the panic trembling in his voice: "Meth—"

A low gurgling growl rattled at his side. He stretched his hand down, and
felt the bristling hairs of Schnorbitz's raised hackles.

Then he too froze in paralysis, as he heard what they had already sensed.

Laughter. Children's laughter, shrill and playful, like demon claws scratching down glass, coming from the darkness all around them, bringing the darkness with them, turning his blood to ice.

Gapp's eyes bulged sightlessly, and he could not breathe. He was shaking from head to foot. A sudden scraping at his side drew his terrified face around. He could see nothing. A further rasping scrape. What—?

A flurry of light danced about, and Gapp realized that Methuselech had lit a torch. The agony of his terror subsided a little. He, Methuselech, Hwald, Finan, and even Schnorbitz now strained their eyes into the dimly illumined woods around them.

Nothing. No children, no floating lights, no ghostly apparitions. Just trees, their bark as pale in the torchlight as dead men's skin. Methuselech swept the burning brand about, but still there was nothing to be seen. And the laughter had gone.

The silence was torn by a strangled gasp from Gapp. The torchlight had briefly alighted upon a face, pale and unnatural, not twenty paces from where they stood, and gazing at them from the space between two trees. Methuselech heard the boy's cry, and brandished the torch in the direction the quaking youth was pointing to.

The face, however, had disappeared.

"Move. Now. Quickly," Methuselech instructed levelly, and no one argued. They cantered through the awful darkness of the woods in the unsteady torchlight without any idea of the direction they were taking. Minutes of this guarded retreat passed. There was no sound of pursuit, but fear, though less intense, still filled their hearts. All Gapp wanted to do was reach the safety of Wrythe, but he knew with sickening certainty that they had no idea which way to go, and were in all probability fleeing instead even deeper into the forest.

Soon they could feel they were heading uphill. Still resisting the urge to flee in panic, the Paranduzes nevertheless plowed up the slope with great speed and effort. Gapp could smell the hot vapor of animal sweat rising from them, could sense their hooves sinking into the deep carpet of pine needles. At this incline he had to lean forward on Finan's back to keep himself from falling backward, but in doing so almost gouged out his eye on the unseen plume of antlers just before his face.

The slope leveled out, and in the light of Methuselech's torch Gapp could see that they had come to an area of limestone karst towers. Ahead was a gap between two such formations, and into this narrow defile they rode.

Just then, and without warning, Hwald reared up and let out an unearthly sound—something between a bellow and a whine, whether in anger, pain, or fear Gapp could not tell. Methuselech was almost pitched from his back. In the ensuing confusion of stamping hooves, panicking cries, and flashes of flame-lit images, Gapp looked up and saw the boy.

A naked boy, perhaps five years old, white and emaciated but unusually hirsute, was perched like a gargoyle partway up the rock face to their right, mere yards away. He—it—was staring down at them, softly singing a childish rhyme to himself. Gapp shuddered in a convulsion; it was not the aberrance of this night-borne apparition that chilled his heart so, but more the look in those eyes. There was nothing feral, cruel or insane in their regard. It was simply the expression of casual interest that a hunter might reveal on witnessing the torment of a terrified prey.

"Go!" Gapp wailed, and spurred Finan on through the defile. Primal terror had taken full possession of him now. Down the cleft between the two karst towers they sped, down and down into blackness. No care had he for his companions, no thought for whether they followed, or even if they yet lived. The whole world was one of blackness, meaningless noise, and horror.

On the two of them sped, guided only by the Parandus's instincts. There was no thought for what lay ahead, no plan beyond flight. Then suddenly a diabolical cry pierced the air right beside Gapp, and a white shape flashed before his eyes. A skritche-owl, harbinger of his death. He was flung sideways from Finan's back as the beast tripped and crashed to the ground. There was a momentary weightlessness as Gapp was hurled through the blackness; for a second that seemed much longer, he truly believed he was dead and his tattered soul was floating through an eternal limbo of darkness.

Then the world smote him with its reality, as he plunged into the freezing black mud of a bog.

Seconds, maybe minutes, passed, till Gapp finally hauled himself from the sucking ooze. Half-concussed, he was dimly aware that he could see clearly again. The darkness had gone, but not because of any torchlight. It was real light, twilight. The light of the sun's last rays. And coming up behind him was Schnorbitz, with Methuselech on the other steed. Finan pushed himself off the ground and joined them, and there they all stood, together again, staring about in bewilderment.

"All right, Methuselech?" Gapp queried, although what he really meant was: *Any ideas about what just happened?!*

In the sudden silence, though, none of them had the faintest clue. In fact now that everything seemed normal again, they were not even sure it *had* happened.

"I . . . suppose we'd better be on our way again, then," said Methuselech. "It really will be dark soon."

" 'Spose so," Gapp agreed. They checked the saddlebags for spillages and wiped themselves down, saying nothing, feeling somewhat odd and still bemused by the surreal quality of their situation.

"Uh, before we go any farther," Methuselech suggested, "I think your dog has something to tell you. . . ."

Gapp looked sharply over at Schnorbitz. He stood motionless, hackles still raised, staring toward a nearby outcrop of rock. At first Gapp could not make out anything there. The hound appeared to be growling at a bare patch of stone, like a cat staring at ghosts above the mantelpiece. But as he squinted, his skin suddenly began to crawl with a fresh sheen of ice; for he could now make out two vague shapes, leaning up against the rock face.

Two people stood, looking back at them, with expressions that were wholly inscrutable. Two normal humans, or as close to normal as one could get in this land. In Fron-Wudu, with its fungal growths and eerie hooting echoes, they probably fitted in perfectly; back in Nordwas, however, they would definitely swivel a few heads.

"*Horse and Hattock!*" Gapp breathed, "Get me out of here! Who *are* these twisted aberrations?"

Both stood well over six-and-a-half feet tall, as gaunt and wan as a withered silver birch, and wore a simple one-piece burlap outer garment, shapeless and drab. One held a sodden clump of earth in one hand, and a bundle of twigs in the other, which he was chewing at idly as he regarded Gapp and his group. The other had what appeared to be a spinal column around her neck, and from a pocket protruded what must surely have been a human femur, with a few holes bored regularly along its length like a flute. Their unusually dome-like heads were almost bald save for the occasional wisp of ginger hair. Their tiny and sand-caked eyes displayed painfully enlarged nictitating membranes.

At first, like the travelers, they made no move, just continued to stare at them in the same way that the devil-boy had just minutes earlier. But then they slowly approached. There did not appear to be any immediate hostility in their demeanor, but neither was there any suggestion of warmth. With those dead eyes, the set of their hard, slitted mouths, and the cheekbones jutting from their faces like the limestone karst towers did from the forest floor all around, they exuded that stony inhumanity that Gapp had witnessed in the refugees from Hawdan Valley years before. There, the winter had been so harsh that the inhabitants had been reduced to eating their own . . . Gapp shuddered at the memory.

"These people are from Wrythe?" he asked doubtfully. Clearly they were not the fierce, noble warriors of legend.

"Back then, they had big red beards, wore bushy musk ox pelts, and were almost as strong as the bears they hunted," Methuselech recalled, staring in disbelief at the two tomb dwellers before him. "—so the old stories tell us."

The Oghain of yore were well documented as having skin as fair as the walrus ivory they loved so much as adornment. These two, however, had the same complexion as a night-watchman in a graveyard—maybe even one of his charges. With skin semi-transparent and blue-veined, one might suppose they now preferred hunting jellyfish to walruses. The only real color either of them had to their flesh was the odd bright red, angry-looking scab upon neck or face. These were the most revolting things Gapp had ever seen growing on a human being, and second only to the Nycra in the mineshaft a month ago. Even the nine-eyed carbuncle that had opened on the back of his brother Ottar's neck a year or so back was less of a visual and olfactory offense than this, and that had been so bad that for several weeks Ottar's head had been forced forward onto his chest. Gapp recalled with distaste that it had leaked so much during the night that when he got up in the morning his pillow would rise with him. While he slept, a constant line of ants wound over the blanket to feed from it, and it had smelled so badly that his mother had been forced to burn dead dogs just to mask the stench.

Methuselech gave the boy a knowing smile, and said, "Welcome to Wrythe."

Gapp's arrival in Wrythe would leave an indelible impression for the rest of his life, however long that might be. Their terrifying experience just prior to this encounter with the two Oghain had snapped the boy fully out of his torpor; what blood Methuselech had left to him now surged powerfully through his veins, and he felt distinctly charged, his senses fully alive.

Following their creepy guides, they proceeded through the forest until they eventually reached the first signs of habitation. Still within the woods, Wrythe had the air of a place that was not quite real, or as Gapp reflected: *not part of our world*. It was an experience not dissimilar to entering another dimension, a phantom realm that did not welcome outsiders.

At first they were led between more karst towers and steep, stony knolls. He noticed the latter contained caves here and there, some closed off with wooden gates or doors, while others were unbarred and open to view. Several had lamps or fires glowing within them, but sputtering and vapid affairs that served only to emphasize the drear aspect of this cheerless place. Various troglodyte figures could be seen huddled in the dank fetor within, each one as pale, insipid and ill-favored as their guides. As the wayfarers progressed through this network of defiles and gullies, they became increasingly aware of hissing noises above them and to either side. Glancing up, they saw unfriendly eyes glaring down at them, and could see other shapes flitting about in the darkness, gibbering sickly.

A wider space opened up around them, barely visible in the last vestige of twilight's gleam. Here they heard other voices, surprisingly cheerful voices, and high-pitched laughter.

Gapp shuddered on recognizing it was the laughter of children. But it was not like before, for this time they were *real* children, *Ogginda* playing a youthful game at the day's ending. Through the gloom and freezing fog only dim images could be seen, but as the newcomers drew closer they could see that they were now walking through a cemetery. The Ogginda—skinny little kids in rags, too preoccupied with their game to notice the newcomers, were darting from headstone to headstone like wraiths.

As they passed by, Gapp watched a group of them gathered off to one side. They appeared to be playing with something on the ground, and were giggling feverishly. Drawing level with them, it could be seen that they were doing something . . . . Gapp was not sure, but it sounded very painful.

A little gray shape suddenly darted out from this group and bit Methuselech savagely on the leg. This was instantly followed by the dull thud of the mercenary's boot against the child's head, and its startled cry was cut off as if smacked against a headstone.

Gapp's head spun round in amazement, but Methuselech did not slow his progress.

"Aren't you going to check if—"

"Better not stop," Methuselech warned. "Must keep up with our guides."

Gapp looked ahead and realized that indeed neither guide had paused, though the female had turned her head to watch the exchange, and was now smiling feebly.

"It's fortunate we met up with these two," Methuselech explained, leaning down from the saddle to wipe his boot. "I doubt we'd have got this far into town without their help. These people are *not at all* as I remember them—remember the stories about them."

Soon, thoroughfares began to appear in the form of single-track lanes, deeply rutted. They were mist laden and empty save for the occasional standing figure that materialized before them, gaunt, shapeless, unmoving. It was so, so quiet that Gapp flinched at the occasional sound of the Paranduzes' hooves crunching the frozen puddles in the ruts.

Then finally the first houses came into sight: dilapidated cabins overgrown with creeping ivy. From their windows came no light, but claw-like fingers could be seen pulling aside net curtains of cobweb, and waxy faces glared at the travelers as they passed.

Gapp felt the same trepidation he had experienced when Yulfric had led him through the deepest, darkest tracts of the forest, felt the same menace as that from the hooting primates on either side. But although the lusterless stare of a hundred dullard eyes watched their every movement, there was no attempt as yet to close in on them, or to hinder their passage, or divert them.

More hovels. More people. Unblinking, unspeaking, unmoving. The outsiders kept close behind their two guides, protected by whatever sanctuary they afforded them, following them dutifully to wherever they were taking them. Gapp kept one hand upon the hefty bronze machete given to him by Ted the Vetter blacksmith, while with the other he grasped Finan's antlers, feeling reassurance in their solidity under their velvet coating.

It was now completely dark: night had fallen in full. The bleary glow of disembodied torches began to appear, and with them more people. As they continued through the streets of Wrythe, Gapp began to notice something about the inhabitants' faces. Though each face looked strange, in the way one would expect in any close, isolated inbred community, here they could be seen falling into two distinctive categories—like clans.

There were the Doll-Faces, of which their guides were fully paid up members. Doll-Face. That was what Gapp had been called by a girl he had once been after, referring to the misshapen wax monstrosities she used to stick pins into.

Then, more disturbingly, there were the ones he dubbed the Wire-Faces. At one point the party was heading toward a large stone building he assumed to be their destination. Gapp dismounted and was just about to step up to the door when there was a sudden moan of alarm from the crowd of onlookers, and his way was barred by two guards.

"Oh . . . my . . . Ghod!" he exclaimed, and found that he had remounted his steed in about three-tenths of a second.

Whereas most Oghain seemed to move around by dragging their feet, the movements of these two were considerably more purposeful. They stalked rather than walked, both wearing long, leather aprons stiffened by a stinking fish oil of sorts, and by deep-soaked, dried blood. Their bare arms were knotted with muscles that looked as hard as iron, and in their shovel-like hands, each held a cheesewire-like garrotte.

But it was their faces that had caused Gapp to remount with such celerity. Jarring in their subhumanity, they looked like the result of some demonic cross-breeding experiment gone hideously awry. Angry little eyes ringed with baggy red flesh smoldered in a face of glistening skin, bound tightly within a crisscross of rusty wires. These contorted the face underneath and bit deeply; in places the skin had begun to grow over the wires, as tree bark will do, given time.

Gapp's mind suddenly reeled in shock and his stomach lurched in nausea. The farther they headed north, the more the world seemed to become like hell, and here in Wrythe they had found hell's very portals.

"They look like the Face-Eaters of Fram Island," Gapp muttered, recalling a darker episode of Wyda-Aescaland's recent past.

"Face-Eaters?"

"The Peladanes managed to capture a group of them once," Gapp explained. "Warlord Artibulus would keep them on hooks, and only bring them in chains out to frighten our enemies."

"I'd say that's the idea here, too. We're clearly not wanted in yonder building. Come, let's follow our guides; there are rather too many people gathering now for my liking."

So they continued through the town, keeping close together, not letting the shuffling horde of followers get too close. Methuselech looked about thoughtfully.

"Wrythe, eh?" he murmured to himself. "Neighborhood's certainly gone downhill since I was last here. . . ."

Ever since they had encountered the pair of locals, not one word had passed between the two groups. Now Methuselech decided to break the silence. He leaned over toward their guides and spoke a few words to the Ogha—the male—in that same droning tongue Gapp had heard him use with the Hauger two nights ago. The Ogha turned to reply in the same language.

Methuselech frowned. "I think he's saying they're taking us to an inn."

"An inn?" Gapp exclaimed. "Are you sure?"

"My knowledge of their language comes from the ancient manuscripts," he explained, "so it's difficult to know exactly what he told me. But I think I'm right."

Gapp was not so sure. "Surprised these people even know what an inn is."

"Actually, the place sounds quite hospitable: wood-paneling, clean sheets, venison on the spit, and a huge samovar of piping hot mulled wine."

"Really?"

"Of course not, you bloody idiot! Probably just an old yurt or a cellar—somewhere they can secure us properly."

"Oh Frigg, they're going to kill us, aren't they? Eat our faces and suck the marrow from our bones! They could do anything they want to us out here."

Soon however, they did arrive at the inn. As Methuselech had guessed, it was little more than a yurt. Between two tall stone buildings lay a gap piled with frozen, frost-covered refuse that was crawling with rats, eyed by a few half-dead dogs too weak to chase them. Just beyond that lay what was to be their quarters: a small, circular, drystone hut roofed with a conical canopy of sealskin that stank even worse than the refuse. Its stone wall rose only about three feet high, and as they picked their way through the discarded bones and rasping dogs, the travelers could see that the hut was partly below ground level. A short flight of steps descended to the door, and once the two guides had shoveled away the refuse that obstructed it, Methuselech, Gapp, and Schnorbitz were led inside, while Hwald and Finan took up guard atop the flight of steps.

The Ogha eventually succeeded in lighting a lamp, then without a single word, simply left them. The Oga hitched up her robe provocatively, then she too walked out.

"A frayed and ragged people inhabiting the frayed and ragged edge of the world," Methuselech tutted, "and gradually coming further undone, thread by thread."

Gapp shivered violently. He was not sure which was the worst: the local people or the place they were in. He looked about at their abode for the night, and grimaced. Freezing cold, utterly drab, and stinking, it seemed more like a public latrine than an inn. The light from the only lamp was dim, the sealskin roof kept fluttering in the wind, and there was not a single stick of furniture. He supposed he should feel grateful they had a roof over their heads for once, but he did not. Icy water covered much of the floor and dripped down the walls, and the only part of the floor free of it was a low dais composed of flag-stones positioned at the far end.

"I think I'd rather be sleeping out in the woods," he muttered, and began to unpack.

Gapp got little sleep that night. It was dank and wholly unpleasant inside the hut, and throughout the night he was plagued by biting insects that dropped from the roof, or by the murmurings of the Oghain hovering outside, who just would not go away. Soon after their arrival, a soft clawing was heard at the door and, on opening it, they had been presented with a few bales of dried rushes to use as bedding. Other than that they had not been disturbed.

Not long after, the Paranduzes came in and joined them, vying for the scant dry space available. Both Hwald and Finan preferred to sleep outdoors, but on this occasion even they chose to make an exception. When Gapp eyed them questioningly, they merely nodded toward the door and shook their heads. Nervousness was evident in their constantly shifting eyes.

Gapp decided to check it out. He pulled open the door a crack and peered outside. Though it was still foggy, by the light of a brazier set up a few yards away he could see a throng of faces staring back at him. Grey-skinned and red-eyed, not one of them moved, and not a word passed between them. Gapp slammed the door shut and fastened it, then swiftly retreated again to the rear of the hut.

"Schnorbitz!" he hissed to the forest-hound. "Come here, boy."

Gapp was only just keeping himself together. Weeks of hardship in the wilds; a twelve-day forced ride with a man who had now become a complete stranger to him; sickness added to disorientation and exhaustion. And now this dark village of the damned with its fungoid denizens.

But among the multitude of fears and worries that were currently crowding his mind, there was one nagging question that would not be stilled.

"Methuselech," he whispered, "do you really think we'll be able to find a silver sword in this primitive place?"

His companion, wrapped up in his own soiled cocoon, replied, "I beg your pardon?"

"Well, I mean, just look at them," Gapp said, gesticulating toward the door and the shambling throng that lurked beyond it. "Silversmithing's a rarity even back home in Nordwas, and these lot look as if they've forgotten even how the wheel works."

But if Gapp had any doubts earlier, the response Methuselech now gave redoubled them. "What are you talking about? Why do you need a silver sword?"

"You—what? . . . a silver sword—to do the job . . . You said so yourself that the folk of Wrythe are renowned silversmiths. How else are we going to . . . you know, do it?"

But Methuselech simply snorted scornfully. "Don't you concern yourself, boy. I'll worry about that."

Gapp, still confused, drew his bedroll tightly about him. But first he made sure Schnorbitz was between him and the stranger at the far side of the dais. As if the dog sensed his fear, it glared hatefully at their companion.

Maybe I'd be safer out there with the freaks, Gapp wondered.

3

The Majestic Head

"We're still alive, then," Gapp murmured when dawn finally broke.

He rose stiffly from his nest and flung the door open to breathe in the cold morning air. The yurt stank like an exotic strain of malignant fungus, and his grimy sweat felt as if it had hardened into scales.

"Oh, they're gone," he noted, and yawned.

The street outside was almost empty, save for a few limping passersby, coughing in the mist. Last night's crowd of silent spectators had presumably dissipated sometime during the newcomers' long sleep, so they were now alone to enjoy the privacy of their little laystall. The air smelled of mist, congealed fat in the frozen gutters, and just a hint of burnt saucepan scrapings.

"Man alive," he breathed, "what a place!"

Just as he was about to go back indoors, he noticed a large tray had been left by the door. It had four bowls of what looked like grey bread with strips of dried skin, a large urn of cabbage water, and a big meaty bone for the dog.

"Breakfast," he announced, not bothering to wonder who had fetched it, and hauled the tray inside.

It was only then that he noticed Methuselech was absent. That did not surprise him, since the mercenary had been fretting for the last twelve days about the importance of arriving here before Nibulus and their other companions. He had probably gone off to inquire from the locals as to their whereabouts. As far as Gapp was concerned, the only important matter right now was the food before him.

It was lukewarm, insipid, and formed a waxy layer on the roof of the mouth, but Gapp and the others gorged themselves enthusiastically. That done, they barred the door again, and went straight back to sleep.

He did not know how long he slept like that, as motionless and cold as a mummified king of old in the stale, fetid stillness of his barrow. The only sounds that drifted through the shady vaults of his half-life were the weeping utterances of a melancholy wind outside, and the occasional gentle clacking together of velvet-sheathed antlers somewhere closer at hand. It felt as if Gapp had been asleep for days when he was finally jolted almost out of his skin by a terrific commotion from Schnorbitz. By the time the boy's wild thrashing hands had ceased their fruitless search for his spectacles, the snarling had quietened to a lower pitch, and above it he could now hear the sound of booted feet crunching upon the frozen crust of household waste outside. The footsteps came closer, then stopped just outside. Both Gapp and his dog stared at the door, not breathing. Then its flimsy collection of rotten planks shook beneath the weight of three kicks so violent that even the comatose Paranduzes now awoke.

It was Methuselech, and for once he was actually smiling.

No, not just smiling, Gapp realized, almost awe-struck. *He's beaming!*

Methuselech was indeed in a somewhat more cheerful humor than was his wont. In addition, he was carrying a large bale of furs and, in spite of their considerable burden, he seemed quite sprightly.

"You look happy," Gapp ventured, trying to modulate the bewilderment in his voice.

"They haven't passed through yet!" Methuselech announced with an uncharacteristic hint of excitement in his voice.

"What, Nibulus and the rest?"

"Exactly. I was speaking with some of the senior burghers of this delightful town before dawn, while you and your fellow sloths were still hibernating, and they've assured me that no one even remotely fitting our friends' description have been seen in the vicinity. Isn't that splendid?"

"Wonderful," Gapp replied dutifully, "but how can you be sure?"

"Oh, the Oghain keep a very tight ship in this town of theirs and, believe me, if any outsiders come anywhere near Wrythe, they do not go unnoticed. Here,"—he flung the bundle of furs down onto the drier part of the floor, and sat down—"cold-weather kit for the days ahead. All paid for, as is our bed and board for the next week."

Gapp noticed that the Asyphe warrior's other golden ear chain had now gone, too. *He really is serious about this, then,* the boy reflected.

"So, what have we got here then?" he said, rummaging through the new acquisitions.

There were hefty, thonged boots made of a thick, oily hide that he had never seen before, and lined with a type of fur as white and soft as a snowflake—so soft in fact that he could not even feel it with his fingertips. There were also mittens of a similar pelt; stiff-hair shirts with a fleecy lining; voluminous brown hoods with attached leather face masks; and the huge, shaggy pelts themselves could serve either as a coat or a bedroll. All felt and smelled of beasts that he could not guess at.

"Sealskin boots, snow hare mitts, saiga antelope shirts, bearskin hoods, and musk-ox coats," Methuselech informed him. "Just the stuff for a cold sea crossing."

Gapp ran his hands over the material, and could well believe that. "Seal, antelope, bear, ox," he said thoughtfully. "Honestly, it's all a big game to you, isn't it?"

Even the centaur-like Hwald and Finan had been provided for—at least, the upper, man-like half of them—and were eagerly going through the heap making little purring sounds of approval. They both had an eye for style as well as quality, and wasted no time in dressing each other up, and striking poses for their own amusement.

Then Gapp suddenly noticed among the pile of skins and pelts something rather out of place. He lifted it out and held it up to study it better in the grey light. It was a blue tabard with three sticks of rhubarb embroidered on its back.

"This looks familiar," he said, half to himself. "Isn't this the emblem of the Seers of Criccadan?"

"Yes, I noticed that among all the other merchandise," Methuselech replied carefully, and fumbled in his robes for something. "And this," he went on, tossing a small metal object to Gapp. "A brooch pin—recognize the design?"

Gapp studied the jeweled pendant, turning it over in his hand. "No," he admitted, "but it's obviously from somewhere far to the south of Wyda-Aescaland."

"The Quiravian chapter of the Shining Circle of Cunnans," Xilvafloese informed him, referring to a very large cult of atheist practitioners of magic dedicated to the eradication of evil and superstition.

"Never heard of them," Gapp sniffed, and tossed it back to him.

"Well, they do exist and, unless this pendant was stolen and brought here by traders, they've probably been this way. Not only that but, while I was checking out this town, I noticed one of the Wire-Faces wearing a Pendonian sallet-helm."

There was a short silence while Gapp let this sink in.

"Seers, Cunnans, and Peladanes," Methuselech said. "Only one reason any of their sort would come here. They're not traders—they're here for the Maw."

Gapp thought about it, then shrugged. "So are we. And don't forget all those reports of other missions heading to Melhus over the last few years."

Methuselech lowered his voice. "Indeed. But I wonder how many of them actually got any farther than Wrythe. Perhaps I'm jumping to conclusions, but it could be that whoever previously owned these items got murdered."

Gapp let out a little laugh, a rather queasy effort that lasted for all of half a second. He had been feeling noticeably better after the lukewarm food and his long sleep under cover for once; besides he could not help but appreciate this rare chance of a conversation with his companion that consisted of anything more than his questions being ignored, sidetracked or his being simply told to shut up. Yet now this rare conversation was taking on a distinctly disagreeable quality.

"I suppose it is a possibility." He shifted uncomfortably. "Guild shirts and badges aren't the sort of things their owners would let go of lightly."

"Quite so. Which is why we mustn't allow the Oghain to suspect for a minute that we're anything other than traders. They're probably already a little suspicious: two men alone, without carts, and with only two steeds."

"D'you think this lot'd really care about anyone going on to Melhus? Even if they remember it still exists? Just look at them; they're not exactly the outward-looking sort, are they? Why the heck *are* they like this, anyway? What could've happened to them to turn them all so . . ." he sought for a simple word which might sum them up quintessentially, "*milky?*"

"Ah, but Melhus was always a place of darkness for the Oghain, and they're not likely to forget what they suffered in ages past, no matter how long that place endures. Yes, I could tell you a thousand-and-one tales of the malicious sport the Rawgrs from the Maw used to have with their forefathers. No wonder, really, that their hatred became so strong—strong enough to form an alliance to topple Drauglir, in the end. Who would have ever believed that of them?"

"Them and the Peladanes," Gapp pointed out.

"Ah yes, the shining warriors, they do have their uses after all, I suppose."

Gapp regarded his companion quizzically, not sure exactly what he meant by this.

"Anyhow," Methuselech went on, "the island is still an evil place for them to this day, and the last thing they want is interfering foreigners stirring up new trouble there. Therefore, unless we can convince them we are genuine traders, there could be trouble for us. These purchases here are enough for a start, but not nearly enough to completely allay their suspicions. Our friends might take weeks to arrive, and if we're to wait for them here any length of time, we're going to need to conduct a lot more business than just this lot. The only trouble is, I don't have anything else to bargain with."

"Are you saying we'll have to leave soon then?" Gapp inquired in dismay. Wrythe might not be the most hospitable place in the world, but it did offer shelter, food, and some small degree of civilization. The very last thing he wanted now was to go back into the wilds, especially so soon after getting here.

"I haven't decided yet," Methuselech replied. "The way I see it, we have two options: Plan A and Plan B."

"Flippineck!" Gapp cried out all of a sudden, and flung the ox pelt he had been handling away from him, shuddering. "Are those things really supposed to have mites the size of crabs in them? That one nearly had my finger off!"

Methuselech stared at him, as if wondering just why he was bothering to explain any of this to the boy. That old familiar reticence returned to his eyes, and he rose to his feet. "We can talk about that another time. I need to meet their chief sometime today, so we'd better get cleaned up. Come on, I'll show you the bathhouse."

Bathhouses were the last thing Gapp expected to find in Wrythe. But bathhouses there were, of a kind, and they turned out to be a luxury hitherto unimagined by the boy. Close to the center of the town there was a huge karst tower riddled with caves and tunnels; and some of these contained natural springs, hot springs that bubbled away constantly like soup and filled the air with the smell of bad eggs.

At the sight of the large pool of green water in the cave Methuselech had led them to, both Hwald and Finan hooted with fervor, and plunged straight in. Schnorbitz wrinkled his nose and shied away, while Methuselech made his way unobtrusively to one of the private cubicles situated at the far end of the cave.

There were no locals present, so Gapp peeled off the oily layers of clothing, and gingerly lowered himself into the water.

"*Oh—my—fanny!*" he cried as the hot water surged up his body, and he grimaced in ecstasy as all the pain, weariness, and grime of the last two weeks were washed away. Steam wafted up his nose and filled his head with the powerful, dizzying aroma of sulphur. Limbs that had stiffened with an aching chill now began to relax, expand, almost unfold. Bubbling jets of magma-heated water pummeled away the rasping layer of chitinous filth from his skin and, as the warmth began to reawaken his blood and send it coursing throughout his body, extremities long forgotten now glowed a tingling pink.

Gapp allowed himself to drift off into a blissful private world of giddying rapture. The deep laughter of the joyful Paranduzes echoed loudly around the cave, but the boy heeded it not, heard it only as if in a dream, or the memory of a faraway land.

Time passed for him in a strange way. Hours became days, weeks became minutes, and years wavered undecidedly between seconds and decades. Time went forward, then backward and, after a spell in which it appeared to move sideways but at a slight diagonal incline, it stopped. The whooping and splashing of the Paranduzes turned into sprays of peach blossom that exploded in the air, cascaded through the purple darkness, and fluttered away on wings made of musical notes.

The boy from Wyda-Aescaland danced after them, and found himself skimming over treetops of brightest vermilion. He smiled at the rainbow birds that swooped through ropes dangling from clouds, and filled his lungs with the heady fragrance of burnt cinnabar. Down he went, through aromatic smoke trails that undulated from the tallest tree of all, and he was in Cyne-Tregva once more. There was Englarielle, Radkin, Ted, and the Vetters, the Cervulice and the Paranduzes. No words did they use, for none were needed; they simply smiled, and welcomed him into their firelit dance. Never before had Gapp felt such an abundance of joy and love; with tears of happiness he was borne away in the warmth of their embrace.

Then the laughter and the music died away and, in the hollow silence that followed, Gapp awoke.

"Oh. How long have I . . . ?"

He looked about himself. Schnorbitz lay at the poolside eyeing him with head cocked, while Hwald and Finan had quietened down and were now washing each other's bodies, languidly but thoroughly.

Gapp stared at them. *I wonder how they feel about all this?* he thought. *They never complain, never offer any opinion, don't really talk. Don't they wonder what it is we're doing, exactly?*

It did seem odd to the boy that such creatures could allow themselves to be taken so far from their home, and by such alien beings as he and Xilvafloese. Again that sense of warmth and love came back to him, and he felt empty and troubled. *Surely they must be dying to be with their own sort again?*

Gapp slipped out of the pool, and tried on his new raiment. After so long wearing clothes that felt and smelled like discarded kipper skin, these thick pelts embraced his body like a bear. He stopped for a moment to admire himself in this outlandish gear *(Flip, what would the family think if they could see me now?)* then he strode over to Methuselech's cubicle.

He was about to knock on the door, but suddenly drew back in alarm. There was a narrow sluice along the floor, which issued from the same cubicle, and coursing along it was the foulest looking bath water Gapp had ever seen. Not simply dirty, this stuff ran a brownish-burgundy color with little white flecks floating on the greasy surface, and smelled of rancid myrrh. From within could just be heard the stifled grunts of the desert man.

Clarty bugger, Gapp thought to himself. *I bet he only came in here to mask his evil pong.*

"Methuselech?" he called out, and tapped gently on the door.

The grunting stopped and, after a pause, Methuselech answered: "What is it, Greyboots?"

"Any chance of telling me about Plans A and B?"

A few moments later, Methuselech emerged wearing his new apparel. He now looked every inch the barbarian *Oghain-Yddiaw* warrior of legend, despite his swarthy complexion.

"We've got what we want," Gapp explained hurriedly, "food and clothes . . . So I was just wondering what we're going to do now: wait for Wintus, or go and meet up with Englarielle and his Vetters? They might have reached the Last Shore already; for all we know they might be camped on the strand waiting for us right now."

Methuselech seemed to be in some pain, and did not answer. He shuffled over to the cave mouth, and sat down, breathing in heavily the wafts of steam that curled up into the cold air outside.

"What's the matter, boy?" he said with a strange, labored slur. "Asking questions all the time . . . poking your nose in . . ." He paused for a moment, eyes closed tightly, and inhaled deeply. Then he looked sideways at his companion, and jabbed his finger into Gapp's temple. "That brain of yours woken up at long last, eh?"

Gapp swatted the intrusive finger away irritably. "I'm just worried about who we're supposed to meet up with. Is it Nibulus or Englarielle? Haven't you talked with Hwald and Finan about that?"

Methuselech slumped back against the rock wall and sighed deeply. For once, Gapp was close enough for his foggy vision to see the man's eyes clearly. They looked, he fancied, much like those of a dead fish, but behind them he thought he could detect a certain hesitancy, or maybe uncertainty.

A moment later, Methuselech appeared to come to a decision.

"About Finwald . . ." he began.

"What about Finwald?" the boy probed attentively.

"Two years ago," Methuselech went on.

"At the forest giant's, yes?"

"You didn't really think he was carrying a dead snake about with him, did you?"

"Of course not!" Gapp snorted, louder than was strictly necessary, then averted his gaze.

Methuselech's eyes, all-seeing, all-knowing, rose to the ceiling. Gapp could see the oily smears of superciliousness floating upon their watery surface without even having to look at him. He did not need this. The only reason he was sitting this close to Fish-man and suffering his pestilential presence was because he wanted answers. He decided now that if all he was going to get was the standard dose of disregard and slight, then he was going to get up immediately and walk out of here without so much as a word or a backward glance.

"So?" he demanded.

"So," Methuselech explained, "he was carrying a weapon. And that's what this whole misadventure is about. Finwald, our affable and modest young Lightbearer, was walking about in Fron-Wudu—alone—with possibly the most powerful weapon in the world at this moment. With a single stroke it could change the course of history."

"History?" the boy gasped. "You mean he intends to try and change the *past?*"

"Gods' Pollux!" Methuselech swore in amazement. "Obviously I was mistaken about your brain waking up."

"Well I don't know, do I," Gapp protested, using six more words than he had resolved to, and completely forgetting to flounce out of the cave.

"It's probably enough for you to merely know that Finwald's precious item is of great importance. Yes, that'll do—just try to remember that. And it is precisely because of this importance that I cannot reveal any more to you. There are certain people—and I'm not talking about just humans here—who would be very interested to discover Finwald's little secret, and should these people ever find you, me or anyone else who knows anything about the aforementioned dead snake, then we will all wish we'd never been born. I wish to protect you, Master Radnar, and at the moment, ignorance is the greatest protection I can offer you. Should your mission, and your knowledge of Finwald, ever become clear to these people I speak of, then the less you know, the better."

"You mean the less I can disclose to them under torture, the better," Gapp corrected him.

"Now you're getting it."

Gapp sat silently, observing a few hens who were stalking around near the mouth of the cave. One of them was drinking from a bowl that someone had left on the ground. It contained a cloudy brown fluid, and had a partial layer of pale scum on top. It reminded Gapp of what his mother's fish pond had looked like when they had found the bloated carcass of a sheep in it one day.

As the bird tilted its head back to swallow, it kept one eye firmly upon the humans that watched it.

"So what do we do now?" Gapp sighed, none the wiser, as usual. "Wait here for Finwald, or go meet the Vetters?"

"As I said, Plan A or Plan B. I still haven't decided yet."

"Well, let's start with Plan A then," Gapp persisted, "meeting Englarielle."

"That's Plan B."

"Plan B! What d'you mean, Plan bloody B?"

"Those Vetters, they're just convenient backup in case I need a strong force in the Maw. It might well be that there's nothing active in there, nothing of any danger to us, in which case of course I—we—could go there alone and complete the job in secrecy. On the other hand, there may be considerable danger there—as I suspect there will be—and in that case we'll need every bodyguard we can get hold of."

He paused, then continued. "But if we can only find Finwald, it'll all be so much simpler."

Gapp did not know which stunned him more, the callousness of the man or his deviousness. To drag the Pride of Cyne-Tregva, fifty trusting, faithful Vetters and their steeds through the worst stretches of Fron-Wudu simply to serve as a contingency plan . . . Methuselech was clearly not the same companion who had traveled with them from Nordwas; of that Gapp was now certain beyond doubt.

"And if we do find Finwald?" he inquired. "What of the Vetterym then?"

"Then they can go home, of course," Methuselech replied, puzzled at the question.

"Right, just like that."

At this, had Methuselech been wearing spectacles, he would no doubt have peered over the top of them at the boy. "Would you prefer, simply to justify their long journey, they got killed in the Maw? This may turn into a conflict to change the whole world, Radnar, make no mistake about that. And in war, people get used."

Of course Gapp did understand much about using people in war. He was after all the esquire to a Peladane. But that seemed like such a long time ago, and he at least was different now.

"In any case," Methuselech went on, "there's not much we can do about it at the moment; Englarielle will still be traveling through the forest, and I can't see him getting to the Last Shore for a while yet. Maybe in a few days. And Nibulus and the rest should take even longer. Whichever way, boy, it looks like we're here for the duration."

"What about Plan A, then?"

"Stall for time, wait until Finwald comes, finish the mission. If we can't wait here any longer, I'll try and leave a message for Nibulus here with the chieftain, and we'll go on and find the Vetters."

"You've met the chief then, have you?"

"Not yet. Those Wire-Faces wouldn't let me see him. Wouldn't let me near their Majestic Head, so they call him. But I've been promised an audience this evening. I've got a special deal I need to talk with him about, something I'm sure he'll find very interesting indeed."

Not more deals! Gapp thought in vexation.

"But that can wait for the moment," Methuselech said, rising stiffly to his feet at last. "I'll tell you about it once we get to the tavern. Come on, let's eat."

Leaving Hwald and Finan to occupy themselves in the bathhouse, Gapp, with Schnorbitz at his side, followed his leader to the tavern. He did not question Methuselech; he knew better than to try to get straight answers from such secretive men. So he contented himself with the thought that they were at least going to an inn, and whatever comforts that promised.

The new Methuselech, however, cared nothing for such earthly pleasures. He strode on, silent with his thoughts, plans, and strategies.

Ah, decisions, decisions! If only he knew where Finwald was now. Could he really risk wasting time here, waiting or hoping for him to come along, when for all he knew he might already be on Melhus Island by now? After all, there was no guarantee he would be coming to Wrythe at all. That damn priest seemed to know so many secrets; perhaps he knew about the ice bridge over the Jagt Straits?

Yes, maybe it would be better to forget about settling his old scores, and just accomplish what he had been yearning to do for over five hundred years.

On the other hand, if he could get hold of that sword, by all that was unholy, he would die a happy man!

Methuselech had still not forgotten or forgiven the Peladane and his rabble.
Bitterly he recalled clawing his way out of the Valley of Sluagh, only to find that
they had abandoned him. Yet it was nothing as petty as human revenge that
burned in his soul; there was a far greater wrong than theirs that needed to be
righted.

Gapp did not have a great deal of experience of ale houses, or indeed anything that might fall into the broad category of night-life. It was not that youths
in Wyda-Aescaland were forbidden to drink; on the contrary, in Nordwas it
was common to see packs of gawky, gangling little pillocks making even greater
fools of themselves in the local taverns than they did in their sobriety. No, it
was just that he was—or had been—the esquire to an important Peladane, and
thus his weekends were always the same. Whereas his peers, after an exciting
afternoon's stone-skimming, would be found pretending to enjoy beer and
making derogatory comments about the local girls (until some huge-buttocked
belle might happen to flash one of them a knowing smile, thus causing him to
spend the rest of the evening in a hopeless, puppy-eyed subservience, until finally getting the elbow and sobbing in a dark alley wiping bile from his acne-
encrusted chin), Gapp would be confined at Wintus Hall serving mead to that
drunken oaf Nibulus and his gaggle of loud, slobbering friends. And then
mopping up their mess the following morning.

So there was, then, more than a flicker of curiosity and anticipation at the
prospect of a night out in Wrythe. It provoked an incongruous juxtaposition of
images. First, he pictured the throng at Wintus Hall, the Peladanes singing,
quaffing, fighting and wenching, faces smeared with pork fat and red with wine
and laughter and heat from the roaring hearth. Silverbacks, one and all. Then
he pictured the silent wall of grey, blank faces standing outside in the fog the
previous night. Try as he might, he just could not put the two images together.

This should be interesting, he thought.

As it transpired, here they did not have taverns in the traditional sense. No
ale, food, music, or fire. The good folk of Wrythe's idea of a night out was apparently to crawl down into one of the communal mushroom cellars and lick
lichen off the walls. There was little light down there except for a few candles,
and a slight purple aura surrounding the Oghain who had been licking all day;
and hardly any sound save the constant rasp of tongue upon brick, and the
occasional moan when some lucky reveler came across a particularly hallucinogenic patch of fungus or some other cryptogamous spore that might temporarily pique their senses.

In one corner, several punters, having apparently gorged themselves to satisfaction already, were now settling down to one of Wrythe's most popular pas-
times: mushroom racing. This involved a considerable degree of concentration
and unearthly self-restraint. Each player would select one of the mushrooms

that sprouted from the gaps between the flagstones, and then keep a careful eye on it—all night. Whoever had chosen the mushroom that grew the tallest by sunrise was the lucky winner.

Judging by the behavior of his companion these two weeks past, it would not have surprised Gapp one bit if Methuselech had joined in with those revelries and felt quite at home there. But Gapp himself maintained a very bad feeling about this whole scene.

As if reading his thoughts, the older man said by way of reassurance: "They sell beer here, too. Just ask one of the cellar maids."

Sure enough, some time after they had descended the slick flight of steps that led in from the street, a servant woman approached the two men. The Oga placed an earthenware bowl firmly into Gapp's palms, then folded his hands around it. Her fingers felt like frozen blindworms, and it was all Gapp could do to stop himself shuddering at their touch, so that he almost lost his grip on the bowl.

Steady, Radnar, he scolded himself. *Don't do anything to offend them; I'm sure they mean well.*

But it only took one glance into the bowl to remind him that they probably did not.

"Isn't this the same stuff we saw the hens drinking earlier?" he asked.

"Oh indeed." Methuselech beamed. "The finest brew in the north. Mmm, haven't tasted this since I was nine!" He took a bowl for himself, and drained it in one go.

Gapp regarded his own with apprehension. He noticed several insects crawling around the rim of the bowl, and when one had the misfortune to fall in, its death throes disturbed the liquid contents, causing a plume of sediment to rise from the depths that gave off a sweet, frowsty odor reminiscent of Traders' Mild, that cheap brew one could purchase at Nordwas's less reputable hostelries.

"What's it called?" he asked, stalling for time. The Oga guessed his meaning and, smiling shyly, replied in a croaking whisper: "Leuccra-ho'i."

Gapp looked at her blankly. Methuselech translated: "Hop juice."

For the next hour the two travelers squatted upon the floor among their whispering or groaning hosts. Methuselech seemed content to drink bowls of hop juice and just stare about himself with a kind of misty-eyed fondness in those sunken eyes of his. Gapp, however, noted with consternation a soft patter of liquid on the flagstones soon after each draft his companion consumed. It seemed almost as though Methuselech's body was leaking.

Eventually, Gapp could stand it no longer. "Meth," he began, trying not to sound too urgent, "couldn't we just proceed to Plan B?"

Xilvafloese surreptitiously wrung the hop juice from the seat of his pants, and gave Gapp a questioning look. "I thought you wanted to be reunited with your friends?"

"Well, yes," Gapp replied, "but I can't really imagine that's going to happen now. Not in the next week or so, anyway. And I hope—no, I fervently pray—we don't have to wait even that long; this place is like some kind of purgatory."

In truth, though he did indeed hold out little hope of ever seeing their old companions again, and despite his yearning to be away from Wrythe, the real reason he wanted to leave now was Methuselech. He trusted him even less than he did the Oghain, and craved the security and companionship of the Vetters. Though he had not shared their acquaintance for long, he trusted them, and in this part of the world they were probably the most normal individuals one would find.

So much for humans, he reflected bitterly.

But Methuselech was not ready to leave just yet. "We'll see how it goes tonight with the chief. The meeting I told you about earlier—"

"Your 'special deal,'" Gapp interrupted sulkily.

"Yes. It might buy us a lot of time and, if we're lucky, without having to put any money up front."

"Go on then, what is it?"

"Marmennill scale," replied Methuselech with a grimace of satisfaction.

Gapp stared blankly before him at one of the Ogha, whose glistening blue tongue was carefully scooping out the feculent dregs of a bowl of hop juice in the same way a doctor might swab the contents of an ulcer.

"Mar-*what*?" he asked distractedly.

Methuselech rolled his eyes. "Marmennill scale, boy. The scale of a Marmennill. Tougher than iron but three times lighter, and worth about fifty times its weight in gold. Used to make armor. Merchants will cross entire continents to acquire it. I've asked for four sacks, about as much as two Paranduzes could be expected to carry. In other words, a perfect cover story, one which should allay their suspicions *and* buy us time. It could take them weeks to gather that quantity of the stuff. Clever, eh?"

Again that feeling of irritation, and the weariness that went with it, surfaced in Gapp. *Marmennills? What the flipp are Marmennills?* He just never stopped, that Xilvafloese, springing bizarre facts upon him out of the blue, talking of matters of which the boy could have no knowledge, and then not explaining how *he* knew.

"What exactly is a Marmennill, then? Some kind of fish?"

Methuselech coughed with mirth, an ugly, dry sound. "You really are a stranger to these parts, aren't you?" he sneered.

"Well, yes actually," Gapp protested, *just as you're supposed to be, too.*

"No, not fish, not exactly," the other explained. "Rather Selkind, the Children of the Waves, a marvel the length of the far north coast, but seldom seen elsewhere. Even here, though, where they are at their most abundant, it is the luckiest of fishermen or whalers that have ever caught one."

"Yes, so what are the chances the Oghain have any of their scales to sell?"

"Next to none, I'd imagine." Methuselech smiled smugly. "It'll take them a *long* time to gather my order. As I said, that's the perfect excuse to hang around here without actually buying anything more."

Gapp eyed him darkly. For someone who was supposed to come from the southern deserts, Methuselech seemed to know an awful lot about the far north. But as ever, he could do nothing but follow the other man's lead, allow himself to be dragged behind the magnetic pull of this most northerly of men.

It was time now for them to meet the Majestic Head, and face whatever that encounter might bring. Gapp called Schnorbitz to his side, took a deep breath, and followed his leader out of the mushroom cellar.

It was beginning to get dark already. As they walked, the young Aescal studied the town about him, and found himself memorizing landmarks, noting streets. He seemed to be mapping the layout of this place in his head, almost as if he were expecting to have to flee from it at any minute. He already had a profound sense of foreboding about what might happen in the chief's hall and, more disturbingly, a sense of powerlessness to stop it. That feeling, so recently awakened in him of being master of his own destiny—ah! under the cold gleam of the setting sun, it had withered like mist. This was the far north, a subarctic wilderness set wholly apart from the rest of the world, and fate governed it entirely.

They returned first to the bath-house to fetch Hwald and Finan. Both creatures were sulky at having to leave the baths, and pointedly took their time in getting dressed in their new pelts. When they were done, however, they picked up their moon spears and followed the two men and the forest hound out into the chill of the evening. There was nobody about and, as the small company made their way up the narrow lane toward the chief's hall, an uneasy feeling once again began to steal into their minds.

"Schnorbitz, what is it, boy?" Gapp called out. The dog had suddenly veered off to the left, trotting, ears erect, up to a large timber bunker to one side of a house.

"Just be a second," he said, and went over to fetch him.

"What's the matter, Schnorbitz?" he asked. The dog's head cocked this way and that, and when Gapp laid a hand on the animal's side, he could feel the tension and the trembling through his whole body. He glanced ahead at Methuselech, who had stopped and was waiting impatiently. Gapp was just about to try to haul the dog away when he heard a sound from within the bunker.

A faint thudding and, almost beyond the range of his hearing, a tiny muffled voice. It was croaky and fey, and reminded him of the horrid little voices when he was trapped in the mines. An icy tremor ran through his body, but he managed to stifle it. Instead, he gently forced Schnorbitz's head away from the little gap he was staring into, and himself peered inside.

It was completely dark in there, but as he strained his eye to see, there came from the gloom a long, strangely echoing whisper, sounding somewhere between a human voice and the gases escaping from a corpse. His eye widened as he noticed a large spider staring straight back at him. It seemed to snicker, winked at him with four of its eyes, then sealed up the peephole with gauze.

The sound of heavy, flapping feet snapped the boy's head around, and he saw two Wire-Faces approaching. They immediately placed themselves between him and the bunker. They did not move, did not make a sound, but the menace of their garrottes was unmistakable.

"Come on, Schnorbitz," Gapp whispered, "time to go."

They rejoined the others, calmly but swiftly, and continued down the street. Gapp glanced behind, and was relieved to see the Wire-Faces were not following. They still stood there, two contorted figures in bloodied aprons, their cheesewires ready in knotted claws.

He hissed into Methuselech's ear: "You really want to stay here for several more weeks?"

Methuselech, however, did not appear at all troubled. "They're probably just the local militia," he suggested, "or maybe the royal guard. Don't fret; the same thing happened to me earlier today when I was shooed away."

"From a timber bunker? What d'you think they keep in those things? It sounded like there was someone in that one back there."

"Not a bunker, no; I was stopped from getting too near to a cabbage patch. There are clearly some places in this town they don't want us to get too close to. Best just respect their wishes. I wouldn't fancy getting into a fight with them."

Gapp did not know whether to believe him. "Why do they have to dress like that, anyway?"

"Those wires crisscrossing their faces? Couldn't say, really. Maybe it gives them comfort."

"You're joking!"

"Comfort of the mind, I mean. They're probably the only inhabitants who ever leave this town—as hunters, rangers, soldiers, I don't know—so they need to bring a part of the forest with them. Stand upon a hill near Nordwas, and you see hills, woods, fields, stretching in all directions, and above everything the sky, unobscured and clear for all to see. But here, stand anywhere in these woods, or on a hill, and look into the distance, it's all seen through a mesh of branches and twigs. They're so used to seeing the outside world in that way, that openness scares them. Like field mice venturing onto the open expanses of a lawn."

"How do you feel about being pushed about by these Wire-Faces? You, a veteran of the crusades?"

Gapp surprised himself with the boldness of his own words. A mere boy just did not ask legendary men like Methuselech Xilvafloese questions regarding their feelings, especially reactions of fear. Surprisingly, Methuselech deigned to reply:

"On the field of battle," he said, though his voice sounded as if it came from somewhere else, "I have done things so terrible not even your master, Nibulus, would believe. I have driven back whole battalions with my power. I have broken bodies, ripped out entrails, and torn off limbs with barely a conscious thought. I have also slain the greatest warriors in single combat."

He paused for reflection. "But all that in war, and when it was over, I would return to my land, and to myself, and be at peace with my neighbors. Then if a city guard should threaten me, even were he a simpleton armed with a bludgeon as blunt as his wits, I would merely do as he wished, and walk away from trouble.

"Because in war you do a warrior's job, but in peace you become just a citizen once more; and that seems right, somehow."

Looking into the veteran's eyes, Gapp found that for once he wholly believed him. Yet was this man he now believed actually Methuselech, or someone completely different? And was this man speaking from his own experiences, or trying to recall someone else's?

"You're not from the desert, are you?" Gapp ventured carefully. "I bet not even Nibulus knows where you're from exactly, or who you really are."

Methuselech raised an eyebrow, but merely replied: "I hope you won't talk like that to the Majestic Head. Straighten up boy, we're nearly here now."

Unlike other buildings in Wrythe, the chief's residence truly was a lesson in geometric squareness and solidity. Like a donjon it squatted, cold and ugly, upon a low hill right on the edge of town. Here the trees grew sparsely, and a raw wind smelling faintly of salt kept at bay the fog that held the rest of the town in its dismal grasp. It was probably also the only building to date back to the time of the Oghain-Yddiaw of old, and as such seemed wholly out of place.

As they approached, the sea breeze caused the scant trees to moan like lost souls. It was difficult to be certain in the near dark, but Gapp thought he caught a glimpse of several hanged bodies swinging from their branches. Reminding himself that he had seen worse things in the Torca village back in Wyda-Aescaland, he wrapped his ruffled pelts about him more closely, and pressed on.

They followed the path up the hill, the vestigial twilight dying with each step they took. Unseen things slithered away through the mud under their feet. Night creatures began to stir. By the time they had reached the top of the hill, night had descended in full, and there before them, only a shade darker than the sky behind it, sat the keep. Silent, and unlit by any welcoming torch or lamp, it awaited them.

"Doesn't seem to be anyone in," Gapp whispered, but no sooner had he uttered the words than some figures materialized from the shadows. Without any sound, they came towards them. Gapp gritted his teeth, but determinedly did not back off. A second later, they were confronted by three Wire-Faces.

"Ghac deu-nhann!" Methuselech snapped impatiently, without slowing his progress, and the sinister guards parted to let him through. Hurriedly the other arrivals followed, and the Wire-Faces silently closed in behind them.

Finally, they reached the keep, and entered. Though they had not realized it before, for no light came from within, the main door was already half open. Into the belly of the keep they walked, Schnorbitz and the Paranduzes only just managing to squeeze their gigantic bulk through, and found it to be as stony and lightless as outside. They could feel rubble on the floor and wet moss on the door jambs, smell the faint odor of decay that hung in the cold air and, from somewhere within its echoing spaces, hear the irregular drip of water into a puddle.

"Shogg me sideways, Meth, what the heck is this?" Gapp hissed as, with arms stretched out before them, they continued their sightless, faltering ingress. Behind them they heard the Wire-Faces following into the entrance chamber with them, then heave on the door to close it. It scraped across wet grit and rubbish on the floor, then slammed to with a dull thud that seemed to echo throughout the whole building.

At a word from one of their unseen guards, they were led stumbling farther across greasy puddles and over rubble and pieces of discarded timber, through to a smaller room. Moments later a few candles sprang to life. These shed a thin light, bestowing upon the Wire-Faces a dull glow and threw their great looming shadows across the walls.

One of them left silently through a side doorway, presumably to announce their arrival. The other two remained exactly where they were, and just watched Gapp and his companions without moving a muscle.

"I really don't like this at all," Gapp whispered, even though he knew his words would not be understood. "These lot look like they might peel our skin off just for a laugh."

"I wouldn't worry about that," Methuselech replied. "We're more than a match for just two of them. Anyway, they're not as bad as the rest of the people around here—at least they've still got some life in them."

"What, you mean they've got a pulse?"

Gapp looked around anxiously. When first told he would be joining Nibulus Wintus on a sacred quest, he had never imagined this might entail standing around in a derelict house on the edge of the world, in near darkness, in the company of beings one might imagine dwelling in the asylums of hell. Out of habit, his roving eyes checked the room for quick escape routes, should the need arise.

Apart from the two doorways at either end of the room, there was a single window, and a large trapdoor in the floor. The window opened onto the dimly lit courtyard around which this keep was built. The trapdoor, partly covered by rubble with a virulent growth of moss feeding on it, was secured by a sturdy metal lock which, Gapp noted, appeared new and shiny.

Schnorbitz had noticed the trapdoor too, and was now giving it the same attention he had the timber bunker earlier.

Just then a muted scream erupted from somewhere on the other side of the inner courtyard, followed by a chorus of children's laughter. All those in the room—save their guards—looked out the window in alarm. Then there came the strangely sinister sound of metal joints squeaking, a clanking noise, followed by the thumping of something heavy upon floorboards.

Gapp's eyes flicked over to the Wire-Faces. Still they did not appear to react.

He coughed casually to gain the attention of Finan, and motioned with his eyes for the Parandus to nonchalantly place himself between Gapp and the two guards. Luckily, Hwald had caught on too and, as soon as the great beasts had blocked the guards' view of him, Gapp slipped out of the window.

Heart beating madly, he padded over the stony surface of the empty courtyard in the rough direction of the noises. There was nobody about, and no faces visible at any of the other windows overlooking the yard. Gapp reached a large, bronze-bound door on the far side, and squinted through the keyhole.

There was plenty of light in the room beyond, at least, but what Gapp was seeing was difficult to make out. Various images danced before his eye: the blurred figures of cavorting children, their skin slicked with sweat and reddened by torchlight, pupils dilated in near-hysterical excitement; the arcs of smoking flame as flambeaux were swept through the air; a man on the floor, his face turned almost inside out with torment; and—Pel save us!—a spray of thick droplets of red raining from floor to ceiling!

Gapp looked away and blinked furiously. Had he really seen what he thought he had? Was his eyesight truly that bad? He put his eye back to the keyhole, and refocused.

As he did so, all sound and movement ceased from within, and Gapp froze. The Ogginda were all staring back at him, as if the stout planks of the door were made only of glass.

He immediately recoiled, and stood by the threshold, trembling with new fear. Still the silence continued. He began to back away slowly. Glancing toward the window he had slipped out through, he saw that Hwald and Finan were still blocking the Wire-Faces' view of him. If he were quick he could probably still make it back inside without his absence being discovered.

Then the childish laughter began anew, only this time he realized they were laughing at him.

An odd thing then happened to Gapp: he began to get angry, very angry. Thoughts of his solitary travels underground came back to him, recollections of the fears he had overcome, ones that might send any normal person into dribbling madness. And here were these yokel *freaks* playing mind games with him! In a sudden surge of fury, he strode up to the door and booted it in.

Instantly, all was silent and dark. With the echo of the torture victim's last cry fading into silence, the room before him brooded with cemetery-like menace. The intruder ignored it, and began feeling along the wall by the door for a torch cresset. As soon as he found one, with his tinderbox, flint, and steel, he set about lighting it. Moments later, the torch was kindled, and Gapp held it aloft.

There they were, the Ogginda, the Children of the Keep, all standing in a line, staring at him. Not a sound did they make, and of their victim there was not a sign. In the awful malevolence of their regard, Gapp's anger evaporated, and he fled.

Just as he reached the threshold, a shape stepped out of the shadows of the courtyard and struck him full in the face. Gapp grunted as he staggered back and hit the stone floor. In the brief moment before he passed out, he beheld an image before him: staring down at him were the Wire-Face who had struck him and the circle of Ogginda gathering around to gloat. His torch was still clasped in his hand, and its dying flame cast their shadows against the ceiling. Except these shadows did not seem to belong to them, but to misshapen creatures with billowing cloaks and horned helmets.

As the torch finally sputtered and died, so did Gapp's consciousness.

Only one man, a nonlocal, *normal* man, bore witness to any of this.

In one corner of the room, a suit of armor stood, antique plate armor of the sort used by the Peladanes five hundred years ago. It was bulky and impossibly heavy, and rusted up so badly that the joints were practically welded together. It would have taken any decent armorer an entire week to dismantle.

But behind the breastplate, a heart was beating out of control, and from within the sallet of the helm, two eyes stared. Wide with terror and red with blood, they gaped as if through windows looking onto the Abyss of Pandemonium, while the man's mouth was frozen in a silent scream after the weeks of horror he had endured since arriving in this town. And from the torture he had just suffered at the hands of the Children of the Keep.

Though still, of course, a nonlocal man, by now his mind was anything but normal.

Although he did not appear so, Methuselech was getting concerned. Gapp had not yet returned, and already the third Wire-Face could be heard coming back. The other two guards had not yet noticed the boy's absence, fortunately, but soon this would no longer be the case. And when they realized that the small foreigner was wandering about freely somewhere inside their Keep—for there was no way he could have got outside it—things would very likely turn ugly. For all of them.

Moments later, the third one did reenter the room. To Methuselech's alarm, he noticed, even in this poor light, blood glistening upon the man's knuckles.

Methuselech maintained his veil of insouciance, but beneath this facade, he was coiled up tight, preparing himself for whatever would come next.

If any of the Wire-Faces did notice that Gapp was gone, they did not show it. Methuselech was beckoned to follow the returning guard up the stairs, presumably on his way to the chief, but all the others remained behind.

Stupid boy! he cursed. What did he have to sneak off like that for anyway?

Forced to leave the Paranduzes and an increasingly agitated Schnorbitz behind, under the watchful eyes of the four remaining guards, and sensing that they were being deliberately separated, Methuselech followed his escort.

Up a large and crumbling spiral staircase he was led, round and round until he finally emerged into the open air again. They had come out onto the parapeted roof of a large turret located right at the top of the keep. The dank closeness left behind him now, Methuselech breathed in raw sea air and, for the first time in many weeks, looked upon a night sky bright with stars, unobscured by fog or forest canopy. Wind-whipped flames crackled in a couple of braziers, while torches sent swarms of sparks writhing up into the blackness above. Over the sounds of burning fuel could just be heard the distant voice of the ocean.

Methuselech glanced around at the turret, but could not see anyone else up there. He peered carefully into the darker areas between the bright flames in an effort to locate the chief. Then he noticed a dark shape at the very far side of the rooftop, and gradually was able to discern the large figure leaning over the crenellation and staring out toward the sea.

Not waiting for a signal from the guard, Methuselech made his way across the rooftop, until he was standing just a few yards away. He was big, that was for sure: at least a foot taller even than any other Oghain. And unlike them, this man was broad. From behind, all Methuselech could make out was a multi-layered funereal robe of burgundy that clothed him from collar to ankle, grey-brown, crinkly hair swept back into a horsetail, and a pair of pale hands. They were like those of the Wire-Faces, but even larger and bonier, and with finger-nails as blue as a hanged man's face. One of them was wrapped around a large drinking vessel, the size and general shape of a human head, but heavily decorated in gold and rubies.

"Uh . . . Majestic Head?" Methuselech called out.

"My name is Yggr," the figure replied in an extraordinarily deep, almost frog-like croak, and turned to look upon his guest.

Methuselech's face did not customarily reveal much expression, as if he feared it might split and fall off. But upon beholding the chief of Wrythe, a very noticeable look of deep puzzlement passed over it. He could not say why, exactly, but there was something very familiar about this Yggr, and it disturbed him greatly.

The face that now regarded him was very long, flat and stony, with skin looking as old, dessicated and chalky as the calcified karst towers that sprouted up all over the area. In fact, it bore a manifest resemblance to a gravestone, or similar monument to days and lives now long past. The only words chiseled into it, the only part of it that spoke anything of what lay within, were the eyes. They were small, pale and watery, like oysters, surrounded by folds of dark skin, but containing within them a pinprick of blackest black that glittered sharply. As Methuselech looked closer, he noticed that one eye was somewhat wider than the other, this one intense and penetrating while its mate was heavy-lidded and languorous. The combination was startlingly beguiling, almost hypnotic since neither eye blinked, not even once, but stared piercingly into his own. He could not remember ever meeting a gaze like that from any man.

"Thank you for allowing me this meeting with you," he said to the chief in perfect Oghain, "to discuss trade."

Still the piercing eyes lanced into his own, the only modification in Yggr's expression being a slight tilt of the head, as if he were considering something carefully. His lips, large and slug-like, the color and texture of chopped liver, curled sardonically at the corners, then parted and again that strange, frog-like voice rolled out.

"And you are from . . . ?"

Even at this distance Methuselech could smell the foulness carried on Yggr's breath. In the capering torchlight he could discern small pieces of dead skin still lodged between his teeth from some long-ago meal.

"My name is Methuselech, from Qaladmir," he replied, omitting the surname which might identify him as a warrior even this far north. "I come from afar to trade in—"

"You speak Oghain rather too well for my liking," Yggr interrupted, and took a step closer. Methuselech sensed immediately that the chief was now more than just suspicious, and cast his eyes down at the floor to avoid further contact. He was beginning to feel decidedly uncomfortable in the presence of this local chief, something which had never happened to him in over five hundred years, and it was a feeling he was finding very difficult to deal with.

"There were two of you," Yggr persisted, coming closer still. This was not mere suspicion, Methuselech realized; he knew there was something wrong with the southerner, and he was searching for the truth, getting closer to it with each step he took.

He's reading my mind! Methuselech thought with unaccustomed panic, though he could not be sure.

"My companion is here too . . . down below. He heard some children playing and went to investigate. It sounded like they might be in some distress."

"What, my brood? I very much doubt it. Look at me when I'm talking to you!"

Methuselech, dumbfounded at this intimidation, found himself taking a step back. He raised his eyes till they rested on the big man's chest. What was it about this Yggr that perturbed him so? The man seemed as old and soggy as a piece of bread left in the rain. Even his clothing looked dank and shabby, as if he had wallowed all day in a fungus patch, and when he ran a hand absently down his robe to smooth out the creases, a cloud of old spores was released like a puffball exploding.

Yggr finally halted less than a yard from Methuselech. He cupped the shorter man's chin in one big hand and raised his head so he was staring straight into his eyes.

"You're local, aren't you?" he accused, with conviction.

There was no point in denying it. "As a child, I lived in the forest south of here," Methuselech lied, "but have spent most of my adult life with my kins-folk in Qaladmir. My parents are traders, and—"

His eyes fixed now upon the drinking vessel the Majestic Head held to his lips. Under the embellishment of gold and rubies it was clear to see now that this cup was in fact a human head, preserved in oil, the cavity in its skull now holding the strong mead that Yggr sipped.

"Drink," he commanded, and held out the head toward Methuselech's mouth.

In the normal course of events, Methuselech would have shoved the cup down this impudent man's throat. Yet, it seemed, through no volition of his own, he felt forced to drink. He parted his lips before the varnished skull bone, and clenched his eyes, as the vile fluid was tipped down his throat.

"That's it," Yggr purred in gloating satisfaction. "Accept the hospitality of Wreca of Helggestre by drinking from his brain-ball."

The liquid was thick and sweet, and much stronger than usual mead. It burned like fire through what was left of Methuselech's system, and he was forced to keep his legs closed tightly lest it leak onto the floor. When he finally opened his eyes, all he could see before him were Yggr's limaceous lips curled in sneering domination. Still Methuselech avoided his tormentor's malefic gaze. He was convinced they had met before; that smile was unmistakable.

Yggr continued to stare into Methuselech's downcast forehead, as if drilling into his brain.

"Wreca of Helggestre," he repeated, still holding the ghastly goblet up to Methuselech's face. "Recognize him? No? You're not a Peladane then, that's for sure. But who exactly are you?"

By now any attempt to keep up the guise of innocent trader was useless. Methuselech had to escape. Bitterly he thought back to his earlier smugness, when he had believed his machinations and contingency plans would be suffi-cient. How had everything gone so wrong so quickly? From deep down within the keep he thought he heard voices raised in ire, and a savage growling. This was quickly followed by several loud thuds and a high-pitched squeal. His mind raced, recalling there was only one Wire-Face between him and the stairs, but—

Suddenly Yggr froze, then, for once, his friable face cracked into a wide, shark-like grin: "My, my, my!" he coughed in disbelief. "Mauglad Yrkeshta, as I live and breathe! We meet again!"

Methuselech's eyes bulged, and he turned to sprint away as fast as a hare. But Yggr already had him by the neck, and swiveled him back around.

"How the world turns!" Yggr whispered with a tremor running through his great frame like a tree in a gale. "Things are finally drawing together, after all these years."

Just then a new presence made itself felt. One of the Children of the Keep had arrived, and approached from behind. Methuselech was as impervious to fear as he was to the effects of the alcohol that was now running down his legs, but, even so, he knew with an absolute conviction that everything, all his plans and even his very existence, was in ruin. It was inescapable.

The Ogginda reached Methuselech and stared up at him as he still dangled helplessly in the iron grip of the Majestic Head. The side of the child's head had split open, and some matter one would not normally expect to find in a human head had leaked from the wound and set into a crust down his neck. The child showed no sign of distress or discomfort, and just continued to regard Methuselech casually.

"Is this the one who crushed your skull?" Yggr asked of his minion. It was only then that Methuselech recognized the boy as the child he had kicked against the headstone the previous day.

"Yes, Daddy," the boy replied.

"Then, when I have finished with him, you may take him to the schoolhouse and play with him."

4

The Stabbur

He woke with a start, and instinctively kicked out. Like a swimmer rising from lightless deeps he gulped in desperate lungfuls of air. Then he opened his eyes wide, and stared about.

It was dark, too dark to discern anything, and so cold he could not feel his extremities. But he was not outside; he could feel wooden flooring beneath his back, sense the closeness of this place, and hear the wind rattling a door upon its hinges nearby. There was also a strange, quiet, continuous sound all about him, one that he could not identify.

His first thoughts were that he was still in the woodcutter's hut. There was that same feel of rank airlessness, and a stale odor that made him want to sneeze. But then his memory returned, and with it the full, awful knowledge of the peril he was in.

He tried to get up, and immediately gasped at the fierce, burning pain that seared every joint in his body. He was bound hand and foot, in such a way that even the slightest attempt at shifting position disabled him with torment. He strained uselessly against his bonds, but whatever bound him was tough and fibrous enough to flay his skin off before it would yield.

"GRITS!" Gapp spat.

But he forced himself to relax, take in his surroundings properly, and put all thoughts of the evil of the keep to the hindmost reaches of his brain.

Minutes passed. Soon the darkness began to lessen as his vision began to adjust. The palest slivers of light could be made out, coming through several cracks in the ceiling. Vague shapes they revealed, their forms only hinted at. Squat, perhaps man-sized, standing all about. Some of them appeared to be wearing hats or helmets. He suddenly froze and drew in a liquid gasp, imagining himself to be in some kind of pagan temple surrounded by its dreadful keepers. Then he realized that, whatever they were, they were not moving at all. Motionless, they could have been statues, or even furniture of some kind.

Again Gapp found himself yearning for his dear old spectacles, ripped so cruelly from his face back in the Jordiske cave in the forest. *Damn this whole region!* he cursed passionately. *Am I fated to spend all my time here in the north trapped in some dark prison or other?*

Gapp shivered. It was not just cold; it was freezing. As his eyes adapted further, he could make out the cloud of breath condensing before his face. This place was far too cold for any dwelling of Man, even men such as these. But whatever sort of place this was, it was sturdily built, for he could feel not a breath of air from the wind that moaned outside.

What was that smell? Gapp inhaled deep, drawing the air over his tongue. There were hints of resin, fermented grain, old meat, and the mold that grows on damp straw. . . . Maybe the smell had something to do with the noise he could hear: a fizzing and popping sound like elderberry mulch turning into wine?

For a long time he was forced to lie thus, unable to move, unable to do anything except try to steel himself against panic, to banish the fears that brushed ghostly fingers against his mind. He seemed in no immediate danger as yet, but lying trussed on the floor, hardly able to see, he felt as vulnerable as an overturned tortoise. And his captors could arrive at any time, and do anything with him that their sick little minds could devise.

Who in Pel's name are they? he wondered. These lands had always been savage, dark and heathen. But from what he had seen of the town, Gapp knew that something terrible had twisted it, infected it with evil and sickness. Normal people did not live like this, or even look like this . . . . It was as if something had emerged from the forest, and so warped the Oghain and their lives that they began to take on the darker qualities of a nightmare. Not suddenly, but over years, decades, even centuries, so gradually that they probably were not even aware of it happening to them.

It all came from the keep, of course. From the hall of the Majestic Head. Gapp had seen both the Doll-Faces and the Wire-Faces—and they were human. Twisted but still human. But those unholy Children of the Keep . . .

Gapp convulsed at the thought, and his brain instinctively denied their existence. He needed to gather all his wits to escape, even if it meant flaying all his flesh off on these bonds and running away through the woods with nothing but a shirtful of sore bones.

Where was Methuselech? Had he been captured too? And what about Schnorbitz, and the Paranduzes? Surely they, all together, could beat a path through the Oghain and flee this town . . . and then plan a rescue attempt? Xilvafloese might not be very interested, but the others would never abandon Gapp. Never let him rot here, floundering at the mercy of those—

No! Don't think about them. Keep focused. Stay calm.

His ears pricked up. *What was that?* A droning noise, muffled but nearby. He held his breath, and listened hard.

The wind? Yes, it moaned like the wind, rose and fell like the wind, but . . . no, not the wind. Voices. Voices, just on the other side of the wall!

Again he held his breath. Moments passed—followed by more moments. And then he heard it again. Yes, voices, clearer now, coming from somewhere beyond where he guessed the door to be.

Gapp strained his ears, hardly daring to breathe. It occurred to him that the voices sounded a little like the Paranduzes. Had they traced him here? His blood pounded faster, and throbbed painfully where the rope dug into his skin.

Minutes passed. There was definitely a conversation going on out there, but still he could not make out whether the voices were human or otherwise.

Suddenly, for what reason he could not tell, every hair on Gapp's body stood up, and his blind stare slowly turned to the opposite side of the room. His eyes—so wide and glassy he might still appear to be wearing his spectacles—fixed upon a patch of floor he could not see, and his whole body tautened like a cable about to snap.

There was someone else, or something, in this room with him, and it was snuffling around like a boar on the scent of truffles.

Gradually, it came closer.

With glazed eyes staring sightlessly up at the infinity of the night sky, the bloodied form of Methuselech was dragged away, leaving a trail across the stone floor of the turret.

Yggr, wiping the slime from his hands and lower arms, watched as it disappeared down the stairwell, the unconscious head bumping upon each step. Then he lit a roll-up, took a long drag, and closed his eyes as the bitter smoke from the dried sprout-leaf filled every last capillary in his brain. His thick lips parted barely enough to let the smoke escape, and he absently watched it snake languidly upward before being snatched away by the wind. He then picked up the skull goblet from the parapet, and drained it in one gulp.

"Thirsty work," he commented, leering at the head.

After another quick drag, he pushed the roll-up into the head's ear hole, and left it gently glowing there. Then lifting the cup level with his eyes, he stared into the expressionless, leathery face as if expecting to see some reaction there.

The dead eyes of Wreca stared back. Yggr regarded them for a moment, then said:

"Alas, poor Wreca, I slew you well!
Your cohorts keen upon their quest were not so bless'd as thou,
Upon that day when darkness fell,

And hath remain'd so until now.
  With but a careless flick of the wrist
  Bodies broke, ten to a stroke,
  They, from this world, into darkness hurl'd, I so artlessly dismiss'd.
But for you, my Wreca, no such brutish haste;
In slow, sweet torture we embraced.
More care I reserv'd, as you deserv'd.
The blade of this artist your shuddering flesh kiss'd,
And as lover's token, your head preserv'd."

Yggr, on seeing the bemusement so apparent in the Wire-Faces nearby, frowned, and stopped. Most of the Oghain assumed their leader's painful attempts at poetry were a form of torture, and they were probably wondering why he had dismissed the prisoner before commencing his recitation.

Yggr's blue fingernail traced the lines of the dead man's eye creases. "Would you call me a bad man, Wreca?" he asked.

He paused to consider his own question. "In my younger days I felt so sure—always up to my elbows in my work. But nowadays it all just seems so . . . *messy*, don't you think?"

He looked at the slug trail of Methuselech's leaking fluids that glistened in the torchlight, then he turned and leaned against the parapet, once again staring out at the sea.

"Well, I suppose it *is* my job to look after this place, but to be honest, Wreca, I'd rather they all just stayed away. It would save me so much unpleasantness. But, if they *do* come, well, they can hardly blame me for doing my job, now, can they? I mean, it's not as if I'm over-zealous or anything. Not like the old days, eh? Back then I'd tear their arms off just for fun. I'd sometimes tear their legs off too. It gave me an enormous sense of well-being. . . ." He smiled at the memory.

"But they still need correcting, these people. Ha! I remember the first correction I ever did. Took me days to pick all the fragments of shattered bone out of my face! Still haven't forgotten, after all this time . . . Ah yes, how he squealed. . . ."

The distant cry of a bird, a forlorn and bodiless sound, was carried upon the wind from somewhere out over the ocean.

Yggr's eyes narrowed. "So many of them recently, too. I just don't know what things are coming to. Ha, yes, of course I do: the time is near. They know it, we know it, and *he* knows it. So near, now. Then he will arise, and the time of reckoning shall begin. Especially for those Peladanes." He paused for thought.

"Talking of Peladanes, it appears I might even have the pleasure of correcting another of them before long. A nice, fat one too, by Mauglad's description—and the son and heir of a warlord, to boot. Yes, it'll be good to go to work on—what was his name? Nibulus? You'll enjoy that, won't you, Wreca, seeing one of your own squirm. Oh, he'll squirm, all right. Like a maggot on a hot plate. I'll milk his gall bladder before his eyes and make him drink it ere death takes him. Drink it from your head, Wreca! Would you like that, eh?"

"I'll stick to mead, if you don't mind," the head replied in a strange mutter.

Yggr spat, and stubbed his cigarette out in Wreca's eye.

He set down the drinking cup, and wandered off down the stairs, thinking. Peladanes! How he despised them and their braying sanctimoniousness, hollow boastfulness, and risible bravado! Coming here in their polished legions as if they owned the place, bawling their incontrovertible wisdom and stomach-churning piety into the faces of the poor, dumb locals. The self-appointed militia of the world. *Ptui!*

What got to Yggr, what truly whitened his knuckles, was how they were so *sure* of themselves, so utterly convinced of their might and invincibility! If they were so ferocious, why did they need the help of the Northmen? If the greatsword of Pel-Adan was the mightiest of arms, why would it suffer the rustic axe of the Oghain-Yddiaw for company?

"But the old alliance, their Fasces, is long dead. Would the Peladanes be so cocksure now without the aid of the Northmen?" Yggr reckoned not, and he himself knew what it was like to face Peladanes in battle. They were no better than dogs: get them on their own, away from the pack, they were as craven as any skulking cur that whimpered and piddled on the floor. *Pathetic!*

All humans were pathetic! Out of all the peoples of the world, it was humanity he despised above all. It would be the disciplined Haugers who would inherit the world before long, and put humans back in the place they deserved to be. Of that he was certain. Or at least would be so were it not for the imminent return of Scathur and his kind.

Yggr reached the bottom of the stair, and, abruptly paused. Something had been troubling him of late, and now he found himself pondering upon it yet again. Over the past few years he had intercepted many parties of adventurers on their way to the Maw—too many for his liking—but while he had been correcting them, not one had confessed to any knowledge of an invasion. No armies, no coalitions: just small groups of never more than thirty foolhardy intruders. Quite often considerably fewer than that. Not at all like the vast hosts of old.

Yes, Yggr was troubled. Despite a lifelong conviction that humans were essentially herd animals, it did seem that in this new world they were beginning to show disturbing signs of individuality. . . .

Well, one way or another that new world was about to change. His torture of Mauglad had revealed much, and this approaching Peladane would soon learn that six men were not much use against Yggr's army.

He pondered for a moment. "What to do now? Watch the children at play with Mauglad, or go and visit the boy?" Or else, he could go and oversee the fun and games that Rind-Head was having with the Paranduzes at this very moment.

"But then," Yggr murmured to himself, as he turned to leave the keep, "maybe I *should* go and pay the brat a visit; the smaller they are, the higher they squeal. . . ."

Back in the stabbur, the snuffling drew even closer, and still Gapp could not see a thing.

Seven yards now . . . six yards . . .

His glaring eyes strove desperately to pick out anything in the darkness. Those pale glimmers of light from the cracks in the ceiling still illumined nothing save the squat urn-like shapes lined along each wall. But it was from the dark aisle in between these lines that the ghastly animal noises came, and no amount of ocular straining could pierce that gloom.

Five yards . . .

Gapp slowly drew in a long breath, then let it out, trying to calm the quaking inside him. *Remember what Wodeman said about hunting in the dark, Don't look directly at your quarry; look slightly to one side and wait till you detect movement.*

But nothing. Utter blackness.

Four yards . . . three yards . . .

Frantically the boy forced himself back against the wall, trying to press his head and the nape of his neck into the cracks between the wooden beams. Panic and heat rose within him, till he could smell the musk of his own sweat.

Two yards . . .

On the other side of the door, completely unaware of the terror that was approaching just yards away from him, the voices started up again. Gapp tried to cry out to them for help, but no sound came. Then suddenly the snuffling stopped, and a moment later was replaced by an evil gurgling. In the terrified boy's mind it evoked images of slitted, hell-red eyes, lolling tongues and bloodied fangs—*a humped back of poisonous bristles, the stench of an overflowing cemetery, and a creature that stood on two legs and laughed insanely.*

The bonds bit deeply into his flesh, and he could feel warm blood trickling down his skin.

The animal sounds ceased abruptly, but the rank smell did not fade. Still it approached until it was almost upon him. Time slowed almost to a standstill, and so did Gapp's heart. With an acuteness that was almost hallucinogenic in its vibrancy, his hearing picked up everything and magnified it tenfold: the fizzing from the jars, as loud as treetops in a gale; the muffled voices outside the door like the bellowing of Ettins in deep valleys; even the wood-boring larvae that hacked their way through the damp walls could, he fancied, be heard laughing at him between greedy mouthfuls.

A low croak, barely audible, bubbled out of Gapp's throat. He so wanted it to be louder, wanted so desperately to call out for salvation.

One yard!

Another croak from Gapp, a little louder but still scarcely more than a whimper. This was like trying to wake from a nightmare. Another croak, almost a moan this time . . . then another, and another, each louder than the last.

Then just as he finally managed to voice a demented howl, the thing was upon him!

But . . . no, it was not upon him. It was beneath him! Gapp's heightened senses detected it as clear as day: the monster was not in the stabbur, but right under the floorboards.

Whoever owned the voices beyond the door had now heard Gapp, and called out sharply. Immediately the presence below him moved away.

Footsteps, heavy and irate, sounded upon the wooden steps outside. A heavy lock rattled noisily, almost deafening after the stillness. Abruptly the door was flung open—and someone stepped inside. With him flowed cold air and the damp smells of the forest, but still very little light.

Gapp held his breath.

All of a sudden, all hell broke loose, and the night was filled with the tearing sounds of animal savagery—stifled grunts of surprise and fear—useless struggle—ruthless laceration—hot spray steaming against the wooden walls—shock—terror. Then two heavy thumps . . .

And, finally, death.

Eyes clenched shut to hold back the tears, and teeth gritted to stifle his cries, Gapp could only wait.

Padded paws made their way softly up the steps; and, without hearing or seeing anything, Gapp felt an animal presence enter the hut. Without haste it moved over, then stopped right behind him. He could smell its stink, and hear the *drip, drip, drip* of something pattering on the wooden floor.

Then came that familiar, worried whine, and Gapp, at last, could relax.

"Schnorbitz . . ." he sighed, and fainted.

When he came to, Gapp found that his bonds had been cut. Or rather, gnawed through. All about him they lay in ragged, spittle-soaked clumps. And there, looking down at him with that particular expression of concern that is unique to dog-kind, stood faithful Schnorbitz.

He was free. Come what may, for the next few minutes at least, Gapp still had a chance. The blood that dripped from the forest hound's mouth was still warm. Scarcely more than a minute could have been wasted while he had lain unconscious; so they still had time before his guards would be discovered.

"Gotta leave!" he hissed as he staggered to his feet and rubbed his chafed skin. *"Gotta get outta town NOW!"*

And never come back.

After his ordeal, Gapp had no plan further than this. He was in no state of mind to give consideration to matters like provisions, exactly where he would go, or even the present circumstances of his companions. The only thought on his mind was rapid and immediate flight. He would run as fast as he could through the accursed town and back into the woods, not stopping until all that remained of this place was a bad dream in his memory. Even starvation in the forest was preferable to remaining here for one instant longer.

He hobbled toward the door as fast as his numb and tingling limbs would carry him. *Pech, it's freezing!* He was dressed only in the saiga shirt that they had left him with when they had taken him prisoner. Everything else they had removed: his own clothes, his gear, his tinderbox, flint and steel; the bastards had even taken back the pelts Methuselech had just bought from them! *Armholes!*

Presumably they had put the shirt on him solely to keep him from freezing to death before they came back to do . . . whatever it was they were keeping him for. It was a warm and sturdy garment, for sure, but apart from that and the sealskin boots that they had neglected to remove, he was naked and horribly vulnerable.

Well, it was all gone now, and that was that. He was leaving. Gapp reeled out of the door blindly, and then, with a cry of surprise, pitched forward into the dark and landed heavily upon the ground.

For a moment he lay stunned, the wind knocked out of him. Then he lurched to his feet, and looked about in panic.

It was dark and still, and there were trees all about. No houses or karst towers, only trees. There was only the faintest smell of that awful town here. He and Schnorbitz seemed to be alone in the forest. He stood shivering in the freezing night, and listened to the sounds that filtered through the woodland. The furtive rustles and sudden squeals of nighttime slaughter were giving way to the hesitant, opening chords of a new dawn's song. Nature's sounds, untainted by humanity.

It was the first night after the new moon, and what scant light managed to penetrate the pre-dawn mist was further diluted through the mesh of trees. All in all there was but the barest glimmer to illuminate his surroundings. But after his time in the stabbur, even this was enough to confirm that they were no longer anywhere close to the town.

Gapp's panic subsided somewhat, and hope of a more substantial kind began to swell in him. Rather than dashing headlong in any direction that presented itself, he allowed himself a few seconds' pause and looked around.

There was indeed no sign, smell, or sound of human habitation wherever he looked, apart from the stabbur itself and the narrow track that cut through the brambly undergrowth toward it. His prison, he saw now, was just a log cabin— some kind of storehouse maybe—raised about three feet off the ground on wooden posts. Crawl space for a forest hound. It had no windows, and only one door, reached by a short ladder of three steps down which he had just tumbled. Though sturdy and secured by locks, it seemed hardly the obvious place to hold prisoners.

They probably don't consider me important enough, Gapp concluded with grim relief, *or that dangerous. It's clearly nowhere near as secure as the keep.*

The keep! Only now did he fully recall what had befallen the night before. *What's happened to the others? Have they been taken prisoner too? And how come Schnorbitz's wandering free?*

He almost wailed in confusion and frustration.

They had to be still in the keep—the donjon. And if he himself had been held captive elsewhere it must be because they wanted to hold all of them in separate locations around the town. Less chance then of them helping each other to escape.

Oh, Yeggeth's Breath, what chance of finding them all? he panicked, then immediately thought: *None, so let's go!* He scanned the trees around to decide which direction to start off in.

His recently reawakened (and by now sharply honed) instinct for survival was kicking in hard. It was not exactly selfishness (he told himself) but he had just been saved by what must surely have been a godsent miracle, and it was ungracious to offend the gods by declining their gifts. Even if that did mean abandoning one's friends.

"Nothing we can do to help 'em now," he pointed out to Schnorbitz. "Come on, dog."

He turned to head off behind the stabbur, in the opposite direction to the track that approached it, and immediately skidded on something slimy.

It was the bodies of the Wire-Faces; he could tell without having to look. Nothing else in this place could be so soft and steaming. He did not even look down at their mangled remains, for he had already had his fill of horror for the moment. But then there was another thing he felt underfoot that caused him to risk a careful peek downward, something long and rigid.

It was a moon-spear, whether Hwald's or Finan's, he could not tell. But there was no doubt this was one of the Paranduzes' huge flint-crescented pole-axes.

Yes, and there was the other one, now he came to look closer. The Wire-Faces had obviously taken these weapons for their own, and had been standing guard at the stabbur door like a couple of palace sentries. It was possibly the spoor of these, rather than Gapp himself, that had drawn the forest hound to this place.

An awful contraction twisted Gapp's guts. This confirmed that Hwald and Finan had been captured also.

But that changed nothing, in fact only served to steel his earlier resolve. He was utterly powerless to help them, and their capture pressed home the absolute necessity to get the heck out of here this instant.

He briefly considered taking one of the moon-spears to protect himself, then immediately dismissed this idea as ludicrous; he would hardly be able to lift the damn thing, let alone wield it. But while he paused to think, something else occurred to him: what to do with the Wire-Faces' corpses. *An unguarded storehouse might not attract the attention of passersby,* he thought, *but two bloodied corpses definitely would.*

"Spend a second to gain a minute," he muttered to himself, and heaved the dead guards each in turn up into the stabbur. Having no time or enough light to find a better hiding place, he lifted the lid off one of the urns and proceeded to tilt it in order to empty its contents. He gasped as the smell hit him.

Whatever had been popping and fizzing in those jars had obviously been doing so for a very long time, but rather than slamming the lid down and looking for empty urns, he decided to find out what was actually inside. In spite of the precious seconds ticking away, he resolved that he would unearth at least one of Wrythe's dark mysteries. It might even shed light on some other of its secrets.

Rolling up his sleeve, and holding his breath, he plunged his right arm in up to the elbow, feeling around. Schnorbitz suddenly whined, his lips curling strangely.

Mere seconds of morbid fascination later, Gapp slammed the lid back down, and fervently wished that he had not been so nosy.

"Pickled people," he uttered, backing away; it was all he could do to resist the urge to bolt out of this crypt of acetic aberration. But people they were; curled up, lifeless, fetus-like, in a saponaceous, effervescent ichor that could only be described as myrrh-gravy.

What in the name of Forn's fetid loincloth is all this *about?* Gapp wondered, aghast. *They preserve their dead in storehouses?*

Five hundred years ago, he had been told, the Oghain had shared certain beliefs with the Torca who resided in the nearby Seter Heights, especially believing in the Circle of Life, the natural cycle of birth, life, death, fertilization and so on. Man was thought of as a natural extension of the land itself, as were animals, plants, and even the sun, wind, and rain. Death was natural: Man's return to the womb of the earth that bore him. This typically soil-based philosophy of the Torca made perfect sense to the Oghain in their harsh environment, and went hand in hand with their notions of the absoluteness of Fate. If a man were to fall ill, suffer serious injury, fall into the sea or go missing in the wilds, no attempt would be made to help him. It was considered a sign that the land no longer needed him; like a leaf in autumn, he had begun the slow process of death. Even if a man inflicted with a fatal malady continued to survive for several months, eating and talking among them, still he would be considered already dead.

So this attempt at preserving the deceased, cheating Father Earth of what was rightfully his, it puzzled Gapp greatly.

It's the influence of the keep, he decided, *or whatever dwells within it.* He could practically smell the perversion of that place, even from here.

But time was fast running out. He had to leave now, unless he wanted to end up in one of those urns himself. It was a sobering thought—and still he had not hidden the dead guards. Swiftly he went from one urn to the next, yanking the lids off and holding his breath against the stench of the myrrh-gravy within. Each one, however, was occupied, like a hive cell of baby grubs nestling snugly in their sweet, creamy oil.

Time, Gapp had decided, had run out completely. Yet there was one thing he could still do before he took to his heels—one last act of purging. Grabbing each urn by the neck, one after the other, he heaved. . . .

Halfway along Nettle Street, Yggr paused in midstride and looked up sharply. Something *untoward* had just happened in the stabbur, he could sense. He clenched his massive fists and continued on his way, with grim intent.

As soon as he was done, Gapp bounded out of the stabbur and gasped in the clean forest air. His eyes were stinging, his legs wobbly with nausea. During his loathsome task he had had to breathe through his mouth to avoid the unbe-lievable ammoniac fetor, but within seconds it felt as if his tongue were coated in drain cleaner. Even out here it reeked enough to wilt the branches of even the sturdiest deodar. But it was worth it; he smiled between shuddering. And now he really was finished with this town.

He wasted no more time. Trusting to Schnorbitz's guidance, he followed the hound's lead, and together they tore off through the woods.

Like unbaptized souls fleeing from the Wild Hunt they ran, leaping over boulders, splashing through streams, toiling up steep banks. No undergrowth was too thick to slow them, no thorns strong enough to snag them. Swift as the hart and silent as the lynx, they sprinted for their lives away from Wrythe for-ever.

Or so Gapp had believed. He suddenly checked his pace as the dim shad-ows of three houses loomed up before them. *What the heck?* Not wanting to lose sight of the hound in this gloom, he continued after him through the gap between two of the houses, then saw that he had been led not deeper into the forest, but back toward the town! They had come out of the forest and over a rutted mud track to a small field.

"Schnorbitz!" he hissed incredulously, glancing all around in extreme agita-tion, expecting to hear at any moment the primate-like moan of some alerted local.

Bur Schnorbitz was equally agitated, and began furiously scrabbling at the earth at the far corner of the field. Great sods of wet soil went flying up behind him, and his eyes were rabid with fervor as he whined and snorted. The forest hound, it must be remembered, was four feet high at the shoulder, and strong enough to pull down a bison, and he was currently tunneling into the earth like a digging machine. Clearly, then, there was not a thing the puny little esquire could do to drag him away and back under the cover of the trees. Gapp had no idea what had got into the dog; all he could do was crouch beside him and keep watch for any sign of the Oghain—or worse.

He momentarily glanced at the ground where Schnorbitz was digging, and there noticed a little wooden pipe about the size of a flute sticking up out of the soil. There were no crops evident in this patch, though the rest of the field sprouted a few sad, worm-eaten cabbages. Then Gapp noticed another pipe, just a few feet away, among a darker patch of freshly dug soil.

A very uneasy feeling arose in him. He hopped over to the nearest pipe, and put his ear to it.

"Oh Ghod!" he cried, and shrank back in dread, landing on his backside. Through the pipe he had heard the sound of frantic breathing. It seemed Schnorbitz was not digging for old bones after all.

Resisting the urge to leg it back into the woods alone, Gapp suddenly heard a muffled voice from underground. Schnorbitz now dug even more frantically, and seconds later the boy's eyes almost popped out when he saw the ground heave. Like a scene from Judgment Day, the earth was giving up its dead. A large hand, grime-covered and blood-smeared, wriggled out of the soil, soon followed by another, and then a huge head, complete with antlers. It spat out the long pipe from its mouth and spluttered fitfully.

"Finan!" Gapp cried, in a mixture of fear and relief.

The half-beast—half-dead, half-buried, and as yet unable to utter anything beyond a strangulated gurgle—struggled madly in his newly dug grave. Maggots, orange-headed and pale-fleshed, writhed through his hair, around his eyes and mouth. As if the covering of soil had not been enough, Finan had been further weighted down by a heavy plowing yoke. Grief and revulsion threatened to send the boy's body into convulsions, and he had to fight hard to control it. But how could he not be moved by the sight of his steed—no, his friend— buried alive in the local maggot patch with the paraphernalia of a draft animal holding him down? It seemed a sick joke that was all too fitting in this town of the twisted. Did his tormentors wish for his Gyger-half to wrench itself free of his beast-half?

As easily as if shaking the life out of a rat, Schnorbitz's teeth bit through the yoke's fastenings. The Parandus desperately lurched from the ground amid a cascade of loam, pebbles and grubs, rising like a conjured earth-elemental to stand proudly in the light of a new dawn.

"Thank Pel-Adan, Cuna, Erce, or whoever," Gapp stammered, only now getting a hold on himself and going to Finan's aid. Several minutes later, Hwald too stood free of his barrow and, for the first time since he had become sundered from Yulfric, Gapp knew he was among true friends.

For once, each Parandus seemed more interested in cleaning himself than the other. Shivering spasmodically, they frantically shook, combed, and swatted their repulsive tormentors off their hides and out of their hair, squashing the ones that had caused them the most discomfort between thumb and forefinger with vengeful relish. In spite of their long ordeal, their blood was up and a fire was in their eyes. As he watched the great beasts cavort in a frenzied dance of twitching madness before him, the young Aescal stood back in awe of their sheer power and ferocity, and gleefully pitied any foe that must now face them in combat.

Nonetheless, all this was taking up precious time, they could do their grooming later. What they most needed to do right now was to get under cover. What they also needed was to get tooled up properly.

"Moon-spears!" Gapp hissed quietly and, miming as best he could, pointed back toward the stabbur where the two spears still lay. That might at least get them going in the right direction.

Then the dull thud of a door opening resounded across the field from one of the nearby houses, magnified in the dead stillness of the dawn. All four of them froze, then whipped their heads round and scanned the middle distance to locate the source.

There was no one to be seen; they were not yet discovered. But night's vestigial veil had already dissolved in the bleary, pastel-grey murk of a new day, and the good folk of Wrythe were rising. Without a moment's further delay, the outsiders disappeared back into the forest.

"What now, for fox-ache!" Gapp hissed impatiently. He stared back at the two Paranduzes who had just collected their moon-spears from amid the two steaming piles of Wire-Head carnage. Hwald and Finan, for some reason, were not following him.

The little group might now be safely out of sight of the houses, and Schnorbitz's nose clearly could not pick up the scent of damp burlap robes or skin sores, but Gapp's fraught nerves were close to snapping permanently.

"*Mmeth . . .*" Finan voiced with difficulty, and followed this up with something spoken in his own tongue that was so unintelligible Gapp at first thought he was trying to dislodge maggots from the back of his throat.

The boy stared blankly. "Right. Meth," he acknowledged with a shrug. He then made as if to go, but was stopped by Hwald's huge hand on his shoulder. He was steered around to find the Gyger face: down close to his own.

"*MMETH,*" Hwald repeated, and jabbed a finger back in the direction they had just come from.

Gapp twisted free of Hwald's grasp and backed away, disbelief rounding his eyes. "You have got to be joking," he protested. But Hwald and Finan remained where they were, and did not look as if they were about to budge an inch.

Gapp began to understand what was going on here, and he did not like it

one bit. In the world of the Parandus, you just did not leave your friends behind, not even if it meant suicide.

And suicide it would be. The trouble was, Gapp considered, looking into
their eyes, it was his suicide, not theirs. Methuselech was, after all, *his* friend.
The Paranduzes, despite their physical strength, did not have the air of those
now determined to mount a rescue bid. The Children of the Keep had over-
powered them, how easily Gapp could not guess, but he needed no sign language or garbled attempts at human speech to tell him that they would not be
fighting those devils again. The dread in their eyes said it all.

However, their present stance conveyed no coercion of him. They themselves were not leaving without "Mmeth," but they would not force Gapp to
help them. The choice was his entirely. Yes, they were making it absolutely
clear that it was his own *moral* choice.

Gapp's blood boiled. They had all just escaped by an enormous, unreason-
able amount of luck, they were free to go and, now they were mere minutes
from certain escape, these two damn *steeds* were expecting him to walk right
back into the dragon's jaws! And just to make an almost predeterminedly
failed attempt at rescuing some benighted, manipulative leper whose purposes
and loyalties were as unfathomable as his true identity, and one who seemed
more a part of this dark, distorted world than even the locals. If they seriously
expected Gapp to acquiesce to a moral code even they were unwilling to follow through, they were in for some long overdue education.

"FINE!" he suddenly cried. "You stay. GOOD! I go. Schnorbitz, we're
off."

And, without so much as a wave good-bye, he vaulted away through the
trees.

Yggr neither spoke nor moved. At that moment all he could do was stare at the
corpses of the two guards, and twitch. This sort of thing just did not happen in
Wrythe. He had arrived only moments earlier to find the guards dead and the
boy gone. His bellow of rage had rung throughout the woods, bringing to the
scene every Wire-Face and Child in town.

It was not that the deaths of two Oghain were any great loss to him. Once
he got them into the Urn they would serve him again anyway. And it was certainly not as if he actually liked these people. On the contrary: he hated them.
The only humans he hated more were Peladanes, and then only because he had
not enjoyed the centuries of revenge upon them that he had with the northmen. What fanned the coals of his ire so was that mere outsiders had taken
their lives, when they were *his* to take. The Majestic Head's twisted tastes in en-
tertainment demanded *living* playthings if it were to really hit the mark.

While the Children tried to stifle their giggling, he now stalked around inside the stabbur. and grimly inspected the ruin within. How had the boy

managed to do all this damage? And, more to the point, why had he attacked the pickled people? They were no threat to him. Such barbarity! Such wanton vandalism! How could they offend him so?

Damn city-folk! he cursed. *They never did understand our ways. . . .*

But as he surveyed the scene, his rage began to diminish. The damage to the pickled folk was not all that serious after all, and dead guards, though at first sight a complete disaster, probably could be sewn together into some semblance of working order again.

No, maybe not so bad after all. Some of the Children had already begun to clean up the blood, their tongues writhing lasciviously over crimson puddles on the frosty ground. Their eyes rolled in delight.

Yggr straightened up and strode back to the door. *Well,* he mused, *the stiffs have been building up a bit lately. Seems like there's not an attic or cellar that isn't crammed with the things, and even the timber bunkers are getting a bit full.* In fact, it was a measure of Wrythe's serious shortage of shelf space that they had resorted to storing their corpses in cabbage fields.

No, he had put it off for long enough. Even before hearing Mauglad's interesting little story earlier, he had been intending to transport another shipment of the Dead over to the Maw. ("The Urn awaits, as ever.") But now, it seemed, the time had finally come when he would set sail for the very last time.

"COME!" he barked. "We find the *boy!*"

And, with that, every Wire-Face and Child lurched off into the gloom, fingers twitching and red tongues flicking.

Yggr watched them go, and smiled. It would not take long. First, bring the young wastrel back and pump him for information. Then go to work on his mind. No need to send *his* corpse to the Urn; far too puny to be of any use. Instead, carve the finest, most exquisite work of art out of his young flesh that Yggr's flagitious soul could contrive.

In fact, why not redecorate the entire keep with him?

Then kill him. And keep that pretty little head. It would be nice to share the long centuries to come with such comeliness.

So much more fun to talk with them after their lives have fled, Yggr thought, *and remind them of just how dead they are!*

Moments later, a series of terrible howls rose into the air and set the trees a-tremble. Two sets of Parandus tracks had been found, leading away from the town into the woods, heading south.

The hunt was on.

The keening of the Children could be heard even within the deepest fastness of the keep. The victim slumped against the wall in the schoolhouse heard it, even above the wailing of the imprisoned child-souls and the rasping protests

of the embittered dead that seeped from the very walls into his head. Manacled, his eyes staring vacantly ahead, and a thin line of discolored drool hanging from his lip, Methuselech had undoubtedly seen better days. But there
was no reaction in him to that dire screeching that subdued every man and
beast for miles around in cowering dread, no recognition in his eyes of its por-
tent. Methuselech's mind had fled, run screaming to a far realm beyond this
awful reality.

Even when he heard footsteps softly pattering across the flagstones
outside—those soft, little children's feet; even when he heard the bar lifting
from the door—such tiny hands, such unearthly strength—still he did not respond. Their work had been interrupted, but Methuselech knew it made no
difference; they would be back soon enough to finish what they had started on
him.

It was only when that voice—urgent, fearful, *human*—finally penetrated his
brain like an astral harpoon setting its barb into the floating leviathan of his
soul, that he slowly drifted back into the real world. Still bewildered and idiot-
faced, he looked up, and saw Gapp Radnar staring back at him.

"Radnar . . ." he breathed hoarsely. "So they killed you too?"

"What?" the boy replied.

Gapp was regarding him intensely. Methuselech could see the terror in his
eyes, the barely checked panic. There was also a presage of despair and an
abundance of doubt. These were things the necromancer recognized so well,
had centuries of experience of. But, for the first time in his long existence, he
also saw concern. Care and concern for him.

He shook his head. This was doing nothing to alleviate his confusion.

"Methuselech," Gapp whispered, "are you all right?"

"All. Write . . ." Methuselech repeated distantly, not understanding the
question.

"Listen to me! Can you walk?" Gapp went on urgently, unwilling or afraid
to touch Methuselech's body, or even inspect it too closely.

Xilva's lower jaw started moving, albeit a little too loosely, but no words
came out.

"That is, could you walk if you weren't manacled to the wall?" Gapp continued, half to himself. He clicked his tongue, at a loss what to do.

He could not complain too much, though; the first part had, after all, been
easy. The time of day could not have proved more fortuitous. Few of the
Oghain had risen yet, and those who had went about heavily attired against the
freezing early morning fog, hooded and cloaked like shambling monks. It had
been easy for the boy's light fingers to acquire such raiment. Thus clothed, he
had smoothly infiltrated Wrythe's murky depths and arrived without incident
at the keep itself, which, due to his own actions at the stabbur, he found unguarded. Slipping nonchalantly through the main door he had had to choke
back a scream when he found Schnorbitz already waiting for him there. How

the animal had guessed his intentions, or managed to arrive without raising the alarm, Gapp did not have time to speculate. They had both arrived at the heart of darkness, and had swift work to do.

"Listen, Xilva," he hissed, "we've got to get you out of here now—those things could be back any minute. Hwald and Finan have drawn them off into the forest, and Schnorbitz's acting as watchdog at the front door, but we've got to act fast. Is there any way I can get you out of these manacles?"

"They removed his bones, you know," said Methuselech dreamily.

"Beg pardon?"

"Him over there. With special knives. Inserted them into his skin, dislocated his joints, separated the flesh, then drew out the bones, one by one. Hardly left a mark. What they couldn't remove, they just dissolved with vibrating tools. Turned his whole body into a boneless lump. We used to try that when we were kids, but could never get it right. They must have perfected the process—that one's still alive."

Gapp had no idea what he was babbling on about, and no time to care. He yanked furiously on the chains, but to no avail.

"The other one they tied to a stake," Methuselech went on, an abstracted look further clouding his eyes. "They tore pieces off him, and threw them to the Wire-Faces. He was still alive as they chewed his flesh."

Ignoring him, Gapp looked about the chamber for something to help him. If this was a true keep, a donjon, he assumed there would be some kind of tool he could use.

"And the last one." The prisoner smirked inanely. "They decided to cook. They heated him up in that suit of armor till he bubbled and smoked. Screamed like a lobster, he did!"

"Just shut up!" Gapp cursed. "Shut the flipp up!"

The boy was on the point of just giving up and leaving. If this really was, as Xilva suggested, a torture chamber, then it was surprisingly lacking in metal implements. Not even an axe or a jimmy to be found. The man was obviously raving.

Then he went cold all over—as the spirit of the Children entered him.

"Did you just say 'suit of armor'?" he asked, dreading Methuselech's answer.

"Over there," the prisoner confirmed, nodding to one corner. Though he had not really registered it at the time, his attention being somewhat diverted by the orgy of blood witnessed last night, Gapp now recalled that he had indeed seen a suit of armor in this room. There it stood, blackened and threatening. Even from here he could smell burnt . . . something. He had to find out for sure.

". . . for weeks encased in a shell of iron," Methuselech was droning, "a metal cocoon . . ."

Gapp drew closer, closer still, until he could feel the heat radiating from it.

Ignoring the repulsion that stuck in his throat, he grabbed the helm's visor and wrenched it open.

"Oh for the love of . . ."

He trailed off. It was like being struck full in the stomach with a flange-headed maul. The poor man's face was now a glistening lump of charred meat, mouth gaping in an eternal scream, looking through him with eyes as dead and white as those of a boiled fish.

Gasping, the youth staggered back. He turned and looked at Methuselech with eyes aged far beyond his years, his face clammy and drained of blood.

"Who *were* those people?" he demanded in disbelief.

Methuselech looked up at him and squinted like a psychotic, then giggled. "The Children have such monstrous appetites."

Gapp took another step back. "They eat them?" he breathed. "All of them?"

"No, not all of them. They usually leave the spines—give them to the Oga to wear. Like jewelry."

"But who were they?"

"Just people like you," Methuselech replied, a little more coherently now. "Adventurers to the Maw. But they never get farther than here. Merchants might pass through unhindered; they're no threat. Your sort, on the other hand . . ."

"*My* sort?" Gapp was on the point of bolting from this place and leaving Xilvafloese alone with all its horrors. But he had to find out.

"I always felt there was something familiar about this place, ever since we arrived. And now I think I know what it reminds me of. You!" He leaned closer. "Who *are* you?"

"I'm the Black Sheep," Methuselech replied. "And I should never have come back."

Gapp ignored this babble. "What business is it of the Majestic Head if people want to go to Melhus anyway?" he demanded. "And how do *you* fit into all this, eh?"

"Yggr and I, we're in the same business. Or rather, we were. I'm the Black Sheep, but he's the Caretaker. We've both been around here for a very long time. In fact, he's always been here . . . and his name's not Yggr; it's Scathur."

Finally, Gapp's legs gave way completely, and he sank to the ground, smitten by the full weight of despair and dread that that name brought upon him.

"We're dead," he whimpered.

"He's an artist," Methuselech murmured, "an artist who wears his victims' blood upon his raiment as a badge of honor, and encourages his wire-faced protégés to do likewise. I once saw him create such a masterpiece out of a man's body that his weeping could be heard throughout the lower levels, mingling in ecstatic rhapsody with the man's screams. He doesn't hate them; he exalts them . . . An artist in rapture, who's even been known to fall in love with his subjects."

Staring deep into Methuselech's eyes, Gapp was suddenly aware of two pairs of eyes looking back at him. There were the eyes of this present persona, this Black Sheep who was talking to him. But there were also the eyes of Methuselech Xilvafloese, that happy-go-lucky friend of Peladanes who (he now had to admit) Gapp had always found one of the more pleasant members of the little band from Nordwas. Either way, Scathur had no love for *him*, either of him. And against every instinct in the boy, Gapp had now come to save him. Pity, and that embryonic spark of loyalty that Hwald and Finan had engendered in him, overcame his misgivings.

"What did they do to you, Xilva?" he whispered.

"They forced me to watch all of it—that atrocity exhibition. Then they gave me a choice: either I gouge out my own eyes, or they burn them out with hot pokers. I have to decide before they return."

Gapp lurched up from the floor with a cry and lunged at the manacles, trying to wrench them off the wall.

"But it's too late!" Methuselech hissed, looking up at the boy in supplication. "I told them everything! Everything! Scathur knows as much about the Quest as do I. About Nibulus, Finwald, *everything!*"

"I really haven't time to worry about any of that at the moment," Gapp said, as he tugged on the manacles. "All I know is that your caretaker and his little friends will be back for their dinner very soon, and I don't intend to end up as pudding."

He gave up pulling on the manacles, and leapt over to a trough where he had noticed some cutlery. He grabbed one of the knives, the nearest one, and was just about to return to his task when something caught his eye. He hopped over to another of the dining implements, and snatched it up.

"My sword!" he gasped.

It was true. The blade they had taken from him, that sturdy little hiltless machete given to him by Ted the Vetter, was once again in his hands. These Children clearly had good taste when it came to stylish kitchenware.

Buoyed by this sudden upturn in his fortunes, Gapp set to working on the irons with renewed vigor. He inserted the pointed tip beneath the metal plate, and levered for all he was worth.

But it was useless: those manacles would never give. And now time had almost run out. Instead, and as a measure of his desperation, Gapp frantically began hauling on Methuselech's arms. He pulled, heaved and twisted, like a maddened terrier with a badger's hind leg, until finally, with a sound like a boiled chicken's carcass being pulled apart, Methuselech's hands came off.

The older man struggled to his feet and lurched off toward the door, the boy still staring in open-mouthed horror at the dismembered hands on the floor.

"Don't worry about them," Methuselech panted. "Let's go!"

Half in a dream, Gapp reeled after him. *Maybe he really is dead, after all,* he thought, as they caught up with Schnorbitz and fled the town.

That was the thing about Methuselech: you never could tell.

5

On the Plain of Fire and Ice

Bolldhe had taken his gloves off for only fifteen seconds, while he took a draft of liquor from his flask. But even that was enough time to freeze his fingers almost solid. With increasing difficulty, he finally managed to get the gloves back on, then leaned back against the rock in relief.

"Six bloody days . . ." he gasped. Six days of traveling across ice and frozen rock since they had parted from Kuthy and Elfswith. Those had been the longest six days of Bolldhe's life. Even for one as well-traveled as he, there was nowhere in the world he could think of that was as brutally inhospitable as this place, nowhere that even came close. Men were not supposed to exist here on this island. That he knew. And, as Bolldhe nursed his frozen digits and gasped in the thin air, he very much doubted they would make it to the other side.

Crossing the frozen sea alone had almost killed them. How in the name of the wee man they had survived that trail, Bolldhe would never know. Perhaps Fate had taken a hand. This far north, that was always a possibility. It was the sort of thing Fate would do, really, now Bolldhe came to think about it: lend them a kindly hand across the causeway, and keep encouraging them on, day after day, prolonging their lives and their misery and dragging them on to an even harsher enviroment until finally cutting them loose and abandoning them to a slow and miserable death. Yes, Fate was just like that. . . .

At first it had been plain sailing. The day had started fine, the ice stretched out as smooth as glass ahead of them, and they could clearly see the headland of Stromm Peninsula that marked the beginning of the island proper, no more than four hours' march away.

But none of them, not even Bolldhe, had any experience of fissures: great, gaping crevasses that opened up suddenly before them, invisible from even a short distance, but too wide to jump, and indeed long enough to force them off their route for miles. First one, then another, then another. As the sun began to sink in the sky, the travelers' anxiety grew. They knew they could not risk spending the night out here on the ice, but there was nothing they could do about it. As their trepidation grew, their good sense lessened, and the risks they took became increasingly reckless.

At one point Nibulus had stood on the very edge of a fissure, the better to gauge the distance across. The ice had groaned in warning as the southern idiot had gawped down into the yawning chasm of blue ice plunging into darkness, and only Bolldhe's shout of alarm had pulled him back, scant seconds before the entire shelf suddenly fell away into the watery depths below.

More care had been taken after that incident, but this had meant a frustrating series of detours and backtracking that resulted in their reaching the headland several hours after nightfall. Those hours had proved the worst: every step could result in a fall to their death, despite being roped together, and they could only guess in what direction they were heading. It had only been the intense cold that had forced them on in such foolish desperation, a chill that none of them had ever experienced before.

That cold, and the voices.

Those voices. Not even in the wasteland south of Myst-Hakel had they felt such unease, such unearthly dread, or heard such warped and soulless keening. As soon as the sun dipped below the horizon, the sounds had started up: long, mournful moans that came from afar, washed over the ice field, reverberated subsonically inside their heads. Maybe they came from the sea, maybe from miles beneath the ice. Perhaps they had come from the air high above. The adventurers would never find out. Nor could they even guess what made them: some great creatures of the ocean depths, or dwellers on the island, alive or dead? There had been undertones of human speech heard chattering on the edge of that wailing. On and on it went, plaguing the frightened travelers' first night on the island.

When finally they had risen again, it had been to a land that was as utterly alien as it was desolate. As the first light began to appear, Melhus slowly revealed itself to them—almost savoring the dismay it induced. Great towering cliffs of lead reached up before them, and stretched away on either side as far as the eye could see. Ragged clusters of boulders, split by the cold and rimed with hoarfrost, lay scattered all about. And, flowing with unnatural slowness from the heights above, came a yellowish-grey vapor that caressed everything in its path with sickly, pestilential fingers, and left an unpleasant dampness that smelled of bad eggs.

The whole day had been spent finding a way up those cliffs to the hinterland beyond. One whole day of frustration, danger, and fear, and a deepening sense of despair that sapped the will of even the strongest among them.

But a way had eventually been found: a series of ledges, slopes and scree banks rather than a path, up which Zhang could be coaxed, pushed, and hauled. So, just before nightfall, they had gained the land beyond the cliffs, and stared in awe at Melhus, the last island at the top of the world.

It was a land of fire and ice, rock and wind, a churning battleground in which these four powerful elements waged ceaseless war against each other, and whose merging energies shattered the entire seething, bubbling crust, sullied the air, and pulverized the chthonic depths beneath. Mountains of blue rock, mere nunataks poking their peaks through mile-thick ice, were whittled and carved into the grotesquely contorted shapes of horn, claw and tooth by the screeching arctic winds, clamped around by the vise-like grip of ice that pushed its searching fingers deep into cracks to split and shatter, while from within, their innards were melted and boiled by fire from hell's own cauldron. In quaking convulsions this would spew out of fissures, melt the ice in seething gouts of steam that would burn the very air, and send rivers of boiling water down into lakes below, that would in turn freeze over. Then the ice would be chiseled into bizarrely shaped points, forming sastrugi oceans of jagged waves, or forests of cold, white spears that forbade any passage. Geysers belched foul-smelling water from magma-heated sinkholes. Gale force winds whipped ice, sparks and ash about in a frenzy, and curled steam into living vortices. Lakes of sulphur and ice-melt sprawled like a yellow, scum-layered regurgitation across the landscape.

Amid all this chaotic, boiling activity, not a sign of life could be seen. During the previous day's journey, the travelers had watched from the ice bridge sundry birds and beasts: darting sea swallows that wheeled over the wind-whipped tops of waves, silver-grey fish that leapt in unison from the water, and the occasional wet-eyed seal cub that was abandoned upon the floe by a mother scared away by these strange new creatures that walked on two legs. But here on the island not even the meanest patch of lichen could endure this hostile environment.

On the afternoon of the first day, the blizzards had blown so fiercely it was almost impossible to see. Had they not encountered Elfswith before, and accepted his arctic clothing, they would not have lasted one day. Those bearskin coats were massive, all-encompassing, and so thick that it felt as if their wearers were swimming through a sea of pure bear-dom. But, even thus clad, the wind somehow managed to find a way through this hairy armor. The pelts would suddenly fly up alarmingly, and continual stops had to be made to resecure them. The blinding snow constantly stung their faces and eyes until they bellowed in frustration and anger; but the wind only laughed all the harder. At one point they had been forced to don their crampons and lash themselves together in a line behind the sturdy Zhang. On another occasion they had shared the exhilarating, once-in-a-lifetime experience of being dragged behind the galloping beast over a smooth frozen lake, thanks to Elfswith's whalebone skates.

During the night, they had almost shared another once-in-a-lifetime experience—they had almost died. Just as Elfswith had promised, fierce winds came "screaming from the very heart of Eisholm, across the flat land where there be no shelter." Only Bolldhe's know-how had saved them that night from death and failure almost upon the very doorstep of Vaagenfjord Maw. Recalling tales he had heard of the reindeer hunters of Hoc-Valdrea, he had directed all of them to use their ice-saws to cut blocks of ice as swiftly as their numbed and breathless bodies could. Fighting against time, exhaustion and the rapidly failing light, they succeeded in constructing a crude igloo that would take the worst force out of the wind. They all piled inside, horse and all, and managed to survive the night by dint of sleeping embarrassingly close to each other.

The following day had seen even worse blizzards. Each step they took was accomplished by dogged perseverance alone, as the desperate, and by this stage, very frightened men had forced themselves onward. Even Zhang, further encumbered by the now unconscious form of Appa, had whinnied from time to time in anguish. Leaning forward at a forty-five degree angle into the gale, all the walkers had followed Wodeman, the only one among them capable of keeping his bearings in this blizzard.

Bolldhe was having a particularly bad time of it. At one point he looked up through the blinding snow to just about make out the stumbling shapes of all his fellow travelers ahead of him. *Ahead?* He had been swearing, almost crying like a child in fury and frustration at the beating he was receiving from the weather, and to see the others all ahead of him made him curse his weakness in every language he knew. That should have been him in the lead, not them! His coarse words, however, were snatched away by the even coarser wind.

But the company had learned something from the previous night's experience, and that evening made sure to establish camp in a spot amid hot springs and clouds of steam. From that night on they set their course by similarly welcoming areas, though always keeping the distinctive cat's-tooth peak of Ravenscairn in their sight as a guide. By the sixth evening of their trek across Melhus, they arrived at the last stretch of the journey.

Bolldhe managed to slip his liquor flask back under his pelt and into its belt pouch without letting in too much cold air. He chafed himself vigorously and tried to stamp some life back into the numb blocks of ice that his feet had become, then gazed around at his surroundings.

As far as the eye could see in every direction it was the same: a flat expanse of white, punctuated by jagged points of ice around which a freezing fog billowed. The light had almost failed, and they could no longer see the pinnacle of Ravenscairn itself, nor any other higher land save the rocky knoll upon which he and Wodeman now stood. Down below, on a patch of steaming black rock just warm enough to hold back the encroaching circle of ice that hemmed it in, he could see the others busily setting up for the night. The blaze of the campfire looked bleary through the fog, but infinitely more reassuring than the disembodied flares of red that could occasionally be seen in the sky from unseen, far-off volcanoes.

During his travels, he had heard many songs and tales of lands so cold even the sea would freeze over, but he had always dismissed that as poetic exaggeration, if not pure fantasy. But he realized now that the skalds had been right all along; for Melhus was a terrible land, yes, terrible beyond belief. Yet there was a fierce pride in Bolldhe's heart also. It was only right that he, Bolldhe the Wanderer, he who had traveled through lands of every extremity in climate and terrain, should finally have made it to the coldest, most inhospitable, most northerly place in the known world.

He turned back to Wodeman and grinned defiantly.

"So?" he asked. "What do we do now?"

The sorcerer had dragged him up to this higher place as soon as their day's journey was over. A quiet, private place, away from the others. He had not explained why to Bolldhe, but certain words had passed between them on the previous days, and Bolldhe had a fair idea of what was about to occur.

"We'll start by taking some of this," Wodeman began, as he extricated a pouch of something herbal from beneath his pelts. "Henbane leaf."

"What's it do?" Bolldhe wrinkled his nose dubiously.

"It's good stuff," the shaman reassured him, his exhaled breath falling to the ground in a shower of whispering crystals. "Helps to free your mind, block out the distractions of the present. Helps set you on the path to your inner consciousness . . . put you in touch with the spirits!"

"Sounds a bit fishy to me," Bolldhe replied. "Not really my thing."

"Suit yourself." Wodeman shrugged, and settled himself down in the shelter of a rock. "Mind if I have some?"

"Why? Are you going to get in touch with your inner consciousness too?"

"No," Wodeman replied simply, and lit up.

Bolldhe waited patiently while the other man puffed his special stuff and giggled a bit, then turned to him to explain.

"We're nearly there, Bolldhe; two days from Ravenscairn at the most. This may be our last opportunity to really talk, before . . ."

"Before entering the Rawgr's lair," Bolldhe finished for him, rather histrionically.

"There's something buried deep within you, something so important it will change the fate of our world," Wodeman continued, slurring his words slightly. "I don't have the slightest clue what it is, and neither does Appa—"

"Or me."

"Right. But we have to know. Or, at the very least, begin to guess . . . I don't know if you're hiding something from us, or whether you really have no idea why it is that you're so special, but we've now run out of time. Important words must come before important deeds, and now is the last chance for us to have them."

He peered closely at Bolldhe, but Bolldhe merely looked at a loss. "I'll do what I can," he said. "But I can't promise you anything."

Wodeman mumbled something under his breath, and shifted himself into a more comfortable position. "You see, what it is . . . If we mortals are lacking in sufficient knowledge, then perhaps we can turn to others who *do* know. Have you ever heard of the *H'urvisg?"*

"H'urvisg," Bolldhe repeated thoughtfully. "Is that anything like 'Urisk'? Half-mortal and half-fey?"

"It could be, in *your* language. H'urvisg are the earth-spirits: they dwell among us but are not of our kind."

"Where I come from, Urisks are no spirits: they're just the bastard spawn of succubus and man," Bolldhe replied, a little annoyed that he had been hauled away from the camp just to be lectured on Caravan People, as his mother rather euphemistically termed them. "They help out villeins, fetch and carry, perform all sorts of tasks, all for no pay, then think they have the right to stick their pointy noses into *our* affairs and give us the benefit of their higher wisdom."

"Mmn, I think we're talking about different beings here, after all. In any case, I can see you're skeptical, but I have to tell you that I have often asked H'urvisg for advice and, whatever you may think of them, they have proved themselves reliable."

"Just a minute," Bolldhe cut in. "Before you start, Wodeman, let me tell you something I've learned from my own life: I've been all over Lindormyn, and encountered many sorcerers of one description or another, and if there's one thing I'm fairly sure of, it's that spirits do not know the minds of men. They don't know our world, our feelings, our motivations, or any of that, even a fraction as well as we do ourselves, so they can have no wisdom or knowledge that could be of any use to us. Whatsoever."

"H'urvisgs are elementals; they are of the very stuff this world is made of," Wodeman insisted. "They may be limited in their depth of knowledge, but potentially unlimited in their release of energy. Their help is in the form of physical emotion, not wordy explanations. If they get a chance to feel what is within you, maybe they can unleash that inner energy of yours, like a volcano about to erupt."

"Maybe they'll just choose not to answer," Bolldhe countered. "*Maybe* they can't be bothered. Divination, or whatever you call it, has no compelling force. Have you ever considered that? In fact, when you think about it, can they even be *trusted?* No one ever claimed they were honest."

"Look, Bolldhe, it's getting bloody cold out here, and I really don't care all that much. These spells of mine are my way—and the way of the Torca, my own people. I don't care to question matters that are so . . ."

"Traditional?" Bolldhe suggested. "Set in stone?"

"Fundamental," Wodeman concluded. "Now shall we get on with this, or would you rather postpone having these words until we are in the Rawgr's own lair?"

Though he did not say so, Bolldhe would indeed rather have such discussions within the relative warmth and shelter of the Maw. He still did not believe there was anything there at all, but deep down gave a sigh. Wodeman's words were all too typical of humanity. The Torca here had previously asserted how openness is preferable to belief, but just listen to the old gasbag now. "Fundamental"? That was as good as admitting that belief itself is stronger than the object of belief. And Bolldhe on his travels had seen and heard of many cults, sciences, and even entire civilizations that were founded on beliefs that were now recognized to be false, yet were still going strong right up to the present.

People and their bloody anchors of faith. Entire lives built up or chained down by pipe smoke visions. And those most miserable people of all, who have no doctrine to start with, so have to invent one, and then disallow anyone—themselves included—to question it.

Thus their civilization is kept together, he surmised, *and I am kept out. . . .*

"Right, well . . . how do we get started?" he asked with a hint of weary resignation.

There was also a trace of resentment in his tone. Why did people fear the truth so much? Why did they always have to defer the responsibility of decision making and self-determination to higher beings? Even in Quiravia, a country famous for its republican ideals, the only decision its self-governing people ever took was in the election of leaders who would make all the decisions for them. The stupid idiots preferred that responsibility should rest on the shoulders of higher beings whom they could subsequently blame for messing things up.

Hu-bloody-manity! Pitiful!

Wodeman closed his eyes, took another long drag from the noxious weed, held it in for a while, then slowly exhaled, some of the smoke wafting straight up Bolldhe's nostrils. A slight dizziness passed over him, and for a brief moment he fancied he could see the smoke curling through Wodeman's beard. The sorcerer's eyes opened and, through the veil of henbane smoke, they regarded Bolldhe like red lanterns.

Then Bolldhe blinked, the moment passed, and the smoke was instantly taken by the wind.

Henbane, he reflected. Yes, it was a henbane derivative that he himself had used on those mad old abbesses way out in Dzhygyn-Erdtse. Now *that* had been a trip worth taking! Way out indeed . . . even though the only effect it had on *himself* was to make him walk around very fast and urinate a lot.

Well, if he gets something out of it, Bolldhe thought, *good on the old sod. It's about time he loosened up as bit.*

"First, I'm going to send you on a journey," Wodeman proclaimed. "You possess goodness in your soul, whatever you may think. Except you bury that soul so deep inside yourself, it's cut off from the cosmos by your hard shell."

"My what?"

"Your skepticism—you wear it around you like a suit of iron, and I'm not very good against iron. It'd be useless for me to try and delve into your soul from without. Maybe no man could get past armor such as yours."

"What *is* the plan, then?"

"Only you yourself stand any chance of discovering what lies within you, but perhaps I can guide you some of the way along that path. But remember: I can only show you the doors; it is you who must open them."

Bolldhe felt he should be smirking at this. But today he just could not manage it. Maybe the thin air was making him emotional. But, even so, it was Wodeman who had saved his life back in Eotunlandt. After reaching the safety of the tunnel he had ridden back out, right under the shadow of a giant's foot. And that took some doing. Yet all he asked for in return was this brief opportunity to perform a divination. He wondered if it was right: his humoring Wodeman like this. This dream-giving was the Torca's sole reason for joining the quest, his divine mission from Erce the earth spirit, to guide Bolldhe by means of visions, and thus allow him to discover for himself how to defeat Drauglir, the potential despoiler of all the land.

Well, it was true Bolldhe hated all the gods—their false promises, their machinations, and especially their mindless followers. One of the reasons he had decided to become a false fortune-teller in the first place was as a way of getting back at all that stuff, laughing at his gullible customers while simultaneously sticking two fingers up at their ridiculous gods. And though Wodeman may have earned at least some of Bolldhe's respect along the way—even to the extent that he sometimes wondered if there might be some validity in the shaman's beliefs—he nevertheless found it hard to credit the power of dreams.

But, despite Bolldhe's disbelief, he had to acknowledge Wodeman's selflessness in the matter; as he wanted nothing for himself, just the chance to help Bolldhe yet further. Surely Bolldhe owed the strange man this much, at least.

He nodded assent, and Wodeman commenced.

"Close your eyes," he purred, "and relax."

"Wodeman, it's cold enough here to freeze the tears in my eyes. I won't be doing any relaxing."

"You will," Wodeman insisted calmly. "Just still your brain, loosen your muscles, and absorb the cold into yourself. It is a part of this land, its very spiritual essence, as natural as the forests around Nordwas. Do not fight it; do not think of it as the enemy; it was here long before the Rawgr, and will be here long after he's gone. So welcome it into yourself. Breathe deeply, think of nothing, just listen to my voice. . . ."

As the sorcerer droned on, Bolldhe's thoughts drifted—as per usual in these situations. He could not focus on anything else but the cold. Despite his promise to go along with this ritual, Wodeman's words went unheeded. Again the shaman had become just a disembodied, lispy mouth floating before

Bolldhe's face. Soon, though, even that image began to fade, and when Bolldhe finally tried to concentrate on the words, he found it impossible. They mingled with the sound of the wind that buffeted his face, became one with it, in a moaning, whistling reverberation like the rushing of an underground stream.

Not once did he feel the urge to walk around fast or urinate.

Yet, after a while Bolldhe noticed that the cold did indeed seem less of a discomfort, and instead more like the refreshing touch of clean, white sheets on a hot summer's night. He began to loosen up.

Funny, really, he thought, *how extremes of temperature can feel so alike: ice against the skin can burn like fire. Hot or cold, it's just a state of mind—*

("—your mind: I direct you, give you the keys to open your mind—")

In fact, the more he thought about that, the warmer it seemed to get. Stifling, really. He broke out into a sweat. *Maybe I should loosen my clothes, peel them off layer by layer . . .*

("—unclasp your suit of iron. Throw it off—")

. . . expose myself to the elements . . .

Melhus receded, and Bolldhe found himself standing in the middle of a courtyard. It was a vast and empty courtyard of hard, grey flagstones that stretched away on all sides, and was encircled by great walls that towered to inconceivable heights. No windows breached this barrier, nor were there any gates or doors; not even the tiniest wicket gate. And not a crack could be seen between the brickwork. Wind howled about the courtyard and shook the ground beneath his feet.

In all of this desolate place, only one thing stood there: a single building dwarfed by the dimensions of the courtyard, but of such striking appearance—

What's that smell? he thought suddenly.

Turning, he saw a gaggle of tumbrel drivers, all standing there just watching him, waiting.

Even here? Bolldhe thought in exasperation. He shook his head and walked on quickly.

Toward the building he headed, and as he drew closer to it, the bizarreness of its design grew so apparent that it began to make his eyes hurt. It incorporated walls topped with an array of stupas, statues, and gargoyles, punctuated with web-spun stained glass windows, and buttressed with rickety lean-tos and even a little shack that was probably a lavatory. Intersecting it were aqueducts engraved with arcane symbols, trailing growths of ivy and henbane, external staircases that seemed to lead to nowhere. And the whole was topped by two mismatching rooftops: a small, stone cupola that was half crumbled like a broken eggshell, and a spiral tower of tarnished bronze. Atop both of these stood a weather vane and between them was slung a grubby clothesline.

The general impression was of a temple built in collusion by every cult in the world, from every era in history, using every design, material and color known to man. A jumbled collection of all Bolldhe's memories, thrown together into one untidy edifice.

As he approached, his feet were snagged in the overgrown weed patch surrounding it. He proceeded more slowly, and perceived an unusually solid looking gatehouse flanking the building, with a rickety, wooden summerhouse to one side of it, and a barrel of stinking oil on the other. Bolldhe walked right up to the gate, and could see that it was heavily barred by a great portcullis of black iron. He looked for a keyhole or lever, but found none. A single lantern burned with a fierce red flame above this iron gate, and above that was arrayed a collection of gargoyles. As he looked closer, Bolldhe realized that each bore an unsettlingly disfigured likeness to one or other of his traveling companions.

The wind was getting colder and sang with a lonely voice, and it was beginning to get dark. Bolldhe approached the portcullis. Having no better plan, he grasped the bars and shook them hard. But the gate remained stubbornly shut, and would not move an inch—

("—not until you can think of a good reason why it should allow you in—")

He took a step back, and thought hard.

"Because it's the only thing to be seen *in* this place," he said aloud, speaking easily once more now that he was using his native tongue. He looked up, and still the lantern burned red. This time, however, the gargoyles were smirking at him, especially the one with the wide brimmed hat, and even the thwarted tumbrel drivers had gathered around to watch the entertaining spectacle of this mad bloody foreigner who talked to gates.

Bolldhe thought again.

"Because it's cold, and I'm feeling lonely," he admitted, hoping this mawkish display of candor would unlock the gate.

Still the lantern burned defiantly red, and by now the gargoyles were laughing so hard that phlegmy water began to spit out of their mouths. The tumbrel drivers were beaming like a line of horse skulls, settling down comfortably in their carts, making the most of the performance.

Bolldhe clicked his tongue in frustration. After a moment of pondering, he suddenly tried again:

"Because it's *my* temple, and I *really* want to go inside."

Red.

"Because if I don't, this whole thing is a waste of time!"

Red, still.

He tried a totally different approach. "I'm going in because I'm the best there is; *the very best*. So open up now!" He strode forward with his chest thrust out confidently, and did not slow until he smacked his forehead hard against the metal bars and landed on his backside.

Bellows of mirth echoed around the courtyard. It sounded as if the entire world was laughing at him. He shook his head, then stood up groggily. Water was splashing down upon his face, and when he looked up he saw that it came from the gargoyles.

No normal man would have been able to show similar restraint under such provocation. But Bolldhe was no normal man: he had been mocked and laughed at in every far corner of Lindormyn, and if anyone could handle it, he could. Nonetheless, this was becoming more than a little frustrating. Just how many good reasons are there in the world to pass through a simple gate? He was also rather dismayed to see that the lantern was now burning an even brighter red than ever.

Then his head began to clear.

"I need to find out exactly what is inside my place here, not for my own sake but for the quest."

At last, the lantern softened to a pale amber. And even the laughter subsided. There was resentment evident in the tumbrel drivers now and, for the first time in his life, Bolldhe began to feel actually intimidated by them. The stench of their unwashed bodies was becoming quite overpowering, reaching toward him like hot gusts of pestilence, till he found himself fighting for breath.

". . . For the sake of the world, then?" he tried.

Back to red.

"No, no, you're right, flame; I'm not doing this for any noble cause. I'm doing it just for myself. Right?"

Finally, the lantern flame shimmered, then changed to a ghostly green. There was a mechanical snap of sound from somewhere inside, and the gate was hauled up in a jarring clamor of turning machinery that drowned the last titterings from both gargoyles and tumbrel drivers.

Bolldhe now found himself inside the temple. He stood in some kind of hall or anteroom, with a fountain set in the middle of the floor, and several closed doors leading off it. It reminded him somewhat of those cloistered quadrangles found in the private homes of the enormously hospitable residents of Bisq'ra Oasis, which he had visited several years ago. Pleasantly cool, with its blue and white tiles, it contained an abundance of green leafed plants in pots. But it was all a little worn, and slightly musty.

Disturbing the dust and dead leaves lying on the floor, he walked over to the fountain and sat on the marble ledge that surrounded it.

"What now, then?" he asked, his voice echoing softly around the hall.

He shivered. This place looked so pleasant, and yet also so old and . . . lonely. The fountain rooms he had been in when he had traveled through the desert had always been so full of kind, friendly faces. All of them interested in him, Bolldhe. Here, though, he was alone, and had no one to show him around the house. He could do it himself, of course, but that was bad manners in these homes. He needed someone. Needed help—

*("—not enough that you need help, but that you admit you need help, and ask
for it—")*

Bolldhe cleared his throat, and called out: "Is anyone there? Is anyone at
home?"

This time the echoes came back to him embarrassingly loudly. Bolldhe
coughed, and called out again. "I say, I could do with a little help here."

As if by magic, a man appeared.

Dressed in the long, pink and gold robes of a monk, he beamed at Bolldhe
so widely that his face seemed to have been fitted with special cheek extensions
just to accommodate such a smile.

"Can I help you, sir?" piped the monk.

Bolldhe leapt to his feet, startled, and found himself bowing low, both arms
extended before him, his right wrist clasped in his left hand in the manner of
the people of Bisq'ra.

"In your house I am reborn," Bolldhe stammered, hoping he had remembered the correct way to address him. It was a long time since he had made use
of such customs, but he was glad of the opportunity to relive memories of a
gentler, more hospitable land.

The monk merely nodded, but his smile softened in genuine warmth. He
came over to stand before Bolldhe. They smiled at each other, though Bolldhe
was well aware of how stilted his must have appeared compared with the
monk's open, natural smile. Bolldhe waited for him to say something, to begin
the proceedings, but the monk seemed quite content to just stand there nodding and smiling.

Bolldhe coughed uneasily. "I don't really know what I'm doing here," he
confessed awkwardly. "I mean, what happens now? Aren't you going to show
me around your house?"

The monk chuckled softly with a shake of his head. "But this is *your* house.
I am just your servant."

Bolldhe felt confused. He suddenly realized that he had absolutely no idea
where he was, how he had got here, or even *who* he was. His memories extended only as far as the courtyard's perimeter wall. He thought harder, and
gradually certain memories did begin to occur to him.

"Everyone was so kind in Bisq'ra," he reminisced fondly, "despite the
harshness of their lives. I just felt comfortable there, and welcome . . . at
home."

"You feel that way here?"

"Well yes, I suppose I do. To be honest, I've never felt more comfortable in
a strange house."

"Well, then." The monk turned to pick up a pewter jug and a cylix. "Perhaps you'd like a drink now."

He leaned over to hold the jug beneath the sparkling gush of the fountain.
The sound of the water hitting the pewter was like the sprinkle of tiny ice-shards

upon crystal. He then poured the water into the cylix, proffering it to Bolldhe, who stared at it noncommittally.

"But you fully trust your own home?" the monk enquired. "Do you truly feel safe here? You cannot proceed further until you are completely comfortable with it. Ah, Bolldhe, it has been so long since you were last here."

Bolldhe, being as innately cautious as they came, had never been one to indulge in leaps of faith. And besides, now that it came to it, the monk's incessant smile was becoming a tad irritating. Nevertheless, he carefully reached out to accept the cylix and, pausing only to take one last look at his companion, drank deeply.

As the crystal clear water flowed down his throat, memories of his early childhood came flooding back to him. He gasped in ecstasy, and now, when he opened his eyes again, all the doors around the hall stood wide open.

"If you no longer fear what is inside yourself," the monk proclaimed happily, "then half the battle is won."

Hearing the changed tone of voice, Bolldhe looked up sharply. The monk, he suddenly realized, was now a woman. He peered at her rounded face, then said: "You're Yorda, aren't you?"

Yorda beamed joyfully, and winked at him.

But Bolldhe was not so sure. "You weren't a monk," he said, "and you didn't even come from Bisq'ra."

"It doesn't matter about that. I'm your Spiritwalker, now."

"But when I knew you, didn't we . . . you know? That is—"

Bolldhe went red, and scratched the back of his neck.

"This temple holds many secrets," Yorda went on, ignoring his comment. "Some of its rooms are light, some dark. I shall guide you certainly, but *you* must tell me where you wish to go."

"All right, let's try climbing that tower," Bolldhe suggested. "To get a good view of this world I'm in."

"As you wish." Yorda turned, and led him through one of the doors.

Up the spiral steps they climbed, up and up, round and round, higher and higher, until they finally emerged onto a viewing platform. The wind was howling loudly up here, bringing with it voices from Bolldhe's past and present, and ever it snatched at his clothes, as if trying to pull him this way and that. Bolldhe ignored it all, and pressed on toward the parapet; he wanted to see how everything looked from up here.

There was nothing but clouds however, a thick brown fog that clung to his skin and smelled of snow. Bolldhe began to feel strangely disturbed, but continued to peer through the fog, trying to see through to the world beyond—

(*"—look for a sign. A rune, or symbol, engraved in the stone about you. Note its form. It will tell you much—"*)

But Bolldhe, being Bolldhe, would not listen to any who would persuade him. Still he tried to pierce the mist with his gaze—

("—the rune! If you cannot see out, then—")

Bolldhe pushed himself away from the parapet abruptly, and returned to Yorda without even looking round at the walls, floor or ceiling of the viewing platform. Together they descended the stairwell. He would not be told.

"If you find you don't like it here, you can leave any time," Yorda said. "Just ring any of these bells, and that will be that."

She was guiding Bolldhe around the upper rooms of the temple, guiding him by the hand. They had left the tower and its platform, and now wandered in plusher surroundings. Down corridors of vaulted ceilings hung with bright silver lanterns they proceeded, treading upon carpets of finest Adt-T'man wool, between ornately carved marble pillars that adorned the walls. The intervening spaces were hung with numerous oil paintings specifically depicting scenes from Bolldhe's life, amid trophies of his travels mounted upon carnelian pedestals, and shelf upon shelf of books.

"What do you mean, 'that will be that'?" he asked.

"Just what I say. If you feel disturbed, ring one of these little bells you see on each window sill, and you'll be out of this temple. That is, if you really do wish to keep wandering around that empty courtyard in the fog, going round and round the perimeter wall without any hope of escape. Now that *would* be a journey of epic proportions." She squeezed his hand, and gazed up into his eyes.

"But what is it, that great yard out there?" Bolldhe asked, studying it through one of the windows. It was not just foggy out there. It was also getting dark, getting late.

And still the tumbrel drivers hovered as if waiting for him, standing silently out there in the fog, unmoving. He shivered, and turned away.

"Your world," she replied—

("—your mind—")

"—What you've made it become."

"I told you before, I feel comfortable in here," Bolldhe insisted. "But up there, on that balcony . . ."

"That is the highest point in the temple," Yorda explained, "the only place where you can view the real world—the world outside—beyond yourself. Do you really believe this quest is all merely about you? You think you're that important?"

But Bolldhe did not bother to respond. He knew he was here to find out about himself, and that he could not help fulfil the quest unless he did just that.

"What are all these books, anyway?" he asked.

"Your life," she replied. "Everything you ever did, every sight, every sound, every thought, all of it written on parchment and bound in leather."

He looked down the length of the corridor, at shelf after shelf after shelf, all crowded with great tomes, stretching out of sight.

"Impressive, isn't it?" Yorda chirped. "Who would have thought that a man of your tender years could have done so much?"

Bolldhe contemplated it all, then said: "No, I reckon that's about right."

He went up to one shelf, and scanned it. "Hmm, seems to be a section missing," he said. "There don't appear to be any records on when I was aged eight."

Yorda remained silent. As she led him on past the bookshelves he felt her fingers intertwine his, and her grip became firmer. They passed a large mirror set into one of the wall spaces between the pillars, and in it was reflected his own image, being led along not by Yorda—nor by a Bisq'ra monk—but by Finwald smiling confidently.

He yanked himself free and stared round at his guide. It was Yorda still but, though she gave no indication that she had noticed his wariness, she did seem more distant and brittle, and she avoided eye contact.

Bolldhe looked ahead in the direction where she was taking him and sighed. This corridor seemed to be going round and round, leading nowhere. He could spend a lifetime reading these books and still remain none the wiser. His Spiritwalker was not really helping him at all.

The tower was no good, he decided. *If I'm ever to find out anything, I need to go down, not up.*

No sooner had this thought sprung into his head than the corridor ahead of him forked. Yorda was no longer holding his hand, but walked on ahead. She turned and beckoned him along the right-hand fork.

"Just a minute," Bolldhe called out to her. "Where does the other way go?"

Yorda looked sad now, and thin, perhaps even a little transparent. "I go this way, not that," she replied in a strangely quiet voice, her eyes cast down.

"But what about the *other* way?" Bolldhe demanded, staying put. "Does it lead downward?"

Yorda reluctantly nodded, and her eyes began to fill with tears. "I go this way, Bolldhe," she repeated, "and I would ask you to come with me. This world is so cold without somebody to share it."

As she spoke, memories of dappled sunlight reflecting off long, shimmering, black hair suddenly came flooding back to Bolldhe. Before his eyes the corridor began to transform into a narrow, leaf-strewn lane, the marble pillars into trees with boughs that arched overhead in a shady, vaulted canopy. There came also the soft murmur of clear water, the contented croaking of a toad in the reeds, the single toll of a shrine bell that drifted across the fields with the smell of incense—and a lump in the throat that would not go away.

Do you want my help, Bolldhe? Do you want . . . me? Which path do you choose?

A part of him had ached to submit to her, to acquiesce to friendship and all its ties, all those years ago. But now he was aware he was just following this past dream like a dumb pack animal. He had walked away then, and he would do the same now. His choice was made.

"Good-bye, Bolldhe," she said, and dissipated into nothing. The bright green and gold of the lane faded to grey . . . and was stone once more. The peaceful sounds of a field in summer were quieted, and the incense snuffed out. He was alone again, with nothing of Yorda but a lingering sadness, and a shadow of wonder at what might have been.

They have no hold on me, he told himself, *and I, no obligation to them. For I am BOLLDHE, and I go my own way.*

Truly alone now, Bolldhe wandered through the winding corridors and secret chambers of his mind with mounting agitation and impatience, forever seeking a way down. Somewhere behind him he could hear the creaking of axles, and the low rumor of tumbrel wheels upon stone, as the air turned rancid, with visions of bad-toothed grins trundling after him. They had found a way in! He quickened his step, keeping his eyes focused dead ahead.

Gradually he managed to work his way down to the lower levels, leaving the sounds and smells of his pursuers behind him. And finally, he came to the cellars.

No, these were not cellars—no cool vaults for fine wines and cold meats. This place had the dank feel of a dungeon. It was a place of rusted iron bars, walls of fingernail-scratched granite smeared with filth, manacles flecked with dried blood and old, ragged skin. The floors were puddled with feculence and scattered with the wretched detritus of human misery: sheets of old parchment scratched with charcoal letters—the diaries of prisoners' final days—and crude idols formed from refuse by shaking hands and desperate minds. Despair flowed like a black vapor and fear, evil and death stalked cackling up and down between the cells.

In one cubicle a single flame hovered in the darkness, shedding no light. As Bolldhe slunk past, it lengthened, solidified, and became a snake with eyes burning magma-red. Held spellbound for a moment, he watched as the reptile expanded, and became a tall, broad-shouldered man wearing a yak hide kirtle and a satin-white coif. Only the apparition's eyes remained the same.

Before he fled, Bolldhe noticed that the red-eyed prisoner's hands were tied, his mouth gagged, and his cell door guarded by shadowy grey-robed sentinels. The despair was at its strongest here, and stank of condemned men's sweat.

Bolldhe blundered on through the darkness until he came to the end of the corridor. There he stopped dead. Before him lay the final cell, its door open wide, and within it, nothing but blackness. This was the blackness of death without hope, final and inescapable. No conviction of faith or any glib philosophizing could stand up to such darkness. Not even the strongest power in the universe could sustain itself as more than a candle's flame against the roaring tempest of that oblivion.

And within that black void was the end of the quest.

Olchor, the father of Drauglir.

It was useless, he knew, but Bolldhe had to keep searching. Frantically he scanned his surroundings, until finally his eyes latched onto another shape. It was a figure, familiar from days long ago, carved in relief upon a manhole cover lying right under his feet. It depicted his erstwhile god Pel-Adan, holding the legendary sword Unferth in both gauntleted hands. Strong and reassuring, Bolldhe grasped at this image with the desperation of a man drowning in quicksand, and heaved the lid off the manhole. Letting it fall upon the stone floor with a heavy clang, without hesitation he dropped himself down into the darkness below.

Out of a bottomless ocean of blackness Bolldhe swam, up through the shallower waters of nausea and disorientation, to find himself spluttering and heaving upon the lonely strand of wakefulness. He raised himself carefully to his feet, clutched his head in agony, and leaned back against the wall.

He opened his eyes cautiously, and winced as bright yellow light pierced into the back of his brain. Slowly, his eyes adjusted till he regained full consciousness.

That was quite a fall he had taken. Quite how far, he did not know, for above him there was now just a low ceiling, with no skylight or vent down which he could have tumbled. Exactly how long he had lain unconscious, he could only guess.

However he had arrived there, he now appeared to be at the end of a long corridor. Behind him was a dead end: a solid stone wall engraved with that same icon of Pel-Adan he had recognized on the manhole cover earlier. There was a difference, though; for this one was considerably larger, and rather than a relief it was an indentation, almost as if he were on the reverse side of the manhole cover, but with the dimensions all wrong.

Bolldhe turned to face the corridor. It was lit by beautifully wrought lanterns, much like those in the upper rooms, but more antique. The corridor itself was like an older design of those above, with a floor of polished stone, a rib-vaulted ceiling, and the finely carved columns and arches of a triforium running along each side. It reminded him of the nave in the temple of Pel-Adan back in his birth place Moel-Bryn, somewhere he had not been for so many years. Even the smells here brought back memories long forgotten: a mixture of clean white linen surplices, polished chain mail, and wax-candle smoke. Faint sounds—more the ghosts of sounds—drifted down the corridor toward him: the strident singing of a choir; the moral exhortations of clerics; the hurried footsteps of a late-arriving Peladane clanking down the aisle; the mewling of the youngest of the congregation; the un-self-conscious flatulence of the eldest; and the impatient sighing of those in-between.

Solid beliefs for solid lives. What was he doing *here*?

Down the nave Bolldhe strode, breathing in the air of his youth. About him he thought he caught glimpses of others his same age then—ten years old— young boys in ill-fitting cuirasses or surplices who seemed to develop an incurable itch the moment they set foot in the temple, and girls of a similar age trying to catch the eye of the dashing young knights.

But the farther he walked, the dimmer became the light. The antique lanterns gave way to naked torches positioned in black cast-iron cressets set along the walls. The polished floor, vaulted ceiling, and triforium were now just plain dressed stone, with more ancient, cruder engravings of the god Pel-Adan etched into the surfaces at intervals. The singing was supplanted by a slow, rhythmic chanting, and the smells were now of damp turf and penned sheep.

Deeper and farther he went, until he entered the cold, subterranean depths of a series of prehistoric caves, lit only by the occasional burning log. Here the images of Pel-Adan were primitive petroglyphs engraved on the surface of boulders, and the only sounds were a low, god-fearing, moaning chant against the beat of hide drums. There was now a pervasive stench of animal skins, blood and sweat.

Stumbling among the stalagmites, Bolldhe continued. He did not pause until he came to a place where there was no light, and no sound. No sound, that is, until he reached a spot which by its very feel he could tell was far more ancient and far deeper than any place he had yet been: the bottom of the well of his deepest memory.

There was the sound of running water. He emerged into a vast underground cavern of dripping limestone and freezing air that smelled of ice. This was the lowest place he could go, the place where he would find that which he sought.

No longer needing any light or any other guidance, Bolldhe slowly walked over to the far side of the cavern. His outstretched hand met with a wall of ice, so hard and thick it might as well have been rock. In his mind, he knew he must somehow get through it. He thought hard.

The never-ending beat of hammer upon anvil . . . across the ice-field . . . smoking fissures . . .

The memory of Elfswith's words chiseled away like tiny knocker hammers at the periphery of Bolldhe's mind. What had he warned them they might meet on Melhus Island?

The fire giants! The Jutul! Of course. In this land of fire and ice it was the only thing that made any sense.

As if in answer to his thoughts, a tremendous ringing of metal upon metal broke out in another section of the cavern, so loud that it sent tremors through the rock. Bolldhe could see the dull glow of fire, a shower of bright orange sparks with every beat that sounded, and the enormous, hulking silhouette of what could only be a Jutul.

He had met a Jutul before, of course: the only Jutul any man was likely to meet. Uch-Toghyz was the armorer-in-chief to K'sar Govdelig IV, the warrior-chief and dromedary magnate of the Drur Hills, that ungovernable land of no-madic herders that separated Vregh-Nahov to the north from Ochtamman to the south. Uch-Toghyz was a singularity: a Jutul who chose not only to mix with non-Jutul, but also to serve in their long-term employ. Having become thus accustomed to living above ground and coming into regular contact with people of diverse race and social status, he had developed a gregariousness and refinement that was remarkably cosmopolitan by Jutul standards. Bolldhe him-self had regularly shared tea on the mezzanine balcony with Uch-Toghyz, get-ting to know much of his disposition, his customs, and his interests.

All of which was now to prove utterly useless of course, as the Jutul were the most solitary, bad tempered, intransigent and mercenary oafs on the face of Lindormyn. Or under it.

"FOKKIN 'ELL, BOY! WADDYA WANT? CAN'T YOU SEE I'M WORKIN', ISN'T IT?" the fire giant bellowed, as Bolldhe tentatively ap-proached.

The Jutul that now strode out of the darkest corner of Bolldhe's deepest memory was definitely not the urbane Uch-Toghyz. No easygoing conversa-tionalist, and with a cough that sounded like a wrench caught in gears, this was a Jutul cast from an entirely different mold.

At ten feet tall and nearly as wide, the fire giant looked more like some heavy industrial machine than a living being. He turned his face to Bolldhe and glared fiercely at him. The creature's pig-like face had metal tusks protruding from the lower jaw, a thick, greasy layer of soot coating his skin, and two glow-ing white eyes rimmed with red, like the fire from a blast furnace. A walrus skin apron pocked with scorch marks and smeared with graphite protected his front, but apart from that he was entirely naked. The hairs on his dark skin looked like steely curls of swarf, and his fingernails and toenails were chisel-like talons.

Bolldhe took a step back, unsure what his next move should be. The Jutul blew an angry puff of steam from his nostrils, then went back to his task. Girder-thick arms swung like pistons with unmalleable purpose, a huge ham-mer and some tongs gripped in gigantic vise-like hands. Bolldhe had no idea how to communicate with such a being; his previous experience of Uch-Toghyz now seemed laughably irrelevant. No tea on the mezzanine would sway *this* lumbering slab of newly-smelted pig iron from his labors—it would be like trying to negotiate with a siege engine. What Bolldhe needed was to lure his at-tention with something precious, appeal to his greed. . . .

But, even if there was any available in this place, Bolldhe knew the Jutul would have little time for gold or gems. What they craved above all else was *magic*.

In exasperation he puzzled: *How can I lay my hands upon something I know nothing of, in a place I don't even understand?*

Maybe Wodeman might know. What was it the sorcerer had advised him? "Expose yourself to the elements."

("—let the H'urvisg unleash your emotion like raw elemental energy—")

Wodeman's words resonated in his mind as loud as they could between the hammerings of the Jutul. But unlike most people, Bolldhe had never been able to believe in something just because it would be advantageous to do so—and he certainly had no belief in the H'urvisg. It was time to finish all this metaphysical codswallop in the only way he knew how.

"Listen, you!" he shouted. "There's a great wall of ice over here, and it's in my way. I want you to thaw—"

The Jutul wheeled around and flame and smoke belched from his mouth.

"THAW, IS IT?" he bellowed. "WELL, THERE'S IMPUDENCE FOR YOU, AN' I DUNNO WHAT!" And with that he picked up his glowing anvil and hurled it straight at Bolldhe.

Even before it had left the giant's fingers, Bolldhe had thrown himself upon the ground. A sudden explosion of elemental fury seethed through the air as the red-hot anvil exploded into the ice wall, destroying both of them. From the Jutul came a roar fit to shake the very foundations of the world. It vibrated with a painful buzz in Bolldhe's ears, then trailed off into hollow silence.

The Jutul was gone—and so was the ice wall.

He leapt to his feet, and stared at the opening in the cave where the ice had been. Slowly, hardly daring to disturb the profound stillness, he approached. Something important, something of the greatest significance for himself and possibly the whole world, was about to happen. He could sense the press of history, all those terrible and wonderful deeds, the deaths and lives of men and all their struggles, and indeed the destiny of men for centuries to come, all *that* he could feel now hinging upon the pivot of this very moment. He was about to step over a threshold—as he had almost done when he had killed Eggledawc Clagfast—and find out something about himself that would change everything forever.

Steadily, almost ceremonially, he paced slowly toward that hole in the wall. As he did so, he heard a faint music, or maybe the sound of the sea, seeming to emerge from the rock itself. He reached the gap, held his breath . . .

And looked through.

Bolldhe stared expressionlessly at what lay before him. Then his eyes widened, his heart began pounding fit to burst, and his lips retracted in a grimace of revulsion and horror.

"Not me . . ." he whispered in disbelief. "I never—not that . . ."

He shook his head in sobbing denial of what he was witnessing. Then his mind snapped, and he tore himself from the hole and hurled himself screaming back the way he had come.

The bells! was all he could think of. *Those silver bells!*

He sped through the same tunnels, tripping over, colliding heavily with the walls, splashing through the puddles on the floor that were already freezing over again. It was a flight spurred by unreasoning insanity in which his only thought was to find the silver bells Yorda had told him about earlier, and exit this nightmare.

But there were none to be found down here, and he charged around the tunnels in ever-decreasing circles of despair.

Where were those blasted tumbrel drivers when you needed them most?

Then, without warning, he came to a dead end. He realized through his panic that he had somehow arrived back at the commencement of this subterranean journey through his mind, at the place where he had dropped through the manhole. But it was all different now; there were no columns, no tiles or engravings like before; it was just another dripping cave of dancing shadows and hollow, watery sounds.

Bolldhe stopped dead. There ahead of him right in the middle of the cave, could be seen a solitary figure, swathed in white garments, squatting by a stream that leaked slickly through the cavern. The face was shrouded beneath a pointed white hood, and its attention was wholly focused on some task it was performing. Bolldhe shivered convulsively, but called out cautiously.

"Yorda?"

Still the figure did not look up, but continued in its task of washing clothes in the water. Bolldhe peered closer, and saw that the stream ran red with blood from the same garments. The smell was like a sluice in an abattoir.

He guessed it was not Yorda.

"Messy devil, aren't you?" issued a voice from beneath the hood.

Definitely not Yorda.

"Who are you?" Bolldhe asked tentatively, not moving from the spot.

Again that voice, like dry twigs being snapped: "I'm old Benne Nighe, and I've got something that belongs to you."

Bolldhe did not budge. Having fled from his awful vision, his courage was completely spent. He began to quiver all over, and sweat beaded his face despite the freezing cold in this subterranean cavern.

"If it's any consolation, I'm not real," the clothes-washing figure assured him, with perhaps the barest hint of mockery.

Fearfully, more out of desperation than courage, Bolldhe finally padded closer. All he wanted now was to exit this awfulness, even if it meant facing more and greater terror to do so. It was an expedient, like forcing one's fingers down one's throat to vomit.

Just two yards off, and keeping the stream between himself and the apparition, Bolldhe stopped. He looked down at the filthy water and bloodied clothes, and straightaway recognized that they were his own.

The figure finally looked up at him, revealing a shriveled, bark-skin Huldre face utterly devoid of even the merest trace of humanity. Eyes white as an empty page suddenly dilated and, before he had the chance even to cry out, they drew him in. From somewhere distant, Bolldhe could hear sounds like a funeral procession, and the crackling of a great fire. Then the Benne Nighe's eyes turned from white to red, and within them Bolldhe could see flames rising, reaching out to consume him.

"Idiot!" she spat. "Coward!"

And Bolldhe was screaming in the fires of his own cremation. . . .

With a wail of anguish, Bolldhe awoke. It was absolutely freezing . . . and he was being attacked by a terrible, leather-faced devil in a white hood. Bolldhe pushed it away with a scream, lurched to his feet, and immediately skidded back onto the icy ground.

"Bolldhe, you idiot!" the figure cursed him. "Get a grip, man!"

He stared up at the devil blankly, not understanding where he was or what was going on.

"The dream, remember?"

"The dream . . ." Bolldhe repeated dumbly. Strong hands held him down, but not ungently. He looked up at the figure above him, and gradually made out—for it was almost dark—that his attacker was only the shaman, and the white hood a layer of snow covering his shaggy hair.

Bolldhe stared about himself to check that this was all real, and spotted the rest of the party going about their business down at the campsite. Never in his life had he experienced such an agony of fondness and a surge of relief as he experienced now, at the sight of such perfect, down-to-earth mundaneness: four men cooking food and setting up camp. He turned over onto his front, plunged his face into the snow, and began sobbing until his whole body shook.

Bolldhe could not forgive himself for breaking down like that. Especially in front of another person. He had never committed such an absurd display before in his life, not even in front of his horse, and now he felt stained, degraded to the level of every other human. He hardly heard Wodeman's words at all as the sorcerer animatedly discussed the dream.

Bolldhe had related every detail of his spiritwalk to Wodeman: the mysterious temple, Yorda, the caves, the Benne Nighe, everything. All, that is, except what he had seen beyond the ice wall. And that was simply because he could not *remember* what he had seen. It had been so terrible that he had recoiled from it, and the ice wall was now firmly back in place.

Who would have thought one's own soul could harbor the greatest terror in the world?

"It's not the first time it's happened," he confessed. "Back in Eotunlandt, when I . . . killed that thief . . ."

"Ah yes, we had all been wondering about that little episode," Wodeman admitted with uncharacteristic delicacy.

"I can't tell you what happened to me at that time, any more than I can tell you what I saw in my vision just now. All I know is that on both occasions the vision was the same . . . but this time it was even stronger."

Wodeman stared at him intently, but held his silence.

"I was eight years old," Bolldhe went on, "a period of my life I seem to have no memories of at all, though normally I remember everything clearly. . . . And what's stranger still is that this gap has never before occurred to me—a part of my life just washed away."

"Locked away," Wodeman corrected him. "Sealed in ice. Something happened to you when you were a child, something so terrible your mind couldn't cope with it. You shut it away, but it has left a mark—an engram, like an inscription on your brain."

"A carving," Bolldhe pointed out, "like all those other carvings."

"Of Pel-Adan."

"Right." Bolldhe shook his head. "That bastard really does know how to leave his mark on a man, doesn't he?"

"You've sensed deep down that your old faith has hurt you more than you can remember, haven't you? Is that why you fled your native country?"

"I didn't flee. Nothing so dramatic. I just left, walked out"

"But the engram is important," Wodeman insisted, "maybe the key. There are so many other things significant in your dream, it's hard to tell which is the most important. The tower? The rune? The Benne Nighe?"

"Yorda?" Bolldhe cut in, and instantly wished he had not.

"Your Spiritwalker may or may not mean anything much. For most people it's just a comfort-figure, someone they trust, something to reassure them."

Bolldhe nodded in assent, glad that that bit was out of the way.

"Some dreamers take the tower, some the deep place," Wodeman explained. "When you chose the tower, I thought you'd see the rune—that would've told us much."

He paused, giving Bolldhe a chance to explain himself, but Bolldhe did not say a thing. *What's he expecting?* he thought, frowning. *An apology?*

Wodeman shrugged. He knew Bolldhe well enough not to pursue closely matters such as these. "Oh well, I don't suppose we'll ever know now—but maybe the important point *is* your refusal to look at it."

"I'm a stubborn, arrogant sod," Bolldhe smiled. "But the Benne Nighe?"

At the mention of that, Wodeman's face looked genuinely pained, an old weather-beaten tramp with ragged hair encrusted with ice, for once every bit like the disenfranchised and destitute old alcoholics that many of his people had become.

"I fear your retreat from the engram may prove to be the finish of you," he admitted heavily, bluntly, "and the Benne Nighe the herald of your death, for that is the only time such spirits choose to visit us. But, then again, perhaps she just stands for death in general."

"Death . . . yes." Bolldhe shivered, a vague memory flitting through his mind, ruffling the back-cloth of his consciousness. "There was much death behind that ice wall. The whole place was awash with blood, and I was right there in the middle of it, like a child staggering through the ruination of the slain. . . ."

He stood up, ready to leave. "I'm finished now," he announced. "I won't be doing any more dreams for you. That's it. But thank you, Wodeman; I feel better now, strangely enough. I just hope you feel adequately repaid for saving my life."

The Torca nodded sadly. He too realized there would be no more dreams. His job—his very reason for coming along on this quest—was finally at an end. It was a relief, really, despite the limited success he had seen. At least now he no longer needed to strive, to rack his brains, or to agonize. And, as he himself said, "At least we can get down to that campfire now; I don't know about you, but I'm bloody freezing up here."

As they made their way down to the camp together, Bolldhe breathed in the air of Melhus. "Just smell it, Wodeman; fire and ice—that's all there is to this land."

"That's what we *need*," Wodeman replied, a little more cheerfully. "Fire and ice are the stuff of creation!"

"Eh?"

"Don't be so dim, Bolldhe. Haven't you heard the old stories? What do you get when those two elements come together?"

Bolldhe thought for a moment. "Tepid slurry?"

"Steam!" *(You cretin!)* "The basis of Creation. According to the beliefs of the Uldachtna tribe, life was created by the steam we see all around us now: warm droplets formed upon the rock, layer upon layer, until they eventually formed the skin of the very first woman. *That* is what we're doing here— *creating.* So don't lose all hope just yet."

But Bolldhe was not so sure. "Actually, Finwald told me fire isn't even an element, just a process of change. But what have I changed into? A devil, judging by what I saw in my engram."

"Devils don't cry, as you did. Only people can do that."

"And baby seals," Bolldhe reminded him, changing the subject quickly. "God, all that dream magic just to thaw a memory! Couldn't I just have held my head up against Appa's kettle, or something?"

Wodeman then, for some reason, stopped dead. "Actually," he said, "there *is* another possibility. It's just come back to me: something Nibulus told us back in that witch Nym Cadog's dungeon, but you weren't there. He told us about something the Peladanes are supposed to have found in Vaagenfjord Maw after the siege. Some great pit of falling souls, he said, like some gateway to hell itself. Somewhere where time and space are missing. Said that there, if a man could brave it, he might find any knowledge he wanted. *Any knowledge in the world . . .* Makes you think, doesn't it?"

But, after a pause, they both grinned and shook their heads. Some things really were a bit too far-fetched to believe.

As they re-entered the camp, Wodeman inquired: "But you do feel something now, don't you?"

"Yes, I suppose so," Bolldhe admitted. "I feel different; happy, now that I've opened up a bit. Maybe even higher spiritually."

And Nibulus, too, was happy as he greeted the returning dream questers, for he, after all these years, had just succeeded in spelling out his full name in the snow with his own urine.

The following day was their last full day of traveling before they reached Vaagenfjord Maw, and every member of the company knew it. Even Appa, who had lain slumped across Zhang's back in varying degrees of consciousness for the entire journey across Melhus. The pinnacle of Ravenscairn now loomed large before them, casting a shadow of silence and sobriety over the travelers. Each in his heart felt that this might be the last day they beheld sunlight, before entering that place, and each of them breathed the chilly air with the appetite of a condemned man. How far away Nordwas seemed now, how long ago since they had set forth beneath the sunlit, wind-rippled banners of Wintus Hall.

As the sun dipped behind Ravenscairn one final time, and the evening sky was lit up by weird and terrifying ribbons of dancing light, they finally reached the road.

"We've come to the End of the World," Appa ranted in moist-eyed horror, "the Head of the Great Dragon Lindormyn! See His fiery breath—it will devour us all!"

But the lights, disturbing though they were, concerned the rest of the company somewhat less than the megaliths. Two lines of standing stones, each three times as tall as an ordinary man and carved in the shape of the grotesquely distorted head of some terrible fiend from the Underworld, marched across the ice field in the direction of Ravenscairn. These formed the road—such as it was—that would take them to the very gates of the Maw. And these heads would be their last, leering companions for the remaining few miles of their journey.

That night they decided to make camp away from the stare of those heads. They chose instead a sheltered spot beneath the overhang of a cliff. As they had done four days ago, they cut blocks of ice to build a protective wall to seal themselves in.

They could not, however, seal themselves away from the fear. Even at this distance waves of dread seemed to emanate from the standing stones, and they could still see regular flashes of that dancing light. But it was the voices that kept them from sleep, as it had done on their first night on the island. Wailing, mournful.

Bolldhe got no sleep at all. The strangeness of this place was draining his soul, as it did for the others, but for him there was something else. Though he had not mentioned it to his companions, he had kept looking back over his shoulder all day long.

Almost as though he sensed they were being followed.

"What in—?" Eorcenwold hissed, then hushed himself. The same voices that were troubling Bolldhe's party many miles to the northwest, and had been having a similar effect upon his own group, suddenly stopped. In the eerie silence that followed, all the thieves held their breath, sweated, and seriously questioned their wisdom in coming to this island in the first place. It was a silence full of growing dread.

Whatever it was those voices belonged to, they seemed to have sensed something. It was almost as if the voices had been quelled.

For an evil presence was out there somewhere in the night, out on the black ocean and, slowly but inexorably, it was approaching the island.

"Get away from me! Get thee hence! Begone, foul deviants!" the red-eyed stranger cursed. He swatted at the malignant little sprites as they flitted about his head and snatched at the yak hide kirtle that billowed around his frame. "Ah, so sorely environ'd am I by hell's arse-belched hobgoblins! Fire and fury, I hate these things. I hate this land, it torments me so!"

Far above the fields of fire and ice did Red Eye fly. He cavorted and twisted like a wind elemental in his struggle to pluck the gamesome, chittering sprites from his tangled hair. They pulled at the coif of white skin he wore on his head, leaving sooty deposits upon its satin, Dhracusian immaculacy. They wrenched at the clasp of his knapsack, essaying to cause the bloodied heads therein to fall out to their ruin below. They fogged the lamp atop his staff and smarted the string of eyes that hung from it. And they spat tarred vitriol at the translucent stones of his chaplet. And ever Red Eye essayed to swat them, to clutch them, to eradicate their contaminating menace from his person. But they were as insubstantial as smoke, and would merely dissipate into wispy tatters of darkness in his grasp, only to reform, cackling, with a wicked phosphorus glow, in front of his face.

It was a losing battle. He was a stranger in a strange land. It galled him in every particle of his being. The whole island of Melhus, it seemed, fixed him from below with its icy glare, its mountains a mass of cruel fangs, its breath black and stinking—the open maw of the World Serpent—and he felt as if he were going mad.

His silent companion hovered nearby. Unmoving, it stood miles above the earth, inscrutable and unharried. A light layer of frost on its gray robe sparkled in the moonlight. Head becowled, it gave no impression of feeling or reaction, but Red Eye suspected it may even have been laughing.

Still flying about like a witch, Red Eye continued to swat. "Of all the most detestable of imps we might have hap'd upon in this most detestable of lands," he cursed, "why had we to meet these smog-breathed, sulphurous *sprites?* These black-souled, bituminous little bastards! O, despicable exhalations of Melhus's deepest and foulest furnace, I entreat thee once more, *get thee hence!*"

"They are what they are," Chance averred impassively, "Spirits of Olchor, the Father of Darkness. And they were here long before Drauglir. This is their home. They belong here."

"They belong in the vats of hell!" Red Eye snapped, infuriated that his Syr companion should remain ignored by the sprites when he himself was so injuriously afflicted by them. "Back to the elements whence they came!" He soared away through the night sky, and disappeared behind a vast, poisonous cloud that basked in a sickly yellow moonglow. Still the swarm of sprites pursued him, squealing gleefully at his torment.

Eventually, Chance reached out a hand, splayed its fingers, and sent forth a pulse of green light into the cloud. From somewhere within could be heard the shrill wailing of agony and astonishment, then the sprites, condensed now into nothing more than smoking droplets of tar, fell in a black, acid rain of despair to the ground.

"Enough capering," the Syr stated. "We need to talk."

"Thank you," the returning deity said breathing heavily, wondering even amid his ire if this might be the first occasion he had ever had cause to thank one of the Skela. Though calmer now, his face was still flushed, the fiery indignation in his eyes but barely quenched by the Syr's intervention.

"We do not have long," Chance informed him. "Others of their kind will arrive very soon, I'd wager."

Red Eye's mind reached out all around him, far and wide, feeling through the reeking caliginosity of Melhus's poison atmosphere for their repugnant presence. There was no immediate sense of evil, but he would take no chances; they would not suffer him for long in their world. "We must speak quickly," he said.

Together they descended, and hovered above the laboring wayfarers, only a mile below now. Any closer would draw more sprite-kind from the earth

"So," Chance intoned, the cowled head nodding toward the six men and the slough-horse who forced their way over the last stretches of Melhus's tundra, "the engram continues to thaw, and Bolldhe begins to guess something about himself. Perhaps now the time for guidance by your priests is at an end."

"If ever it started," Red Eye snorted. "Bolldhe may have divined the great virtue in Finwald, may even have esteemed his fortitude at times, but always has he mistrusted the man's innate furtiveness. And as for Appa, the lukewarm counsel of that one has fallen on stony ears from the outset, and now, near dead on his feet, the aged cleric has become scant more than bootless impedimenta. Yet of all the priests that might have swayed Bolldhe, it is not one of my servants, but Erce's, who has edified Bolldhe the most—Wodeman the dream-sorcerer, he alone who pauses to wonder if his presence on the quest has been of any avail."

"But will this be to your benefit or your destruction? The flamberge has been placed in Bolldhe's hands, the murderousness awoken in his soul, and the proselytizing efforts of your two priests has so far only made him even more of a god-hater. He has the sword in his hands, but it is he himself that has become the most volatile weapon—thanks to the efforts of those around him. For though they do not realize it they have, each and every one of them, forged a weapon, to some extent or another. But it remains to be seen how it will be returned to them—hilt first or blade."

"Bolldhe abhors the flamberge. The sword is the symbol of all he loathes, especially after the Peladane's mercenary confession in the cave. Yet Bolldhe is also the ficklest of men. He abandoned the quest in the marshes on scant more than a whim, yet returned to them at only the entreaty of a *dream.* He turned against them a second time, betraying such worthy company to affiliate with thieves—almost doing Appa to death in the process. Yet despite this grossest of perfidies, still he voices no contrition nor begs for absolution, but in his heart seeks yet further betrayals. Almost a third time did he forsake them, tempted as he was to enroll with the Tivor, abandoning the quest in favor of mere adventure."

"Yes, indeed, the ficklest of men; and such a one is your Chosen. Who can tell what fancy might take him at the final moment. He is like a seed blown upon the wind."

"And one which may even yet find soil in which to flourish."

Chance hesitated, then replied: "Here in this land of frozen stone?"

"Amid frozen stone is Bolldhe in his element. The frozen engram is the key, and the stone beneath, that is Bolldhe's granite, which may yet see him through."

Red Eye sent his sight out all over this northern land, a lighthouse beam piercing the darkness, to glimpse those struggling mortals upon whose actions the futures of the immortals now depended. Now, however, his attention turned from Bolldhe to Methuselech and Gapp, to Kuthy and Elfswith, and to the Thieves of Tyvenborg.

"Unforeseen by me, many pieces have now been placed upon the board, and the game is not what it was. The Peladane's boy, the Peladane's friend, the Tivor, and the Tyvenborgers—who amongst the gods could have predicted that? Who even among the Skela? You, Chance? Or your brother, Fate? Even Time?"

Chance remained silent, its face invisible within the darkness of its grey cowl.

Red Eye went on. "The belief was mine that Methuselech, when he fell— and later the boy too—had been wiped from the board forever. And yet they return—"

"With a vengeance," Chance added.

"Assuredly it is vengeance that impels Mauglad on so."

"And Mauglad who drives on his host body—and the boy."

"But I wonder how likely it ever was, Chance," Red Eye said, looking side-long at the Syr, "that anyone should ever have ventured into the Valley of Slu-agh, so remote, so hidden, and so fearful. And not only entered, but to have fallen, *and* survived, yet wounded enough to suffer the spirit that languished there to take hold . . ."

Chance, however, remained as inscrutable as ever. "Eventually it would have happened. My brother Time is patient."

"*Eventually* even mountains turn to dust." Red Eye scoffed, "but it has come to pass *now*, at exactly this moment, these days, and to one of Finwald's mission, of all people. Well, whether or not you or your brother Fate admit such abetment in this matter, you have my gratitude. I am even tempted to postulate that it was one of you two who guided young Gapp along his way also, bearing dispatch of Finwald's occult weapon to Mauglad. Had it not been so, Mauglad would have contented himself with merely finishing his own personal business in the Maw. As it is, however, he now does my work, though he may not con-sider it thus. Such a catalyst the boy has been! And so nourishing, to boot. To-gether they have come far—*I* have come far—and but a little farther, and Mauglad will be able to drive a pole in the spokes of Fate's wheels for good. Oh yes, I have much to thank you for, my dear Syr."

"You have come far indeed," Chance agreed, "but along which path? It seems to us that the closer you come to the Rawgr, the closer you come to his methods. You do realize what is happening to you, do you not? Pitting a ser-vant of your enemy against one of your own? Finwald, do not forget, is still a good man, and Mauglad is still evil."

"Mauglad is out for himself, pure and simple," Red Eye disagreed, "in this, not at variance to Bolldhe. And who can admonish them, after such tribula-tions as they have endured?"

"They are neutral, then, the pair of them. So is that what you finally admit to becoming? The god of neutrality?"

"Perhaps in neutrality do I have my only hope at this dark hour. In naught can I now have surety."

"But you are, are you not, the cunnan? Cuna, the knowing god?"

"Yet still just a god," Cuna admitted. "You can hardly expect me to be om-niscient. Unlike you and your council, all I can do is guess, and what now I guess is that mayhap Mauglad will make good if Bolldhe does not."

"So Mauglad is your Plan B, then?"

"Exactly."

"And where have we heard *that* before?"

"Exactly."

Cuna, as he had done on countless thousands of occasions down the millennia, tried to see through the blackness within Chance's cowl, to bring to bear the full power of his all-seeing eyes against that impenetrable veil, to see for once what expression the Syr might be wearing on its face. To see if there was even a glimmer of irritation there at his chiding. But he knew it was use-less. It probably did not even possess a face.

Cuna knew so little about the Skela: Chance, Fate, Time, and the rest. They had not been there when he had first arrived in the world. Nor had needed to be. Cuna had come to a world new with promise, a world of light, of youth, of a multitudinous variety of peoples. He had walked among them, talked with them, and found that he had power—power over people. They looked up to him in fear at first, as they did with those of his ilk: Olchor, Erce, Luttra, all the others. They had called them gods, whatever that meant.

Cuna had enjoyed the power. But he had not wanted the sort of mastery that was Olchor's desire. Cuna wanted rather to guide, to mold, to lead the way as a torchbearer. So the wars had begun. The wars of the gods. Even now the evening skies turned red in remembrance of the blood that had flowed in those days. And so the Skela had arrived, the Keepers of Balance. And suddenly the gods found themselves beyond the mortal veil.

Talking with people had been easy before. But no longer. Now, portents and dreams were the only speech permitted betwixt gods and people.

If Chance had sensed Cuna's sadness, it did not show it as it went on: "And do not discount Scathur yet, either. He is on the move after all these years of caretaking, hot on their trail. I do not deign to reveal whether he catches up with Bolldhe or Mauglad, but latterly an air of conceit hangs about my brother Fate."

Cuna hesitated. Had the Syr's response been just that little bit trenchant? It had certainly sounded so, but was such a thing possible for one of the Skela?

"What's this?" Cuna chided. "Was that a hint? Is it possible that, after all the centuries, one of the mighty Skela deigns to—*Oh hell, here they come again! Let us be gone!*"

The discussion, such as it had been, was over. The ancient spirits of Melhus were once again issuing from the land, a seething, black gout of gaseous efflu-ent that belched from cracks in the turbulent surface, and swarmed upward to harangue the Alien. Cuna immediately soared away from the rapidly ap-proaching sprites, and disappeared, leaving Chance alone.

The Syr pondered the god's question as its robes fluttered in the turmoil. "Perhaps, indeed. Anything can happen."

The Dead Raise the Living

Two days earlier, on the day before Wodeman had sent Bolldhe into the ramshackle temple of his own soul, Kuthy, Elfswith, and Ceawlin arrived at Wrythe.

As the clawed tips of the wyvern's outstretched wings sliced through the cold air, leaving streamers of vortices in their wake, both riders could see coming into view ahead of them the familiar scattering of limestone karst towers that thrust up from the dark forest canopy way below. After many hours of freezing, aching flight, this sight truly was a relief. But as they soared on, lowering gently toward where they knew the town lay, and the massed trees came into closer view, an unsettling anxiety began to take hold. The treetops now flashing by directly beneath them had always appeared black, crooked and mist-laden, as if the whole forest were interwoven with giant cobwebs. But this time, there was something else down there that was seriously knotting each traveler's stomach into a tight bunch of dread.

Kuthy, never the most fanciful of men, did not like it at all. Something, he could tell, was happening down there in that sick little papule of a town, something important, something big, portentous enough to give him fleeting, prescient visions of dragons pouring from the black storm clouds of the World's Last Twilight.

He shook his head to clear it of such imbecilic fancies, and glanced at his companion in front of him. Again he shook his head, this time in annoyance. He himself had been clinging desperately to the crest running along Ceawlin's back for the past several hours, gripping her flanks with his legs until they were well past aching. Even his headgear had wrapped its appendages tightly around Kuthy's head in an effort to stay put. Yet there was Elfswith, casually sitting sidesaddle upon Ceawlin's neck as if he were perched on a five-bar gate, watching the cows come home on a summer's eve.

Cocky little swine! Kuthy thought. Despite his usual nonchalance in all things challenging, he was now approaching the limits of his endurance, so to see Elfswith having such an easy time during this ordeal . . . well, it just wasn't right, that's all.

Then again, I am *only human,* he reminded himself.

As they descended farther, skimming lightly over the treetops, Kuthy could hear the wet slap of slick, grey leaves against the wyvern's hind feet. They were coming in to land.

Briefly Kuthy's mind went back to the Peladane and his funny little expedition. He'd seen so many like them recently; plume-headed errants bound for the Maw, Righters-of-Wrong, Looters-of-Loot, Stirrers-of-Shite . . . Something was definitely up, he had no doubt. He had even toyed a few times with the idea of continuing his travels with Wintus & Company into the Maw itself. Might even be something there of advantage to him . . .

But no—that place had died centuries ago, and Kuthy Tivor did not deign to go sifting through dust like some morbid old grave robber. No, as far as he and Elfswith were concerned the only possibilities in this part of the world would likely be found in the scabrous little hamlet they were flying over right now. There were many secrets here that he and his companion had yet to uncover, so it was just as well they'd made sure the Peladane and his meddlers would steer well clear of the place.

As it happened, on that day they waved good-bye to Wintus's band upon the ice bridge leading to Melhus, he and Elfswith had not continued directly on to Wrythe as they had claimed they would. That was just a small white lie, for they had still had a few things to arrange before they got there. No, they had only accompanied the travelers to the causeway to make sure the little pests did actually go that way, and not later decide to head west to the town instead.

Certainly they did not want any more daft Southerners stirring up trouble in Wrythe, and possibly getting themselves killed there—or worse. No, that little white lie might even have saved their lives.

So, after seeing them off, he and Elfswith had simply flown straight back to the cave, where they spent the next three days finishing off their preparations. Only today had been spent flying here—a long, exhausting day, which would take its toll on Kuthy's old bones (and eardrums) for the next few days to come, he was sure.

"Let's hope the bathhouses are still open," he called out to Elfswith, his voice hoarse above the screaming wind, "and the temperature well up."

"Something's certainly up," Elfswith replied in that scratchy, metallic little voice of his. Without explaining further, the half-Huldre pointed down toward the town, whose outlying cave houses and cabbage patches were now coming into view.

Kuthy followed the little man's finger, and his innards revolved sickly with fear. He gripped, white-knuckled, to the bony crest-plate along Ceawlin's back so hard that he drew blood. But he did not even notice it as it streaked in ragged red lines across the crest-plate like windblown raindrops on a window pane, for his entire attention was upon the birds.

So many of them. Wheeling above the treetops, as far as the town extended. Screeching in that way birds do when held captive between a predator's needle-sharp teeth. Flying around chaotically, insanely, terrified.

Kuthy quickly brought his fear under control, but studied the flocks of panicked avians darkly. "I never did like the way the birds round these parts fly," he murmured to himself, the words instantly whipped away by the rushing wind.

Though he could not possibly have heard him, Elfswith replied: "What, in reverse?"

Sure enough, as they both gazed down and around, many of the birds did indeed seem to be flying backward in their terror. Ceawlin lazily extended her neck and gulped one up as it came past, disappearing backward down the wyvern's gullet.

Though his initial fear was now checked, Kuthy could not stem the rising tide of disquiet still growing in him at every beat of Ceawlin's wings. It was beneath his dignity to admit to fear, he knew, but on this day he was feeling genuinely scared. He had always known there was something wrong about this place, of course; its twisted, inbred, fungus-licking inhabitants with their drab garments and their dead eyes; the kids, too, who seemed more like devils than humans; those various bunkers and storehouses that were always so closely guarded by the Wire-Faces. But most of all, the Majestic Head, that fish-eyed, burgundy-clad ghoul that ruled from his sepulchral keep on the hill. Something had *always* been wrong about Wrythe. Yet it was precisely this aberrance, this beyond-the-realm-of-normality uniqueness, that continued to draw Kuthy and Elfswith back here, time and again. They had never unearthed its secrets, and maybe never would, but it was places like this that were Kuthy's and Elfswith's business. And so they came.

Today, that wrongness reached out to Kuthy like an enormous threatening black hand.

Ceawlin's immense tail dipped, the yellow poison sac now pointing toward the town as if in defiance, and her wings turned into the wind, billowing like the sails of a ship. Straightaway the force of arrested momentum pinioned Kuthy painfully against the crest on her back.

And then they were landing.

Directly below them lay a wide clearing, the frozen mud patch of a cabbage field. As they dropped almost vertically (*I wish she wouldn't do that!* thought Kuthy, gripping tenaciously) it could now be seen that this field, normally as dead and deserted as a cemetery, was a-crawl with moving figures. All over the field, silent Oghain lurched, maggot-pale in the late afternoon's wan light, clawing away at the frozen earth with uncharacteristic fervor. It was almost as if they were being controlled by some remote, chuckling puppet master. Around the field's periphery, lurking in darkness beneath the trees, could just be seen the motionless shapes of Wire-Faces looking on.

Suddenly gripped by acute panic, Kuthy almost bawled out to Ceawlin not to land there. Within two seconds the feeling had left him, but he wondered at it. He had faced up to so many dangers in this world (some even outside it) things no ordinary person would even understand, that this sudden inexplicable terror was distinctly odd.

Wings beating the air madly, Ceawlin finally touched down. Immediately over a dozen Wire-Faces detached themselves from the cover of the trees and loped toward them. The three strangers looked about them in consternation, neither passenger dismounting just yet.

The Wire-Faces formed a rough circle around the newcomers, though they kept some distance—namely, striking distance from the wyvern's stinger. Both Kuthy and Elfswith were more than a little perturbed by their unwelcoming stance. Normally the town's militia kept out of their way, only keeping an eye on them from a distance as they went about their strange business. The three travelers were well known in Wrythe, though hardly welcomed, but had never before been received in so hostile a manner.

By now, eighteen guards in all had left the Doll-Faces to do their grubbing unsupervised, and stood around the three arrivals in a silent circle, red eyes glaring, big hands twitching at the cheesewires held taut between them.

"Yep," Elfswith concluded, "something's definitely up."

As they were escorted through the town, Kuthy and Elfswith stared around in bewilderment at the signs of hurried activity all about. The place was in an uproar. Wherever they looked they could see fields being scrabbled through for things to be unearthed, timber-bunkers unsealed and plundered of their contents, storehouses and stabburs ransacked; and all of this proceeding at a frenzied pace the like of which had probably not been seen in Wrythe since the long-past days of the Fasces. The Doll-Faces, who normally appeared incapable of showing any emotion, now bore expressions that were drawn tight with fear. Not even in the fungus cellars on a particularly damp and fruitful night were they ever this animated. Now they shuffled about as fast as they could, under the unblinking glare of their overseers, fulfilling the task of hauling their unearthed burdens about.

"Any ideas what's going on, Elfswith?" Kuthy asked as they were herded along. Both men's curiosity as to what was being lugged about with such urgency was frustrated by the fact that their escort was guiding them by a deliberately circuitous route that always kept them well away from the toiling Oghain.

"Well, I really couldn't say, my man," Elfswith replied in a singsong tone that did not suit the dark mood of the place one bit. "Stone pitchers big enough to hold a man, wooden crates the size of a coffin? Oilskin-wrapped bundles suspiciously *man-sized*? Could be anything, really."

Kuthy forced a grin. "Yes, these Northerners really do know how to have a good time."

But, beneath his jest, he felt as though he should be shuddering. Watching them at work, lumbering about like zombies freshly disturbed from the grave, he again experienced that sense of *ragnarok*. His earlier vision of dragons screaming through the storm clouds was now enhancd by images of glaciers rolling over all the lands, damned souls wailing in despair, *the dead rising from their graves to walk the earth upon the Last Day.*

No, shuddering was too gentle a word. Kuthy felt himself more *squirm*. Squirm in a place deep within his soul, a place he normally kept locked away from his everyday thoughts. On previous visits to Wrythe he had merely laughed in scorn at the Oghain, contemptuous of their half-lives up here in the land of the dead. But today things were troubling him greatly, and those recurrent *ragnarok* thoughts would not let go of him. Kuthy was neither a spiritual nor compassionate man, but here in this place, the last town in the world, where the very air was steeped in the inevitability of the End of All Life, he was unexpectedly moved to an altogether different mood.

Such lives! he reflected, as the dome-headed graveyard people tramped their way through this perpetual fog. *Such terrible lives!*

Then, out of the blue and with a suddenness that jolted him, he thought of Appa. The mad old priest Appa who stank permanently of ewe-butter and rapped his ring against his amulet with the untiring obsessiveness of the asylum-dweller. Someone of his inner strength and beliefs, his missionary zeal, what if he were to settle here? Could he not do something for these people, with his patient teaching, his care?

But Appa was now on Melhus—a place so much worse than here. He was probably dead already. Deader even than an Oghain.

If only I could see how they're getting on over there. . . .

They were led on through Wrythe, past the dark avenue of rowan trees on the north side of town. Here, where the road led down to the small dock situated a few miles away, the Oghain with their heavy containers were particularly numerous, all carrying their burdens down to the sea. All so careful not to spill whatever comprised their precious cargo.

Watching their progress with interest, Kuthy and his companions were led farther on, right through the town until they reached the keep. Approaching it, resembling a giant gravestone looming blackly against a sky contorted with sunset-reddened storm clouds, Kuthy again had that brief, prescient foreboding of the end of the world. Here as it ever had been, was the source of Wrythe's warping.

"Oh look!" his diminutive companion suddenly chirped. "They've taken down all the hanged people." He sounded almost disappointed, as if he felt they had lent the place a certain atmosphere.

On past the harvested trees, bereft now of their macabre decorations, they continued, and as they had done on previous visits, passed through the rotten mouth of the keep's main door to stand waiting politely in the guest room.

Within minutes an enraged bellow sounded from the battlements above and, three to four seconds later, the Wire-Face who had gone to announce their presence came tumbling head-over-heels back down the steps. Whereupon the three guests were summarily shown the way out.

"Somehow I doubt we'll get any business done here this time," Kuthy said in irritation. "The Maj-Head really seems hacked off about something."

"We're certainly not wanted here at the moment," Elfswith agreed, as they were led back downhill to a secure lodging place where they could be easily watched. "But I didn't come all this way for nothing. I say we just lie low for a while, wait till things calm down. He's a nice old bloke really—he's bound to be in a better mood by tomorrow."

Kuthy, his heart still troubled, scowled. "*I* say we clear out as fast as we can. Ugly Town grows uglier. We can always come back in a few days' time when it's cooled down a bit. In the meantime, how about a quick flight over Melhus? We could see how our boys are getting on."

Elfswith looked at his old friend with horror. "You going soft in the head? Who gives a damn about them? Besides, you're in no shape for that. *I* could do it. *You* couldn't. Not just like that. Your're already frozen half-solid. I say, while we're here, let's make good use of the place. How does a nice hot bath sound to you?"

The bathhouse was warm, pleasant, and calm—in short, everything that the town outside was not—and, exactly as Gapp had done just over twenty-four hours earlier, Kuthy and Elfswith almost cried out in rapture as the heat enveloped their bodies and jets of sulphurous water pummeled their skin. The two bathers sank into its hedonistic embrace up to their necks. For long minutes they simply sat there and enjoyed the luxury of this place, breathing in the potent fumes and staring up at the contorted rock formations of the cave roof above them.

The state of Ugly Town concerned them little for the present, and two such as they had little need for caution. Their clothes and weapons were stashed right behind them on the ledge, while Ceawlin was on guard over near the cave entrance. Ever watchful, she did not share her companions' current serenity in this place, and stalked about in the water, eyeing it suspiciously, like a giant wading bird. The bathhouse echoed stonily with a quality of half-sleep. Lazily the two men let their minds drift. After a while, even Kuthy's headgear extended one of its tendrils to test the water, then slipped off his head and sculled off on its own.

"All we need now," Kuthy sighed luxuriantly as the opiate vapors curled up his nose and further permeated his softening brain, "is a little gentle background music."

"Your wish is my command," Elfswith purred, and absently reached behind his head and groped for his baggy overcoat. His tiny hand disappeared into a breast pocket, and resurfaced with a long, brightly shining trombone. He put it to his lips, rolled his eyes up into his head, then blasted out a few bars of the most hellish clamor Kuthy had ever heard, filling the cave with an earsplitting din. Ceawlin leapt back in fright, and tumbled into the water in a melee of flailing wings and spume. Kuthy's headgear quickly retreated beneath the surface, and even the few Oghain still outside wailed in terror, dropping their mysterious burdens upon the frozen earth, and loped off into the dark safety of the trees.

Later, when they were finally ready to move, Kuthy and Elfswith returned to discussing Wrythe. That their business here would have to be put off, maybe even forgotten completely, was obvious. Between languid scrubbings and the occasional fanfare-like scale progression from Elfswith's trombone that would cause Ceawlin's ears to flatten, the two adventurers debated at length on the subject, but without reaching any satisfactory conclusion.

Suddenly, Yggr himself strode in. He did not bother to greet them, not even in his customarily icy way, but just marched along the ledge, his shadow, cast by one of the wall torches, lengthening menacingly toward them. In spite of themselves, both travelers' hearts skipped a beat. Even Ceawlin hesitated momentarily, before wading over to join her companions. As he approached, the hollow crunch of Yggr's boots upon gritty stone sounded like the tramp of some war god upon the skulls of the fallen.

And then he was upon them. That familiar, calcified tombstone blankness still defined his visage, but it now seemed somewhat flakier, as though the magma of ire surging beneath its crust was causing tiny cracks to appear. *Who could say what might happen if he became truly angry*, Kuthy wondered. Would the tombstone shatter completely? And what black hell of saprogenic corruption would then be revealed to the world?

"Can I help you?" Elfswith inquired politely. "We *are* having a bath, here, you know."

Yggr's dead-oyster eyes were dark and unfathomable. For just a second he stared at Kuthy—now hatless—seeing for the first time his terrible secret. Then without preamble, he growled: "You don't know anything about any other foreigners snooping round these parts recently, I suppose?"

Kuthy thought his voice sounded like the belch of a giant toad, sick from eating too much quicksand. "How recently?" Kuthy replied cagily.

Yggr's blue-nailed fingers clenched into massive fists. *"Recently,"* he reiterated stonily.

"... Oh, *'recently',"* Elfswith cut in, rather too glibly for Kuthy's comfort. On his own, this big guy was probably an equal match for him—maybe even for Elfswith—but even above the sulphur he could smell a lot of Wire-Faces close by.

"We met a few humans farther off to the east," Kuthy replied, not wanting to reveal too much, but reluctant to lie, especially to *those* eyes.

"Heading where?"

"Really couldn't say. They were up in the mountains. Probably lost."

"Did they look like Peladanes? Or possibly two men, one robed like a desert man, the other small and skinny, both riding antler-heads?"

Replying truthfully to the second question, Kuthy said, "absolutely not." He had not got a clue or a care about these last two, but his thoughts were flying out to Wintus's group upon the ice; looking up into Yggr's eyes, he was so grateful not to be in their place. The Majestic Head had no mercy for any caught near Melhus.

Yggr continued to stare into his eyes. They stared back. Then abruptly, he turned. "Thank you for your help," he said. "And make sure you do not leave your quarters tonight—for any reason. In the morning . . . well, in the morning we'll be gone. You can do whatever you like then."

Just as he was about to leave, he stopped and stared down at Elfswith, a hint of puzzlement on his impassive features. He had noticed the band of leopard-spots blemishing Elfswith's skin, the very same ones that Bolldhe had noticed the day they first encountered him in the Giant Mountains. Now, with his entire torso exposed, they could be seen to continue all the way down the little man's chest.

Elfswith stared back defiantly. "Birthmark," he offered weakly.

Yggr frowned. On a face such as his, that was hardly necessary, but he frowned nonetheless. And then he was gone.

The heavy reverberation of his footsteps receded through the limestone vaults, then abandoned the karst tower to an empty silence that those left in the cave were reluctant to fill.

A droplet of water plopped into the pool, and the two bathers dared breathe out once more, resting their heads back against the ledge and staring contemplatively into space. Kuthy's hat slithered back up to its customary resting place.

"How the heavenly hell does the Maj know about Fatty Peladane and his friends?" Elfswith murmured, keeping his voice low in case spies lurked in the vicinity. "I know Yggr's scouts roam far and wide, but surely not as far as the Giant Mountains?"

"Perhaps his spies are monitoring the ice bridge these days," Kuthy suggested. Elfswith stared at him and frowned. "Like you said," Kuthy continued, "something's up now that Yggr's on the move."

Elfswith pursed his lips. "Possible," he replied, "since he guards Melhus against intruders—"

"The whole of *Wrythe* guards Melhus against intruders," Kuthy corrected. "That's all this town exists for, if you ask me. Probably been the case ever since the days of the Fasces and . . ."

He trailed off as his mind traveled back to that time half a millennium ago, and he started to recall every single piece of information he had ever learned about then, and all the years since. Eventually he concluded: "I wonder whose side Yggr is on?"

"Makes no difference to us." Elfswith shrugged. "We're on neither."

"True, but this is all getting a bit . . ." Kuthy paused, thinking once again of those fiery stormclouds. ". . . interesting," he finished lamely. "A lot of people headed to the Maw these days."

"Yes, including two men riding antler-heads," Elfswith suddenly added. "What was the description of them? *'One robed like a desert man, the other small and skinny'.'"* He looked hard into his companion's eyes.

Kuthy finished the sentence for him: "How many desert men come this far north? What was the name Wintus used of that mercenary friend of his? Methuselech?"

"Something like that. And a small, skinny one—Fatty's esquire? But didn't they die early on in their journey?"

"Way back," Kuthy agreed. "But their bodies were never actually seen."

They pondered long and hard, about the Peladane's group mainly, but also about Yggr, the greatest mystery of these lands, the self-appointed guardian of Melhus, now loading up his boats.

"Maybe we ought to make this our business," Kuthy suggested.

Elfswith eyed him, and absently blew on his trombone.

The following morning they awoke to find the town strangely quiet. Not the customary contented quiet of the graveyard, but a kind of hollow quiet, and a resonating echo as of something just departed. Indeed, that same oppression that had always been the very essence of Wrythe seemed now to have magically lifted.

Elfswith peered out between the moldy shutters of their lodging to look upon the morning. There was a mist-clogged lane outside, with the odd Doll-Face wandering about. It all looked much the same as it ever did. But, as he continued to watch, it occurred to Elfswith that even the mist somehow felt cleaner upon this fresh morning.

And also, he noticed how the wanderings of the locals appeared to have become so distinctly *aimless.* They had always moved about slowly, vacantly, like somnambulists, but nevertheless with some purpose. But this morning, they appeared bewildered, bereft of direction, abandoned, as if the strings to their puppet master had been cut.

Also, sometime during the night their Wire-Face guards had disappeared.

"Kuthy!" Elfswith yelled over his shoulder. "I do believe the Maj has genuinely done a bunk."

It was true. As the three of them explored the town later, it became clear that every single Wire-Face had gone. Only the aimless citizens had been left to their own devices. And even up at the keep there was no sign either of Yggr or his foul little Ogginda devils. They had all simply gone, quitting the town as if they intended never to return.

They searched the keep thoroughly, but found it as empty and derelict as if it had been abandoned hundreds of years ago. There was nothing there at all. All those secrets Kuthy and Elfswith had hoped to discover were just gone, as if Yggr and his darkness had never been present.

It was an old Doll-Face who eventually explained. After slapping her repeatedly across her lumpen visage, she appeared to regain some kind of clarity, albeit troubled. She told them how the Majestic Head had set sail for Melhus "with the sleeping ones," taking his brood and the Wire-Faces with him. The only Wire-Faces he had not taken were the ones in the search party that he had sent off yesterday.

"Search party?" Elfswith asked.

Indeed. It seemed that as soon as the two foreigners—the desert man and the pale boy—had escaped on antler-heads, Lord Yggr had sent after them a large pack of their hand-picked hunters under the command of the Wire-Face champion Rind Head, all freshly fed upon raw sea slug and eel pout.

"This desert man," Kuthy pressed her, "his name wasn't Methuselech was it?"

No. His name was Mauglad. Mauglad Yrkeshta.

After a short pause of stunned silence, both Kuthy and Elfswith stared at each other, beamed in recognition and cried: "BINGO!" They then slapped the Doll-Face once more, leapt straight onto Ceawlin's back, and took to the air again.

After snuffling around like a badger for several minutes, the leader of the Wire-Face pack lifted his snout from the patch of freshly disturbed earth, and slowly turned his head to face toward the northeast.

Yes, he confirmed, they had definitely gone that way. They had taken the direction *all* intruders eventually took.

Toward Melhus.

He licked some soil from his nose and tasted it. Antler-head, no doubt about that; their scent was unmistakable. He glared after him hatefully. *Filthy little tricksters!* They had sent him off on a wild detour south, trying to deceive him into believing that they were escaping the region altogether.

But they had not reckoned with the tracking skills of Rind Head. And now the hunt was on in earnest.

Had they known how swiftly Rind Head and his pack could travel, and just how hard on their tail they were already, Gapp and his companions would never have paused to spend the night with the Uldachtna nomads.

Their flight had started as a terrified and desperate escape attempt to get away from Wrythe, and a day and a half later it was equally chaotic, constantly slowed by uncertainties and conflicting opinions—not to mention hunger, disorientation, and exhaustion. In short, it was still very much a panic-stricken rout, and one likely destined for a very bloody conclusion.

They had begun with a nightmare shuffle through the awakening streets of Wrythe, both men hooded and cloaked in the monk-like raiment of the locals, and clumsily trying to mimic their ponderous, shambling gait while at the same time desperate to escape this awful place as fast as possible. After the siren-like alarm call the Children had raised with their screeching it had been all that the fugitives could do to curb their panic and not simply bolt. The Ogginda's growling and keening seemed to be all around them, down every lane and behind every fence, their pursuers searching, sniffing, closing in with every second. Gapp and Methuselech had expected at any moment to hear scratchy little voices at their side, see something small but terrible step out into the street before them, or feel the heavy clamp of big hands upon their shoulders followed by the steely bite of a garrotte around the neck.

It had been horrible. It was only the myrmidonic presence of Schnorbitz that had delivered them from the heart of darkness in that most terrible hour. For all the while the forest hound had never left them, staying close, but keeping always in the shadows, out of sight of the enemy. While the two fugitives were forced to keep their heads bowed and their eyes firmly to the ground, by barely heard whines and whimpers Schnorbitz had guided them through the tightening net of pursuers, and finally, almost beyond belief, back under the relative cover of the forest.

Then had followed the flight of reckless insanity through the ripping thorns and sucking bogs of the woodlands extending east of Wrythe. It had been a headlong dash into the unknown, with the terror of Yggr and his fiends driving them faster and ever farther than they would have believed possible. For mile after mile they had lunged after Schnorbitz, without any clue where he was taking them. Eventually, after many hours, Gapp had simply collapsed in gasps of exhaustion and tears of relief once he heard the gallop of hefty hooves and those droning Parandus voices approaching fast from their right.

Hwald and Finan had proved themselves admirably. The false trail had been successfully laid, and their pursuers would be heading south for some time yet. With luck that would distract them long enough for the fugitives to put a good distance between them and the horrors that stalked them.

From then on, they had continued east, all throughout the day, as fast as the debilitated Paranduzes could manage. Even when the last, cold rays of a weak sun winked out completely, they carried on, not stopping once during the night, but stumbling through a bad dream of sickness, confusion, and fear that seemed to have no end. Both men's cold-weather gear had been seized from them, and the Oghain robes they had stolen to replace them were wholly inadequate against the terrible chill of the night.

As dawn approached, cold and drear ahead of them, still they toiled on-ward, for hour after hellish hour.

The only aim for most of them was to get away from Wrythe in whichever direction offered easiest passage through the dense forest. Only on the insistence of Methuselech had they been steered northeast, toward the coast, finally emerging from the forest into this dismal land of bare rocky cliffs, black, stony beaches, and stinking sea wrack.

But they were far from being out of difficulty yet. To a barren, largely unknown land they had come, with an uncertain destination and an even vaguer purpose. They were all on their last legs, and starving.

It was an opportune encounter with the Uldachtna nomads that saved them. Toward the evening of the second day, they came across a small group of hunters who were fortunately human, and seemed neither hostile nor too surprised at seeing Hwald and Finan. Best of all, they turned out to be Torca.

The Uldachtna tribe of the Torca race migrated up through the northern reaches of the forests of Fron-Wudu every autumn as far as the Seter Heights. Gapp recalled Wodeman making mention of this people. In their stories they remembered Drauglir, the shaman had claimed, and referred to him as *Kelet,* the Devourer of Whales.

This particular family was currently making a short detour north to the coast in order to forage for shellfish. They had been in the spot for several days already, having erected a few of their bowl-shaped, antler-crowned yurts upon the scrubby grassland lying between the strand and the edge of the forest.

A hospitable people, renowned for their generosity, they had welcomed even Hwald and Finan into their camp without hesitation. There the Torca provided them all with the best they could offer in safety, warmth, and comfort for the night. It was certainly the safest they had felt since leaving Cyne-Tregva, though the warmth and comfort were relative. As guests of honor Methuselech and Gapp (with his hound) shared a yurt with the patriarch and his several wives, while the Paranduzes took up their customary ever-watchful position outside. The shelter was cramped, and lightless save for a single ozocerite candle that succeeded only in illuminating the thick brown smog immediately surrounding it, and a seal oil lamp with translucent fish skin for glass. The earth floor had already become a packed-down tar of walrus oil, elk hair, and crushed mollusk shell. The pervading fug stank of old sweat, horsehair blankets, plaited wolf skin ropes, cold mutton grease, and a choking smoke that never dissipated. Even when Wife Number One opened the smoke-hole with a stick, the wind merely drove it back into their eyes and lungs.

Furthermore, as soon as the sun went down, they were plagued by a merciless swarm of biting midges.

But in compensation the Torca also provided them with a veritable banquet of mutton, beans, and wild garlic, all washed down with fermented goat's milk.

But there was something equally comforting they provided; and that was hon-est, simple company. This last did at least as much to revitalize Gapp as did the food and warmth. How long it felt since he had enjoyed the company of normal people, people of his own kind, *humans*. For the Oghain he considered to be something less than subhuman, and Methuselech was not much better nowadays.

Only now did Gapp's thoughts turn once again to their current leader. That there was something dreadfully amiss about him went without saying; the man was falling apart more obviously as each day passed. For Gapp, the flight had been bad enough, but at least he still possessed hands to grip onto his steed's antlers; Methuselech, however, had managed only by enmeshing his handless stumps among Hwald's rearward tines. It was a sick and pitiful sight to behold.

But, now that he came to think about it, what was really preoccupying the boy this night was Xilva's deepening reticence. He had never been forthcom-ing about his plans, but now he seemed to have retreated even further. What, before Wrythe, had appeared as uncivil aloofness now seemed more like complete mental withdrawal.

As far as both body and mind were concerned, Methuselech Xilvafloese was apparently drawing to some sort of close.

In the course of that same night, the Torca provided some information that lit the first flame of real hope in the hearts of their guests for a very long time. For, two days earlier, they had seen a large encampment of rather strange creaures farther along the coast—not more than a day's travel away.

Two types of creature there were, the patriarch informed them, but whether man or beast he could not tell, for even at a distance he could see they were like nothing he had ever encountered before in his life. (*Or anyone else's*, Gapp imagined, thinking back to that most isolated and unheard-of forest realm.) The smaller ones, it seemed, were about Gapp's size and build, and were at least partly clothed, but were otherwise covered head to foot in curly brown hair and, in addition to this, possessed weasel-like faces and long tails. The larger ones, though, reminded the Torca a little of Hwald and Finan here, though they went on just two legs—like a deer's hind pair—and had a long single horn instead of antlers. And though they had tails like that of the Parandus, theirs lacked the cluster of spikes at the end.

To the Uldachtna wanderers, they might as well have been devils come straight from Melhus Island.

Gapp and Methuselech looked at each other through the lambent ozocerite glow, and sighed with relief.

Methuselech demanded to know where exactly these creatures had been seen, and from the reply he received it seemed these new creatures were camped pretty much where he had instructed Englarielle to lead his Vetter army.

For Gapp this news produced a surge of joy. In spite of the dull sense of fear that still haunted him, he felt lightheartedly excited at the thought of being reunited with Englarielle and the others after all he had been through. Not even the midges and smoke could dampen his relief.

For Methuselech though, things were entirely different. He suffered the excited prattling of his companion with the glazed and suffering look of a parent. He continually declined the Torca's offer of food with unaccustomed politeness and as much firmness as he dared, and placed himself firmly in the midst of the reeking smoke, the better to mask his growing stench of decay.

For him, it was to be a very long night.

Despite the boy's optimistic wittering, Methuselech realized they were far from safe. He knew Scathur too well and within days, possibly hours, this whole area would be teeming with Oghain, all out for his blood (such as it was). And already he felt so weak. If Scathur arrived during the night, he was done for.

But if they did make it through to the morning, he should, by then, be refuelled. And, if he could once again wrap his arm stumps around Hwald's antlers for a few hours more, and just sit tight, they would arrive at the Black Shore, and the worst of the danger would be behind him.

This body may be a pathetic sack of mushroom fodder with only a few days left in it, but if I can haul it as far as the Black Shore, then at last I can use my real powers . . .

His body was increasingly rebelling against the spirit that dwelt within it, rejecting it and trying to destroy it in any way it could. But they were already so close now, and he still had Radnar there as a little self-propelled bag of fresh blood.

There was also the chance of reinforcements close at hand. Yet, even without the Vetters, he might still make it. Make it back home.

If only they made it through the night.

The rose glow of the sun's first rays came slanting over the eastern horizon, and cast long, xiphoid shadows behind the yurts. It was a bitterly cold morning, still quiet and reluctant to get going. Even the sea was sluggish as it listlessly rinsed the stony beach.

Gapp awoke in a fit of coughing, and flung the uncured saiga-pelt covers from his itching body and crawled outside between the two walrus tusks that framed the felt door flaps of the yurt. He stretched his cramped body and breathed great gulps of the blessedly clean air deep into his smoke-tarred lungs. Then he stood pondering silently in the dawn chill.

For once, he realized, he felt surprisingly relaxed and rested. Not drained or dizzy, as was usual recently, but properly refreshed in the way one should feel after a good night's sleep. That food had been wonderful, and despite the primitive conditions in the yurt, he had slept deeply. No dreams of bats or leeches sucking his lifeblood.

Yes, he was decidedly feeling ready to be off. Even Methuselech looked a little more human, that is to say, slightly less of a cadaver. The only one in the camp, in fact, who seemed drained and off-color was the plumpest of the patriarch's wives, the one who had slept closest to Methuselech.

After a hurried breakfast they effusively thanked their hosts and bade them farewell, then set out again along the coast. All were eager to quickly put more distance between them and the threat from the west, and the icy sea breeze served to add yet more zest to their journey.

At last, by early afternoon, they spotted several thin columns of smoke rising into the air, and two hours later they were finally reunited with the Vetters. A strangled hooting went up from the Paranduzes, and in a mad clatter of flying pebbles and spray of sand they galloped at full speed down toward the encampment laid out on the strand.

Vetter and Cervulus alike came charging toward Methuselech and his group, the Vetters sprinting nimbly along, their ratlike tails pointing straight up in the air, and their much larger companions bobbing along with that strange gait of theirs, shaking the ground under their powerful three-toed hooves. Even the Vetter sentries, who had been perching atop the odd sea stack around this area, now came gliding toward them on their ratlike arm membranes.

"Thank you!" Gapp beamed as he stared into Englarielle's big, apple-green eyes and clasping his clawed little hand in his own. "Only you could have done it!"

He did not really know what he was saying, and was sure the Vetters had not a clue either, but the words came bubbling straight from his heart, and the feeling behind them, at least, could not be misunderstood.

All of them were there: the Cynen Englarielle, the Vetter Radkin who had originally found Gapp, Ted the blacksmith, the captains, and about two-score others, with one Cervulus mount for each Vetter. All one hundred of them crowded around the newcomers eagerly, and for a time it felt as if they were all on holiday; all they wished to do now was sing, dance, feast, and catch up on news.

The bad news that Methuselech no longer had any hands, however, would have to wait. He was still considered by the Vetters a superior being, but that might not last for long once they witnessed his handicap; for impairment of any kind in Vetter society was likely to warrant a fast-track ticket to the cutting slab. He therefore kept his stumps firmly concealed within his Oghain robe.

As far as the good folk of Cyne-Tregva were concerned, however happy they were to see the arrivals, they were not in the least bit surprised. Having been promised a rendezvous here, they had accepted that without any doubt. Now that they were all safely together again, that seemed to be that: mission accomplished. Their laughter and music rang out, welcoming fires were built higher, sending even denser plumes of smoke up into the heavens, and the story-telling began.

Methuselech was too tired to argue. He could see any attempts to drag them on eastward now would simply fall upon deaf ears. The Vetters wanted to celebrate, and that was just what they would do. He was forced into translating the various stories for all to hear, though he did so with disappointing brevity. Continually looking over his shoulder toward the forest, he could not properly concentrate.

Well, they had at least brought some decent weaponry with them, he was relieved to see, and not simply their workaday hunting equipment. It did appear that they would be well prepared should they encounter any resistance within the Maw. Each of them had brought along one of those Jordiske-scapula machetes, plus several quivers of quartz-tipped throwing darts the size of an arrow. And the Cervulice were armed even more formidably, each of them having a pair of long sabres that were heavier at one end and made from a flexible wood coated with a specially-treated amber that both toughened them and rendered them as sharp as glass. Many of them had also been kitted out with crude leather tabards hung with small plates of metal.

Nevertheless, this was the Last Shore; he knew it well and it did not welcome happiness. They were all hopelessly exposed here, yet it would take a lot to instill any sense of urgency in them while they remained in this euphoric mood. Methuselech could feel the heat of Scathur's anger on the nape of his neck, increasing with every minute they wasted here.

"Radnar," he hissed, "we've got to get them away from here right now. It's not safe."

The atmosphere of celebration had temporarily wiped away Gapp's fear of Wrythe, but the shadow of that place now returned to him on hearing Methuselech's voice.

"Yes of course." He nodded. "But where do we go?"

Methuselech held his eye, and murmured: "To Melhus."

"What, today?"

"Yes, today! Don't you understand? *He* is not far behind us."

Englarielle and the nearest Vetters quieted down, unsure as to what their friend's sudden retort might mean.

Gapp lowered his head. "I understand fully," he responded. "But we still haven't got a boat."

"Leave the details to me," Methuselech said, and moved away through the carousing throng. "I know a way, but you must help me get these—oh my life, they've found us already!"

All turned to follow his widening gaze. There at the top of a ridge overlooking the beach, stood five malign black silhouettes. They did not move, but just stood there watching at the now silent company. Two more came up from behind to join the line, one at either end . . . then two more.

"No more talk," Methuselech urged. "We're off—now!"

There was a hurried scramble for weapons as growling Vetters and gabbling Cervulice cut short their celebrations to face this new threat. Methuselech meanwhile clambered up onto Hwald who snorted and began moaning in wide-eyed dread. Gapp similarly wasted no time in vaulting onto Finan. All four, plus a snarling slavering Schnorbitz, were about to start off when Englarielle, with his ridiculous antique helm rammed down upon his head, leapt right in front of the two Paranduzes and halted them.

"Uaiah nauiraeavi waunou!" he cried shrilly, clearly confused as to why nine—now thirteen—they were still coming—strangers were such a threat to over a hundred. The Cervulice, too, appeared more than ready for a fight, each twirling his twin swords in the air and making stabbing motions with the black, sabrelike horn on his forehead.

But still they came: sixteen of them now. Hwald bellowed something to Englarielle, and whatever this was, it finally seemed to do the trick. The four who had suffered so badly at Wrythe had no idea how many Wire-Faces there might be, but the very air now stank of Scathur. They could sense his vile presence all around, in the dark clouds, the leaden sea, the whispering wind; they could almost see his evil darkening the air, blowing from the west in a pall. They were not going to wait to find out how many others there were, even if it meant deserting their Vetter friends.

Straight onto the backs of their mounts the Vetters sprang, seating themselves each on that hefty, protruding Cervulus rump while firmly grasping a good handful of leonine mane. Then, charging along as though the very flames of hell licked at their heels, the whole company fled. Even the confused and disappointed Cynen and his captains. The Cervulice even went down on all fours, using their great arms as an extra pair of legs for added speed. And it was a long time before any of them looked back.

As they rode, Methuselech continually cried out for them to keep their eyes peeled for any seaweed deposited by the high tide. Gapp looked at him in puzzlement, wondering if he had finally tipped over the edge of madness. But he saw in the man's eyes no insanity, just unbelievable desperation as he bounced about atop the thundering Parandus with his concealed forearms wrapped about its antlers.

He's holding that body of his together by will alone, Gapp marveled. *Or perhaps something else is?*

When they finally halted, it was twilight. They all looked around at this place Methuselech had brought them to. Not one of them uttered a sound; this place definitely did not feel good to them.

A thick gray fog had rolled in from the sea, gradually eating up the stars and blotting out the moon. It glided around them, beading clothes, skin, and fur with a loathsome dew, invading every crevice with clammy fingers; the breath from the Serpent at the World's Ending, infecting them, petrifying them, making them a part of its world. Sly waves lapped slickly against oily rocks before slithering back into the unknown. Deep, sonorous calls could be heard somewhere out there, how far off they could not guess.

The Vetters' pointed ear tips trembled. It was now unnervingly quiet. They had foolishly made too much noise in their arrival, and knew now that this strange land was aware of them, was listening to them.

Before two days ago, Gapp Radnar had never actually seen the sea. He had heard about it all his life, of course, so much so in fact that his first sight of it was something of a letdown. Here it was sluggish and had an unpleasant look about it. Nothing at all like the stirring promises of the sagas. But for Englarielle's folk, never even having heard about it before, it might as well have been another dimension, too big for comprehension.

And what back there had at first sight filled them with awe, here seemed alien and terrible. For the ocean had taken on a decidedly darker aspect to that it wore just a few miles west. In fact, it now scared them witless. They felt as if they had arrived at the very edge of the world, and were gazing out at the blackness of the void beyond, wherein dwelt the Serpents of the Poison Sea.

He did not know what lent it this foreboding air, but something told Gapp that they had at last arrived at Xilva's special place.

The fog swirled all around them now. In wreaths and wispy tatters it rolled toward them out of the sea, muffling what little sound there was among them. It engulfed them wholly and cut them off from their own world. Gapp was reminded of the stories of U'throst, an underwater Huldre-land that rose out of the sea from time to time. Many were the accounts of ordinary men wandering the well-trodden paths of their coastal home, only to find themselves passing through a strange fog and emerging into that strange land. Even then, he had never enjoyed listening to those stories.

"Xilva?" he called out, unsure where his companion was.

His question fell dead.

"Xilva!" he hissed, "where are we?"

A voice sounded from somewhere nearby, or possibly from inside his head. "The Black Shore," it murmured.

"Where are you?"

"The Black Shore," the voice repeated. "It lies between the sea and the line of weed left by the high tide. This is a refuge for Huldre, and here may we pass into their world, and emerge on to Melhus."

"What are you talking about?"

"It's been a long time since I had any dealings with Jagt—a long, long time. But if Chance has the whim to smile on us on this day, I may be able to secure our passage."

Methuselech closed his eyes, and then simply ignored the company.

Gapp wrapped his Oghain robe tightly about him, and gazed out over the flat, lifeless grey of the Jagt Straits. Though now the twilight and the fog combined made it hard to see farther than ten yards, just half an hour ago they had enjoyed a clear view many miles out into the ocean, and had seen no boat, raft, or ship, or indeed anything at all, upon its surface. He turned back to Methuselech, who was facing out to sea with a look of intense concentration on his face.

"But there's nothing there," the boy protested, trying hard not to sound as if he thought his companion was insane (which he did). He had no wish to antagonize this lunatic, especially now that he had begun to move his shrouded stumps about in a peculiar, trancelike manner reminiscent of those gin-crazed Torca vagrants in Lower Kettle Bazaar back in Nordwas, who would suddenly decide to dance, glassy-eyed, with their arms waving vaguely.

"There will be," Methuselech murmured, still gesturing. "Trust me. I'm a necromancer."

Gapp ground his heels into the grit in frustration. Why had he followed the creepy old specter this far? He looked around at the familiar faces of the Vetters, the Paranduzes, and the Cervulice ranged all around him. They were clearly fearful, it was true, but their fear was induced by this place and the rumor of the horrors that were on their tail. Of Methuselech himself, however, there was not a trace of distrust in their eyes at all.

It seemed to Gapp that Englarielle, even though he was high chief of Cyne-Tregva, considered Methuselech to be the leader here, and trusted him as blindly and faithfully as a prophet, or even a god. Though he was as intensely curious as any of them as to what the great one was up to, it never occurred to Englarielle to question Methuselech's motives.

Gapp could not decide which irked him the most, Methuselech's reticence or the naiveté of an entire community. Or perhaps he was most annoyed by the fact that he was going along with it just as dumbly as they were.

In any case, things did not bode well.

Then Methuselech opened his mouth wide, and from it blasted a sound as loud, deep, and reverberating as a foghorn.

Just as the screeching of the Children had oppressed every citizen in Wrythe two days ago, so did Methuselech's trumpeting wail now flatten all those anywhere near him onto the ground in cowering dismay.

"Wuih!" Gapp breathed, ducking also. "I never expected that!"

Then without warning, the air changed. Or *something* changed. There was now a definite otherworld presence close at hand. As Gapp strained to see through the enveloping murk, he could suddenly discern a darker shape out there upon the sea. Slowly, noiselessly, it approached them, gradually growing more distinct.

It was a figure—could it be a man?—that floated upon the waves, or even upon the fog above them. Some of the Cervulice snorted and backed away. The others held their ground, but could be heard panting heavily, occasionally stamping their great velvety toes into the sand.

Methuselech ceased his incantation, and stood silently waiting, swaying slightly. Gapp edged surreptitiously away from him, and continued to watch the approaching figure.

It traveled upon a round platform, he could see now. At first it appeared to be some kind of coracle, but as it drifted closer it was revealed to be no boat but a disc of floating ice, like a tiny ice floe, carved with grotesque reliefs and draped with sludge-grey seaweed.

Gapp felt increasingly agitated with each passing second. Whoever Methuselech was underneath it all, hadn't he just confessed to them he was a necromancer? And didn't *they* summon the dead? But as the floating figure beached upon the sand, it became more and more apparent that it was far from dead. It might not be part of the human world but it was very much alive.

So if the dead are summoned by living necromancers, surely the living then are summoned by—?

"Bilge!" the boy muttered to himself. "Old Xilva can hardly raise his arms, let alone anything else."

Then a soft voice drifted toward him upon the still air. At first he assumed it to be that of the newcomer, till it became clear it was Methuselech's. No longer hoarse, his voice now sounded as velvety-smooth as an altar cloth, entering Gapp's mind directly rather than through his ears.

"This is Jagt, the pilot of the waves," that voice intoned, "and no, rest assured, he is not dead."

Jagt now stood before them on the strand, and all sound was stilled as he began to speak.

"Your day is long gone, Mauglad." He addressed Methuselech in a tone as profound yet unvoiced as the gale that shudders the timbers. "Drauglir died an age ago, along with all his spawn. His halls ring hollow with empty air now."

Jagt stood tall before Methuselech, unbowed by the power of the necromancer whose same power had summoned him here. Of the rest of the throng he remained as heedless as he was unmindful of the glamour he induced in them. In the dark it was difficult to clearly make out anything of his form, but Gapp was aware of a tall figure clad in a trailing mantle of grey-green seaweed. Oddly-jointed limbs there were, one of which held a staff fashioned from barnacle-encrusted driftwood. Between curtains of matted sea grass hair could be glimpsed a pale face whose skin reminded him of a jellyfish, running with water constantly, bulging and palpitating. Of this slick visage, all that could be discerned were two lifeless fish eyes.

Gapp was as unprepared for this apparition as any of them there, save Methuselech. But like the necromancer's words, those of Jagt permeated into the consciousness of all there, and Gapp could understand every one. And in his mind now came a surge of joy on hearing what Jagt had just said.

"Drauglir died an age ago."

Gapp's body stiffened with inner excitement at the news.

Jagt washed up against the line of wrack that marked the periphery of Huldre-Home—beyond this he would not pass—and gazed upon his summoner with scantly disguised loathing. He was a creature of the sea, and had no love of the land, nor anything that dwelt upon its two-dimensional surface. But here, along this narrow belt of wrack-strewn strand that Methuselech termed the Black Shore, he was still within his realm, and walked with the flowing ease of one comfortably in his element.

"You're in the wrong place and time, black conjurer," Jagt hissed. "There's nothing for you here now. Get back to your cow dung sepulcher; let the earth plants infiltrate their roots into you and feed upon your dessicated flesh. Go now, just GO!"

"Say what you will," Methuselech responded in that silken mellifluence that spoke to the mind rather than to the ears, "for all the good it'll do. You know as well as I that you have no power to refuse me. I have the binding over you, and you *will* do as I bid."

Huldre and necromancer held each other with their eyes, unmoving.

"For all its size," Methuselech continued, "your ocean might as well now be a puddle of piss in a cowshed. I can hook you out as easily as a boy plucks mussels from a rock pool at low tide. Though you might skulk hiding in the deepest, iciest cracks in the ocean floor, it will avail you nothing, for even there I can burn you like a lobster in a pot, or shrivel you like an eel thrown upon a bonfire. The only difference being that *your* torment would last considerably longer than theirs."

Between these two great powers the night air crackled with tension. None watching dared make a sound. Then abruptly, Schnorbitz broke wind. It was not loud, but it broke the suspense of the moment, and caused the hound's head to spin round in surprise at his own posterior, as dogs do.

Jagt's secondary eyelids drew over those blank fishy eyes, turning them white. He did not move, but it was clear to all watching that he had been brought to heel. Shambling rather than drifting now, he turned and walked back into the sea.

"Come," Methuselech rasped, in his real voice again, "follow him quickly; his power will get you all across to Melhus only if you stay close to him. Let's go!"

None of them knew what was going on, but such was the force of Methuselech's exhortation that all found themselves charging without hesitation into the sea. Spray flew about as fifty mounted Vetters floundered about in an element that was baffling to them, but none cried out in alarm.

Gapp stood like a frozen pillar upon the strand, a singular point of immobility amid that whirling commotion, that unthinking herd that stampeded headlong into the freezing grey oblivion. His world, never quite in phase with reality since he had met again the one that called itself Methuselech, had now collapsed into meaningless chaos—a melee of leaping, plunging, horn-headed demons that screeched insanely in that white fury of sea spray.

He had only this minute received the joyous news that Drauglir was truly dead, and that they could all go home again and never return to this Badland again. *So what were they all doing now?* It ceased to make any sense to him at all, and he felt like shouting out to them that they were all heading in the wrong direction.

But even if they had decided rationally that they must follow their spectral leader over to Melhus, it still made no sense. This was for them their first advent to the sea, something which was to them otherworldly, terrifying, too immense to comprehend. Every nerve ending in Gapp's warm oversensitive flesh drew back, repelled by the mere thought of contact with that freezing, salt-poisoned element. That was not their world; theirs was one of loamy earth, warm air, sun on leaf, and it ended here on this beach. To merely sail upon the surface of the ocean was a risk undertaken only by the bravest of heroes; but to plunge *beneath* it was nothing less than equivalent to throwing oneself over the edge of the world.

Yet there they were, following the lead of the Methuselech-thing, himself as rotten as the sick air of this place, plunging mindlessly over the edge of the world.

He was alone now. The last of the Vetterym had just submerged from sight.

How is it that they can do such a thing but I can't? he asked. *It's as alien to them as it is to me—more so, in fact. Am I still such a coward after all I've been through?*

Then a howl that turned his bones to jelly erupted from behind him. The Wire-Faces had arrived! Over two-score of them, already charging down to where he stood alone by the water's edge, their garrottes almost singing in anticipation of flaying him alive.

After the briefest moment of frozen terror, he scurried down to the water and flung himself into the mercy of the sea—or of Jagt, or the necromancer. A second later, he, too, was off the edge of the world.

"*God's Pollux!*" he gasped as the freezing water clamped around his torso, squeezing the air from his lungs. For a moment of blind panic he believed the sea had frozen solid around him upon first contact, and was attempting to crush the life out of him—as if caught in a Marmennill's icy grasp—as his punishment for entering this alien world. For several seconds he thrashed about in despair, and truly believed he was about to perish.

Then the strangest, most unexpected thing happened.

He found he really *had* entered another world. A suddenly quiet world, where all the noise and commotion of sea spume and his own panicked gurgling were gone, and where the cold, though undiminished, caused him no discomfort at all. As Bolldhe, miles to the east, discovered under the influence of Wodeman's spell, even extreme cold could be accepted into oneself, and become as natural as breathing.

But breathing, Gapp realized with astonishment, was not of this world. He neither held his breath nor took water in through gills, for breathing was simply not a necessity anymore.

Suspended there, he looked around himself in bafflement. The ocean that from land had appeared as dead and colorless as stagnant ditch water now swirled with a thousand different sea-hues; every shade of grey between iceberg-white and shark's-eye-black appeared around him, from the scintillating silver of a mackerel's belly through to the dark blue-grey of a dolphin's back, and all bespeckled with the bright, shimmering, ever changing hues of a rainbow. Gapp had never imagined mere water could be so dazzlingly colorful. This was something not even the skalds had sung about.

Not only this but the boy also found to his wonderment that he could actually see the patterns the water made: every swirl and eddy from the tiniest vortex caused by the twitch of a minnow's tail, to the rise and fall of warmer or colder water, and on to the vastness of the tide itself. If he ever returned to Nordwas, he would have to have a few words in the skalds' ears before they thought about their next composition.

If he ever did return to that flat, drab world, that is.

Through the grinding of remote icebergs and the haunting whale song that echoed with aching sadness throughout the ocean, Gapp became dimly aware that Jagt and the company were somewhere ahead of him, a distant flurry of movement. How far away, though, he could not tell, for in this new world relative dimensions in both space and time were unfathomable, and held little interest for the boy. Nevertheless, with a quick flick of his feet, he soared after them, darting through the water with eel-like fluidity, faster than he could have believed, and with effortless ease and grace.

Pearlflower and starblossom exploded into color around him, and sang with the chorus of a million silver bells. The very ocean and its wondrous inhabitants seemed to smile with him in exultation and exuberance: langorous whales; spear-nosed narwhal; battalions of mandarin shellfish, each as big as a Sailam horse, that marched in lines over the sea bed; sly Marmennill with scales that glistened electric-turquoise and psychedelic-yellow; forests of multicolored sea grass expanding and contracting with each breath, swirling like a drowned maiden's hair; creatures that flew upon vast wings; tiny specks of incandescence that surged as one in shoals of billions, changing color with each turn.

Almost immediately, it seemed, Gapp was back with the main company. He could feel the giddy ecstasy of the Vetters emanating in waves of blue electricity toward him, like new souls awakened into life on the First Day of the world. No longer riding their steeds, they now swam with the playful fluidity of otters, their large, splayed feet working like flippers. Through them, among them, twisting and turning, wide-eyed Paranduzes and Cervulice galloped upon finlike hooves like a herd of sleekly glistening Hippocampi. Schnorbitz, too, wriggled through the water like a great seal, enjoying every moment of this brilliant new game. Even Methuselech was among their number, a black, poison spine that darted harpoon-fast at the head of the throng.

And then there was Jagt.

Gapp gaped. It *was* Jagt, and yet a Jagt that was as different to his former manifestation as it was possible to imagine. Now that he was in his own element, that grotesque figure that had appeared so out of place upon the strand flowed with the grace and beauty of one wholly at one with his world. Gone was the pale, jellied complexion, replaced by a skin as white, hard, and shining as the smoothest pearl, and glowing with an inner light that shone from a high, noble forehead. With the unhurried grace of one as deep and ancient as he, Jagt swam, cloak billowing around him like a manta ray, his clothes that had looked at first like greyish seaweed now swirling and furling every shade of green and blue. Even his staff, formerly a rotten stick scabbed with dead limpets, was now a fine black cane inlaid with mother-of-pearl, long as a narwhal horn.

A high, song-like voice keened through the depths all about, and Gapp realized that Jagt was talking to them. Here, his voice sounded infinitely more musical than it had seemed on land. And though there was no normal comprehension of the individual words or sounds he uttered, again, all gathered there could understand what was being said, just as one comprehends the message a composer conveys through his music.

U'throst, it seemed, awaited them; through that marine Huldre-realm they had to pass if they were to reach their destination.

Gapp was already too glamored by this world to feel any trepidation. As Bolldhe and his companions had done three weeks ago on entering Eotunlandt, Gapp felt nothing but breathtaking renewal, the pure joy of a child, a second birth. This was his baptism into Huldre, and ever after he would yearn to return to its cold embrace.

Had he thought about it, however, he would have detected a certain slyness in Jagt's voice, knowing, cold and dark as the ocean's depths, *unfeeling* . . . Exactly how much hold did Methuselech's binding spell really have on him?

But evil? Who could tell? Is a fish evil? Who could know what thoughts lay in the heart of Jagt, if he even *possessed* a heart?

Meanwhile, U'throst still called. Down they plummeted, spiraling deep through a whirlpool that could not be resisted, awesome and—for the first time on the voyage so far—frightening in its power. Down through a great hole in the sea bed, twisting and twirling so fast the land-dwellers felt their frail bodies might at any moment come apart . . .

. . . Along tunnels of grinding ice . . .

. . . Speeding through vast underground caverns that teemed with the wraith-like shapes of pulsating, translucent medusae; lunging, multilegged monsters with scissorlike mandibles; leviathans that rolled overhead so vast their size and shape could not be guessed . . .

... And amid fey denizens with faces that were almost human, but were sharply pointed, made of hard, dark-green shell, with eyes that poured forth beams of yellow light, and expressions of such ghastly malice they could never be tolerated on land. With pincers bigger than their own bodies they snapped at the intruders, but Jagt's power kept them at bay.

Now they cavorted through pillars of rock covered in needle-sharp spears of rainbow hued crystal, faster, faster, faster still, a hyperdive through the aquakaleidoscope of the galaxy. A dull humming filled Gapp's ears till he began to feel his eardrums might burst. Now, all sight became a meaningless blur of color and light. It was impossible to tell even in which direction they were headed.

On and on it went, until soon even Time gave up, took a bow, and fled, back to the surface where its services might be better appreciated.

Then it became dark and very, very cold. Time may have drifted back, slowly, hesitantly, still unsure whether it was wanted or not. That sense of Huldre gradually dissipated, and they could now feel they were heading upward.

Up, up, up, but getting ever slower, losing momentum. A tight, uncomfortable feeling began to grip their chests, and with it came the first sensations of panic.

And pain.

All light now faded, all glamour, all warmth, until they realized with awful clarity that they were beneath the ocean—the real ocean—and Jagt had abandoned them. They had been cast adrift in the ocean depths far beneath the sea bed.

With vengeful glee Jagt, the pilot of the waves who leaves no trace of those he lures to his dungeons, slammed the door of Huldre-Home on them, issuing one last cry that was clearer than anything he had spoken to them earlier:

"And don't come back!"

They would not be coming back that way. Not ever. The door was closed and would not be reopened.

No trace.

The sea, that oily, dead sea that lapped onto the Black Shore, erased every footprint, every last sign of Gapp and the others ever setting foot on that beach, then slid back toward the depths with a whisper that might have been laughter.

"No trace," Kuthy brooded. "No trace at all."

"Like they stepped over that line of seaweed and simply ceased to exist," Elfswith agreed. He carefully picked up a rubbery frond of glistening bladder-wrack on the tip of his pencil, scrutinized it, then dropped it into a small glass jar. This he sealed tightly, and put into a pocket.

"Sample?" Kuthy inquired.

"Supper," Elfswith corrected.

It was forty-eight hours since Kuthy and Elfswith had left Wrythe. On that same day, they had risen above the trees upon the wyvern's back and surveyed the forest below for many hours. The sun had disappeared early, and they had been forced to adjourn their search. Perched in hammocks, they had spent the night among the treetops.

The next day, however, the keen eyes of Ceawlin had spotted a group of Wire-Faces ("The search-party!") heading northeast, and so they too had swung round and headed for the coast. There they had spent the remaining hours of daylight searching the coast, but then heading back to Wrythe, on the supposition that Methuselech intended to double back and steal a boat. But they had found nothing, no trace of the ones they sought, so spent a second night in frustration, this time camping upon the beach.

It was only upon this third day, waking at dawn, that they had noticed the line of smoke rising far to the east. Not long after, they arrived at the nomad camp, by now nothing more than a smoking ruin of burnt-up yurts, scattered and wailing herd beasts, and neatly decapitated Uldachtna-Torca. None had been spared by the Wire-Faces and their garrottes.

An hour later they had caught up with the marauders. Rind Head and his band had provided *excellent* target practice for them, till over forty garrottes now lay rusting at the water's edge. And an hour after *that,* here they were at the Black Shore. In the sand, the tracks of Methuselech's company had been easy to follow.

Until now.

"Well, whatever it was old Mauglad was up to, whatever secret he had, it looks like he's taken it with him into a very deep grave," Kuthy proclaimed solemnly. "Seems hard to believe. . . ."

"Too hard," Elfswith replied. "Mauglad died—what, six hundred years ago? The body of that desert friend of Nibulus may be crab food now, but Mauglad's spirit is still around somewhere, I guarantee."

"Searching for a new host, yes," Kuthy agreed. "What I don't get is why it's taken him over five hundred years to return. What was keeping him so long?"

"Something, obviously; we'll probably never know. But his soul is here now, and he won't stop till he reaches Vaagenfjord Maw. That was his home for countless years; it made him what he is, and he knows more about it than anyone. Whatever he intends to do, I think he'll do it very soon. Something big. Something *way* beyond the capability of all these hopeless adventurers coming here over the years.

"Come on, Kuthy. We'd better get going!"

7

The Maw, the Merrier

Thus came to an end the search of Kuthy and Elfswith for Mauglad Yrkeshta—or Methuselech, or whoever/whatever it was that had somehow succeeded in causing an entire army of Tregvans to plunge after it into the death-cold ocean off the Last Shore. For the time being, at least. The thoughts of those two searchers for the Hidden Mysteries now focused upon those Methuselech had traveled with from Wyda-Aescaland. And so they took to the air once again, headed for the ice bridge where they had parted company seven days ago; and from there, probably, on over Melhus and, if necessary, all the way to the Maw itself. Elfswith, it had to be said, had little confidence in the southerners' ability, expecting to find, if anything at all, no more than a few sorry, snow-cloaked lumps of frozen meat huddled upon the ice. Kuthy on the other hand could not settle the knot of anticipation in his stomach that he had borne ever since they had flown to Wrythe. He for one was convinced that *interesting times* lay ahead, and that it all pointed to the Maw.

So the game was set and ordained, and all the players finally converged that same day upon the Maw.

Kuthy and Elfswith upon the great wyvern, soaring high above the Last Shore.

Bolldhe, Finwald, Appa, Wodeman, Nibulus, and Paulus, tramping along the last mile of the statue-head road.

Scathur, still sailing across the ocean with his Children, his Wire-Faces, and his precious pickled people.

And the Thieves of Tyvenborg, perhaps a day's journey behind Bolldhe, steadily approaching Ravenscairn.

But what of Vaagenfjord Maw itself, that magnetic pole that inexorably drew all who bore iron to the north? What thoughts or secrets still lay within its stony fastness? Was it really awaiting them, chuckling from deep within its hellish chambers that had not seen any light for five hundred years? Or was it truly as lifeless as it appeared?

At exactly the same time Kuthy, Elfswith, and Ceawlin lifted off from that dismal beach into a sky that was yellow-grey in the bleary mid-morning light, Bolldhe and his companions were coming to the end of the statue-head road, at last to look upon their final, long-sought destination.

The road itself, they had refused to tread. It was the work of the enemy, and as such they would not avail themselves of its aid, even were it to speed them on to *his* destruction. Instead they forced themselves through deep snow and over jagged rock, using the lines of statues only as a guide, a pointer to their goal. All the while, ice and ash howled through the air, and the ground rumbled to the anger of distant volcanoes, selfish giants simmering in fury at the presence of intruders in the secret garden of Melhus.

But there was another reason why they avoided the road. For in truth none of them was willing to walk all those miles under the silent gaze of those grotesque, ice-furrowed Rawgr heads. Put simply, the road repelled them. More than that, it appalled them.

For the last couple of miles, however, it had cut steeply downhill between two high cliffs of steep, hoarfrosted rock and, with no other way available to them, the company had at last been forced to make use of it. They averted their eyes from the leering regard of the statues, keeping their attention firmly upon the ground immediately at their feet. Here at least the ice was not the same impediment it had been while journeying off-road, but they still had to brace themselves against the cruel blast of arctic wind that howled up the cutting from the northern sea beyond.

Then the road swung around west, and so, before long continued its curve over to the left, until it almost led back upon itself, heading south, and the company found themselves staring, at long last, down into the very fjord itself. They had arrived at the summit of the eastern cliff of Vaagenfjord. Perhaps four thousand feet below them lay the dark waters of the inlet, while over on the other side, the western cliff faced them directly, grey and sheer, a wall of rock rising from the lowest waters to the highest skies.

The road was now no more than a cliff path, and ran not along the rim of the cliff, but against its sheer face, gradually leading diagonally downward. This was the route that would take them down all the way to their final destination.

And there, miles ahead of them and far below, the fjord ended against a black wall that, though from here it was nothing but a small dark patch in the distance, they knew to be the Maw itself.

They halted, battered by the wind, and peered at it through the sleet. After nearly eleven weeks of hard journeying, there it was, the end of the road. For a very long time, despite the freezing winds that snapped at their bearskins, the travelers could only stand and stare.

"It looks so small." Nibulus, the first to finally speak, sounded uncharacteristically thoughtful.

"And so empty . . . so dead," Paulus added, though what senses the Nahovian possessed that would tell him this at such a distance, none there could guess.

The relief in their voices, however uncertain, was unmistakable. The terrible crossing of Melhus was over, and by the looks of it, so was the danger. For them, the Maw really did appear dead.

Seated upon Zhang's back, Appa let out a long, heartfelt moan of relief, and closed his eyes tightly. All thoughts of Rawgr and quest now receded far from his mind, further and further. His ordeal upon the plain of fire and ice seemed finally over. He clutched his talisman, and began to shake with sobs.

The other mage-priest, Finwald, on the other hand, stared impassively at that little black smudge ahead of them, his feelings masked. And for Wodeman too, it was different, again; he seemed to have something on his mind that was troubling him, and though none of his companions could tell it, this had nothing to do with either the crossing or what lay ahead within the Maw. What was perturbing him was a matter that had preoccupied him ever since learning of Bolldhe's soul-journey on the ice field.

And Bolldhe, he who was considered by some to be the central player in this game, what thoughts lay behind his silent gaze as he beheld his destiny?

Of all of them, he was the only one who felt like turning back, simply heading back up to the ice field and leaving this place far behind. Like Kuthy, he was neither a fanciful nor a superstitious man, but, again like Kuthy, there were certain visions of Fate that now crowded around the edge of his waking mind. After all these months of stony disbelief and contemptuous laughter, now that he actually stood there facing that dark patch at the head of the fjord, it seemed far from "small" and "dead" to him. He could sense that something *bad* was going to happen; maybe tomorrow, maybe today, maybe even in the next hour or so.

But all he said was, "It's waiting for us," and left it at that.

Without pausing a second longer, Nibulus led the way down the cliff path. For months he had thought about this, imagining the moment when he would retrace the footsteps of his heroic ancestors right to this very point, at Vaagenfjord, and begin the last march unto the very gates of the Maw. On the long days and nights of the journey that had led him here, he had often wondered what it would feel like, what passions or fears would stir in his breast upon first setting eyes on that great defile that led to the Great Defiler. But, now that it came to it, he and his men were so tired, frozen, and browbeaten by the terrible crossing that all he felt now was an overwhelming desire to get lower down and out of the wind.

So they descended into Vaagenfjord.

The farther they progressed, the more the wind began to be left behind them. Or rather above, for it still reverberated powerfully in the rock all around them. But the sound of its icy, demonic screeching remained in higher places, up there at the roof of the island, and troubled them no more. In this they took some comfort, hearing the wind, yet not feeling its life-sapping breath—as any traveler will do on reaching home and listening to it rattle harmlessly around his house while he is safely in the warmth.

The ice upon the pathway, too, lessened, growing patchier, and upon the rock face to one side it had even less purchase. Thus the fjord grew blessedly darker to their reddened eyes, a small mercy after a week of snow glare.

The chill of both body and soul began to thaw.

The company continued on down. Gradually, as they studied their new surroundings, they became aware of something unexpected. Holes began to appear in the cliff face, not natural cavities, but carved with tools; regularly spaced vertical slits about six inches wide and three feet in height.

"Arrow slits!" Nibulus declared. "Look, hundreds of them!"

Not only arrow slits, but below the path they could make out narrow ledges, balconies, and sills, their edges curving slightly upward. All of these were shaped to fit the contours of the rock so that from below they would appear merely as natural outcroppings of stone. In effect, they were carefully camouflaged.

Seen from above, however, it appeared as though the entire fjord were one vast honeycombed fortress wall. Even the windows and doorways opening from chambers inside the cliff were plainly visible.

Nibulus halted the group, and drew forth the Chronicle.

"It says here that, on that day as the fleet sailed up the fjord . . .

"Ther cam from above a sudden rayne of arrews and speres that forsoth was so dens and thickly clustr'd that we coulde no longer see even the lite of daye . . .

"I'd imagine there's more than a crumb of exaggeration there," he interjected, "but anyway . . .

". . . alle spouting from the very stone of the cliffes, yet no archer nor any wight 'pon those cliffs was ther seen.

And ther'upon as we helde our shieldes above us that we myte yet holde back this rayne of Helle, so cam a falle of rock to smite us. Many dyed upon that moment, and no small number of vessels did founder, rock-stryken. T'wer as iffe the very rock, the very Isle itself, wer rejekting uss.

"Pel-Adan save us, it must have been terrible."

Nibulus closed the book, silent in his thoughts, for once even he seeming reverential.

Bolldhe peered down into the shadowy, blue-misted depths of the fjord, and shivered. Poetic exaggeration or not, that cannot have been a good day for any warrior. All those longships and xebecs, so low in the water under the weight of so many Peladanes in their immensely heavy field-plate armor, crawling so slowly up the fjord, utterly open to attack from above, and yet not a single target for them to fire back at. He reflected upon his good fortune that today they were approaching from above.

(*And five hundred years after all the enemy have been slain,* he tried to reassure himself.)

"All this here now explains the 'rayne of Helle,'" Nibulus considered, "but it also shows how unbelievably *open* the place is. We've always been taught the entire place was sealed off."

"Yes," Finwald concurred, frowning. "And it explains how all those previous looting parties gained entry, too. I'll be surprised if there's a single flagstone left intact inside. Come on, let's get a move on."

A move on was duly got. The path leveled out somewhat, and led them alongside a smoother cliff side that was punctuated with even more holes. No arrow slits this time, but windows and doorways that led into dark chambers cut into the rock. They peered inside the first one they came to, a small, rough-hewn room, but saw within it nothing more than a pile of boulders. Directly outside this chamber on a crudely semicircular sill that jutted out over the drop, lay what they at first imagined to be the fossilized remains of some great, smitten beast whose days had long since passed. But on closer inspection it turned out to be an ice-covered pile of wooden beams and metal cogs, the shattered ruin of some enormous rock-hurling artillery weapon, its timbers petrified and its metal parts rusted into the rock.

Now and again they would pass small quarries excavated on their left. These would all have grooves cut across the path, to join a chute leading down a steep incline and thence over the edge of the cliff.

"Just one small group of men—or a pair of ogres—could've kept a constant stream of boulders rolling from here down these chutes to crash upon our ships below." Nibulus winced. "How even one vessel made it through, I'll never know. They must have been *formidable*, the fighting men in those days, the like of which we can scarcely imagine."

For the first time since he had met the man, Bolldhe saw that the Peladane was looking almost cowed. There was undeniable pride in his voice, but it was the humble pride of admiration, and it bordered on awe. *Maybe he's beginning to realize just what it takes to be a* real *Peladane,* Bolldhe thought, *and not just the shadow of their ancestors that today's sorry lot have become. And who can blame him here? By Pel-Adan, it almost makes me proud of my old religion!*

Other openings, other chambers followed. None was particularly large, nor did they reveal connecting passages that might lead deeper into the fortress, and though each cavity was briefly searched, none contained aught but scattered fish bones and other, fouler-smelling filth.

"What creatures still live in these roosts, I wonder?" Wodeman speculated. Certainly this was the first sign of life they had seen since they had crossed the causeway onto Melhus.

They pressed on.

Finwald narrowed his lips in bewilderment; again came that worry about how open the place was. Like the others, he had somehow imagined that there would be only one way into the Maw, one great, brazen portal of immeasurable strength to deny access to any intruder that might come this way. Unlike the others, though, Finwald did not appear reassured that the whole place looked so dead.

But as the windows and doors became so numerous, so too did the darkness in all their hearts. The wind, though a spent force down here, nevertheless moaned spectrally throughout the hollow chambers, sometimes causing a slither of loose stones from above, and more than once the travelers were convinced it carried ill voices upon it: a stony cackling, a far-off yammering, or a ghostly, discordant whistling.

"What d'you make of it, Wodeman?" Nibulus asked the shaman, who walked ahead of the group. "Is this natural?"

But Wodeman was distant, preoccupied still with his private thoughts, and merely shrugged. "I'm not of this land," he replied vaguely.

"At least it doesn't stink of Rawgr," Appa put in. "I have a nose for— *CUNA SAVE US, WHAT IS THAT ABOMINATION?*"

They had already noticed a scraping sound, and immediately followed the old priest's bulging gaze upward. There, not ten feet above their heads and crawling down the rock face toward them, was the most revolting . . . *bird?* . . . any of them had ever seen, heard of, or even dreamt about in their more feverish nightmares. Though it looked like a newly hatched chick, all naked, veiny, and shriveled, it must have spanned at least six feet. With batlike wings ending in bony, hooked claws, it pulled itself down the cliff surface, flapping its way forward with a repulsive, leathery, scratching noise. When it opened its pink-grey beak to caw evilly at them, they could see within its mouth four rows of sharp, black teeth.

Fortunately there was only one of the things, and it was both slow and awkward. For once, Nibulus remembered Methuselech's bow. It took him mere seconds to rip it from its fastenings on the horse, fit an arrow, and while the others left him to it and hastened on down the path, let fly straight at the beast's huge, swiveling eyeball.

The arrow struck the rock at least a foot away from its left wing tip, and shattered into splinters. With a cry of surprise, Nibulus saw the creature, now only an arm's length away, suddenly detach itself from the cliff and fall upon him. In the second before he leapt back, he saw that it possessed no legs, but it was still by only an inch that he managed to avoid the noisome shroud of bird-flesh that sought to envelop him. Scrabbling madly away in horror, he rejoined the others farther down the path, and they all hurried on their way.

They continued for several miles without encountering any more of the winged creatures. The air became even stiller, the light gloomier, and the path narrower with each mile that passed. Zhang, normally as tough and stolid as any of them, was becoming increasingly agitated, and several times simply stopped dead, casting his head about this way and that while raising his snout to smell and taste the air.

"Look! What's that ahead?"

Wodeman, taking the lead now as usual, whispered back to them, and pointed out something ahead of them on the path. *What was it? Smoke?* they wondered in trepidation. *Someone's campfire, perhaps? Another party of adventurers following the same path?*

But no, this was steam. Steam bubbling from a crevice in the rock just around the next corner. It was not quite a geyser, but clouds of noxious vapor billowed fiercely from the cliff and out over the path. Even from a distance they could hear a fierce gurgling hiss as lava-heated gas met the cold air and condensed into droplets that spat out over the path, covering it with a slick yellow scum. It was as if a hateful serpent trapped within was spitting its venom out into a world it could not reach.

Wodeman went first again. He ventured out close to the very edge of the drop, treading carefully flat-footed upon its slippery surface, risking a fall rather than the touch of that steam. It was not fear of being scalded, but rather the unnatural smell that seemed to unsettle him.

Sure-footedly, he reached the other side, turned, and waited. Paulus went next, without care or hesitation, for he had no fear of burning or poisonous liquids. Then went Finwald. He pulled his bearskin collar up over his ears and tilted his wide-brimmed hat toward the steam, then keeping well away from the drop, darted nimbly through the spitting cloud.

"Take the horse through now, Bolldhe," Nibulus ordered, fitting an arrow to the string of the bow he still clutched. "I'll guard the rear in case any weirdling comes along. And be very careful; we don't want to lose Zhang."

Bolldhe nodded, gripped the horse by the reins, and—with Appa still mounted on top—took up position to one side. Hearing a certain note in Nibulus's voice, he felt his throat constrict oddly; the Peladane's concern was not simply for the baggage the horse carried, or the priest who sat on top of him, but for Zhang himself. During this quest, they had all grown very fond of their beast of burden and especially on this last, cruellest part of the journey, while trekking across Melhus. They would not, any of them, lose him now.

As a final precaution, Appa hoisted his left leg up out of the way of the steam, and sat mounted sidesaddle. This meant he was directly facing the horrendous drop just inches away from him, and also had a considerably more tenuous grip.

"Ready?" Bolldhe asked him. Appa nodded.

So, placing himself also dangerously close to the edge of the cliff, Bolldhe propelled the three of them into the cloud of steam.

Out the other side they emerged, partly scalded and gasping. The ordeal was over almost as soon as it had started.

No sooner did they slow down to wait for Nibulus, than a terrific clattering broke out immediately beside them. Visions of rock-falls or armies of darkness clashing spear against shield flashed through Bolldhe's mind that instant. He froze, his whole world filled with dark, flapping shapes, then realized that it was only a flock of birds. Disturbed by the travelers, they came pouring out of an unseen window right alongside the steaming fissure.

He observed, with startling clarity, a flurry of leathery wings, toothed beaks, *six* legs . . . Zhang rearing with a snort of panic . . . and Appa being pitched off the horse's back.

The priest wailed in terror as he flew backward through the air, only to be yanked back like a rag doll, as his foot snared in one of the straps used to lash down the baggage, and dangled helplessly from the stamping, panicked horse, his head hitting the ground sharply.

Bolldhe instantly tightened his grasp on the reins, then realized with horror that Zhang was shifting outward, nudging him toward the edge.

"Get back, you idiot horse!" he yelled, loosing the reins quickly and pushing hard against the animal's flank.

Then Zhang finally bolted, dragging Appa, screaming shrilly, down the path after him by the foot. Bolldhe teetered on the edge, swayed a moment, then disappeared over into the abyss . . .

. . . "NO!" cried Red Eye in a voice that filled the entire fjord with a crack of thunder, at the same time flinging his arms out, as if to push the tumbling man back onto the path.

"Don't you dare!" came the voice of Fate, a voice without sound that caused no thunder, but was still immeasurably more powerful. Red Eye gasped in pain, and snatched his hands back.

Bolldhe, after an unreal moment in which it seemed the fjord around him exploded with thunder, and he himself was held miraculously suspended in midair, now plunged on down the steep slope of the cliff. It was not a sheer drop, but not far off it. Smoothly, impossibly fast, with no rough edges of rock to snag or slow him, he careered downward.

Boulder chute! The thought came to him in a flash. He was barreling down one of those steep grooves used in olden days to send boulders crashing onto vessels below.

Time slowed sickeningly, and Bolldhe the human cannonball became strangely aware of everything around him. His eyes widened, his lips curled back, and a hoarse moan issued weakly. The edge of the cliff raced toward him; he had just one second to do something, or face certain death.

Instinct took over. Kicking out savagely at one side of the chute, Bolldhe somehow succeeded in flipping himself onto his belly. At the same time, his hand found the leather-bound grip of the grapnel—Elfswith's gift—slung at his side. Then, just as he yanked it from his belt, his one remaining second ran out.

The scraping rock was no longer beneath him; Bolldhe was in midair with nothing below him but a thousand-foot drop to the water below.

The grapnel came down, bit hard, sending sparks and rock dust into the air—

And found purchase right on the up-curved lip of the chute.

With a bone-wrenching tug that almost ripped his arm from its socket, Bolldhe came to a swinging, swaying halt.

How long he hung there, he could not tell. Time seemed to have stopped altogether, and the world became very still. Everything was as a dim, puzzling dream.

It was quiet down here as he hung by one arm from the grapnel, with only the peaceful sound of the wind floating down the fjord. For a moment he fancied he was back on the Tabernacle Plains, gradually rising from slumber inside the shelter of a nomad's tent, listening dreamily to the muffled but comforting sound of the breeze outside as it snapped burlap covers hither and thither, soughed through the tall grasses, and moaned through the treetops of some distant forest.

Lazily, only faintly aware of the dull pain in his arm, he swung around, and found himself facing the Maw. Whether it was some fancy of his desperate brain, or the gods taunting him with one last, clear view of that which he would never reach now, it appeared to him with the clarity allowed only to the dying; every wall, gate, portcullis, balustrade, buttress and tower could he see in detail—as clear as the Gates of Death to a dying man.

Then he became aware of a dry, tickling feeling running over his face, almost as if he were being caressed with a feather. But his eyes stung, and the sound of some commotion began to be heard. Louder it became, and the stinging sensation increased. Then once more time came gate-crashing noisily into his reverie, and he was back.

The dry tickling turned out to be a rivulet of sand, runing down the chute and onto his head, and the hubbub was the voices of his companions, shouting in panic somewhere above. The very next instant he felt a hefty blow land on his left shoulder. He cried out in pain, let go of the grapnel . . .

. . . but did not fall. Something was tugging him slowly but firmly up by his thick garments. It was Nibulus's grapnel that had been hurled blindly over the edge of the chute on the end of its rope. Somehow Chance or Fate had guided it true, smacking it into the heavy pelts Bolldhe kept fastened about his person, and now, suspended precariously, the choking traveler was hauled up, back over the lip of the chute, and up onto the cliff path.

Nibulus helped him to his feet, and eyed him up and down, shaking his head in disbelief that Bolldhe was still with them.

"Nifty with that hook, weren't you?" Bolldhe wheezed, panting heavily.

"Not half as quick as you," Nibulus responded.

Neither said another word, for no words were needed. There was a look of mutual admiration in the eyes of both of them, for they would both now go down in legend as the-fastest-grapnel-hook-in-the-north.

Finwald was not quite so calm and collected, however. He sat on the pathway with his back to the cliff wall, his face buried in his hands, rocking back and forth like a lunatic.

Of the others, there was not a sign.

"C'mon, Bolldhe," Nibulus suggested, "better go and see where that horse of yours has taken the little guy."

It was not long before they caught up with the others. Wodeman, the fastest among them, had sprinted hare-like after the terrified animal, with Paulus close behind, both desperate to halt the horse before he charged straight off the edge of the path, taking all their precious baggage with him.

As it happened, they need not have worried about Zhang, or the baggage: he was a slough-horse, and no amount of panic would have sent *him* toppling off the path. When they caught up with him, he was just standing there, swishing his tail and looking about rather sheepishly, as if having decided that it was rather silly to have overreacted like that after all.

Appa, though, was another matter. The old man was sprawled on his back upon the ground, kicking furiously at the strap that still held his foot. Whether it was due simply to the shock, or because he felt Melhus to be so far out of Lord Cuna's jurisdiction that it did not matter, he was letting rip with the juiciest and foulest curses his long years had taught him.

It took a full five minutes for the others to calm him down. His body fortunately had been shielded from the worst of the ordeal by the pelts that he always kept tied so tightly about his person with lengths of hairy string. His head, however, was a mass of cuts, grazes, and bumps that were going purple even now, and swelled visibly with each minute that passed.

"Bloody, bloody, bloody animal!" he ranted at the horse (who looked innocently down at the little old man as if to say: *Who? me?*) "I'll bloody walk from now on!"

It had been a miraculous escape, and not only for Bolldhe and Appa. That horse, now casually looking about for something to eat, carried every bit of food they had, all their rations for the next ten days. Even if all went well for them in the Maw, they knew that they would have to hunt for more before getting off Melhus. They should surely be able to lay their hands on some seal meat once they reached the causeway, but before that—well, Bolldhe worried that it might be his dear old friend Zhang for the pot. He could not hope to hold back men like Nibulus or Paulus, with their fighting skills. And after this little episode, he wondered just how far their affection for the pack animal actually went.

Maybe it won't come to that, he tried to reassure himself. *Perhaps some of them will die in the Maw, and there'll be more rations to go around.*

He looked to Wodeman, hoping to find in those green-brown eyes some measure of sympathy for their loyal beast of burden. But all he saw there was a glint of ice.

So on they went. By now, they were a good deal lower, and at last they began to discern the sound of the sea below. It had a disturbing quality to it, like the murmur of unquiet souls. Now and again it would be punctuated by the shrill, strangulated cawing of the six-legged birds that wheeled around looking for heaven-knew-what food might be found amid this desolation.

Once, they saw one of the larger, legless birds circling the empty expanse above the water, at a level with themselves. It, too, saw them, and moving in a wide curve—for they truly were the least agile of birds—it winged straight toward them. Luckily, even at this distance it did not have a tight enough turning circle, and crumpled into the cliff face several yards behind them. Laughing, they turned to look, expecting to see the creature lying dead, or at least dazed, upon the pathway. But apparently, that was how these foul avians landed. Having no legs allowing them to perch on the rock face, they instead dived straight at the cliff, and simply stuck to it like a lump of grey-black putty, using their wings to crawl forward in whatever direction—up, down, or across—they wanted.

Curling their lips in distaste, the travelers hastened on.

The path now forked, one branch continuing at a gentle downward slope, while the other plunged more steeply down below that.

"Nibulus?" Wodeman called back.

After a pause, the Peladane replied: "The lower ones, I reckon; the sooner we get down off this cliff, the better—we're far too exposed here. Bolldhe, think that *Aht-Kazar* of yours can manage it without tripping over its hooves?"

Bolldhe frowned worriedly at the Peladane's derogatory reference to his steed. "Aht-Kazar" was the term used by the sedentary dwellers of the Tabernacle Plains (they, alone, who hunted horses) to describe Zhang's kind. In their tongue, it meant "coarse horse."

But Zhang did not miss a step. And once, when Nibulus lost his own footing on the scree and skidded uncontrollably down the steep path, it was only the "coarse horse's" solid backside that blocked the Peladane from carrying on over the edge and joining his ancestors in their watery tomb at the bottom of the fjord.

After this, the path leveled out a little, but grew alarmingly narrow, hardly wider than a goat track. And it looked unstable, liable to crumble beneath them like the dried bones of a corpse.

"Seems the closer we get to that damn fortress," Appa ranted, "the deader everything becomes. Looks like it's sucked the very life out of the ground itself."

"Go back and try the other way, Nibulus?" Finwald suggested.

"No, I don't want to waste any more time. It'll be nightfall by the time we reach the Maw if we fiddle around here much longer. And I don't fancy scrambling up that steep bit behind us. Let's just carry on and if it gets really bad we can always turn back—maybe spend the night in one of those old guardhouses or whatever."

As they went on, they were forced to shoulder much of Zhang's baggage themselves, and pile the rest of it up higher on his back so as to make the load no wider than his unburdened flanks. Thus adjusted, they let him pick his own way forward, while they flattened themselves against the cliff—almost like those no-legged cliff-hugging atrocities—and worked their way onward, gripping the rock with un-gloved hands.

The extra weight they carried threatened at any moment to topple them backward over the edge, and it was at this time that the wind, hardly noticed until now, suddenly grew stronger. It pulled at them as if trying to pluck them from their precarious perch and send them plummeting the same way the rock crumbling underfoot was going. Tenaciously they held on, their eyes closed, and negotiated their way forward by feel alone.

"This is madness!" stammered Appa, the slowest and most ungainly of them all. Paulus, two places behind him, spat in contempt and occasionally tried to shove Finwald on quicker with curses and threats. Even Zhang, who alone of them was born to this, was wide-eyed with fear.

The closer they drew to the Maw, it seemed, the closer Death grinned at them in welcome.

It was not long after that when something else was grinning at them, something altogether more immediately tangible than death.

Still flattening himself against the rock face, Appa paused briefly to draw a few breaths. He rested his chin against the cold stone, glanced up, then cried out in fear of what was lurking immediately above him.

The company froze, followed his gaze upward, then they too froze in dread and revulsion.

It was a spider, but the like of which none of them had ever beheld before.

Long, multi-jointed legs it possessed, partially covered in thick, spiny, white hairs that now bristled in anger. On every joint of the legs was a gap of naked pink flesh that crawled with ticks and throbbed sickeningly. Its two foremost legs were raised toward Appa, as if feeling for him, and from the mass of mandibles and eyes that made up its face came a thin wailing, followed by an almost cat-like hiss. Grey-yellow liquid began dripping from its open jaws onto the pathway, where it began to smoke and stink horribly.

"Polar spider," Bolldhe breathed, as if he had actually encountered one before. "Get away from there, Appa, before it pounces!"

The polar spider suddenly vibrated its abdomen rapidly for a moment, a truly menacing sound, then it began its crawling descent. All the while it kept growling threats in a hateful, gurgling squall that kept Appa standing petrified.

"For Jugg's sake, can we just get on?" Nibulus growled impatiently, putting his gloves back on and squashing the little arachnid's abdomen under his thumb.

They continued down the steep path, stopping only for a moment as Nibulus, flinching with pain, scraped the bristling mess off his gloved thumb. It had begun to burn through the thick leather and, as he wiped it onto the rock, they could smell the pungent, rotten odor of the insect's disintegrating remains.

Minutes later they reached a stretch of path that was thankfully a little wider, more regular, and actually provided steps. These were clearly discernible even beneath a crusty layer of detritus from the last five hundred years, and along this section appeared another series of wide-open doorways and windows. From these empty rooms emerged a whistling wind, as they went deeper than the chambers they had passed earlier that day. Nevertheless the company pressed on, preferring to head for the Maw's main entrance, rather than risk investigating these eerie roosts just now.

"If we can't find a way in down below," Nibulus reassured them, "we can always come back and try these places instead."

But a way leading right down to the main gate was not to be found. To their dismay, they reached a section of the path that had simply crumbled away. It recommenced farther along, they could see, but there was a fifty-foot gap, and was the same distance lower down as well. Ignominiously forced to backtrack, they were only about twenty yards from the first of the chambers when Paulus cried out a warning.

"Stupid damn Peladane, why did you have to kill that spider? The smell's drawn its entire family!"

Bolldhe, leaning dangerously out over the drop in his effort to see past the horse, the Peladane, the two priests, and the mercenary, screwed up his eyes to see what lay beyond. Then they opened wide in a stare of disbelief. There, a few yards beyond the first doorway, the cliff was alive with movement. The way the Nahovian had announced it, Bolldhe had expected to see the whole rock face a-crawl with a white blanket of spiderkind—slowly creeping and leaping toward them. But there were not thousands, nor even hundreds, just a few dozen.

Except those were a few dozen *fully-grown* polar spiders, each one the size of a large lobster, each one growling like a rabid cur, and advancing with horrible deliberation toward the baby-killers dithering on the narrow pathway.

". . . Oh . . ." was all Bolldhe managed.

No way back, forward, up or down. They were trapped. Strung out along this narrow path, soon they would be swamped one by one. None there knew for sure just how dangerous these creatures were, but no one with a half-ounce of imagination could deny they were an abominable sight, and at all costs, to be avoided. Paulus, realizing he would be the first under attack, wasted not a second in sprinting toward the cover of the nearest doorway.

There was, of course, nothing else for it, so the rest of the company followed him without hesitation.

Paulus was one of the nimblest among them. Haring along the path, he made it to the door easily, ducking his head and disappearing inside. Finwald came next, and succeeded in gaining the chamber only by slashing wildly at the first of the spiders to attack. Luckily his sword-cane hit it squarely, the blade sinking into its cluster of mandibles and eyes. It penetrated only an inch or two, however, and reverberated so strongly it almost fell from the priest's grasp. By the gods, these things were tough!

For the others, however, it would not be so easy. Appa had frozen in fear, knowing he would never be able to drag his old bones up that path fast enough to gain the chamber. Meanwhile, for the others there was not enough space to squeeze past him.

"Just get a bloody move on, will you!" Nibulus bellowed, red-raced with frustration. Without waiting for a response, he simply lifted the little man up by the waist, held him in front of him like a large shield or pavise, then charged forward up the path. Behind followed Zhang, Bolldhe, and Wodeman in hot pursuit.

Screaming weakly, the old man was for the second time that day propelled along the same path by a much bigger being. The first of the adult spiders had reached the doorway, gurgling murderously, and some had already even entered, going after Paulus and Finwald. By the time Nibulus reached it, the entire door frame was crawling with the eight-legged demons. Appa's eyes and mouth widened in terror the closer they got, then with a grunt of disbelief he was hurled bodily through the opening. He landed upon the cold stone floor with an impact that drove the wind from him, then writhed in horror in the darkness, with several spiders now attached to him. Others were swarming over his crow's beak staff where it had clattered to the ground.

Paulus was far too busy gleefully skewering arachnids to come to Appa's aid, but a second later Nibulus entered and, with Finwald's help, set about kicking or raking the foul creatures from the screeching priest's bucking body.

Seconds later the desperate yet strangely muted grunts of this battle were joined by a low whinny of fear, as Zhang lurched awkwardly through the doorway. The baggage, piled high on his back, had roughly scraped several spiders into the chamber with him across the stone door jambs, and the acrid stench of their wreckage now filled the stale air.

Bolldhe and Wodeman were yet to be seen, but could be heard shouting and cursing in fury outside.

The hateful chittering of one of Appa's assailants was silenced as Nibulus's boot smashed into its face and sent it flying through the air, pale legs flailing madly. It crunched against the far wall, then folded up like a closing flower. Appa, weaponless, had seized another by its scrabbling forelegs, and was whining feebly as his two runny eyes stared into the spider's eight mephitic ones, trying desperately to hold it at bay just inches away from his face. At the same time Finwald was trying carefully to stab a third spider that had folded its limbs around Appa's thigh. He was no swordsman, and did not wish to sink his blade into the priest by mistake.

"Stop faffing about, you pillock!" yelled Nibulus at Finwald, who was indeed, it had to be said, faffing about. At this, the mage-priest steeled himself, put his trust in Lord Cuna, then hacked his weapon straight into the creature's abdomen. He yanked the blade sideways, in a two-handed wrench and, with a hiss, the monster's legs contracted around Appa's thigh in a death grip. As it expired, its abdomen split in two, and brown, rice-like fluid soaked the old man beneath it.

Amid the slicing and dicing, the hacking and kicking, the cries of fear and disgust in the dark, Bolldhe and Wodeman appeared. Bolldhe, unable to use his flamberge now that there was a still-wriggling spider impaled upon it, had simply dropped the weapon and its burden by the door and charged straight through the skirmish into the welcoming black depths beyond. His only concern was to get as far away from these hideous things as possible.

Wodeman, though, had a weapon better suited for this sort of task. Ignoring the new-fangled iron implement Elfswith had given him, the shaman reverted instinctively to his quarterstaff. As he ducked and dodged the pouncing enemy he dextrously and methodically flicked one spider after another over the cliff side to plummet, legs a-flail, into the gorge. His trusty staff truly came into its own that day.

But still they came, and eventually the shaman was forced to retreat from the seething onslaught of white-bristled monstrosities to join his comrades inside the chamber. By then each had succeeded in dispatching the last of the foe that clung to him, miraculously without suffering any punctures from those dripping fangs. Amid yells of panic and revulsion, they gradually retreated deeper into the chamber, blindly following Bolldhe to wherever he had disappeared in the dark. Meanwhile the creeping, hissing horde continued to pour in through the door and window openings behind them.

Just then a bright flame flared in the darkness, and there he was, Bolldhe, holding up the lantern he had been desperately trying to light. They charged after him, but were instantly checked by a loud cry of horror behind them. They turned and saw Finwald, glowing strangely in the xienne-light. Still by the doorway, he was now trying to snatch up Flametongue from the floor where Bolldhe had abandoned it. The entire door frame by now was a heaving mass of polar spiders.

There are such things as agility and skill. There are such things as strength and bravery, too. There is also desperation, and devil-may-care abandon in the face of impossible odds. There is even downright insanity . . .

. . . And then there was Finwald. The prime mover in this whole mad enterprise, he alone of those present would have attempted to rescue the flamberge from the surging tide of death that swarmed into the chamber.

None there could understand how he managed it. But manage it he did. "And now," he warbled insanely as he sprinted toward them, "we GO!" Without stopping, he charged right through them, and was first to follow Bolldhe into the passage leading deep into the cliff-fortress beyond.

To try escaping from the spiders by heading deeper into lightless and confined spaces may have seemed like the ultimate folly. Those monsters could see in the dark, could crawl securely upon every surface, and furthermore knew the territory well. But now the travelers were here, they had little choice but to press on.

"Shine that lantern back here," Nibulus growled angrily. "I can't see a damn thing."

He kicked at a rock that he had just stumbled over, sending it clattering away down some side-tunnel. In possession of the lantern, however, Bolldhe was now temporarily the leader, and he had no intention of slowing down—even if it meant leaving the others behind. The pattering and hissing of the rapidly approaching swarm of death was creeping closer with every second, and though that reminder was dreadful enough for any of them, for Bolldhe it held even greater terror. For him it sounded horribly like the swell of the rising tide in a sea cave, and for some unknown reason this sound provoked a shudder to his very soul.

"Come back here, you coward!" the Peladane cursed, and plunged almost blindly after the gradually receding light as it bobbed away down the passage.

The lantern's beam soon fell upon the petrified wooden planks of an ancient door. It was stoutly built, banded with bronze that had melded over time into the wood, and was so old that it appeared almost like the stone of the walls. Bolldhe did not hesitate. He threw himself straight at it, putting all his weight behind his shoulder, then crumpled to the floor in a daze. He had succeeded in shifting it about as much as those no-legged birds shifted the cliff face they habitually slapped against.

Fortunately, Zhang was right behind him, and the slough-horse was considerably heavier, more solid, and even more terrified of spiders than his master. Under his repeated onslaught, hinges that had not been used for five centuries squealed in vociferous protest as the portal was battered open, and Zhang plunged through the doorway. Immediately the whole company—including a groggy Bolldhe—piled in after him, just as the tide of spiders came leaping and skittering round the corner.

As soon as Finwald, the last in the line, had picked up the fallen lantern and himself darted through, Nibulus and Paulus put their whole weight against the door, and heaved it shut. Even with their combined strength it hardly moved, but with tortured effort they managed to get it shut just before the spiders reached them.

Wedging it into place with a fallen lintel, they heard a series of dull thumps from the other side, followed by an uproar of eerie, thwarted, squealing protest. The monsters would not get through that in a hurry.

The company finally dared to release its breath.

"*Now* where are we?" Appa stammered, on the verge of collapse. The old man had been dragged bumping along a rocky path by a panicking horse, used as a human shield, hurled through a blanket of polar spiders—one of which was still attached to his leg—and soaked through with a thick, meaty gunge that had spilled from the one Finwald had sliced. And he had lost his beloved staff. Even now it was back there being filthed-over by those things. All this, too, on top of that terrible, weeklong trek across Melhus.

The old man was alive, but he had definitely seen better days.

In answer to his question, Bolldhe snatched the lantern from Finwald and shone it around. While Appa endeavored to prise the dead spider off his thigh, they looked around at the apparently empty rough-hewn cave where they were now cowering. Clearly a sizeable chamber, its confines stretched beyond the lantern's range. Indeed, their voices did not fall so flat here, and there was a definite movement of air.

"There have to be openings not far ahead," Wodeman assured them. "Can't you smell the seawater from them? If we keep close to this wall on our right, we should be out of here soon."

They had to trust to the Torca's uncanny sense of direction. In any case, they had little choice. There was a macabre, insidious scratching still coming from behind the door, like ghosts behind the wood paneling of a mansion, so they knew there was no going back that way. But the freshness of the air in here did at least give them the impression they were still within reach of the outside world, and were not simply journeying ever deeper into the mountainside.

A wet crunching sound came from near the door. They all turned to see Finwald hauling the flamberge from the nasty ruin of the spider it had impaled. With a grimace of disgust, he curtly thrust the sword back into Bolldhe's hand.

"For gods' sake, Bolldhe," he breathed in exasperation, "d'you think you could just hold on to it for once? Or would you rather someone else carried it?"

Bolldhe took the weapon with neither word nor expression, and slid it under his belt without cleaning it. Glaring at the priest, he took hold of Zhang's reins in one hand, the lantern in the other, and once again set off, leading the way.

Several minutes later, they emerged from the caverns and into daylight again. There were no spiders to be seen here, and they realized that they had emerged farther along up the higher of the two paths, not far now from the head of the fjord. Continuing along this alternative route took them finally, and without further mishap, right down to the harbor that directly fronted the Maw.

They had arrived at last. Their journey was finally, unbelievably, at an end. And it was no longer fear of polar spiders, raptorial predators, nor any other twisted denizens of the fjord that blanched their faces and widened their eyes. For now they stood right before Vaagenfjord Maw itself—and this is where the fear *really* began.

For now, the great looming wall of the Maw was mercifully veiled from sight behind a thick shroud of sea fog. It was not far off, they could sense, a dark menace awaiting them yet somewhere beyond that lowering miasma. But for the moment they could only avert their eyes and turn their attention away. They chose instead to focus upon the harbor spread all around them.

The chill fog fastened the entire area in an uncanny stillness. Not a thing moved; hardly a sound could be heard. In such cemeterial quiet the company felt like mean, shabby intruders, small, exposed and resented. They paced along through the disquieting hush, eyeing each shadowy form that emerged from the gloom as they progressed: ruined battlements, empty storehouses, abandoned barracks. The ground was littered with frost-split boulders, treacherous puddles of ice, rusted and moldering remains of broken artillery weapons, and other such debris.

Sometimes one or other of the searchers would snag a foot on lengths of grey-red, rock-like mineral that might once have been iron weapons, but were now returning to the stone. Occasionally they encountered evidence of more recent intruders: various familiar tools, well rusted but still usable; leather bags stiff and empty; the crumpled remains of old banners that not so long ago would have dazzled the eye in brilliant, silken colors, but which now resembled a pile of old handkerchiefs clogging up a drain.

Also, they found barrels, still in fairly good condition, now empty of food, but retaining vestigial smells of the provender they had once stored.

This complex was a lot larger than any of them had expected, and in its heyday must have been as busy as a nest of ants in the summer. Now however, it stank of a thousand different kinds of decay, the stench held in place against the tugging winds by the high cliffs rising all around.

But eventually they arrived at the sea walls, and stared out at the dismal scene before them. About a dozen quays there were, long, black fingers of crumbling stone that thrust out into the listless water. The intervening sea was clogged with lumps of yellowy ice and a particularly noisome strain of seaweed the color and texture of spilled brains. Rising out of this blanket of bad skin, several masts thrust up, leaning sadly, the ships below them having long ago foundered. Their blackened timber was caked with a type of frost that resembled a fine scabbing of necrotizing fungus, and the rigging hung limp and dripping, like the ragged garments of a hanged man.

Needless to say, these were the remains of the ships that had visited the Maw more recently. The Rawgr's fleet had been destroyed centuries before, of course, and the only Peladane or Oghain-Yddiaw ships that remained were now strewn across the seabed farther out in the fjord, little more than scatterings of barnacle-encrusted, half-disintegrated timbers lying deep beneath the lifeless, salty water. These remnants rested among the boulders that had sunk them, their only company the odd pale bone, fragments of rusted armor, gossamer-thin ghosts of sweethearts' scarves, or the long-sullied gold of lovers' keepsakes.

As they gazed out over the water, the six new arrivals at the Maw fancied they could half-hear the songs of the warrior ghosts still remaining—those unlucky souls who had never gone home to a hero's welcome and the cheer of a warm longhouse. They were not sad songs, but slow, simple, stirring melodies that were made all the more tragic by the haunting, discordant harmonies that overlay them. Like the ruins of the harbor all about, they carried an air of terrible sadness, and the finality of death.

Wordlessly the six men and the lone horse made their way along one of the quays, from where they regarded the only ship in the harbor that was still even partly afloat. There was a faint hope within them that it might remain serviceable enough to get them off this island, if only just as far as the mainland nearby. None of them could bear the thought of a recrossing of that terrible ice field. However, on closer inspection they found the vessel to be so low in the water, and tilted at such an unfortunate angle, that it was plain to even the most desperately optimistic that it would never sail again.

"What d'you reckon, Paulus?" Nibulus asked. "Seen anything like it before?"

The hull was so wide as to be almost square, the prow was remarkably short, and there was no telltale figurehead or sign upon it that might give any clue to its origin. This was simply a large craft of a very plain, utilitarian design, a simple merchant's ship intended for carrying cargo rather than undertaking exploration or engaging in warfare. Clearly whichever crew had sailed it was expecting a large haul of plunder.

"Could be from anywhere," Paulus sniffed. "But that's of no concern to us. Whoever they were, they died just like all the others."

"My opinion exactly, and . . ." Nibulus replied, but Paulus had already strode away, leaving Nibulus alone to blink after him despondently.

Died like all the others, right, Bolldhe pondered. *And what of us?*

He came up behind the Peladane and studied the vessel more closely. "Doesn't look that old, does it?" he assessed. "And it's cold enough to preserve rations well. What do you say, shall we have a look?"

"A bit risky," Nibulus replied. But like all the others, he was keen to postpone the inevitable task they had come all this way to undertake, and any excuse would do. "Go on then, let's give it a go. There must still be some cabins that aren't submerged."

They lashed themselves together by a length of rope tied around each of their waists, in case one of them should slip on the steeply inclined and icy deck—or fall through it. The others shuffled together on the quayside, and stood watching, curlers of steam rising from their nostrils.

The two men stepped up from the quayside onto the gunwale that was tilted down toward them, hurled their grapnels till they snared on the opposite side, then began hauling themselves cautiously up the sloping deck. This was hard going, for the wooden planking was as slick as an ice rink. But various remnants of mast, spar, or rigging had become frozen onto the deck, and provided convenient footholds. Bolldhe was first to reach the deckhouse and booted the rotten door into splinters. Then, lantern gripped in his teeth, he slipped inside. Nibulus followed close behind, and also disappeared from sight.

The onlookers waited, chafing themselves against the icy cold.

Hollow footsteps and scrapings could be heard from within, accompanied by the occasional slide or bump. But no voices yet. Still the others waited.

Silence. A long silence. There was no movement at all from within. For all this time the four men on the quay stood watching, their attention focused upon that jagged, black hole where the door had been. But there was nothing further to see or hear. It was as though the ship had eaten their companions.

Appa stamped his numbed feet in agitation. He did not like this at all. He was just about to cry out to them, when a small barrel appeared at the doorway, teetered for a second as it rested against the jamb, then slid down the deck towards them. The four men leapt back in fright as it crunched against the gunwale, almost punching its way through the decayed timber. A moment later, a second container appeared, and followed its mate. And then a third.

Immediately after, an extremely pale face peered out of the doorway.

Bolldhe hoisted himself up out of the deckhouse and, without hesitating for even a second, almost dived out of the door and slid on his front down the sloping deck to join the barrels. He did not stop to hand the containers to his waiting companions, but instead simply left them where they were, leapt from the ship, and walked off down the quayside without a word.

Nibulus too emerged from the darkness below. He disengaged the grappling hooks, slid down the deck on his back, and helped Paulus transfer the containers to the quay. The Peladane was obviously not in quite so much of a hurry as Bolldhe had been, but he too wore a very grim countenance, and said little.

There had not been much left to search through, apparently, but the two men had succeeded in salvaging a small tub of ghee, a chest of tsampa, and an entire puncheon of drel-sil. All was frozen solid, and once defrosted would probably prove edible.

"Shine *on*, you crazy goblin!" Wodeman beamed. "There's enough here to last us for weeks!"

It was true. Here, in the last place on Lindormyn they would have hoped to find sustenance, they had managed to unearth a bountiful supply of fat, barley flour, dried meat, sweet potatoes, rice and beet sugar. It was the first real stroke of good fortune the company had met with since encountering Elfswith. Yet to see the looks on the faces of the two men who had discovered this haul, one could be forgiven for thinking they had instead come face-to-face with their own Benne Nighe.

Neither Bolldhe nor Nibulus would talk further of what they had witnessed below decks, and none of the others pressed them on this matter. It was getting late, so they decided to search the rest of the harbor for somewhere they could store their equipment and new supplies, and safely stable Zhang. They searched carefully and methodically, even exploring some of the rooms tunneled directly into the rock face of the fjord.

Yet again, Finwald marveled at how unsecured it all was. "Weren't the Peladanes supposed to have sealed it all off after the siege was over?" he said in astonishment.

"According to the books, yes," Nibulus agreed, "but a determined robber will always find a way in."

"Luckily for us," Finwald replied. Nibulus was right; most of the original doors to these numerous rooms had either been prised open, or had holes knocked into them just wide enough for a thief to squeeze through, or had simply been battered down. The company explored most of them, and found all had been ransacked. Naturally anything of obvious value would have been plundered by the victors five hundred years ago, but subsequent raiding parties had stripped away floor tiles, ornate columns, carved stone fittings; anything, in fact, that bore the mark of Vaagenfjord Maw and so could fetch a price on the relic-collectors' market.

Traces of old campfires there were too, and musty, filthy blankets, possibly only a few years or months old. As they searched, the company wondered if any such adventurers were still lurking about even now.

At length they found one small, freestanding building intact enough to use as a base. An unremarkable but sturdy edifice, it had probably served as a storehouse for Drauglir's fishing fleet. (Though the Rawgr and his netherworld company might not require normal nourishment, such mortals as worked in his service definitely did.) This shed appeared to have escaped the worst ravages of the siege—and of Time—and most importantly it stood about as far away from the Maw itself as it was possible for them to get. Here they gratefully stabled Zhang, and stored their newfound supplies.

With the help of Elfswith's ice-axes and a good fire, they had soon defrosted and cooked some of their food to satisfaction. And then, oh how they gorged themselves! The food may have tasted rather faded and more than a little bitter, but it was wholesome, and brought out a red cheer in their faces that tingled exquisitely. For a time, the nightmare of the journey, the weirdness of Vaagenfjord, and the horrors that might await them still within the Rawgr's fastness were thrust far from their thoughts, and they feasted as enthusiastically as if they were in a tavern back in Nordwas. The ghee was particularly welcome, as they now used it to smear their raw, chapped faces and hands against the intense cold.

After their feast, they slept. This was the first proper shelter they had enjoyed since leaving Elfswith's cave; it was almost warm and, after the unbelievable hardships of the past week, they slept long and deep. Not even thoughts of what they were to face on the morrow intruded into their exhausted slumber.

At least, that was how it went for the ones who had not explored the ship—those four lucky men who had not seen what Nibulus and Bolldhe had seen down in the deckhouse.

For Nibulus, a seasoned campaigner who had witnessed many an atrocity on many occasions—much of it perpetrated at the hands of his own men—it had chilled him enough to take the edge off his appetite, and now keep his sleep light, fitful, and troubled. For Bolldhe, on the other hand, this night was proving both very long and very strange.

Inside the galley, they had found somebody, or some *bodies,* for it was difficult to say how many. Those hanging, frozen lumps of what had once been people were plastered all over the walls, ceiling, and fittings. Moreover, there were things that had been done to that flesh—certain processes—that Bolldhe simply could not believe.

What had done it, he wondered, and why? A wild beast, no matter how savage, would not have caused such carnage, nor been so wasteful. And even a Jotun—an ice giant—though chaotic and cruel enough, would have lacked the imagination and manual dexterity for those ingenious processes. No, there had been evil of the greatest magnitude at work: an almost artistic hand behind its devilish intricacy that to Bolldhe's glazed eyes bore the hallmark of . . . of what he could only describe as "correction."

Neither he nor Wintus had yet spoken a word of this to the others. For how could they now, at this late stage? The fear pervading the company was already deleterious enough, without them knowing what he and the Peladane now realized: that Vaagenfjord Maw was far from empty and dead, but contained an evil the like of which none of them had ever imagined even in their worst nightmares.

All night long his brain was churning, replaying over and over what he had witnessed. All night he drifted between wakefulness and a half-sleep, never really sure which was which, always alert to the sounds of the harbor outside, sounds he was convinced were meant for his ears only. Sometime during the night he heard a low moaning drift from the quay. It could have been the wind, of course, that same wind surely responsible for the galley door of the lone ship rattling so urgently and loudly upon its hinges.

A sudden crash—after which the door stopped rattling. That must have been a powerful gust indeed, but would the wind also cause the rhythmic creaking of deck boards that followed? A creaking that sounded so much like footsteps? Footsteps that descended onto the quay. Now it seemed to be stealthily approaching the very building they sheltered inside, heading unerringly through the freezing fog and darkness toward them? And surely no wind would make those scratching noises at the door . . . just like the spiders back in the tunnel . . . or something from the ship coming to reclaim the food that they had stolen? Bolldhe could no longer be sure now what was real and what was a figment of his dreams. Yes, it was a very long night indeed for Bolldhe.

But morning did come, of a sort. Dawn crawled with sluggish reluctance from blankets of grey, slithering weakly and hesitantly into a world that was frigid, vaporous, and hateful. For Bolldhe it was a morning without any relief from the horrors that had stalked through his feverish imagination. His eyes were red from insomnia and his face grey-wan with dread.

Not a word was spoken. The company prepared their second meal in this place, ate it in an absorbed silence, and carefully avoided all eye contact. The torpid air around them was steeped with the rank odors of stale musk, horse flatulence, rotten fish, and burnt drel-sil. A relentless chill had taken hold of them all, causing them to shake incessantly even as they pushed spoonfuls of warm food into their mouths.

They made this meal last as long as they could, for they all knew what must inevitably follow. But there was no putting it off. As the final mouthfuls of what might be their last breakfast were forced down dry throats, the silence in the hut deepened further still.

Nibulus licked his bowl clean, stared into it for a moment, then with great deliberation, placed it on the floor. The others stopped whatever they were doing to watch as he solemnly drew himself up to his full height, looked each one of them in the eye in turn, then let out a deep, almost deflating, soul-felt sigh.

"Come on then," he said at last in a voice that was unusually high-pitched and unsteady. "Let's get on with it."

He went over to the door, heaved away the barrels they had placed up against it, kicked away all the makeshift wedges, and opened it wide. A grey fog rolled in, bringing with it darkness rather than light.

Without another word, the Peladane strode outside and his men followed as boldly as they could manage. Each of them carried torches and rations a-plenty for the days ahead. Bolldhe went last, and tarried just long enough to run a trembling hand over Zhang's fleecy neck. He could not bear to look the beast in the eye, however, and after the briefest hesitation followed the others, slamming the door behind him.

Then they were there. Out of the shroud of fog, the Maw came at them, and one by one the travelers' footsteps faltered, then stopped, till they just stood gaping upward.

Before them, stretching out on either side and soaring up sheer to immeasurable heights, stood the black, ice-frosted face of Vaagenfjord Maw. It was a wall of rock, in truth a vast cliff, but a cliff that had been shaped—chiseled by countless minions over the centuries—until a fortress-wall regularity was evident. It was not smooth, however, for this was natural rock, and its surface was scored by great furrows, or gouged with hollows, and twisted by strange outcroppings that covered it like carbuncles riddling the skin of a giant. Between clouds of fog these nodules of stone would appear, staring down at the little questers below. In the fascinated minds of the men from the south, they would take on the semblance of hideous fiends and loathsome gargoyles, before again being cloaked by the fog. And when next revealed in another gap in the fog, it would appear they had multiplied, joined now by diabolic companions that had skittered down from higher places to glare at the intruders below.

Farther up could be seen rows of windows: great architraved and embrasured black oblongs about twenty feet high, arranged in ranks that stretched almost the entire width of the fortress. Between these openings, massive horns of rock jutted out, too smooth and pointed to be natural. They seemed to serve no purpose other than emphasizing the impression that this entire wall marked the boundary between the World of the Living and the Underworld of Rawgrkind.

Truly this was an abode befitting the mightiest of Darkangels. A far cry from the forlorn ruination and decay of the harbor that sprawled before it, Vaagenfjord Maw seemed a bastion of indomitable, hell-wrought strength that laughed at men's puny efforts to destroy it. In fact, so inconceivably massive it was that it seemed to possess its own field of gravity, which even now pulled the errants in toward it with an irresistible force, as if to crush them into nonexistence at its stony heart. Before it, they were—what were they?—they were six tiny ants that had wandered too far from their nest.

And there, at the base of the cliff, right at its center, was the gate. A colossal aperture whose mighty doors had been cast down and lay now shattered upon the crumbled steps that led up to it, this gaping hole was utterly, utterly black. Indeed it was the blackness of complete oblivion, the end of all things—of light, life, even time. It looked exactly what it was:

The Gateway to Hell.

The Peladane looked round at his men appraisingly. "Well?" he asked, trying to clear a dryness from his throat. "What do you think?"

The question was unspecific, but thereby he hoped to gauge the mettle of these men who would accompany him into this dread place. In particular, he wanted to hear what Bolldhe had to say.

But Bolldhe was without speech. All he could think was: *Go in there? We might as well try to pass through the sun, or drink the ocean dry!*

None other of the company returned their leader's regard, either. They all looked pale and tiny, their white, bony little faces peering out from amid the shaggy bulk of their bearskins, looking for all the world like a straggle of schoolchildren in toggled, hooded coats who had inadvertently strayed out of their own territory to find themselves suddenly in the presence of the local hard kids from the wrong side of town. Both Appa and Wodeman cast their glances down, and would say or do nothing. Paulus ignored the Peladane's look and just stared all about him. Only Finwald was prepared to say anything, and that was merely a weak "I never imagined . . . In all these years, I thought . . ." But he did not actually answer the question.

Vaagenfjord Maw, meanwhile, loomed silent over them. A thin wind whistled around its wall, its broken door, its vacant windows, causing a tremor to run through the ancient stone. The wall stared down at them blankly, but they could all sense in that strange tremor a feeling of anticipation. There was a definite sense of *waiting*. It had waited for half a millennium already, suffered the onslaught of the Peladanes, shrugged off the irritation of subsequent raiding parties, and upon this day, at long last, things were about to happen.

Step by step the company ascended the steps up to the Gate. Their boots echoed menacingly in the sudden hush that descended. Step by step they drew closer to that darkness, until finally they were upon the threshold, its gaping mouth set to envelop their whole world.

Nothing moved by that Gate, not even the wind, and the fog did not dare enter. For wind and fog are of *this* world, and it seemed to Bolldhe and the company that nothing of *this* world could penetrate the Maw. They hesitated for a long moment, and wondered just how they could bring themselves to step into that blackness ahead.

There, ready poised, stood Nibulus. He had left his bearskins behind in the outhouse, and was clad at last in his full suit of magnificent tengriite armor. His head was encased in the dragon-crested helm, but his face as yet unshielded by the sallet. The grim visage of the god Pel-Adan glared out from the newly polished plastron of red tengriite that covered his chest, and over it all flowed the green Ulleanh cloak, mantled about the shoulders by a black-hemmed, gold-braided, white surplice. His greatsword Unferth he bore over his right shoulder.

By his side stood Paulus. The crows' feathers adorning his cowl were well greased with ghee so that they now shone with a plume-like defiance. He too had discarded his bearskins, but retained a saiga-pelt jerkin beneath his coat.

Behind these two fighters, followed Wodeman, Finwald, and Appa. Each now bore the tulwar Elfswith had given them. Ending in a squared rather than pointed tip, those swords had a short, heavy, sabre-like blade that was good for decapitation. Though easy to use after even scant training, they looked markedly out of place in the hands of these three priests.

Last came Bolldhe. In his left hand he held the unhooded, already kindled xienne-lantern, while in the other he gripped the flamberge as though his life depended on it. He stared up and around at the mighty pillars flanking the blackness before them. To his surprise, now that they were so close, he found that their columns had been scrawled with graffiti, though none of it in any script he could understand.

Then Nibulus continued: "This is it, gentlemen. We've arrived. And, now it comes down to it, I have to admit I don't understand what in all Lindormyn we're doing here. . . . It all just seems to have happened, doesn't it? Well, we're here now, so I suppose we'd better go and slay a Rawgr, or something."

He glanced up at the graffiti. "As you can see, this place is no stranger to looting parties—looks like half the northern world has been coming and going here at the Maw at some time or another. Some made it back home, so we've heard, others were not so lucky. I—we don't know what befell them, but at least we can be fairly sure there truly is something bad in there. I realize this clearly now, and am sorry I doubted it before." He nodded to the two mage-priests apologetically.

"And, by the looks of it, we're almost certainly the smallest group to have ever ventured here. So why should we succeed where others failed? What, when it comes down to it, is so bloody marvelous about us? Well, the truth is, I'm afraid, that we are weak, weaker even than they. But I ask you to remember this one thing: these people who now litter the Maw with their dirty bones, they came here solely for personal gain. We, I hope, are trying to achieve something better than that. While our numbers may be small, our true purpose must be our strength. We've got a mission here, and we must not let our fear get the better of us—as it did so many of these other poor souls.

"Remember: fear, if terrible enough, can turn a man's soul inside out and rob him of his true self. I've witnessed this myself, so many times. We must not allow such fear to destroy us, for there is no character within the terrified man."

All five then looked at the Peladane in a different light. On this journey they had shared so much, experiences both terrifying and wondrous. Yet, despite this, it was as if they had remained six strangers who walked the same road for only as long as it suited each his own particular purpose. A team they had never been, nor their objectives ever united.

But now, after the ordeal of Melhus, that weeklong test of endurance, that torture of body and mind, something had changed within them, between them. None could have made it across this terrible land on his own; it had been a union—a harmony of six souls—that had got them across, dependent even on sharing the heat of each others' bodies.

Six disparate entities had entered the ice field of Melhus; a single team had left it.

This Nibulus who addressed them now was no longer a mere Peladane, all polished armor and arrogance, a jumped-up loudmouth who claimed leadership as a right of his inherited status. He was simply a man, an ordinary bloke like they. Gone was the crass, jovial adventurer they had rode out with from Nordwas. Gone too was the cynical businessman who had revealed his true purpose to them back in the Giant Mountains. Here was a man whom they could really follow, and they, his team.

And this pronouncement was not the standard, glib oration of the Thegne, a mere string of mellifluous blandishments to rouse the troops before sending them off to do battle; it was simple, honest truth, man to man. Though he was not aware of it, Nibulus Wintus had thrown off his magnificent tengriite, and revealed the real man beneath.

"Right," he said firmly, "let's go and cut us some Rawgr-fillet."

Finally, one by one, the company from Nordwas entered the Maw.

Beneath a lead-grey sky, heavy with the smell of storm clouds, nothing moved. A dead calm had settled upon the sea, and there was not the slightest breath of wind.

At the same moment that Nibulus was leading his men into the Maw, out on the water many miles behind them, something was approaching. The first of it to glide into view was a sail, a single triangle of gold cloth bearing the effigy of a coiled red dragon. Limply it hung from the mast, for there was no wind to fill it. Then, as the craft drew closer, the hull could be seen, narrow, sleek, razor sharp, its high dragon-prow slicing through the black water as if hurled by expert hands. Silently, smoothly, purposefully it came, planing the waves in an effortless glissade. With a patience as calm as the sea, it did not have to hasten, for like death itself it knew it would bag its prey sooner or later.

As finally the vessel came into full view, it became apparent that no oarsmen were at work. With a power that was not of this world it was propelled forward over the Lobster's Heath.

Upon its deck, an army of Wire-Faces stood unmoving. Feet planted firmly apart, garrottes held stretched taut before them in the usual manner, bloodied aprons barely fluttering, they stared ahead of them and did not utter a word. Above them, swinging from yard, forestay, topmast shrouds and ratlines, and giggling feverishly, the Children of the Keep played, the only things moving on the ship.

And in the middle of all this, his back to the mast, as silent and unmoving as the Wire-Faces, sat Scathur himself. Gone was the moldering burgundy robe of his days in the keep. He now wore a voluminous coat of pale cream adorned with black flecks that could have been either ermine or snow-lion. Like a barbarian king upon his throne he appeared, one elbow resting on his knee, the hand cupping his chin, while in the other hand he grasped a huge, twelve-foot-long Bardische. This greatest of all axes was forged from adamantite, its two blades curving out like the horns of a devil.

Not even the barest shade of expression flickered across his stony visage, save perhaps for the steely, unflinching purpose in his eyes. Scathur had already covered most of the distance lying between Wrythe and Melhus, and his eyes never left the point where he knew Vaagenfjord Maw opened onto the sea.

Like death itself, Scathur was inescapable, and he was coming for them.

Finally—after all these years—coming home.

Brains screamed in blind panic; lungs burned in torment; bodies contorted and limbs thrashed at the freezing water that enveloped them. No thoughts were in their minds save the exigency of reaching air. Survival instinct had taken possession, and propelled them ever upward.

Upward. What a joke. Jagt had abandoned them deep beneath the sea, below even the seabed, and within seconds they would now fill their lungs with freezing water, flail about in agonized frenzy, then die. But even knowing all this, still their instinct drove them upward to a surface that was not there.

But then, without warning and beyond expectation, they did reach the surface. One after another, each head broke from the water with a howling gasp of agony, the air screaming into his lungs. There, in darkness and confusion, the whole throng thrashed about in frenzy.

Jagt, of course, had not betrayed them. How could he defy the binding spell that Methuselech had placed upon him? No, he had played his part; he had delivered them to Melhus, and it was only this last mean trick of his that had left them still underwater while mere yards from the surface—one final, spiteful stab to shake their composure and remind them of their place in the world.

With water streaming down his forehead and into his eyes, Gapp choked with violent sobs as he tried to tread water. He had been ripped cruelly from the ecstatic beauty and warmth of U'throst into this pitch dark world of freezing, spluttering, echoing mayhem, and his Ohgain robe was so heavily sodden with water it might as well have been an anchor tied to him. Though at first relief had elevated him beyond reckoning, now he foundered in panic. A Vetter's hand raked him straight across the eyes as the poor creature tried to swim, and Gapp cried out in shock, swallowing a mouthful of disgusting brine in the process. He tried to see something, anything, which might suggest to him a direction in which to swim, but here it was absolutely without light.

Nighttime? But there're no stars . . . And we were only down there for . . .

Now that he thought about it, he had no idea how long they had been under the sea. It had seemed like only a few moments, but there had still been a little light when he had stood upon the Black Shore. Just where the ruddy heck-fire had he ended up this time?

"*Radnarr,*" hissed a voice nearby, cutting through the gurgling cacophony all around, "*follow me. Jus' swim.*"

It was Methuselech's voice and, having no other plan at that moment, the boy followed. Amid the gulping, gasping and swallowing, the heaving of constricted esophagus, the spluttered sluicing of pharynx, and the clamor of lamentable sobbing, Gapp dragged himself through the spume of noxious, seething water. The *U'throst-effect* was now reversed, in that what seemed to last forever was actually all over in a very short span of time. Before long the whole company had hauled itself up onto a stone shelf. All who had entered the water also emerged from it. Whether man, dog, Parandus, Vetter, or Cervulus, Jagt had delivered them to Melhus without a single casualty.

"Where are we?" Gapp stammered between the violent spasms that shook his entire body.

He was lying upon the hard, rough stone floor of a large, echoing cavern, in absolute darkness. Along with all the others here, he was still hacking up toxic seawater, while trembling with a chill that had soaked into his very bones. He had wrung out his garments, and had sandwiched himself between Schnorbitz and Finan for warmth. The sound of coughing and intermittent moans could be heard all around, and the fearful bewilderment created a tangible menace that drew all of them to huddle together, and stare sightlessly out at the impenetrable darkness. What *was* this place?

For a long moment there was no answer. Gapp assumed Methuselech had not heard him. Then from somewhere indeterminate in the cavern came the voice: "*Un'erneathth Mellhhuss,*" it soughed, "*b'neathth the very hheart o' Vaa'enfor' Mhawr . . .*"

All there instantly froze—and Gapp spasmed as if he had been stroked by the damp robe of the Reaper. The voice bubbled hoarsely into silence, and Schnorbitz growled savagely.

It was Methuselech, for sure, but a Methuselech that had fallen even further into decay and ruin during their sea-passage. His voice whispered reverberantly like a sigh from ancient tombs deep beneath the ground, insubstantial and wraith-like, as if his body were now a mere carapace of old skin, worm-eaten and hollow. Muted though it was, it nevertheless cut through every other sound, and filled the cavern.

"Methuselech?"

"*Resst,*" the voice breathed again. "*Musst resst . . . there iss no dangerr dow' hhere . . . Resstawhillle.*"

It spoke no more.

No danger! Gapp screamed inside his head, his skin crawling as if he lay in a coffinful of maggots, *No bloody danger? Have I ever been in more danger than now? Caught between miles of sea-tunnel below and the "heart of Vaagenfjord Maw" above us, and here in this lightless hole with something that was once a man but is now . . . whatever it is. Have I ever been in more danger?*

He thought back to his time in the stabbur; to his capture by the Jordiske; his ordeal in the mines; and, immediately before that, his imprisonment in Nym-Cadog's witchly realm. Now, squeezed between the Rawgr and the deep black sea, Gapp's breath began to come in short bursts, and his mind fought against the panic that threatened to engulf him.

He held on to Schnorbitz, that wonderful canine friend who had rescued him, on two occasions already, from what had appeared to be inescapable death, held onto him tightly. And Schnorbitz, understanding the boy's suffering, nuzzled him back.

Gradually, Gapp regained some measure of self-control.

Yes, I have been in worse situations, he thought, *'cause this time I'm among friends.*

Gapp never did find out how long they had spent in Jagt's domain. It had felt like mere minutes, but he had heard enough stories of Huldre-Home to assume better. For instance, there was a man in Nordwas who had disappeared years before Gapp had been born, only to reappear unexpectedly a full twenty years later. Much to the amazement of his relatives, he appeared not to have aged a day. When questioned about his disappearance, he scratched his head vaguely, and told them that he had wandered into a land that was like a dream, a dream that he could hardly remember, but—so it seemed to him—one that had lasted for only a matter of days.

In truth, Gapp and his group had been submerged in Jagt's world for well over a day. Meanwhile, a long way above them, Bolldhe and his companions were settling down to their last supper in the storehouse. And at this very moment, a long way above Bolldhe, a straggling line of thirteen travelers was approaching Ravenscairn.

It was as black as the deepest trench of the ocean in here. The air was the same as had been here five hundred years ago, had not stirred in all that time, still smelled faintly of Scathur's breath. The entire place was without life, movement or sound.

But into this deadness, had anyone or anything been there to perceive it, a faint sound did, upon this day, occur. Indistinct at first, the sound gradually grew until it could be identified as footsteps: the muffled fall of many feet, softened further by the deep snow lying outside.

From without, voices could now be heard, ill-defined, murmuring, rising and falling like the erratic gusts of a far-off wind, but deadened by the thickness of the stone portal. A long silence ensued. It was the silence of contemplation, expectancy. Searching.

Then came the first thud, a blow that was dull but heavy enough to cause the first reverberation of air inside here since the Rawgrs' captain had last departed from this place. Profound, resonant. Ringing.

The silence returned. Soon it was broken by a scratching, as of metal upon stone. This went on for quite some time, a patient sound but at the same time insistent, purposeful. Probing.

Then came the rhythmic patter of many feet rapidly approaching as one, and immediately a second thud. This one was more determined, and succeeded in dislodging a scatter of ancient grains of stone from the cracks between door and jamb. The footsteps retreated and, seconds later, charged again. This third impact was stronger still, and was accompanied by an ox-like grunt so deep it could only be felt, not heard.

Moments later, a third charge came, and with it the determined cry of many voices. Finally, with a terrific blow that sent a deep quaking throughout the stone walls of this chamber, the door crashed open, and with that came the helmeted head of Klijjver the herd-giant.

For five hundred years this same room had been sealed up as tight as a coffin, and now at last the stuffy, sulphurous air was blasted away as an icy wind, the tree-trunk-like bulk of Klijjver, and the eight chargers who carried him horizontally, burst into the secret place.

Down a steep flight of steps that they had not expected, but that lay directly inside the door, the ram-raiders tumbled, yelling in panic. Just as Gapp, Methuselech and the Vetters had broken into the Maw in a confusion of pain and desperate gasps, so too did the Thieves of Tyvenborg. Only *they* had entered from the opposite direction. Cursing and yelping as they went, when at last they came to a stop, the thieves lay in a tangled pile of flapping limbs at the bottom of the stairs. Some moaned in pain, others were silent and did not move. The remainder were bawling and gesticulating in anger and fear. For none of them had any idea exactly where they were or what lurked below them in the darkness.

"What's down there?" came a small, broken voice from the top of the stairs. Though fierce winds now howled through the doorway from the night outside, those of the thieves who were too small to bear the battering-giant still did not dare enter. Brecca's anxious little prune-face peered fearfully from the cover of his frost-stiffened hood, his gaze trying to pierce the darkness. It was he who had loosened the door in the first instance, and who called out now.

"*We* are, you stunted little shite," roared Cuthwulf, from the top of the pile. "Get that light on us quickly."

As the resourceful Stone-Hauger Brecca fumbled with the makeshift lantern that he had fashioned out of spare parts a week ago, Cuthwulf lurched to his feet, felt around for the steps, and then pounded back up to the open door.

"Give that here, you prat!" he cursed, and snatched the lantern from Brecca's hands. The Hauger flinched away, and stood obediently off to one side.

In all honesty Cuthwulf was not annoyed with the Hauger; the thieves' crafty little locksmith had, after months of seeming nothing more than a burden, finally come into his own and proved his worth. He had succeeded both in finding the secret door and also unlocking it. At long last he was earning some of the respect he deserved.

But Cuthwulf, youngest of their leader's brothers and perhaps not the most stable of men, felt naked without his voulge. Like the other ram-raiders he had left the pole-weapon outside, and was rather shaken, to say the least. He also had little patience with the Hauger. And besides, over the long months the thieves had been together they had got used to victimizing the little guy, and long-established traditions did not die easily. He turned his back on Brecca, and, lantern held out before him, descended once again into the pit—albeit with considerably less celerity than before.

"And shut that pissing door!" he yelled back savagely.

The little folk, Brecca, Flekki, Khurghan, and Grini, wasted no time in picking up the discarded weaponry, equipment, and supplies, before bustling in out of the freezing cold. Cuthwulf shone the lantern around revealing that they were now in a large room—a cave really—that had been excavated from the rock. High up in one corner was the door they had entered through, closed firmly now against the fierce elements outside. The faces of the four little folk, who had now hauled all the weapons and baggage in with them, glowed yellow and sickly in the lantern's beam as they stared anxiously back down at Cuthwulf while they waited silently by the door.

Brother number two, Cuthwulf, now focused the lantern downward. From the door itself, a rock-hewn flight of steps descended steeply across one wall, leading down to the heap of thieves at the bottom. A single archway exited the room below, but—to everyone's immense relief—there was no one (or no thing) else in there with them.

With the howling wind and desperate cold now shut firmly behind the stone entrance door, they finally breathed a sigh of relief, and began to take stock of their new situation. Cuthwulf's brothers—the leader Eorcenwold and his lieutenant Oswiu Garoticca—still lay prostrate upon the floor, unmoving, eyes closed, but at least still visibly breathing. They had been at the head of the charge through the entrance, so they and Klijjver finished up at the bottom of the pile. Klijjver, as hulking and solid a Tusse as could be found throughout the north, looked fine, and just sat there in the corner with a rather blank expression.

And then there were the others—Hlessi the acid-haired Grell, Cerddu-Sungnir the multiweaponed half-Grell, Dolen the alabaster-faced Dhracus, and the two humans Aelldryc and Raedgifu. Though groaning loudly and clutching at their battered bodies, they were only superficially hurt.

They had made it. Made it to the cat's tooth pinnacle of Ravenscairn. Made it to Vaagenfjord Maw.

Though it was still bitterly cold in here, after the last twelve days they had endured, it felt almost like an oven. Finally out of the blasting wind, their weather-ravaged faces began to glow hotly, joyfully remembering warmth, and their fingers tingled painfully as the blood now pumped back into them.

It had been an ordeal such as none of them had ever envisioned. After emerging from that dreadful tunnel in the Giant Mountains, with its lych-candles and ghostly voices, they had hastened on through the early hours of the night, trying to put as much distance between themselves and that nightmare place as possible. For two days they had wandered through those mountains, almost dying of cold. Most of their arctic gear and supplies had been abandoned in Eotunlandt—now presumably flattened by some giant's foot—so the Tyvenborgers were none too well prepared for their journey. It had only been Eorcenwold's determined leadership that had held them all together.

But on the third day, fortunately, Khurghan the Polg, most excellent of that nomadic race's hunters, had spotted and brought down a great Monoceros with one arrow-like cast of his assegai spear, and they had devoured it like a pack of ravenous wolves. The healer Flekki, the other Hauger in the party, had rendered its rump-fat into a viscous jelly that would adhere to the skin all day, providing a salve for their badly chapped hands and faces.

From a higher vantage point, the maps they had brought with them from the Thieves' Mountain now began to make more sense, and with the guidance of Cuthwulf—the only one of them who had ever traveled in arctic places—they had three days later managed to reach the sea.

They had ended up not at the ice bridge used by Bolldhe a week earlier, but rather a small cove lying to the east of it. Luck had again come their way then, for they happened upon a small party of Torca whalers from the Odnuig Estuary. These small, rather subdued men in their tiny boat had been most accommodating, eventually—mainly due to the persuasive methods of Brother Oswiu Garoticca, cleric-assassin of Cardinal Saloth Alchwych—and they had obligingly agreed to hand over all their pelts and supplies. Some of them were so keen to see the Tyvenborgers on their way that they had even donated their few personal valuables to the cause. Such nice folk.

So, after a week upon the ice, Eorcenwold's party had finally arrived. The crossing itself had been horrendous, so bad that Eorcenwold had subsequently questioned his own decision not to requisition the whalers' boat, cram the best of his men into it, and attempt to sail right around the coast of Melhus and arrive by the fjord. But instead they had chosen to stick together, and thus they continued.

Great had been their relief then, when they at last reached Ravenscairn, and even greater their relief when the door yielded to their onslaught.

Eorcenwold and Oswiu were slowly regaining consciousness. For a while Oswiu remained flat on his back and did nothing but blink like an idiot.

Eorcenwold however, then raised the pair of them to their feet. Flekki quickly checked them over for damage, then nodded. "Nothing broken, nothing split; I pronounce you well and fit," she chirped in her strange singsong croak.

"Yes, thank you, little Hauger," Eorcenwold said. "You too, Brecca, well done."

Brecca managed a quick gurgling laugh, his neck glowing blue with embarrassment. Eorcenwold's eyes, if not his mouth, were smiling at their skillful locksmith with a kind of respect. Yes, at long last, Brecca had proven his worth. Adjusting the great shield upon his back, and hefting the other onto his right arm, the Hauger set his jaw defiantly. He had justified his presence here, but now his work was only beginning. They had come here for plunder, like everyone else, but unlike all those other fools, the Thieves of Tyvenborg knew where to find it.

For they possessed the one and only thing that could get mere mortals inside the inner reaches of the Maw. They had with them *The Testament of Khuc*.

It was about four years ago now that a party of thieves had journeyed from Tyvenborg to the Maw, lured, as so many others were, by a resurgence of interest in the Darkangel Drauglir. That had been a larger group than Eorcenwold's, and was made up mainly of Grell and half-Grell. Previous groups had rarely got beyond the outer reaches of the Maw, which were by now derelict and entirely plundered of anything valuable. So, Grell being what they were, i.e. possibly the most pernicious, brutish, and ill-favored race in Lyndormyn, these previous bandits had come armed with an arsenal of hammers, mattocks, and pickaxes, with the intention of simply bludgeoning their way through to the inner levels. For it was here, in these deeper places, they were convinced lay the fabled secret rooms that even the searching Peladanes had never found. The Maw was unbelievably huge, everyone knew, and the Peladanes—though they had ransacked the place with a thoroughness only their sort could achieve—had not possessed the expertise of thieves in discovering secret rooms. Or indeed the food supplies to sustain them a long time in searching.

So the Grells had set to work with their tools and with their brawn, a steaming industrial demolition machine driven by the hot coals of unlimited greed. But after weeks of frenzied work, severe privation, and a continual but unspecific sense of fear that was slowly driving them mad, though they indeed smashed their rude way into some hitherto undiscovered chambers and retrieved a little loot, they had never managed to penetrate the inner places where supposedly lay the "real good stuff."

But there was one thing that they had found, one very small, mean-looking item discovered in among a pile of old rags and bones that huddled in the corner of a secluded room near the dock. Almost overlooked, it was a rolled-up bundle of oiled leather, ancient and withered, and, when they opened it up, it appeared to be a collection of vellum sheets, all covered in writing.

None of the thieves had the patience, wit, nor even the desire to read what was inscribed on these fragile fragments. They were partly disintegrated, barely legible, and in a tongue they possessed no knowledge of. But what had caused them to fetch it home with them was that, in among the writing, there were also *diagrams.*

So, months later, this document had arrived safely at Tyvenborg, and before long fell into the hands of Brother Oswiu Garoticca. Guessing its significance, Oswiu had paid a considerable amount of money for it, and very soon he had arranged for the fragments to be translated by the Tyvenborg Chapter of Seers.

It transpired that these sheets were not vellum, but simply scraps of soft leather, cut or torn from old clothing into the semblance of writing sheets. And the writing was not writing at all, but *engraving* probably performed with some crude, improvised tool unsuitable for the task. Like the snapped shard of a broken knife? It must have taken the scribe some days to set this all down, clearly driven by no small amount of desperation to pen his last words before death finally took him.

The entire document was in the old tongue of the Oghain. This was an obscure language even by the seers' standards and, what with the decrepitude of the leather, had also been very difficult to read. So the translation was, by the seers' own admission, somewhat patchy and open to misinterpretation. But, if it was authentic, then that would date it to the time of the Fasces. Moreover, it had apparently been inscribed by one of the very Oghain-Yddiaw who had fought at the siege five hundred years ago.

And it went like this:

"FRIEND—can I call you friend? For we have never met, nor ever will, but in these my final hours I have a yearning for friendship such as I have never before known in my life, nor even <illegible>. And you, whoever you are—sweet, beautiful, living person—are the last one to whom I may speak. So you will forgive my presumption, I hope, and suffer me to address you 'Friend.'

(Alternatively, I could call you 'acquaintance.')

Whatever. FRIEND, I am dying, alone and in the dark, utterly forsaken in this awful {hell} that is deserted by men. But, alas, not by Evil. For the Evil yet lives on. I alone may know this, for I alone have seen it.

The shining warriors, they believe in their pride that they have defeated the Rawgr and all his <stain>. And of Drauglir that is true, for I myself have beheld his gargantuan, lifeless husk with my own eyes. But there is one yet that has not perished, and skulks now within the peak above the Rawgr's Hall. For upon Scathur, that {crude remark} captain of hell, I have also looked, though still I can hardly believe it.

But what has brought me to this lonely end, this most miserable, frozen starvation in which my only comfort is setting down this my final testament?

What folly could have taken hold of me so? For I, Khuc of Wrythe, did not become Akynn~Lord of the East Jarl by such dire recklessness. But it is true that, in the days after Drauglir was slain by his own captain, while the Lords of the South went about their destructive business, I alone of the Yd-diaw stayed behind, though all my people had been {sent home?} by the High Warlord. Whether it was in recognition of my high rank, or finally yielding to my eloquent persuasions, the Peladanes did finally allow me to stay on while they searched the enemy's stronghold.

And, oh, what I found there! Scathur, we had all heard, on being caught in the very act of slaying his own master, had fled the Rawgr's Hall before the grim horde that issued from Lord Bloodnose's mighty <hole>. Up the great flue that ascended from the infernal fire-pit he disappeared, like a thief in the night, climbing the rungs set into the stone, but, with a terrible strength in his pernicious fingers, wrenching them out beneath him as he climbed. And as he tore each out, he would hurl it down on the heads of his eager pursuers, who therefore had no way of climbing after.

Scathur had made good his escape. By the time the Peladanes had re-set the rungs and climbed after him, he had of course eluded them. At the top of the rungs the flue inclined around so that it ran almost level. But this passage was now blocked by a succession of {mod. equiv: 'great stone blocks'} lowered from cavities set at intervals in the passage roof. By ex-tracting the rungs, Scathur had gained himself the time to reach the far end of the flue and set into motion a crafty mechanism that deposited these huge obstacles.

For many days I tarried there, assisting where allowed, while yearning to find out more. And when finally those blocks had all been levered up back into their cavities, and there re-set, and held, there was naturally no sign of the dark fugitive. The flue ended by opening into Smaulka~Degernerth, the great Hall of Fire. There was nothing to be seen save the sheer drop to the river of searing magma running below and a ceiling of rock above. No escape, it seemed, not even for a Rawgr. Such heat there was even up there, that none could endure long enough to properly examine the ledge from which {it was assumed} Scathur had hurled himself, perishing in the fire rather than suffering himself to be taken by the enemy.

None could endure, that is, save I. No, I do not boast, for it was this, my strength, my determination, that led me to my undoing. Had I been less tenacious, you, Friend, would not be reading these same words now.

Yet what was I to do or say? Would Scathur have devised this elaborate escape way simply to end his own existence in the fire pit? I thought not. I knew he was up there somewhere. Heedless of the danger and the agony of heat and the noxious fumes I had to endure there, I slipped back out onto the ledge when none was looking.

True to my reckoning, I found a way. It was at first only a few {hand-holds?} along the rock, with a great drop below straight into the white-hot death. But resolute I was, and I followed it, though burning my hands terribly as I scrambled along.

Crying in pain I continued, until—Gyyrdznakh be praised—after but a minute or two I came to a hidden path. This narrow ledge was mere yards away from the flue's exit, but, around a protrusion of rock, was out of sight of any who stood upon the flue ledge itself.

Along this new path I made my way up, until shortly I had reached the very roof of the Hall of Fire. Hastening, for I was now in such pain, I followed a new passageway as it plunged into the cooler darkness. Thence, heading up and up, I came unto the chamber that I now know lies within the very peak of {Ravenscairn}.

I grow weak. My hands barely grip. I must be brief if I am to finish ere I fade. A small chamber lay at the head of the passage. No one in it. A door on the other side. Open. Ice~wind cooled me. I went out. Outside again at last. Top of Melhus. Snowfield. Night time. Walked some way, sucking in the air. So sick with heat and fumes. Collapsed. Asleep. When awoke, still night. Almost dead with cold. Door now closed. Looked in, saw Scathur sobbing in ruination. He saw me not. But how <Tobacco burn. Sorry about that. Will refund> *Fled in terror.*

Weak. Bad lungs. Could hardly walk. Wandered for days. Each night near killed me. Trapped foul birds for food with <unknown word—poss. a form of archaic harpoon> *so kept alive. Many days later found way down fjord to harbor. All ships, all Peladanes, gone. Only myself. Tried to catch fish, bird, but so weak.*

Now, I hardly think right. Will die soon. Whoever you are, whenever you are, I send love down the years, across continents, and a message of great import . . ." <illegible from here on>

So there you have it. *The Testament of Khuc*, complete with diagrams of the portal into Ravenscairn, and the path to the very heart of Ymla-Myrrdhain, Drauglir's inner keep. Indeed, to the very chamber in which he had died. If he could believe its authenticity, Brother Oswiu Garoticca had in his possession the only known record of a secret way into Ymla-Myrrdhain, a way now known only to himself, to a group of aging, quill-fingered seers, and an Akynn-Lord who had died five hundred years ago.

A secret way! A thing craved by generations of looters ever since the Peladanes had sealed off the inner keep.

But it was not solely by the contrivance of the Peladanes that Ymla-Myrrdhain was cut off from the world. Of the few groups who had recently gained access to the Maw, none had apparently gone very deep. Always they had been forced back by some obstacle or another—or they had simply never returned. It was therefore widely believed that some great power had been re-awakened to guard the inner places, some dark entity that was so much more insurmountable than the mere physical earthworks and barricades of the Peladanes.

But here, maybe, provided a way. And that is why the Tyvenborgers had come.

Eorcenwold, as always, proved the leader. Few people even of the Thieves' Mountain would follow one such as Oswiu Garoticca, that black-souled, pig-faced and slug-breathed necrophiliac. In any case, Eorcenwold was, in his own unremarkable way, one of Tyvenborg's finest. He may not have been the strongest, brightest, most dextrous, or charismatic man in the Mountain, and was by no means the tallest. But he was a solid bloke, solid in both body and mind, and people trusted him. He listened to people, asked their advice, and was not too proud to admit when he was wrong. And though he had a voice that could peel bark off a tree at fifty paces, or shout a lammergeyer out of the sky, he was no bully; what he did, he did to get the job done.

Cuthwulf and AFinwald were automatically included in this expedition, of course. AFinwald could be a bit slow: her head was too tiny to contain a size-able brain, and her massive hips gave her an awkward, un-thiefly gait similar to that of a torpid lizard climbing up a mud bank in the chill of an early morning. And her brother Cuthwulf possessed a mean streak that sometimes perturbed even Garoticca. But they were both *family,* and their loyalty was thus ensured.

As was that of Klijjver. His was an interesting story. Tusse—or herd-giant—society, though mainly nomadic, was divided into many castes, each of them deriving from whichever animal they herded. The highest caste, the Dhurgh-nagh, herded the Red Bison, that most prized, near-deified beast that featured in all inherited aspects of pan-Tusse culture, from their most ancient and hal-lowed myths, down to the humble bison-head toggles the children wore on their kirtles.

Klijjver, however, came from the Boyles, the very lowest caste, and they herded dogs. Their livelihood, such as it was, derived from dog-meat (which was stringy and tended to bite back several days later), dog-sausages (dog-intestines filled with dog-blood and dog-nail-clippings), and most famously, dog-dairy products: thin dog-milk, bitter dog-yoghurt, and hard dog-cheese.

Dog-cheese was their speciality; it had evolved a culture all of its own, and was dear to the Boyles. Lupers' Hill was the venue for the annual dog-cheese-rolling games, an event in which a large piece of cheese would be rolled down the frighteningly steep western slope of the hill, and wild young braves would chase it with reckless abandon in the hope of catching it before it reached the bottom, and thus gain the coveted prize. This would have been an exciting and heart-stopping event had they rolled rounds of cheese, and not wedges, as they did.

Boyle life was a hard one. They were both pariah and feared, particularly the over-sized Klijjver. It was on one occasion after he had been trying to sell dog-crackling at a human settlement near Hrefna that Klijjver had first met Eorcenwold. The poor Tusse had been driven out of town with pitchforks and grain-flails by enraged villagers chanting: "Man's best friend! Man's best friend!" These were good, decent village folk who knew that a dog's lot was not the pot but rather the post by the farm gate, to which they would be chained all day and night, especially in the winter. Anyway, even the nine-foot-tall Klijjver had been terrified and it had only been the muzzle of Eorcenwold's blunderbuss suddenly staring them in the faces that had persuaded the good folk to return quietly to their homes.

Such an act had guaranteed him Klijjver's loyalty for life.

Cerddu-Sungnir the half-Grell had come along at Cuthwulf's invitation, and he in turn had invited Hlessi. Cerddu-Sungnir possessed possibly the most bizarre and lethal arsenal in all of Tyvenborg, and Hlessi was just plain nasty, so the pair of them were about as close to Cuthwulf's heart as he could hope for. As for the others, they had been chosen for their various specific skills. They were a mixed bag to be sure, but unlike the party from Nordwas, they had just one purpose to unify them, and one leader to bind them.

The Thieves of Tyvenborg; a careful blend of strength, skill, stealth, psionics, and vicious, bloodcurdling savagery. And they had now almost reached Drauglir's Chamber.

So, within the space of twenty-four hours, no less than five separate parties entered the Maw. From the sea cave far below, late in the evening, emerged Methuselech and his army. From the mountains high above, a little later, arrived the Tyvenborgers. From the front gate, approached at dawn the following day, the men from Nordwas. From the sea, later that day, sailed Scathur and his host. And from the air, later still, Kuthy, Elfswith, and Ceawlin flew in.

Each and every group entering with an entirely different motivation.

Yes, it seemed Vaagenfjord Maw really was *the* place to be, that season.

8

Knackered

The instant Bolldhe stepped over the threshold into Vaagenfjord Maw, his sword burst into flames.

"Soddin' hell!" he cried out fearfully, at the same time tossing the weapon away from him as though it were a viper. The others too almost leapt out of their skins at his cry of alarm, then swept up their weapons, and crouched defensively.

All stared at the burning flamberge as it clanged noisily upon the black flagstones, flickered for an instant, then was extinguished.

Miles away, out on the dark ocean, Scathur suddenly leapt to his feet, and gripped the haft of his Bardische in trembling hands. His eyes bulged out of their leathery folds, but still he stood with his glowering gaze fixed on *that* spot. The headland of Vaagenfjord was still not in sight, and would not be for several hours, though the coast of Melhus drifted slowly by on their right. But Scathur did not need eyes to recognize what had just befallen.

The enemy, he knew, had just entered the Maw.

With the metallic clang of the sword still echoing far into the great chamber, the company stood stock-still upon the threshold, staring at the weapon in shock. For a long while, no one dared move. They just stood there openmouthed, not even sure—now that Flametongue was back to normal—that they had really just seen what they imagined they had seen.

At length the silence was broken by Bolldhe, one small voice in the yawning immensity of that place.

"What, in the name of Cuna's celestial hole, was *that* all about?" he bleated weakly, and glared round at Finwald and his companions.

Blank stare, dumb expressions—they did not know either.

Then Finwald went over to the sword, and carefully picked it up. His long fingers enfolded the hilt, pale grey over black. There was a look of unconcealed admiration, almost reverence, in his eyes as he held it up before him. A slight breath escaped his lips.

"A magic blade, now beyond any doubt," he whispered in awe, then turned to Bolldhe. "As I said when you first found it—didn't I?"

He proffered it, two-handed, to Bolldhe.

"I tell you, this is destiny. We were *meant* to find Flametongue. Or else it was meant to find us."

"What are you going on about?" Bolldhe replied sickly.

"Don't you see?" the mage-priest insisted. "That fire—like the voice of a prophet roaring through the halls of kings—it's as good as announcing to us its purpose in destroying the Rawgr. Was there ever a surer sign?"

"Well, yes, actually," Bolldhe replied with a hint of his former scorn. "I could think of quite a few." And reached out to take the weapon.

As soon as he touched the flamberge, a vision flashed into his mind. It was the same vision he had experienced on first touching the sword back in Myst-Hakel, the vision of a desolate heath, the cliff, and the distant stranger looking out over a troubled sea. This time, however, it held him longer. He drew closer to the figure, closer still, until he was near enough to make out its wind-ruffled clothes, occult-black and swirling like silken banners upon a battlefield.

Bolldhe then blinked . . . and his companions stood before him, regarding him intently. He was back at the Maw.

He drew a weary hand down across his face, and breathed in deeply, unsteadily.

"To hell with this," he muttered in his own language, then in a louder voice said: "Don't just hang around then, Nibulus. Take us in."

Over the threshold they stepped, into the darkness of Vaagenfjord Maw, and left the world of light behind them.

Their torches created a sphere of sickly yellow light around them, but illuminated nothing beyond that. Even Bolldhe's lantern beam revealed only stone floor, featureless save for the occasional puddle of partially frozen black water, silted with the grime of centuries. Just how big was this hall? As the men progressed further, they soon began to feel ever more timorous, as though they had become just a pathetic little globe of weak light floating in an eternity of black space; a lone firefly lost and blown far from its kind deep into the night. One puff of black wind and they might be extinguished, like a naked candle flame in a gale.

Six tiny specks of life in a place where no life was meant to be.

They continued on and on, and still the cavernous hall did not end. It was as if whoever had designed the Maw had decided that its "front porch" should leave none entering this place in any doubt as to the vast eternity of blackness of Drauglir's realm. Never had there been, in any of their lives, such a tangible feeling of abandonment. They had cast themselves adrift into the void, where there was *nothing,* no light, no life, not even time. Just an emptiness, and with it an awful desolation that clamped its wet, black hands around the windpipe of each and reached down deep inside them, filling them with hopelessness.

Yet on they went. They could still feel the ground beneath them, but numbly, as if it were not real, just as the frostbitten walker perceives not the firm texture of ground beneath him, but merely the dull weight of his bones upon insensitive feet. The blackness, too, was closing in around them even more intensely, robbing them of more than just their sight. Even sound grew muted, for though they could all sense the vast, cavernous space around them, still the scrape of their booted feet across the damp, gravelly floor developed a flatness reminiscent of the melancholy tramp of pallbearers.

Senses, it seemed, were unwelcome intruders here, reminders of life and movement, those qualities that belonged outside. Even the air seemed deadened: freezing, with the close, airless chill of the grave. The sepulchral gloom of this vast atrium transmuted everything into a condition which the intruders just knew was not right.

Eventually their feeble sphere of illumination touched upon a raised lip of stone. It was the first step of a vast stairway that seemed, in their dream-like bemusement, to span the entire width of the underworld lying before them.

"According to Gwyllch," Nibulus whispered, "there was indeed a great stairway that led up to the passages of the Great Concourse."

Not allowing them to check their pace, he led them on up. They all marveled at the sheer steepness of this stony terrace. Each riser was as high as a gravestone, and every bit as crumbling. Whereas Paulus had only moderate difficulty in managing with each step, Appa had to use both hands to pull himself up, gripping gecko-like to the stone for dear life. Before even reaching the tenth step, they could sense they had ascended higher than the average house in Nordwas; by the thirtieth, they had left the floor far below. Hearts pounding with the effort, their fear of the Maw was now being pushed to one side of their minds by the more immediately threatening fear of falling, for if they were to lose their footing here, the only thing to stop their rapid descent would be the unforgiving ground far below.

"Made it," Paulus called back, the first to reach the top. "Bolldhe, where are you? Bring that lantern up here quick!"

"Wait for me!" a panicked voice whimpered from below. "Shine it down here!"

As each of them in turn gained the uppermost step, they sat down or squatted, gasping to regain their breath.

"Pel's Bells!" Bolldhe gasped in awe. "How could anyone manage to *fight* their way up here?"

"And in heavy iron field-plate, too," Nibulus agreed in a hushed voice. "The Peladanes of those days were true heroes, every one. Their faith made them unstoppable."

For once, Bolldhe could not disagree.

There was naturally a kind of relief that they had gained the top of the stairs without mishap, but now that sense of panic that Nibulus had warned them about earlier bore down on all of them from somewhere ahead, from somewhere out there in the crushing darkness beyond their puny illumination.

But there was nothing for it now but to go on. Nibulus could not allow them to stop for a second longer than necessary, not permitting them to let fear or doubt falter their resolve.

The next few minutes were spent searching the wide area at the top of the stairs. Several passageways led off from there, either keeping level or sloping up or down, some heading back to run along the galleries above the Great Hall, others running deeper into the castle. For now, though, the company carefully searched this area immediately before them before going on. Gwyllch's chronicle was a detailed one, to be sure, but it was primarily heroic in inspiration, and he had never really intended anyone to use it as a guidebook, let alone a map. But they had to be sure of taking the correct way right from the very start. Any alternative might be disastrous.

"Looks like whoever came here recently ran into a spot of trouble," Nibulus commented grimly. He reached down and picked up a metallic object from the floor. "Bolldhe? Paulus? Either of you seen one of these before?"

The company gathered round to inspect his find. It was a Quiravian falchion, a light and elegant sword customarily worn by the wealthy merchant types who paraded about town. It had the letters "Y," "E," and "N" engraved upon its blade in fine, flowing, Quiravian script.

"Not at all the sort of blade you'd expect to find in a place like this," Paulus commented. "Beautiful workmanship, true, but not exactly heavy-duty."

"Not the sort of blade one leaves behind lightly, either," Bolldhe added.

"There's been fighting here in the last few months," Nibulus agreed. "This falchion's hardly even rusted."

True enough, as they searched the stair-top, they began to find other evidence of conflict: broken or discarded weaponry, torn rags, the tracks of boots skidding upon the flagstones.

But no bodies. Not even parts of bodies, nor the clothes, nor the armor they must have worn. It was as if they had discarded everything they held and simply run away in blind terror. *Extreme* terror, judging by the fact that they had not only dropped their weapons but also their torches. *What could cause such fear that men would drop their only source of light?*

"Keep together," the Peladane ordered, his voice as steady as he could manage. No one argued.

Suddenly Wodeman hissed harshly, holding up his hand.

"Listen," he whispered. Everyone froze.

At first it seemed only the nature-priest was able to hear anything. Soon, however, they too could discern it, far-off, barely audible, terribly feeble, but undeniably there: a sobbing, child-like and horribly forlorn, so similar to the voice they had heard in the tunnel leading out of Eotunlandt. It iced the blood in their veins and immobilized them utterly.

"Wind?" Finwald stammered, pleadingly.

No one replied, because they all realized the truth. It could not be the wind, for here there was no breath of air at all. This was a dead place, and movement was against the rules. Still the crying continued, somewhere out there in the dark, rising and falling, sometimes sputtering and failing. Bolldhe felt its awful wretchedness draining the very life-force inside him.

Nibulus, characteristically, set his jaw and gripped his sword firmly with both hands. Steadily, he began to advance.

"Nibulus!" Appa bleated. "What do you think you're doing?"

"My job," the Peladane announced as he proceeded. "What we came all this way to do. *That* is the enemy and *this* is Unferth, and I believe the time has come for them to get acquainted."

"But—" Bolldhe began.

"Remember the Heroes of the Fasces, Pendonian," Nibulus cut in. "Let our faith make us unstoppable, too." The tone of his voice brooked no dissent; the Peladane was at last going in to meet the enemy.

They had no choice. Squeezing their hilts, they padded after him.

Closer, closer. The stifled, high-pitched sobs continued—the only sound in that place, for the travelers stole along upon silent feet.

And then it stopped; cut off in an instant, as if finally it was aware of them.

"The light!" Nibulus hissed. "Shine it ahead of me!"

Bolldhe thrust his lantern out to light their leader's way, and more swiftly now they proceeded.

"We startled it?" Finwald whispered. "Is . . . d'you think whatever's there, it's afraid of us?"

Nibulus shot the trailing priest a grim look, silencing him. *Afraid of us?* he considered, as if such a thing might be possible in this abyss they were walking through. "This way, quick," he urged. And with more haste and less stealth they hurried on in the vague direction from which the sobbing came.

Here the passage became narrower, the air even closer, with a sealed-crypt deadness to it. The beam of the lantern danced over the stone walls that were gradually closing in on either side. They were blotched as if diseased, dungeon-grey and dank. The floor beneath their feet was littered with the discarded remnants of previous questers to the Maw.

Then Appa choked: "What in the sweet Lord's name is this?"

He whimpered in horrified disbelief as the lantern beam flickered unsurely over walls only now coming into view. The entire crumbling surface of stone in this part of the passage was marked by what appeared to be sharp striations, cutting deep and ragged, but it was only when they inspected these closer they realized with horror that the walls had in fact been scored by monstrous claws. To the minds of every man there, the words of the old Peladane from Wrache returned: *"Great rending sounds as of some terrible talon could we hear upon the door, and a hammering upon all the shutters so strong it was only Faith that held them from splintering asunder . . ."*

The beam now visibly trembled in Bolldhe's hand as it lingered reluctantly upon the other hellish images that some demented, anti-human mind had daubed on the walls. All around, in some dark, glistening and disturbingly sticky substance, were smeared twisted stick figures of things that could have been human, or Rawgr, or some awful fiend from the Pit. A sense of utter madness hung heavy in the air, and again Bolldhe began to dredge up memories of black blood boiling inside his brain. Things were definitely starting to happen to him, and he very much doubted that mere faith, should he possess any, would be able to arrest this process.

"Never mind that stuff!" Nibulus snapped, as Appa lingered by the graffiti in morbid fixation. At the same time, the Peladane's harsh command jolted Bolldhe from those strange pinpricks of memory.

Then another voice murmured into his ear. "Keep Flametongue ready."

It was Finwald, hovering just behind him. Bolldhe felt the priest's hand fold around his elbow, soft and trembling, its coldness somehow penetrating even his thick garment. Then Finwald moved on ahead of him.

Bolldhe was confused. Something had just gone dreadfully wrong, and he was desperately struggling to cope with it in his mind. For Finwald was now several paces in front of him, yet his hand still clung to Bolldhe's elbow.

He looked down at it, and saw that it was not Finwald's after all. This hand was corpse-thin, with old, grey, skin that stretched taut over swollen knuckles and bulbous veins. The fingers looked more like bird claws, and ended in blackened, broken nails.

With a liquid whine half-caught in his throat, Bolldhe turned his head, slowly as if in reverie. And saw the face at his shoulder. It was the ash-pale, vesicant visage of something that had emerged from purgatorial pits, streaked with a palette of filth, and pitted with the dead, sunken eyes of one that had witnessed carnage inconceivable.

Then it opened its mouth horrendously wide, and screamed.

In that stone-splitting keen could be heard the howling of the torture chamber, the lamentation of the damned, the wailing of war victims, women, children, the old and the crippled who fled before the berserk stampede of horsemen, fell beneath spear and hoof, were herded into burning buildings, strung up, pierced through, roasted alive over bonfires, hacked into pieces like meat on a butcher's slab.

(Bolldhe was suddenly eight years old again, and giggled with the same

dementia as the howling face before him. The graffiti upon the walls leapt out at him, caught in the lantern's beam, cavorting before his eyes like the whiplash of viscera; and he understood it all so well.)

. . . Then his mind deserted him, and fell into a deep void where blackness and that awful keening sound were his only companions.

". . . about Bolldhe . . . for his own good . . . stay with us, or do we send him away . . . must decide quickly . . ."

Voices swimming through the purple vortices of his madness. The smell of polished armor; clean, leaf-bright Ulleanhs; sunshine on temple lawns.

". . . hard world, hard choices . . . burden . . . man, not a boy!"

Who was it? So hard to think. Voices from a long, long time ago.

". . . do we stay with him or leave him here? We must decide quickly."

Clearer now, as Bolldhe's derangement began to dissipate. Familiar voices. Not his parents—more recent. Blue armor covered in grime; mold-green Ulleanh; the blood red of a single torch in the cold night.

"Bolldhe, snap out of it," a voice hissed urgently, right in his face. "We've got to decide what to do. Is he—what's the matter with him?"

Rough hands shook him, and he finally managed to focus on the figure before him. It was Nibulus, his big face silhouetted by the torch he held above him. "At last! Come on, old son, it's time to go. You'll be all right; she didn't do anything serious to you."

"She?"

"Probably just the shock. Got to admit, that scared the shit out of us all. Even me."

Bolldhe paused, then with a gasp he lurched forward, grabbed his lantern where it had been set on the floor, and snapped the brass and silk cylinder up into its leather sleeve, transforming it to focus a narrow beam. He cast the light about, and almost at once it fell on a huddled scarecrow that knelt on the floor, surrounded by the rest of the company.

Bolldhe's face screwed up. "Who is she?" The woman—if woman it was—rocked back and forth, staring ahead vacantly, her claw-like hands making an odd, feeble swatting motion before her ravaged face. Both mage-priests and the sorcerer were tending to her, while above her stood Paulus with his sword poised ready.

"Quiravian adventuress, from what we can gather," Nibulus replied scornfully. "You know the sort: merchants' daughters, all money and spare time. Hang out with the gangs, run with the dacoits—do anything to shock. Seems this one was shagging a Grell, too. A *Grell,* for Jugg's sake! Can you believe it?"

Bolldhe could believe it. On his travels he had encountered many such women in the more affluent cities: rich, bored, and squeaky clean. Started every sentence with the word "actually" or whatever the equivalent was in their tongue. He had even heard of some employing *sarcasm* tutors. Yes, Bolldhe knew their sort well. Indeed, it was from women such as this that much of his income as an oracle derived.

"What's she told you so far?" he asked, listening to the awkward phonemes and dancing intonations of Finwald as the priest tried to communicate with her.

"She hasn't said much at all yet. Sounds pretty garbled to me, and I'm not sure how much Finwald's getting out of her, either. It's been a long time since he's heard any Quiravian spoken."

They went over to her, and Bolldhe held the unsheathed lantern closer to her face. He stared into those blank, lacteal eyes, and was struck by how closely they resembled poached oysters—pale, runny, and twice as stinking. Her skin looked like old parchment, all the youth and elasticity drained from it, its natural deep-brown Quiravian tone now yellowed and sickly.

His gaze dropped to her garments, and he pursed his lips. Maybe she had indeed once been a young adventuress, the daughter of a wealthy merchant, loaded to the ears with amethyst and arrogance, up for fun no matter the risk. But now the rich brown leather and luxuriant hyrax and civet fur of her perfectly tailored traveling garb more closely resembled what they really were: the tattered skins of dead animals, grimy and decaying.

"Sure she's an adventuress?" Bolldhe asked doubtfully. "Looks a bit old for that to me."

"Nineteen years of age, so Finwald says." Nibulus clicked his tongue. "Battle shock, starvation, terror . . . I've seen many cases like hers before, but never this bad . . . Must've really been through the mangle, this one."

"But what's she doing here?"

"What do any of her sort do here?" Nibulus scoffed, for a second reverting to his Peladane persona. "Same as all the others, those types back home who like to walk around Lower Kettle Bazaar dressed as Olchorian priestesses and—"

"Then they start believing they truly have The Power," Appa cut in ruefully. "Always pushing the limits to their extremes."

They all stared down at her in silence. This place was evil and sick, and very very dangerous. Yet none of them could help but feel strangely consoled at seeing the utter devastation of this silly little rich girl before them. They knew this was wrong, of course, but there was something perversely reassuring in knowing that they were not actually the most ridiculous and puny group of questers to have ever entered the Maw. Not anymore.

"Women, eh," Nibulus said in his most sagacious tones. "Takes all sorts, I suppose. . . . Have you found out how long she's been here, Finwald?"

"And what happened to her companions?" added Paulus.

"Do we even know the poor child's name?" asked Appa.

"Weeks or months," Finwald replied. "She doesn't seem to know how long ago it's been since her arrival, but she arrived here with a whole crowd: her brother, her friends, her lover, the Grell, and a fair number of pretty tough-sounding swords for hire, too. So I wouldn't laugh too hard yet, lads. Oh, and her name's Yen."

Y-E-N. The letters inscribed upon the falchion they had found. Only the way Finwald pronounced it, it sounded more like "Ian."

"*Ian?*" Nibulus repeated. "That's a *name* in her country?"

"She was attacked by something," Finwald continued, "but she won't say what. The mercenaries were either slaughtered or fled, and her Grell lover-boy legged it without so much as a backward glance. Little brother was eaten, devoured from the face downward: nice clothes, hairbrush, nail file, and all. Apparently he'd won nearly every tourney award going—had all the badges sewn onto his tabard. Pity he couldn't fight in a real situation."

"What about the ship?" Bolldhe asked, remembering with dread the half-sunk wreck that he and Nibulus had explored—and its grisly contents.

"Hers, I think," Finwald supposed. "She won't talk about it, though." And here he gave both Bolldhe and Nibulus a hard stare. "It scares her to death."

Probably saw what we saw, Bolldhe guessed. *Maybe that was her lover. . . . I'm not surprised she's kept away.* But neither he nor the Peladane deigned to elaborate.

"Lucky for us that she stayed away from it, though," Finwald went on. "Otherwise there'd have been none of that food left for us. She's been living on fish heads, lichen, and polar spiderlings all the while."

"So what do we do now?" Wodeman demanded. "We can't just leave her here."

"Absolutely," Bolldhe agreed. "I'm not having her creeping round here, jumping out on us like that."

"I'll take her out of here, then," Wodeman volunteered, "take her back to our storehouse. She can stay there till we get back. Wait for me here. I shouldn't be too long."

"You'll be all right on your own?" Nibulus asked, more than a little surprised.

"He'll have to be," Paulus grumbled. "I'm not going all the way back just for her sake."

"And I'd rather not tackle those stairs again unless I really have to," Appa added, apologetically.

"Come on, then, you," said Wodeman, dragging the confused woman with him. "I'll see you in a bit."

As a wounded hunting cat flees from a quarry that turns suddenly to gouge it, so Wodeman staggered away from the Maw. Like the sobbing woman he dragged behind him, he was sick with fear and despair, scantly more than a frightened animal himself. Though born of the forest, like all forest creatures he had often known terror. There had been times in his life when he had stumbled through woodlands lamentable and drear, when swamp mist rose chill and damp to befoul the night air, and out of darkness came voices of things of which even he had no ken.

Out of the gateway he reeled, dizzy with disorientation, and gulped in the cleaner, salty air of the real world. Above him the cliffs swam vertiginously, and the gargoyles seemed to cackle at his failure. But he did not pause long; he propelled the woman roughly before him, and together they reached the relative haven of the hut on the dock.

He heaved the door open, thrust his charge inside, and quickly followed her. It was dark in there, and now smelled not dissimilar to an elephant house. From the corner came a whinnying and stamping of hooves from Zhang, and a fresh gust of warm flatus to add to the already mulchy fug. Wodeman immediately set his torch in a bracket in the wall, lit another two, and rolled the heaviest provisions barrel against the door. Only when that was done did he finally collapse to his knees and pause to catch his breath.

"Four dreams!" he choked acrimoniously. "Four stupid dreams! All this way, all the pain and . . . and *soul-death,* and that's all I get to give to him!"

His green-brown eyes broiled with the intensity of his anguish, and he hugged his knees, silently cursing everything in the universe.

The woman, meanwhile, stood flattened against the wall, staring at him in fear. She had pressed herself into a gap between two sacks, too witless to think of looking for a weapon. After a while, she too slumped to the floor, and continued to eye the sorcerer cautiously, whimpering softly to herself.

Without wasting a moment longer, Wodeman wrenched the leather bag from his belt and, after fumbling with the drawstrings, spilled its contents upon the floor.

Hungrily, desperately, he stared down at them.

His eyes widened. He blinked hard, and looked again. *What the . . . ?*

Perhaps it was a shared vision of their imagination, but to both himself and the woman it seemed as if the whole room around them now faded into blackness, till all that could be seen—maybe all that there actually was now—was the circle of orange torchlight around the floor immediately at his knees. But what had previously been the ancient, frost-cracked flagstones of the storehouse floor now appeared to have become the dried-up earth of a stream bank somewhere in the woods, green with hazel-filtered sunlight, an alder wood bowl resting just to one side.

As it faded, the shaman nodded in recognition of the vision's significance. Yes, of course: he had cast his runes for the very last time.

Of all the runes that had fallen from the bag, only two lay faceup. They stared up at him from their final resting place, on a bone-hard floor on their island at the end of the world. Like dead men's teeth they lay and, like death it-self, nothing could now be changed.

The Beast and *Death*.

"Erce!" he swore, and immediately snatched up the offending runes and hurled them against the wall.

His dreams—those visions sent from Erce, channeled through himself, to enlighten Bolldhe—were now done, already given. That, Bolldhe had made quite clear upon the ice field. And now there was nothing else for Wodeman to do, no reason for him to be here on the quest anymore. Like an old, worn-out slipper, he had served his purpose, and now all that remained to him was slow decomposition on a rubbish dump. Despite his relative safety out here, he al-most envied his fellow travelers inside the Maw.

But he did at least still have his runes, if only they would be allowed to teach him one last message. Scrabbling like a beggar whose bowl has spilt its meager copper zlats in the dirt, Wodeman gathered the runes up in his chapped fin-gers and thrust them back into their bag. This time he shook them up, drew out a small handful, and cast them again.

The small circle of torchlight drew in even closer upon the precious runes. Again, only two of them landed faceup.

The Beast, and *Death*, again.

Wodeman's eyes widened into a couple of hot moist circles. Had he not just thrown those two away? He leapt over to where they had landed earlier, and searched every inch of the vicinity.

Gone. Not bounced away, or fallen beneath a crate. Simply *gone* . . .

Taking no chances, Wodeman carefully removed those objectionable tiles, placed them well to one side, then cast his runes for a third time.

Six fell now, but only two faceup.

The Beast, and *Death*.

Wodeman cried out in horror and scrambled away from the circle of light. His breath quickened, till he was sweating hotly beneath his furs. The woman began to moan, and Zhang, eyes rolling, joined her.

His heart like an engine thumping in his chest, Wodeman crawled forward. *The Beast* and *Death* were still there, for real, but those two that he had just put aside had vanished. The Torca cursed himself for ever letting himself believe he could force a different outcome here. In his arrogance he had actually thought he could help change the course of the world. He realized now beyond doubt that he should never have left his familiar woods. This place of ice and stone mocked him, and soon it would crush the life from him.

Suddenly angry, whether at Erce or Olchor, or even at Bolldhe, he was not sure, Wodeman again scooped the runes back into the bag and, without bothering to shake it, he tipped them *all* out as he had done the first time.

The Beast and *Death*.

Again he tried—the same. And again—the same.

And again and again and again, the low gurgle in his throat rising in pitch as each increasingly panicky casting resulted in *the same*.

Then with a resounding blast and a brilliant flash of green light, the whole set of runes exploded.

A minute later, when the sorcerer finally crawled out from behind a large kilderkin, he simply stared at the place where his beloved runes had been, and whispered: "By the holy hagbut of Winfloeta, they've never done *that* before!"

The crunch of teeth on something hard broke the spell, and his gaze was drawn over to where the woman still huddled. She had not taken her eyes from the shaman all this time, but now, sensing the worst was over, she had scooped a handful of uncooked rice into her mouth and was eating it noisily.

Wodeman sighed. Of course, he should have known: there was never any getting away from it. His four dream-spells for guiding Bolldhe were done, and now his continued presence here was next to useless. But there was still one thing he could do, *had* to do. One final spell he could cast—perhaps his most powerful.

But could he really do that? After all they had suffered together, and all they had taken from him, it would be the basest betrayal imaginable. But also, the very definition of sacrifice.

The north. Fate's domain. Just as iron is drawn in its direction, or migrating wyverns are guided by its pull, so too do Fate's iron chains pull tighter on men's lives. It is said that the farther a man goes north, the greater the influence of Fate. This maxim was known by people of every region, realm, race, or religion in Lindormyn.

And here today, in this little hut, stood Fate. It did not have to be there, of course; it already knew what would happen, what *had* to happen. But it liked to be there anyway. just to watch. Fate was like that: assured, some said, and more than a tad conceited. So there it stood in the storehouse, its grey robes hanging stiff and starched as a high priest's cope, wearing that engraved stone tablet suspended as ever on a black chain round its neck.

It could never be proved, of course, but there were those who claimed the words inscribed upon Fate's token read: "*Told You So.*"

But Zhang knew nothing of Fate. He was a horse. All he knew in his simple animal brain was that it was bloody cold in here, and the food was crap. He wished they could go to a warmer place, with *grass* and proper smells, and he fervently hoped they were not going to stay here forever. Zhang was naturally glad to get in out of the weather's worst excesses, and he was unutterably grateful for the chance of a rest; nevertheless, he ardently wished his friend were here now instead of these two. Who the breeder was he could not guess—she did not smell too good, which made him jittery. Even the red, friendly one was behaving very oddly at the moment. Usually he was nice; he understood Zhang, gave him things he liked when he wanted them, and made him feel better when things were not right. But Zhang had not at all liked those lights and noises just now, and it was his view that the red one ought to make it up to him somehow.

Ah, here he came now—and he was holding something in one hand. The other he lifted to stroke Zhang's muzzle, and pat him firmly on the neck. Yes, this was more like it. Good old red one pressed his hairy face against Zhang's long snout, and breathed his moist human air into the Adt-T'man's nostrils.

Still the stroking continued, moving round to his withers, soft and luxurious, sending a slight shudder along the little horse's flanks. Closer now, the human's face was pushed against his muzzle. Ah, this was *nice,* this he could really get into—

NAY!

A searing slash of pain ripped across his throat, and suddenly the air was bright with the smell of hot blood. Lots of it. His blood. *Nay!* What was happening? What . . .

. . . The red one! It was the red one! What had he done? *What had he done!* Zhang whinnied in fear and pain, and staggered backwards on legs that were suddenly so weak. The red one had done something awful . . . He was not his friend after all . . . Zhang wanted his real friend . . .

But where was he? He must come back instantly and put things right. Now! Now *stop the world spinning . . .*

Weaker still, his legs folded beneath him, and he sank to the floor. He felt the flagstones smack sharply against the side of his face. But there was little pain now . . . just dull confusion, a sense of betrayal, and fear.

He felt a pool of warm wetness against his cheek, and the smell of his blood was stronger. But the light began to dim from bright orange to dark red, and everything became blurred.

Where was his friend?

The last thing Zhang saw, as that circle of red light contracted, was a pair of little stone things with scratches on them; the things that the bad one had thrown against the wall.

They stared at him, faceup.

But Zhang could not read them.

The Beast was Dead.

9

Down in the Ground Where the Dead Ones Walk

"Stop horsing around, Wodeman, and tell us what you've done!"

Wodeman was back inside the Tomb, deprived of his sky, his earth, of light, the very air, even of some normal sense of time. The graffiti scrawls of dementia seemed to be dancing ever more insanely upon the walls: he was scared, exhausted, and his guilt felt like a skeleton under the floorboards, an old sin he thought well hidden. And like those dirty bones, he prayed this terrible crime would remain so, and not be discovered by the nag's unhappy owner.

Wodeman almost wished that he had never made it this far, but had instead died up there somewhere on the ice. What had at first seemed a terrible necessity, now just seemed terrible. In fact, here in the unreality of Vaagenfjord Maw, he began to wonder whether he had actually committed the dreadful deed at all. But the horse's blood was still wet upon his face, its reek like the putrefaction of his own soul. And, try as he might, he could not deny what he had done.

"Wodeman!" Finwald said firmly. "We don't mind doing this if it makes you feel better. At this moment, we're frankly not even interested in what purpose it serves. All we want to know is where did you get it from? Whose blood is it?"

Only a little of Zhang's blood had he used on himself; he had needed its power straightaway to grant him the strength to reenter the Maw, to descend into the clay, into that black place where all life ended. The rest of the blood he had brought along for his comrades.

Most of the vocal, somatic or material components of the sorcerer's spells were of more symbolic significance than anything else. This fact he knew for himself. But the spell he had performed at the storehouse, his final spell, had nothing to do with symbolic gestures. No placebo this, for the blood sacrifice of a loved one—and Zhang truly had become loved, respected and valued almost above all others during the crossing of Melhus—could render real, palpable, physical power to those who accepted it, those who smeared its life-force upon their faces. For they would be wearing it as their oblation to the gods, their defiance of the enemy. Those who had made this sacrifice—and that included all here, for it was their loss—would be granted by Erce a bounty of vigor, stamina, mental focus, and courage the like of which no amount of months-old frozen food, Peladanic oratory, or thin Cunaistic prayers could supply.

He had done it for them—for the whole world, if it came to that. And if he now felt sick with guilt and sorrow for the Adt-T'man he had personally betrayed, that was his burden to bear.

"What have you done with the Quiravienne, the woman?" demanded the Peladane.

"Nothing!" Wodeman protested. "This blood is mine. It is my sacrif—"

But he then caught sight of Bolldhe, and could not finish the sentence.

"What I *meant,*" Nibulus went on, regarding the shaman doubtfully, "is have you taken care of her, made sure she's warm, safe, got food?"

"She's fine," Wodeman blurted out, conscious of how monumentally unconvincing he must sound. "As fine as can be expected, anyway. And I gave her back her falchion for protection." This was awful, Wodeman thought. No, not awful, *unbearable.* Was it not bad enough that he had committed the worst betrayal of his life, without piling lie upon lie like this? For even now in his guilt, he could not suppress the notion that if the madwoman had her falchion back, it would be that much easier to frame her for the horse's death.

"We're wasting our time," Bolldhe cut in. "Look, just give the bloody stuff here, and let's get on!"

The shaman watched in nauseous fascination as Bolldhe tipped a few drops of his own horse's blood out of Wodeman's waterskin, and unceremoniously daubed it across his face.

"There!" he said, handing it on to the others. "Happy now?"

"Never felt better," Wodeman croaked, and on into the Maw they all continued.

How dark can dark become? How absolute is absolute? And if darkness can be absolute, what lies beyond that? This the company were now to discover as they continued down ever deeper into the Maw.

"I thought you said we were supposed to be heading upward!" Bolldhe hissed in a vexation of ill-concealed fear. "Up to the Chamber of Drauglir!"

"That's what they all think," Nibulus replied without slowing. "But unless you want to end up like the rest of them—that madwoman or her pretty, dead friends—you'll ignore hearsay and concentrate on what *I* say. Or, rather, what the book says."

This sermon truly annoyed Bolldhe. Their leader guarded that damn chronicle jealously, never letting anyone else in on its secrets. *Typical Peladane,* he thought in exasperation. *Always like to hold the keys to heaven . . . or hell.*

They were already alarmingly deep inside the Maw. Countless halls, chambers, and passageways they had passed through. Past long-abandoned kitchens and through soldiers' living quarters with their endless ranks of stone sleeping platforms, empty now yet still ringing faintly with the chink of bronze upon stone; between the breeding pits for fat-rich seals, filled now with black, stagnant water and the ghost-echoes of underwater voices; and sneaking swiftly past the numerous shrines of Olchor, and other such places of punishment where the vats had long ago been drained and the fires gone out, but where the air was still rank with the stench of blood and heavy with the blackness of torture.

Down, ever down . . .

But Finwald was in accord with their leader. "I myself have studied manuscripts hinting at such: to go inward, one must go *down*."

So down they had gone, down a long tunnel, a particularly low-ceilinged and narrow tunnel, tube-like and winding, which gave the explorers the impression they were slipping down some gigantic artery leading to the heart of a monstrous beast. Or even, judging by the smell that proliferated the further they descended, to its bowels.

Gwyllch's chronicle spoke of a number of such tunnels, many of which had been used by the Peladane scouts and light infantry to gain swifter entry to the places deeper in. Using these tunnels meant that those soldiers of long ago had bypassed the worst of the fighting, and thus had arrived at the inner reaches hours before the main force. This also meant, of course, that they were the first to get themselves slaughtered by the dreadful denizens that lurked within, but as Gwyllch blithely noted:

"*. . . you cann't hav yore kaikke and eate itte.*"

This sinuous artery finally opened out into a large place. A very large place. Though there were still no echoes nor any movement of air, they could nevertheless sense an enormous space about them. Indeed, they appeared to have arrived at the lip of some immense pit. Bolldhe's lantern, even set on narrow beam, illuminated nothing down there beyond the encompassing wall of the abyss, and they all knew instinctively that, wherever it was that they had come to, it must surely now be the lowest, deepest place in the whole of Vaagenfjord Maw—well below even the level of the sea.

From this pit rose the most sickening, life-draining fetor that any of them had ever been forced to breathe. It was as though the earth, no longer able to contain the vileness of its deepest, darkest secret, had broken the crust of its millennia-old, scabbed-over plague pits to disgorge the pestilential decay therein. Down there it lay, stretching away like some vast subterranean lake, and down there they had to go.

A series of crumbling stairways, flue-like chutes, and sheer drops (for which Elfswith's ropes and hooks proved necessary) eventually brought the men, coughing and retching, to the very bottom of the pit. And it was here, down where the air itself seemed compressed by the weight of so much rock above them, that they found out what lies on the other side of absolute darkness.

It was a kind of anti-light; not merely an absence of light, but a negative force that actually drained much of the illumination from their feeble torches. Even Bolldhe's lantern was next to useless, as its faint gleam, thin as watery milk, bled away from it in trailing wisps.

"Stay very close together," the Peladane commanded, his voice sounding strange and barely audible, "and keep your left hand always on the wall. If this place is the Trough—the Moghol—that Gwyllch writes about, then we need to follow it for about an hour or so. Do that, and then we'll almost be at the inner keep."

They waded, knee-deep, through water now, an oily, brackish stuff that tried ever to hold them or suck them under, and which left a crusty, slightly wriggling deposit upon their breeches. The hems of their cloaks and furs trailed behind them heavily, getting clogged with the scum that floated upon the surface, and with nearly every other step they stumbled on things that crunched beneath their boots and issued bubbles of evil gas.

Despite their dread, the company was surprised to find they had the fortitude to persevere. Perhaps Wodeman's mysterious blood-spell was proving efficacious after all. For this place was surely the worst by far that any of them had chanced upon in their entire lives. They did not merely feel as if buried alive in some ancient crypt in a necropolis; this was far deeper, more primordial, as though they had tunneled their way down to the lowest level of the underworld itself, the uttermost Abode of the Dead. Like the shades of the departed that wander bodiless through the labyrinth of hell, they appeared to each other ill-defined and not quite real, and all they could hear above the swirl of water was their own breath, increasingly labored as dark fear and the weight of the island above pressed in on them.

Time stretched out, distorted, and still they strove on. Each of them began to feel, insidiously pervading their reason, an unspoken fear that they were not alone down here. At first, the unsure wheeze of each other's breathing was all that they had been aware of, but now it seemed that the exhalations of others were joining them, and the farther they walked, the more breathing they could hear. It could have been an echo of their own, but that would be impossible in such leaden air.

It was undoubtedly the voices of the dead, awakened to animation by the breathing of the living, and responding in mimicry. They were all around them, following them, *joining* them.

And below that, the almost subsonic breathing of something so much larger—something monstrous, something so much deeper, which wrapped itself around them, penetrating armor and clothes, sunk into the pores and shivered under their skin.

From here there could be no point in turning back, so on they trudged, doggedly placing one foot in front of the other, blanking out their fears, wild imaginings, hearing, even consciousness. On and on through the Dead Place. At times came the ghosts of sounds from a distance that was impossible to judge. The squeaking of . . . bats? No, not bats, more like metal joints—or sometimes a heavier squeaking like the sound of poleaxes being dragged across a stone floor because they were too heavy to be carried. Sounds that did not make any sense in this submerged world.

At some later time when it began to occur to them that they had been down here too long to ever hope to rejoin the living, Wodeman made a rattling noise in his throat and bade them to halt. They all remained stock-still and listened.

. . . *rap, rappitty-pat-tap, rap-rappitty-pat-tap, rap-rappitty-pat-tap* . . .

The company had been losing all sense of time, all sense of direction, all sense of reality—yet finally the dream-like monotony of their progress was punctuated. For something, at last, was happening.

. . . *rap-rappitty-pat-tap, rap-rappitty-pat-tap, rap-rappitty-pat-tap* . . .

Some kind of drumbeat? Maybe a tattoo . . .

"Nibulus!" Bolldhe whispered, high-pitched with fear. "Does your book have anything to say about . . . that?"

But no answer came back to him. Nibulus, like all of them, stayed motionless and silent. For an age, it felt, the company stood there, reluctant to speak, even to think. As before, they blanked out all imaginings, but to doggedly place one foot before the other was now no longer an option. All they could do was stand and listen.

Bolldhe carefully raised a hand to his face to wipe away the sweat that clogged his eyebrows. As he did so, his fingers brushed against the blood smeared on his brow. Wodeman's blood. *Mad old hermit, did he really imagine it would make any difference here?*

Then, for no apparent reason, into his mind trotted the image of his horse. He could smell the beast's muskiness, feel that congenial shoving—gentle but insistent—of his muzzle against Bolldhe's shoulder in the mornings—the warm glow of Zhang, his only true friend in the world.

Thank Fate or Chance you're safely out of this, old mate, he thought as he stood knee-deep in foul water, eyes straining through the darkness, while listening to sounds that should not be there.

The others of the company, too, found themselves thinking of Zhang, of his playful affection, his sense of humor; the companion who would never betray them, and had been their strength and inspiration out on the ice field.

The sheer character of that tough little beast! But above all, they recalled the way he would never, ever, give up, but would forge on resolutely, until death took him.

As one, their fingers moved to touch the blood Wodeman had marked them with and, though they knew not why, a new strength infused them. In this, their hour of deepest fear, they could all draw upon this new seed of courage, and once again push on one step at a time. Even Appa was revitalized, helped along with Finwald's hand for support.

Now Bolldhe began to understand what made their little party so unique, why they alone would succeed where all others had failed. They had Nibulus with his chronicle, Finwald with his years of research, and now Wodeman's strange gift of blood. How many other questing groups had ever possessed even one of these advantages?

But it was not to last. Closer still the drumbeat sounded, until suddenly Wodeman let out a small croak and pointed ahead. The company stared through disbelieving eyes as a whole line of figures swam into view.

It was blacker than black down here, yet they were aureoled in a pale, spectral luminosity that surrounded them like a gas lamp in the fog: a column of soldiers marching toward them. Tattered robes were worn proudly over armor that still gleamed between rips, punctures, and dark, viscid smears. Singed beards and ragged, greasy hair had been roughly combed and straightened, and a fierce light smoldered in their tired eyes. Now the slow, stirring melody of their song could be heard, but sounded muffled by the deadness of this Trough or the passing of centuries beneath the water. Their feet, though trampling ankle-deep through water, made only the hollow sound of hobnailed leather clumping upon dry stone, and caused no ripples.

As they came closer, the sighs of the Dead rose all around them as a troubled and babbling chorus. Closer still, now louder of song and brighter of eye. Then abruptly the head of the column turned and began to march toward the wall. One by one the lost patrol disappeared through the rocky side of the Trough and as each one vanished, dimmer glowed their aureole and quieter became their song.

But the sighing of the Dead did not hush; indeed it grew stronger, more urgent, *hungrier*, as each ghostly soldier faded into the wall of rock. Finally, there was but one left of them: one disagreeable man-at-arms who had less radiance but more substance. He sought to follow his comrades into their evanescence, but instead smote his helmeted head against the wall with a dull clang and a sharp yelp of pain.

He turned, and eyes that were yellow and inhuman fell upon the six watchers who stood rooted to the spot. A malefic grin twisted his features, and then he came for them.

There was a fluttering of light, a brief confusion of shadows and, with a weak fizzing sound, the lantern went out.

"No! Not now," Bolldhe whined in his own tongue, and frantically pumped the xienne rod to rekindle the flame. But the fuel, it seemed, had run out.

"Find another xienne stick," Appa gasped. But it was far too late for that.

"Charge!" roared the Peladane, released at last from his limbo of stillness, and stormed ahead. Unable either to turn back or stay, there was only one way now to go. Without a sliver of vacillation his men sprang after him. Whereupon the howling cacophony of the Moghol erupted around them.

Just as fish will rise from the stagnant depths of a pond on a midge-filled summer's evening, the Dead were coming up to feed.

Appa was the first, he who—as the oldest—was closest to them. In bug-eyed terror he let out a childlike squeal, as clawed, steel-hard hands lunged out of the mire to fasten in his bearskin. He was swung round and almost yanked off his feet, as the Dead tried to pull him under, but at the last moment Finwald managed to catch hold of one arm. Still the deathly hands would not let go, and though heaving with all his might, there was nothing Finwald could do to stop them dragging the screaming priest down among them.

Shadowy faces, barely visible, came at them from out of the darkness, bodies reared up in fountains of vile black water with savage, hacking bellows, and amid the screams of despair from both priests, Paulus appeared from behind. With a casual backswing he passed his blade through the wrists of the clutching hands, severing them with surgical precision even in the dark.

He did not stop to offer further help, but neither did the priests tarry, for the Dead were exploding from the water all around. In and out of their vision flashed nightmare images as torches were swung about as wildly as weapons. The cries of the hunted, the wailing of the Dead, the fury of the seething water: through all this mayhem the travelers fled for their lives.

With a torch brandished in his left hand, and his right hand holding Unferth over his shoulder, Nibulus charged. Two ghoulish faces that were almost all mouth lunged at him. Without hesitation, he jammed his torch into the mouth of one with such force it punched clean through the back of its skull. At the other he lashed out with one iron-capped boot, and even in the absence of any light now it fortunately connected, hurling the snapped cadaver back through the air to splinter against the wall. With both hands free now, though totally blind, Nibulus plunged on through the Trough, scything his greatsword before him like a threshing machine.

Though not sure which direction he was heading, all his men could do was follow the sound of his charge, and hope that by some miracle Bolldhe could fumble a new xienne-rod into the lantern while simultaneously floundering ahead as fast as he could move.

Of all of them, Wodeman probably had the least difficulty. The moment they were attacked, instinct took control and he was at last freed from fear. The animal finding itself trapped is then at its most dangerous, and the wolf-man fought tooth and claw, not even thinking of the tulwar dangling uselessly from his hemp belt. Where his eyes could not see, his other senses took over, and in a snake-quick, frenzied dance of flailing limbs and head-butts he ducked, dodged, sidestepped, and swerved his way after the charging Peladane.

Whether Fate or Chance held any sway in the underworld was a question debated by philosophers for centuries. But it felt as if *something* was on their side that day, for, beyond all expectation, the company from the south emerged from the Moghol, in one piece.

Even in his blind panic, Bolldhe managed to realize that luck would favor impetuosity only so long. He slowed himself down long enough to slide a fresh recharge of xienne out of his belt pouch and into the lanten's aperture. Pumping fast, he soon had it lit again and shone it ahead—the only direction he was interested in.

Among the vague forms that lumbered through the anti-light, his desperate gaze picked out his companions, rapidly receding before him—and he pelted after them. They had managed to do as ordered and keep to the wall, so were soon all together again within the lantern-light, and heading in the direction they wanted to be going.

With the moans of the Dead slipping farther behind them, the darkness gradually seemed to become thinner. It was not that they could see anything beyond the radius of the lantern, but just that the *negative* light seemed less potent here. As did the stench.

Also, the water level was gradually subsiding.

About an hour later they emerged from the sucking ooze, and at last beheld, like a beacon high above them, a shaft of orange light: Smaulka-Degernerth, the great Hall of Fire.

They had come to the end of the Moghol.

Dolen Catscaul brushed away the single red tear that welled in her eye, and bit hard on her grey lower lip.

Steady, old girl, she scolded herself mentally, as she fought to keep control. *No time for weakness, now.*

With a show of finality and purpose (that was as unconvincing to her companions as it was to herself) she slid both of her knives into their scabbards, hoisted her pack onto her shoulders, and stood ready to go.

There was a subdued and serious air throughout the chamber as the thieves went about their preparations. Calmly and efficiently they checked their equipment, made sure everything was in its correct place, and fastened things down. All this without fuss or dalliance. The stony room, cramped and unventilated, smelled strongly of sweat and rustled quietly with the hushed to-ing and fro-ing of the adventurers. In the light from the various torches and lanterns, their huge and distorted shadows moved upon the walls and ceiling like demons going about their dreadful business.

But the Dhracus's heart was not in it. She had left that back in Eotunlandt with the blood-drained shell of her swain.

Eggledawc! she wept inwardly. Why was she still here, with these strangers, now that he was gone?

With a mental discipline few humans would possess, she went through three seconds of breathing exercises, then calmly pushed the weighty lump of her tragedy down, far down inside her, and was in perfect control once more.

Swiftly and methodically she cast her black eyes over her fellows, appraising them. They were not such a bad lot, really, she told herself. Since that tragic day in Eotunlandt they had changed somehow, had behaved differently toward her. Whereas previously they would keep their distance, these days they would often come forward to offer their help. This was especially noticeable during that long, horrendous crossing of the island, and Dolen was touched by their unexpected thoughtfulness. She had had no shortage of offers to warm her body with theirs. Indeed, it seemed to her that they had almost been fighting among themselves to get close to her. . . .

Her thoughts were interrupted by a sudden harsh voice.

"Right, are we all ready?" demanded Eorcenwold, while his sister AFinwald snapped a dozen dragon's teeth, one by one, into the appropriate hoops in his bandoleer. He looked his company over. They were ready, of course, as always. For they were Tyvenborgers.

"Good, then let's get on with it. We've got a lot of ground to cover."

He folded his big hand firmly over AFinwald's shoulder. "All right, sis?" he asked. She nodded solidly, unmasking none of the fear that threatened to snap her nerves like a jib-stay, and returned his gesture. As any true sister of Eorcenwold should.

He turned back to his men. "Remember, that place down there'll probably be like nothing we've ever imagined, and we'll doubtless find some pretty weird stuff, one way or another. But don't you be letting it get to you—there's nothing alive here anymore, nothing which can hurt you. Apart from the traps. So stay close to me and Brecca. Stay *alert* and for Nokk's sake don't get jumpy, all right?"

Dolen's face was a mask, chalk-white and without expression, as she listened to the words of their leader. But she had been watching the other thieves as they readied themselves for the descent—sharpening their blades, practicing fighting moves, securing shield and armor; if there truly was "nothing alive here anymore," then what exactly were they preparing for?

But there was no time to ponder that now. His morning star held ready, Eorcenwold was heading over to the arched tunnel that dropped down through the stony bulk of Ravenscairn, The others parted to let him pass, looked each other in the eye without speaking.

"Klijjver," he ordered, "you're behind me. Let's go."

"It's getting hotter," Brecca repined in that fussy little midget-Haug voice of his. "I tell you, it's getting—"

"Hotter, yes, we know." Oswiu cut him off. "If Khuc's sketch is right, we're probably about five minutes away from the greatest caveful of white-hot volcano juice in Lindormyn—of course it's getting hotter!"

Brecca the Stone-Hauger became very silent. He kept close to Eorcenwold's side, and scanned the surfaces of walls, ceiling, and floor as they made their progress on down the tunnel. In the narrow and stifling confines of the passage, moods were turning acetic, one might even say waspish, and Brecca's somewhat self-evident observations were not being well received. He scraped his noduled fingers around his neck beneath his hood, and flicked a spray of salty sweat against the wall beside him.

"Eorcenwold," he hissed, "it really is getting—"

The leader silenced him with one sharply raised finger. "Not another word," he hissed. "Eyes open, mouth shut . . . unless you spot any traps."

Brecca was confused, but did not wish to risk further contempt, admonishment, or death threats by asking questions. Did Eorcenwold want him to shut his eyes if he saw a trap, he wondered.

Within minutes, however, he had no need to concern himself with informing his companions about the heat, for even to Brecca it became obvious they must all know by now. Rounding a bend in the tunnel, they reeled back as a wave of heat swept over them, filling their lungs with unwholesome fumes and causing every one of them to cough and retch. It was as if someone had just hauled open the doors of a blast furnace.

Without waiting to be told, the thieves reached into their pockets and each pulled forth a mask. The *topengk* was a marvelously well crafted and wonderfully light, padded mask of silk and voile that entirely covered mouth and nose, filtering all noxious vapors yet allowing the wearer to breathe freely. With these firmly in place, the thieves pulled their hoods tightly about their heads, and pressed on.

The dull red glow brightened to a livid orange, the temperature soared, and minutes later they emerged from the tunnel onto the unsheltered upper ledge. Like Khuc before them, they had arrived at Smaulka-Degernerth.

Little did they see of that infernal, subterranean cauldron; they were not here to admire the view. This was thieving at its most extreme, and the frisson of the situation was like an electric whipcord across the back or a baluchitherium-goad up the behind. They all knew exactly what they had to do, and wasted not one second in doing it. Piton hammers, pegs, and ropes were produced in a trice, lines were hammered in and secured swiftly and efficiently, rock surfaces were scrutinized adeptly, and without a moment's delay, Grini the Boggart was harnessed up and swung bodily over the edge.

As the lightest, most agile and above all most dispensable member of their party, Grini had been volunteered for the heroic task of locating the ledge at the top of the flue, and securing a line to it. What had not been foreseen was that, as the hairiest member of the party, he was also the one most likely to combust. Luckily however, it was only a slightly singed (though more than slightly hysterical) Grini who achieved the applauded task of locating the handholds that Khuc had painstakingly chronicled five hundred years previously. Growling, and salivating profusely, the hirsute little homunculus succeeded in a remarkably brief amount of time in scrambling over to the other side.

A tug on his end of the rope told the others he had now fastened it, and one by one, with a safety rope harnessing them, the thieves followed him. As they scrambled along, they too sweated abundantly; for to them, clinging onto the jagged rock face, this whole place felt as if it were alive, a gigantic, quaking monster that sent its anger and heat and hatred in diabolic pulses through the trembling stone. Rapidly but dextrously the thieves made their way around the burning rock face to the ledge where Grini awaited them.

Not wasting a second, they almost dived into the darkness of a tunnel: the same flue that Scathur had used to escape his pursuers all those centuries ago.

And, almost too good to believe, it was all just as Khuc had promised. There were the great stone blocks above them, re-set by the Peladanes into their cavities in the tunnel roof. Over there was the "crafty mechanism" by which Scathur had set them in motion. And there, leading down at a slight angle, was the open passageway that would lead them, if their luck continued this way, to the Chamber of Drauglir itself.

Farther along the tunnel they plunged, gratefully gasping in the cooler air within.

Chink-chink-chink.

The faint sound of boot upon rung gradually increased within the Chamber. It stopped. Voices, hushed but urgent, whispered down the flue. A light flickered erratically, shyly, wanting to discover but not be discovered. Slowly it descended, until it could be identified as a lamp dangling at the end of a rope, its beam turning in random circles around the Chamber.

A few dislodged granules of powdered stone drifted down, like a light dusting of snow on a winter's eve. It was followed by a sparkling, bauble-bright mirror of polished silver attached to a long telescopic rod. This, the Eye of Tyvenborg, took up position by the lamp, following the beam's every turn.

After a while a hooded head, small as a child's but wrinkled as an old man's, appeared upside down, and eyes wide with wonder peered into the Chamber.

"No one's home!" hissed Brecca.

Seconds later the much larger head of Eorcenwold appeared beside it, also upside down; and this was followed by the even larger head of Klijjver, the Tusse's small iron cap still clamped fast upon his huge pate.

With an adroit twist, Eorcenwold landed feet first upon the floor, followed quickly by Brecca, and then the herd-giant. Despite their ungainly appearance, each one dropped as lightly as a snowflake. The area immediately by the shaft's emergence was swiftly scanned by expert eyes and, at a word from their leader, more lights descended from the flue, each in the grip of a thief, and began spreading outward into the hall. A weapon was held ready in each thief's other hand.

A gradually widening area of floor was checked for traps, but with a speed and efficiency that did not allow time for any fearful thoughts to gain hold. The Thieves of Tyvenborg were professionals, here to do a job they would not abandon unless confronted with an extremely persuasive reason.

But in spite of such adeptness, each one of them could not suppress the notion that they perhaps should not be so deep within the Maw. The Chamber of Drauglir was not for such as they. Religion hung heavy in the air, reeking of blood and the fires of hell, and every thieving step they took upon its marble floor was a sacrilege against both good and evil.

There was a definite presence: perhaps the evil that had once dwelt here yet remained, permeated into the stone itself, too potent to ever dissipate. Or perhaps it was the assembled souls of all those who had suffered and died here.

Dolen was the first to feel it. For her, it was the strongest. The prescience of her race, the Dhracus, could not be blinkered by the orders of her leader. She stood apart from her companions, her torch limp in her hand, as images and emotions from the past flowed in thick, crimson rivulets into her gaping mind.

There heaped before her were people-piles, men reduced to slabs of living, screaming meat. There also stood Scathur, offering up this mangled sacrifice of human bodies and human minds, his eyes sightless in shuddering rapture as he uttered the words of his subjugation to the master. His language was mushroom-flavored, his musings poppy-wrought, the shower of bursting flesh as sweet as fragrant rain upon his face. To him the ruin of men was an intoxication both infernal and divine, their clamorous supplication as sweet as the pipes, beauteous as the harp. Human-stuff—flesh, liquid, sound, and soul—he proffered, collapsed onto his knees now, arms outstretched and dripping, gazing glassy-eyed up the marbled ziggurat that pulsed with dark, abysmal power.

Dolen could not bring herself to follow that gaze upward, for she knew something lurked at the utmost pinnacle of that altar, something of such monstrous evil that, were she to behold it, would melt her brain like candlewax.

Instantly she snapped back to the present.

"Eorcenwold," she called out, as calmly as she could. "I think we'd better leave this place. Right now."

Thus, for the first time in five hundred years, was the Chamber of Drauglir breached. And abandoned, too, with quite surprising haste. The thieves had no need of the Dhracus's prescience to sense the clinging vestiges of evil that floated like gossamer in the air.

In any case, they had no reason to linger here, for they had finally reached Ymla-Myrrdhain, the inner keep, and had only to find the secret places the Peladanes had missed last time, then ransack this sanctum of all its valuables.

Without further delay, the Tyvenborgers slipped out of the door.

Out of the fog of late afternoon the longship came drifting. Barely a sound could be heard as it glided down the fjord. Like the half-submerged remains of the broken vessels, locked in their icy graves all around, its simple sail hung limp, and upon its deck not a soul moved, nor from its rowlocks any oar heaved. Less noise even than those creaking wrecks it made and, in the grey half-light, of less substance did it appear. As neatly as a scalpel slices a fish, its dragon-throated prow furled back the scum of ice that clogged the water, until neatly, almost ceremonially, it slid into anchor beside the wharf.

At about the same time as Bolldhe and his companions were fleeing the Moghol, Scathur set foot once more upon the rock of Melhus. The merest pressure of his boots splintered the ice beneath them, melting it and turning it yellow with sulphur. Eyes aflame with incendiary malevolence, and fingers tightened around the haft of his Bardische, he surveyed the area swiftly, then rapped the pole twice upon the ground.

Only then did his silent crew stir to life. Needing no verbal orders, the Wire-Faces furiously set about their task of unloading the containers of pickled people. Casks, crates, barrels, bunkers, pitchers, and puncheons, all were lowered onto the dock and dragged off toward the hungry mouth of the waiting Maw. The Children of the Keep, squealing and jabbering, swung from ratline and brace or leapt down from the masthead. Some sprang over the gunwales and skittered over the ice, to spread out across the dock. Others took up position guarding the paths that wound up into the cliffs. A few remained on the ship.

Scathur stood silently by, overseeing the operation, saying nothing. He was leaving the Children behind to guard this only exit from the Maw, should any humans try to double back and escape. His Wire-Faces he was taking with him: half of them to drag the pickled people to the Moghol, and then tip them into the Urn. The rest would go on ahead with him and hunt the enemy.

He could probably do it himself alone, of course. But there was always a chance the enemy had come prepared for him, might prove too much for him. If there was one lesson his defeat that last time had taught him, it was to always be prepared for the worst. The Wire-Faces that he had brought along should be enough, he deemed. But even if they were not, he had his backup behind him in the form of the Dead. There was an entire legion waiting in the Trough already, and there would be even more once the Urn was emptied.

And if even they were still not enough, there was always Lubang-Nagar and its guardian. No one had ever got past that one.

Scathur pursed his swollen lips, and slid his tongue out to taste the air. There was blood on it. Fresh blood . . . but it was not human. He scoured the harbor with his eyes . . .

And located the storehouse. Its door lay open, swinging slightly in the breeze. He sniffed hard, and then smelled it: human sweat, fear-enriched and sweet with promise. *Female* sweat, too—that would be a novelty: breeders made a different noise altogether, and it was one not displeasing to his ears.

Noiselessly he paced over to the little hut, and disappeared within.

10

Disgorg'd 'Pon Our Rankes an Ichor So Foulle

"As the stagges who, inne a lyne, reste thieyr chinns 'pon eche othres' rumpe to cross the rivver, soe too didde eche of us hav neede to suport hys commrayde for alle to sirvyve. Lernyng allso from the beests that didde huddel togethyr agaynst the eis-stormes, we then cam togethyr inne lynes three deepe, the outer lyne holdyng sheeldes agaynst the fyr, while thieyr commraydes maid swyft thieyr way to the iner keep. And wen we were assayl'd from the Hel-Houndes that from the fyr cam, why, those brayve menne on the out-syde simplie felle, and felle in legeons, for littel combat could ther be inne that heet. And inne fallyng they did bild a walle of slayne, a dyk of ded agaynst the flammes . . ."

"So that's the plan, is it?" said Bolldhe, as Nibulus concluded the latest chapter from the Chronicle. "I could be wrong, but I'd hazard a guess that Bloodnose had *considerably* more men than *six* . . . Exactly how many volunteers did you want to fall in legions?"

Nibulus wiped his face with his Ulleanh and tried to blink the sweat from his eyes. The heat was quite unbelievable; in his armor he felt he was being poached in his own juices, like a lobster in a pot.

The climb from the Moghol had been dreadful, and despite the horse-strength that they unwittingly drew from their slain Zhang, it was with the direst dismay that the company clambered up the last slope of the Trough to approach Smaulka-Degernerth, the great Hall of Fire. From blackness, cold, and fear, they had come to the ovens of hell, and panic gripped them as they struggled to breathe.

Appa had wailed in despair upon beholding the infernal place they had reached. A cavern immeasurable it was, a subterranean realm of bewildering, god-like proportions, a living tunnel scooped from earth's bowels by the ancient wars of leviathans, where cold grey stone had become green-black glass in the heat of the white-hot torrent that poured through it. The roof was lost somewhere way up there amid a smog of churning gases and emissions. Towering, ribbed walls, curving away out of sight into whatever terrible abyss lay beyond, gleamed with a vitreous sheen; melted, fragmented, folded, and contorted into shapes that appeared to scream in torment after eons of fire.

They stood upon a wide ledge like a road running around the outer rim of this immense cavern tunnel. It was wide enough to drive three carts along, side by side, but the innermost edge, farthest from the wall, was crumbling and treacherous, as if shrinking away from the trench of magma that ran beneath it. Even here, still at the entrance, the ground beneath their feet quaked as if they stood above some gigantic, entombed god who struggled in perpetual anguish. Geysers of molten rock constantly spouted from the river of fire, clouds of toxic gases spiraled like foul efreets, and flares of orange, red and white light seared their eyeballs.

"Oh come on, Bolldhe," Nibulus shouted. "At least there are no hell-hounds to assail us."

So on they went, leaving the Trough of the Dead behind them, to staunchly face whatever fresh peril this hall of fire might hold in store for them. Of all of them, only Appa now still wore his bearskin.

Steadily they marched, for neither haste nor delay was possible in that heat. They kept as close to the wall side as they could, shrinking away from the fiery Trough below and hugging what meager shadow was provided. The rock itself was too hot to touch with the bare hand, though they longed to collapse against it for support.

Their gear became an increasing burden, and they ached to hurl down their weapons, which weighed heaviest upon them. But nothing more could be safely left behind now. No one spoke, nor even opened their mouths for fear of swallowing more of those hot gases. A slowly rising panic began to enfold them, and both sickness and claustrophobia tightened their grasp. But still they trudged on, for it was either continue or die.

After just one hour of this terrible trek, Appa could stand it no longer. He tore off his besodden bearskin and hurled it to the ground. Underneath, his grey cloak was heavy with sweat, which now began to steam. He cried out in anguish, in part because his bared arms began to blister, but also because it seemed to him that he had willingly walked into the realm of the Evil One, and would languish in the agony of burning for all eternity. Hastily he rolled down his sleeves against the furnace-like glare, then scurried ahead of them in a fit of reckless hysteria.

"Leave him!" ordered Nibulus. "He won't get far."

Sure enough, minutes later they caught up with the old man, collapsed facedown upon the obsidian road, unconscious.

"Any of your blood left, Wodeman," Nibulus inquired.

"A little," the shaman rasped, "though I had hoped to keep it, till we reached the final place."

"We won't reach anywhere unless we have it now," Bolldhe choked. "C'mon, just give it here!"

Wodeman extracted the waterskin from beneath his pelts, and very carefully measured out a ration of blood for each companion, squeezing it drop by drop into their desperate, outstretched palms. They daubed themselves like ravenous beggars, and once again grew calm. Finwald smeared some of his share on Appa's brow before applying it to his own, and once they had all received the secret blessing of Zhang, Wodeman managed to rip open the waterskin and wipe a last smear from its inside onto the old priest's mouth.

Appa, regaining consciousness, was raised to his feet and after a pause, plodded on ahead of the company.

This is ridiculous! Gapp fumed as he dragged his aching bones up the stairs. *Completely stupid! Can't they see that? We're a hundred-strong, and yet we follow that . . .* thing *up into Flipp-knows-where! What is he now anyway, other than a wet shell of dying skin? He shouldn't by rights be even able to stand up, let alone force his way up these steps!*

After they had sufficiently recovered from Jagt's little jest, they had looked around and found they were in a sea cave of sorts. There was no light whatsoever, nor did any of them have any means of making any. It was a treacherous place, a black pit of knife-sharp rock, aggressive crustaceans with pincers as powerful as they were toxic, and slippery slopes that might pitch even the most careful walker into the freezing sea. Because of these hazards, and the utter strangeness of the place, no one had felt much inclined to move, to search for a way out, or do anything but huddle together in mutual protection.

The legion of Cyne-Tregva were only now beginning to find out what such glorious quests really involved, and clearly they were enjoying this their first adventure as little as Gapp was.

So once again the entire company was obliged to put its trust in Methusclech. There was, he informed them, only one exit: a flight of steps that wound steeply upward. It would lead them from the freezing blackness of this cave up to a wide hall where light and warmth awaited them. No matter how dubious this all sounded to the young Aescal, the Vetters at least were soon right behind the old spook.

So up they all went, one hand holding on to the one in front, the other feeling the wall, and groping their way up blindly. Gapp deliberately lagged behind, preferring to leave at least a dozen Vetters between himself and their soggy leader. Schnorbitz remained at his side always, and behind him he could feel the reassuring presence of the Paranduzes. The slippery steps were narrow, uneven, and each tread worn almost porcelain smooth in the middle. They did not tunnel directly up through the bedrock of the island, but instead seemed to run around the sea cavern's wall, spiraling up higher and higher and higher, till the company felt as if they were scaling the walls of a giant well.

On and on they went, yet the blackness showed no sign of lessening, and before long they were all too cold even to feel anything. Only the sounds reminded them that they were still alive: the constant drumming of velvet-shod or fleshy feet, the occasional slip or slither, an odd grunt as a Cervulus-horn accidentally pricked the buttocks of whoever was in front. And, gradually dwindling below them, they could still hear the muffled rumbling of the sea.

The exhausted boy imagined they sometimes passed beneath arches of rock, and occasionally over bridges. But no matter how far they climbed, it continued to be unrelentingly cold, and dripping, and dark. He did not know how much longer he could keep going like this, and dully wondered how long it would be until he lost his footing through sheer exhaustion or disorientation, and toppled over the edge into the void.

Then something at last broke the monotony.

What the—? What's he doing up there? Is he . . . laughing?

There came, from some place above, one of the most sinister sounds that Gapp had ever heard. It was *like* a laugh but, carried down through the dank air of Hell's Well, it arrived in his ears sounding more like the deranged gurgling of a nocturnal, swamp-prowling lunatic.

It was Xilvafloese, of course, but a Xilvafloese that was losing more and more of himself with each minute that passed.

To be honest, Gapp was hardly in the stablest state of mind himself, but was he really hearing two voices issuing from the one man? It really did sound as if Xilva was now talking in two voices. One was the awful, hollow whisper of the awful, hollow thing he had become; the other was his previous voice, almost as it had sounded back at Wintus Hall. These two voices would call out, whispering urgently as if to something far above them, or at other times would rasp out to the empty void of the stairwell, and, as Gapp believed, would be answered by whatever floated about in that vacuum.

It was weird, so weird. There were sounds coming from everywhere now: the creak of wooden masts, the distant calling of seafarers, a rapid clicking and high-pitched whistling like that of the fabulous marine beasts in U'throst. Yet these did not appear to come from anywhere in particular, and reinforced the boy's conviction that he was losing his mind.

Then the voice called down to him directly, and Gapp's legs finally gave way beneath him. If anything at all around him was real, then that terrible voice must surely belong to Drauglir himself, summoning him to his Chamber.

Caught between the Rawgr and the deep black sea . . .

The sudden stillness of the company all around him confirmed to Gapp that he was not the only one to hear it. Too weak and dithery to protest, he was hauled up the steps by the Vetters, passed from one pair of furry hands to the next, until he found himself breathing in the same foul air that surrounded Methuselech.

"*C'n you ssmell it?*" that disembodied voice whispered, "*the Lake o' Fffire?*"

"Smell?"

"*Br'mssstone,*" it continued. "*The Lake o' Fffire.*"

Gapp, now that he concentrated, found that he could indeed smell something reminding him of fire and sulphur.

"*We nnear the grea' lava-dyke,*" Methuselech hissed, gripping the boy by the shoulder with brittle fingers and propelling him forward. "*Ourr fin'l d'sstina'on . . . where you c'n meet yourr fffrenns once mhorre, an' I c'n fffinissh it once 'nf'ralll!*

"*'Tis herre where Boll' muss come—i' iss the ohhnly way.*"

At the head of his army, Scathur pounded through the gates of Vaagenfjord Maw, his eyes narrowed to slits, steam venting from his nostrils. The shaggy cloak of white fur ruffled listlessly about him as he went, and the Bardische he held in both hands before him, crossways like a quarterstaff.

Damn breeder! he boiled in frustration. *But she can't get far. I'll get her when this is all over, and when I do, I'll turn her inside out!*

The woman, whoever she was, had clearly got wind of his arrival, and had fled the quayside hut before Scathur's ship had even come into harbor. She was probably skulking in one of the artillery caves back along the fjord, if she was not already running for her life up toward the ice field. Scathur had considered sending one of the Children after her, but right now he had more pressing business to attend to, and might have need of every Rawgr, Wire-Face, or dead man available to him.

The Wire-Faces trooped in after their captain, following him into the darkness of the Maw bearing neither lantern nor torch. The freezing sea fog of late afternoon twisted around them and beaded their aprons, stiffened with cold now as well as oil and blood. As ever they moved without words and with only the barest sound of feet slapping upon stone.

Scathur sniffed the air, but did not slow. Without deviation or delay he marched his troop straight up the wide staircase, and on into the narrower confines where the debris of the last pack of thieves still remained. Through this area, with its recent stench of female, they went, and without hesitation plunged on into the inner reaches. The scent of his quarry was easy to follow, for bitter smoke and fear-infused sweat befouled the stony purity of his Master's abode.

The farther they went, though, the more urgent became their pace, for it began to appear that these latest invaders were penetrating to the deeper levels more swiftly than any of the previous raiders. Scathur grew increasingly unsettled. It was clear that this group was not bothering to explore the outer reaches, but was heading instead straight for the heart of the Maw. Had his soul not been so black with hatred, Scathur might have felt a certain twinge of admiration for them. This lot were certainly not messing about. Did they have some inside information?

Soon they were descending into the Moghul itself, and there was a sudden creaking of metallic callipers and a stirring of the black waters as the Dead rose up all about them in the dark, moaning in greeting. Along the Trough, Wrythe's army now waded, and all the time the Dead lurched out to join them and swell their numbers.

But inevitably the Dead fell behind Scathur and his army, for they were slow-moving, and he refused to tarry. The light from the Hall of Fire was even now coming into view, and it was there Scathur knew his quarry would have tried to head. *Not long now*, he thought eagerly. *They must be around here somewhere.*

But they were not. For as Scathur approached the Urn, it became apparent that these new trespassers had actually survived the Moghul! Unutterable curses polluted the dim orange light around him. *They had survived the Trough of the Dead!*

That had never happened before—not once in five hundred years.

The captain of Vaagenfjord Maw was becoming genuinely worried now, and barked out commands for his men to climb more quickly. There could be no delay now. He could not even afford to await the arrival of the emburdened rear guard, and to watch them tip the pickled people into the Urn. And there was certainly no time to stay and witness the emergence of the freshly reanimated dead from its depths. The mysterious enemy could not be far from the tunnel leading to the inner keep by now.

Belching threats of eternal torture at his Wire-Faces, Scathur drove his army as fast as possible on up to Smaulka-Degernerth. With tongues lolling from their open mouths, they hared off in hot pursuit of Bolldhe and his company.

The final stretch of the hunt had begun.

Just as they had spent their first hour in Smaulka-Degernerth, the company persevered, for many long hours. How many hours, they could not tell, for their minds had only enough space to focus on the single task of placing one foot in front of the other. Everything else—their pain, nausea, thirst, exhaustion, even consciousness of who they were and why they were here—was thrust aside.

Yet into their somnambulistic torpor swam now and then images of some gigantic horned devil, some wolf-headed colossus with skin as gleaming and scalding as newly forged iron, which might surely rise from that dread pit of fire immediately to their right, filling the entire hall and reaching out for them inescapably with soot-blackened talons.

But the great hall of Smaulka-Degernerth did not go on forever. Curving imperceptibly but relentlessly around to the right, it did eventually come round nearly full circle and was, in effect, a huge moat that almost entirely surrounded the inner keep of Ymla-Myrrdhain. For that wall of stone that lay just on the other side of the river of fire, that glowing surface of rock which they had first beheld upon entering this mighty cavern, and remained in sight all this time, was in fact the outer wall of Drauglir's central bastion. However, even if a way could be found to cross that wide channel of swiftly flowing liquid stone, there seemed to be nothing on the other side but a blank wall of rock; no opening for doorway or window, no battlements or ledges, not even the meagerest of arrow-slits along its entire length. Just mile after mile of solid, unbreachable rock.

After a time that might well have been measured by the slide of glaciers or the leveling of mountains, a time of pouring sweat, ragged throat and blinded eye, Bolldhe finally lifted his gaze from the smoking toe caps of his boots, and through the black, oily mask that coated his face, stared upon what lay ahead.

The Hall of Fire, this great fissure along which they journeyed deep beneath the earth, came at last to an end.

Through the blinding glare and a blizzard of chemicals, distance and dimension were difficult to gauge, but it seemed to Bolldhe that they had about a mile farther to go before they reached the end. This last stretch saw the ledge they followed begin to narrow slightly, and to gradually slope downward. Closer to the surface of the moat it descended, until both walls of the tunnel curved in toward the other and met, and through a large doorway in this wall, the ledge disappeared and continued into darkness.

The river of fire, running fast and thick along this narrower channel, flowed on through a great archway, and disappeared down a gargantuan chute, like a fiery waterfall descending into the very foundations of Lindormyn.

Bolldhe's soul surged, for he had no heed of what perils might lurk within that dark portal, so glad he was that surcease from this fiery tribulation was at hand. Mouth clamped shut, he shook Nibulus's shoulder roughly and pointed out to him the doorway: a black oblong whose very darkness promised such blissful coolness. Nibulus, too, glanced up, croaked in astonishment, and eagerly waved the company on.

Jolted from their mental stupor, they staggered ahead on this last lap of the race, heedless of all else in their haste to plunge their tortured bodies into that blessed darkness.

But though it had smothered their thoughts and cauterized their senses, the hours of travel in that terrible place had not eroded away all survival instinct. Appa, despite his immense relief, suddenly felt something behind him, and glanced back the way they had come.

He slowed, then came to a stop. What was it he was looking at? Through the commotion of elements and the curtain of sweat before his eyes, Appa could not be at all sure what he was seeing, but it was almost as if the ledge farther back, where they had been walking only minutes before, was somehow shifting . . . no, *running* would be a better word.

Appa continued to stare, his fast-disappearing friends forgotten for the moment. Could it be that the very road upon which they had just traveled was now *melting* behind them? For there was definite movement upon its surface, some kind of frenetic torrent, a—

"Oh Cuna . . ."

Appa stood paralyzed where he had stopped to look back, a new pillar of salt to join the fiery elements of that place, and forever bear testimony to his folly. He could not even think to turn and run, or call out to his companions. All he could do was stare. For, perhaps a few hundred yards away and closing fast, a long column of figures was marching toward him with dreadful purpose. Heads lowered, their manner murderous, and with glints of fire reflecting blood-red from the jagged shards of metal they bore and the wires that crisscrossed their faces, the guardians of Vaagenfjord Maw bore down on the intruders. What they were, and where they had come from, Appa did not know, for they did not *look* like the Dead; yet they were led by Death itself, a tall warrior cloaked in bone-white, who held a massive poleaxe in both hands.

Appa stood as though his legs were held fast in quicksand. All his faculties had packed up, abandoning him to his fate. All, that is, except for one instinct that now screamed in his brain. *Evil has arrived, and you are going to die!*

That was enough for the frail Lightbearer. With a cry, he wrenched himself out of his paralysis and leapt after his companions, yelling out as loud as his lungs could manage.

"THEY ARE COMING! IT'S ALL UP! THE HORDE OF DARKNESS! *THEY ARE COMING!*"

The first the others knew about the impending danger was when their little grey stickman—who only hours ago had lain almost dead from the heat and his own exhaustion—now burst through their midst from behind, almost spinning them around on their heels, and sprinted on toward the doorway, still wailing in madness. As one, they whirled around to look behind them, knowing that whatever it was he was running from was bound to be bad.

It was indeed. The enemy had at long last arrived. Their true enemy. No shuffling tomb guardians or vestigial shades of evil, no traps contrived of spear, pitfall or exploding glyph. The dire host that loped toward them was very much alive.

A second or two of eye-widening incredulity, then all five of them were ignominiously following the priest. The animal roar of what sounded like a thousand snarling berserkers rose up behind them and ignited the cavern with searing flashes of fire-hued lightning. Along the ledge they surged in frenzied pursuit of their prey, and Vaagenfjord Maw once again licked its lips in anticipation of war.

But there were others also in that same place, and at that same time. Not the Tyvenborgers, for they had been for some time now preoccupied with their pilfering and plundering. It was Methuselech and the Cyne-Tregva company who lurked in the shadows beyond the doorway, for many hours awaiting the arrival of the travelers from Nordwas.

For it was here, Methuselech knew, that Bolldhe, Finwald, and their companions had to come if they were to gain entry to Ymla-Myrrdhain. None save he knew of the secret way up from the sea cave.

It was a long tunnel that sloped steeply up from the doorway in the hall of fire. There strange sounds whispered hollowly and shadows danced against the dim, red glow radiating from the magma beyond. The Drake Tunnel it was called—Lubang-Nagar, in the language of Rawgrs—and it was here that had taken place the worst of the fighting five hundred years ago.

Horrendous beyond belief had been the carnage, for this narrow but vital artery that flowed with the blood and entrails of both defenders and attackers was the only ingress to Ymla-Myrrdhain, and the place where neither side could, or would, fall back. Here within this cramped oven, men died in their hundreds, as much from heat, asphyxiation and the press of their comrades, as from sword, claw or flame.

And here again, an entire age of men later, the forces of Pel-Adan and Ol-chor would be once again reunited—albeit in greatly reduced numbers.

Gapp, still sick from the sea voyage, the steep climb, and the proximity of Methuselech's disintegrating shell, crouched with the rest of the company in stuffy darkness at the upper end of the Drake Tunnel, staring down its length toward the ember-like glow at the far end.

He longed to be away from this place, this pointless vigil, this madness, for he knew in his heart there would be no joyous arrival of his old comrades. They were gone long ago, either lost in the wilderness or dead. Or they had done what he himself should have done ages ago, and simply gone off home. But where else could he go? And what *was* Methuselech thinking? Gapp turned his gaze away from the burning light at the end of the tunnel, that spot on which all eyes were fixed, to find himself looking into the glaucous fish eyes of Methuselech.

But there was no humanity to be detected there: just two opaque discs that reflected the redness while giving it a silvery sheen. Those eyes would surely look at nothing else now. They were sunken, dried up, unblinking.

A sudden coldness crept up through the boy's innards. Was Xilva actually still alive? It had always been a moot point, of course, but here, now, the man looked so still—in fact *stiff.*

Then the chill intensified, but not from fear. There was something happening now, something in the air itself. It was a sensation, a power, that could be felt in the hair and on the skin. As Gapp continued to stare, he saw Methuselech's hair, normally so lank and straggly these days that it resembled washed-up sea grass, was now beginning to animate: there was no other word for it. Methuselech's hair was starting to rise as if it were possessed by the spirit of the man who was finally departing its corpse.

He looked down at the backs of his own hands, for he felt the hairs stand up there too. A quick glance around at Schnorbitz, Hwald, Finan, Englarielle, all the others, confirmed that they too were experiencing this bizarre phenomenon.

The air of Lubang-Nagar was coming alive—and it bristled with energy.

Following the priest, the five men fled stumbling along the last stretch of the ledge toward the portal. Their bodies burned from within and without, and breathing was a self-inflicted torture as they gasped in lungful after lungful of scalding air down throats already inflamed. But that doorway, the black gash in the glassy skin of the red rock face ahead, was beckoning to them with an oasis-like allure, becoming the only thing that any of them could think about.

Bolldhe, again, was last in line. Into his mind flashed a sudden sequence of jarring memories: images of snow-shawled mountains, the feel of upland turf beneath his feet, the smell of sultry late-summer air. But there was no earth-shaking pounding of a giant's footfall here; just the growing clamor of hooting, bawling, growling Ogha, a living "Enginne of Distruction" that was gaining on him with every second. The doorway was still far off, and he and the others had only seconds to go before they would inevitably begin to slow down.

Suddenly he came upon Nibulus. The Peladane had come to a halt, and was now standing legs apart in the middle of the ledge, facing toward the enemy. He had pulled something out of a large pouch hanging at his side, and was hastily fumbling with both it and his sword. The leader was badly out of breath, barely able to keep himself upright, and an evil green discharge exuded from one corner of his mouth, yet it seemed that he was about to confront the oncoming horde all by himself. As Bolldhe approached, he looked up and their gazes met. Neither could breathe properly, let alone speak, but the Peladane's eyes were incontrovertible in their command. *Go on without me,* they demanded. *I'll hold them back with the Thresher.*

Bolldhe obeyed this silent instruction, and continued on past their leader without even slowing pace.

The Thresher! he thought, recalling that amazing chain extension for the Peladane's greatsword. If Nibulus managed to bring that to bear, maybe they could make the doorway after all. Hope rekindled in his heart, Bolldhe then eased off, and twisted his head around to witness the awful destruction wrought by Kuw Dachs' flail weapon.

Immediately hot tears stung his eyes. For there stood Nibulus, a black silhouette all alone upon the ledge, swinging the pendulous weight of his Greatsword around in ever-widening circles at the end of the razor-studded chain of the Thresher. His emerald-green Ulleanh swirled about him like a war banner and, from some deep well of fortitude that yet remained, he succeeded in summoning up a roar of defiance against the onrushing legion.

But they did not even slow. They seemed unmindful of his heroic stance, un-cowed by his iron wall of flailing death. For they were captained by Death Itself, and ever swifter they charged down upon their foe. Their phantom-sheeted leader surged ahead of them, his robe streaming out behind like the shroud of a revenant, his Bardische held out lance-like before him.

Their eyes met, the captain's and the Peladane's, and it was only then that Nibulus realized that he was about to die. For, looking into those eyes he knew he had been singled out, because he was the one wearing the Ulleanh. He was therefore the one marked out as a Peladane, and it was for him alone now that the Darkangel was coming. His defiant roaring ebbed away sickly, and died.

Bolldhe turned away. *He's gone,* he thought briefly, and ran on. The heat and the horror crushed in upon him as he staggered ahead, and he felt his heart and lungs must burst from his chest at any moment.

An instant later, everything changed. A wave of electrical energy rolled up out of the river of fire, and transformed the very air about them. Hair, beards, even the wool fibers in their clothes, all rose up crackling as if alive. The bubbling and steaming stilled, and the howling blood cries of the Wire-Faces transformed into a wail of terror.

Bolldhe's legs buckled beneath him, and he pitched forward onto the jagged obsidian surface of the ledge. For a moment he lay there half-stunned and bleeding, and everything was still. All sound receded from his tiny world save the pounding in his ribcage and his empty retching. Then the dreadful commotion began once more: an escalated seething of the swelling magma, the panic-stricken shrieks of the Ogha, and a new voice—the triumphant and demonic laughter of their leader.

And then, a sound that rose above all else: a monstrous screech that set the cavern's very foundations a-quake, and which splintered every icicle of glassy rock. Men dropped their weapons and covered their ears, cowering upon the ground in a paroxysm of petrified impotence.

Bolldhe, after a moment, raised his head from the floor in a daze of horror, and squinted through the thick, black pall of smog that now belched from the dyke. Disoriented, he turned this way then that in befuddled panic, at a loss what to do next. Then his streaming eyes discerned the shades of men stumbling through the choking pall: the enemy fleeing in the madness of their fear; their leader cursing them but refusing to pursue; and his own companions flattening themselves against the wall and staring aghast at the thing that had just risen from the river of fire.

To the Oghain it was known as the Fyr-Draikke, the Bringer of the End of All; their own ragnarok. As one, they ran screaming back the way they had come, fleeing from the vast hall in uncontrollable dread. Some, in the blindness of their panic, blundered over the edge of the path, and tumbled, gaping in terror, into the orange-white magma below.

For Scathur, though, this apparition was Gruddna, the Great Sentinel, the

final and absolute defense against any that might dare try entering Ymla-
Myrrdhain. Had any pillagers ever come through the Moghul alive, and further
managed to endure the heat of Smaulka-Degernerth, then this is what they
would encounter next. And nothing or no one that came from outside
Drauglir's realm had any power against it.

Let the Ogha run. Scathur smirked, as his eyes watered in feverish lust. *I'll
have no need of them any more.*

From its home in Lindormyn's breast, it had risen, up the chute that sluiced
the river of fire, to darken the cavern with its apocalyptic awfulness. Yet it was
not in itself a creature of fire, but a vast, foul, undead thing that might once
have been a Wyrm. Gigantic wings, tattered, and limp as the cannon-blasted
sails of long-sunken galleons, stretched out to fill the hall, and from its pinions
were draped skeletal corpses from yesteryear whose blood poured over bone
and gristle. For such hostages that had been "spiked upon pinions' claw," no
escape from torment had been granted, no soft worms to nuzzle their flesh, no
cool embrace of hungry marsh to draw them down and away from the burning
light.

Barely concealed was the broken framework of bones beneath stretched
folds of skin, in patches hard and leathery, in other places softened to a jelly-
like slime, but all black, and running with putrefaction and drenched with the
blood of its corpselike adornments. Within this splintered skeleton, organs
pumped and churned, swollen with dark green ichor potent enough to dissolve
stone, and rotten to the core. And throughout its body, horned and razor-
toothed maggots the size of eels squirmed in frenzy.

The monster rose from the dyke in slow, foul-smelling wingbeats. Its massive head reared up on a serpentine neck that bristled with lethally venomous
spines, seeking out the enemy it was to destroy. It was a head that was nearly all
mouth; what little hide there remained on its lengthy snout was wrinkled with
malice, and its blackened teeth dripped suppuration from its festering gums.
As it turned its gaze upon the men on the ledge, they saw in its featureless eyes
only a mindless hunger for world destruction, and they were smitten with total
petrifaction.

Further it rose in the air, its viscera trailing beneath it just as it had done on
that historic day five hundred years ago. Never once did it take its awful stare
from its prey. Then, as Scathur howled in jubilation, it deposited its entire sodden bulk upon the ledge just before the doorway. It had blocked their
escape—and now came for them.

"NO!" Methuselech cried. *"THAT IDIOT, WHAT HAS HE DONE? OH, BY
ALL THE ELDER POWERS, MY SOUL!!"*

Vetters and Cervulice scrambled away from their leader, finally repelled by
the sudden and terrible mania in his tone. He lurched to his feet, then with a
curse of fury collapsed forward onto the ground. That sudden violent move-

ment had snapped both his legs, yet he floundered upon the floor still trying to haul his body forward with his hand-less forearms. Gapp and Englarielle stared at each other in shock, then looked back dumbfounded at the broken man-thing before them.

"Seelva?" Englarielle whimpered in total confusion.

The cry of the Fyr-Draikke had roared like a screaming hurricane up the tunnel of Lubang-Nagar, flattening all therein to the ground in abject terror. But there was a power of greater subtlety and more immediacy here also, housed in the disintegrating ruin of Xilvafloese's corpse.

From that place of fire at the end of the tunnel continued the thrashing and bellowing of Gruddna, but amid this could just be detected the sound of another's voice, equally dreadful and exultant. The company in the tunnel remained paralyzed and impotent, incapable even of fleeing. Yet still the corpse of Methuselech crawled onwards, leaving a slimy trail of itself on the floor, heedless to all else but the exigency of its purpose.

The keep all about them quaked, static surged and crackled in the air, magma churned in its molten trough and flared gouts of fire against the stone walls, and the cries of the Darkangels blackened the world. And it was amid this chaos that Gapp suddenly focused upon the putrid heap that was Xilva as it jerked and slithered down the tunnel. And an image—no, a recollection—switched on in his mind: a moonlit figure among the trees, poison-eyed, ring-bedecked, a long mace at its side, and a bat's nose sniffing for blood . . . leeches crawling toward him!

"Mauglad!" he breathed, and Gapp, at last, began to understand.

He could not explain why, but as he rubbed the itchy scarring on his wrists from which Mauglad had drunk so frequently, he now guessed that the spirit possessing Methuselech's body all this time was not evil, was not in league with the Rawgr after all. It had been allied once, as was clear from its knowledge and understanding of this place, but that had been a long time ago—before Drauglir had cast it out, before Drauglir had himself been cast down. Now, after such endless, empty days of banishment in the deep and desolate ravines of the wilderness, the houseless shade of Mauglad Yrkeshta had at last contrived to come home. Not to rise up and gather power once again, but simply to sleep, to put an end to all those centuries of its unwanted, abhorrent existence. How could anything that so yearned to cease from being, that had striven so hard for a merciful release from this world, be either good or evil?

Well, if it's death he wants, Gapp thought, *he'll certainly find it down there!* Though not knowing how the spirit of Maugland could embrace true death, he guessed that confronting whatever monster lurked down there would probably do the trick.

On, slowly, down Lubang-Nagar did Mauglad crawl, little more than a slug upon a vast stretch of dry earth. At that speed the monster would surely be gone by the time he arrived.

A voice suddenly hissed back up the tunnel:*"Radnarrr . . . help me."*

Then Gapp became enraged. Fear, sickness, and exhaustion had frayed his sanity to tearing point, and he boiled with an anger the like of which he had never known before.

"You want to go?" he raged at the corpse. "You really want to go down there? Good! Then I'll help you. Oh yes, I'll help you, all right!"

He charged down the slope to where Mauglad struggled to advance, and yanked him up by the arm, propelling him toward the fiery portal below. At long last he would be rid of his slaver!

A noise behind him caused Gapp to pause. It was Englarielle. The Vetter was clearly clueless as to just what else was going on in this mad world, but at least understood that the leader of this enterprise needed his help. Grabbing Mauglad's other arm, he slung it over his shoulder, and the three of them stumbled onward.

"Th' sssword . . . !"

Words bubbled amid the oily discharge that leaked from Mauglad's mouth. *"Th' sswor'! Let no' the tall captain gain th' sswor'. Tell Bolld' or Finwa—"*

And then his lower jaw fell off.

"Yeah, yeah," Gapp muttered in irritation, and together they staggered on down Lubang-Nagar.

So it was that, after six weeks of separation, the two groups from Nordwas were finally reunited. Here, amid the fires of hell and the evil that raged deep within the earth beneath an ice-gripped island at the top of the world, they once again looked upon each other.

Over the splintered shards of obsidian the Fyr-Draikke dragged its trail of gore, tramping toward Appa, the closest to the doorway. Paralyzed, the little grey man could do nothing but stare helplessly at the grisly hell-spawn that bore down upon him. As it approached, his face contorted with an expression that would have better suited a bawling infant, and a thin cry like a steaming kettle began to issue from his lips. Unable to move, his companions, strung out along the ledge, could only gape, weapons dangling uselessly from limp hands, as Gruddna finally closed in upon the old priest.

But a new power now entered the Hall of Fire, and it seemed that the whole of Melhus Island shifted upon its axis. Sensing this potency, the Draikke screamed in frustration and wheeled around, its great tail smiting against the rock wall above Appa's head and showering him with scree.

There in the doorway, for all to see, stood Mauglad Yrkeshta, sometime High Necromancer of Vaagenfjord Maw, but clad in the crumbling husk of Methuselech Xilvafloese. And to either side of him, holding him up, stood Gapp Radnar of Nordwas, and Englarielle Rampunculus, Cynen of the Vetterym.

Appa collapsed beneath the shower of stone. Wodeman, closest to him, fell to his knees. Bolldhe and Nibulus, further back along the ledge, sensed the transformation in the air, but could not begin to guess what was happening. And Paulus and Finwald, they who alone were close enough to see who had entered, screwed up their faces in total bewilderment.

But Scathur realized only too well who it was. Though himself too far away to see clearly, he understood fully who had returned from the dead to stand among them once again.

"You!" he cried, fear entering his voice for the first time in centuries. Then, after only the fleetest whisper of vacillation, he charged toward the Peladane—the bearer of the sword.

Gruddna, meanwhile, appeared in some state of confusion. Grunting in beast-like savagery, it writhed and thrashed at the air as though assailed by an invisible tormentor. The corpses that dangled from its pinions became animated and gyrated in an obscene dance of death; they moaned in a hollow, desperately forlorn elegy, a threnodic lament that echoed the discordant harmonies of wind in far-off tunnels, and their rotten fluids rained all about in a grey-brown diffusion.

The monster staggered closer to the river of fire, then reeled back from the very edge of the dyke. Then in a sudden spasm it flung back its head and sent forth a howl of such fury, pain, and despair that great fissures split through the roof of the cavern, and all, even Scathur, were leveled to the ground as reeds before a tempest.

All except Mauglad—though the two who had supported him here now cowered in the shadows, their burden, now abandoned kneeling upon the floor, remained unbowed. His handless wrists held together in the manner of one in prayer, Mauglad appeared calm within the eye of the hurricane that raged all around him. He moaned wordless incantations from the ruin of his mouth, and the painful effort of his concentration was deeply chiseled into every fold and line in his face.

The Fyr-Draikke gathered itself up and sprang toward its tormentor, desiring only to smear this wretched intruder across the cavern floor into an oily, black stain. But Gruddna was now a creature of the undead, and over even this colossal manifestation of world-ending horror, the necromancer held mastery. Both Fyr-Draikke and black priest screamed in torturous conflict, their voices and power intertwining, fusing, spiraling through the air, canceling each other out. Only Mauglad had potency enough to face this leviathan that Scathur had brought back into the world. But it was a struggle that was rapidly destroying them both.

"Nibulus!"

The warning came from someone somewhere and, just in time, the Peladane heaved himself from the ground where he had collapsed, and turned to see the white-robed captain coming straight for him. He immediately leapt to his feet, grabbed his greatsword from where it lay on the path, and stood his ground once again.

Behind him, Paulus had also gathered his wits, and suddenly bounded over the trembling forms of Finwald and Wodeman, splayed on the ground, with sword held high. Viper-fast, he ducked under the sweep of the Fyr-Draikke's massive tail, rolled beneath its contorting belly and, with a savage snarl, arced his bastard blade deep into that mess of cold, churning vitals.

A hoarse cough exploded from Gruddna's throat, the trophy corpses flew from its pinions, and its entire body buckled. A freezing gust of soul-wind screamed out of Methuselech's collapsing form, bowled Gapp and the Cynen over, and wailed its way up along Lubang-Nagar. And Methuselech's eyes, his own once again, stared through the carnage and fire to pick out the shape of his friend Nibulus. With a resounding cry that came from his soul rather than his broken form, he uttered his final words: *"Death to the Green Ones!"* And, at last, died.

Then the air folded in upon itself, and their world exploded into a noiseless void of blinding light.

When sight and sound were returned to them, the company awoke to their senses with a choking cry, and looked about in panic.

The Fyr-Draikke was now still, nothing more than a steaming pile of offal upon the ledge. Its trophy corpses were busily legging it off in all directions. Methuselech's body was gone, simply not there, though the stone doorjambs adjacent and the floor beneath them were decidedly darker and stickier than before.

And Scathur, who had once believed his master's chambers unassailable by any, now glanced around in genuine fear, standing as he was amid these strange new enemies that had somehow managed to breach all his defenses. Who these foes were he could not imagine, but he did know that this was not a fight for himself, alone, with neither his Wire-Faces nor the Children in sight. Hesitating for not one second, he fled the cavern as swiftly as he could.

The unseen eyes of the Skela focused upon Bolldhe as he picked up Flametongue from the ground, and walked dazedly toward the doorway.

"Looks like Plan B failed, then?" one of them suggested to the fire-eyed figure nearby—who merely nodded ruefully, and disappeared.

11

Stained-Glass Demons

It was to be a reunion that none had expected, nor even imagined. And after it had occurred, there was scant certainty among the seven travellers that it actually had occurred at all. For at that time, they had just been snatched from fire, havoc and unimaginable horror, and these moments they were experiencing now were more precious than any reunion.

As the undoing of the Fyr-Draikke spread its melting wreckage across the rock, the six men had staggered out of the boiling cauldron of Smaulka-Degernerth to plunge through the doorway at last. Up the steep incline of Lubang-Nagar they had toiled, not even letting their exhaustion halt them until the worst of that insufferable heat was behind them. Then, gasping, cascading with sweat, and shaking as from a seizure, they gulped the cooler air deep into their scalded lungs, and reveled in the soothing darkness into which they had been delivered. For the first time that day, they had realized beyond doubt that they were still alive.

Nibulus lay sprawled on the ground retching with exhaustion. What with the tengriite armor and the burden of his sword Unferth, his encumbrance had been the greatest by far. He was now so completely spent that he could not even begin removing the armor that entombed him in its roasting grasp.

After a while, he succeeded in opening his eyes, then raised his head sufficiently to peer around at this new place they had come to. Someone had managed to get Bolldhe's lantern both alight and set on wide focus, so the tunnel around them was lit up by a little sphere of soft, yellow light.

Incredibly, they were all still alive, he realized, in spite of everything that had been set against them. The Fyr-Draikke was destroyed, that horrifying captain and his host, whoever or whatever they were, had fled, and—if his reckoning was correct—they had actually succeeded in making it all the way to Ymla-Myrrdhain. He was so astonished he might have laughed out loud.

Might have laughed, had it not been for the torment that he could see in his men's eyes. Around him they huddled, eyes hollow and staring, dumb with shock. Blow upon blow of torment had been heaped on them, and this was their first chance to dwell on it.

Both Bolldhe and Finwald had apparently given in to their hysteria. In the case of Bolldhe, this manifested itself in an anguished shuddering of the body, and a sightless stare, while Finwald was sobbing openly. Nibulus's own throat began to spasm as he looked on. He had witnessed these reactions before on the battlefield, and knew well what they were going through.

Wodeman was not so easy to read. There was a frown on his face, and he kept prodding himself all over. Though Nibulus did not realize it, the shaman was actually trying to convince himself that he was actually still here, still among the living. All of him. It was said among the Torca that if a man should travel too far from his homeland, or experience too much fear, his soul might depart his body and wander the earth until such time as it might be located by one of those with the Seeing, and be encouraged to return to its body. If either of these were true, Wodeman pondered, then his soul must be halfway across the Giant Mountains by now.

As for Appa, how that scorched old moth had managed to survive, Nibulus would never know. Maybe there was some truth in this Lightbearing stuff after all. But what a sorry state the old priest was in, to be sure. Though one hand was still closed limply around his talisman, for once he was not chanting or rapping it against his ring. He was clearly too far gone, too shocked to do anything but whimper and sob, and stare emptily into oblivion.

Nibulus squeezed his eyes shut against the tears. *Pel-Adan, how they had all suffered!* The fire previously in his men's eyes had dimmed like an arctic sun dipping beneath the grey waters of the ocean. And it would be some time before the first glimmers of a new dawn might herald the sparking of fresh courage within them.

Nibulus's lingering gaze moved on, and it was then that his grief was frozen out of him by a vision of his dead esquire with some twisted little demon by his side. Both of them were staring intently at him, not a dozen feet away.

For such was how they appeared. Nibulus was too far from the doorway to see clearly who stood there. Memories of the Moghul, that Trough where dead men walk again, were still too fresh in his mind for reaching any but the most obvious conclusion. Apparently, Nibulus and his troop had struggled through those terrible places to experience an even greater evil in Ymla-Myrrdhain where dwelt the worst horrors of the underworld. This emaciated, filth-caked, subhuman ghoul with its sunken eyes and stench of night soil could not be the real Gapp Radnar, any more than was the sick and animalistic parody of a human that squatted beside him.

"I saw you die," he whispered. But even as he said it, he realized how inaccurate that was.

As if reading his thoughts, the boy spoke, as he moved forward: "You may have seen me fall, but you did not see me die."

The voice was the same. The eyes, too, though hungry and unhinged. And this hairy little imp with the outsized helmet by his side had the air of one who had shared their suffering of evil, not one who dealt it out.

"Radnar?" Nibulus murmured, half in a dream.

Gapp neither nodded nor smiled. "*Mister* Radnar, to you," he replied, then reached out towards Nibulus, clasped his hands round an arm, and helped him to his feet.

Gapp stared about himself, giddy with the storm of feelings that were churning through his insides: wondrous joy, paralyzing horror, dizzying relief, confusion, fear, and tragedy. But most of all, amazement. He felt like one who has finally woken from a months-long sleep and the nightmares that stalked through it.

My old mates! he cried silently to himself. *Thought them gone beyond any hope. Who could've believed that the Mauglad-ghoul's promises would actually come true?*

An urgent tug at his arm brought his attention back to his companion, the Vetter chief. He turned to Englarielle, saw the questioning look on his face, and by way of response could only shrug.

"Don't ask me, friend," he said after a moment. "I haven't got a clue what's going on either."

He wished dearly that he could understand Vetter, or that Polgrim patois he had heard him use with Xilva so often. But Xilva was now gone beyond recall, and with him had gone their only leader, their direction and their purpose. Utterly at a loss now, the Vetter chief clasped hands with the boy, staring into his eyes in supplication. *What do I tell my people now?* he seemed to be entreating.

All Gapp could do was gesticulate for the Cynen to head back up the tunnel to rejoin the Tregvans, and wait for him there. *Best if he keeps his lot out of sight until my own lot have recovered*, he reasoned, They've suffered enough without having an army of outlandish Cyne-Tregvans in this devilish place.

"What in Gwyllch's name was *that* thing?" the Peladane breathed, pointing after the departing Vetter with a shudder.

"Captain of my army," Gapp boasted.

He looked Nibulus directly in the eye (probably for the first time in his entire life). As Nibulus looked back at him, there was wonder in the Peladane's regard, wonder at first over the simple fact that Gapp was still alive. And then, as it sunk in, nothing less than awe that he was *here,* of all places. How in all the world the lad had managed to make his way here, past all the terrors and dangers that they themselves had come through, Nibulus could not begin to imagine. And with an *army,* he said? There was a surge of pride in the Peladane's heart; he had clearly taught his esquire well.

"So, you finally caught up with us, then," he said to his servant.

Gapp laughed. It was just a quick laugh, but it was the first one he had given for an entire age, it seemed. And it felt so good. Now, at long last in the company of his friends again—*normal* people, for once—he could laugh, and smile, maybe relax a little. In short, return to his normal self. It was a wonderful feeling, and did more to revive him than any medicine.

"It's good to see you all, Nibulus." he replied. "It really is. I never believed we'd meet again."

"And yet you came here?"

"Only because of him." He jerked his thumb toward a dark stain on the walls, back near the tunnel entrance.

"Him?" Nibulus was puzzled.

"Methuselech," Finwald choked, still gagging at the memory.

Methuselech? Nibulus wondered.

Just then, dragging footsteps began to be heard further down in the darkness. Nibulus and all the others turned and peered down the passage, frozen into sudden immobility.

"It can't be!"

"It's that ghost-cloak with the poleaxe come back to get us!"

Sure enough, a tall, robed figure was emerging from the darkness—a black shadow, approaching them with slow but determined pace.

Then Paulus came fully into view, and they relaxed.

He was carrying something. It appeared to be a lump of meat about the size, shape, and texture of a set of bagpipes. But as soon as he rejoined them in the circle of lamplight, the whole company drew back in revulsion, uttering oaths of dismay at this, the vilest of their number.

"Paulus!" cried Nibulus in disbelief. "Why *do* you do it? Why must you always be so disgusting?"

The Nahovian sat down heavily, uncaring of their repugnance. Humming merrily, he began tying into knots the tubes of the gallbladder he had just hacked from its previous owner.

"Each to his own," he replied, secretly smirking. "You never know—it might come in handy before the day is out."

They shook their heads, not even wanting to imagine what use the mercenary might find for a rotten Fyr-Draikke's gall bladder.

"Still," Nibulus admitted. "I suppose you of all here have earned the right to claim the Hero's Portion. How could you find the courage to go up against that . . . *thing* when all others were laid low? Not even the Peladanes of old dared attack it singly. Truly the spirit of Gwyllch dwells strongly within you, Odf Uglekort!"

Paulus's eye met those of the Peladane. He was speechless. Never, to his knowledge, had Nibulus accorded anyone so high an accolade as that. But it was then, in his moment of silence, that Paulus noticed Gapp for the first time. His body stiffened, and his expression was utterly aghast.

". . . You!" he whispered in disbelief.

". . . Me," Gapp confirmed, puzzled.

Paulus just stared—and stared. Like all of them, he had believed the boy to be dead, long ago buried deep beneath the Rainflats. But, unlike the others, Paulus knew the boy had not died in Nym-Cadog's well. Ignoring its plea for help, he had been the last to hear Gapp's voice, rising from deep in the silver mine near Myst-Hakel. For several minutes of guilty shock, all he could do was gape.

Gapp smiled nervously. "All right, then, Paulus?" he said awkwardly by way of greeting. He wondered if this was the first time he had actually spoken to the mercenary, unable as he was to recall any previous occasion.

Paulus continued to stare hard, as if trying to read Gapp's soul. Did the boy realize how he had betrayed him?

But after a further moment of close scrutiny, he felt satisfied; the boy did not have a clue.

"Fine. You?" he replied, and went back to tying off his gallbladder.

"We have to leave now," Nibulus announced suddenly. "That ermine-clad fiend with the huge axe is still out there somewhere. The army he brought with him fled from the Fyr-Draikke, not from us. Once he's rounded them up again, they'll be back."

"It's Scathur," Gapp informed them, unexpectedly.

"Scathur?" Nibulus echoed. "*The* Scathur? Don't talk excrement, boy."

"It's Scathur, I tell you!" Gapp snapped, angry all of a sudden. His voice strove to sound manly, but was still constricted by the midget-tones of adolescence. Nevertheless, his defiance was enough. Everyone looked up, startled.

"It's Scathur," Gapp repeated, his voice calmer now that he had their attention. "I've never seen him, but I have felt him. And I've definitely seen enough of those Wire-Faces to last me a lifetime." He ignored their puzzled looks and pressed on. "Well, I've brought my own army—I'll introduce you in a minute—but he's got much worse things up his sleeve than just Wire-Faces. Yes, Nibulus, you're right, we *do* have to leave. Right now."

How, who, where, when, why, and what? Those were the questions. There were, in fact, a thousand questions to be asked, on both sides, but no one wanted to tarry here in this tunnel that reeked of such ancient horror—and so close to the enemy and the new horror it would bring. So they gathered up their equipment, and followed the boy up the passageway, deferring any urge for enlightenment till they had found somewhere they could hole up in whatever safety and concealment was offered in this place.

Suddenly, an enormous hell-hound stood blocking the passage ahead and growling at them demonically.

Then Gapp was calling out to this ferocious guardian of Lubang-Nagar: "Here, boy! Schnorbitz!"

Next two antler-heads came up from behind, to stand beside the hound.

Then, finally, the return of the hairy little imp with the outsized helmet, bringing with him about fifty other hairy look-alikes, also heavily armed.

All this was going to take some time to assimilate. And the questions kept piling up.

Unlike *The Testament of Khuc*, Gwyllch's chronicle contained within it no floor plans, maps, or diagrams. Its writer had been a little preoccupied when he had come this way, and had somewhat inconsiderately omitted much of the cartographic detail they would have found useful at this point. There was, thus, nothing to guide them toward any convenient spot nearby where they could rest, talk, and try to regain that portion of their wits that still remained to them.

So, with Nibulus leading the way, they now entered the inner keep of Ymla-Myrrdhain altogether blindly.

What was this place they had come to? Was it in Lindormyn? Was it hell? For as soon as they ventured beyond that chamber at the top of Lubang-Nagar, they realized that they had entered an area entirely different from those they had journeyed through so far. The dereliction of the outer halls, the utter blackness of the Moghul, the fiery commotion of Smaulka-Degernerth, all these had been as different from each other as it was possible to be.

But Ymla-Myrrdhain, this final manifestation of Vaagenfjord Maw, was like nothing any of them had ever imagined. In the outer Maw, their souls had been chilled; in the Hall of Fire, they had been seared; in the Trough, they had seemingly been sucked down into the mud. Here, however, the effect upon their souls was alluring, bewitching, and insidiously disturbing all at once.

The first thing they noticed was the light being reflected from their lanterns and torches. After the darkness of the Drake Tunnel, this place fairly shimmered with illumination and color. As Bolldhe played his lantern about, light sprang to life from a thousand different surfaces which, even after the beam had passed on, would yet glow for a while with a soft but evanescent luminosity. It might glitter but it was also strangely subdued, and in redder torchlight it looked as if a fine spray of blood were falling slowly through the air.

Floors, which sloped at illogical angles, were paved with purple and turquoise marble that still retained a flawless sheen despite the despoliation of both Peladanes and time. These floors were shot through with veins of cobaltite that, in the flickering lantern's beam appeared to throb with a pulse as though they carried a lifeblood of mercury to some vast and unnatural heart.

Walls, too, were set in bizarre, perhaps even impossible geometry, so that it became difficult to discern the difference between near and far, up and down, or right and left. Many were covered in glassy panels that depicted images of nature, grossly perverted, and other themes that were darker still.

All about them rose columns. Some had no base below, and appeared to hang suspended above the floor. But there were also plinths with no column above, which—though fashioned from marble—had over the centuries developed the semblance of rotting, fungoid tree stumps. Both these, and the great carvings of deranged, screaming flowers reeked with a sickly, putrid fetor mingling with the cardamom incense that still hung heavy in the air. Throughout it all there ran a hint of whispering, and lesser scents aroused the hackles of more than just the forest hound.

Passage, chamber, hall, or pit, they all seemed to run together into one. There would be nowhere in this antechamber to hell that they could call safe, so before long they simply stopped where they were. At what was possibly the end of a huge open hall, they finally made camp.

Within the pale radius of Bolldhe's lantern, the newly united army of invaders to the Maw was now assembled. Standing, squatting or sitting in a rough circle, this company of strangers regarded each other with mutual curiosity. In the middle of them sat Gapp, flanked by Schnorbitz on one side and Englarielle on the other, with Finan behind him. Facing these four were ranged the other humans, staring blankly at their former dogsbody and the unusual company he now kept.

"You've obviously been busy during your absence," Nibulus said at last. "Would you care to introduce us to your new friends?"

Gapp had picked up very little of the Polg trading-tongue that the Tregvans had habitually used with Methuselech. But he was the only link between the two groups, and now found himself in the unenviable position of translator. After so many weeks under the domination of Mauglad Yrkeshta, during which time he had been little more than a necromancer's witless vassal, he was finding it very difficult to think for himself. But Mauglad was destroyed now—Gapp himself had helped him down that road—and he was "Mister Radnar" now. He had not dragged himself from a watery grave in the caves beneath Fron-Wudu for nothing, and the patronizing tone of the Peladane now did as much as his release from the will of the black priest to stir anger in him anew.

"Sure," he replied testily. "Nibulus, this is Englarielle Rampunculus, king of the army of Cyne-Tregva that I've enlisted for this campaign. Englarielle: this is Nibulus Wintus, a fat oaf I used to work for."

Gapp did not try to translate this for the Vetterym; it had been for his former questmates' ears only. In actual fact, it caused considerably less of a reaction among them than he had hoped. Considering what the Peladane's group had just been through, there was very little left in the world that could have surprised them. And as for Wintus, he simply gave the boy a rather weary look.

If anyone, it was Gapp who was surprised; six weeks previously, the Peladane would have swatted his esquire halfway to the ocean for making a remark like that.

Gapp shrugged, and got the further civilities underway. Apart from the leaders of each party, namely Nibulus and Englarielle, he did not bother to introduce anyone else by name. He realized that none there would be able to recall any new names, even if they were in a state to care about such things.

As far as the Tregvans were concerned, Gapp imagined, Mauglad already had told Englarielle a bit about the party from Nordwas and their mission, and that would have to suffice. There was not any way Gapp could begin to elaborate on what may already have been said. What he urgently needed to do, though, was assure them that these humans were effectively taking over from their friend "Seelva," so that nothing really had changed. Apart from the fact that Xilvafloese, their ex-leader and sole reason for their being here, now decorated the doorway of Lubang-Nagar in a darker shade of grey.

He sighed tiredly. "This isn't going to be easy."

He looked around at the expectant faces of the Vetters, the Cervulice, and even the two Paranduzes. Hwald was having a particularly bad time of it. They were all clearly at a loss. *Hardly surprising*, Gapp mused, *considering their leader has just exploded—and without even bothering to explain why*. Having plunged into a world so far beyond their understanding, now that the progenitor of this whole misadventure—that one piece of rotten driftwood that had been keeping their heads above water—was dead, their disorientation and fear threatened to pull them down into an ocean of madness.

In exasperation, Gapp gave up and simply jabbed a finger repeatedly at Nibulus, while shouting in Polg: "Erjar mycel, Seelva cynen, nosa cynen narru!" *This big warrior, Methuselech's leader, now our new leader.*

That seemed to do the trick. The Tregvans henceforth clung on to this simple fact with fervor. They had a new boss, and that was all they needed, or wanted, to know.

Gapp gradually calmed down a little. Now at last there would be the chance to have serious words with his old companions, tell them what had befallen him since their parting, catch up on what they had been doing, and maybe work out between them exactly what had happened to Methuselech.

Nibulus, being Nibulus, told his story first. In a low, euphonious voice that he believed lent him the qualities of an akynn, the Peladane related everything that had befallen them since Gapp had disappeared down the well in the witch Nym-Cadog's realm. Reaching the town of Myst-Hakel, the fight in the silver mine and the finding of the sword Flametongue, meeting Kuthy, the journey through Eotunlandt, Elfswith and Ceawlin, Melhus Island, and finally now, the Maw. It was all an incredible story, in spite of the Peladane's bombastic narration, and one which confirmed Gapp's anxiety about the pickled people he had seen hoarded in the stabbur.

But there was one thing his former master talked of that had drawn the boy's ear above all else. And that was the mention of Flametongue.

Dead snake in a bag, eh? he reflected, and it was only then that he recalled the words Mauglad had spoken in anger outside the woodcutter's hut: "Finwald's *sword* must not enter the Maw."

About this matter, he held his tongue for the moment, for he guessed that things would *really* happen once he let *that* cat out of the bag. He instead brought them up to date with his own adventures: from the moment he had plunged into the dark and freezing waters of Nym's well to his eventual emergence from the dark and freezing waters of the sea cave just below them now. Unlike Nibulus, that reverer of Gwyllch, however, he had no need to employ bardic mellifluence or statesmanlike grandiloquence in his telling. The deeds alone were enough to awe his audience, and at long last, at very last, Gapp Radnar beheld in their eyes something he had awaited for months, *years,* even: *respect.* Respect, recognition, and perhaps even reverence for this young man whom when last seen was only a boy. It was only now, after all that they too had been through, that they were able to appreciate the magnitude of his experiences, and wonder that he had survived to be here with them now.

So they were seven again. Yet uppermost in their minds was the thought that they had been so nearly the full eight again. The subject of Methuselech Xilvaflocse, inevitably, came round. Particularly after Gapp's disturbing revelations.

Nibulus explored it with them, step by step. There was a hollow tone to his voice, a tired flatness, and a distinct lack of euphony this time as he spoke. He had already done his private mourning for his friend, and there was no fund of real grief left inside him. Just sickness, confusion, and an overwhelming desire to have done with this campaign once and for all, the worst one he had ever been part of.

"Xilva," he began, "having already been wounded by the wolf pack, took a fall into a pit in the mountains. But what came out? What can recover *in days* from wounds such as those he received from the wolves *and* the fall?"

"And to come after us all that way on his own," Finwald continued. "I ask you, what manner of man or devil are we talking about here?"

Nibulus was becoming increasingly agitated, but this was a situation that for once he could not solve simply by an outburst of anger. In exasperation he repeated his question: "So, what *did* come out of the valley, then?"

"Not Methuselech Xilvafloese, that's for sure," Bolldhe stated bluntly.

"Then can anyone here tell me what kind of creature or spirit could resemble our friend so closely?" Nibulus enquired.

"Maybe it was an Abyssian," Wodeman suggested, his voice barely more than a whisper.

"Aye, an Abyssian," Paulus agreed. "Such deceit as this would as like as not derive from that filthy breed of Huldre! Well-known are they in my land. They incarcerate our people in their unholy cells, and then take on their semblance. Then they walk among us, talk among us, eating, drinking, sharing our lives, sharing our wives, and all the time *laughing* at us!"

"For how long can they do this?" Appa asked, shivering.

"And *why?*" demanded Nibulus.

"Why?" Paulus repeated, surprised at the question. "Why does any Huldre do anything it does? And as for how long, well, for just however long they want. Who can tell? We are only able to see them for what they truly are when they *want* us to. Never before. Perhaps they eventually tire of their sick sport, and return to their realm to gloat with their kind."

"And the people they mimic?" Nibulus asked. "After the Abyssian has returned to Huldre-Home?"

"They are then released from its thrall," Paulus admitted, fiddling with the knotted tubes of his gallbladder. "Some have simply sprung from the tree bole, or boulder, where they have been held, and they remember nothing of their imprisonment. But by then, of course, they have a lot of explaining to do, a lot to answer for, as the Huldre has meanwhile sown pernicious mischief into the framework of their life."

Gapp, interesting though this all was, tried to cut in. "I don't think he was a shape-changer. As I've already said—"

"What you said," Nibulus persisted, "is that he behaved differently to before. Paulus, what do you know of these Abyssians' art, their performance, and their guile? Do they attempt to closely impersonate the characteristics of those they supplant too?"

"They try to resemble them in every way they can," Paulus explained. "They even do so when they take on the guise of an animal."

"They do that too?"

"Indeed," Wodeman confirmed, with a nod at Paulus. "I myself have known such cases in Nordwas. Usually they masquerade as farm animals. Some seem to enjoy being ridden, others have a yen for being milked. Or they may pretend to be the household dog—you know, getting in really close with the family, but without the extra bother of having to pass themselves off as a human."

"And is there some way you can tell it's not really your own dog at all?"

"Well, the Abyssian will attempt to mimic the one it has ousted in every way," Wodeman explained. "Such a false dog, for example, might continue to torment cats, gnaw on bones, roll on dead things—"

"Greet women from behind," added Paulus with distaste.

"Exactly," Wodeman continued. "All those practices the Huldre take such pleasure from in their true form. But no matter what they become, their spirit remains Huldre, so if observed for long enough, certain discrepancies may be noticed. In the case of a dog, then, though they would never do anything a dog wouldn't do, like read a book, or use a latrine, it may be noticed that in certain ways dogs do generally behave, the changeling doesn't."

"Such as?"

Wodeman scratched his head. "Well . . . I suppose you'd never see them licking their privy parts, or anything like that."

"Really?" Nibulus replied, surprised. "That's the first thing I'd want to do."

"Listen to me!" Gapp interrupted. "He wasn't a blooding shape-changer, all right? He behaved *nothing* like Xilva, I'm telling you."

"Why, what was he like, then?"

"You all know what he was like back then. He was . . . I don't know, joyous, I suppose, and full of life. Always a bit of a laugh. But when I met him again afterward, well, he probably didn't even know what laughter was. He was so serious all the time, so intense—so *obsessed.* And very, very strange, too. He hardly spoke to me at all, and when he did . . . well, I was so confused, so drained, I hardly took any of it in. But there was one thing he kept going on about: justice. He seemed obsessed with *justice.*"

"Justice?" Finwald repeated. "For whom?"

"I couldn't make head nor tail of it, but it was the need for justice that drove him on so. And he knew things, too, things Xilva wouldn't have known, I'm sure. He spoke Polgrim, and he was fluent in the Wrythe-people's speech. He knew exactly who the Majestic Head was. He knew things about this land that not even Nibulus knows.

"And he had power. Such power! He stood on a beach and summoned, *compelled* that Jagt-thing I told you about. Imagine! And you all saw what he did to that monster."

Nibulus's eyes suddenly lit up. "In that case, maybe the real Methuselech is still alive after all. Perhaps he's still back in the mountains, or maybe he recovered enough to make his way to Myst-Hakel—or else back to that Torca village."

"What?" Bolldhe scolded. "You think he crawled from that terrible pit? Then dragged himself all alone out of the mountains? Don't be so bloody stupid!"

"Maybe he's still imprisoned in the Abyssian's boulder, or tree bole, or wherever else he was put," suggested Paulus darkly.

"Will you listen to me!" Gapp exclaimed. "There was no Abyssian. There never was! I *saw* Methuselech in those eyes occasionally, sometimes heard his voice, his *real* voice, speaking from within his body. You yourself heard his last war cry, Nibulus. That was truly *him*! But he wasn't the only one in there. I've got scars here on my wrists from where the other thing drank my blood, just trying to keep Xilva's body fresh and alive. And by the time we met up with you lot, that body was looking more like one you'd see swinging from a gibbet after a fortnight. I'm sorry, Nibulus, but Methuselech's dead. His soul may have been in there along with Mauglad's, but it was Mauglad who was pulling the strings."

Nibulus was finally silent then, and for a while, so were the others. Then, gradually, before their very eyes, the Peladane appeared to diminish, to almost shrink in to himself, and his jaw softened in a way none of them had witnessed before. He had grieved the loss of his good friend once already and, now that his sudden new hope had been crushed by the boy's words, he must grieve a second, and final, time.

"Mauglad?" It was Finwald who broke the silence.

Gapp turned to him. He had not mentioned the name earlier, and wondered why he had done so now. It was, after all, a name he had only ever come across in his dreams, in the nightmares he had suffered while riding through Fron-Wudu with the Methuselech-thing. But there had been a note in Finwald's voice as he had uttered that name. A definite note. And now that it came to it, maybe the time had come at last for Finwald to tell them what exactly was going on here.

"Mauglad, yes," Gapp responded. "Why, Finwald? Friend of yours, is he?"

Finwald regarded the boy through narrowed eyes. *What the Frigg was that supposed to mean?* But, like Gapp, he too wanted answers.

"It's a name I've come across in my research, yes," Finwald admitted. "He was a great power here once, though who or what he was, I don't know. There simply are no details, only fleeting references. About one who was once great, but fell from power; possibly thrown from power . . ."

"So what happened to him?" Nibulus demanded, clearly irritated by the priest's knowing something he himself did not.

Finwald shook his head. "I've no idea. I hardly know anything more than you do. I'm theorizing only."

Oh really? thought Gapp, scrutinizing the priest in the weird light that altered the lines of his face.

"All I do know is that there are no records of Mauglad's presence at the Siege. The references to him date back to an earlier time—and then they simply finish. It's as if he, or it, vanished without trace."

"Power struggle between rivals?" suggested Bolldhe.

"Could be," Finwald confirmed. "The servants of Olchor have always been aspiring, competitive, jealous and, above all, resentful. Maybe it was Scathur who brought about this Mauglad's downfall. Maybe Drauglir himself."

"You've never mentioned any of this before," Nibulus said suspiciously.

"No need to. As I said, Mauglad seems to have vanished long before the days of the Fasces. He has nothing to do with our business here—or so I thought."

"What do you think his enemies did to him, then?"

"Exactly what, I can only guess. Slain, expunged, held in perpetual torture—you tell me. In any case, one way or another, his soul appears to have found its way into our poor Xilvafloese."

Gapp shivered in a sudden spasm of cold. He had the uncomfortable feeling they were being watched. That freezing gust of wind that had cannoned past him from Methuselech's expiring corpse to fly on up Lubang-Nagar, now came back to him in a flash.

"His soul is then as damned as the worst of heretics," Nibulus seethed, and his face burned purple with wrath. He tried to choke down his feelings before continuing. "So this Mauglad gets himself killed somehow, and hundreds of years later, his soul ends up inside Xilva? There's got to be more to it than that."

Finwald's brow was creased deeply in thought. He eventually cleared his throat. "Mauglad's soul could have been banished, I suppose. Cast out of the Maw, far far away where it could cause no mischief. For the presence here of a soul of a former power within Vaagenfjord Maw would not lie still easily, and would remain a great danger to all who had abused it."

"They could have bound him to a task, of course," Appa proposed, "something that would have occupied every moment of his time for all eternity."

They all turned to the old man, who squatted near the lantern, his glassy eyes fixed upon its glow with a faraway look of complete distraction.

"I have heard of many such stories," he continued. "A long time ago in the Blighted Heathlands there lived a moonraker who caused much darkness with his evil and foolish ways. Eventually he was captured by the villagers, who drowned him in the very mere upon which he so loved to practice his arts. But his ghost arose and brought down a fearful and continuous unrest upon the villagers who had slain him. It was my own father who eventually had to deal with him." At this the assembled audience murmured with impatience, for they felt this was no place to be listening to the old goat's tall stories. But Finwald waved them to be still, and they listened.

"My father placed a curse on the moonraker's soul," Appa went on, "binding it to the task of draining the mere whose moon-reflection it used to rake. It was a hopeless task, of course, for the lake was bottomless and, not only that, the ghost was allowed only a tea strainer to accomplish its work. But it was *compelled*, so had no choice but to stick to its task. And thus it continues to this day, the ghost knowing it can never finish, and the villagers untroubled by its hauntings."

How much of this tale was true, and not merely the ramblings of an old man, none there knew, but it was sufficient to prompt the inevitable wisdom from Bolldhe.

"I've heard that story in just about every tavern I've ever visited, in one form or another, and I've often wondered exactly which one was the evildoer, the ghost who gives people the odd fright now and again, or the holy man who puts such a curse upon it."

"Yes, and what about those villagers?" Wodeman pointed out. "They were *murderers*."

Appa shrugged. "I must admit, it does seem overly cruel to make the ghost use a tea strainer," he conceded. "But when you think about it, if the lake really is bottomless, it hardly matters what implement is used. In fact, if the ghost is never *ever* going to empty it, then a tea strainer is actually better than, say, a great big bucket, because at least it's lighter to handle."

Finwald was beginning to regret indulging his brother-in-faith. "It really doesn't matter," he said impatiently. "The point is, the troublesome spirit was given a task that kept it out of the way eternally. It's a perpetual banishment of sorts."

"In my land," Paulus cut in, "it is said the spirits of murderers must suffer an eternity of being killed and killed again, thus forced to endure the agonies that they inflicted on others, and with the despair of knowing they must go through it again and again until Time itself dies."

"Yes, I imagine they would say that in your land," Finwald commented. "Does anything *pleasant* ever happen where you come from?"

"That place in the mountains where Xilvafloese fell," Paulus went on, ignoring the priest. "Where he *changed*—I think I know its name."

"Really?"

"To the east of the Blue Mountains lie the Polgrim Hunting Grounds," Paulus explained, "and it is said by the Polgrim themselves that within the northern reaches of the mountains there lies a valley of great evil and darkness. It is a place that the living would never willingly enter, for none even among the great heroes could endure such dread as is in that place. And there dwell the souls of the damned, doomed to languish there forever beyond the reach of the living. They call it the Valley of Sluagh."

Bolldhe snorted. It always made him laugh when the Nahovian started prattling in that way. He was just about to accuse him of having made that up on the spot, when he suddenly remembered that poem Paulus had recited to him just after Methuselech's fall. This poem, risible though it was, contained within its poorly-translated stanzas the same word "Sluagh."

Maybe Paulus does know something we don't?

Finwald, also, was slow to dismiss the Nahovian's words. "It makes sense," he admitted. "If a soul must be banished, best to send it where no living being would dare venture."

"No living being save one who hasn't a clue what he's doing," growled Nibulus, "one not fully awake, or too sick to stop himself."

"Poor Xilva," Finwald cursed, "he was probably the only living thing ever to have been brought down into that place. Such a terrible stroke of misfortune."

"But good fortune for Mauglad," Wodeman concluded. "His first chance, after all that time, of being rehoused in a fresh vehicle of flesh, and one that was already heading back home, as it were."

"And now he is home, somewhere close around here," Appa said quietly. "Cuna save us all!"

"But why?" demanded Nibulus. "What's his purpose?"

"And whose side is he on?" Finwald wondered.

"Certainly not Scathur's," Gapp insisted. "You should have seen the state he was in when I rescued him from the keep. As he said himself, he's considered the Black Sheep and he's out for justice. And if he can drag Xilva's crumbling corpse all the way from that Sluagh Valley to here—*can you imagine how much that must have hurt?*—he's not going to give up too easily."

The assembled company nodded thoughtfully, and pondered at length upon all that had been said. There were so many questions about this whole matter regarding Methuselech. So many questions, and as yet few answers. But there was a feeling in the air that this discussion had gone as far as it could go, at least for the time being, and that it was perhaps time for them to get on their way.

But just as they began to rise and prepare themselves, Gapp suddenly called out: "Before we go, there is just one small matter I'd like to clear up—if I could have your attention for just one minute. Finwald, I wonder if you could tell us, is this the first time you've journeyed to the Maw?"

The mage-priest stopped dead in his tracks.

"I beg your pardon?" he replied.

Everyone else paused too, even the Vetters, when they recognized the sudden note of tension in his voice.

Looks like I've got your attention then, Gapp thought, and suppressed a grim smile. He had been waiting so long for this moment.

They were all staring at Finwald now, for he had not yet answered the boy's question.

"Well, no, I suppose . . ." Finwald stammered. "I mean yes, of course it is."

Appa's eyes narrowed, as he stared hard at his fellow Lightbearer. "Finwald?" he prompted in puzzlement.

Gapp shrugged. "Oh all right, it's just that I've suddenly remembered some other things Mauglad said to me during our time together. I told you earlier how obsessed he was, didn't I? Well, he certainly seemed obsessed about one thing: to reach this place before *you* did, Finwald. Or at least to intercept you before you arrived."

"Me?" Finwald tried to say but his throat had somehow dried up, and all that came out was a half-squeak.

"Yes, there was one very odd thing he said back in Cyne-Tregva," Gapp continued, "that, if we didn't meet up with you in Wrythe, we'd just have to do the job ourselves, which meant getting a silver sword made in the town. But then, after we arrived, he seemed to have forgotten that whole thing about silver swords, or maybe didn't think it was important anymore—and then there was all this stuff about Plan A and Plan B, and Marmennill scales, and . . . I don't know, but he was obviously changing strategy as and when it suited him—"

"Boy!" Nibulus yelled, his voice barging through Gapp's prattling. "Cut to the chase!"

"With or without the sword, he was heading this way anyway. But when I told him Yulfric's story, he really did become obsessed."

"Yulfric's story?" Appa asked, and studied his brother mage-priest's aura intensely.

Though the room was crypt cold, Finwald's pale face was clammy with sweat.

"Yes, Yulfric the forest-giant, remember? You see, Yulfric told me he knew Finwald," Gapp informed them. "He'd met him a while back, stumbling half-dead through the forest, heading northward, with a sword. Isn't that right, Finwald? On some kind of preaching mission to Wrythe, weren't you?"

Finwald was now rigid.

" 'So long, and thanks for all the venison,' " Gapp quoted, " and signed, 'Finwald.' That's what you wrote in that book you gave him, didn't you, Finwald? That book you gave him along with your meditation-wheel."

The circle of listeners tightened noose-like around the mute priest.

"And it was this sword that was uppermost in Mauglad's mind as he drove us on and on through the forest. A sword he claimed was the most powerful weapon in the world, one that could change history with one stroke—a sword that, at all costs, must not be allowed to enter the Maw. And do you know what this sword looked like, gentlemen? Why, apparently, it looked very much like a snake. Sort of *wavy*, you know?"

"Get on with it!" Nibulus scolded him, clearly irritated at the boy's histrionics.

But Gapp had already said all he would: his part of the storytelling was done. It was now up to the mage-priest to draw his tale to a close.

"Finwald?" Nibulus said levelly, hating every moment of this attack on his friend, but determined to get to the bottom of it nonetheless. "Care to explain, old mate?"

Finwald apparently did not. He just stood there, unmoving, in exactly the same position he had adopted two minutes ago.

"Finwald," Nibulus repeated softly, but more menacing for all that, "would you care to tell us more about Bolldhe's sword?"

He approached the priest slowly, with deliberation. So too did the others of his small company, these men who had traveled with him so far and through such pain. And as they closed on Finwald, they could recognize it in his eyes, in his trembling lower lip, in that stance of a trapped animal: they could hear it in his breath, even smell it from his pores:

He had deceived them.

"Finwald?" Nibulus inquired in a voice that began softly but ended in a growl. "For the third time, would you please care to enlighten us as to what the *hell* you've dragged us into!"

"I . . . *can't!*" was all the terrified man could manage.

"You will," hissed Bolldhe, and extended the flamberge towards Finwald until its tip almost touched the man's eyeball.

Finwald's stare now went from Bolldhe to focus on the sword point less than an inch from his face. Then an unexpected calm came over him. He opened his mouth as if about to explain, but then refocused his gaze upon Bolldhe.

"I really can't," he repeated, some measure of the old control now restored to his tone. "It cannot be revealed. But believe me, Bolldhe, when I tell you that you, or at least one of us here, must use Flametongue on Drauglir."

"Finwald, stop this!" Appa cursed in frustration. "Why are you deceiving us?"

"I am deceiving no one."

"I can feel your untruth as surely as I can see you standing before me now!" Appa spat. "What is all this nonsense?"

Bolldhe suddenly withdrew the flamberge, slid it back into his belt, and carefully but firmly took Finwald's tulwar away from him.

"I reckon *I'll* be using this thing from now on," he told the priest. "I don't think I can trust that flamberge any more than I can trust you."

Bolldhe snapped his lantern up into its sleeve, and directed the strong, narrow beam directly into the mage-priest's face. Finwald flinched under the light, almost recoiling, but he tried nevertheless to out-face the company. And they stared back at him. They stared at him hard. It was only in the harsh glare of that lamp that they could study his face in any detail. And what they now saw there stilled them, puzzled them, even shocked them.

Like them, Finwald had come through some rather extreme situations to arrive here. But unlike themselves, he had constantly faced and overcome these trials without even the slightest faltering of his resolve. Yet, now looking upon him closely, they saw for the first time a strange anguish in the priest's eyes, and a hopelessness in the set of his mouth that they had never witnessed before. It was as if they were seeing each taut nerve of his courage stretch to its limit, and one by one, snap.

For the first time since any of them had ever known him, Finwald had clearly lost control—of everything.

All of a sudden, Schnorbitz leapt up and whirled around to stare into the darkness they had forgotten still surrounded them. The low rumor of his growl set the air around him pulsing, his nose dilated and snuffled frantically, and ice once again clamped around the entire company's hearts.

Don't say they're back already! they prayed to their separate gods. *Please don't say they're back!*

The Vetters and their steeds now also picked up the scents that had spun Schnorbitz's attention around, and without a word being spoken, without any apparent fear or hesitation, they began to draw closer to any of their kind who bore the torches distributed to them by the humans. In separate groups the Vetters then spread out, and softly paced towards the place where they could sense their new enemy waited.

In awe at their new allies' courage, the men still held back. But they knew there was nothing else for it. Weapons were taken up, straps refastened, tattered nerves secured, and any thoughts that this was all happening far too soon after their last ordeal, battened down fast. Every human soul in that chamber—including the now-disarmed Finwald with Paulus's bastard sword at his back—readied themselves, and followed the Vetters.

With the searchlight beam of Bolldhe's lantern lighting his way from close behind, Schnorbitz padded with dreadful purpose down the cavernous hall ahead of them. There were no noises to be heard yet, but others with keener noses than the humans were becoming increasingly tense.

Radkin and Ted pushed their way through the throng to locate their young friend Gapp. The Vetter blacksmith grasped Gapp's wrist firmly, and hauled his arm up to see what the boy was holding. In the light from a torch, the bronze machete shone with a dull gleam, the blacksmith's signature just visible on its blade.

"Yes," Gapp whispered, "I never go anywhere without it."

Ted nodded in approval and patted the lad roughly on the shoulder. He then put his mouth to the boy's ear, and whispered: *"Mycel-Haug."*

Gapp's eyes met those of the Peladane. "They've detected humans," he translated for him.

"Scathur's Wire-fellows," Nibulus whispered, then began creeping forward, till Radkin tugged at his arm.

"Dorcht-wela," he trilled, and imitated the thumbs-up sign he had seen Gapp use now and again.

"Encouraging news," Gapp reported. "He says there aren't many."

"Good, but can he smell other things?" hissed Nibulus. "Dead things maybe, or that Scathur?"

Gapp translated as best he could, but the two Vetters were becoming a little confused. They were not sure now what smells they were picking up.

"Move!" Nibulus commanded in a louder voice, and marched on ahead of the company.

The lantern now began to pick out strange shapes from the darkness around them in this unfamiliar hall. There were niobium pulpits in the likeness of winged fiends, around which the very air itself swirled in shades of violet and gold. There were idols of netherworld denizens engaged in unspeakable acts of violent copulation. Here and there were stairways that spiraled upward unto the loftier reaches of the hall, only to stop dead, leading nowhere. Some of them even emerged horizontally out of the walls; others still hung upside down from the ceiling.

Edging the chamber now was a kind of nave arcade, or ambulatory, the upper level of which was a clerestory punctuated with lunettes, through which poured an infernal light that came from some unknown source. Below ran a walkway that had been smashed in places by the invading Peladanes; yet it could be seen that, unlike the plinths they'd passed earlier, which had rotted, this appeared to be *healing,* with fresh, pink marble growing out in rounded stumps to bridge the gaps.

And below this ambulatory, supporting the entire structure, were columns that looked for all the world like membranes, which smelled of old blood and appeared to pulsate before their very eyes.

"There are toadstools in the woods back home that can turn a man's mind inside out if eaten raw," Wodeman whispered to the old priest at his side. "But none that I know of that could beget nightmares such as this."

Carefully the whole company pressed on, eyes straining, weapons at the ready.

Suddenly Bolldhe said: "Isn't that a pair of hips sticking out on either side behind that pillar?"

They all stared. Sure enough, Aelldryc, the tiny-headed but massively hipped sister of Eorcenwold, had been detected. Though all twelve of her cohorts had selected pillars broad enough to hide their bulk, only one of her gender could have been both vain and deluded enough to believe that a twelve-inch-diameter column might conceal her twenty-four-inch-wide hips.

Nibulus nodded. "I'd recognize those bolster-like pins anywhere," he whispered. "Seems like our friends from Tyvenborg don't know when to stop."

"You know anything about this little ambush, Finwald?" Nibulus hissed into the priest's ear.

Finwald, with a blade at his neck now, moaned in what sounded like genuine disbelief. "How in Cuna's name did they get in here?" he breathed.

"I don't know." Nibulus grinned evilly. "But I know which way they're leaving. . . ."

"What are you going to do?" wheezed Appa. He still had nightmares about those thieves, and was not sure what he wanted done about them, holy man's conscience or no.

Nibulus glanced over to the mercenary. "Kill every last one of them," he said coldly. "Right, Paulus?"

The mercenary's single eye twitched, and he nodded his immediate and wholehearted assent. Englarielle, too, though he knew nothing of these newcomers, signaled his willingness and that of all his people. Now, at last, they could do something they understood, something the Vetters were good at. Without a sound, they almost slid up onto their steeds.

"And this time," Nibulus went on, "we have our own army."

"Wait a minute!" Appa croaked. "We can't just—"

"DEATH TO THE TYVENBORG BASTARDS!" Nibulus roared, and the company surged forward, taking up his cry.

A second later, a stocky figure stepped out of concealment with a blunderbuss braced on his shoulder. In the next instant the entire chamber exploded with a terrible thunderclap of noise. Many there were flattened to the ground or glued to the spot by the blast alone. Nibulus was knocked off balance when a fragment of shot rang off his pauldron, and two of the Cervulice doubled over with strangled cries of pain, throwing their startled riders. But three less fortunate Vettersteed, having taken the full force of the discharge, went down in a spume of blood and flying tissue, dead before they had time even to scream. Their unseated riders would not be getting up again that day, or any other.

Before anyone had time to gather their wits or even grasp what had just happened, the rest of Eorcenwold's band stepped out from behind whichever pillar, plinth or pulpit had been shielding them. Cerddu-Sungnir the half-Grell leaned casually with one shoulder against his column and let fly a volley of five quarrels from his crossbow. Hlessi the Grell loped forward and flung one of his throwing axes in a lightning-fast overarm spin. With a flick of his wrist, Khurghan the Polg sent his double-bladed haladie boomeranging into the advancing enemy. Meanwhile, Flekki the River-Hauger had flung three of her poison chakrams.

At the same time AFinwald, their disproportionately shaped giveaway, appeared at her brother's side and began pouring a flask of some sticky green liquid over the stock of her brother's musket while he firmly gripped it at arms' length. A veritable steam-demon of noxious, green vapor billowed into the air, enveloping the two of them.

The effect of the ensuing missile discharge was devastating. A tide of the Peladane's allied force went down in that first salvo, it seemed. But Nibulus's voice bellowed as a raging buffalo, and his followers were propeled with even greater madness of battle against the enemy.

With neither haste nor apparent fear, the Tyvenborgers withdrew. They had come for plunder, not battle. Not one of their number had been harmed, and they intended to keep it that way. Ghost-silent and swift as hares, they vanished into the darkness beyond.

"Bitch-born scum!" Nibulus yelled at their backs. "Toerags!" But none that carried torches could keep up with him. Though incensed by this unprovoked attack, Nibulus was a seasoned enough soldier not to head alone into that darkness against such an enemy. Instead he almost ripped the bow off his back, fitted an arrow to it quicker than even he would have believed possible, and then let fly into the gloom.

It was a wild shot, and served mainly to assuage his impotent fury. Nevertheless, Nibulus could not help punching the air in triumph when he heard a scream issuing from the darkness. It was a very small victory, to be sure, but that did not abate Nibulus's battle-joy one bit. His beaming red face glowed with satisfaction as he shouted out further orders:

"Appa, sort out the wounded! Bolldhe, get that lantern over here, and stick with me from now on! Paulus . . . Paulus—where the hell's that sneaky little priest got to?"

Where, indeed?

Not even Finwald himself really knew where he was. Or what he was doing. Or how in the name of Cuna's Almighty Eye-staff everything had fallen apart so completely in the space of mere minutes! Years of careful work laid to waste by something so tiny and unforeseen!

That boy! he wept bitterly. *That snot! That smarmy, short-arsed, know-it-all little puke-brat! Why the hell couldn't he have just stayed dead?*

But, no, Gapp Radnar, the least among them, had not stayed dead. He had somehow survived where others greater than himself would likely have perished. Furthermore, he had, beyond all reasonable probability, stumbled across a small part of Finwald's secret. And if that were not enough, the boy had managed to drag his worthless little carcass all the way here to the inner sanctum of Vaagenfjord Maw just to start telling tales!

Reeling with disbelief at how unfairly things had turned out, Finwald stumbled on blindly, heading away from his companions. *That he had traveled all this way with them, only to fail right at the end!* But fail he had. For what could he possibly do now? The game was up for him, as far as that lot were concerned; there was absolutely no going back to join them now. Their voices were already fading behind him, fading into his past, and here in this blackness he was completely, utterly alone, and completely, utterly without any plan.

It was as though the entire world, his world, had winked out of existence, and he was now the only thing floating about in an eternity of space.

Nauseous with fear, disrepair, and disorientation, and not least from the vile and unnatural fragrances that clogged the air, Finwald blundered on through the heavily-scented darkness.

What am I to do? What can I possibly do now?

The voices behind him gradually faded to nothing. It was then the voices ahead of him began to be heard.

Got to form a new plan. Cannot give up yet, he told himself.

His scheme had come wholly undone, but there had to be something else he could do. There had to be.

The voices ahead of him grew louder, and it did not seem as if they were aware of their silent, torchless pursuer. Farther they continued, somehow drawing him on as a distant lighthouse summons a drowning swimmer in a dark, stormy sea. Then the beginnings of a new plan did indeed start to form in Finwald's head.

Flametongue was out of his grasp now. He could only hope, *pray,* that Bolldhe, or somebody, would use the sword as Finwald had instructed. But for himself it was vital that he find himself some new companions.

After all, he reasoned as he sped noiselessly after the escaping thieves, *if Bolldhe could switch sides so easily, as he almost did back in Eotunlandt, then why can't I?*

Ignoring the dark all around him, Finwald plunged on towards whatever Chance had in store for him.

The thief lay facedown upon the ground, teeth clenched in a silent grimace of agony, as blood welled from the deeply embedded arrow. It was pitch-dark here, without the meanest hint of light to see by; but the Tyvenborger could feel only too well that familiar sensation of nausea spinning the whole world around.

Damn those Peladanes! the thief cursed, spitting blood in between chokes and gasps. It had been such a perfect hit-and-run, too. Who would have thought such a lucky shot was possible? And the rest of the thieves had just carried on, disappearing into the secret places whence they had emerged, not realizing yet that one of their number had fallen.

Got to get up! Got to get out of here! Hvitakreust, *the pain . . .*

Then the thief stiffened in fear. The agony, the disappearing Tyvenborgers, the approaching enemies, everything was suddenly forgotten, everything save the abysmal blackness of this pit and the new presence that drifted out of it.

Oh, you've fallen down, a silken thread-like voice hissed, with a humorless leer on its nonexistent lips. *Here, let me help you up. . . .*

The thief stiffened even more, extremities feeling as if they were about to snap off like icicles. Head throbbing painfully, there followed a stomach-heaving sensation as of a red-hot needle passing into the brain, but without actually penetrating either skin or bone. Thereupon the presence began eagerly searching about for the thoughts that lay therein. Searching with all the delicacy of a boar rooting for acorns in the loam.

The thief's mind screamed out in indignant protest, *Get out! Get out! Get out of me!* and it fought with every last ounce of determination and typically Tyvenborgian savagery to rid itself of this unspeakable intrusion. Eyes tightly shut, fingers clenched claw-like, the victim stifled the grunts that tried to force their way out through gritted and bloody teeth. Yet all the while the intruding shade howled with laughter at these puny attempts at resistance.

It was, of course, useless. The spirit of Mauglad Yrkeshta now clung like a limpet to the inside of the Tyvenborger's skull, and nothing in the world could be done about it: the new possession was completed.

Ah, good, still alive then, Mauglad purred in a tone that suggested fine silver strands of cobweb being stroked by a spider's claw. *But thankfully not too much alive.*

Possession. Dominion over the dying, a hold over the half-alive, sovereignty over the semi-dead. Not so alive, so *vital,* that they could resist, yet alive enough to inhabit—for though Mauglad might raise, summon or even direct the dead, their empty husks and empty minds were no good to him if he wanted to take possession.

But when the opportunity did arise, well, it was not to be passed up, and could be so immensely gratifying to one such as he. To dwell in the flesh-case of one caught between both worlds, to inhabit this halfway house, it somehow reconciled Life and Death in such a satisfying way.

Yes, possession; it was a holistic experience indeed, yet also one that was so wholly steeped in revenge, the sweetest turning of the tables imaginable.

For centuries Mauglad's soul had wandered the dark crevices of Sluagh Valley, forever howling out towards the north: *Kill me! Kill me! Slay my body and let me be at peace!* For he knew from suffering this unceasing perdition in limbo, that the body that had once been his—his real body—had not been laid to rest. Soulless now, a vacant shell, just another tool for the use of the Rawgr, it walked in dark places where its owner could not go. *Such heinous blasphemy!* And until his original body was destroyed, the soul of Mauglad Yrkeshta would simply go on, and on, forever condemned to wander in grinding bitterness and self-torment.

To Mauglad when he had been alive, death had always been the most dreadful terror. It was something he had taken the greatest pleasure in inflicting on others, but that he had taken great care in avoiding himself, at *all* costs. There were some who claimed that every different type of creature on Lindormyn had developed in their own way purely as a result of this obsessive, unceasing struggle to avoid death. In fact, for most, life itself was little more than a continuous escape from death, the struggle to survive no matter what.

How naïve this all seemed now to Mauglad, who would do anything to end his endless existence.

Then all of a sudden Methuselech had happened along, straying unconscious on horseback into the shunned depths of the Sluagh. Deep into his dying mind had Mauglad probed, laying bare its contents. Oh yes, what a veritable diamond mine of information *he* had been!

Then Mauglad's new shell, a battered and unreasonably alive reanimation of Methuselech's former self, had pulled itself out of its prison of stone, stood jerkily upright upon damaged feet, and smiled thinly.

"Well, well, well," it had said, "so Drauglir has fallen! I never would have believed it possible. It certainly never would have happened if *I'd* still been around. Well, we'll just have to see what we can do to put things right, won't we, my friend Methuselech, eh?"

So too did the Tyvenborger now begin to suffer, as Xilvafloese had done. A numbness began to seep outward from the brain along every nerve, like an early frost penetrating the soil, driving the warmth before it, obtunding the senses, until all that remained of the body's former mind was a small piece of consciousness locked up now as if in an old and battered trunk shut away in some dusty, cobweb-hung attic of the brain.

The Mauglad-thing reached awkwardly around its back and, with clumsy new fingers, wrenched the arrow out and cast it away into the darkness.

Such strength! it thought, marveling at this fine new body after so long in Methuselech's rotting carcass.

"Right," it rasped to itself, "let's get this over with once and for all."

"Only the soul-dead would ever betray their friends," Nibulus cursed above the screams of the maimed and dying, unable to believe what had just happened. The loss of several of their new allies within just a few seconds was bad enough, especially as they had not even been given a sporting chance to retaliate. But the absconding of the mage-priest had shaken him badly. His grief at losing Xilvafloese for the second time was still keenly felt but, now the Asyphe had gone for good, out of all those remaining Nibulus had counted only Finwald as a genuine friend.

But there was little sympathy to be found among his company. The blunderbuss had killed three Cervulice and one Vetter, and left two others writhing in pain; four other Vetters had been badly wounded by crossbow bolts; the throwing axe had lodged itself deep into the sternum of a very dead Cervulus; Flekki's three poisoned chakrams had each found a target, namely Wodeman and two further Cervulice; and the Polg's haladie had sliced the head clean off another Vetter, before returning to its grinning wielder.

"Oh, come off it, boy, you should be used to betrayal by now!" Appa growled at Nibulus. Splashed liberally with blood and, with Englarielle's help, struggling to restrain those he was attempting to heal, his lower jaw had resumed its customary doglike protrusion. He was in no mood for the Peladane's sudden fit of righteousness.

". . . Isn't that right, Bolldhe?" he added trenchantly.

Bolldhe, also kneeling by his side, did not look up from his task of holding the lantern steady over patients the priest was working on. "Only the dead are beyond betraying their friends," he agreed readily. "People under threat are capable of doing anything to survive."

Nibulus looked around bitterly. There were six dead and six injured, plus three (including Wodeman) who were rigid with paralysis from the poison inflicted by the chakrams. For the time being, no one was going anywhere, revenge or not.

"What d'you think those people want?" Gapp asked, visibly shaken by the carnage all around. "Are they going to keep out of our way now, d'you reckon, or are they going to pick us off one by one?"

"They're here for loot, pure and simple," stated Nibulus, "but I don't want to chance a repeat performance of *this* bloody mess. They'll pay for this with their lives, I swear—one way or another. But there's not much we can do till Wodeman snaps out of it. I'm not going on without him—we've lost enough of our number in the last hour or so as it is."

Paulus stepped forward, black with suppressed fury. "The priest was my charge," he said to Nibulus. "I want him back."

"Well, tough!" Nibulus retorted bluntly. "Unless you can see in the dark."

"Finwald can't," the Nahovian countered, "leastways, not as well as I. And I move faster."

The Peladane considered this point for a moment. "We certainly can't allow him to run around loose in this place," he admitted. "Pel-Adan only knows what he might get up to. But go *quietly,* Paulus, all right? You can never tell what that one's capable of, once he's cornered."

"He's not evil, if that's what you're saying," Appa called over to them between salient gouts of arterial spray. "Even when he bolted, I could sense no evil in him. Deceit, yes, but no evil."

"Thanks for that reassurance, Appa," Nibulus grunted, "but all that tells me is to watch my back with you as well. Paulus, if you can fetch that bastard back before he brings all hell down on us, then go. *Now.*"

Finwald fled up the spiral stairs in the wake of the thieves. There was light here, of a fashion, for the fire from the channel found its way along narrow ducts to kindle a muted redness out of the marble walls. The whole stair-shaft whispered with distorted echoes, among which he was sure he could pick out faintly the slapping of many feet on a stone surface somewhere above. His jaw, shapely and refined though it was, was set as tight as a bear trap, and his movements, swift and light, were those of a hunter. Despite the unforeseen setbacks, Finwald was as resolute as ever.

He nimbly leapt up the glass-smooth winders of the staircase, with only the lightest whisper of robe-cloth against stone. He was fleet, sure-footed and determined, but under it all, his mind was close to exploding.

Everything was coming undone, and the full extent of this undoing had not yet sunk in. But Finwald was "a man of singular purpose, driven by great need," and as always, he simply would not allow himself to fail. He would focus his prodigious concentration upon first locating the thieves, and once he had persuaded them not to kill him outright, he would call every last ounce of eloquence, bribery, trickery, and even intimidation to somehow get them to go along with his plans.

What exactly those plans would be, however, he was still not sure. And how he was going to bring his eloquence to bear when he did not even speak their language, remained at the moment a complete mystery. He would have to deal with those problems if and when . . .

He stopped dead and flattened himself against the wall. He had heard something below him. *Damn,* there it was again! Someone or something was climbing the stairs after him.

Onwards and upwards he climbed, now choosing speed over stealth. *This shouldn't be happening,* he thought as he climbed. *I'm not a bad man—Why is this happening to me?*

Oh, how the world turned! It could not have been even three weeks ago now when he had stood upon the blue-hazed meads of Eotunlandt and looked on in a horror of incredulity as Bolldhe offered his allegiance to the cutthroats of the Thieves' Mountain; stood over Appa with the Fossegrim-poisoned voulge poised above the old man's outstretched neck. How Finwald had fumed! How his insides had boiled with righteous indignation at this lowest of treacheries!

Yet here he was now, doing exactly the same. Not on an impulse born of self-preservation, as in Bollde's case, for Finwald's life was probably not even threatened by his former companions. But he had defected knowingly, deliberately, and relentlessly, refusing to look his conscience in the eye. Oh, how the world turned, indeed. . . .

The sudden rustling of an overcoat, the slight squeak of leather, and the soft patter of rapidly approaching feet spun Finwald round again. He fearfully approached the parapet, trying to still the heavy panting that shook his frame, and leaned over to peer down into the stairwell.

His panting was arrested in a choking whimper, and his labored heart seemed to stop pounding. There below him, the surest and most chilling vision of night-spawned vengeance spiraled up the stairs towards him. Greatcoat billowing out in languid ripples to caress the scarlet gypsum of the wall, the feathered cowl masking his visage in the manner of an assassin, and bastard-blade held out in front like a divining rod that tracked a liquid altogether thicker than water, Paulus was coming for him.

When Finwald's heart started to beat again, all thoughts and machinations, all feelings of compunction, self-pity, and failure evaporated in the furnace of his terror. He turned and ran as fast as ever he could.

Up and up the steps he wound, with the vicious Nahovian closing fast behind him. "C'mere, you wanker!" Paulus growled, without any hint of breathlessness. Still upwards the priest stumbled, running for his life, for he had no doubt in his mind that the mercenary, now let off his leash, fully intended to kill him.

His lungs had nothing but fire in them and his legs were about to buckle, when the stairs finally came out onto a landing. Leaning heavily against the massive balustrade, Finwald swiftly scanned his new surroundings. Either way the long passage reached back into darkness, and was lined on both sides by a row of heavy brass doors.

One of which was slightly ajar.

"I've got you now," Paulus simmered, just yards behind him. Without a second's delay, Finwald slipped through the welcoming doorway, just an instant before his pursuer gained the landing. Noiselessly he swung the heavy door to behind him till it almost closed, leaving just a crack through which he could peer.

Here came Paulus now, a great black, stalking bird of prey against the dull ember glow emanating from the stair shaft. Had he seen where Finwald had gone? His faceless cowl swung this way and that as he crouched watchfully on the landing.

Oh Cuna! Finwald quailed, *he's coming this way!*

As Paulus approached the same doorway, Finwald stumbled away from it back into the darkness of the room. It was almost pitch-black in here, with only a bare sliver of illumination from the crack in the door. He had no idea where to run next, or what to do.

Then the heavy boot of Paulus crashed against the door. With a reverberating clangor it slowly swung wide open, and the tall predator slipped inside. He did not come straight for Finwald, for he had not spotted him yet. Instead, he disappeared off to one side, and was swallowed up by the darkness.

Reprieve! Finwald thought. If he could keep his footfalls silent, he might make it back to the door before Paulus noticed him. Stock-still for the moment, he waited for the ghoulish mercenary's footsteps to recede. There they went, pad-pad-padding away into a deeper corner of the room. Finwald breathed in deep, offered up a prayer to Cuna, and readied himself—he had to get this right. There could be no false move if he were to get out of this alive.

Then, just as he was about to break for the door, a horrible scuffling sound broke out. Finwald's mind screamed in panic, and paralysis took him.

The scuffling was terrifying. There were no words or shouting, just strangled grunts, and the desperate gasps of those locked in a struggle to the death. As he stood there immobilized, images of his persecutor being torn limb from limb by nightmare creatures ran through Finwald's brain. Then a sickening scream of agony sliced through the heavy stillness of the chamber, followed by the deafening clang of iron upon stone as Paulus's sword clattered upon the floor at Finwald's feet.

He stared at it lying in the glow from the corridor. The blade was slick with blood, but even in near-darkness it did not look a normal red.

That was enough for Finwald. He sprang for the open doorway, but just as he was about to fly through, something huge stepped in front of it, blocking out the light. Finwald smacked straight into this leviathan with a force that sent him staggering backward to collapse upon the floor. It was like colliding with an armored war-bison.

Lights from torches, lanterns, and other cleverer devices sprang out of the surrounding darkness, and in a hazy muddle Finwald looked all about.

"Of course," he breathed in relief. "It had to be."

He had caught up with the Tyvenborgers.

But Finwald had little to feel relieved about. By running from his own group like that, he had demolished and incinerated every bridge along the river, and cast himself hopelessly adrift. For there could be no reconciliation now, not now, not ever. He had run from his own people—who had been both escort and friend to him—only to throw himself at the mercy of the most savage and deadly bunch of cutthroats he had ever clapped eyes on. As he looked upon their impassive faces, and their assortment of ingenious flesh-rending tools (all now casually pointing at him) the old expression *"Out of the frying pan . . ."* sprang quickly to mind.

Perhaps I was a trifle rash? he reflected.

He looked from the bleeding, semi-conscious form of Paulus sprawled on the floor nearby, to the squat thief-sergeant who returned his stare with undisguised disdain. It was only then that it occurred to Finwald that the Tyvenborgers would not even realize he was running from his former companions. For all they knew, he and Paulus were simply the first who had caught up with them. And how on earth was he going to explain all this to them, when he could not speak a word of their language?

How, indeed. For now, he could do nothing. Rough fingers enmeshed themselves in his long hair from behind, and he was dragged away, along with the insensible Nahovian, out of this same room, down the passage, along several others passages, up many flights of stairs, and through lightless places that did not seem to be a part of this or any other world. The farther up they went, the less real it all seemed, until Finwald began to form the impression that somewhere along the line he had already been slain, and that this was where he was condemned to wander for the rest of eternity.

Though he did not realize it, the thieves were deliberately bringing him to the mid-levels of Ymla-Myrrdhain, and their latest hideout. In all the time they had spent in the inner keep so far, the Tyvenborgers had only succeeded in finding one secret room, and even that had contained little in the way of treasure. Nevertheless, because it seemed reasonably safe to them, it now served as their base.

Eorcenwold and his band of picaroons were clearly not the sensitive sort, Finwald realized as soon as he was thrust into their chosen room. For of all the chambers he had looked upon in Vaagenfjord Maw, this surely had to be the most warped. Though they appeared completely unaffected, to him it seemed a visual and olfactory transgression. It felt in fact as if he had stepped right into some disturbing dream: a vision of the aberrant, a nightmare in purple and green, a chamber for demons to dream in.

What was this unearthly place?

Drapes of glistening, sickly mauve hung like wet skin from the walls, all the while undulating strangely as if something lurked behind them. Between these could be seen alternately great mirrors that reached from floor to ceiling and pictures of vicious delights similar to those in the great hall downstairs. These images, however, were of such revolting, intensified atrocity that merely a half-glance at them caused Finwald to avert his eyes out of fear of losing his sanity.

Huge candles of black wax stood around, ensconced in pricket candle-sticks. In place of rugs, strewn about the floor were the pelts of flayed humans, Haugers and giants, some with the heads still intact, snarling in pickled pain.

The chamber was dominated by a giant four-poster bed. The twisted spinal columns of huge unknown creatures served as the posts, supporting a cornice that looked to be the upper shell of an enormous, virulent green turtle. From this hung a crumpled, black leather valance and matching hangings. Covers of burgundy and ermine-white were spread out over the mattress, and two crossed Bardisches hung above the headboard. To the right was a fabulously ornate bedside cabinet with a pewter bowl on it. Beneath it was a pair of slippers with finely stitched apertures to accommodate claws.

Beneath the bed could just be seen the head of some defeated champion. Its jaws had been dislocated and the mouth grotesquely widened, the entire contents of the skull scooped out, and the whole ghastly item resting on a brass hoop with three legs, so it could serve as a chamber pot.

Finwald felt a certain sense of familiarity as he beheld all this. Had he been told something about this place before? By that old eremite in the green jacket, all those years ago . . . ?

Nothing in this ghastly room appeared to have decayed or moldered, or indeed been affected by the passing of time in any discernible way. It was as if it had been spared the ravages of the ages, and instead had about it an air of patient expectancy. Yet there was also a queerness that pervaded all. There had been too much raw flesh, burning, and incense in here for it to ever wholly dissipate.

"Set him down over there," Eorcenwold instructed, indicating Paulus. "And bring the other one to me."

Finwald was surrounded by several of the brigands, and forced to kneel on his hands. Eorcenwold approached him and stared at him intensely with those big, round eyes. Earnestly, he began: "Right, you lanky streak of piss, I think it's time you started explaining yourself."

The mage-priest, of course, did not understand a word of this, but there was something surprisingly comforting in the stocky little thug's tone. It was so down-to-earth, so human, so *normal,* that it did a great deal to bring Finwald back to the real world of men, from the weirdness of this soul-cloying chamber. And, anyway, despite the company he kept, Eorcenwold did not look like the kind of man who would murder someone casually.

Finwald's disciplined mind now focused exclusively upon his blessings: *a) Paulus is no longer a threat, b) I've found the ones I've been looking for, and c) they haven't killed me yet.*

Now comes the hard part. . . .

Thus began Finwald's lengthy and desperate attempt to save his own life. He began by trying to communicate with sign language. It seemed a straightforward enough message at first: he had run away from his old company, he wished to join the Tyvenborgers, and great treasures awaited them both if they would but agree.

The more he tried, however, the clearer it became that they had not got the faintest idea what he was trying to convey to them. Finwald found himself repeating the same hand signals over and again, just the same only more emphatically, till desperation began to fog his concentration. Then he did the worst thing possible in that strange place. Looking imploringly from one thief to the next, his eyes inadvertently fell upon one of the mirrors that lined the wall.

From where he knelt, he could see in this mirror the reflections of several of his captors' backs. This in itself would not have been particularly remarkable, since the mirror was behind them. What was alarming, however, was that although the thieves themselves did not move, in the mirror their reflections appeared to be turning around.

Finwald's eyes almost popped out of his skull. He quickly tore his gaze away from the mirror, and concentrated it upon the thieves themselves. They were still there as before, regarding him with slightly puzzled amusement. Then he glanced again in the mirror, which should have reflected the backs of their heads, but instead he could see their faces, grinning at him directly. Grinning sinfully—and now laughing.

As the Lightbearer stared in horrified beguilement, their reflected heads began to expand. Bigger and fatter they swelled, fed by grotesque, blue, pumping arteries that bulged like frantically wriggling tapeworms beneath the skin. Long, dark bristles started extruding from that same skin, their eyes shrunk and narrowed, their mouths warped into heavy snouts, while two brutal, ripping tusks slid up from the lower jaw, and began dripping with the innocent blood of all the races of Lindormyn.

Within seconds this disfigurement was complete: there stood the thieves, their bodies now crowned with the wagging, monstrous heads of swine, which regarded him with odious, porcine mirth.

Eorcenwold shoved him impatiently, but for some reason Finwald found himself now unable to concentrate on his hand signals.

Once more he tore his gaze from the offending mirror, in an effort to recommence his crucial communication, but found that he was now looking at other mirrors farther along the wall. In these, he could make out the reflections of other thieves: Oswiu, Dolen, and Raedgifu. Raedgifu, he of the fine silks and voluminous leather trousers, occupied a whole mirror all by himself, having expanded to push the thieves nearest to him out to the edge of the glass and beyond the frame. His reflection, with an extremely vainglorious and lackadaisical countenance, stared out of that mirror toward another mirror on the opposite wall, each self-satisfied image enjoying what it saw in an endless repetition of reflected comeliness.

Dolen on the other hand was less favorably reflected, her face now a ghastly mask of loathing blackened by the flames of the hate that consumed her from within. And as for Oswiu Garoticca, bizarrely he appeared as a skeleton with a Kh'is dagger hovering inside his ribcage.

Then there was one mirror each for himself and Paulus. The recumbent mercenary, currently propped against a carved wooden screen and breathing heavily, was shown as a naked old man hunched up in his bed, fondling himself lasciviously.

Finwald found himself staring at a reflection of himself that wore several faces, all of them the brilliant hue of new grass.

Vanity mirrors, he noted, and dropped his gaze. *What personal sins would this room's previous occupant have gazed upon in admiration, I wonder?*

Back to the matter at hand, Finwald took a deep breath, and again attempted to sway his captors. The thieves however, by their very nature impulsive and inclined to lash out on a whim, were visibly losing what little patience they possessed, and the Lightbearer began to fluster. Raedgifu stepped forward and thrust his face embarrassingly close to Finwald's, appraising him carefully. Finwald did not dare return his gaze, could not guess what he was up to, and the fear grew in him that this dandified rogue intended to teach the captive the "tricks of the trade," as the Peladanes euphemistically put it.

Eventually, to Finwald's immense relief, Raedgifu sniffed haughtily, and backed away. Then with a casual flick of the wrist as though whipping a silk kerchief out of his breast pocket, he brought his cat-o'-nine-tails round and smote Finwald full in the face.

The priest reeled back in shock and agony, then collapsed upon the floor with a shriek. The room, and all in it, turned red as blood poured into his eyes. His sight swimming in nausea, the red room began to blur, and spin, and he inhaled deeply to prevent voiding his stomach. But the acrid stench of this corrupt chamber did nothing to help, and within moments his vision totally faded.

Though he did not realize it, Finwald had fallen into a swoon. In front of him the entire room seemed to distort. The thieves themselves were transformed into those Rawgrs and fiends depicted by the statues in the hall below, and even larger ones stepped out of the mirrors and stalked about, conversing in their own diabolic tongue. The chamber pot waddled, growling, out from under the bed, its mouth full of Rawgr's waste, and suddenly it multiplied into a whole swarm of chamber pots, gargling on their contents. They began leaping up and down irately upon their three-clawed brass feet, before charging forward ready to vomit their cargo upon him . . .

Finwald felt the revoltingly greasy splash of liquid on his face—and awoke to find Flekki standing over him with a flask. With an almost child-like cry of relief, he hauled himself onto his knees and stared up at the leering visages that surrounded him.

But it was useless. He had failed, and he would die. Surely the only reason he had survived this long was because he did not share their language. Otherwise, they would have tortured all the information they wanted out of him long ago.

Khurghan, indeed, was all for handing him over to Grini, as the Boggart had not eaten for a while, and was becoming difficult to handle. Finwald glanced over at AFinwald, and wondered about using his old charm to elicit a female's support. But as she stared expressionlessly back at him, all that entered his head was: *By the gods, she's got massive hips!*

Of all of them, only the Dhracus offered him a glimmer of hope. From his companions' very first encounter with the Tyvenborgers, they had learned about her mind-tricks, and though he did not properly understand how they worked, that was now the only way Finwald could think of communicating his desperate message.

Sensing herself in his thoughts, Dolen stepped forward to stand before the kneeling man, and began searching his mind.

Those eyes! Finwald winced in repulsion, staring up into the Dhracus's soulless, glistening black orbs. There was an intensity and potency within them beyond anything he had observed in any other person he had ever met. But most of all, they were utterly unreadable. This was not going to be an easy task at all.

"Paulus," Finwald murmured to her (softly enough so that his former companion might not hear), and pointed to the Nahovian as he still slumped against the screen. Then he went on to concentrate on the image of himself being chased by the mercenary up the stairs. Concentration, fortunately, was something Finwald was still a master of.

He looked up hopefully, but the Dhracus merely shrugged.

Finwald tensed with anxiety. *What's the matter, can't she read my thoughts?* Then he remembered something Kuthy Tivor had once said about her kind: *"It is their cousins in Ghouhlem that possess the psionic art. Those from Godtha are mere apprentices."*

Maybe she's an empath, he wondered. *Maybe she's better with emotions than with thoughts or images. . . .*

So he drew upon his considerable imaginative ability, and focused upon the feelings he had experienced during his recent flight from Paulus. The animal terror . . . the desperation . . . the near-hopelessness . . .

Again he looked up, hardly daring to hope.

And released his breath in a sigh of relief. Dolen was nodding her understanding. She now turned and murmured something to Eorcenwold, who raised his eyebrows with interest, and the other thieves backed off a little.

Thank you! Finwald breathed. He did not need to be an empath to sense an easing of their hostility.

Next he focused all his thoughts and emotions upon *cunning* information and *greed* for treasure. . . .

It was a painstaking process, fraught with infuriating setbacks, constant misunderstandings, and an impatience that was threatening at any minute to tear the whole process apart. Because empathy has its limits, even for a Dhracus. But, despite these problems, Finwald believed that he and the ghost-faced woman were finally coming to an understanding.

Or so he believed. But the trouble with empaths, unfortunately, is that they can only ever be receivers, never transmitters. Dolen had still not been able to fully get her own message across.

Finwald did have one thing going for him, though. The thieves, it seemed, had not as yet been overly successful in their quest for riches. Gaining ingress was one thing; locating the goods was quite another. And this entire place, frankly, scared the pants off them. They were not going to leave until they had got at least something to make their journey here worthwhile, but neither were they going to stay in this Rawgr-pit for a second longer than necessary.

This strange newcomer, though, clearly knew a lot more about Vaagenfjord Maw than they did. How fortuitously timely. In addition, he was compliant, *very* eager to please and, above all, *alone*. So rather than being the threat he had at first appeared when arriving among them, this funny little man was now beginning to resemble a gift sent from whatever gods smiled on them.

But first, he would have to prove himself.

"No!" he cried out in protest. "Absolutely not! I can't!"

It had taken a while for the Dhracus to get her point across—quite possibly because the mage-priest was subconsciously refusing to believe it. But now that he knew what the test for his change of allegiance was to be, his newly regained self-control was disintegrating into fragments all about him.

It was Eotunlandt all over again. This time, however, he was to play the role Bolldhe had performed. A sacrifice was now demanded and, as luck would have it, the Tyvenborgers had just the right victim to hand.

My sweet Lord Cuna, Finwald railed internally. *That it should come to this!*

Just as Bolldhe had stared in disbelief at the back of old Appa's neck laid out before him, so too did Finwald now look down upon the battered and bound form of Paulus. And just as Bolldhe had then done, so too did Finwald now think: *How the hell did I get myself into this?*

How indeed? Had the shaman been here now, perhaps he would have been able to assist Finwald in searching for his answers within his soul, just as he had done back then with Bolldhe on the plain of fire and ice. On that occasion, Bolldhe had journeyed down, deep down into his past, further and further, until he had reached the deepest and most ancient place of his soul, wherein lay the answers.

For Finwald, however, it was a journey in exactly the opposite direction. Up, up and up unto the highest chamber of Ymla-Myrrdhain. Up, up and up, from his earliest childhood memories to the awful present that he now found himself in:

His mother, that vole-faced old hag with a mouth so big and a tongue so sharp she could have circumcised a fully-grown baluchitherium. Oh, what a great mother she had been! He had fed on the milk of human kindness from the flattest-chested woman in the whole desert region, and even then, had to wait at the end of the queue behind her clients.

Passed like a parcel then from mother to alchemist, Pashta-Maeva by name. Possibly the oddest man in Qaladmir, he of the lateral thought, the singularity of purpose, the consuming obsession and, of greatest significance, the monumental collection of literature. All in all, the perfect greenhouse for Finwald's intellect, curiosity, and inexplicable feelings of vocation . . .

. . . The finding of the sword . . . other mentors . . .

. . . Then a mentor of an entirely different kind. Appa, the Lightbearer from the north, had arrived in the boy's life at precisely the right moment. For young Finwald's constant searching was by this stage leading him down altogether darker paths; and he had been on the point of stepping over that black threshold beyond which no light shone. But just then Appa had arrived, and Finwald had been truly *illuminated*. Yes, Appa had given Finwald his long sought after sense of purpose which had filled that void that had been draining away his very soul. For this, Finwald would be eternally grateful to the old priest. Because he knew that same void was not waiting for just *anything* to fill it; no, that void had been opened in him for one specific purpose. It was awaiting Cuna.

And, finally, their journey together to the north, a journey to light, a journey to lands where the summer days swallowed up the night inside him. He had snapped shut his alchemical tomes, waved good-bye to a hopping mad and fist-shaking Pashta-Maeva, turned his back on the city of Qaladmir, and rejected the Olchorian darkness that had been beckoning him so patiently, so seductively, all that time. He had swapped obsession for discipline, and it was this discipline that would in time set him on a course taking him even farther north still, as far towards that light as it was possible to go—driving him on beyond the endurance of all but The Called.

All that, then, leading to this. Murder. Plain and simple. The culmination of Finwald's life, all that enlightenment, discipline, and study, all the careful preparations, the subtle arrangements, the clever machinations, all leading him—by Fate or by Chance—to this simple, black or white choice that was laid before him now. Should he throw everything—his own life included—down the drain, or should he continue Cuna's work, while murdering his companion in order to do so?

For murder it most definitely would be. Finwald could call to mind a thousand-and-one alternative words for it, had he wanted to, but there was no getting away from the truth of it. He was about to become another Bolldhe: he was about to step over that hidden threshold.

The chamber they were in then came sharply back into focus. The bed, the mirrors, the wet skin drapes, even the slippers and the torture chamber pot. That earlier feeling of having been told about this place during his research grew into a sureness in Finwald's mind. Or, if he was not *exactly* sure, then at least he could make an intelligent guess, for there could not be many rooms in Vaagenfjord Maw like this one.

And if his guess proved well-founded, then there should be an adjoining room, that contained something that just might save Paulus's life.

He made his decision.

"I'm going to get you out of here, Paulus," he said to the stony faced, but now recovered Nahovian. "But you must do exactly as I say."

You must do exactly as I say. But of course. That was always the way with Finwald. He had to be the one ever in control. Appa had often laughed at the skillful methods Finwald would use to get what he wanted. But that joke had turned bitter, and no one was laughing now.

"Stand back," he motioned to the thieves. They did so without hesitation, eager to see what cunning devices this magician was about to employ in order to kill his friend.

Finwald rummaged about in his inside pockets, and soon extracted two small items. The first, a small stick of yellow chalk, he used to draw a collection of odd symbols, like a chart, upon the stone floor. The second, a needle of some unknown blue metal, he placed exactly in the center of this chart.

Cuthwulf started forward with his voulge, but Eorcenwold yanked him back, glaring at him testily.

Finwald then closed his eyes, breathed deeply, and focused all his concentration. Before long, a look of relaxation smoothed the deep lines in his face that were etched with his own blood. Strange sounds issued from his lips, as silky and languid as if breathed out upon swirls of smoke.

He was using the ancient and occult tongue of the Quiravian thaumaturgists, a coven that had numbered hundreds of thousands of adherents at the zenith of its influence, but which had all but died out now. It had taken Finwald years to uncover its deepest secrets, and he was immensely proud of himself for mastering them. More importantly still, he loved the way his own voice sounded when he uttered the words. The simple spell he was employing now did not need to be spoken in any particular tongue, but to Finwald it always sounded so powerful and mystery-laden, which enabled him to focus better.

Roughly translated, it meant: Magic of Earth, let me Know the Way to the Rawgr.

Almost immediately the needle began to quiver, humming slightly, and glowing. As it slowly turned, all eyes in the room followed it. Round it moved, taking its time, until finally it came to rest, ceased humming, and was once again a plain blue needle.

"The bed," Finwald announced, seeing where the needle pointed. "Of course—typical Rawgr, always on top of their work."

He turned to Eorcenwold and indicated to him the locksmith of the party. Eorcenwold nodded, and the little Hauger immediately got to work. Within minutes the cunning thief had found a small obsidian panel on the headboard which, when pressed with the palm of one hand, opened a section of the wall where previously one of the vanity mirrors had been located. The mirror did not slide back, or open like a door; it simply shifted itself to another dimension.

Finwald was impressed. He had never seen anything like that before. But he was a little concerned at the thieves' lack of similar wonder; they looked as pleased as a party of sots who have just found the key to the wine cellar door, but the magic itself clearly did not impress them. Held securely, with his arms behind his back and Cuthwulf's voulge at his throat, Finwald was frog-marched through this open portal at the head of the line. As the others filed in behind him, dragging Paulus along with them, they all stared around at this latest discovery.

"Pox!" swore Eorcenwold. "Is this all?"

Finwald, however, had entered the room with an air of reverence, even awe, for he alone of them viewed the place through the eyes of a magician. There would be no plunder here, he knew, yet for him it held greater wonder than the most glittering, gold-strewn and jewel-bedecked treasure room of any tomb of kings.

It was a small room, barely large enough to hold the fifteen intruders who now occupied it. The ceiling was low, so low that Klijjver was bent almost double, the floor and walls were plain, and there was no furniture or indeed any other item to be seen. The only feature at all, in fact, was a large stained glass window that almost entirely occupied the far wall.

"What manner of place is this he's brought us to?" Oswiu growled into his brother's ear. He for one had picked up on the arcane resonances from the great window.

"Yes," Cuthwulf agreed, "I seem to remember something about performing a sacrifice."

The window truly was quite riveting, though. There was no resisting it. One could not be in that room more than a minute without gazing at it transfixed. A hot blood-red, the deepest shade of green, and the dark blue of the clearest evening sky, spangled with the glittering silver of starlight, it glowed with a light that came from within, and none could guess what lay on its other side. Even from several yards away, it could be seen that this was not fashioned from ordinary glass—if glass it was at all. Those who approached it and studied it up close saw that there was not the slightest reflection of light from their lanterns upon its surface. If anything, it appeared to absorb the light, as it did their steaming breath, and even, to a certain extent, the sound of their voices.

But it was the images upon this window that drew their eyes to it compulsively. Had these images not been so ugly, they might have instantly glamored the thieves. As it was, all of them in that room found themselves drawn to it and repulsed at the same time, resulting in a morbid beguilement that kept bringing their eyes back to it.

Even Finwald, the only one among them who had been expecting something like this, was not fully prepared for the effect these depictions had upon him. For he had seen them before, only minutes ago. These were the fiends from his recent swoon, those which had stepped from the vanity mirrors to stalk about in his head.

Some appeared as beast and man melding into one, the most brutish features of both coming to the fore. Others more resembled the dead, or the reanimated, bearing various body parts of insects, or of the vilest creatures that lurked in the deepest, lightless trenches of the ocean.

"Not very realistic, are they?" Cerddu-Sungnir commented, but the disdain in his voice was clearly an affectation.

Of all of them, only Eorcenwold appeared unmoved. He was a practical, earthy and, above all, unimaginative man. He could not be frightened by anything that was not real. Alone, he walked up to the window, drew level with what was probably the most sickeningly horrendous fiend in the entire imagery, and just stared at it openly. Finwald held his breath, expecting something to happen.

But it did not. No hand reached out of the glass to clutch the thief's throat, nor tentacles to pull him in. The fiend did not even turn round to stare back at this impudent rogue. Eorcenwold was so sure of himself that, even if it had done so, he probably would have out-stared it anyway.

Paulus was then shoved to the fore. The thieves did not have a clue how this sacrifice would unfold, but they were almost giddy with anticipation. They backed up against the doorway, while Finwald was goaded forward with Cuthwulf's voulge almost piercing the back of his neck. Just the two of them stood there facing Paulus, the rumor of projectile weapons being extracted or loaded causing a strange rippling sound behind him.

Finwald took a long, intense look at Paulus. The man from the forests of Vregh-Nahov, this greatest warrior of their company, formerly so tall and menacing, so steeped in death, now knelt before him, disarmed, wrist-bound and still half-dazed from the beating he had received. It seemed now to Finwald that the stained glass window's light glowed more strongly, but far from bathing the room in its colors, it actually drained what light was left in there. Dimmer and dimmer became the room, until all Finwald could see was the crouched silhouette of his former ally against the bilious hues of the demon-glass.

The air throbbed with a power that reminded Finwald of that heavy breathing they had heard in the Moghul, that subsonic growl of something very big that shivered their bones to the marrow. The stone of the chamber pulsed as though it was alive, and the entire keep purred with expectation. All the priest could do was stare at Paulus's one eye. It was the only point of light in his crumpled shadow, possibly the only indication of the dark hatred yet seething within.

"Well?" came a voice from the black shape of the prisoner.

Finwald was shaking now, shaking from a sorrow far deeper than he would have ever guessed possible.

"If you could just get me my sword back," Paulus suggested calmly, "we could both get back to join the others."

The grief inside Finwald then froze and, as Paulus began rising to his feet, an inexplicable anger flared in him. *Did this idiot seriously believe that the thieves would simply stand by and allow Finwald to walk out of the room, retrieve the mercenary's sword, come back in and hand it to Paulus, then the two of them could fight their way through this pack, return to the Peladane, and everything would be just as it was before?* It was clearly time to put him in the picture.

"I can get you out of this without any fighting," whispered the priest with ice in his veins. Then he charged at the mercenary with every ounce of the madness that had taken hold of his brain. Full into Paulus he drove himself, and hurled the startled man backward. There was a sudden radiance of color, a kind of sucking sound, and an instant later, Paulus fell straight into the window behind him. It did not shatter, it did not crack, but with an air of horrible glee it snatched at the falling man and absorbed him.

Eorcenwold and his followers gasped in fear and revulsion, and their weapons turned to aim at the window itself. Finwald broke out into a sweat like a basted goose on a spit, and took a couple of faltering steps back toward them. The burning, laughing colors of the stained glass reached out and sparkled as reflections in the tears in his eyes: the green of sickness, the red of foully diseased blood, and the icy blue of pitiless cruelty. Horror there was also in those saucer-shaped eyes, horror not just at what had occurred, but at the atrocity he had committed; for he had known what would happen all along.

And then, as they all watched spellbound, a new shade joined the three existing colors in the glass.

Black.

Paulus Flatulus, or rather a stylized depiction of him in the same ecclesiastical design, now appeared along with the other figures in the stained-glass window. Frozen, upon his knees among the fiends, with one arm held up in defense, he became a part of the greater picture.

As the horrified onlookers stared, they could just about hear his voice, high-pitched and screaming, a thin wail as if carried upon the wind from far, far away.

Unknown words in a mortified tone lashed out at Finwald from Eorcenwold's mouth. The mage-priest did not recognize them, but understood their meaning well enough. He turned to the company before him, and, not caring whether they understood or not, announced:

"You wanted your sacrifice. Well, I hope you're satisfied. He's in *their* world now."

12

Tomes of Power

"Mind your head, Kuthy," Elfswith cried above the howl of air rushing in their ears. "We're going underground!"

Elfswith stood upright on the wyvern's neck, and leaned forward into the wind with a look of insane glee spreading across his face. Kuthy clung on for all he was worth, his cap appendages wrapping themselves tightly around his neck. Then Ceawlin tucked her wings right in to her sides, leveled her body right out from beak to stinger, and like some shimmering black arrow, streaked on over the ice.

Through tightly slitted eyes, streaming with tears from the cold, Kuthy could just make out the yawning black chasm that rent the ice field before them. He could scarcely breathe, and his body felt as if it was being stabbed all over with icicles, but he had never felt so exhilarated and alive in all his life.

Then, with a scream of mad excitement from Elfswith that sounded like the whistle of a steaming kettle, they plunged almost vertically into the freezing fog of the fjord. They had entered at the head of the ravine, and now fell down past the balustrades, corbels, and gonfalons of Vaagenfjord Maw's frosted epicarp towards the dock below.

"Watch out for those bloody kids!" Kuthy roared above the tempest of air currents that threatened to tear him from the back of the wyvern.

The ground had suddenly zoomed into view, and sure enough, directly below them could be seen the Children of the Keep. They were spread out at various points among the wharves, outhouses, and pathways, but for the most part, they were gathered around the main gate. In the second or two given to Kuthy to observe them, they appeared as no more than a bunch of mischievous brats playing hide-and-seek in the schoolyard, their attention focused excitedly and impatiently upon the entrance. Evidently they were not expecting invaders from *outside,* and certainly not from above.

Squeals of alarm, swiftly transformed into deep bellows of demonic fury, followed the wyvern-riders as they swooped right through the gateway, spinning a number of the little fiends around like tops, then carried on into the darkness ahead.

"Keep going!" Kuthy howled, gesturing rudely at the angry Children. He did not dare look behind him at the dwindling rectangle of daylight that framed the irate Rawgrs (now leaping up and down and shaking their fists at the impertinent marauders who had barged right through their midst). Had he done so, he would have noticed that they were not, in fact, giving pursuit. Their orders had been to guard the gate from escapees, and for such as them, orders were as unbreachable as a pentacle of warding, or a physical barrier.

"Right, good idea, Kuthy," Elfswith called back sarcastically, as they sped on into the blackness of the hall.

Though unable to see in the dark, both he and Ceawlin did seem to possess an almost bat-like ability to find their way in places where others would be completely disoriented. This talent was a strange amalgam of all five of their senses, and allowed them to fly on unerringly—though at a greatly reduced speed. Now, gliding through the great underground vaults of the Maw, instead of resembling a speeding black arrow, they more resembled the giant invisible fliers of Fron-Wudu, those ghostly, sylvan manta-rays that winged their silent way through the darkest reaches of the forest.

Keenest among these confined senses, now, was smell. The scent of human was unmistakable.

"Seems like our old friends were here a while ago," Elfswith reported. "If Ceawlin's right, they're about twelve hours—maybe a whole day—ahead of us."

"Shouldn't take too long to catch up with them, then," Kuthy replied.

They followed that scent to a place where the passages became too constricted to continue travelling by wing. Ceawlin alighted and set her passengers down, and the three of them now began exploring on foot the narrow place where Yen, the female survivor from the previous band of adventurers, had been discovered. The stench from her lair had drawn Ceawlin straight here almost as soon as the wyvern had flown into the hall, and once they were here, it was not difficult to follow their predecessors' spoor.

Thus they made swift progress and, in a fraction of the time it had taken the humans to get this far, Kuthy, Elfswith, and Ceawlin finally made it to the Moghul.

As they stood on the lip of the pit and stared down into the murk below, Kuthy wrinkled his nose in utter disgust.

"What is it about these places that people find so intriguing?" he demanded. "Just what is the attraction?"

"We have to head down there," Elfswith stated reluctantly. "This is where the others came—though how we're supposed to keep track of a scent in that morass . . ."

"*Excrement!* I *hate* tomb-raiding!"

They remounted the wyvern, and gripped hard onto her flanks—and their own stomachs—as she dropped straight down into the Trough, like a stone thrown into a well. Even as they plunged, it quickly became apparent that this abode of the dead was anything but dead. Their ears were soon greeted by the commotion of what seemed an entire army wading through the watery filth at the bottom. Leveling out sharply, Ceawlin glided well above these ghostly marchers.

"*The dead that walk,*" Elfswith announced. "Judging by the smell, I think we've finally discovered Yggr's precious cargo."

"Smell" was an understatement. Even to Kuthy's limited olfactory perception it smelled as if the whole undercroft of Melhus was crawling with the dead.

"They can't be here," he said of the Peladane and his men. "Not still alive, anyway."

"Well, I'm certainly not going to search for them down among that lot.*" Elfswith shuddered. "Come on, let's see where this place leads to; there's always the chance old Fatty and his crew passed through before this lot arrived."

So, continuing the only way they could, the three soon beheld that grail-like beacon of orange light gleaming up ahead, just as Nibulus's company had done earlier. They wasted no time in soaring up towards it.

It was there that they once again came upon Wire-Faces.

By this time the flight of Scathur's henchmen from the Fyr-Draikke had slowed somewhat from a mad sprint of screaming panic to a progress of exhausted but steady determination. Though their blind terror had largely faded, their faces were still drawn with trauma as one by one they doggedly swung themselves over the edge of the pit, and began the long climb down into the Trough.

Only to see another dragon materialize from the darkness ahead of them.

"What in the name of Blessed Elspeth is going on here?" Elfswith chittered, severely puzzled, and swung Ceawlin sharply upwards into the hall of Smaulka-Degernerth. As she went she swung her talons up in an arc, and smote the two leading Ogha, who stood gaping at her with death in their wire-bitten faces, hurling them right back over the dyke into the river of fire. They both hit the lava at the same moment, and a steaming gout of evaporating grease billowed up for just a second at the spot where they had landed.

As the wyvern soared above them, a fresh chorus of apocalyptic wailing immediately rose from the fleeing Wire-Faces.

"God, it's hot in here!" Kuthy exclaimed, throwing up an arm to cover his eyes.

"It is a bit," agreed Elfswith, and took out a pair of dark-tinted spectacles from his breast pocket.

They both stared wide-eyed at the infernal place they had come to. Maybe tomb-raiding was not so boring after all.

"Any ideas what's happening, Elfswith?" Kuthy called out, as the Wire-Faces flattened themselves in terror upon the road below them, or milled around like ants amid the ruin of their broken anthill.

"It looks to me," Elfswith shouted back, "that your Peladane friends are rather scarier than we thought. Come on, I'm dying to get to the bottom of this."

They continued along the Hall of Fire, all the while passing above Wire-Faces who were hastening the other way.

Before long the last stragglers of the routed Wire-Face army were behind them, staggering about the ledge like drunks or smoking like charred squibs. The way ahead was now clear, but, far from continuing as fast as they could in order to leave this awful place behind them, Elfswith reined Ceawlin to a halt, and bade her land upon the burning road.

"What're you doing?" Kuthy exclaimed, between choking gasps. "Carry on! It can't be far till the end, now."

"Exactly," replied the little man, somewhat more calmly, as he slid off Ceawlin's back and walked over to the edge of the dike. "And what then, more fire? I don't think so. I can't imagine the inner reaches of Drauglir's realm are going to be lit up all the way like this just for our convenience. Sooner or later we'll need something to see with."

He extracted a strange little cylinder from one pocket. It appeared to be made of a glass-like substance, but something told Kuthy it was more than just that. Elfswith lowered it on its chain into the lava dike, and swung it around a little, looking for all the world like a ragamuffin fishing for tadpoles in the local pond. Presently, he hauled it back up, and thrust it into Kuthy's grasp.

"Gak!" Kuthy exclaimed, immediately recoiling and letting it drop upon the ground. But the thing was not hot. Despite being immersed in, and filled with, the glowing white-hot magma, it was merely warm to the touch.

Elfswith grinned. He picked the cylinder up and placed it inside a leather sleeve, thus hooding its brilliant light.

"Lava lantern," he explained.

It was just as he was preparing to remount Ceawlin that they saw, striding toward them with his ermine robe streaming out and the fires of Hell's Ditch crackling behind him, the Majestic Head.

After the defeat of Gruddna the Fyr-Draikke and the flight of his cowardly Wire-Faces, Scathur was not feeling his usual self. It had to be said that his usual self was not particularly agreeable at the best of times, but now the nor-mal tombstone coldness of the chieftain of Wrythe had finally been burnt through by the magma of ire that churned within, and swirls of black hatred drifted from ear hole and nostril. He still had not caught up with his fleeing army, but even when he had rounded up those pathetic worms again, he would not be nearly done. For things had got severely out of hand, and Scathur realized he would have need of every soldier he could muster. He would not march on his foe again until the dead had been thawed out.

In addition, he ruminated as he pounded onward, he would have to send back a message for the Children to follow on.

The very last thing he expected to see now was the wyvern team.

"You!" he cried in astonishment, and smoke steamed from every vent in his body.

"Us," Elfswith confirmed awkwardly, then turned to Kuthy. "D'you think he's pleased to see us?"

Kuthy remained seated on the wyvern, who was now backing away, stinger held high and poison dribbling.

"You disgusting little *IMP!*" Scathur railed at Elfswith as he came on.

"I wouldn't bet on it," Kuthy replied to his friend's question.

"You son of a succubus!" Scathur roared, getting nearer.

Elfswith, for once, was momentarily taken aback. "You know my mother?" he exclaimed.

Even the Rawgr captain hesitated a little at this.

Elfswith recovered, and called out: "Uh, Maj, I don't suppose you've found those foreigners you were asking us about, have you?"

Scathur glowered, and set about closing what little remained of the gap between them. Slowly but steadily he paced forward, and as he did so his left hand went up behind his back, took hold of the Bardische that was suspended there and, in one smooth movement, swung it around before him in a two-handed grip. The twin axe blades curved wickedly, like the horns of some great prehistoric herd-beast, honed to a sharpness that nothing could withstand. As the Rawgr approached them, the mirror-perfection of those blades transformed to a glistening blood-red, streaming and glowing with heat. Droplets of dark brown formed on their surfaces and trickled down, a kind of pre-hack lubricant that, even at this distance, caused the dead to stir and the Wire-Faces to pause in their flight.

The Bardische of Scathur, after centuries in retirement, was now about to go back to work.

"Oh, I've got one just like that," Elfswith chirped. "Here, I'll show you."

He rummaged through one of his inside pockets, till Kuthy suddenly grabbed him by the coat, yanked him up onto the wyvern, and slapped Ceawlin's flank, all in one smooth maneuver. In a flurry of wings, she lifted vertically off the road, just a moment before Scathur reached them. As he swung his poleaxe uselessly up toward them, the three objects of his wrath soared away along the Hall of Fire.

"Where in Pel's name have those two got to?" Nibulus growled, barely able to contain his frustration. "They should've been back here ages ago!"

He snatched Bolldhe's lantern from his hand, and used it to scrutinize every square inch of the stair-hall they waited in, every glistening and varicose-veined marble surface.

"Are you sure they even came this way?" Gapp demanded. "Schnorbitz doesn't seem to have picked up any scent yet."

"Of course I'm not bloody sure!" Nibulus shouted. "Nobody actually saw where they went, did they!"

"Perhaps we should go back to the pillar-hall where we started, and then allow our redoubtable hound to locate their trail from the beginning," Appa suggested rather meekly.

"Shut up!" Nibulus hissed, rounding on them all. " 'Redoubtable hound,' my arse! What's the matter with you? You trying to take that traitorous bastard's place by talking pretentious pox like him? We've been walking for hours now and we're *not* going back . . . even if we knew the way. So just keep that crumbly little cakehole of yours *sealed!"*

He slapped the lantern back into Bolldhe's hand, hefted Unferth again, and led the silent company on up the stairway, his mouth clamped shut into an angry little slit.

He realized the truth of it, of course, but was too furious to admit it. Once again, his anger had got the better of him. What had occurred when they had encountered the Tyvenborgers had shaken his already overstretched nerves. Like all of them, he was not used to journeying through ice, fire, and the dark places of the dead. Nor was he in any way prepared for attacks by undead dragons. But the Finwald incident, well, that was something that just did not happen to the son of Artibulus Wintus. The loss of good comrades was already well-known to him, and hunger, thirst, and exhaustion had become familiar companions upon the road of his life. Ambush by the private armies of robber barons had occurred, too; and he had grown accustomed to charging headlong into battle against a typhoon of arrows, quarrels, and spears. But the inexplicable actions of Finwald . . . He still could not quite believe the man to be a traitor who had strung them along from the very beginning. There *had* to be a good reason for his incomprehensible actions. There always was . . .

If only Paulus would return, then maybe all of this could be sorted out.

But he had not returned and, once Wodeman and the two Cervulice had shaken off their chakram-induced paralysis, Nibulus had decided that they could wait there no longer. Something clearly had happened to the mercenary, and in his growing impatience the Peladane had suddenly lost his temper and ordered the remaining party onward.

All except the four Vetters and two Cervulice that had been wounded in the thieves' ambush. They now lay, hiding in the shadows near Lubang-Nagar, waiting for their comrades to return, should they ever do so, and meanwhile keeping vigil over the bodies of the slain.

Abruptly, Nibulus was shaken from his cogitation by the changed timbre of Wodeman's voice. He had not been listening to the shaman, and thus did not catch his actual words. But it was the tone of the man's voice that brought him back to the present so sharply. It was that same tone Wodeman had used when they had heard the fey sounds in the tunnel leading out of Eotunlandt.

As it had done then, it chilled Nibulus to the soul.

"I think we're getting close," Wodeman repeated. "Can't you feel the difference in the air?"

Yes. Now that he thought about it, the Peladane could. They all could. They had ascended to a much higher part of Ymla-Myrrdhain, and the enchantment here was even more palpable.

"Stop!" hissed Nibulus. They swiftly obeyed. Englarielle, just behind him and to one side, sent word down the line for all his followers to be still. Within seconds, stillness there was.

Every ear listened. None even dared breathe.

For long moments they waited, but no sound could be heard. Whatever had caused the Peladane to react so, it was gone now. Following his guidance, they resumed their progress along yet another new passageway.

At first, the only sounds were those normally to be heard from a marching troop. But moments later, other sounds began to stir around them: mutterings that were barely audible, never heard if one listened out for them, only when not concentrating, like faint movements perceived only from the corner of the eye. Whispers ran along behind the walls to either side; metal squealed across stone; a low voice whistled like the wind gusting through the deep dungeons of an old castle, the echoes of a slamming door, but without the actual slam itself; the sudden flurry of leathery wings; the clicking of talons—or bones—over a marble floor.

But these sounds were only hinted at, and not even the keenest of hearing among them could tell if they came from some distant part of the keep, or right beside him, from above, below, in front or behind, or even from inside his own head.

They bunched together even tighter, their weapons gripped in hands that were becoming increasingly shaky.

A long time passed in such trepidation. As has been mentioned, *The Chronicle of Gwyllch* was not written as a guidebook or set of directions, so it offered nothing specific to go on. It was nonetheless accurate in describing the feel of the place, which was what Nibulus was using to guide them.

Still the strange noises continued, however, and seemed to be getting stronger. Joining them now were the nervous mutterings of the Vetters hindmost in the line. They were becoming very unhappy about something, and were beginning to push forward against those in front of them.

"Nibulus," Wodeman hissed, "I think there's—"

"I'm well aware that there is something following us," Nibulus enunciated tersely. "Believe it or not, *I* have ears too."

Everyone in the company was getting jumpy, and something had to be done soon. But Nibulus was little prepared for dealing with an enemy such as this. It was not a foe one could tackle with weapons.

"If only we had some of that pitch-scented cloth—" Bolldhe whispered.

"What?" Nibulus snapped at him.

"That cloth Kuthy used when we were leaving Eotunlandt," Bolldhe explained, "when we heard the ghost-battles, and that kid screaming. What we can't hear, can't scare us."

Nibulus stared at him with incredulity. "That is probably the stupidest thing you've said on this entire journey," he rejoined. "We are *not* stopping up our ears!"

"Kuthy knew a lot of wise things," Appa pointed out.

"Not about *this* place," Nibulus retorted. "He'd never even been here and—"

The words stopped dead in his throat, as they all froze, staring about, seeking confirmation in each other's eyes that they were not the only ones who had heard it. A strange kind of fluttering, as before, only this time, unlike the ghost-mutterings behind the walls, there was a definite sense of physicality to this. Furthermore, they could now hear where it originated: from behind them, just along the passageway.

The enemy was upon them.

"Down this way!" Nibulus urged his host in a voice that was not quite a whisper but at the same time not quite a shout, then fled as fast as he could. He was driven partly by the need to find a more strategic place in which to stand and fight, but in his haste there was more than a hint of barely suppressed panic too.

The entire army poured down the passageway after their leader, wild-eyed and snorting with terror, jostling each other in increasing panic to get past their slower comrades. Soon a kind of wailing could be heard from the unfortunate Vetters to the rear, and this rapidly spread up the line.

As the fluttering commotion drew nearer, within seconds all control had deserted them, and they stampeded in total disorder from the horror that was about to overwhelm them.

The noise, whatever it was, suddenly reached the back of the line, and terror-stricken screams pierced the air. Amid a light-show of flailing torches, something very large came rushing on over their heads, the beat of its wings felling them in its wake.

Like a wind devil, on it came, passing the entire line, and heading for the leaders. At the last moment Nibulus and his vanguard flung themselves to the ground with a cry, and the great winged devil soared overhead, its claws missing them only by inches.

"Stand up!" Nibulus cried, having used the momentum of his dive to roll over and up on to his feet again, sword at the ready.

"Get some light over here!" he snarled at the tangle of bodies around him, then yelled blindly into the darkness ahead: "Come on then you bastards!"

In the briefest of moments, man and beast scrambled to their feet. Torches were swept up again, and they spaced themselves out as best they could, weapons gripped tightly, ready to stand and fight. There could be no such blind routs again.

They all stared into the blackness while Bolldhe fumbled with his lantern, and listened to the sounds coming from somewhere ahead. It sounded as though the winged devil had collided into a wall, but even now was coming back for them. Talons clicked upon the glassy floor, wings ruffled loudly, and a voice that sounded like two voices melded together was babbling in a demonic gibberish that almost had recognizable words in it.

Then there was a sudden snap, and a great fire-red eye opened before them, bobbing this way and that, drawing closer, as if searching them out. Appa moaned in terror.

"Got it!" Bolldhe hissed, and finally swung his lantern up. The apertured sleeve clicked down, the beam narrowed, and intensified, then it lanced into the darkness ahead.

"Oh, sweet Cuna above!" yammered a hysterical Appa. "It's Rumbletyts of the Three Heads!!"

A collective sigh arose among the men from the south.

"No it isn't," said Bolldhe, as he slid the tulwar back under his belt. "It's just Kuthy and his funny friends."

"By my god!" Nibulus panted, his face nearly black with fury as he marched up to confront the wyvern-team. "I'll kill you for that—I'll *kill* you!"

"And it's terribly agreeable to see you too, Nib," Kuthy greeted him, amiably, though loosening the swordbreaker from its clasp at his belt.

"Don't give me any of that shite," Nibulus growled, "or so help me, I'll give you such a thrashing you'll never be able to forget what it is to face a Peladane when his dander is up!"

Just for the effect he slammed down the boar's-head sallet on his helm, and blew steam through the snout vents. But both Kuthy and Elfswith knew it was an empty threat, and walked on past the fuming Peladane to greet the rest of the group.

They were met with a mixture of feelings. Whereas Bolldhe and Wodeman simply breathed a deep sigh of relief, Appa seemed to share Nibulus's anger, and was jumping up and down like a frog, speechless in his rage, and making

some kind of eccentric gesture with his hand as if he were flinging imaginary
ordure at them. His other hand was, more characteristically, tapping his ring
against his amulet faster than a woodpecker's beak.

Gapp had never met the trio until now, and just gawped, chuckling a little
hysterically, while reflecting on how understated his companions' descriptions
of them had been. Schnorbitz, by his side, growled with rabid slavering.

The Vetters, Cervulice, and Paranduzes, however, surged forward and
crowded around with intense curiosity. They had never even heard of a wyvern
before and, once it became clear that these newcomers were not Rawgrs after
all, swarmed around them like schoolchildren, almost mobbing them in their
fascination and eagerness to stare and touch, their terror wholly forgotten.

And, for their part, it had to be said that Kuthy and Elfswith for once reciprocated the curiosity. Though they had heard stories, neither had ever seen Vetters or Cervulice before, and while Ceawlin, cocking her head on her
snake-like neck, stalked about eyeing these strange musty beasts cautiously, her
riders returned the Tregvans' scrutiny with reciprocated interest.

"Have you ever seen anything *like* them before?" Kuthy asked Elfswith excitedly, studying one of the Vetters closely. The Vetter himself kept looking
from Kuthy to Gapp and back again, realizing with increasing awe that their
friend Gapp belonged to the same race as this prodigy who rode fabulous
dragons through castle tunnels!

"No." Elfswith shook his head. "But we *have* seen their tracks. . . . Take a
gander at their feet; look anything like those prints we saw back on the
beach?"

"Got to be," Kuthy agreed after, studying them carefully. "So where are the
other two they were with?"

Elfswith nodded, scanning the throng for the desert mercenary Xilva and
the esquire, when he suddenly became aware of a furtive little hand beneath his
coat. Radkin, the boldest of Vetters, had managed to slip in among the three of
them unnoticed. Something about Elfswith had caught his eye, and he wanted
to make a closer examination. Before Elfswith realized what was happening,
Radkin had slipped his hand up inside the coat, wrapped his bony fingers
around something encountered there, and hauled out a long and wriggling ap-
pendage for all to see.

Cries of amazement and (in the case of the Vetters) approval met this revelation. Englarielle even swept his own out to compare sizes.

Elfswith's tail had at last been revealed to all.

"Right, that does it!" Nibulus snapped, and strode right up to the little
man. For once he was not intimidated by the tail-flicking wyvern; they had just
recently survived far worse dragons than she. He squared up to Kuthy, while
glaring down at Elfswith.

"No more horse shit, Tivor," he said levelly. "Just tell me straight: *who* are
you, *what* is he, and why the *Pox* are you both here now?"

Sensing a fight, Englarielle's army chattered excitedly among themselves, and while those nearest drew back to give the humans space, those behind pushed forward eagerly to get a better view.

Kuthy turned from Nibulus to Elfswith, staring down into his strangely flecked yellow eyes with a look of inevitability, as if asking: *Are you going to tell them or shall I?*

Elfswith glanced ruefully down at his exposed tail, then returned Kuthy's gaze, as he spoke to him in a tongue known only to the pair of them: "Don't suppose you know the Aescalandian for 'birth-mark,' do you?"

Kuthy's eyes lifted to the heavens, and he turned back to the exasperated Peladane.

"He's a bard," he confessed. "A bard, all right? Of singular lineage."

The listeners waited silently, expectantly, for Kuthy to continue. Everyone knew what bards were. Solitary wandering minstrels, they traveled from village to village, farm to farm, taking on the most mundane and repetitive jobs imaginable, and apparently would be quite happy and content with this toil, before inevitably moving on. Some said they lived thus in order to retain their close links with the earth while their heads were up in the clouds, for if they did not keep themselves grounded somehow, their souls might fly off and never return. Others maintained that the exact opposite was true, that it was the mindless monotony of the work they undertook that allowed their minds to wander free and untrammeled, and thus alight upon whatever inspiration might be floating about in the cosmos.

Yes, bards were familiar to all and, though they were all a little strange, this still did not explain Elfswith's tail, nor any other of his mysterious little peculiarities. It was an explanation of that "singular lineage" that they were now waiting for.

Elfswith nodded. "My mother was a succubus, and my father a human. A Lightbearer, actually, from Venna."

The company was quite taken aback, yet the truth of Elfswith's claim was plain for all to see in his eyes. Nevertheless, they were not sure which was the more incredible, the fact that Elfswith was born of a succubus, or that there actually were Lightbearers in the sleaze-pit of Venna.

"Goes some way to explaining why he's so mixed-up," Kuthy confided to Nibulus, "so at odds with himself."

Nibulus just stared at the floor, and continued thus for quite some time. "So we've been sharing the company of a *Huldre,*" he said in irate disbelief. "This just gets better and better."

Elfswith picked some dirt from his fingernails, then turned to Nibulus: "You made it here then, Fatty. Looks like I've lost my bet with Kuthy—"

"—*Don't* even talk to me, you!" Nibulus commanded, raising his hand and refusing to even look at the Bard. "I have *nothing* to say to you. Nothing at all."

He gave all his attention instead to Kuthy, and focused on him every last mote of the vexation and grief that was unraveling him from inside. At length, he said, "I thought you were supposed to be going to Wrythe?"

"We were," Kuthy replied. "We did. And that's why we're here. Nibulus, listen, we've found out something you really ought to know. Something about those two friends of yours, the ones you said died down south." He looked again around at the company, trying to see if there were any humans here he had not seen before.

Nibulus grinned acidly. "If you came all the way here just to tell us about those two," he said in cold satisfaction, "then I'm glad to inform you that you've wasted your time. *Radnar!*"

Gapp, as usual seemingly invisible to the human eye—even the Tivor's keen, searching ones—now stepped forward. Both Kuthy and Elfswith scrutinized the youth before them closely. That he was alive did not surprise them; the presence here of the Vetters had already confirmed their sea passage had been successful. Nevertheless, there was a glint of bemusement in their regard as they appraised the boy.

Gapp openly returned their scrutiny. Kuthy nodded at him in acknowledgment. "So what's your secret?" he asked in a tone that was both circumspect and reticent, for he was not sure what to make of this incongruity standing in front of him. "Yours—and that of your private little army here? Just how long *can* you hold your breath?"

Gapp blinked. "Beg your pardon?"

"We trailed you all the way from Wrythe to the Last Shore," Elfswith explained, "right up to the point where your tracks disappeared into the sea. That's quite a trick, and it's not often myself and my friend here are impressed."

"Oh that," Gapp sniffed. "I suppose I have my methods."

Kuthy grinned. *Cocky little toss-pot,* he thought, seeing easily through the youngster's affected nonchalance to the glowing pride beneath.

"Oh right," he replied, "forget it then. So where's your friend, then? This "desert man" we've been hearing so much about? Seems he's quite in demand these days."

Gapp rested the machete blade against his shoulder. "Splattered all over the sides of that great doorway back there. Why, was there something you wanted to ask him?"

Not quite so clever now, are you, fellows? the boy thought with an inward smile as he perceived the sudden darkening of the two errant adventurers' expressions.

"Is this true?" Elfswith demanded, turning to the Peladane.

"Redecorating the entrance to Lubang-Nagar even as we speak," Nibulus confirmed, sharing his esquire's satisfaction in pissing on their bonfire. "Yes, he blew up, just like that—spontaneous explosion. Happens all the time, apparently."

Neither Kuthy nor Elfswith actually slapped his hands against his face in horror. Nor did they draw their fingers down their cheeks in the customary gesture of frustration. Nevertheless, their manner said it all. Mauglad Yrkeshta, and indeed their entire reason for coming to this pit, was, apparently, no more.

Elfswith quietly but neatly summed up their feelings in one word.

"Bugger!" he said, and sighed deeply.

This was not the place to stand around talking, they knew. Here they were, a disarrayed bunch of wayfarers in a wide-open corridor high up in the mid-levels of Ymla-Myrrdhain, the residence of evil. All could sense the nearness of the Chamber of Drauglir, and all were aware of the presence of hell about them. Nevertheless, there were things that needed to be said, questions that had to be answered, and matters that were crying out to be cleared up before anyone was going anywhere.

So, briefly and without elaboration, the tales were told. Nibulus spoke of the dead and the ermine-clad warrior that some believed to be Scathur. He told of the desert man and his battle with the Fyr-Draikke. Also, the surprise arrival of Gapp and the Tregvans, and the subsequent revelation concerning the flamberge. And finally, the thieves' ambush, and the defection of Finwald from their company. To all of this, both the newcomers listened carefully, not interrupting even once.

Thus it was that Kuthy and Elfswith finally learned the true identity of Yggr, the Majestic Head; he who had held such strange sway over Wrythe, and had done so for longer than anyone could remember; he whom they themselves had known for many years, and during all that time without appearing to age a day.

And now that they came to think about it, it was he who just days ago had loomed over them while they were naked and defenseless in a bath. It was a sobering thought.

But so too was the tale of Mauglad's end. Sobering and bitter. When the story was done, Kuthy deemed it time to tell tales of his own.

"Mauglad Yrkeshta was once the High Necromancer of Vaagenfjord Maw," he enlightened them, "and seems to have ranked alongside Scathur in the hierarchy here. Well, perhaps not quite as high, for Mauglad was only a human—if you can count one as abominable as that 'human'—whereas Scathur was . . . *is* of Rawgrkind. One of the three original Avatars of Olchor, Scathur was the warrior, the captain of Drauglir's forces, while Mauglad presided over ritual and unholy worship. But in their different ways, both were priests to Drauglir; for to serve the Rawgr is to worship him.

"As the Darkangel, Scathur was naturally always going to be number one. Rawgrs have much greater power than ordinary people. However, humans— especially ones of Mauglad's particular quality—have a potential intelligence and discipline beyond that belonging to any of the Rawgr world. And if our sort can lay our hands on their power somehow . . . well, who can say?"

The company now looked at the soldier of fortune and his bardic companion in a very new light. This was the first time the strange duo had revealed even a hint of their purposes, and the Peladane's group was not sure quite how to take it.

"And you? *You* seek this power?" Wodeman questioned them darkly.

"We seek answers," Elfswith responded (rather evasively, some there thought). "Who knows what secrets might be revealed if only we could get to talk with one possessing such power over the dead."

"Life and death," Bolldhe put in, "breaking the chains of this world and of Time. Your business, right?"

Kuthy looked at Bolldhe in surprise. "Finwald told you I said that, did he? I'm rather disappointed in him; I thought he'd be better at keeping secrets."

"He tries," Appa commented.

"Well, our concern was never really with Melhus, as such. We left that to you lot. It was always Wrythe that interested us."

"But it's only in the last week that we've realized the two are one and the same," Elfswith added.

"There's always been that connection, though," Nibulus pointed out, "ever since Lord Bloodnose decreed that Wrythe was to be the caretaker of Melhus."

"The caretaker?" Gapp interrupted. "That's a name we've been hearing a lot about recently, isn't it?"

"Right," Nibulus agreed. "Meth—I mean Mauglad, described Scathur as the caretaker."

"And as the 'tall captain,'" Gapp added, then lowered his voice to a hollow hiss, in imitation of Mauglad: *"Let no' the tall captain gain th' sswor' . . ."*

"Not hard to guess which sword he was talking about," Bolldhe decided. The weapon he now bore was the tulwar he had confiscated from Finwald, but Flametongue he still kept with him, strapped securely to his back. This he now unfastened and, though they had seen it before, he held it out for Kuthy and Elfswith to examine.

"Our only weapon against the Rawgr, according to Finwald," Bolldhe continued, "though coming from him, that hardly tells us much."

The eyes of Kuthy and Elfswith sparkled, both icy blue and yellow, as they looked upon the flamberge.

"Mmm," said Kuthy, "so what's your plan, then? You still intend to use it?"

"What's yours?" Nibulus cut in. "You still haven't explained why you're here."

"That's because we don't know," Elfswith stated. "Not yet, anyhow. But we will, when the time's right. Always the way, isn't it, Kuthy?"

"For certes," Kuthy agreed. "And if the likes of Scathur—and maybe even Mauglad, for that matter—are still about—"

"Then Vaagenfjord Maw is clearly the place to be these days," Elfswith finished for him, and playfully swatted Nibulus with his tail.

The Peladane and his group could do nothing but stare at these two most enigmatic characters. Devil-red in the lava lantern's light and appearing as insouciant in this place as though they belonged here, it was as if the whole thing were just a game to them. The questers, on the other hand, had endured so very much to get from Nordwas to here. They were dizzy with exhaustion from their journey, traumatized from their horrendous experiences in the Maw, sick with fear, and soul-darkened with the very real anticipation of death. The only spirit that remained within them was that of sheer dogged determination; there was no longer even the slightest vestige of adventurousness or curiosity. They were here simply because they had to be.

Yet in front of them stood these two singularities, a legendary hero of men on the one side and his half-Huldre partner on the other, both apparently tagging along with them out of nothing more than their interest in the outcome.

It was left to Wodeman, who had held his tongue throughout, to sum it all up:

"It's by strange chance that we all come together in this place, so far along our journey, to become one just before the end. And despite all that's passed between us, I don't believe there's one among us who isn't glad that we've found ourselves together now. I'd hazard a guess that you three will prove more than handy in a fight, and probably still have many more surprises up your capacious sleeves to marvel us with. And if we can find our two absent friends along the way, then none of us could ask for more, for we'll then be as ready as ever we can to fight the Rawgr.

"But for now, we simply can't continue any longer without sleep. We *have* to find some place where we can rest and regain our strength before the final confrontation. Come, Master Wintus, lead us somewhere where we can get our heads down safely for a few hours. I for one am absolutely shattered."

The devilry was stronger up here. The higher they ascended, the denser it became. From the lowest pits of Ymla-Myrrdhain it rose like a red steam, snaking its way in wispy feelers up the stairwells and through murder-holes, gaining more and more substance as it came, until finally it could rise no further. Here in the highest places, it coagulated into a thick and choking evil that swam in cackling spirals around its master's chambers.

This was all a bit much for the Tyvenborgers, it had to be said. Despite their unique and redoubtable expertise, they were still, when it came down to it, nothing more than thieves, and as such they were here for loot, plain and simple. They may have been prepared for the "pretty weird stuff" Eorcenwold had promised them, but up here, where the air whispered with phantasms and throbbed with a dormant malice, their trusted leader's sworn affirmation that there was nothing alive to hurt them, was now gravely brought into question.

They and their captive guide Finwald were currently heading along a corridor that seemed to go on forever, and which had a palpably vise-like quality to
it. It must have reached up forty feet high or more, but was so narrow only two
could walk abreast. The lurid marble of the previous levels had given way to a
kind of green-black obsidian which swallowed almost all the light from their
lamps so that they now stole along like true burglars in the night, with naught
but the pathetically diminished glow of their more powerful lanterns bobbing
will-o'-the-wisp-like, down the passage. Down this slit, this mere fault line running through a mass of obsidian, they paced as silently as their skill would allow, but even such footpad-lightness of tread counted for little here, as every
tiny noise they made was sharpened and amplified so that they sounded like an
army of metallic lobsters clicking their way along a glass tube.

Finwald, too, had known better times. As they proceeded, the mage-priest's
arm was clutched tight by the giant Klijjver, in a grip that only a team of oxen
would prise open. And just like a team of oxen returning after a hard day's
work did the herd-giant now smell, rank with multitudinous layers of dried
sweat forming an extra shell over his already tough hide.

If this were not bad enough, Khurghan had taken the added precaution of
chaining Grini to their captive. The feral Boggart sat upon Finwald's shoulders, growling down at him, with his rancid, hairy legs wrapped around his
neck.

But despite this parlous situation, Finwald was beginning to feel in control
once more. A captive he might be, but as far as he was concerned, his captors
were doing just what he wanted them to. They had already almost completed
the task he had planned for them: through their thievish expertise and greed
(and *his* long years of research) they were now drawing inexorably closer to the
heart of Vaagenfjord Maw, to the very place which Finwald had dreamed of for
so long.

And then we'll see who the prisoners are, he thought secretly.

A stinking breath of air was exhaled up the passageway towards them,
carrying with it a tomb coldness, and an ethereal panting sound as of a great,
ghostly hound. Finwald suddenly recalled the story told at the Moot by the soldier of Wrache: an account of the Black Dog that had ravaged his home village,
which some believed to be the spirit of Drauglir himself.

Well, Finwald was not sure what he now believed; he was not even sure he
was hearing the sound at all. But below it could be heard, only by those per-
ceptive enough, what sounded like a whispered, cult-like chanting. As they approached, every step bringing them closer to this potential menace, fear oozed
out of every pore in the thieves' skin, feeding Finwald's sense of mastery with
each warm, salty drop.

Their weapons were already out, and gripped tightly in damp palms, but
now Finwald could hear the furtive rustling of other weapons also being readied: the singing slide of blade from sheath; the loosening of throwing weapons

from their fastenings; the jangle of flail-chains; the slow, muted ratcheting of a crossbow's gear-wheels; the soft, steady click of a dragontooth into a gun chamber.

The anticipation, the fear, he too could feel it. *Almost there,* Finwald repeated over and over in his mind. *Almost there . . .*

And eventually, this longest of corridors did come to an end. But as its narrow confines opened into some enormous space beyond, they could only wonder at exactly what manner of place the passage had delivered them to.

Gone were the glass-smooth, geometric surfaces of earlier. Here there were no regular walls or floor, or ceiling. It was more like an immense natural cavern, though there was nothing natural about the aura that pervaded this place. A sense of perversion and wrongness emanated potently from the hidden midst of the vast cavern. It was a place set aside from the rest of the world, a separate dimension it seemed, out of place with the time and reality they were familiar with. At no other point during all their time on this island had any of the bold thieves felt more strongly like intruders.

But an altogether different look passed over the face of the priest. Those big black eyes of his visibly swelled in size, quivering slightly at the edges.

So here I am at last, he spoke to himself in solemn wonder. *The Gateway to the Underworld!*

There was not much to see yet, for their strangely diminished lamps could illuminate their immediate surroundings only. But they were nevertheless aware of a dim light of some unknown color in here. It swirled about upon the winds of ether, here and there, near or far, high up above or way down below, teasingly revealing parts of the cavern to them for just seconds at a time before moving on. In the higher places it illumined outcrops or perches that no stair or passage led to. Down below could be seen walkways and ledges that at first glance appeared to teem with armies of underworld dwellers, but if stared at closely, turned out to be empty. Invisible things could be heard scuttling all around, the sound of their scraping appendages, taloned pinions, and popping suckers hinting at entire legions of creatures that crawled, clawed, or slithered their way about the walls at any angle they chose.

From here, more strongly than ever before, emerged that death-cold black wind, howling out of the vast pit, bringing with it a stench of corruption and sickness. From here too could be heard, more manifestly, that eldritch breathing, panting, and chanting.

At exactly the point where the passage opened into this place, the floor dropped away toward the depths. It sloped steeply down about a hundred yards or so, until it reached a level but narrow ledge, nothing more than an unbalustraded platform of stone, that curved right around the pit and disappeared into the darkness on either side beyond the reach of the swirling light.

Without hesitation, for he was keen to get a move on, Eorcenwold hissed out his orders. This was all just as the mage-priest had described to them in the diagram he had sketched earlier. The thieves immediately busied themselves with straps and slender ropes, then divided themselves into three groups. While Oswiu, Klijjver, Grini and Brecca stayed behind to guard Finwald, the two other groups without hesitation slid down to the ledge, and there separated. Eorcenwold and his sister led Khurghan and Dolen around to the left; Cuthwulf led the rest of them to the right.

From where he stood, Finwald could just make out the two clusters of lamp beams widening in an arc after the groups split up and headed their separate ways. At first their light would occasionally pick out mysterious shapes along the walkway, but soon they became too dim to discern.

Back at the top of the slope, where Finwald was, nobody spoke a word. As the minutes passed, the air around them grew colder, crystalizing their sweat, and both thieves and captive alike grew ever more agitated. Finwald became a little disconcerted at the feeling (or rather *lack* of feeling) in his arm that was still gripped, with increasing firmness, by the herd-giant. He was also becoming decidedly more disconcerted at having Grini's noxious proximity at the back of his neck.

The tension was getting to all of them.

Within minutes, however, Cuthwulf's group could be seen returning from the right. They reached the bottom of the slope and called up to Oswiu in urgent whispers, gesturing back to where they had just been. Finwald did not understand a word of their report, but he was reassured to hear no increase of fear in Cuthwulf's voice. Moreover, since they did not appear to be running away from anything they had recounted, that alone surely had to be a good sign.

So far so good, Finwald comforted himself.

Now, while Brother Number One was left all alone holding the ropes at the head of the slope, Grini was finally unchained from Finwald, and together with Klijjver and Brecca, they made their way down towards the ledge.

As they scrambled down the slope, Finwald began to feel panic taking hold of him, and expected at any minute to lose all control and break into screaming convulsions. The ropes felt thread-thin, and ready to snap, and the lumpy, uneven rock beneath his soles shot pulses of horrible power up his legs and into his brain. It occurred to him that he was surely sliding with the other sinners down into the pit of hell itself.

But the steel in his character that had been with him for so many years managed to hold firm, and within moments he felt his feet land abruptly upon the ledge itself. There he paused with the others, in total silence, keeping safely from the edge and refusing to even think about what lay down in that pit which loomed just inches away.

A short while later the strangely colored beams of several lanterns could be seen reaching out along the ledge path leading to the left. Slowly they came closer, so slowly that those who bore them might have been pushing their way through deep water. Minutes later, the second group rejoined them, and there was a brief whispered exchange between the two brothers.

Eorcenwold pointed back along the left-hand path, sounding disappointed, and yet at the same time noticeably relieved. Cuthwulf, on the other hand, sounded highly excited but at the same time horribly nervous as he gestured back toward the right.

Immediately, the entire group turned and moved off toward the right path. There was a noticeable quickness in their pace as they hastened off to whatever destination Fate had in store for them, for they could all sense the nearness of their goal. The ledge grew narrower and more slippery, its uneven surface bulging erratically underfoot. Slender, twisted pillars of amethyst thrust from the very edge of the pit and spiralled up into the darkness above. Whenever they had to pass close to one of these, it would begin to glow from within with a sickly violet, and throb. At one point Khurghan inadvertently pricked one of them with the tip of his assegai, and instantly it contracted away from him with a hiss, and shuddered like a prodded jellyfish.

Soon they had rounded perhaps a quarter of the circumference of this huge cavern, and came to the point that Cuthwulf's group had reached. Finwald peered hard out into the yawning space, his eyes searching fervidly. . . .

Then his heart almost bounced into his throat as he finally laid eyes upon what he had been searching for.

It was a walkway, similar to the one on which they now trod, about two feet wide and just as slick and perilous. But this one jutted straight out across the gaping void and, more worryingly, appeared to be suspended without any support from either above or below. The thieves ran their lantern beams slowly along its undulating length, picking out every bulge and swelling, until they lighted upon the rounded platform at its far end.

A sudden rumor of fear went up, which was swiftly quelled by Cuthwulf and his group. For at the end of the walkway stood the zircon statue of a winged and horned Rawgr, lurking like a sick murderer in the night, sprouting it seemed from the very stuff of which the walkway was formed.

Exactly as the scrolls described! Finwald was thrilled, thinking back to the strange old eremite with the green jacket, back in Qaladmir all those years ago. *At last!*

Though he was prodded forward at spear-point, the priest needed no goading. He got down upon all fours, and proceeded to crawl along the walkway, heading out over the horrendous void. Though moving with utmost caution, he nonetheless felt a surge of adrenaline through every vein in his body, and he had to restrain himself from leaping up and racing ahead in the madness of his excitement.

There was only one other upon the walkway. Right behind him came Grini, tied by the ankles to an umbilical rope held by Klijjver, who himself stood safely upon the ledge with the others. It was not that Finwald could hear or even smell the Boggart, for the ethereal wind from below grew stronger and more malodorous with each step; but he knew he was still there, through feeling the saliva from Grini's tusks spatter now and again upon the bare skin of his ankles.

Finwald focused his gaze upon the churning gloom ahead of him. The threatening shape of the zircon statue drew closer, the wind howled up from the abyss in increasing foulness, but, surprisingly, Finwald felt the going get easier. Puzzled at first, he soon realized that he was becoming physically lighter. The closer he crawled toward the center of the cavern, the less gravity seemed to affect him. The end of the walkway was now only yards away, its grim occupant grinning stonily back at him. As Finwald propelled himself forward upon his fingertips, just like a swimmer in shallow water, the Boggart began growling in that liquid way of his that betrayed terror and bewilderment. The voices of the thieves floated out to them, as though from the depths of a mountain chasm.

Then with a sudden lunge, Finwald flew towards the Rawgr statue. As the writhing eddies of the black wind around him howled to a squealing zenith, he just about managed to grasp the effigy by its horns. Legs flailing in the air, body floating weightlessly, he held on tightly lest he be snatched away into that swirling, keening limbo around him. The zircon image was freezing and, as he pulled himself closer to it, Finwald could feel the skin of his face sticking to its surface.

Just as he was painfully peeling himself free, he suddenly felt the slap of a large hand on his shoulder. In his terror he almost let go. Twisting around urgently, Finwald saw the big round face of Eorcenwold shimmer into view. On his knees, the thief-sergeant frantically jabbed a stubby finger at the air, and directed a questioning look at the mage-priest. Finwald nodded vigorously and, noticing the bewilderment of the Tyvenborgers, began to laugh.

One of the first things I'll have to do when I get hold of the tomes, he thought to himself as he studied the comically befuddled visage of the thief, *is to obtain the power of tongues. Even his thievish cant!*

Again he succumbed to laughter.

Eorcenwold's face darkened like a blood-blister about to burst. He was beside himself with fury at the Lightbearer's asinine behavior. He snarled out words that were quickly carried away by the wind and more Tyvenborgers began to join them, also perilously clinging to the walkway. Shinnying up behind their leader with increasing alarm, each of them appeared as startled as Finwald had been by this new sensation of weightlessness. But having almost reached the end of his time with them, Finwald already felt himself well beyond their reach.

As he continued to float about, anchored only by his hands as they clung to the freezing zircon, he looked around in wonderment. Here at the very center of the Maw, there were no dimensions, no up or down. But magic was all around: the air crackled with it. It swam about in eddying swirls, caused his hair to toss madly and his teeth to ache. His beloved hat, after convulsing increasingly violently upon its tether around his neck, was finally ripped off by the gale, spinning away into the emptiness. Finwald could have sworn he heard it screaming in panic as it went. Then, with a final squeal of terror, it disintegrated into a thousand burning, wriggling threads.

Legions of souls, it seemed, flew around in howling madness before being sucked down by the vortices into the Underworld below: Peladanes, Oghain, and others that were even less human. Then before the mage-priest floated visions of faraway places he could not possibly know, of events that might have happened long ago, might be happening right now, or might be yet to take place. Other visions involved his own life: his childhood, his days of apprenticeship under Pashta-Maeva, his time in Nordwas, the journey of the past few months. All shifted in the air about him, like magic lantern images cast by the candlelight of his mind onto the black felt of oblivion around him, spinning faster, faster, and faster . . .

. . . Until one vision clarified: Bolldhe, flamberge strapped to his back, walking down a wide hallway that echoed with the memory of battle, heading to a door at the far end. He noticed this great door had a huge hole blasted through it, still smoldering, reeking of smoke, hanging upon tortured hinges . . .

. . . About to crash to the ground.

Finwald snapped himself back to reality with a jolt.

No more time, he cursed, and swung round to face the thieves. With one hand he still held onto the Rawgr-statue, while with the other he yanked out his old silver torch amulet from within his raiment. He let it dangle free, weightlessly, before him from its chain, and fixed Eorcenwold with an uncompromising glare. He pointed first to the amulet, then to the thief-sergeant before him. Then, with his little finger, he indicated each link in the chain, then pointed similarly to each of the thieves.

Finally, he jerked his thumb over his shoulder toward the abyss behind. It was clear what he wanted—a floating, human chain.

Eorcenwold's eyes, already wide, widened even further, till Finwald wondered if they might slip out of the baggy red folds of skin that contained them and float away upon their gluey nerve strings. Eorcenwold shook his head at the priest, reached over to tap the torch amulet, then pointed to Finwald instead.

Finwald feigned an expression of extreme disaster, but inwardly he was chuckling. *One born every minute,* he reflected, then nodded his head in mock-reluctant assent. With his free hand, Eorcenwold grasped the wide-eyed, uncomprehending Grini by the ankle, and yanked the gibbering Boggart from his perch, extending him toward the mage-priest. Before anything foolish could occur, Finwald took the flailing creature's hand and wrapped it firmly around his own ankle.

Then, with one swift backward glance to check that he was still linked se-curely, Finwald released his hold on the statue.

Like a maggot cast out on a fishing line, he floated off into the void. Further and further he went as one-by-one the thieves fed out the line. Within minutes all were swimming in this same astral sea, each holding onto the one in front by his ankles, and all ultimately anchored to the zircon bollard by the massive weight of the herd-giant, remaining on the spot.

It was one of those experiences that so rarely occur in life, and though Fin-wald felt he should be making the most of it, there was something about the timelessness, the non-dimensionality and undulatory movement of this place that caused his mind to wander. Perhaps it was like being under the ocean amid a storm; while up on the surface the gale rages tempestuously, far below all is just depth and powerful feelings. He found himself gazing back at the thieves, and could not suppress a chuckle at the terrified expressions on their oafish faces, their eyes dancing about in their sockets and their mouths idiot-wide in maelstrom-engulfed screams.

It's no use your howling, he laughed to himself. *We're way past the point of words.*

But there was one word that did reach him. Whether she had the most pen-etrating voice, or the most forceful mind, Finwald could not tell, but he was sure the Dhracus had managed to transmit that word to him.

Sophistra!

It was just one word, but it was soaked in contempt and infused with ha-tred. Finwald's laughter died in his throat, and suddenly he did not feel quite so sure of himself anymore.

Sophistra, legerdemainer—*conjuror*! Bloody flux, how he despised those words being applied to him! It was like being compared to that blue-skinned freak Paulus Fatuus, from the Levansy Theatre Company back in Nordwas, who capered about for the amusement of drunken, leering, slobbering cretins, singing for his supper, and pulling rabbits out of his backside! Now *he* was a conjuror. But what really galled Finwald was that the Dhracus was so close to the truth. What was he, then, if not exactly that? "Sparky" the other boys used to call him back in Qaladmir. Good grief, was that any better than being dubbed "conjuror"?

Finwald drifted further and further out—always further out than anyone else. Yes, he reflected absently as he swam through the air, he *was* a "further out" kind of person, really, wasn't he? Further, more advanced, less limited than others.

But then Finwald scowled. He knew in himself that there was something very flat, something very linear, about his "knowing." He could quickly find his way from stage one to stage two and three and so on right the way up to a hun-dred. But Wodeman, he realized, knew nothing of stages two to ninety-nine. He did not need to, for he could hop from one to a hundred without the bother of negotiating all the ponderous stages in between. It was like crossing a lake by stepping-stones in the fog; Finwald could see only the next stone before him, whereas Wodeman's eyes could penetrate the fog and see all the way to the opposite shore. Finwald may have known the charts, sigils, incantations, and substances of magic, just as a mapmaker knows the layout of the land, but Wodeman *lived* in that land as a real place.

Face it, Finwald, he sighed, *you just don't have that type of genius, do you?*

It seemed so natural and simple for the shaman: to Wodeman, magic was just Erce, and Erce was magic. What was it he had said once? *"Whatever Erce is, he can't be imprisoned by leather-bound parchment."* He could only be perceived by those who lived in him, right? Yes, that was always the way, wasn't it? That was just typical of his sort of priest. Appa was much the same, for he would teach that magic simply *flowed* from Cuna. And for him that was enough. But for Finwald himself, magic was . . . What was it? It was a part of alchemy that he was trying to fit into Cunaism. And so far the two were not comfortable bedfellows.

Admit it, Finwald. He frowned. *You just aren't the simple type, are you?*

He continued to float in the howling firmament. *What am I, then?* he pondered, though he knew it was far too late to start asking questions like that. *Am I a priest of Cuna, or am I some kind of mutated alchemist? And can the two ever be reconciled?*

Years ago, when he had first met Appa, everything had seemed so clear, so easy to understand. He had opened his heart to Cuna, truly opened his heart, embraced his message warmly, and had thrived. But during the years that followed, during all those long days and nights as he had pondered his faith, especially in the early hours before dawn when the mind cannot tell lies to itself, Finwald began to realize, deep down, that his was a faith without deep roots, because he had never fully understood its core meaning.

Be honest with yourself, Finwald, he told himself. *You're just not solid. You've never had any real oneness of purpose, have you?*

Perhaps if he had simply accepted it all, as did the others of his order, things would have been different. But blind faith would never be for him; he was of a different essence. Always he must study and probe, questioning everything. Too intellectually aloof to just discuss his faith with other priests, Finwald, in his focus on his solitary studies had become more driven, more intense, almost obsessive. And with never anyone to argue with him, well . . .

On the other hand, Pashta the alchemist had referred to him as his "disciple." Finwald could study for an entire day and night, without sleep. Nevertheless, it was abundantly clear to Finwald that of the two, it was Pashta who was the more gifted: his best ideas would often come to him in the middle of a dream, or while cutting his toenails. In short, he would be *inspired.*

Don't lie to yourself, Finwald thought, grimacing. *You were just never the intuitive type, were you?*

Then Finwald grew angry with himself, crying out to the darkness all around him: "Face the truth, Finwald, for once. This quest was never about faith, or knowledge, or understanding—it's only ever been about one thing: power!"

And with that, arms outstretched, he plunged, hungrily, down into the void.

Falling through darkness, tempest-flavored and laced with insanity; jabbering souls sine-waving through the Primal Chaos and burning with an inner chryso-prase radiance; lurching maw sloshing with narceine-tanged bile; quicksilver blood corpuscles pumping at the speed of thought along frozen carotid arteries of virulent lapis lazuli, before bursting into lotus bloom in the brain; the mind splin-tered by the clanging of quartz bells in the cupola of the Yttrium Chapel; naked mortals hooked through the lip with copper wire, dangling from stratospheric globes; sailing over a forest canopy of offal stench, swarm-ridden cryptomeria; sailing, trailing, limb-flailing, face-paling, harpooned from a whaling boat, float-ing through novae of multi-hued brilliance exploding from the dark before rain-curtained eyes propped open by shards of zinc . . .

. . . searching for power at the Gateway to Hell.

Flekki the Hauger had on occasions experienced this same sensation while concocting her creative little spikenard unguents in her badly ventilated cellar by the riverbank. It was similar also to the soul-voyage undertaken by Grini when he had first acquired his shamanistic powers. This was *almost* how Dolen Catscaul had felt when she had projected her mind into the empty house of her dead swain's skull at the grassy knoll in Eotunlandt where Bolldhe had mur-dered him. And it was very close to the way Klijjver spent his dreams after a heavy supper of dog-cheese.

Alchemics, narcotics, psionics, cheese-antics. It all boiled down to much the same in the end. So why were they becoming so hysterical this time? What was all the fuss about? What exactly was so terrible about floating, in a living chain linked hand to ankle, in the screaming darkness above the Gateway to Hell?

Finwald regarded the Tyvenborgers with detachment as they writhed like skewered bait dangling above a melee of ravenous pike; saw how, as the line corkscrewed uncontrollably, the veins in their forearms bulged, skin seemed to turn inside out and bones were almost twisted apart; looked at his own laugh-able form at the end of the line, wearing its ridiculous expression of rapture. All perceived as though he were studying a scene with a scrying glass.

He did not care—not about those people, not about anything much any-more. He already had what he had come for, and the problems of the world now seemed just so mundane.

Ever since his hands had closed around those precious tomes, felt their pulsing animation wriggling beneath hot devilskin covers, smelled their sul-phurous sigh breathe out of the pages, nothing else had mattered any longer.

It had been so easy. Far easier than he had ever imagined. For in Hell's Hole one could be anywhere within the bower of Olchor that one desired, grab anything one wanted, even the Tomes of Power that belonged to the father of Drauglir himself, he alone who had true mastery over the Rawgr.

An odd look crossed the small man's face, and he tilted his head back a fraction. Beneath the greasy collar, turned up at the back, his nape-fur prickled. Then his pupils narrowed to chromatic blue slits rimmed with cobaltite.

". . . Elfswith?"

The half-Huldre did not appear to hear Kuthy at first, and remained seated up against the wall listening for something. Then he turned to his partner and stared into his eyes, seeming for a moment to forget where he was or what he had been doing.

Elfswith's eyes cleared. "Nothing," he replied. "Just thought I heard something."

A fair way above them still, Finwald had just gained possession of the tomes from the Hole, and the resonances of his actions had sent vibrations along the strands of the web to any of those nearby who could pick up on such things.

"Where was I?" he muttered, then finally noticed the krummhorn that he was still holding to his lips. "Ah yes," he said, and began to blow into it.

Hours earlier they had chanced upon this hall. It was a small chapel in which the floors and walls were black with the residue of centuries of bloody sacrifices, and the ceiling dripped with resinous stalactite-like formations from the near-ceaseless emissions of the cardamom braziers. As the papery mass of a wasps' nest gradually engulfs the timbers of the attic in which it is built, so too did these stinking protuberances almost entirely mask the stone ornamentation up above: vaulting corbels, arched braces, hammer beams, and purlins, all carved into the likenesses of fiends that leered down in relish at the ghastly scenes below. And at the opposite end of the chapel to the one where the company was camped, stood an altar in the shape of a great tree, de-crowned, contorted, and flayed of most of its bark, with no leaf nor any branches save the main limbs, which had been twisted off to all sides. From these hung the effigies of sacrificial victims, and upon spears thrust through the bole, similarly pathetic remains or parts of people had been spiked. The craftsmanship was beyond doubt, but the effect all rather troubling to the eye.

It was a terrible place to seek rest, but it was the best they could find. Most of them had simply sunk to the floor and gone to sleep immediately, and were curled up in varying states of slumber even now. Some drifted between restless waking and troubled half-sleep, while others remained dead to the world through sheer exhaustion.

During this unquiet recumbency, various scouting expeditions had been sent to try and locate the two missing members of the party. None of the company from Nordwas had felt up to this, but the Vetters and Cervulice seemed much hardier, and proved expert at padding around silently and sniffing out trails. So far, none of these reconnaisances had turned up anything, but it was only a matter of time.

Elfswith, in the meantime, was growing a trifle restless, and the sprite in him was sorely in need of distraction. He half-lidded his eyes, inhaled long and deeply, then let his weed-soured breath weave its piquant magic over the double-reed of the krummhorn. The ancient woodland tone of the pipe, with its tremulous earth-deep vibrato, bardic melody, and pagan rhythm, resounded from wall to wall, floor to ceiling, and filled the derelict chapel with a beauty and power that did more to heal the company's scourged souls than any sleep, or stirring oratory. Those who were still awake sat or lay transported for a time into another place far from here, and just let his music fill their bodies and minds with bright colors, smells of childhood, and greater depths of emotion than any of them had felt for a long time. Even the sleeping ones slept more soundly, and peacefully.

But the old evil that still lingered in this temple of profanity was permeated deeply into the resinous stone, and rather than soothe, Elfswith's music seemed to awaken it. His trilling notes set up a new resonance in the air and caused the fiendish corbels up above to growl and whine among themselves, cackling blackly, and spitting down on the travelers below. Soon a whole chorus of diabolic moaning and hissing could be heard from the lofty ceiling, a choir of the inanimate, the unholy, and the undead all giving full voice to their disapproval of the bard's playing.

Elfswith instantly ceased playing, and stared upwards. The chorus of grumbling continued for a moment, then began to ebb away. Within seconds, all was silent once more.

The half-Huldre regarded his krummhorn with wide eyes, while his overcoat turned as white as a snow fox. He and Kuthy glanced at each other, and he gingerly slipped the horn back into a pocket.

"This horn can replicate the calls of over a thousand beasts and birds," he said, "and I can even make it speak in a hundred languages. But I swear to you, Kuthy, it's never produced *that* effect before!"

Elfswith sealed the pocket shut, and instantly his coat thawed out to a seal-grey slush.

He looked around and studied his present company. Apart from Kuthy, Ceawlin and himself, only a couple of Vetters, one Cervulus and the Paranduzes were still awake. Hwald and Finan sat apart from the main company, legs folded beneath them, and were rather bizarrely engaged in the ritual of oiling each other's bodies. Elfswith stared hard, thinking he must have seen this wrong but, no, there they were, contentedly smearing handfuls of aromatic oil over every square inch of each other's torso. It was something they apparently always did before going into battle.

Suddenly the chapel door opened, and two Vetters came skittering across the floor toward the slumped form of their leader. Without even glancing at the humans that lay snoring upon the floor, they blew softly into Englarielle's face (the Vetter way of waking each other up) and gently prodded him with their tails.

The large green eyes of the chief flicked open as if he had not been sleeping at all. In muted but urgent tones the two new arrivals announced something to him, and pointed anxiously at the sleeping humans nearby.

The chief's ear tips trembled, and he leapt to his feet.

"Something's up," Kuthy said, and reached for his sword.

"R'rrahdnar!" said Englarielle, shaking Gapp violently by the shoulder (the Vetter way of waking humans). *"Porluss nos lyael dha fley-tregva!"* And he sharply gesticulated upwards.

Gapp was immediately wide awake, and turned to shake the Peladane violently.

"Nibulus, wake up, will you!" he hissed into the groggy man's face.

" 'Sa time?" Nibulus slurred, barely able to awaken.

"No such thing as time in this place," Gapp grumbled, still shaking him.

With a gargantuan burst of willpower Nibulus managed to open his eyes fully, then raised himself into a sitting position. "What's going on?" he demanded as those all around him began to stir.

"The Vetters," Gapp hissed. "Those scouts who went out earlier—they've just found Paulus!"

Of the half dozen or so Vetters that had dared essay the higher levels, only one pair had succeeded in picking up the spoor of Paulus and the priest. This had drawn them to the demon bedchamber, and it was here they discovered the Nahovian's bastard-sword, discarded upon the four-poster bed. Now, in that secret little side room, they stood with their chieftain, the five men from Nordwas, with Kuthy, Elfswith, and Schnorbitz, all in complete silence, all rigid with shock, all illuminated by the bilious light of green, red, and blue. The rest of the troop had stayed outside, either in the passageway or in the main chamber, and their whispered growls—amplified in the silence, but strangely distorted—echoed around the room like a throng of souls calling from the phantom realm.

"Paulus?" the Peladane breathed in shock.

There, still within the demon-glass, knelt the black shape of Paulus, one arm flung up in defense, terror in his face and surrounded by monsters.

Those present who had traveled all these long, long miles with the mercenary could now only stare. From their faces, it was clear that their minds were struggling: caught between the morbid beguilement experienced by any who beheld this window, and by the confused jumble of thoughts as they tried to understand exactly what it was that they were staring at.

The first to break the stillness was Wodeman. He reached out and, very hesitantly, tapped Nibulus upon the shoulder. Unable still to tear his eyes away from the garish scene before him, he murmured: "Peladane, just who is this Paulus that you brought along with us?"

Nibulus eyed the shaman sharply, and a chill enveloped all of them.

" 'What,' not 'who,' " corrected Bolldhe from somewhere behind.

"And how old is he?" Appa hissed, before the Peladane could get a word in. "This window must be *centuries* old!"

"He is Odf Uglekort, mercenary of Vregh-Nahov," snapped Nibulus, caught in the disarray of his thoughts and feelings, "and he's no more than five years older than me. All right?"

"So what's he doing in that ancient picture?" Kuthy demanded, though he knew the answer was hardly likely to be known to Nibulus. Again, they stared.

"What is this place?" Nibulus breathed, and the sibilance of his utterance whispered all around the room.

"Listen!" Gapp hissed, and pointed to Englarielle.

The Vetter had approached the window, and was both sniffing the ground where Paulus had knelt, and pointing one ear towards the glass itself. They all edged closer, and listened carefully.

Then an expression of slow, reluctant understanding that turned to utter horror creased their faces. For, just as Finwald had done earlier, they could now hear the voice of their lost companion, a sparse moaning carried upon a wind from far, far away.

"No! *No!"* Appa whispered. "It can't be. Please, anything but that!"

"Get him out of there, quick!" Gapp stammered in rising panic.

"How?" Nibulus demanded.

"Just get him out!"

The boy backed away as images of that awful torture chamber from which he had rescued Methuselech now spilled out from his suppressed memory to blacken his mind, and his stomach heaved. The others too picked up on the horror he felt, and soon it infected the entire room. They looked longingly to the door as their one chance of escaping the hysteria that threatened. The Vetters whined and growled, and curled their lips in fear.

"What can they be *doing* to him in there!?" Appa whimpered, fumbling for his amulet.

"Appa!" Nibulus barked at him. "Tell us what this is!"

"I don't know!" the old man howled, and began pounding the amulet with his ring again, clearly losing control.

Elfswith's voice, deadly serious for once, cut through their panic: "Wintus! Listen to me! Does that chronicle of yours mention anything about this?"

Nibulus stared at him in bewilderment for a moment, then shook his head. "There's no mention of *this* kind of devilment," he replied, "or anything like it. I . . . I don't think they ever came upon this place."

"Some kind of elemental Rawgr, or portal," Kuthy began surmising. "A way into their world . . . or a part of it . . . ?"

"Just smash the bloody thing!" Bolldhe growled. "We'll take the consequences—"

"No!" Appa cried, but could elaborate no further.

"Is it really glass, that we can smash?" Kuthy snapped. "I don't think so. And even if we could, would he then come out?"

"A-And would he still be looking like that?" Gapp stuttered, with his back now pressed flat up against the far wall. Schnorbitz at his side looked increasingly wild. "I mean, all flat and sharp, and . . . *ecclesiastical?*"

"And if he does come out," Wodeman stammered, "will he be followed by those others?"

"We must try!" Bolldhe cried. "We *must!* We cannot allow this to go on! If the pain they can heap on us here in *this* world is so bad, whatever would it be like over in *theirs?*"

"But is he worth the risk?" Kuthy demanded. "You all know what kind of person he is—or was. No one wants him to suffer, but ask yourselves . . ."

But Bolldhe had had enough of asking, had had enough of debate. Above all, he had had more than enough of suffering, his own as well as Paulus's. He marched directly up to the window and whipped out the tulwar he had taken from Finwald.

Cries of protest came from behind him, followed by a flurry of movement, but none of them was quick enough. In one swift move, Bolldhe raked the sword down in a diagonal stroke that sliced into the fabric of the window.

There was a chorus of stunned gasps—and a startled grunt from Bolldhe as he felt himself being almost yanked in by his sword arm. After a moment of silence, there was a brief hiss, little more than the fizzle of a dying squib, then nothing. The stained glass window remained as before.

Everyone's eyes dropped to the smoking remains of the tulwar Bolldhe still held in his shaking hand. The hilt itself was undamaged, but only an inch of blade still survived. That part of the sword that had entered the demon-glass, however, was simply not there. All that remained was a smoking residue of liquefied metal that dripped onto the floor.

"You *idiot!*" Kuthy let out a tremulous sigh. "What d'you think you were doing?"

The others likewise were stupefied by Bolldhe's action; they could hardly believe what he had just done. Nibulus straightaway stepped forward in order to pull Bolldhe back from the window. But, far from being deterred, Bolldhe sprang away from the advancing Peladane, then reached quickly behind his back and tore Flametongue from its fastenings. In almost the same movement he swung the blade around and, with a snarl that seemed to say *"Sod you!"* to the horrified onlookers he plunged that also deep into the evil image.

As soon as the flamberge struck, all color and light drained from the glass, and the room was plunged into darkness. The earsplitting clash of demonic forces from within the window could be heard as one awful sound made up of many: the wet thrashing of tentacles; the hiss of acid drying upon scorched flesh; the mad wing-beating of a songbird in a burning cage; the splintering of twisted exoskeletons. Behind it all was also the shrill, tortured screaming from multi-voiced, unimaginable beings beyond.

The stonework all around them lurched and quivered as if it would tear itself apart. The trembling grew worse and worse, until with a general cry of alarm, all there began to collapse, one by one, to the floor.

Then, with an ear-splitting sound that flattened the tall ears of the Vetters against their skulls, the window exploded.

There was a burst of brilliant light that burned the tricolor tones of the picture deep into the retinae of everyone there, a violent scission between the two worlds, and finally a gout of ectoplasm disgorged itself from the exploding window, drenching everyone that cowered within the room.

Exclamations of horror and disgust filled the air. Human, Vetter, and Cervulus picked themselves off the floor, and stared down at the iridescent fiend-filth that steamed and undulated like reanimated tuberculous matter upon their clothing or naked skin. They writhed about in abhorrence and revulsion, ridding themselves of the vile stuff as a dog shakes off water.

"Stupid bloody idiot!" Nibulus cursed Bolldhe, who just stood there looking totally stunned. "What d'you want to go and do that for?"

Amid all this activity, none thought to look at the space where the stained glass image had been. But as the company came to realize that this fluid was not of their own world and was already rising from them in trailing wisps of mucus-green vapor, their attention now refocused upon the wall where the window had been.

And the bundle of smoking black rags that huddled before it.

"Paulus!" they cried, and just stood there unable to move.

13

Like a Sigh from the Crypt

"Paulus? . . . *Odf!* . . . Is that you?"

Bolldhe was now alone in the darkening chamber, alone with whatever it was that had come out of the demon-glass. The light of the unholy picture had gone, smashed forever, and the only illumination here now was the diminishing torchlight of those departing. For the rest of the company were backing out of the room, either slowly and carefully or simply stumbling out in dread. All their weapons were out, trained on the smoking pile of rags at the far end of the room.

A hoarse exhalation could be faintly heard from the heap of black clothing, though none could be sure if it was human.

"Bolldhe," Nibulus said in a low voice, "hadn't you better see to it?"

His tone was unambiguous: Bolldhe had freed it, so Bolldhe must now deal with it. No one else offered to help, in agreement, it seemed, with the Peladane, and all were waiting for Bolldhe to get on with it.

There was no way out, nothing else for it then. Bolldhe blanked all doubt from his mind, and started moving toward the huddle on the floor. Cautiously he extended a foot toward it, whereupon everyone held their breath. He prodded it with the toe of his boot, and the doorway behind him rustled with the sound of the watching throng hastily backing off.

"Careful, careful!" Nibulus growled a warning.

The pile of rags did not stir, but that strange breathing continued as before. Again Bolldhe prodded it, this time with the tip of his flamberge. The untidy shape rolled over with a moan and with a horrible scraping, chitinous sound. Instantly the onlookers flinched, and the torchlight receded further. The scraping continued.

Then Bolldhe relaxed. Even in the paltry light cast from outside the room, he could now make out the source of the scraping; it was caused by the brass studs of Paulus's familiar cape brushing the floor.

"It's all right, you can come back in now," Bolldhe called out to his cowering companions. "It's him."

What had Paulus suffered in there?

He was among them once more, all in one piece and without a mark on him. Though a little off balance and unsure, he stood on his own two feet. His clothes were still smoking a little, and he was just staring round at them one by one.

There was not a hint of recognition in the mercenary's eyes, no understanding nor any sign of intelligence. Paulus regarded his fellows with vacant eyes, opening and shutting his mouth without words. That former air of death that had always surrounded him now seemed more like an air of *dead*. And exactly how, they all wondered, could a seven-foot-tall man suddenly appear so small?

Clutching his hand, Bolldhe led him out of the smaller room and into the bedchamber proper. All eyes were fixed upon him, but only his human companions would approach. Appa began to inspect him closely, prodding with the tip of his tulwar, and even placing his holy torch talisman upon the Nahovian's skin to see if he would recoil. Wodeman sniffed at him suspiciously as a dog might sniff a wounded rodent on the road, ready to bolt at the first sign of movement. Even Gapp tried to get closer, but found himself held back by the strong forest hound's powerful teeth enmeshed in his Oghain robe.

"What happened to you?" Nibulus said in awe. "What happened, Paulus?"

"And what of Finwald?" Appa joined in.

But their interrogation was useless, as they soon realized beyond doubt. There was nothing left in Paulus. His mind had gone off to some place where they could not reach it. And it might never return.

Nibulus had seen this sort of thing before among his own soldiers, those twilit souls that rocked back and forth upon the benches lining the corridors of the Wintus Hall almshouse. Their death mask visages drooling, or grinning in mortification, empty eyes staring sightlessly from cavernous sockets.

"Here!" He strode over to the bed and grabbed the bastard sword that still lay there. "Maybe he'd remember something of his old vigor if he held his sword once again."

He thrust the hilt of the weapon into Paulus's hand and folded the mercenary's fingers around it. The company stood back to await the transformation, but in Paulus's flaccid grip the sword drooped briefly, and clattered upon the floor.

"Then again . . ." Nibulus scowled.

They were all at a loss. What were they to do? Paulus, their former champion

swordsman, was as good as destroyed. And on top of that, they still had no further information on Finwald.

"So what now?" Bolldhe asked, glad that it was not he that had to make the
decisions here.

Nibulus tapped his boot irately upon the floor, inches from where Paulus's
hand-and-a-half sword now lay, and studied the hollow man before him. Eventually he simply shrugged. "You might as well have his sword too, Bolldhe.
Come on, let's just take him with us and get on with it."

So many colors, so many images! All these sounds, feelings—such things as he
had never experienced or even *imagined* before. All floating around him like
glowing baubles, not only near but as far as the eye could see, as far as the soul
could reach. It was a veritable kaleidoscope of spinning sensations, experiences . . . *knowledge.* And Finwald, the mage-priest from the south, was standing right at its very nucleus.

He was flicking through the tomes, leaf after leaf, absorbing their essence at
the rate of one page per second. It seemed to him that all the knowledge in the
world was his, here at hand, and all he had to do was reach out and touch it. It
was fascinating beyond any prior expectation, utterly and unbelievably absorbing, far more incredibly wonderful than he had ever dreamt in even his most
far-fetched fantasies.

But there was so much of it! If he wished to learn of history, science, even
alchemy, his finger had only to alight upon the appropriate sphere, and all
the knowledge retained therein would be his. But subsequently that same
sphere would explode into a billion fragments, like an expanding universe,
each one of them a tiny atom of that greater knowledge, yet each one a planet-
sized library in itself.

This might take him longer than he had anticipated.

The thieves were staring at him, even talking to him. They filled the scope
of his real vision, yet he was not thinking about them. Had he tried, he would
not have been able to even recall their names, or indeed distinguish one from
another. In some distant part of his mind that had once cared about such
things, he was aware that they appeared confounded, flummoxed, even exasperated with him. He was also aware how he must look, standing there gazing
back at them with a thin, fixed, smile on his face.

Yet, he still had business to attend to here. He could not stand around all
day grinning like an imbecile. Again, he went back to the tomes. His finger
reached out—

Drauglir, Chamber of: *pictures, images, each from many different viewpoints,
from many different times in the past, each conveying a different aspect or feeling
of the subject, the Chamber of Drauglir. So much information, such a rapid succession of images and thoughts, too much for the little man to assimilate, to register,*

to cope with; Finwald found himself spinning into a swoon out of which he knew he might not awaken. . . .

No. Too complicated. Far too much for him to absorb at this stage. Try something else. . . .

VAAGENFJORD MAW, Denizens of: *little pulses of light, some great, some small, some motionless, some on the move, and all different colors depending on . . . depending on what? Size? Gender? . . . No, on type—species . . . Have to sort that one out later. Not too much later, though. Right now, where's Bolldhe? That's the question. Or, more to the point, where's Flametongue?*

Searching . . . searching . . .

Hellfire! *There they are, only moments away from reaching the Chamber of Drauglir! Vetters, Cervulice, Paranduzes, a hound, a wyvern, a half-Huldre, And humans—one carrying Flametongue . . . But what're those? A whole army, just behind them and closing fast. There must be hundreds . . .*

That was it. No more time left. It was now or never. Finwald extended his hand and snatched at:

LANGUAGES, Modern: *Ah, that's handy! Each language is represented by an icon, a symbol. Let's see now: Venn, Rhelman, Findic . . . What damn language do they speak anyway?! Ah, of course, Cant.*

Searching . . . searching . . .

Damn, not even listed here! Just an icon of a pink embryo, all wrinkled and moist. Barbarian Tyvenborgers, their language was at that time too young to have developed. Just how long ago had these tomes been written? Useless thieves, just what did they think they were doing here, anyway? They were more like a bunch of bawdy, drunken oafs spilling out of a tavern on some alcohol-fueled dare than men on a quest.

Ah, here's one: GODTHAN.

Didn't someone once mention to him that the Dhracus came from Godtha? Without hesitation Finwald selected her language.

"Drauglir's Chamber," he suddenly rapped out in flawless Godthan. "Been there yet?"

Dolen would have turned even paler if she could have done. Things had been bizarre enough since she and her fellows had ventured underground, but nothing had prepared her for the shock of hearing this human suddenly speak her language.

". . . ?"

"Come on, come on! Have you been there or haven't you?"

"We've . . . yes, I suppose. We came in that way."

Her answer finished lamely, her mouth still working but no words coming out. "Show me then. As fast as possible."

The Dhracus jabbered out something in Cant, the uncouth syllables tripping over each other in their haste to exit her mouth. Finwald found himself instantly staring down the flared bore of Eorcenwold's blunderbuss, simultaneously hearing the indignant uproar of the other enraged thieves and the drawing of knife, spear, and missile.

For a second he just stood there, taken somewhat aback by this colorful reaction, and aware how, after all, his attention was now totally focused on the thieves. He realized that he could actually *smell* their anger, that hot, yellow-brown secretion that poured from liver into duodenum, taste the salt of their sweat and the metallic, mordant magic upon their weapons, feel the bright expectancy throbbing in their brains.

Their words, *"we're going that way anyway, but not till you've shown us the loot,"* spoken in a language he had not yet accessed, meant little to him however. But their tone was unmistakable, and Finwald did not like it. He touched another glowing bauble in the tome, and immediately his entire body shivered under the sensation of this latest spell to be discovered.

A word—just *one word*—was all it had taken; one incantation of admittedly formidable pronunciation, and he could then feel an aura of protection pulse into life around him, like oil-steeped kindling leaping suddenly into flame. To the onlookers it was invisible, but to Finwald it felt as if he was enveloped in a cocoon crackling with rainbow-hued energy, a suit of impenetrable armor that encased him wholly, the only possible chink being the risk of a temporary lapse in his concentration.

The vestige of the child in him giggled with the thrill of it all, as the tingling sensation ran over every inch of his body like a swarm of ants causing him to twitch and squirm. But most of all he was laughing at what he had achieved, how far he had come, and where he now stood in the world.

Time to try this out, he decided mischievously.

Just as it had taken but one word to awaken the spell, so too did it take but one gesture to test it out: two fingers raised in the appropriate manner, with just the right amount of impertinence, right in the face of the thief-sergeant himself.

"THAT DOES IT!" Eorcenwold cried in outrage, and his finger squeezed the trigger of the blunderbuss. The dog spring was released, hammering the serpent into the pan, and the needle lanced straight into the fleshy nerve ending of the dragon tooth that nestled there waiting in the chamber . . .

. . . And the entire cavern almost expanded with the force that exploded from the gun.

When their eyes had recovered from the blinding flash of detonated dragon tooth, the thieves turned back in slavering anticipation to look upon the headless, shoulderless, and possibly even chestless corpse of the Lightbearer. However, though the muzzle had been aimed directly at his head, mere inches from his face, he still stood there, as intact and unharmed as any of them, altogether unaffected (save perhaps for the blown-back hair, and the kind of expression normally seen on a dog with its head poked out the window of a rapidly moving carriage) by that most devastating weapon in the thieves' arsenal.

The reverberations of the shot continued to bounce back and forth around the cavern, until eventually swallowed up by the abyss below. Eorcenwold's large eyes were now dilated to plate-like proportions, and he stood there motionless, unable to do a thing. It was only the timely reaction of his sister who had remembered to douse the stock of his weapon with that same cold green liquid coolant, that saved them all from now being blasted apart by the overheating blunderbuss.

"Finger must've slipped," Eorcenwold stammered unconvincingly.

Finwald smiled magnanimously, savored the looks in their eyes, the *awe* that was so appropriate, so fulfilling for him.

Then he snapped his fingers, and all hell, it seemed, broke loose.

The stone floor all around them exploded like a minefield, as a host of the dead sprang up from their graves below. Wire-haired banshees spun like dervishes out of the walls bearing whips of scarlet acid, and the walls themselves, whence these horrors emerged, melted into a boiling mud that formed huge faces which whooped and slobbered in derision, then lashed at the terrified thieves with serpentine tongues. The ground began to shake with the tread of rusty bismuth giants that leered down imbecilically and reached for them with coracle-sized mantraps in their hands. Then a tornado of fire, wreathed with crackling lightning, suddenly appeared in the air, and from its howling cone flew terrible Rawgrs bearing arquebuses the size of cannons.

None of which existed, of course, but if there was one thing Finwald needed right now, it was urgency. This he now attained, as all the thieves instantly fled the cavern in screaming terror, any thought of loot entirely forgotten in their haste to return to the Chamber of Drauglir and flee this place forever.

That's it, you slope-headed bastards. Finwald smirked to himself. *See how you like being the little guys for a change. . . .*

Still smiling, he followed them.

Finwald's monitoring of his old companions' progress—those little pulses of light—had not been wrong. For here they were; Bolldhe, Nibulus and the others, with the wyvern-team and the horde of Cyne-Tregva, just moments away from reaching the Chamber of Drauglir. They had finally gained the uppermost level, and were at that very moment retracing the footsteps taken by Scathur on that momentous day five centuries ago, as he had marched along the corridor, past his terrified men, on his way to give that report to his master.

Here the corridors were at their loftiest, rising higher even than the lantern beam could reach, and were buttressed by tusk-like columns that appeared to have thrust up through miles of the earth's crust from the depths of the Place Below. Whenever the intruders brushed against them, the walls of rock crackled and hummed with a crystalline energy, or rang like metal being struck. Indeed the surrounding rock seemed more like iron than stone, its weight compressing the air till the ears popped and the brain began to ache. This sense of pressure seemed to be increasing the farther they went, producing cracks in the flagstones, ripples running like columns of ants along the walls, and tiny flakes of stone to drift like dead, dried skin from the ceiling. Little glints of light constantly winked at the travelers as they passed, as if the walls had eyes following their progress.

On they continued along the same corridor. All could sense an increasing tension, though its source was not yet clear. The Vetters seemed more aware of this than the others, and would constantly gaze up at things the humans could not see, like a cat suddenly staring up at a blank patch on the wall. Before long, though, even the humans started doing likewise, for they too could now hear the strange sounds that were causing the Vetter ears to tingle.

As silent as the rest, Bolldhe stared all around as he walked. As the principal source of illumination, he should have been concentrating on lighting the others' path. But he found himself increasingly fascinated by the noises that came from the rock face on either side. They reminded him of his mother's house all those years ago, when as a child he had cowered beneath his blankets in dread as he had listened to the nocturnal scurrying of rodents in the spaces between the walls. In the dead stillness of the night, broken only by the gentle moan of the wind through the woods beyond the town's stockade wall, or by the occasional tapping of a gate against its post, these furtive scrapings and sudden sprintings of vermin had always sounded too loud to come simply from the rats or mice he knew they must be. In his child's mind they had evoked visions of black and beastly night bred horrors that might reach out at any moment to snatch him from under his covers and draw him into their narrow world between the daubed lath walls, there to remain forever hunted by nightmare creatures, calling out in vain to his mother who would never be able to hear him.

Looking about now, Bolldhe very much doubted that these massive, buttressed walls had any pockets of nice, warm, insulating air beyond them. And any creatures therein would be genuine monsters, and not merely imagined.

"Hold that bloody lamp steady, will you!" hissed Nibulus suddenly.

Bolldhe frowned. It was precisely at times such as these, when he had greatest need of alertness and focus, that he often found his mind wandering. But almost immediately he found his thoughts drifting again as he considered the present company.

Next to him, at the head of the line, strode the Peladane, Nibulus Wintus. Strong as a red bison, fierce as a stag in the rutting season, but at the end of the day, about as imaginative as a sheep. *Just why,* Bolldhe wondered, did he think he was here? The man was as clueless as he himself was. What kind of man other than a Peladane could be so fatuous as to come to a place such as this for no reason other than "it's what we do"?

Wodeman on the other hand, at least that one *knew* how useless he was.

Now that all that "playing mentor" rubbish was behind him, he was just another bloke with a bit of sharp metal in his trembling hand.

Then there was Bolldhe's other supposed mentor, that mad old ascetic with a body and mind about as firm and vigorous as his jabbering lower lip. His brittle old skeleton may have hauled his bones this far, but there was very little gristle remaining to hold them together by this stage in the game. Now there, if any, was a man driven by purpose.

Well, Bolldhe reflected, *if he's going to teach me anything, he'd better do it soon.*

He was just beginning to muse upon the debilitated Paulus, and the enigmatic Gapp who was now leading him along by the hand, when his thoughts were interrupted by a tug at his sleeve. He looked down and saw that it was Appa.

"Bolldhe," he whispered, "do you feel it too?"

He felt it. He had been hoping that his musings might have managed to block it out but, no, he could feel it. That pressure, that almost audible tension that filled their heads like a swarm of angry wasps, and waxing with each minute that passed. Bolldhe looked around and saw that the Vetters and their steeds were also greatly troubled by it, some of them flattening their long ears against the sides of their head, and occasionally one of them would shake his head vigorously as if to dislodge this new discomfort from it.

Appa leaned closer to whisper in his ear. "It's coming from behind us."

A huge weight suddenly oppressed Bolldhe's soul, and almost dragged him to his knees. Until now he had concentrated on dealing with his fear of going *forward,* to whatever awaited them; now, though, he really did feel utterly trapped, as did obviously the Vetters who were now continually looking behind them and moaning in dread. Caught between the Rawgr in front and his army behind, Bolldhe thrust his hand out to grasp the old man's shoulder, as if to hold himself up, or to draw on whatever reserve of fortitude the mage-priest might provide.

The panic kept rising in him, and he began to breathe heavily. This was worse than in the Moghul, worse even than Smaulka-Degernerth. And Bolldhe was beginning to suspect why. That sleep they had taken earlier, though it had done them all a world of good, had also robbed them of something. Of what precisely, at first Bolldhe did not know, but then it occurred to him that it was the blood. Yes, the power of Wodeman's blood-spell. But what exactly had that all been about?

Whatever the shaman had done for them, it was gone now, and without it they had only themselves to rely on. For Bolldhe, this was the way it had always been, and, he supposed, the way it always would be. But as for the others, well, he did not have to be an expert to see that they were beginning to fall apart. The heavy sweat, the breathing, those skittering eyes . . . their courage was spinning toward the snapping point upon its last fraying thread.

"Light!" hissed Nibulus, and instantly Bolldhe's wavering lantern beam snapped around to focus ahead.

Directly ahead of them, something was blocking the corridor. Bolldhe, wandering along as if in a dream, continued forward until he realized he was on his own. All the others had simply stopped in their tracks. Then he heard a couple of familiar footfalls draw near, and the clicking tread of Ceawlin.

"What's up?" came Kuthy's voice, reassuringly dispassionate.

"It . . . it's a door," stammered Bolldhe.

"Come on then," Elfswith muttered testily. "Nothing scary about doors."

With the wyvern-team, Bolldhe advanced carefully, blood thumping in his head, until the trembling shaft of lantern light could pick out the obstacle in detail. It was a huge door, wrought of adamantine steel and engraved with silver images of the fires of the Abyss. Yet it hung askew upon ancient hinges, and a great hole appeared to have been blasted through it. Elfswith approached it with uncharacteristic wariness, and ran an investigative finger along the molten edge, studying the magic-scarred surface.

Then he turned and looked Bolldhe full in the eye.

"Looks like we've arrived," he whispered, his voice like a sigh from the crypt.

14

A Breath From the Tomb

Under the dream . . . Bolldhe thought in dread, though he did not understand what he meant by this. *Under the dream?* He swayed vertiginously to one side as his legs weakened beneath him.

Something was definitely approaching from behind. Something, or some things. Bolldhe could feel them. Whatever they were, they were not close enough to be heard, but they were approaching with a speed sufficient to drive the cold air of the corridor on before them. As the crypt-chill of its passage sighed over them, one by one in rapid succession, the company's torches winked out.

Or so it seemed to Bolldhe. For none of his immediate companions was reacting. There were no cries of fear, no hurried fumbling for tinderbox, flint or steel; not even when the xienne-flame of his own lantern—which supposedly could not fail—also blew out.

And then they were submerged in total, tomb-sealed darkness.

Bolldhe croaked. The sound of his voice echoed in the strange silence that now closed around him.

So silent it was suddenly. And empty, totally empty. For Bolldhe perceived, with a ghastly realization, that he was now utterly alone in this place.

Where've they gone? Where are they?

And why did it feel so cold in here all of a sudden? So icy!

Now, finally, he began to understand. It was because he was *under the dream.*

Bolldhe had suffered recurring nightmares for so long that he was almost accustomed to them. He had previously supposed that they had no meaning, for as a fake seer he felt a knowing disdain for all that. But he did realize they had a source, and it was this he had never been able to understand. In fact, it often made him beg the question: *was there something deeply wrong with him?*

But that was not all, for beneath these habitual nightmares, he could sense, lay the *real* horror. There was always the feeling that the bad dream he was experiencing was merely the exit point of a deeper and much more terrible dream, a tiny hint of what had gone before, something he could not remember.

This dream beneath the dream, Bolldhe feared, must be so terrible that, were he to confront it openly, it would surely fracture his mind.

Standing now before the great door of the Chamber of Drauglir, looking through the ragged hole that the magic-users of five hundred years ago had blasted into it, Bolldhe felt he was hovering upon the edge of that immense pit that lay beneath his nightmares, staring into its compelling but unbearable blackness, as if dragged here in shackles to stand face to face with his own worst dread. No way back now: trapped between an enemy that bore down on him from behind, and the enemy waiting in that black pit before him.

This is it, then, he thought, sick with fear. *This is what's been waiting for me all my life.* And this, he knew, would be what ended his life. For it was his own death he could sense in the freezing, silent darkness of the limbo he was now caught in.

Reaching out in panic, his groping fingers curled around the rough edge of the hole blasted in the door. But, instead of the molten steel he expected, it felt more like melted ice.

Then there was a sound, the faintest murmuring that he could just barely discern above the trembling of his own breath: running water, dripping limestone, and with it, the smell of underground caves.

Bolldhe's scalp stiffened, and he felt his hair frost over.

Within the Chamber of Drauglir something was walking about. He leapt back in shock, but when he looked again, it was gone. From this position he had not been able to see much, but he had definitely seen a pair of legs move across his view; naked, filthy, skinny legs that glowed with a pale green phosphorescence in that impenetrable darkness.

He was no longer in Vaagenfjord Maw, of that Bolldhe was certain. He had long ago run away from the Benne Nighe of his soul journey, up on the ice field, and now she had caught up with him at last. She had led him back to her stony caverns and the bloodied waters of her stream.

He was back in his dream world, facing the pit of his deepest and darkest memory.

And then came that faint, resonant music, just as there had been in his spirit-walk; but this was a resonance not of sound but of *time,* a re-echoing of times long gone.

And with that music came pictures, pictures forming out of the darkness all around him, a succession of images faintly etched in varying shades of grey, each one of them grainy and troubled: a multitude of soldiery, an entire

battalion of them sprouting spears and banners, surrounding him, pressing in
upon him, towering over him; old men looking down at him, fear and despair
in their eyes; children too, grubby boys the same age as he, watching him in bewildered silence. And striking electric-black shadows upon white in one glaring monochrome frieze, the intense, luminous discharge of vaporizing magic
pouring from the wands of the magic-users against the portal they faced.

One of the taller boys, a glassy-eyed youth of about fifteen, was staring at
Bolldhe with a worried frown. Next to him stood one of the old men, surely
the oldest and smallest one there among the Fasces. Turning from Bolldhe to
this quaking veteran, the boy spoke in a puzzled voice:

"What's the matter with him?"

"He's always going off like this." The old man sighed in exasperation. "Always at the worst possible moment, too, and . . . Just what is that damn rumpus
about back there?"

In the subdued hush, the boy whispered, "Maybe he's dying . . ."

The old man did not seem impressed. "Bolldhe!" he hissed. "Snap out of it,
d'you hear? There's something happening at the rear. The Vetters are getting
agitated. Come on, there's no reason to wait any longer; this is it, the end.
We've got to finish it now. Aren't you going to *do* something?"

"Do what?" Bolldhe stammered, wondering just why he was answering this
question from a ghost out of the past.

The old man leaned over and cupped Bolldhe's face in his death-cold
hands. He gazed imploringly into his eyes, and said earnestly, "Bolldhe, just do
whatever it is you must. I can ask for nothing more now."

Then both he and the boy stood back from him, pointing toward the shattered doorway.

Bolldhe could not enter, of course. How could he enter a place that held
within it all the evil and fear that existed in the entire world? But neither could
he wrench his gaze away from it, and he continued staring through the hole at
the blackness that lay within.

"Come on you lot, *move!*" came a harsh voice from behind him, and immediately two powerful, gauntleted hands rudely shoved Bolldhe in the back.
In horror, but unable to stop himself, he was propelled straight through the
hole.

"No!" he wailed like a soul hurled into hell, and staggered headfirst into the
Chamber.

A pestilence of panic poured in upon him from all sides, and a plague cloud
of nausea condensed around him. Bolldhe stood naked in the Chamber of
Drauglir, alone save for the underdream that had finally come to claim his soul.

No . . . not alone. For as he stared about in an effort to locate the door and
make his escape, he saw that there were other boys hovering around him.
Again, they were etched in varying shades of grey and again they surrounded
him—but this time ducking, feinting, darting around as if in play. Inexplicably,

Bolldhe felt an odd tingle of excitement starting to grow within him. Without understanding, he found himself joining in with their game of tag, charging about and giggling hysterically.

. . . As if he too had been there—he himself—at the siege of Vaagenfjord Maw, five-hundred years ago . . .

Others were now entering the Chamber, behind him. A legion of soldiers marched in to the steady tattoo of two-score side drums, peremptorily brushing aside the old men and boys. One of them, an aging drum major with cold, pale eyes and a helmet resembling a lobster, glanced at Bolldhe and said, "It's all right, kid, we're here now."

The siege had begun in earnest. The beat quickened. More entered. Some were bearing torches, and gradually the darkness was repelled. On into the Chamber the entire company marched. The drum major was joined by someone riding a scaly hippogriff. The yellow-eyed rider placed a krummhorn to his lips and blasted out a shrill fanfare, whereupon, to the ecstatic roar of the throng, the mighty Warlord himself strode in. Appa's distorted face swam into view, then started backing away, hauling Bolldhe and the glazed-eyed boy out of the path of the vanguard elite as they escorted their leader in. Haloed in a blue metallic lustre, the Warlord carried the greatsword of Pel-Adan in one hand and a book in the other. Up to a lectern he swaggered, placed the book upon it, and with a flourish, opened the cover.

The book flew up out of his hands, its fluttering pages a flock of startled birds. Amid their clamor, out of the pages sprang Gwyllch, a brutish sergeant with pox-ridden skin, yet arrayed in fine armor and with bejeweled golden rings upon his talons. While the pages danced, he thrust his hand beneath his habergeon, rummaged about, and brought out a flat slate etched with runes. This he held up for the Peladane chief to see. It was a headstone with a name engraved upon it, which he suddenly hurled at his master. Missing him by inches, it exploded against the wall with a moist slap like rupturing flesh.

Further into the vast Chamber they were pushed, the place filling with clamor as it also filled up with soldiers. The fluttering pages increased their commotion, breaking loose, and began to fly about the hall, until their earsplitting howl was like a swarm of locusts. Bolldhe noticed a tugging at his hand, which felt pathetically feeble and debilitated, and looking down saw Paulus Flatulus. Small now, smaller than the youngest child there. Like a puppy he was staring up at Bolldhe with his single eye full of entreaty, out of his mind with fear.

"What can I do?" Bolldhe whispered, helpless with fear himself.

He could not stand witnessing such pain, and began to look away. But there was something coming into view ahead of them that he could not bear to look at either. For they were finally drawing near to the ziggurat, a great pyramid of black marble that loomed in the center of the Chamber, throbbing with a dormant but insufferable menace.

On towards it they were compelled, and still a tumult of pages flew about, like dead leaves cavorting upon the bleak wind of autumn's passing—leaf after leaf of history unfolding from half a millennium ago right up to the present moment. Heads down, eyes slitted, the company pressed on, ziggurat-bound. Like a lost multitude trudging through freezing pre-dawn fog they advanced, limbs turgid, extremities numbed. Bolldhe was aware that at his side walked the little old man, the Paulus child and the glazed-eyed youth, keeping close, maybe for his comfort or for their own. Beyond these three it seemed only vague shadows shuffled about in the gloom.

A deep, purring growl at the youth's side. A rattling intake of breath from the old man. The child's grip on Bolldhe's hand tightening. A harsh whisper in his ear:

"Schnorbitz's smelled something! We're not alone in here."

At that point, the beat of the side drums doubled in tempo. On past the ziggurat they were led, the whole army swinging round to follow Schnorbitz, now a ghostly Black Dog, the harbinger of destruction. Bolldhe realized in increasing alarm that he was now caught in the spearhead of the phalanx, with the rest of his company close behind and eagerly goading him on. The two time sequences blurred into each other and, through this dual reality Bolldhe staggered, and was pushed, ever onward into the dark.

Still the legion pressed from behind, and still the hound led them further into the unknown. Within moments, Bolldhe realized they must be nearing the far side of the vast hall, for a wall loomed right ahead. The hound was growling savagely, raising hackles on all within earshot. High-pitched shouting could be heard meanwhile from the rear of the column, where the Vetters' increasing panic was infecting them all.

Closer still they approached, until a black empty square in the wall could be discerned. Finally they stopped, all of them, and stared ahead in silence.

"The flue," the Peladane's voice announced thickly. Schnorbitz tensed, ready to spring.

What Bolldhe saw next may or may not have been genuine, for he had no way any longer of knowing what was real. But what he himself saw, the rest of the company saw also, for reality, reverie, and illusion had now become inseparable.

There, within the fireplace lurked a throng of shapes, silent and unmoving. Huge black shapes the size of ogres with one among them that was taller still. As the invaders gaped, great blades of fire leapt up, surrounding them, igniting them, illuminating them in a blood-red glare. Giants they must have been, or fiends, for still they stood motionless amid the flames, their ash-white hair streaming about them in that furnace. Clad in ancient, ornate armor of heavy bronze plate, each bore an immense poleaxe whose blades curved like the antlers of a devil. Both armor and weapons soon glowed with a fierce heat mirrored in ghastly, featureless, inhuman eyes that were all that could be seen behind the shifting curtains of hair. Then the tallest one stepped out to meet them, and the nightmare descended in full.

It was Scathur himself.

Dreams made flesh. Two events, one present and one long past, both running along parallel paths, screaming along blindly like runaway horses. And with Bolldhe caught between them, trying to hold his skull together against their shattering din. Pyrotechnics: raw power unleashed, crackling and screaming into the dark air. A rawgric howling of fury. A tsunami of missiles. A vision of Zhang screaming, the little horse being devoured by a green-eyed wolf that drank his blood. From behind Bolldhe, warriors charged forward, swarmed around him. Tall as antler-headed forest giants, they stampeded past him upon cloven hooves, charged on to assail the Darkangel.

The fog was swept away, and clearly now Bolldhe could see the Chamber of Drauglir in all its diabolic magnificence. From its glass-smooth floor of black and violet marble, up the ornately contorted pillars that ribbed the towering walls, to the hellish canopy of glowing faces—souls of the sacrificed—that spanned the ceiling far above, all could now be seen in such glaring detail that it hurt the eye.

But that earsplitting, locust-like din of earlier now increased in volume until it filled this entire world, grinding through Bolldhe's skull as a chainsaw through teeth. Clutching his head in horror lest it burst asunder, he could only stagger about insanely. But through the rent in his head—imagined or real—the vision that had transfixed him since entering this place now poured out, unfettered. The canopy of souls shrieked as they swirled around, and disappeared in a vortex; the ribcage walls crumbled into decrepitude; shining floors dulled back into the dusty dereliction they really were; and at last Bolldhe's dream came crashing down around him in a pandemonium of screaming, human or otherwise.

"Bolldhe!" a decrepit voice squealed, as the withered little face of the oldest of men now filled his vision. "It's an ambush! We're trapped!"

"Appa?" Bolldhe mumbled, once again seeing the old priest clearly. But a deep voice beside him deluged any other exhortations from the mage-priest:

"RETREAT! RETREAT! BACK TO THE PYRAMID!"

The company needed no further urging. As one, they turned and took to their heels after the Peladane as he headed towards the ziggurat. Paulus let go of Bolldhe's hand and tore after them, followed immediately by Appa. Even Gapp abandoned him, leaping onto Schnorbitz's back and riding off in hot pursuit.

"Wait!" Bolldhe cried, lurching after the departing horde. "We've got to get out of here now!"

"We can't; we're cut off," Appa called back hysterically. "The entire host of the Maw is coming through the main door!"

Bolldhe could barely think straight, for his vision had left him befuddled.

But he instinctively joined the rout that was now sprinting away in panic. With Paulus's sword in one hand and his own lantern in the other, he hared after the skittering shapes before him, catching up with the hindmost of the throng just as they reached the wide base of the ziggurat.

Up the diamond-hard steps they swarmed, torches waving, lanterns dancing, none daring to look back at what they could now hear filling up the Chamber. Bolldhe was among them, bounding up the steps like an antelope—the swiftest and nimblest of them. Now that his head had cleared, his mind concentrated upon doing what he was best at: looking after himself.

He was aware of little during this frenzied flight, as the enemy poured in around them. Instinct had taken control, and there was no room for thoughts or feelings, not even fear. All he could now see in the flashes of wildly swinging lamplight were the moving feet—bare, booted or velvet-clad—immediately before him. All he could hear was the commotion of hands and feet scrambling desperately up those steps, tier after tier. But as he ascended further to where the press was at its thickest, forcing his way through the throng of those weaker than himself, there eventually arose another sound. It was like the rushing of the tide over shingle, the approach of a swarm of hornets through the forest, the first tremors of an earthquake, then finally the rumbling that presages a stampede of bison.

The horde behind them advanced entirely without voice. No shouting, no idle taunts, no threats or oaths. But there were other much subtler sounds: the rustle of clothing and the slap of foot upon stone, the jangle of metal, the squeaking of joints, the snap and flutter of leathery wings. All these came separately to Bolldhe's ears, and drained his bladder as he climbed.

Just what is it we face? He gagged in horror.

Then the voice of the Peladane, yelling above the clamor: "No more, no farther. This is it! There is nowhere left to run!"

So, still shoving, tripping, and moaning, the company finally turned to stare in horror at what had gathered below.

What had, when they had first entered this place, been an empty floor, a vast lake of glassy smoothness that mirrored the glow of their torches, was now a heaving, discolored mass that still flooded into the chamber through the wide-open doors, like sewage through sluice gates.

On the right flank approached a score of figures that towered above the rest. Whether alive or dead, human or otherwise, it could not be determined, for they were draped from the neck down in robes of burgundy and gold, each head wholly encased in a brass helmet bearing a grotesque visage with a long spear-blade curving out from its mouth. Into the battle they carried great thuribles on heavy black chains, and these they swung about their heads as they came on. They belched a thick smog that choked out all light nearby, save for a dull glow of the fire within, like the blanketed flare of lightning amid storm-clouds.

On the left flank proceeded similar tall figures, but these were shrouded in white, with voluminous cowls of ash-grey that hid their faces. No thuribles this time, but bronze bells almost as large as cauldrons. These they pealed continually, doublehanded, filling the air with a doom-laden clamor that sapped the spirit of all enemies who heard it.

And between these two wings advanced the army that Scathur had summoned. Toward the rear marched the host from Wrythe, in their scores. By their bloody aprons and garrottes—not to mention their eager, loping gait—it could be recognized that these were Wire-Faces, but they had covered their heads with freakish bag-like hoods that had only small holes cut out for the eyes.

Among their number stalked the pack leaders, for once foregoing their trusty cheese-wires in favor of "tzerbuchjer." In times of greatest need the Wire-Face elite would wield these long weapons of blunt wood edged with a serrated blade composed of bone-slivers, ripping teeth, and shards of quartz. In their language, the word meant "tenderizer," which was possibly the closest their race had ever come to humor.

Clearly they meant business, more so now than ever. For after their earlier cowardice at Lubang-Nagar they were shamed beyond belief, but not beyond redemption. And with tzerbuchjer in hand they would rip this redemption in hot, red gouts from the steaming insides of their foe.

But before these, and vastly outnumbering them, shuffled the dead. Herded from the Trough, their ranks had been augmented by the pickled people from Wrythe, that had so recently clawed their way with renewed animation from the Urn. As a solid, crawling blanket of damp flesh they appeared, and even from this distance the stench was overpowering.

As Bolldhe stared, he noticed a small figure scuttling ahead of the approaching army. It ran in a most peculiar way, wholly unlike those who followed. There was something in its gait that caused Bolldhe to train his lantern beam upon this solitary figure, whereupon his realization that this was Appa smote Bolldhe with a harrowing grief.

His eyes wide with mortal terror, arms flailing in his pathetic efforts to mount the slippery steps, the elderly mage-priest would be the first to fall.

There was no one eager to help him, for they were all about to face the same fate. Paulus, somewhere up at the top of the ziggurat, was screaming hysterically like a child; curled up on a marble tier with his hands over his ears, he was reciprocating in uncontrollable spasms, his mind completely gone. Nibulus was furiously striving for space to swing his greatsword, thrusting the frightened and bewildered Vetters out of his way. To one side stood Wodeman, one hand over his face, muttering something unintelligible in a shaky voice.

The army of darkness came crashing on to the lower tiers of the ziggurat, surrounding it as a wave surges around a rock. Then up they came. The company shrank back, pressing further to the summit, like ants swarming up their anthill to escape the rising waters.

"Hold the line steady! Hold the line steady!" Nibulus called above the apocalyptic chaos, as though there was any line to hold steady in the first place.

The Peladane, brandishing Unferth two-handed above his head, glanced over to meet Bolldhe's eyes, and gave him a final nod. There were no words to be said. Bolldhe noticed also Gapp and Schnorbitz nearby. Neither showed any sign of emotion other than complete concentration.

A pall of black thurible smoke rolled up towards them ahead of the army. Thick and stinking, it caused the eyes to smart and the stomach to heave. Suddenly from its depths, the first figure emerged. A ragged figure, plunging upward toward them, with two others close on its heels. There was a flurry of sounds as all weapons were raised in defense: the Vetters' quartz-tipped darts and hiltless machetes, and the Cervulice's amber-coated wooden sabres, held one in each hand.

Bolldhe gazed down the steps at their foremost assailant, and realized in shock that it was Appa. He was desperately hauling himself up the great risers, with two animate corpses shambling after him, their broken mouths agape in a permanent silent scream. There was barely any strength left in the priest, and it was only the mind's last few seconds of self-preservation that impelled him on. It reminded Bolldhe of once watching a rabbit, badly mauled and with its hind leg broken, scrabble through the briars, away from the pack that snapped at its heels, to the safety of its burrow.

Then the dead reached out, and hauled him back.

Bolldhe cried out, but just then there was a repeated hiss through the air about him, and the two dead fell back, releasing their prey. Each was now barbed with several Vetter darts, and one by an arrow from Methuselech's bow.

Once again the Peladane had hit the mark. With a flourish, Nibulus returned the bow to its place hung across his back, and rehefted his greatsword. There was the ghost of a smile on his face, and even the sheen of a tear in his eye that seemed to say: *That one's for you, Xilva.*

Seconds later the terrified priest plunged up through their ranks, and did not stop till he had collapsed onto one of the upper tiers.

Terrible noises rose toward them through the dense fog of incense. Though they could still see nothing, the confrontation was merely seconds away.

"Brace yourselves!" Nibulus exhorted. "Brace yourselves!"

The muffled noise of battle engaged suddenly broke out from the far side of the ziggurat—a terrible squawking, accompanied by the screaming of Vetters and Cervulice.

"Brace yourselves!" Nibulus roared, took one last swig of sloe gin, then slammed his visor down.

And then the dead emerged.

The smog had now risen almost to where the front line of the company stood waiting, and thus they had only an instant in which to glimpse their enemy.

But it was an instant sufficient to freeze that image permanently upon their souls.

Out of the black pall surged the spawn of hell's lowest ditch, rising to feed upon the living. Ruined hide, gas-bloated guts, flaps of peeling skin hanging loose off filthy bones, up the last steps they dragged their blasphemous carcasses. Some looked relatively fresh, spry even, compared with the oldest among them. Others, though, were so ancient that their brittle bones had to be held together within an external framework of metallic splints, whose rusted joints squealed painfully with each movement. There were those that had perished while hunting, their faces gouged by antler, tooth or horn, or their chests crushed under three-toed hooves. There were others that had fallen in battle, or simply died under the executioner's tools of trade, their heads or limbs now crudely stitched back on and held in place with rods, nails, and clamps. Many had suffered terribly before death finally took them, as could be seen from the contorted masks of torment forever frozen upon their faces. But there were also those who had died in their beds, for though they advanced with twitching fingers, their eyes remained closed as though in a peaceful sleep.

But in the forefront were the most physically degraded, no more than lumps of sundry bodies sewn together as one; part flesh, part metal; legs where arms should be; external pipes and organs swinging free. Some even had animal parts grafted on to fill in where not enough human could be salvaged.

Among them walked the children, the slick, pale skin pocked with blue, old sores of some ravaging pestilence, others wrapped around with the filth-caked remnants of balding sable bandages. Charms had been lovingly pinned to their shrouds to see them on their way. But now, slack-jawed and with unseeing eyes rimmed with a yellow crust, they approached with nets and sharp little knives, propelled onward by the unseen captain behind them.

The first wave, the cannon fodder, driven ahead to soften up the enemy. As usual.

All around the ziggurat, the quartz-tipped darts of the Vetterim sang repeatedly through the air. Hundreds of arrow-sized projectiles, volley after volley, thudded into the oncoming ranks of the dead. Some fell, as the connection between heart and brain severed, but mostly they still came on, skewered, but basically unharmed. Not for nothing had Scathur sent the dead in first.

Then with a sigh like a thousand death rattles—the first utterance heard from them that day—they were upon their waiting prey. Nets were thrown, screams of terror went up, Vetter, Cervulus, and human alike surged around in chaos. Reaching out with split and blackened talons the dead sought to rip, to rend, to grapple, grasp, and gouge.

Hell had come to them at last.

They gasped for breath. They stumbled and fell, picked themselves up in an instant. They knocked themselves almost senseless against low lintels, or winded themselves in collision against stone balustrades. But, most of all, they *ran*.

Down narrow stairs, along galleries and triforia, over pits and through tunnels, the Thieves of Tyvenborg sprinted. The terrible priest was still close behind them, and the nightmare creatures he had evoked came screaming alongside him. Their mission to the Maw had turned to ruin and disaster, and nothing short of death would keep them here longer.

On, down toward the Chamber of Drauglir they stumbled. It was their only exit now, their sole hope of salvation.

Mauglad ran with them, among them, *in* them. Or in one of them, at least.

Asdtaga, how this new body could run! So much better than that slimy bag of flesh he had been forced to make do with until recently. This new host of his moved along at such a great pace that the necromancer felt as if he were being bounced about in the back of a runaway wagon.

It irked him, however, to have to run like this. He did not fear the Lightbearer, neither him nor his amateurish sound and light show. He might have laughed in scorn, in fact, had it not been for the very real chance that this wretched priest might actually succeed in his mission. The silly man may not have been evil, but that did not make him any less dangerous.

Mauglad had now existed for over six hundred years, for most of that time as a fleshless spirit keening its lamentations of loss and bitterness around the dank, grey passages of Sluagh. In all that time the human feelings in him had dried up, withered and turned to dust. All that there was left of him, all that he *was,* down through all the centuries of Sluagh, was *awareness.* And now that he approached, after eons of banishment, the hall of that devil who had caused him such damnation, Mauglad Yrkeshta became very *aware* indeed.

And what Mauglad was aware of now, what was uppermost in his thoughts, was the necessity for *extreme* haste. Not to evade the pursuing Finwald, but because he simply must not—*could not*—be beaten to that Chamber by Bolldhe and the terrible weapon he so blithely wore strapped upon his back.

But running just below the surface of this seething torrent of dread were underlying currents of self-opprobrium that would not go away. *Why had he not acted earlier, when he first had the opportunity?* Back there in the pillared hall, when he had first appropriated this new host, he had been so *near!* For a matter of mere *yards* had separated him from his goal. *Yards!*

But, in truth he knew he had taken the right decision in heading off the other way to join up with the thieves. For how close could he have got to Bolldhe while wearing the body of one of the Tyvenborgers, their now bitterest enemies, who had just struck down several of their number? He would have been cut down in a second, silenced before even having the chance to reason with them.

Then there persisted the nagging thought that he could have revealed the crucial truth to these companions, could have told them of the Sword. Told

them everything. But why would the thieves believe the word of a ghost—
especially one that had just stolen the body of one of their own companions?

So on he pounded beside them, drawing great drafts of that familiar sickly
air into these capacious new lungs, revelling in the strength and fluidity of this
powerful meat-chariot. For, bizarrely, these brigands with their superior skill,
muscle, firepower and sheer viciousness were probably Mauglad's best remaining chance now—his one and final hope.

"Now!" Nibulus thundered, and at long last did what he had come here to do,
and led his men into battle.

The dead were slow and, yes, their prey not so passive. The Peladane himself was a captain through and through, and there was no gainsaying the command in that voice. Rather than cower back until those black claws were at
their throats, the besieged—man and beast alike—now lashed out at the enemy with every last ounce of ferocity their fear had inspired in them.

Heads flew into the air like pinecones tossed in a gale. But the dead came
on mindlessly, not even raising an arm to defend themselves. In the forefront of
the defense, the dragon-crested, boar-faced Lord of Metal fought; with a
sweep of his massive greatsword, Nibulus swept the heads off three dead,
imbedded his iron-shod boot into the throat of a fourth as he swung round
with the momentum, then brought his sword back in a return swing. The first
four had not even finished falling before Unferth had sliced clean through the
necks of the next three.

Machete held high, Gapp let out a shrill challenge. Then both he and
Schnorbitz plunged headlong into the melee, in an animal frenzy of tooth and
blade. While Gapp lunged, hacked and stabbed in a berserk fury, and crushed
the spilt contents of heads into a mire that was as grey as the boots that trampled them, Schnorbitz flung the broken carcasses of the enemy all about him
with the ease of a terrier in a barrel of rats. As a team they worked, the forest
hound's speed, power, and savagery impossible to counter, the boy picking off
those that sought to swarm over him from the sides.

Wodeman, too, rediscovered his courage at that hour. Refusing to let his recent guilt drain his vigor any longer, he now used it to stoke the furnace of his
rage. For a moment he gripped the hilt of the alien, iron tulwar he now carried,
fingers searching out for its soul. Then he threw back his head in a howl and
launched himself into the pack that harried him.

For the Vetterim too, the spell of horror that had so long held them now
faded. Reanimated dead or not, it made no difference to them any longer—the
swarm slithering up toward them became simply Jordiske. The old enemy. And
they had weathered hundreds of years of dealing with that.

"*Siall Nurr Auoist!*" Englarielle shrieked, and brought his ancient Polgrim
gyag-axe down upon his assailant in a blow that cleaved through bone and rotten meat from skull to breastbone. An accord of warbling howls united with

the Cynen's war cry, as his folk followed him into battle. Swift as the blood-eyed weasel and inflamed by a wrath begotten from centuries of persecution, the Vetters descended on their opponents. The swords they had fashioned from the scapulae of the hated Jordiske cut deep into soft flesh and through brittle bone, and under this onslaught the dead flew apart.

The Cervulice, too, at last brought their weapons to bear. They were forty-six strong, each armed with a pair of long, glass-sharp amber-wood sabres, and terrible, black ivory horns jutting from their forehead. They had every advantage of height, weight and sheer belligerence, and the loss of the four comrades taken from them by the brigands still brought angry tears to their eyes. Blow after blow they now rained down upon the stinking pestilence below them.

But it was under the weight of Hwald and Finan that the greatest number were put down. Side by side they stood, proudest of the Treegard, and before this pair of threshing machines the dead could only fall, and fall in their dozens. Deep into their ranks the Paranduzes waded, tossing the burst remains of corpses high into the air with their antlers, entirely obliterating skulls beneath their mace-like tail spikes, and building a dyke of carnage around them with every scything sweep of their flint-headed moon-spears.

It was a sight that rekindled some of that dark fire in Bolldhe, as yet holding back, and stirred the murky waters of the madness inside him. With a calmness that seemed entirely inappropriate to the situation, he turned and handed his precious lantern to one of the Cervulice poised on the tier above. Then, with Paulus's sword still grasped in his right hand, with his left he reached behind his back and drew out Flametongue.

A germ of giddy excitement tingled somewhere inside him, and he brought the flamberge up to gaze in wonder at its acerbic sharpness.

The shade of a laugh flickered across his soul, and an instant later he was hauling the Vetters out of his way, and revelling in the glory of "the slice."

At the first sight of the onslaught of hell's legion, many there—even those of the hardest mettle—had cried out in dread. Some began shaking violently, and had had hardly the fortitude to grasp their weapons, while others simply loosed their bladders. In Paulus's case, he had lain curled up in a terrified ball upon one of the uppermost steps, rocking back and forth and wailing uncontrollably.

Even Kuthy, on the other side of the ziggurat, had not remained entirely unaffected. For he had raised his eyebrows, not one but *both* of them.

"Lot of them," he observed.

"But three of us," Elfswith pointed out, encouragingly.

"Three against hundreds, though," Kuthy remarked. "Thousands, maybe."

"That many?" Elfswith exclaimed, clearly perturbed by this news. Then he shook his head. "Wherever are we going to bury them all?"

Kuthy glanced briefly at his strange friend, then rolled his head around to loosen up his neck muscles. "Might need something a bit special for this one," he suggested, noticing that the bard had not yet drawn a weapon.

Elfswith could only agree.

"Ah, I think I've got just the thing." From one of his inside pockets he extracted something highly unusual. Quickly disentangling it from the comb and the piece of old string that it had got caught up in, Elfswith shook out the most amazing weapon anyone there had ever beheld.

Its haft, the length of his arm, was carved from fluted ivory and inlaid with swirls of gold, glowing from inside with the pale fire of enchantment. From either end of this instrument sprang a fabulous blade in the shape of a peacock feather. The rachis, or spine, was of the most slender and flexible spring steel, and from both edges of these two blades extended a thousand webbed vanes of tengriite razors that sang with a clear sharpness and shimmered with a scintillating effulgence. Whether this weapon was a spear, a flail or a sword was impossible to say, but it appeared to combine the best features of all three: the reach of the spear, the flexibility of the flail, and the cutting lengths of the sharpest of sabres. "Xem-pu" he had named it—"the Peacock"—and it was the proudest treasure of Elfswith's mysterious arsenal.

Even with the blue wisps of pocket lint that still clung to it.

"Respect." Kuthy grinned in consummate approval.

"Respect," Elfswith agreed. Then he hefted Xem-pu, and turned to face the approaching masses.

"Time to get those pennies back on your eyelids, boys," he called out to the dead. Then with a final, deep breath, he, Kuthy and Ceawlin stormed into battle like a miniature tempest.

Ceawlin spread her wings before the enemy in deadly invitation: less of a wyvern now than an angel of death, the winged corpse-chooser come finally to the battlefield to take her spoils. Pinions down, she came at them silently, a slithering engine of destruction driving full into their midst and hurling them back upon those that tried to follow from behind. While her claws ripped asunder long-dead matter and that terrible beak set about its murderous work, her snake-like tail suddenly flailed all that dared get in the way behind her.

Off to one side fought Elfswith, just beyond her wingtips' reach, but his was an altogether different battle. Exactly what manner of combat ensued between him and the groping cadavers could hardly be understood, let alone described, by the un-fey. It looked less like a battle than a frenetic day at a meat-processing plant. With the sound of a whirlwind, he moved through them at an impossible speed, in a seemingly chaotic vortex of slashing razors as the singing blades of the peacock spear twisted to a tune no human wrist could compose. The pupils of his eyes had narrowed to cat-like slits. His coat had turned a hellish, pygmy-shrew black. His hair rose, crackling with power, like a living thing, animated by the heat of his inhuman ardor, dancing and writhing along with the searing choir of the Xem-pu's thousand lethal vanes. And limbs, heads and entire torsos went spinning away from this frenzied grass cutter that whirled among them.

Dispensing the ultimate cure to their mortal woes, Elfswith finished the job death itself had not been able to.

But it was Kuthy, the lagger-behind, the canny survivor, the scorner of his own numerous legends, the holder-of-coats for those he sent into battle, who was the first of the three to draw grey matter on that day. Appa, by now near the top of the ziggurat, gasping for breath and wild-eyed in disbelief at his unending ordeal, heard the sudden onslaught and stared down to where these three now fought side by side. At first he believed he must be witnessing a suicide charge of the despairing. But as the moments went by and still they had not fallen—instead, appeared to be cutting a swath through the enemy—he began to realize what was happening.

The legend comes to life before my eyes, he thought, *here at the very end.*

Bit by bit, the mage-priest's fear-madness lifted, and he felt his heart strangely becalmed. Had he witnessed Kuthy's sword yet draw blood—even be unsheathed—in all the time they had known him? But unsheathed it was now, and the beauty and elegance of its actions continued to write the legend of the Tivor in characters that flowed like the finest, most exquisitely penned calligraphy.

Though beset by a multitude, Kuthy's martial skills flowed without effort. Feint forward to draw enemy on—skip back—blur of metal: two dead left standing without heads. Slash—backward somersault over other dead that swarm in behind him from all sides—another slash—another backward somersault: two more down. Leg sweep to fell three—continue in same movement to a spin that brings him to face the other way—half-second triple stab: six more tallied. Backward somersault to land on one's shoulders—triple slash from there—twist thighs to snap a neck—and off into the melee again.

Economy of movement, nothing wasted: it was as if he had rehearsed his every move, and those of his enemies, beforehand. There was nothing around him that Kuthy's senses did not pick up.

To all those fighting alongside this legendary trio, new hope and courage were brought, till they fought with a madness that in itself was worthy of a legend.

It was a desperate battle, a lightning counter strike that had finally opened the floodgates and purged the company of so much dammed-up fear. It was as insane as it was valiant, and had the heart of a dragon. But inevitably, it was no more than the final skirmish before the rout. For though they were slow, and of awkward gait, and climbed a steep slope, the dead were many, so very many, pressing in on them in a thick crush driven by a single will. They broke continually upon the ranks of the beleaguered defenders, like a great, slow harbor wave, and no amount of bravery or insanity could ultimately hold them back.

There were no words of encouragement—whether they be vehement orders, valiant oration, or vicious oaths—that Nibulus or Englarielle could use to help stem the force of such overwhelming numbers.

For a time neither side could do much but waver back and forth. There was no room to swing the larger weapons that might have held the enemy for a time, yet nowhere for the defenders themselves to retreat to. Eventually both sides were pressed so tightly that all they could do was shove. There were no cries of pain or anger even, just grunting and gasping.

But slowly the enemy's weight of numbers pushed their adversaries further in on themselves. They were being squeezed upward from every side so tightly now that it seemed they must surely explode like an enormous pustule. It was only the mounting dyke of their slain that had slowed the advance of the dead thus far, but even that had grown so bloated it was in danger of landsliding backward beneath its own weight.

Then one voice was raised that all could hear: a feeble sobbing born of despair.

"Oh, sweet Lord Cuna," Appa mewled, "where are you now?"

As if the old priest's cry had been some kind of announcement, the Wire-Faces finally arrived. Through the thickening pall of smoke rolling up from the thuribles below, they appeared as gaunt and monstrous shadows, spawned of the smoke itself, their only discernible features being eyes that burned as red as the torch fire they mirrored.

Over the heads of the dead they leapt, storm-cloud-demons of the thuribles' fire, striking down with tzerbuchjer-lightning. Tearing off their hoods, they pulled closer their prey to embrace them with sweet garrotte, face to face. That these were no longer truly human could indeed be seen, if truly human they had ever been, for in their lust for blood they had let their own, as if they resented the stuff of life to flow in their cold veins. So impressed by the dead they were, that they had further tightened the wires around their heads, which now cut deeply into the flesh, in some cases to the bone, the better to emulate their new comrades. Thus their faces were masks of blood whose steady dripping freshly emblazoned their aprons.

Squeals of agony rose on every side as, for the first time, Englarielle's followers became acquainted with the cheesewires of the leaping Oghain—squeals swiftly cut off in a liquid choke as the garrottes bit deeply into their necks. Beneath the attentions of these deranged assassins, both Vetter and Cervulus went down in a hideous thrashing of limbs.

"Get the freaks! Get those freaks!" Nibulus screamed, as he became aware of what was happening. He scrambled backward up to the step behind him, leaving his place in the line to be filled by a hefty Cervulus, and plowed his way through the throng, battering aside Vetters and even trampling them underfoot as he struggled to come to their aid.

Quick as vipers and agile as tree-rats though they might be, the Vetterim

were crushed together in a solid pack, unable to move. Their legendary tough-
ness availed them little against shining wires that cut right to the bones of the
neck or flayed the entire face from the skull, nor against the tzerbuchjers that
ripped and crushed defenseless flesh.

In among them the tall Cervulice strove to impale these leaping lords of
wire-faced dementia upon their spear-like horns, or to pull them down,
snarling like snared badgers, from their head-dancing perches. Under the
splayed hooves of the Vettersteed they were trampled, and their bodies speared
with Jordiske bones by the enraged Vetters clustering around.

Among these latter were Radkin and Ted, whose eyes blazed as red as their
fur, which was sodden with the blood of those they slew. It was a frenzied
struggle they were currently embroiled in as they grappled with a high-leaping
Wire-Face in an effort to keep him close to the ground. No savagery was
spared, as fingers, toes, teeth, and tails were brought to bear, but after tortured
moments, the tzerbuchjer, still in its owner's steely grip, was gradually swiveled
around and forced back up toward the Ogha's own face.

Ted was right on top of him now, and straining with every sinew of his
blacksmith's frame to push the lethal instrument's jagged edge closer to the
wire-encased flesh. Their faces were now so close he was forced to inhale the
carrion-infected breath directly from the enemy's lungs into his own. But as
he stared into those inflamed eyes, even now at the point of dying, he recognized neither pain nor fear, no vestige of mercy, love, or humanity. For these
Wire-Face elite were brothers in arms, whose arms would embrace only death.

If it's death you love so much, Ted swore, *then who am I to stand in your
way. . . .*

And slowly, ever so slowly, the sharpened bones and teeth that adorned the
tzerbuchjer mingled with those of its bearer.

But for every one they skewered, and every one the Vetters hauled down and
overwhelmed, another two Wire-Faces would leap over the heads of the advancing foe, and begin afresh. And as the besieged stared up at them in dismay,
there arrived another source of agony and death, only this time from below.

Kids. Not the Children of the Keep, but zombi-brats, crawling between
their legs and stabbing upward with rusty knives. Death from above, death
from below, and death from all around, an entire new chorus of screams filled
the hall, and the army of defenders began to crumble.

"Bastards!" Nibulus was crying. "Bastards! Bastards!" And with each im-
precation, he sent further dead to their destruction. Still caught in the thick of
the assailed Vetterim, the Peladane had no room to wield Unferth, and was
lashing out instead with gauntleted fist, elbowspike and iron-tipped boot. He
was now possessed by an uncontrollable fury he had never known possible, till
steam seemed to blow hot and red from the nostrils of the boar-visor masking
his face.

But, in all his bellicose career, Nibulus had never slain children. Certainly he had sent entire battalions in to sack cities, knowing in a reluctant part of his mind that no mercy would be shown to its inhabitants, of whatever tender years. Once inside the breached walls, his green-cloaked knights errant, his noble defenders of the faith, would become merely joyful bulge-eyed rapists, and guzzlers of human blood.

But having to stare down into the dead eyes of those undead imps, as they brought their rusty little knives up into the vitals of his comrades, Nibulus knew that this truly was hell he had descended into. These were the ghosts of every child he had allowed to die: vengeful, merciless revenants, ice-cold spirits that merely returned the blades of the murderers into their guilty owners' own flesh.

Had those eyes of theirs shifted but once to fix the Thegne in a reproachful glare, he would have broken down and succumbed to their knives, bled tears of pity for what once they had been. But there was not one flicker of recrimination to be seen, and for that small mercy at least, Nibulus was thankful. As he continued putting these children to sleep forever, rather than an act of brutality it felt to him more like an act of long overdue mercy.

Thus the defenders fought, and thus they died, for it was a losing battle, and could not be otherwise. Further up the ziggurat they were pushed, for they were now far fewer. They trampled and slipped upon the bodies of their own fallen as they ascended, and left behind the remains of others, making even higher the wall of slain. The air thickened with censer fumes, the wail of the dying, the snapping of bones, and the despairing yammer of those few who had breath enough in their lungs to manage it.

At the very top, gasping for breath, stomach heaving, Paulus yammered along with them. Like a wounded rat, he had wedged himself into a corner of the altar, and lay choking in a spasm of terror.

No one could begin to guess what was unfolding in his mind, for no one had been to the place where he had been; or where he was now, or where he felt he was going to. For, as he had writhed up there upon the very altar of Drauglir, once more an explosion of shattering glass had suddenly filled his head. Red, blue, and green swam before his eyes, then blackness, cold, still, and complete. Down a long tunnel his soul had sped. A journey through long centuries, and out to the days beyond. And at the end of it, bizarrely, the single small figure of Radnar. The boy turned slowly to regard the newcomer, and Paulus saw that his eyes were glassy with petrifaction. Within them, he could see a vision of the hell that approached all of them within the Chamber.

Shadows flickering against the roof of a flame-red cave . . . figures beneath it, their hair matted and slick with steaming blood . . . rising from the depths of a river of magma. And above it all, the ghost of a sound: the distorted laughter of children playing out in the woods.

A connection? Like Paulus, the boy had been incarcerated by Rawgrkind and, just as the boy did, so too did Paulus now feel their dread presence. So close. Mere minutes away.

The Children of the Keep are coming . . .

It was into the pandemonium of the failing battle that a new evil strode. Amid the escalating clangor of those awful tolling bells, and the deranged screeching of the Wire-Faces that rose now to a frenzied crescendo, the smog parted, divided into two by a Rawgr-wind to form a narrow corridor that climbed the ziggurat from base to apex. And, ascending the steps leading up this passage, swaggering like a god, Scathur finally came into their midst.

They parted for him, the regiment of the damned, backing away in haste to line the smogless aisle and howl in jubilant supplication. Up the steps of his master's altar he trod, and with each step he took, his pale robe furled back to reveal what lay beneath. A habergeon of polished yttrium he wore, each scale wrought in the likeness of a flame. But these were flames that appeared to writhe and constantly change shape, so that this Rawgr armor appeared to be made of real fire. And in each flaming scale could be seen the tortured faces of the victims he had sacrificed, for Scathur would have his loved ones close to him at this his hour of victory.

His head turned slightly and, though at this distance none of the company could see clearly his eyes, Nibulus sensed beyond doubt that Scathur was looking directly at him. Then the Darkangel's Bardische appeared. He did not draw it out from concealment; neither did it magically materialize in his hands; it was simply there. Power and pestilence ran along its length, and its gleaming axe-heads whined in expectation, sweated with red-brown lubrication.

Nobody, nothing, stood now between Scathur and the Peladane. For five hundred years he had waited for this moment, half a millennium of pure hatred compressed by the rock of this island, forged into something inconceivably terrible by the fire, hardened by the ice into a coldness that was the antithesis of life. Now at last the tables were turned, and the Rawgr would drive out the Peladane.

Slowly, relentlessly, he ascended.

15

Last Leave-taking for the Lost

On down the long hallway they ran, the long, final hallway that led to the Chamber of Drauglir. In a ragged and strung out line—Dolen well out in front, Brecca right behind at the rear—the Thieves of Tyvenborg tore along, almost reaching the very limit of their stamina. And still the phantasms of Finwald snapped at their heels.

Mauglad Yrkeshta's meat-chariot pounded along as keenly as ever, but there was something bothering him now, something of which he was becoming increasingly *aware*. Those revolting little evocations of the mage-priest that continued to pop out of the air like impudent blisters were still occurring as before—but a change had taken place. For, in the corridor, the conjuror's illusions were no longer emanating purely from himself, the original source, behind them, herding them onward like scourged dogs, but from all around them. . . .

Yes, there was a power in this passageway. There always had been, he recalled, even back in *his* day. It was a power capable of producing illusions matching those of the priest way behind them.

Illusions from behind, illusions from all around? But there was more: it was all very muddled, and there was no way he could be sure, but to Mauglad it seemed that there might be yet another, *third,* power source helping create these phantasms, one that was neither behind them nor around them but, rather, right in front of them:

The Chamber of Drauglir itself.

There, of course, had lain the greatest source of power in the whole of Vaagenfjord Maw. But why would it now produce such illusions? What purpose could that serve? Were they mere reflections of the Lightbearer's magic lantern tricks, stirred into glowing life once more by Finwald's reawakening of the tomes, humming in accord with sympathetic resonance? For, as Mauglad drew nearer, it became increasingly clear that there were sounds of pandemonium coming from the Chamber. Sounds of evil, sounds of death . . . sounds of conflict.

It then occurred to him: *Unholy god, these are no illusions! The Sword has arrived before we have! The battle has already begun!*

For Mauglad, he whose very soul was at direst risk here, there was no longer need for Finwald to crack the whip. Mauglad now charged ahead so madly that he reopened the wound the arrow had made in his current host's back and trailed blood behind him.

The sword the sword the sword the sword the sword the sword!

It became the one thought in Mauglad's awareness. In effect, that thought was all that he was now, during those infinite seconds as, trailing blood, he streaked, along the black passage, a fallen angel plummeting through the lightless void of eternity.

No thoughts of what might happen if he failed—for that was unthinkable. No thoughts of regret at what he might have done earlier, for that was past. Mauglad just ran, and as he ran the noises of battle waxed ever louder in his ears. Though aware of these, there was no room in his thoughts for them.

The surge of armies. The crackle of arcane power. The howling of Rawgrs. And one voice rising above all else: the roaring of Scathur.

The doors raced up toward him, those blasted-down portals of twisted and molten metal, with black smoke billowing out through them.

The screams of the exultant and the despairing, so loud now they reverberated within his borrowed skull.

Closer. Closer.

Then he was through. Plunging into the pall of smoke. Through the door, into the Chamber. Into the battle . . .

. . . And the silence rang as loudly in his head as did the sound of his heart's beating.

For there was nothing here. No battle, no people, no noise, no light. It was as still as the graveyard it had been for the last five hundred years. The battle was over, finished, cleared up. As finished as Mauglad's soul. He had arrived too late.

The sound of rapidly approaching footsteps seeped into his consciousness. Seconds later the thieves arrived, and slowed to a stop just as he had done. In confusion they fumbled for their lamps, for the fires of Finwald's spells had gone out.

Finwald's spells! That's all it was! Mauglad realized suddenly, hardly daring to believe this revelation that flooded into the abyss of his despair. Finwald's spells, and the sympathetic resonance they had set up from the Chamber.

Moments later, Finwald himself stepped through the doorway, and peered about in wonder. Then he noticed the varying expressions on the thieves' faces, and a glint appeared in his eyes.

He winked at them.

He had reached his destination, and needed no illusions anymore.

"Hope I didn't scare you boys too much," he said softly, then looked around for a comfortable place to await Bolldhe and his company.

Perhaps they should have been angry. And perhaps they were. But Finwald's aura of protection was raised again, and there was nothing they could do about it. In any case, relief now overrode any feelings of exasperation they may have harbored and, without hesitation, the thieves hared off as swiftly as possible towards the flue. They had had as much of Vaagenfjord Maw as they could take, and their only thoughts now were of immediate and speedy escape.

Finwald watched them go, and his inner smile finally managed to reach his lips. He reached out a hand towards them and, with the words "Here's one I prepared earlier," sent out a bolt of white light from his fingertips toward the departing thieves, just as they reached the great fire pit. Through their midst it snaked, continued straight up the flue, and then disappeared. There was a surge of burning power and a moment later every metal rung that had been clamped into the stone now came clattering down in a din that rang harshly throughout the Chamber.

The thieves, picking themselves up from the floor where they had dived, stared incredulously at the white-hot rungs that lay in a useless pile before them, then turned and faced Finwald, who now strode past them.

"Sorry, gentlemen," he began conversationally, not bothering to look at them, "but I've still got some work for you yet."

Finwald hesitated in midstride, shaking his head as if to clear it, and blinked once, twice. *Such a mindsurge!* he thought, still marveling at the power within him. But he straightened himself out, and became himself again after only a moment. He might have been high on magic, his brain effervescent and his extremities tingling with the new power that was all his, but he was not so drunk with it as to lose touch with the situation at hand. He had magic to do very soon now, magic of the highest magnitude, and he would need every scrap of concentration to master it. There could be no distractions whatsoever.

For what he had in mind, he would first need protection. In this, at least, his situation had not altered. Had not altered in years. In this present predicament, the thieves were the best—the only—protection available. They were far from perfect, he knew only too well, and it might indeed be that they would fail him. But now they were all he had. He would have preferred to continue using his Aura of Protection, of course. But that required concentration too, and he could not manage to concentrate on two spells at once.

Suddenly he pricked up his ears. A second later the Dhracus sensed it too, and a moment further, all the thieves were looking back toward the door by which they had entered.

Footsteps in the dark.

"Here they come," the mage-priest announced. "Best we be about our business."

He paused for a second, and studied the thieves closely, probably more closely than at any time since their first encounter in Eotunlandt.

Just look at them, he noted. *They're not just hiding—they're* huddling! *Perhaps I overdid it a little with my illusions . . .*

That was always going to be the trouble with this tome-magic, Finwald reflected. It was a little like progressing from rowing a simple coracle to steering a trireme—at least, to begin with.

A strange warbling from Dolen's throat (that might have been a chuckle) caused them all to start. A second later a weird whispering breathed through the darkness toward them. Holding themselves absolutely still, they listened, not knowing who or what it was out there.

After a moment they heard it again, and could just about make out what looked from this distance to be a reed-thin beam of pale light, coming from where they guessed they themselves had entered the Chamber.

Moments passed, then all of a sudden there came a terrible wailing of "NO!!" that reverberated towards them in vertiginous waves that rose and fell, misshapen by the air in this place that seemed to have the power to warp even sound.

My old mates, Finwald reminded himself, smoothing down the shudder that rippled from toes to hair. *And that, I would guess, was Bolldhe. Couldn't have timed it better.*

He turned back to the thieves, and noticed that they were all pressed against the rear wall with a solid determination *not* to move. But he also noted how they had their weapons drawn, and held steady before them. Like cornered rats, they had the air of those intending to sell their lives dearly.

Finwald pondered. *Probably best not to push it any further now,* he deemed. *Not until I have to. Don't suppose it would do any harm to risk waiting for the old crew right here; it's probably as good a place as any.*

He took his place among the thieves and, though they recoiled from this dreadful warlock who had brought such terror into their lives, still they made no move to leave the fire pit. It seemed to Finwald that they feared whatever was outside there even more than they feared him.

Huddled tightly into the fire pit, they waited and listened, and—as much as possible—gathered the tatters of their courage about them.

So it was that Bolldhe found them. No "huge black shapes the size of ogres," no ash-haired poleaxe-Rawgrs dancing amid the flames. No Scathur. Just the Thieves of Tyvenborg and their sorcerous new leader, their aura mutated by the devilry herein.

Just grab the flamberge, give it to Eorcenwold, and then he can do the job! Finwald's mind screamed, now so giddy he could hardly stand or breathe.

With determination, deliberation, and a purpose strong enough to "beshiver the ice of the Wyrld's Boundes," he stepped out of the fire pit and came for Bolldhe.

But he had been too slow, too careful. For at just the moment he became aware of the sudden presence of Scathur and his army, so too did Bolldhe. All it took was that one second of instinctive hesitation and a glance toward the door, and when he looked back at Bolldhe, the man was staggering away from him with his hands over his ears, away toward the ziggurat.

Too late . . . !

The sound of a multitude fast approaching the Chamber swelled the air, the Peladane's men disappeared into the darkness, and the priest of Cuna—the Tomebearer—stood transfixed, unable to make a decision. Cursing through thinned lips, he retreated back into the fire pit.

Nibulus had not seen the Tyvenborgers. At least he had not seen them in their true form, for like all those of the company who had approached the fire pit, the bewitchment of the Chamber lay heavy upon his eyes, his mind and his soul, and his perception of them was as ogrish spirits that arose mantled in the flames of hell.

But though he had not recognized them, there had been something else in the air (possibly the sour smell of leather jerkins steeped in layer upon layer of rancid sweat) that had sown unconsciously in his brain a tiny image of the thieves.

Whether he recalled it now, here in the bedlam of conflict, upon the very point of their destruction as the Rawgr captain came for them up the steps, he could not be sure. But something did call to Nibulus's mind the damp and florid face of Eorcenwold, and that great, cavernous mouth with its bawling voice of command. That was a voice that could not be disobeyed, a loud-roaring one that might melt glaciers, hold back the tide, awake the dead . . . or even halt them in their tracks.

So as Nibulus viewed the carnage all around him, the writhing sea of dead, the inhuman hatred of the Wire-Faces, the sickening gush of blood and the maddened dance of death of those whose faces were being ripped off, it finally struck him: if there was but one time in his life to prove himself the Thegne he was expected to be, one focal point to all his training, his expertise, and his bloodline, one chance to earn his people's respect, not to mention his pay, then this was it. And if there was one way to do so, he realized, it was to cast off his pride and bellow just like a thief.

Leaping back up to the next tier of the ziggurat, he ripped the Thresher from its belt hoops, and, despite the insane press of surging bodies around him, somehow managed to slip it over the crossguard of Unferth. Then, filling his lungs with acrid air, filling his face with boiling blood, and filling his soul with every last atom of passion, he let fly the war cry that was in his heart:

"Slaughter them! Wipe them out! Obliterate all! Butcher! Kill! Destroy! Maim! Crush! ANNIHILATE!! . . . For the love of god: BREAK THAT SCUM!"

As war cries go, it might not have won any awards, but it captured the gist of what the Peladane was trying to get across and, as such, did the trick. It cut through the clamor, the terror and despair, it swept aside differences in faith, language and even species, and was immediately taken up by all those within earshot, whether they understood the words or not.

It was then that it happened, then that it *really* happened. For, Aescal or Tregvan, north or south, beast or man, hands were clasped across the divide and all were one. Every man, Vetter, Cervulus and Parandus then bellowed out the war cry with every last flicker of ardor in their soul: "BREAK THAT SCUM! BREAK THAT SCUM! BREAK THAT SCUM!"

"AND NOW," the Peladane howled in maddened jubilation, *"KILL THE BASTARDS!"*

That was it. Nibulus the son of Artibulus had succeeded. Down from their skulking perch his army descended, rallying around his lofty dragon helm, weapons raised high and eyes red with fury, and they drove into the enemy like a juggernaut. Sword, axe and spear hammered down relentlessly upon the withered foe, hurling them back down toward their captain, who now floundered in their current, wondering just what could have gone wrong.

As they smote with berserk passion, the defenders screamed their blood song of defiance, screamed out their love for life, screamed till their hearts must surely burst and fiery blood spray from their mouths. And it seemed that a multitude of voices cried out with them, the voice of the entire world of all peoples of Lindormyn—the small, the ordinary, the forgotten—that suffer injustice daily and endure the grinding despair of helplessness that is its bedmate, but who now rose up and roared a chorus of absolute defiance, of refusal to simply lie down and suffer any more.

Uttering a throaty bellow, the Peladane swung the chain of the Thresher around his head with all his might, and joined in with his followers. How he excelled. As he swept the new weapon contrived by Kuw Dachs in rapidly widening circles through the smoke until the choking pall fled in blackened slivers, he went through every oath he knew in less than ten seconds, from religious profanities, through to lavatorial expletives, sexual obscenities, and finally to the strange weather-based curses that he had heard so often when he was campaigning abroad. Then, tilting its chain slightly, he finally brought the Thresher to bear. On and on he swung it, roaring like a dragon, all the time his green Ulleanh flying around his shoulders. In their scores the enemy went down like wheat before the harvester.

Then out of the black pall of fire-tinged smog plunged the flying wyvern, enkindled by the heat of the Peladane's oaths, and her wings unfolded to smite the Oghain with a nightmare memory of the Fyr-Draikke. Swooping low, she came at them with open beak and ripping talon, and upon her back sat the twin stormriders of their apocalypse: Elfswith with winnowing blade and Kuthy with reaping bow. Like a plowshare the half-Huldre furrowed the enemy's ranks, while his companion sent arrows in unending succession into their harried midst. Between them these three swept through the maggot horde in a wide swath, clearing a path for the Peladane and his men to continue the harvest.

Braced against the riptide that threatened to overwhelm him as his army surged back down beneath this terrible onslaught, Scathur stared upward in disbelief. It came to him then that the power of fear he held such store by could, in fact, be overridden and turned back upon itself. For it is one thing to use fear to drive folk, but quite another to steer them with it.

As Finwald, too, was discovering at exactly that moment. His illusions had cracked a whip of terror that the thieves absolutely would not defy, so that the only thought in their heads had been immediate flight. But, now that he had cut off their escape, did the fool mage-priest truly believe they would simply reassemble under his orders and charge into battle?

No, he really *had* overdone it with his phantasms, had overterrorized them, and here they now huddled in the fire pit, unable to consider a thing save to stare aghast at the nightmare scene of fire, smoke and swooping shapes before them—trapped in this mean little space until such time as one or more of the enemy might turn and notice them.

. . . *Which will happen at any second,* Eorcenwold thought, his face ruddy with exhaustion, fear and anger. *But it* can't *happen! We have to find a better place than this to make our stand!*

It was the Peladane's war chant then (the passion rather than the words) that provided just the trigger Eorcenwold needed. He turned to face his thieves, and to him all faces turned. In their eyes they begged for a solution, a way out of all this nightmare, but in his eyes they beheld only profound sorrow, and perhaps a plea for their forgiveness.

"*Wizzerd!*" he barked at Finwald. "Think you could be of any use here—for a change?"

But before he had even finished the challenge, a glow emanated from the fingers of the mage, and touched upon the weapons of the thieves. All of a sudden all weapons leapt in the hands of their wielders as though with a life of their own, and a radiant power surged through them. They lengthened, grew barbs, hummed with a new sharpness, and positively screamed in newfound bloodthirst.

Then, as if imbued with some residual overspill of enchantment that newly radiated from their weapons, the thieves felt a thrill of excitement run through their entire bodies, so intense it left them gasping for breath.

So for the last time, one very last time, the voice of Eorcenwold sounded loud and clear.

"To the Peladane!"

And with that, his morning star in one hand and blunderbuss in the other, the thief-sergeant turned and loped out to meet the enemy.

"We can't!" whined Raedgifu in disbelief. "We can't!" And his protest was echoed by Brecca, but it was too late. A bell toller, one of those calamitous fiends that had been deafening everyone throughout the hall, was closest to their leader's path, and it was with immense satisfaction to all that Eorcenwold, with one clean sweep of his enhanced star, did not just take its head off but disintegrated it entirely.

The other thieves' fear was then blasted away as though by a wind from heaven. Like an enraged bull-baluchitherium, Klijjver hurled himself after his leader, outpaced him and led the charge. His massive armored bulk broke upon the foe like a battering ram and, with super-maul and wonder-bhuj tossing them into the air on either side, the herd-giant of the Boyles steamrollered his way through the enemy ranks. All followed in his terrible wake, fast filling the cleft that Klijjver cleaved.

None could stand in their way. Nobody, nothing, whether man, beast, Rawgr or the dead, had expected an attack from the fireplace. And though these were professional thieves more accustomed to working by stealth than through head-on confrontations, the war cry of the small army marooned on the ziggurat had brought out the soldier in them all, and on through the legion of hell they hacked, slashed, bludgeoned and booted.

Just as the voice of their leader had propelled them on toward the thick of the fighting, so the blunderbuss of Eorcenwold—now an automatic—cleared their way. Klijjver, tiny eyes ablaze, could not be stopped by those before him; his momentum kept carrying him on, fueled by the bitterness of years of victimization, and by the impassioned cheering of his comrades swarming behind him. But he could still be pulled down from either side if enough enemy could pile onto him. It was upon these to his left that Eorcenwold, still running, loosed the devastating cannon fire of his dragontooth musket. No less than a dozen of the dead were hurled back instantly, their long-dead flesh disintegrating as they went.

And upon those to the right, Cerddu-Sungnir loosed an entire volley of quarrels from his five-shot. Not content with one body each, the spiralling quarrels tore through the shattering frames of those they entered first, and burst out their backs to continue their devastating flight through several more, stopping only after five or six, then exploding inside the last victim. He too did not stop, but clambered over the corpses as they fell, smashing the empty crossbow into splinters against the exploding head of a thurible-bearer, and in the same instant swept out with his two-handed, diamond-glowing axe, and went to work.

Behind these three the rest of the Tyvenborg company charged. Flekki's most lethal chakrams spun into selected Wire-Face necks; Hlessi's last two throwing axes clove the heads of two more; Khurghan's Haladie of Returning wove its spell of decapitation among the dead. And though Finwald, his visage scab-red with exasperation, ran along with them crying: *"Go to Bolldhe! Forget the others!"* they were having none of it. A united vanguard that lanced into Scathur's army from the rear, they climbed over the fallen and falling, reaching ever for new missiles or different weapons as they ran, and, with eldritch enchantment and sheer brutality, struck down all that stood in their path.

It may have been the mage's theurgy that had driven them to this place, but it was to the Peladane's standard that they now rallied. For those taproom slobs, the stale ale of earlier days now flowed through their veins like fiery red wine of the finest and most lauded vintage. Thieves no longer, they fought magnificently.

Most of them, at any rate. For in some the flame of ardor burned paler and even now they sought refuge in the chimney. While Eorcenwold led his men out, both Brecca and Raedgifu had stayed absolutely put. Raedgifu had simply stood there motionless, transfixed in a paralysis of disbelief at what was happening around him. But the diminutive Brecca had not dallied for a further second; he knew only too well the limitations of his body, especially his legs, and had instantly scampered back up the flue.

There was one small hollow there, little more than an indentation in the irregular stonework, a place in the corner where someone small and nimble might hold himself with both arms and legs braced against the walls of the shaft, and hopefully not be seen. The stunted locksmith, ever alert for escape routes, had noted it on his way down here, when they had first arrived in the Maw, and without hesitation he now hauled himself back up to it.

The first Raedgifu knew of this was when he heard a clatter of iron-banded wood behind him. Brecca had dumped his two shields, too large and cumbersome for such fly-climbing, and was even now scrambling to get in the right position.

Though he could not see the Stone-Hauger, could in fact see hardly anything in this near-darkness, the mere thought of there being still some way of getting even a few feet away from this scene caused hope to flare in Raedgifu's desperate brain. At once he was himself again, leaping and scrabbling about in the flue in an effort to follow this same route to sanctuary . . . and seconds later his hand happened to land upon a booted foot.

Brecca's mind seized up with terror, for he thought it at first to be one of the dead, and kicked out at the cold hand that grasped him, lunging in spasmodic revulsion.

"Come 'ere, you," came a hate-filled hiss from Raedgifu in the darkness below.

But Brecca was beyond any consideration for his fellow thief. Squeezing his shoulder blades into the stonework to brace himself, he reached down to the

lanyard of his adze, yanked it from its belt hoop, and hacked down at the offending hand with an animal grunt.

Raedgifu cried out in agony and fell back into the pit, only to land noisily
upon Brecca's discarded shields. Instantly a hundred slitted red eyes swung
round to focus upon him and, with a drum-beating of death-horror pounding
in his brain, he realized the game was up.

In an instant Raedgifu was off after his fast-disappearing mates, his pole-
flail whirring before him. But it was hope without hope. Black, dead claws
reached out to him from every side, snatched at him, became enmeshed in his
fine, baggy silks, then ripped, tore and twisted until his clothes were pulled off
him in tatters. Still lunging on and lashing with his howling electric pole-flail,
he still endeavored to force his way through the sea of dead flesh toward the
island-like ziggurat looming ahead, like a bad swimmer in shark infested waters reaching out imploringly for the shore.

Then a silent scream wrenched his jaws wide, as broken teeth clamped vise-
like around his privates and wrenched. In seconds he was dragged under, and
the seething grey waters of death closed over him.

Even Klijjver's momentum began to slow, beset now by no less than four of the
dead. They clung on and scrabbled at his iron carapace, trying feverishly to get
at the living meat inside. Behind him, the morning star of Eorcenwold and the
axe of Cerddu-Sungnir still crushed and hewed. But those behind them that no
longer enjoyed the luxury of such space in which to maneuver, used their boots
to kick upward and fracture pelvises, their fists to punch clean through shattered sternums, their foreheads to cave in splintering skulls. Despite that,
slowly, they were increasingly crushed in on themselves.

It was all coming to an end—for some sooner than others. Hlessi suddenly
gave a snarl of fear as he found himself entangled in a net, just such as he himself carried. Though the three spiked balls of his flail continued to pulp heads
like rotten tubers, the mesh bit deeper into his blue-black skin and he was finally hauled from the wedge of thieves into the reaching arms of the horde.
Hlessi stood no chance: within seconds his acid-green hair was dyed red with
the lifeblood belching from his mouth, while his body was pincushioned by the
rusty little knives of the dead children.

Into this, their darkest hour, Scathur himself now arrived. The tide of his
army had swept him far back, surging against him as both Peladane and thief-
sergeant hurled them down from the ziggurat. Now a fury such as he had not
felt for five hundred years boiled as a white light from the fissures that latticed
his hide, lighting up the Chamber in a furnace-like glare. His eyes had become
featureless globes of inhuman, weeping blackness, his white robes rippling and
snapping as if blasted by an arctic wind, and the screeching from the soul-faces
in his habergeon scales swelled in a rhapsody of torture, like the flue-pipes of
the Organ of the Underworld.

The dragonroar that shuddered from those peeled-back lips caused the floor to quake and the marble to crack as he came on, tearing through the flesh of his own army to get at his foe. Those great hands of his closed over the heads of dead and Wire-Face alike, plucked them from the throng, and flung them, necks broken and heads ablaze with Rawgr-fire, out of his path. And when still that was not enough to clear a path, he hefted his enormous Bardische doubled-handed, and swept it before him, side to side, in an unstoppable crescent that severed bodies at each stroke. Scathur did not stop until he reared up at last before the first of his adversaries.

". . . oh . . ." was all Eorcenwold could manage, and his hair shriveled in the heat that rose up before him (and, oddly, from behind him, too.)

Scathur lifted the Bardische high above his head, and ululated in bliss.

But the stroke never fell. For, out of all the thieves, it was Grini that came to their leader's salvation. All hair and teeth, the screaming little Boggart sprang from the midst of the Tyvenborgers, and with lightning speed raked his steely tiger-claws across the Rawgr-captain's face, before rebounding off his chest and landing back amid the thief-pack again.

It was a vicious swipe that might have ripped the face off any normal man. In Scathur's case, though, it did little more than score the outer crust of his hide. But at least it had faltered his axe-blow.

Ha! Might as well have a go, too, thought Cerddu-Sungnir. *If I'm going to die, I can at least go down knowing I've had a pop at that big bastard.*

A second later, the red-rimmed eyes of the half-Grell stared up, through his helm's face-shield, to meet those of the Rawgr.

"Preying Mortis!" he roared, and plunged the blade from his wrist straight into Scathur's left eye.

Scathur grunted in surprise, faltering again, and, with a laugh, Cerddu-Sungnir continued on after Klijjver.

Flekki too did her bit, driving her weapon straight into the ankle beneath Scathur's habergeon as she passed, before herself pouncing after the half-Grell. She was immediately followed by Finwald, who held up a palm, muttered something, and sent a shaft of blue light directly into the empty eye socket that the blade had excavated.

Squealing like a hundred pigs on fire, Scathur doubled over in pain, a thick, greasy smoke pouring from every orifice in his head, and dropped his Bardische.

Grinning widely, Finwald ran on, crying, "To Bolldhe! To Bolldhe!"

The tomes were strong within this mage, and his aura was sufficient to keep both Wire-Face and dead at bay. In a surge that propelled them up the lower tiers of the ziggurat, it was beginning to look as if the Tyvenborgers might make it after all.

"Keep close to the priest!" Mauglad shouted from the thief he was inhabiting. "Go to Bolldhe!" For he was every bit as desperate to get to Flametongue as Finwald was.

Collapsed on his knees in the middle of a wide circle, Scathur raised his smoking head. Through his remaining eye he watched in disbelief as the ragged troop of impudent little rogues passed him by without even sparing him a glance—indeed as though he were nothing more than a beggar in the gutter.

("Your blunderbuss!" came the voice of Eorcenwold's sister from somewhere.)

Except for one. Scathur blinked, and saw that one of the vagabonds yet remained. This squat and unremarkable man that stood before him appeared to be proffering him something. A gift, perhaps? A token of fealty? While his missing eye was in the process of regenerating itself, he was momentarily befuddled, and could not grasp what was happening at all.

("It's going t' blow!"came the same voice again.)

"Hold this a minute, will you," the man said, handing the pipe-thing to Scathur. Then he promptly fled to the ziggurat.

Scathur did not know who Aelldryc was. He was not aware that she wore a flask of sticky green liquid on her belt, either. And he had not the slightest clue what "coolant" was.

The ensuing explosion came as a bit of a surprise to him, too.

In a rapidly expanding circle, they fell, all who were in the Chamber. Those farthest away merely tumbled; those closer were knocked right off their feet; while the ones nearest to Scathur—and there were many—simply flew apart under the force of the residual energy that had been building up in the chamber of Eorcenwold's blunderbuss.

For those who were spared the worst of the blast, the sound of it was as a white light that exploded inside their heads. In the dazed hush of deafness, shock and nausea that ensued, the defenders picked themselves up and stared about in wonder.

Radiating out from Scathur himself, all the thurible smoke had been blasted away—as had many of the thurible-bearers. The marble floor within this circle was scattered with bodies and body parts, some deathly still, some twitching. Many of the dead had been sheared in half by the explosion but, moaning eerily in the sudden quiet, their top halves continued clawing their way towards the ziggurat.

Others too were stirring to life, and once more began to advance upon their prey. With dismay, the company saw that Scathur was among these, though on his knees now and appearing barely able to move. That long, tombstone face of his was horrendously scarred, smoke-blackened, and grotesquely rearranged. Even the myriad faces within his armor scales wore a look of stunned surprise. His cloak was now no more than a few threads that clung still to his brooch pin, yet for the most part the Rawgr captain still appeared to be in one piece.

And he still had his legions, though greatly depleted, so the battle was far from over. But more significantly, there was a curious warping in the air that told Scathur reinforcements of a very *particular* kind were on the way. For, like the Nahovian who writhed in horror atop the ziggurat, he could sense the approach of his Children. And when *they* arrived, it would all be over. All of it.

But for now, he waved a hand and, with a hacking snarl, sent forth his response.

A score or so of fleet-footed dead pushed their way through the throng, coming for the enemy with a vengeance. There was something in the way they moved, something purposeful, something wrong that caused the human foe to stare at each other worriedly. Flekki reached for her pouch and sent one chakram spinning from her hand toward the nearest encroacher. It hit the creature directly in its bloated, wobbling stomach, and instantly the dead thing erupted in a loud, moist burst of flying meat and bone shrapnel.

Though nowhere near as devastating as the blunderbuss, this explosion nevertheless bowled over those that were nearest to it, and caused all the others to flinch away in shock.

As a pall of creosote-scented smoke descended upon them in purple wisps, Nibulus looked up. "You have got to be joking. . . ." he breathed.

An instant later he was back on his feet, and as he once again ripped the bow from his back, he cried out: "Bring those things down, NOW!"

No further order was necessary. Everyone knew they had but seconds in which to save themselves. Those who had missiles used them. Those who did not, pulled back. Three more exploding dead were detonated at a safe distance, but still the others approached with alarming swiftness, even though stuck with chakrams, arrows or Vetter-darts. Englarielle's spike-balled bola wrapped itself around the legs of a fourth one, bringing it crashing and leg-mangled to the floor so that, though still primed, it was mercifully immobilized.

But some others were bound to get through, and the very next moment the first of them lurched awkwardly into the recoiling ranks of huddled Vetters.

Exploding dead. Exploding Vetters. Screams of terror rising afresh. Bodies opened like crimson flowers unfolding to a riotous sun. Roars of jubilation from the army that came up behind. Heroes hurling themselves down the steps, tackling the oil-glutted dead to the ground ere they could reach their fellows, sacrificing themselves without a second thought.

Both ways the exploding dead now flew, for their foes were *alive* and strong and desperate. Hwald, Finan, Klijjver and Nibulus, together these four hurled this new menace right back down where they came from, to explode in the midst of their own ranks.

It was amid this barrage of fleshy eruptions that Nibulus now fought his final battle. He was no longer in Vaagenfjord Maw, but fought now beneath the blazing skies of his earlier years, upon that desert sand that thirsted so for men's blood, even though this red and glistening marble floor was too sated by centuries of atrocity to drink his offerings. The clamor, the bells, the smoke, the blood and the hatred, all now faded within the Peladane's mind, and in their stead came to the soul of Nibulus Wintus the pipes of Pendonium, the earth-trembling pounding of war drums, and the deep-throated chorus of the Knights of Pel-Adan. It seemed to him that the spirits of those who had fought in this very place those long ages past stirred again from their sleep to gaze upon their comrade, the Heir of Wintus, and to sing for him, their beloved son. And his soul soared higher at that moment than it ever had before, or ever would again.

The Thresher now abandoned, Nibulus hefted his greatsword for one last time, and launched himself into the thick of the enemy. Something pre-Peladane, pagan, *primeval,* burned inside his breast, and he knew that he would fight on and on and on, till death took him. Because there was something in the blood of his people, those countless generations who had lived, fought and died for centuries long before they had worshipped Pel-Adan, that made hope unimportant and victory irrelevant. And even when they knew they were about to die, they would continue fighting regardless, to the last.

He cared not to which gods he now offered this hecatomb, for fighting had become everything. All piety, rank and arrogance had fallen away from Nibulus, and he finally understood what it was to be a warrior—to love not the greatsword, the shining tengriite or the victory, but to love those you fight for, though your death might never be known to them, and no hymn ever be sung in your honor.

Paulus understood it too. Finally, here at the end, he understood.

He had stopped rocking back and forth. His strength, his tears, even his madness, all were spent. *He* was spent. All that was left to him now was to choke out these great rasping sobs, and stare at the hell below him through a single eye red with weeping. Weeping like the infant he had once been, all those years ago, left alone in the cold cabin in the forests of Vregh-Nahov to bawl himself dry, while staring helplessly up through the mist at the loathsome invertebrates that would crawl around on the ceiling, or drop down upon his face to burrow, and to feed.

Here, too, he was once again utterly alone. Once again, utterly ignored by his people, ignored by all except those that would feed upon him. Those comrades nearby might brush past him, leap over him, but none of the defenders, be they Eorcenwold's, Englarielle's, or even his own company, would *look* at him. For he was no longer of any concern to the living. Just as it had been in his homeland long ago. For there, if one was dying of some illness, though one might still consort with one's own people, eat with them, talk to them, nevertheless one would be considered already dead, and ignored accordingly, just as with any other bothersome ghost.

Words reechoed in Paulus's mind, the words of Nibulus when they had stood at the gates of the Maw: *". . . Fear, if terrible enough, can turn the soul inside out, and rob anyone of their true self . . . there is no character left within the terrified man . . ."*

It was so true. All it took was one look at him to see that Paulus was already dead, the spirit within him flown. How could he just lie there and weep? How could he thus betray them? Had he not striven so hard to break through the constraints of his brutal Nahovian culture, to rise above that inhuman darkness and nurture his own fate?

More words came back to him, spoken just after Finwald's treachery, and this time those of Bolldhe as well as the Peladane.

". . . Only the soul-dead would betray their friends."

No. *"Only the dead are beyond betraying their friends . . ."*

"Yes," Paulus stammered aloud between his sobs. "And I'm so truly dead."

Thus prostrated, he looked upon Wintus, saw the way he fought, knew the things he thought. And so he understood. He understood what was surging through the man's soul, that love that was driving both body and mind so much further than should be humanly possible.

Not only Wintus, but the others also: Hwald and Finan, their manes frothy with saliva, the veins on their necks swollen, while walrus-bellowing loud enough to crack the marble floor; seven races of thieves, from lowly Boggart to mighty Tusse, yet not a difference between them, but all acting as one unit, watching out for each other's backs; Gapp, Schnorbitz and Englarielle fighting side by side to their very last breath; Cervulice torn down, yet shielding Vetters with their own ripped flesh even as they fell. For, though mortally wounded, *they* fought on.

Not even the old priest would pause for breath: his wiry, stick-like frame braced like frozen hawthorn against an arctic gale, he fought on like one from a saga, his tulwar lancing ungraciously but surely into the bodies of any that leapt towards him.

Something in the way they fought, something in the way they died . . .

Paulus's tormented soul became still then, and through his one eye he saw—*really* saw, for the first time—their beauty. Such beauty that, had he any tears left to give, he would have wept anew.

They despised him, he knew. Though they had thought their hilarious little jest a secret, he knew—had always known—that they called him "Flatulus" behind his back. But that did not matter, for he had been all his life *"without partner, lover, family or friend."* But here and now, as far as he was concerned, they were his friends.

So it was that Paulus now raised himself to his feet, adjusted his cowl, and smoothed out its feathers. Then his hand reached beneath his coat, and closed around the knotted tubes of the Fyr-Draikke's gall bladder that was still tied at his belt.

"It's all right, lads," he whispered. "I'm here now." And with that, he vaulted into the fray.

Nobody really saw what Paulus did next, and they would have understood little of it even if they had. All they knew was that the seemingly demented victim of the stained glass demons was suddenly among them again, pushing his way through and spraying their enemy with the foulest, most offensive stench any of them had ever known. They had no idea where it came from, but there was death in that smell, the very essence of maggot-ridden corpse meat, and with it an acrid mordancy that made the eyes sting and the teeth hurt.

Down the steps this lunatic thrust his way and, all the while, from the rubbery bag under his arm he sent forth this corrosion in inky jets upon the skin of the enemy. Like ants in a frying pan the dead instantly shrivelled, smoked and fell; as did the Wire-Faces, but with considerably more commotion.

By the time he had emptied his bladder and shaken off the last drops, he had burnt a pathway clear through to Bolldhe. On his knees now and supporting himself with one bloody arm clenching the tier above him, Bolldhe did desperate battle. He was under attack from a grotesquely corpulent dead man, whose folds of cold, grey, nodule-encrusted blubber made him look as if he was wearing the remains of some vast sea mammal that had been found washed up on the strand—or at least the parts the gulls had avoided. Too large and clumsy to bring its hands to bear, this monster was nevertheless in danger of smothering Bolldhe, who had no chance of hurling it away from him.

A ruinous side kick with the blade of Paulus's booted foot crushed the dead thing's head entirely, and sent it flopping back between its shoulder blades like the hood of a coat. It swayed, back and forth, then it tumbled forward. Bolldhe wailed weakly as he was crushed beneath the cold, rubbery bulk of his adversary.

"Bolldhe!" Paulus yelled. "Are you all right?"

"Mnmf!" Bolldhe responded in obvious distress.

Paulus had no time to pause. He could not haul the oleaginous leviathan from Bolldhe, so decided in the heat of the moment that Bolldhe was probably safer exactly where he lay; he could still breathe, after a fashion, and was fairly well shielded from any further attack.

"I'll just take this for now," Paulus said, and prised his bastard sword from the fingers of Bolldhe's right hand. Bolldhe just stared at him, eyes wide with incredulity and reproach, but he could say nothing and do even less.

"Right," the Nahovian breathed to himself, looking around. "Let's show them some *real* fighting. . . ."

Paulus had always taken his martial career seriously, and strove ever to improve himself in its execution. He did not consider this hubris; it was simply that he was contemptuous of sloppy work. Whereas others of less professional pride might hack away like apprentice butchers, Paulus had always been one to experiment with different methods of killing. When he had first started out, there had been a certain gratification in the "clean de-cap" or "two-man-impale," and for those of lesser caliber this might have remained sufficient. For

Paulus, however, they were mere essays in the craft. To his mind, one simply could not beat the Spinal Wrench, the Mouth-to-Heart Penetration, or the Brain-Fingerpunch. He was "Death on Two Legs," so they said, the Dark One, the Raven-Glutter of the Battlefield, and this reputation he felt honor bound to uphold.

Well, just how much of his mind—let alone his pride or conscientiousness—the stained glass demons had left him, not even he knew as yet. But there was still undeniably a certain style that was uniquely "Paulus" as he now went about his work. For a time, as he thrust, swept, parried and countered, Paulus was his old self once more, and everything he had ever learned in his long years as a swordsman he put into busy use. It was probably the last chance he would ever have.

For every half dozen or so that fell directly to his sword, at least one would receive extra coaching, free of charge, in a more hands-on approach.

"Remember!" he cried, "focus on nothing, and see all," and promptly kicked both eyes out of a dead man's ear holes.

"Aim not at your opponent, but *through* him," as his fist burst out the back of another's soggy head.

"Breathe out when you release your stroke," to one Wire-Face, while ripping the spine and lungs right out of his back.

"And though you may be harried by many," he added as he snatched the still-pumping organ from a bell ringer's demolished ribcage, "always take heart."

"Here concludes the lesson—now, you try the same on me."

His was a lesson in combat that was as astounding as it was sickening, but it was a lesson that went completely unnoticed by any others, so occupied were they in their own combat. They would never know how savagely yet excellently he fought on that day. Neither would they know what he was about to do next, nor why. For it was neither dead nor Oghain that Paulus was really looking for. They were mere obstacles in his way. Bigger fish the Nahovian sought now, for those nightmare stained glass visions still played before his eyes.

As he had lain there quaking in madness atop Drauglir's altar, his mind had been propelled into the fire pit, up the flue, and out into the great Hall of Fire, Smaulka-Degernerth. There his travelling spirit had stared down at what lay below: something of which only he could have a presentiment.

The Children of the Keep. Approaching rapidly. Almost upon them.

No one but he knew of their imminence, so no one could ever know his true intentions at this moment. Neither would they ever know, or even be able to comprehend, exactly how he managed to do what he did next.

Suddenly a canopy of vast wings swept over him and beat him down to his knees. The screech of dragonkind, the report of arrows, the seething of a metallic whirlwind . . . and the wyvern team passed overhead. They turned for a second pass, and without hesitation Paulus seized his chance. He quickly sheathed his sword, launched himself through the air, and landed full upon Ceawlin's back as she sailed past for another strafe.

A squawk of surprise. A grunt. The sudden scrabble of hands. And then Elfswith was falling into the sea of dead.

A stony bellow of triumph from the Majestic Head below them.

"IDIOT!" Kuthy yelled in horror, but he did not hesitate either. Abandoning his bow and unsheathing his sword, he backflipped off the wyvern, and followed his undersized friend into the seething melee.

Paulus was well aware how it must appear to the others; his grabbing of the sword from a stricken Bolldhe, then abandoning him, his hijacking the wyvern after ejecting her riders, then forcing her to take him out of the Chamber at full speed, deserting the battle. But there was no other way. The task at hand took everything he had, all his quickness, skill and ruthlessness, and the task ahead would doubtless require even more. There was room now for neither doubt nor vacillation.

Though she twisted and writhed, bucked and heaved, there was no dislodging the Nahovian. He clung on like a tick, one hand clenched hard into her windpipe, his other arm wrapped around her neck, which was now glowing a burning blue with fury. At one point she even turned totally upside down. But, anticipating this, Paulus held on with both arms and dangled in midair, the heel caps of his boots cracking against dead heads as they passed over them.

Then came the angry creature's stinger, as it inevitably had to. But this too was anticipated, and Paulus moved quicker. As he felt her back muscles tense, with only one arm around the wyvern's neck he reached out with his other, just in time to catch her tail as it lanced toward him, and grabbed it mere inches below the lethal poison sac.

He wasted not a second in twisting it so hard he could feel the sacrum vertebra pop out. Ceawlin let out a distinctly un-wyvern-like roar that sounded more like a stallion at stud, and her tail whipped away, the sac now dangling limp as a broken flower head. A second later Paulus had his diamond punch dagger out and pressed sharply against her neck.

"You'll not try that again, bitch!" Paulus hissed. "Or anything else, for that matter!"

The clinging mercenary had the distinct impression he could sense her feelings and thoughts. At this close range, there certainly did seem to be strong resonances emanating from the beast. And what he could sense from her now was *yielding*. Hatred and frustration still, also, but mainly yielding.

As they circled through the air above the battle, Paulus remembered the empathy with which Elfswith and Ceawlin seemingly communicated. Concentrating as strongly as he could, he sent a clear message lancet-sharp into her brain:

That hole over there! Take me, NOW!

It seemed to do the trick. Strangely acquiescent now, Ceawlin did as she was bid. There was no mistaking her fury at being commissioned thus, and taken away from her beleaguered friends, but neither was there any mistaking the extremely sharp blade currently pressed against her carotid artery.

So, wings folded flat against her flanks, tail straight out behind her, secondary eyelids closed against the wind, and violet spittle streaming back along her neck, Ceawlin sped as fast as an arrow towards the fire pit. A chorus of howls and an unfolding forest of lunging arms arose from the dead army as she dived. Paulus braced himself and closed his eyes tightly, for the terror in him had returned, and threatened to rip the soul out of him just as the air was torn from his lungs.

Then they were through. Hardly slowing a wing beat, Ceawlin changed direction in midair and shot straight up the flue. There was a cry of terror behind as Brecca was knocked off his hidden perch to tumble down into the fire pit below, but Paulus hardly registered it. He was clinging on for all his life, his heels smacking with terrible force against the stonework as they streaked upward.

What happened next felt like nothing he had ever experienced before, save perhaps during his soul-journey only minutes earlier. It seemed to him that his ballista-ascent through darkness suddenly veered off through spiralling planes of nausea, until he and the wyvern hurtled on along the level towards a mouth of fire.

Closer it came, that incandescent rectangle of light, approaching so fast he had not even enough time to steel himself.

Then, with a gasp of hot air that seared the very skin of his windpipe, both raptor and captor shot out of the tunnel and into the open once more.

Oh, to be back in Smaulka-Degernerth again! Back in the Hall of Fire. How he had missed its suffocating air, the blinding glare of its magma flare. High above the river of lava he soared, so high, so close to the cavern's roof that the brass studs of his cape struck sparks against the hot, blackened rock as the wyvern brushed him past it.

Then Ceawlin brought herself to a halt with a great billowing of her wings, and hovered there in the sulphurous air. Still beating those enormous wings, she craned her neck back to fix her eyes upon her abductor, who was still somehow managing to hold the punch-dagger to her artery. And in her slitted, mazarine eyes there appeared to burn the question: *Well? What now?*

But Paulus did not return her gaze. Through streaming eyes he was looking down upon this vision of hell below him, down to the source of that infernal heat that formed the very essence of this place. For, as soon as he had emerged into the cavern, that sense of a dread presence had once more overwhelmed him—and now, finally, he saw them.

Monsters, pure evil—Rawgrs in the shape of children—emerging from the river of fire to claw their way up the rock face toward the flue. Though he had never seen them before, he had spent long enough trapped in the

Rawgr-dimension to recognize their kind. Their name, spoken by the esquire but a short time ago, filled his mind: *the Children of the Keep.*

Even from this distance they sensed him, and the malignity of their raised stare struck him with such potency that he cried out in shock and almost toppled from his mount. As it was, Paulus faltered, and the punch-dagger slipped from his hand and fell, glistening with ruby brightness, down toward the lava.

That was all Ceawlin needed. If wyverns could, she would have smirked. Without waiting to find out what her hijacker wanted of her, she turned tail and shot back to the tunnel. She folded her wings back to disappear down the hole again, but this time flew as close to the lintel of the flue-exit as she could, in an effort to scrape the irritating (but now no longer threatening) little tick from her back as she went.

No need, anyway, for Paulus had already thrown himself from her, and landed heavily upon the ledge. The wind was driven from him, and his head swam with giddiness and dread, and the abysmal fumes he was compelled to inhale. But she had served her purpose, and he was happy enough to see her disappear back the way they had come, back to her friends, back to where she could be of more use.

Now he forced himself to his feet, and stood unsteadily by the tunnel mouth. Turning back, he stared in fear at the lip of the drop over which, very soon now, the Hell-Children would haul themselves.

He had summoned them, the overseer of their brood. By the shortest route they came, for neither moat of magma nor rampart of rock could hinder them. Soon, they would rejoin their captain, screaming down the flue in a tempest of fire. And when that happened, it would, as Scathur had so rightly pointed out, be all over. *All of it.*

The only thing that now stood in their way was Paulus Flatulus. It was for this that he had come. Alone. Just as it had always been for him. But it was only here and now that he finally knew just what it is to be truly, utterly alone.

I'd never have got a decent tree-hanging, anyway, he thought with forced humor, recalling his words at the inn at Myst-Hakel. *For what wild creature would be desperate enough to partake of my rotting flesh?*

Forced humor, indeed. For, if but one wish could have been granted him in this, his last moment, Paulus in his breaking heart yearned so terribly that it might be this: that by some grace of the spirits of his clans, one, just *one,* of his people might witness his passing, and the manner which he had chosen for it. Then perhaps they might have said of him: "Surely here was one worthy of the greatest of tree-hangings."

A hideous scream echoed up from the abyss, and slapped Paulus around the face with its impact. He had no time now for such thoughts, but neither did he have a *plan!* He drew his sword, stared into its glassy surface, and saw his own terrified visage mirrored within.

Who was he fooling! Against just one of those monsters below he would have little chance. He might be able to delay it for a minute or two, but against the *horde* that approached, even he, the greatest swordsman of the Nahov, would not be able to hold them back for more than a few seconds. And time was what his comrades needed, if Bolldhe was to do whatever it was he was supposed to.

Paulus looked about desperately. What he was looking for he did not know, and would not know until he found it. But there was always something a warrior could do in the scant moments left to him before he was assailed, some kind of preparation which might tip the scales, no matter how meagerly. An alcove, perhaps? Some small screen to jump out from? Or maybe—and this demonstrated just how desperate he was—he could bring the old and crumbling masonry down with his sword to block the tunnel?

But looking about him for just three seconds was all it took to cause his heart to sink. Old this place was, for sure, but crumbling? It would take an entire foundry of Jutul to make so much as a dent in this stonework.

A second scream sounded. This time so much closer. Paulus's knees began to give.

. . . should I hide? . . .

Then his eyes fell upon an object sticking out of the wall.

What is it? A torch cresset? A sword hilt jammed into the stonework?

Propelled forward by Fate, it seemed, Paulus came to the enigmatic little bar that protruded at an acute angle from the wall, and he stared at it, an ominous precognition growing in his heart.

He knew nothing of *The Testament of Khuc*, but he needed to be neither a loremaster nor artisan of stone to realize what it was he was looking at:

A lever. "*. . . the crafty mechanism that lowered these obstacles . . .*"

For a moment his heart ceased to beat and his vision blurred, as his mind took in the enormity of what he beheld.

I've succeeded! he seethed, jubilation and despair vying for space in his overflowing soul. *Oh, hell and damnation, I've succeeded. . . .*

A third terrible scream reverberated through the air and the stone. The Children were now just below the lip; he had only seconds left to him. He reached out for the lever, and his hand folded around it, and he pulled . . .

It moved! It was stiff, and squealed with a noise like front teeth scraping down a brick wall, but it did move. Immediately Paulus withdrew his hand, and shuddered at the sound. Or the thought.

Just testing, he said to himself, *just testing . . .*

One quick tug, and it would give. The stone blocks set in motion five centuries ago would once again come down, sealing the passage.

Sealing his own fate.

A child's face, its features split by the blackness within it, appeared over the rim. Paulus's hand shot back to the lever and grasped it firmly, determinedly.

His gorge rose in a sickness of horror. He could not do it. Despite all he had done so far to bring him to just this end, he could not bring himself to seal himself in here with those . . .

The sacrifice of his comrades came back to him; the selfless heroism of Englarielle's folk, the heart-lifting sortie of the Tyvenborgers, but most of all, the magnificence of the Peladane's last stand, and what it had awoken in Paulus himself. Just as the "pipes of Pendonium" had sounded in Nibulus's mind, so too did the gentle flutes of Vregh-Nahov now come to Paulus. That single, pure note that could rise clear above the tramp of armies or the burning of villages, rise above all the evil of the world as a diamond tear coursing down through the filth on a smoke-grimed face. And underlying this note, words from the past, muffled yet mellifluous, were recited in elegiac intonation:

". . . heroes were only heroes for how they died, not how they lived. They could be the biggest shits in the seven counties, and yet if they died a hero's death, the skalds would sing their praises for all eternity . . ."

". . . But," Paulus breathed tremulously, "only if one's death is witnessed."

More Ogginda-Rawgr faces appeared, each one more soured with unholy destructiveness than the last, and hauled themselves over the lip—

To wander among the moss-clad trees of his home in spring, breathe deep the fragrance of their immaculate blossom.

RUN! FLEE! NO SONGS WILL BE SUNG IF NO ONE EVER KNOWS!

His eyes crazed with fear, guts weighted as though by a boulder, his grip tightened till blood was squeezed from the fingernails.

But still he could not do it.

Warmth and light in that cold misty cabin, a family to fill it, a meal to share, a drink with friends . . . One to say they would never leave him, but would, no matter what happened, bear him to safety when all was done.

Warmth and light on his face: the infernal conflagration of the Rawgrs as they sprinted for him, almost upon him now. His eyes filled with tears, his mind filled with a picture, a picture of his companions from Nordwas, they who had ever spurned him, they who would forever believe him a coward and deserter.

Swallowing hard, he uttered his final words: "I'm the best friend you ever had . . ." Then he wrenched the lever down hard.

Blocks rumbled down, fiends screamed in jabbering vexation, and Odf Uglekort hefted his bastard sword for one final time.

Bloodied and screaming, in pain, confusion and fear: thus we enter this world. And thus we depart it.

Ceawlin screamed her way back down the flue for all she was worth, and Brecca also cried out in terror again. He had just succeeded in scrambling back up to his alcove, when the wyvern came hurtling down and smote him from his perch a second time.

As he landed upon his clattering shields yet again, Ceawlin swept from the fire pit in a mad rush of unfurling wings, extending talons and steaming nostrils, and sped back to where Elfswith had fallen from her. Frantically the jeweled eyes of the wyvern swept around as she flew, trying to pierce through the dense, writhing swarm of the enemy, trying to locate only her friends. She knew exactly where Elfswith had tumbled off, but now she saw with horror there was nothing there but a sludge-hued tide of long-dead flesh, a heaving mass of grey pressing ever onward.

A shrill cry shuddered from her throat, and her terrible claws resumed the destruction where they had left off.

But something had happened above them all that brought about a change in the atmosphere. That earlier feeling of the approach of something inconceivably evil, that sense of imminent destruction, now eased off, then ceased altogether. There had been a series of loud impacts coming from somewhere up the flue, a dull but immensely heavy pounding that had rocked the entire Chamber, followed by a distant screeching of such thwarted fury that, though muffled to the point of near-inaudibility, had caused all those therein to momentarily falter.

But then it had passed and, for a while at least, the air felt lighter and cleaner.

A strangled bellowing of exasperation erupted from the throat of Scathur as he stumbled and heaved his way through his army. His body had been marred greatly, but yet held together, and now that he sensed his Children were being forced to take the long way around, the will that drove him onward was refueled by a great rage that would not be stanched.

That was my *trick!* he seethed. *How DARE they!*

He had been thwarted yet again, and this time moreover by his own mechanisms. But it mattered little, for in a moment he would reach the Peladane, and then he would have the flamberge. Even in this damaged state, nothing could stop him.

So he came on, bits of flesh falling away from him with each ponderous movement that his body made. The Bardische was now a crutch rather than a weapon.

Finally he reached his quarry.

"PELADANE!" he roared, and loomed up to tower over the human warrior. Before Nibulus could do anything but cry out in shock, one monstrous hand was clamped around his throat, and squeezing so hard that his eyeballs almost popped out.

"I've got you now, you squirmy little maggot!" Scathur wheezed. "I'VE GOT YOU! Oh, how I shall . . ."

He hesitated then, because his gaze had just fallen upon the greatsword that Nibulus had let fall from his fingers.

"What's *that?!*" Scathur growled, clearly confused.

Nibulus, even realizing that the moment of his death had arrived, fixed the Rawgr-captain with a gaze heavily weighted with contempt. "It's called a 'sword,'" he choked defiantly.

"But it's straight!" Scathur protested.

". . . Yes. It's a novelty sword."

"It should be flame-shaped!" Scathur howled.

Then Nibulus grinned, despite his predicament. For only now did he realize how Finwald had been right about the flamberge all along. It clearly *was* some kind of significant weapon. With his last few seconds of life he therefore knew he must buy Bolldhe some extra time. He managed a shrug, and replied, "Yes, I pointed that out to my armorer, but, well, what can you do?"

The eyelids of the Darkangel narrowed into little fleshy slits, and white-hot furnaces built up behind them. His groping fingers forced their way into the Peladane's gagging mouth, and were just about to do something truly awful . . . when he was distracted. Something—*someone*—had just flown past him, as though catapulted from below, to land on a higher level.

Was that the bard? Scathur wondered. *Didn't I just dismember him only a moment ago?*

That had always been Scathur's problem: far too confident in his ability to destroy others through fear and torture. It was just this failing, then, that was returned to him in full as Kuthy, coming up behind him, slipped his temple-sword beneath Scathur's habergeon, and rammed the entire length of the blade right up his diabolical arse.

Elfswith, clutching the treacly cavity in his shoulder where his arm used to be, lay sprawled upon one of the higher tiers where Kuthy had hurled him. He had landed with an awful crunch upon the step, and immediately realized with dismay that he had broken the two hard-boiled eggs he'd been saving for later. Nevertheless, as he looked down and saw what Kuthy had just done, he managed a smile.

Who would have thought that one of Kuthy's nature would dive into a whirlpool of enemies just to save a friend? Especially a friend whose arm had just been sliced off by Scathur and therefore appeared beyond any hope of salvation? Especially since, in the process, his strangely appendaged headgear, that which he *never* removed in public, had been wrenched off to display Kuthy's awful secret beneath: the most appalling frizzy bush of bright ginger hair ever to have sprouted from the head of a human.

Who, either, would have believed even the great Tivor capable of hurling their foe back repeatedly, grabbing the little man by the lapels, then running back to the ziggurat *over the top of the dead's heads*, like negotiating so many stepping-stones? And still have the strength left to hurl his friend several yards farther up to a safer position, then finally stick his sword up a Rawgr's bum?

The chalky menhir of Scathur's face quaked as if convulsed by a tremor, fragments of it breaking away and landsliding down his basaltic skin. Cracks began to appear, crisscrossing its surface in veins of bubo-purple. Those watery little oyster eyes churned, swelled and seethed, rose out of their sockets in the manner of an overflowing drain, and sulphurous spittle began boiling out from his quivering and labrose mouth. Then, without any further warning, the entire surface of his gravestone visage split apart, fell away and, with the jabbering of a thousand fiends, an oily black melee of fibrillating, chitinous appendages burst forth.

As Scathur's head emptied its contents, so too did Nibulus's stomach, and the Bardische finally clattered to the floor.

Still in spasm, Scathur hurled himself down from the ziggurat and staggered away. His army halted in their business and parted ranks to let him pass. In confusion, for they knew not what this could mean, they watched as he fled the Chamber, screaming still, while depositing behind him a trail of steaming puddles upon the marble. And, once he was gone, they milled about like ants that have lost their queen, while the defenders enjoyed a lifesaving gasp of air.

Nibulus gratefully accepted Kuthy's hand, and was hauled to his feet. "Nice one, mate." He grinned, and once again hefted Unferth.

Nice one, indeed, Finwald concurred, then turned back to continue his search for Bolldhe. The *über-Rawgr* was out of his hair at last, and his child-like minions—whom Finwald had been sensing so horribly close at hand—seemed by some miracle to have been deflected for a time.

But things were still pretty desperate, and were becoming more so with each minute that passed. So many of his allies had already fallen, and the enemy, despite its huge losses, still outnumbered them many times over. Before Finwald's very eyes, Cuthwulf was being dragged down by a pack of crazed predators. His Fossegrim-poisoned voulge had turned black the blood of as many Oghain as it had beheaded, and in the process built an entire ramp of their twitching and deflating bodies upon the steps before his feet. But he was set upon from all sides, and had reached the end of his strength. Finwald, momentarily transfixed, could only stare as bone-hard fingers and arms wiry with corded strength sought out Brother Number Two's trembling flesh, gripped, twisted, and pulled it away. The last the mage saw of him was his mouth, barely discernible now in the red pulp of his face, spitting out curses of terror as his eyes stared blindly into space.

It's all falling apart around my ears, Finwald swore, and he realized it would not be long before the end.

So do it. Now!

It was a terrible risk, but he had no choice. He let loose his concentration, and allowed his aura of protection to fall away from him. Thus freed, he could send his mind forth to seek out Bolldhe and, more importantly, Flametongue.

But before he had the chance to even draw breath, the horde was upon him

too, lunging, surging and lashing out. He was suddenly jostled with such vio-
lence that it was all he could do to concentrate upon merely staying afloat.

This is useless, Finwald fumed. Even surrounded by the Tyvenborgers he
could not hope to bring his concentration to bear. What he needed was something instant, something powerful, something to take the heat off him for a while,
and get the enemy off his back long enough for him to locate the flamberge.

Then a word popped into his head—or more precisely, a Word of Power.
Yes, that was what he needed. Instant, infallible and immensely potent, it was
an incantation as yet far above his level of mastery, or even his understanding,
but it was the one thing, the *only* thing, that might yet buy him the time he so
desperately needed.

His extremities tingled with forbidden excitement as this thought took
hold. *The Word of Power,* he pronounced to himself experimentally. *Yes, why
not. It's either that, or death for us all.*

Like a dark, threatening tower, he appeared to rise up, and power swirled
about him. His mind went out again, and waves of wizardry resonated through
him, whipping his clothes about, animating his hair and fluttering his eyelids.
He could feel such enormity of magical energy around him and within him, so
close, almost his! Ah, such mastery!

Then he saw *him.* After all these years, he actually saw him, floating in the
air just yards away.

Cuna, his god, with the Skela all around him.

Finwald could not help but smirk; his god was speaking, trying urgently to
talk with him, to plead with him. But no words came out. He was simply opening and closing his mouth like a netted fish.

If ever there had been a time for soul-searching, Finawald realized then, it
must surely be now. But, then, what would be the point of that, as he probably
would not even find one?

With still the trace of a smile on his lips, Finwald dismissed his god,
mouthing the words: "I'll see you when I'm ready."

His spine now tingled with an iciness that felt like ghosts dancing on his
soul. Then, with one outstretched finger, he touched a Word:

Bad Eye to his Enemies.

Composed of sorcerous light, he saw the sigils appear before him in the
smoky air, glowering, knowing, alive. Their magic laid fingers around his soul,
and stroked with sybaritic effleurage. The mage gasped, and felt himself swell.
Heart beating, palms slick, eyes aglow with expectation, he finally uttered the
Word of Blindness . . .

The sigils faded as swiftly as the smile of a harlot when her job is done and her magic no longer needed. Finwald opened his eyes.

"...no...!" he breathed, and the magic fell right out of his world.

His squad had become a collapsing seawall, a folding deck of cards, swept down in screaming confusion and terror by the onrushing deluge of enemies. Everyone, man, beast or otherwise, staggered back against the tier risers and flailed about blindly, their strokes wild and slued, their eyes running freely with foul fluids the same color as the Word sigils.

Yet their enemies remained completely unaffected, and burrowed into them with renewed glee. Vetter after Vetter went down, and many a strong Cervulus too, unable to defend themselves. Within seconds all would be lost, and Finwald stared on helplessly, almost unable to breathe. His soul was crushed under the weight of his guilt.

Until another Word popped into his view, glowing even more brightly than the one before. Without a second's thought, he enunciated it, for it was his—their—only chance:

Poisoned Chaos of the Mind. The Word of Insanity.

His lips peeled back and his teeth glistened. This spell was different, a Word of an altogether stronger language. It drained power out of him, and it took something else, too; Finwald felt dimmed somehow, his skin turning gauze-thin and his blood just that little bit cooler. Into this vacancy, too, something new fingered its way....

Then the Word blasted forth from his brain, so much more powerful than the one before, and his breath came rank and black in the foulness of its passage. Straightaway his legs gave beneath him, and Finwald fell to his knees. He clutched his head in the severest agitation, and did not dare look up. But the strange cries that now filled his ears soon compelled him to raise his head from his chest and unclench his veiny eyelids.

In the throes of some terrible fit the defenders on the ziggurat now cavorted wildly. Without care or thought for whom they struck, or who struck them, they howled and writhed and lashed out in complete lunacy, as if their very souls were on fire.

For some, especially the strongest of them, this proved unexpectedly fortunate, for the insanity that filled their brains also gave them new strength. Maddened like a raging berserker, Nibulus pitched headlong into the enemy and clove a path deep through their ranks, before finally disappearing from sight. Ceawlin, Hwald and Finan scattered the dead like so many autumn leaves to an over-excited child. Klijjver appeared to have transmogrified from Tusse to

Jutul, and grinned dementedly as he hammered both living and dead flesh upon his anvil.

And Dolen's madness manifested itself uniquely; her hair stood out like the spines of a sea urchin as psychosis boiled within her Dhracus brain, then poured out, channelled through her dagger, and exploded straight into her foe. A living swarm of her nightmare horrors wriggled out, clamped onto the heads of the Wire-Faces, drove mandibles in deep, and winkled the very life from them in cackling hysteria.

For others it did not have such a fortunate effect. Schnorbitz, slavering and drooling, let out a howl such as he had never uttered in his life, not even as a puppy, then cowered away helplessly even as a Wire-Face aimed a tzerbuchjer directly at the hound's skull. Elfswith, meanwhile, was slowly but relentlessly beating his own brains out on the marble step upon which he sprawled. Eorcenwold swung his morning star all around him, and laughed uncontrollably as it took the back of his sister's head off, releasing the cerebral contents in a sluggish cascade down her back. And Cynen Englarielle finally disintegrated in a fountain of blood under the sudden frenzied hacking of Kuthy.

Appa simply collapsed, struck upon the head by the backswing of Wodeman's tulwar. Finwald stared into the old man's glazed eyes as he fell supine upon the steps just at his feet, and saw reflected there the utter madness that had surely possessed Finwald himself, ever since he had first beheld Flametongue. For what else, if not the greatest folly, could have caused him to behave the way he had all these years, or to dream those impossible dreams that had filled his head for so long?

Finwald had lost that which he craved above all else: *control.* Lost control of his charges, of the magic, of the situation and, yes, even of his own mind. Only then did a memory return to him. . . . What was it the shaman had said?

"You can't do evil magic without harming yourself."

Too damn right. Too damn late! For he had let the evil in, *invited* it in, and even now the third Word of Power was forming in the air. He did not want it, would have done anything to thrust it away. But he was powerless to resist it. As he stared into the wells of dementia that Appa's eyes had become, Finwald's religion came back to him; the beloved plainsong of the ascetics, the simple healing of the mage-priests, and behind it all, the all-pervading Face of Cuna, whose red eyes were lidless orbs of radiant energy hot enough to consume souls; pools of castigation with neither stye nor macula.

But the Word was complete.

No thoughts flashed through Finwald's mind. No scheme, stratagem nor revelation. There simply was not the time. He flung himself down next to Appa, clasped him urgently to his breast, and as the Word began erupting from him, focused it straight through the old priest's head.

He had already figured out his mistake. Not just the fact that he had got everything so horribly, unforgivably wrong, but the Words themselves. The last sigil was the key: the Enemy. Words of Power not against the enemy of the caster, but of the Tomes, of him that had written them in the first place.

And what did Finwald hope to achieve by this last act? He could not foil the Word, could do nothing to impede it, for it was within him and had been for even longer than he realized. He could repress it no more than a woman in labor can hold in her emerging child, or a drunkard grit his teeth to stem the rising of his stomach.

It was at best a desperate prayer for absolution, albeit one without any real hope.

The Word of Death.

A gout of black light exploded between the two mage-priests and hurled them away from each other like two repelled lodestones. Between them this anti-light left a gap of nothingness that drew the eyes of all onlookers toward it so forcefully that they almost extruded from their sockets. Immediately there came a great, hollow sucking as of the dispelling of an Air Elemental, then all that remained in the space where the priests had been was the ruined marble of the ziggurat, cracked and desiccated, its luster and color drained utterly, and rimed with a light frosting.

The battle faltered. For a second, while they all adjusted to this new reality, there was a weighty hush in which no one fought, cried, or even breathed.

Then the Word-smitten were whole again, quite whole, both blindness and insanity lifted from them and sucked into the vortex of anti-magic. Finwald's last act, desperate and unconsidered though it was, had succeeded in dispelling the Words of Power. That evil could not penetrate the soul of a truly good man, even one as caught up in brainstorm as was Appa, and so had rebounded upon its caster.

While the survivors recovered their senses, their weapons, and their positions—and pretty damn quickly, too—Appa rolled over and squinted hard through the bilious coruscation in his eyes, trying to locate his brother-in-faith in the darkness beyond the blasted marble.

There! His eyes locked onto a movement, drawn to it by a guttural cry that rose in pitch and fear till it warbled hysterically, and just went on and on. A figure in Finwald's clothes lurched up from the mound of dead, a smoking ghoul rising from the pyres of the battle-slain. Fingers no more than the twigs of a lightning struck tree clawed frantically at its face, now grey and befouled, oozing blood from every orifice and pore. A forked tongue of tumorous pulsation disgorged between a mantrap of urine-brown fangs, and suppurated with a cold, oily venom. As the screaming reached a pitch exceeding that of even the most deranged of the Word's victims, it turned to stare straight at Appa, and its eyes simply melted and ran down its face.

It could stand no more. Amid howls of direst anguish, the apparition bounded down the steps and plunged into the throng. All recoiled before it, for none there possessed the strength or disposition to dare resist it.

So departed Finwald, mage-priest of Cuna, fleeing the Chamber, abandoning the quest, renouncing his humanity, vanishing from their lives forever. And behind him he left nothing but the echoes of his torment . . . and a very bad smell.

Released from their madness, the defenders realized just how few they were. Released from their blindness, they could see just how many of their enemies still remained. Their strength was depleted, the lungfuls of breath left to them numbered and dwindling rapidly, and hope dissipated to nothing. Englarielle was dead, Wintus lost, and no leader or savior was there to aid them in their final moments. Step by step they were pushed back up the ziggurat, and with each rise they climbed, more of their number fell.

Of all of them, only Mauglad retained any hope. Though he was still no nearer to locating either the flamberge or his original body, he intuitively felt that neither could be far away now. Moreover, he *liked* this new body he had chosen. It was truly remarkable, so sleek, so well-oiled, so *potent.* True, given the chance he would have opted for the gleaming kettle-copper hair he had sported in real life instead of this awful dull black. But at least the skin was to his liking; death-pale suited the necromancer in him far better than the bilge-brown tone of his erstwhile host, and what better than a ghost-like visage in this life, he had often mused, to prepare a man for an eternity of such a look in the next?

One weapon in each hand, Mauglad went hunting. His Tyvenborg companions neither aided nor hindered him, and he was free to go about his business as he wished.

He then stopped dead amid the chaos, and trembled as a graveyard lily in a wintry gust of wind. His black eyes bulged from their sockets, and a skull-like grin spread across his features.

There, finally, his old body: scant yards away and getting closer by the second.

My life! he gawped. *What a magnificent specimen!*

It was not merely boastful pride, for this was no ordinary foot soldier of the dead that approached. From toe to pate, the contorted cadaver loomed at least three feet above the rank and file (reminding Mauglad trenchantly of the manner of his death) and was made taller still by the antler-like sprouting of petrified branches that had been grafted onto the top of its skull. Other features that Mauglad did not recall his original body possessing included a second pair of arms (wielding scythe-like weapons), a narwhal horn as a codpiece down below, and—most arresting of all—two faces side by side upon its head. The first of these he recognized instantly as his own face, and he winced to see how unkind Time had been to it. The second, however, was the greatest insult of all, for this face was that of a lesser Rawgr he had habitually bullied during his days in office. It had clearly been culled and flayed almost immediately after Mauglad's own execution, for in the infernal heat it had partly melted its co-face, and both now ran together in an eternal kiss of death. Neither looked especially happy about it.

Six hundred years, six interminable centuries of banishment—and all about to end beneath the wrecking hands of Mauglad Yrkeshta.

"Do not, Mauglad. I forbid you!" Cuna thundered in fury, as if he had any authority in this matter. "Stand back from yourself. You have work yet to do: *Kill the Rawgr!*"

Several grey-robed figures materialized out of the thurible smoke. Floating upon its haze, they drifted up to Cuna.

"Plan B still on, then?" one inquired politely.

Cuna ignored them, and continued raging at the thief-clad spirit, yet knowing that it could never, ever, hear him.

But Mauglad did hesitate, Cuna noticed, transfixed between the wings of a dilemma Cuna knew only too well. He had suffered for so *long* in Sluagh, and could not bear to do so for any longer. Here was a chance—nay, a certainty—of ending it *all* this instant: just destroy his old body there, and merciful release would be his.

But it was this very purgatory suffered at the design of Drauglir that stayed his hand now; for how could he be truly released when there was such lust for vengeance still within him, unfulfilled? Mauglad vacillated. Should he risk failure, and a return to another kind of Sluagh that might *never* end this time, simply to gain a revenge he could only savor for mere moments? Or should he take the easy way out?

Khurghan decided that for him. The Polg came out of nowhere and, as Mauglad and Cuna stared on in disbelief, punched his spear straight into the melt-face corpse's heart.

"DAMN YOU, YOU LITTLE RUNT!" roared Mauglad, "HE IS NOT THINE TO SLAY!" And, without a second's further delay, he jammed his magical dagger squarely into the base of the Polg's spine, and ripped it up clear to his skull.

Khurghan came apart in an explosion of blood, entrails and shattered ribs. He had not even the time to scream before his distended eyeballs glazed over and his body spread out upon the steps.

Mauglad ignored him, and regarded his old body. It was tottering, still speared through by the assegai, but it would not fall ultimately until brain and heart were separated. *Good,* thought Mauglad; it would last a while yet—long enough for what he had in mind. But only if it did not get attacked by anyone else. He wasted no time, and Mauglad's former days in the torture pits came back to him in an instant as, expertly, almost joyfully, he set his knife to work.

The blade was no purpose-made bone-dislocator, to be sure, but it took only moments to wrench both legs and all four arms from the feebly struggling corpse that had once been himself.

"There!" he said in satisfaction. "As easy as pulling my own hands off." All there was left to do was rip its lower jaw off, and then it would be a threat to no one, therefore a target no longer.

That done, Mauglad turned to leave, but then turned back on an after-thought. Gripping firmly, he snapped the narwhal horn off, and flung it as far away as possible.

"You can kiss good-bye to that, too," he said and, with Khurghan's blood and bone-shards still masking his face, stalked off to find Flametongue.

But Mauglad had no need to conceal his identity any longer.

Her mask of gore having been wiped away by six long fingers, the ghost-pale face of Dolen Catscaul peered about her. The first thing she saw was Brother Oswiu Garoticca, and she could see that he was up to something.

From what she could make out between the chaos of leaping figures, he was busy grappling with what appeared to be some large sea mammal unaccount-ably washed up on the ziggurat. Something huge, grey and oleaginous, at any rate. Though his back was turned to her, it was him for sure. She could see the three runes—Torch, Erce and Death's Head—glowing menacingly upon his cloak.

Whether this hitherto unmanifested sartorial phenomenon was caused by the censer flare, the Chamber itself, or some inner enchantment, Dolen did not know, but there was definitely something about the glowing runes that the dead did not like. They swarmed around him, they swarmed past him, some even leapt over him; but none would interfere with him at his work.

Yes, but what's he doing?

There was something lying beneath the grey mass of blubber that he was trying to get at. No, not something, *someone.* A man was trapped beneath the weight of an enormously rotund dead man, and it appeared that he was doggedly fighting Oswiu off. Yes, there was Oswiu, knife in one hand, while with the other he was trying desperately to snatch something the trapped man was grasping tight. It was a minor struggle that looked almost comical com-pared with the butchery going on around it, and yet it seemed to Dolen that the eyes of all the heavens were focused upon it, as if it were the most impor-tant contest being waged at this moment in the entire world.

Oswiu lunged again with the knife, but somehow the trapped man caught the wrist that held it, and guided it deep into the dead man. Straight into that enormous gut it went, and Oswiu's hand went with it, right up to the wrist. Then out came the hand again, minus the blade, and immediately the whole vast bulk deflated and sluiced out a nightmarish eructation of grey fluids and vapor.

The heavens' focusing crystallized further, till Dolen was sure she could even hear what the gods were saying to each other.

Cuna's rapidly dwindling confidence in Bolldhe was now at its lowest ebb. His teeth were gritted in despair, and the light from his red eyes glowed only dimly through the fingers of the hand he clasped over them.

One of the Skela drifted up closer from behind, and whispered in his ear: "So my Lord, if there were one wish we could grant you at this hour . . ."

Cuna stared hard at the Syr, then wheeled away in despair. It was a despair that could not be compared in any measure to that felt by mankind, for it was almighty, and immortal.

And then, with an unexpectedness that surprised even himself, Cuna cried out to Oswiu in thunderous proclamation: "KILL BOLLDHE! KILL HIM NOW, AND DO IT YOURSELF!"

Oswiu did not hear this. Not even Dolen heard it, though she did sense a definite stench of duplicity and betrayal in the ether. What she did hear, however, was the feeble voice of Bolldhe—*that most abhorrent of voices, the murdering scum!*—crying out in desperation.

And what she also now sensed, her Dhracus brain screeching a warning in its every cell, was how the soul of Mauglad Yrkeshta currently inhabited the body of the not-yet-dead Oswiu Garoticca.

Mauglad wavered a second, and wondered if it really was worth trying to search through those undulating folds of dead fat for his Kh'is dagger. Then he reached a decision.

To hell with it. I'll use the miter.

Once again, Bolldhe found himself being assailed by the terrible Miter of Smiting. Again, by some incredible stroke of luck more than by skill, he managed to catch the descending weapon by the haft. Nevertheless, as he and the Oswiu-thing grappled furiously, both clutching the awful skin-searing implement tight, he realized it must be seconds only before once again his face felt its kiss. And this time it would boil his entire head.

"GO ON, MAUGLAD!" Cuna cried, *"WHAT ARE YOU WAITING FOR?!"*

Yes, what are you waiting for? Dolen wondered. *Just kill the bastard!*

The face of her dead swain, Eggledawc, whom Bolldhe had murdered, swam into the void between her and the two men who fought. Red tears began welling in her eyes, and her brain steamed madly. Yet she found herself giggling all of a sudden, for Eorcenwold's Brother Number One looked so ridiculous now, a man alive only because of an ill-fitting soul that possessed him, blood flowing now only feebly from the reopened arrow wound in his back, and all the while trying to belt the hell out of the single arm that protruded from beneath the mountain of grey blubber on the step—like a man trying to club a seal out on the ice.

The floating face of her dead love faded, only to be replaced by that of Bolldhe. She had been unconscious when he had lifted her to safety on his horse's back, but she had felt something of gratitude even in her state of senselessness, and with some surprise had learned later how the stolid stranger had risked almost certain death to save her.

Her soul now burned with such inner conflict . . . but there was no time for such thoughts, for regrets, for love, hate, forgiveness or vengeance. No time even for decisions.

With a howl that bowled back the dead that were descending upon her, Dolen cried out: *"But you killed my boyfriend!"*

(Eorcenwold, bounding up the steps for his last stand, glanced fleetingly down at her as he passed. There were many things he might have expected someone to say in their final moments, but that certainly was not one that sprang to *his* mind.)

Bolldhe snarled in pain as a hefty boot pinned his sword arm to the floor. The square, brutish face of the cleric-assassin filled his vision; stringy black hair drooped over pale, wet skin whose every crease and fold had its own tale of cruelty to tell. Thick lips puckered in a smile of death, as Bolldhe gazed back into those eyes, so tiny yet yawning with blackness, eyes that hosted no soul.

In the very last second before his head would be bludgeoned into seething jelly, Bolldhe wondered what, in truth, he was staring at. Was this indeed Brother Number One, or did he perceive some other entity that lurked in the void behind those eyes?

Or was this simply the Face of Death, that which all men see in the second before they wink out of existence?

But the blow did not fall, nor did Bolldhe die just then. Instead, he saw the death-visage before him transform into a mask of bewilderment and pain. With a paroxysm that set the iron scales of his doublet a-jangle, Oswiu coughed a discharge of bloody maggots straight into Bolldhe's face, then slowly turned around to see who or what had punctured him so rudely.

As the big man lurched sideways, he revealed to Bolldhe another pale face also helmed in black hair. It was Dolen Catscaul, and she had thrust her dagger deep into Oswiu's heart.

"Bitch!" he snarled, and—far from dead—struck her with a backhanded swing of his miter that knocked the teeth from her mouth and crumpled her to

the floor. There was a stench of burning meat that Bolldhe instantly recognized, before Oswiu grabbed hold of him, heaved him out from under the corpulent corpse and, with one boot pinning him to the marble, raised the miter with both hands high above his head.

In that moment, with his rune-cloak unfurling behind him and his weapon held up to point towards the ziggurat's apex, Oswiu resembled in every aspect the necromancer that dwelt within him, now offering up an unholy talisman in supplication to the Rawgr.

But the Dhracus, though direly afflicted, had not quite perished, and the black potency of the miter that had driven all strength from Bolldhe three weeks previously served only to unleash the full fury inside her brain.

In an instant her power went forth, hooked into the mind of another, and dragged him straight back to her just like a lined fish. The body of Oswiu would not be slain while *he* yet abided within him, not with the paltry injury she had inflicted upon it. She had need, therefore, of greater strength. So it was that, before he had the chance to bring that final blow to bear, the last words Oswiu/Mauglad would hear were the two that Dolen now purred to him ominously.

"Meet Klijjver."

An instant later, the borrowed thief's head simply vanished, crushed into a spray of red vapor and flying maggots as Klijjver brought his massive maul down again and again and again. In a fit of psionically agitated madness, the huge Tusse continued to rain down blows even after his enemy's neck had been rammed deep into the ribcage.

Thus, Brother Oswiu Garoticca, Mauglad-possessed and Meat-Kloven cleric-assassin of the Order of Cardinal Saloth Alchwych, was finally allowed to die, his body still kicking and spasming upon the steps long after his soul had fled.

Both of them.

Klijjver looked distinctly puzzled. He was not sure why he had just milled the top half of Eorcenwold's brother into something resembling damson mulch—it was, after all, not the kind of thing he made a habit of—but he hoped there was a good reason for it. With a slight shake of his tiny head, he turned and headed up the ziggurat to rejoin his leader for the last stand, and sincerely hoped Eorcenwold had not seen what he had just done.

Dolen was left behind. She dragged herself over to where Bolldhe lay, avoiding Oswiu's nether half as it cavorted still upon the steps. Amid the charred and popping wreckage of her once-fair face shone now a smile of such unblemished clarity and beneficence that it was plain to anyone of sound mental state that her deed had finally purified her soul. Freed of the invasive loathing that had sullied her spirit for so long, she was returned to the wholeness of being that was her very essence. She looked down upon Bolldhe as he languished in stupefaction and, with red tears streaking her face, offered him her hand.

But Bolldhe was not now of sound mental state. All he saw above him was another murderous Tyvenborger, whose face had been transfigured into a ghastly echo of those chaos-spawn that rampaged all around. For the scorched and stinking skin was beginning to melt from her cheekbones, and fresh blood oozed from her coal-black eyes like some monstrous apparition in his darkest nightmares.

If that was not dire enough, a new presage of hell now entered the Chamber. It was in strict accordance with the equipoise at the center of Oswiu's cult: if one as evil as Mauglad should depart, another equivalent of evil should enter. Thus the Children of the Keep had finally entered Lubang-Nagar, and would be upon them in a matter of minutes.

"Bolldhe!" came the desperate whine of Appa from somewhere above. *"You've got to do it now!"*

As Bolldhe recoiled from the twitching female hand that reached out for him, his own hand fell upon the hilt of Flametongue.

"Got . . . to do it . . . now . . ." he repeated, then swept up the flamberge and, with a savage grunt, thrust it straight up through Dolen's jaw and into her skull.

Her body became instantly as rigid as her smile, then trembled as softly as a butterfly pierced through with a pin. Thoughts of her beloved Eggledawc flashed through her mind one last time, then she went limp and sagged upon the spike that had impaled her. As her body slackened, so too did the smile, allowing the blood to well forth from a heart that was utterly, utterly broken.

Bolldhe's mind began to regain some measure of rationality. He lurched to his feet, and stared down at the Dhracus pinioned on the end of his blade. He still did not know what she had been up to just then, but whatever it was, he guessed he had probably overreacted again.

Yet he had no time to be sorry, for the last of the Cervulice were stampeding up the great steps behind him, and the dead and the Wire-Faces both came shrieking after them. It was time to go up. Up to the top. Time to *"do it now."* Bolldhe braced his boot firmly against the Dhracus's jaw, and yanked the sword from her skull. He delayed not even long enough to see her lifeless corpse slump to the floor, but turned and heaved himself up on to the next tier.

Just before he reached the top, he turned and looked back. There below him lay a scene that no amount of rational thought could fully take in. Throughout the battle, all that fought had become progressively redder and redder, drenched with the blood of their foe, their comrades, and even themselves, till it was difficult to tell who was who, what was what, and who still had any flesh left on them to bleed from. In the end, it seemed, they had all become one and the same, a single entity of sharp tooth and raw meat, one that was inexorably eating itself to total destruction.

Then, at that very same moment, the engram in Bolldhe's mind flared up and melted the ice wall—and, at last, he remembered.

16

Bolldhe the Great

Darkness. Silence. It is cold here, and smells of swamp mist. Nothing moves, nothing stirs. There is only deadness.

Eventually, after a time that cannot be gauged by the living, there comes the faintest of sounds: a soft night wind stirs unseen boughs; a skritche-owl cries, far away. Then the stealthy chink of chainmail, barely heard, far, far away. It gets louder. With it, the muted sound of footsteps, some heavy-booted and confident, others light and less sure, softly crunching the ice that patches the frozen mud on the rutted path.

The pale glow in the east deepens; a red sun breaks over the Rampart Mountains, slants across hillock and field, spreads a ruby-sprinkled gauze over dew-blanketed grass as dawn's sanguine light trickles into a world unwilling to awake.

Voices in the mist, furtive, conspiratorial. But no birds herald this new day. The air is tainted by the reek of rain-doused embers, and of newly spilled blood.

Shadows materialize from the mist, a dozen or more, some large, some small. Over the broken-down gate of the croft they step, snag their cloaks upon the thistles, pick their way over the carcasses that lie contorted and steaming in the early morning chill. Some of the fallen are animals, others humans.

They stand there: the boys rigid, uncomprehending, speechless; the men chafing their arms and stamping their feet. The leader steps forward, impatient, irritable, and hacks phlegm onto the mud by the nearest corpse. He would rather be in bed with his doxy, but has work to do here first.

He jabs a finger into the nearest boy's temple. "You. Fetch embers, wood. Get a fire going." Another he motions into the croft, charged with bringing pots. A third he sends to get water.

He then turns toward the rising sun, and his scarred face glows afire. It is a hard, cruel face, but also, on this bitter morning, a bored face. The boys go about their tasks wordlessly, some in haste, some reluctantly, but all in a daze of shock. It is the first time they have beheld a scene of murder. It is the first lesson of a long, long day.

One boy does not move. Will not move. He stares down at the corpses, axe-cloven and manure-smeared, and they stare back.

The sergeant sees him, and yells: "You! Bladder!"

"Bolldhe, sir," the boy corrects him.

"Baldazar, then," the sergeant amends. "What by zounds d'you think you're doing? This isn't a pissin' leave-day!"

"They're my cousins, sir," the boy states.

"What?"

"My cousins. You've killed my cousins."

The sergeant hesitates a moment, then snorts. "As far as you're concerned, boy, they're just the enemy. Now the sooner you can cut 'em up and cook 'em, the sooner we can get some breakfast."

I was eight years old, Bolldhe murmured to himself upon the steps of the zig-gurat. *Just eight. And that's what they did to me. To all of us. Those crofters hadn't even done anything . . .*

Brutalize them. Inure them. Make them do *whatever* they were ordered to.

. . . And it worked. For a while at least, we wanted to eat our enemies, consume them utterly and shit them out into the latrine. That's the way they do it, those Peladanes, always engineering people's minds. . . .

That was why he hated them so.

But, then, that was why *all* the boys hated them. What made Bolldhe so different?

His vision focused. That . . . that "Breakfast at the Croft" was not, however, the scene he had looked upon in the ice cave of his soul journey. Even that atrocity, he realized with mounting horror, was not the core of his engram; it was merely lurking on the periphery. For, looking now upon the churning flesh-shredder that the Chamber had become, he realized that that which lay dormant in his memory, that childhood horror that had burnt itself onto his brain then sealed itself off, was so much worse. And it was down into this seething core of suppressed memory, this dream beneath the dream, he must now go.

Weeks later, the same company of soldierlings had been taken out into the field, and set against a gang of marauding picaroons that had holed up in the sea caves of the northern straits. It was all a setup, of course: while the Peladanes themselves had waited at the escape tunnel, the boys were sent straight through the front door: cannon fodder to be slaughtered, a mere distraction while the Thegne sent his men in the back way to do the real job.

It was a good enough plan, and by the time the Peladanes reached the scene, their greed-bright eyes gleamed. The picaroons lay dead, together with the boys, either sprawled across the rocks or floating off in frothing circles of red spume. And the bounty glittered in barrels and chests all about.

But, as so often happens in war, things did not go quite as planned. Too late they realized that one boy had survived. One furtive little waif that flitted as a pale ghost through the dark recesses of the cave. One whose sight had had that much more time than theirs to adjust to the darkness. And one by one they fell, those proud and shining warriors. They fell to the sly little blade that struck out from the darkness, pierced from behind, and coughed blood and spittle, and shat in their breeches.

Thus they found him, days later, still in the caves: the sole survivor. Atop the mound of dead and dying, befouled beyond belief, sat Bolldhe. His glazed eyes stared back at them with laughter; his hands were sticky with blood, and he was unable to speak for the pumping offal stuffed in his mouth.

Whether dead or just wounded, in his present state it had not mattered. They were meat, they were warm, and he had gorged upon them even as they writhed.

Such savagery dormant within him it was that he had seen behind the ice wall. Such it was that had sent him screaming through the tunnels of his own mind begging for deliverance and expiation. And such unbridled bloodlust it was that had possessed him when he had murdered Eggledawc Clagfast, the Dhracus's swain.

Well, compared to what he was witnessing now, was it really so bad after all? Was it that childhood horror alone that made him so different, so unique that only he among mortals could fulfill this quest? No, there must be something else, some other reason. . . .

Why had he alone survived the raid on the picaroons? He alone of all his youthful brothers in arms? Indeed, what was it that had impelled him to go off like that, years later, on an endless journey that would take him around the world?

He reflected on this for a moment, and the answer came to him.

Granite.

That's what they had said: there had always been granite in his soul, right from birth. And the more the Peladanes had tried to crush that granite in order to get at the iron they sought—that more malleable ore that was the very cornerstone of their world—the harder the granite fought back. In the end, the only weapon they had succeeded in forging was that knife they later received in their backs.

By the time the searchers had found him, it was all over. He could never be the same again. Not after that. He hated the Peladanes even when he was rescued by them, hated their authority, despised their machinations, spurned their

care and even their pity. There was no longer any place for him in Pendonium.
He had to leave. So he had done so, and to this day had remained an exile, dis-
placed, a permanent outsider. And that long, long journey had hardened him
yet more, drawn his armor of granite closer about himself, built up his stony
curtain walls, continued the hardening process the Peladanes had begun.

But see? They were controlling him *still,* directing him from the other side
of the world—or even the other side of the grave.

So this is what he had become, then: a life so extraordinary, so unique. This
nature of his, somehow, was what was needed to fulfill the quest. And now that
Finwald, the whole cause of this enterprise, had turned on them (or whatever
he had done), nobody even knew what the hell the quest was anymore—if
there genuinely even was a quest.

Well, Bolldhe was still none the wiser as to what unique act he was supposed to perform. But, sword in hand, he turned anyway and headed up to the
top of the ziggurat, for he still had a battle to win.

It was a strange and totally unexpected thing that happened to Gapp just then.
As he and Schnorbitz were busy grappling with the windpipes of the Wire-
Faces that were trying to flay their skin off, something out of the blue occurred
to him. It was, in fact, nothing short of a revelation. For Gapp Radnar, the least
among them, had just then realized the secret of Drauglir, understood fully
what it was Finwald had been up to and, most importantly, knew exactly how
to succeed in the quest.

Lying on his back still, with Schnorbitz's hind claws ripping at his chest and
a Wire-Face struggling frenziedly above him, Gapp somehow managed to
twist his head round, and cried out as loudly as he could:

"Bolldhe! I know what it is you must do! It's all so simple. . . ."

And the words of his revelation came flowing from his mouth like the
golden, sparkling notes of honey-flavored music.

But tragically, inevitably, he was as usual completely ignored. Bolldhe did
not even bother to glance at him as he continued pushing his way through the
last of the Vetters to reach the top.

"FINE!" croaked Gapp, after the disappearing figure. "Do it your own
bloody way!"

It was a sarcophagus. A monstrous, octagonal vault that the Peladanes had
constructed to seal over the remains of that which none would touch. In effect
an armored, flesh-eating spider, pervaded with foul gases, enshrouded with the
very blackness of Olchor himself, of death without hope.

Alone—because none other would dare approach—Bolldhe stood before
it.

Each of its eight walls was as high as Bolldhe was tall. Formidable, daunt-
ing, terrifying, so leaden and dense that it appeared to him as the very axis

around which Vaagenfjord Maw turned. Yet for all its size and intimidating appearance, it had been fashioned by Peladanes, and thus was inevitably made of iron. And iron does not last forever. It took just three hacks and two hefty kicks, and Bolldhe had knocked a sizeable hole through the crumbling metal.

A cry immediately went up from the dead, and from some distance away but closing fast, the Children's keening could be heard. They could now all sense Drauglir's presence, his imminence. Bolldhe had no time to waste. So, flamberge in hand, he entered the vault, and was instantly engulfed in blackness . . .

. . . And emerged, blinking, from the engram-cave at the very deepest part of his soul-house.

"What?!"

Yes, it was true: Bolldhe had come out of that very cave in which he had witnessed himself wallowing in such crimson abomination. He had emerged from the gap where the ice wall had been shattered by the fire-giant. There before him now stood a familiar figure, sweeping up the swarf and coke that the Jutul had left behind on the floor.

"Yorda?"

She looked up sharply, almost in alarm, then relaxed when she saw who it was.

"Oh, hello, it's you again," she said. "What are you doing back here?"

She stared at him for a moment, then when he did not reply, went back to work.

Bolldhe felt understandably befuddled. He was still reeling from the battle, and now nothing in his world made any sense at all.

Have to think quickly, he determined. *I'm here in the tomb, or still in my trance up on the ice field . . . or in some other dream somewhere—sometime—else, or . . . Or else I'm . . .* dead?

"You're inside the tomb," Yorda informed him without looking up from her work. "No need to start losing it."

"Oh. Oh that's all right then," he replied bitterly. "So long as we're both agreed on that."

Why am I talking to her anyway? She's not even real!

"Yorda, I've got just seconds to deal with the Rawgr. I can't go on skulking around in here, trying to figure out the meaning of my life."

"Why not?" she replied, somewhat distractedly. "At least you're safe in here."

"Oh, am I really? And what about the others?"

"Yes? What about the others? Don't tell me you've picked this moment, of all moments, to start *caring* about people! Well, have you?"

"Yorda! I really don't have time for this right now. Just tell me what's going on."

"It's your head, Bolldhe," she replied. "Just yours. There's no one else in here with you. Not even that shaman of yours. If *you* can't answer your own questions, then that's your lot, I'm afraid. And as for Time, well, you don't need to worry about *him.* That one won't lay a finger on you in here. At least, not for some time. . . ."

Bolldhe shook his head, then threw his hands up in utter bewilderment. "I've got to get back. Got to get to the tomb—to finish this *insanity* somehow."

He turned and marched straight back into the engram-cave, then halted. There was no cave any longer. Just a stone wall. All that remained was a vague picture, a far-off image upon the stone of the battle still raging in the Chamber, all dull orange light and indistinct figures cavorting through the smoke.

He turned back and glared at Yorda.

"What's up now?" she asked impatiently. "I thought you had to get back? I thought you didn't want to figure out the meaning of your life?"

He was fuming. "Where's my battle gone to? Where's my tomb? Where's my engram? And . . . why the hell are *you* doing the sweeping up? You never used to bother with it when I knew you . . . You were a lot nicer, too."

She grinned knowingly. "Must be the company I keep. But to answer your questions, your battle's outside your head. If you want to get back to it, you'll have to go *up* . . . You know the way. Your engram you can find upstairs, too, on the bookshelves of your memory, only it's not an engram anymore, is it? And as for me sweeping up, well, someone's got to clean up this place before closing time, and let's face it, Bolldhe, there ain't exactly many other people in here to choose from. . . ."

At that moment, Bolldhe wished, more acutely than ever before, that he had never met that damn shaman in the first place. *He* had started all this; it was all *his* doing! He wished the furry old sod had choked on his pork crackling back at the Chase Inn in Nordwas. And despite the assurances of his soul-guide here—if that was what she even was—Bolldhe still did feel Time breathing down his neck. That grey-robed Skela had become like an impatient marketplace hag behind him in the queue, urging him on politely but insistently with an umbrella handle in his back. There was not any way he could start trying to figure things out; not here, not now. Back up on the ice field, time was exactly what he had plenty of, time in abundance, a veritable cornucopia of the stuff in which to still his brain, loosen his muscles, and let enlightenment flow into him.

But now he had no choice.

"Right!" he snapped. "Let's get on with it, then. C'mon you, we're going upstairs—and you can put that broom down for a start."

So he stormed off through the caves with Yorda in tow. She seemed reluctant to leave her broom behind, especially now that the place was so dilapidated and crumbling. But Bolldhe knew breeders well enough, and was not about to put up with any of this. They ran together as fast as thought, up

through the levels of the early churches, until in no time at all they were striding up the aisle of the Peladane temple.

There was an old, musty smell to it now, and it was empty of people, save
for one hooded priest that shuffled about in the darkness of a transept, his san-
dals scuffing through the hymn sheets that lay scattered upon the dusty flagstones. Yorda had clearly not been here before, and her eyes were wide with
wonder. Or was it fear? While Bolldhe tried to locate the manhole cover at the
pommel of the temple, she stared around her.

"It's big, isn't it?" she noted.

"*What?*"

"Rather bigger than I'd have expected from you, Bolldhe."

Bolldhe frowned irritably. "Yes I suppose it is," he admitted, still searching
the walls for the relief of Pel-Adan that he desperately sought.

"Must mean a lot to you still, after all these long years," she persisted.
"Even *I* can smell the wistfulness here. . . ."

"Crap!" Bolldhe spat. "Just look at it: it's *narrow*, and *sword-shaped*, and
has no *windows*. I've been everywhere, seen everything—far more than any of
the rustics that built this place could ever even imagine. You think this could
mean anything to me now? I can smell in here the fetor of blind acceptance,
willing ignorance, in every dusty manual. Fear hovers over this place in every
curl of candle smoke. This dank hole's shut away down here for a good reason.
I'm not hanging round any longer than I have to. I'm going *up*, to where life
is."

"Yet you carry a sword. Are you so sure those Peladanes don't still direct
you from the grave? Are you sure you don't actually *want* to be directed?"

Bolldhe looked down at the sword at his belt. "At least this one isn't
straight," he muttered, unsure whether this had any significance at all.

"Ah, here it is," he announced, and without ceremony booted open the
door at the far end of the temple.

Just as he was about to pass through, holding the door open for Yorda,
Bolldhe caught sight again of the shuffling priest in the transept. The figure
looked up at him, revealing the face of the Benne Nighe. So she had remained
here still, though her caves and bloodied laundry were gone. Winking at
Bolldhe and pointing at Yorda, she placed her left hand in the crook of her
right arm, then drove the arm up in a rather rude gesture.

"Pathetic!" Bolldhe cussed, and slammed the door in her face.

They were now back in the dungeons. As soon as they arrived there, both
Bolldhe and Yorda retched convulsively. If it had seemed a revolting, terrible
place the first time round, it was doubly so now. It felt as if an entire century
had passed since Bolldhe had last come this way, another hundred years of misery, terror and despair. The rusted iron bars had splintered into jagged points
and been twisted round to form half-obscured forms of diabolical horror; the

nail scratches on the walls had become more frenzied, describing symbols that only the worst cases of psychosis could dream up; the excrement smearings were now augmented by heavy daubings of viscera, some heaped in great, cold mounds in darkened corners; and diseased blood exuded in a steady stream from countless cracks in the stonework.

From the blackness of every cage, it seemed, there came the low, shuddering cackle of deranged voices, though not a soul could be seen, and to this overall malaise was added an unmistakable reverberation through the foundations of this vile place. The bars, such as they were, were even now starting to creak beneath the weight from above, and fragments of stone had begun falling to the floor.

Bolldhe stared on, sick with terror, and could not move a step. Even Yorda had blanched, and was clutching his arm in dread.

"You . . . you're not going through there, surely?" she whispered.

"It's starting to come down already," was all Bolldhe could manage. "We haven't got long after all."

"But you're not going *through*," she insisted, "are you? Bolldhe? Come on, let's get back to the temple."

Bolldhe did not reply, nor yet move, though Yorda tried to pull him back. There appeared now in every cage a disembodied mouth, teeth like miniature dripping gravestones and lips caked with sores, hovering in the blackness and continuing the cackles heard before.

"They want me to go back," he whispered.

He closed his eyes, tried to block out the awful noises and, with an awesome force of will, took his first step forward into the dungeon.

Instantly all the floating mouths gaped and screamed in an anguish of death-agony. Bolldhe's knees buckled in sudden nausea and terror, and it was only revulsion at the miasma of filth and gore upon the ground that kept him from collapsing upon it. Still the mouths screamed and, as Bolldhe lurched forward into a faltering run, he was sure he could discern the voices of his comrades in those screams. And still the reverberation of the cell block went on.

I'm too late! he gasped as he ran on. *I'm too late, and they're dying back there! Oh god, what must they be suffering?*

"Bolldhe, look!" Yorda screamed, her terror reaching its zenith, and seized hold of him by the arm, almost dragging him to the ground. He gasped at her inhuman strength, then looked up to see what she was wailing about.

Two cells, facing each other across the gangway. In one, the yak-kirtled man with the magma-red eyes, howling out to Bolldhe to take the flamberge and strike down the Rawgr. In the other, the open cell that contained Blackness, Death Without Hope, the Father of Drauglir. It was silent, as one might have expected from Death, for it knew it would win eventually, one way or another.

Two cells, two choices. Death to the Rawgr in one easy stroke, or Death to mankind, without light at the end—an easy way out?

But this was not the place to make decisions. Sprinting as fast as the abattoir floor would allow him, Bolldhe fled the dungeons.

The worst of the horror was mercifully behind them, but the shaking and rumbling continued as before. Indeed, if anything, it was getting worse, and it soon became clear that it was spreading through the entire soul-house.

They were in the corridor now, the plush passageway that spiralled its way round the mid-levels of the house. Unlike last time, however, when it had been a place of elegance and fine light, now it was in disorder, like the collapse of an empire. The lanterns, their silver tarnished to black, jangled violently upon their ceiling hooks or came flying off to smash into shards against window or floor. The books, those volumes of Bolldhe's life neatly stacked in endless lines, rattled upon their shelves in an extreme of agitation, or came tumbling down upon the glass strewn carpet, despairing souls hurling themselves from the burning tower.

The corridor itself appeared to be warping. The pillars writhed as though alive and in pain, and the fine glass windows exploded inward.

"This is where we parted company last time," Yorda reminded Bolldhe and, despite all the horror he had been through and the madness that continued still, he winced painfully at the memory. Without slowing, he reached down and grasped her hand tightly, for it seemed to him that he had never before had such need of company as he did now.

Together they ran, hand in hand, while all around them heaven and earth collided in a maelstrom of upheaval. Bolldhe hardly even paused when he came to the shelves that had been empty at the age of eight, and which were now contentedly, almost smugly, filled with a series of fat tomes that were bound in garish leather made from the blood-drenched and steaming skins of freshly sacrificed soldierlings.

He ran on, and could now see that he was drawing near to the corridor's end. A door wrought of chalcedony and jasper swung open ahead. Then suddenly one book flew out and struck him on the side of the head, and landed on the floor, *open*, its pages riffling violently in a demon-wind. He did not stop, but bounded over it in one leap and continued on to the door that awaited him. But as he turned to propel Yorda through before him, his eyes could not help being drawn back to that book, and what hovered above it now.

It did not seem to be a part of this place, somehow. It had the feel of something that had been thrust into the soul-house from outside. Yorda sensed it, and her eyes dilated with horror. Frantically she essayed to haul Bolldhe away. But he lingered for a moment, and stared in fascination.

Between its mad flutterings Bolldhe could make out that the picture on the cover was of his old comrade Gapp Radnar, an imploring expression fixed upon his visage. Above the book hovered a young girl, who now stilled the rippling pages with one hand, while in the other she held a lancet. Staring closer, despite the protestations of Yorda, Bolldhe saw that the pages she now held the book open at included a picture of some kind. An *ecorche*, a map of the human body, a three-dimensional cut-out diagram depicting the layers of anatomy—skin, musculature, organs, bones—each of which could be lifted or folded back to reveal what lay beneath. As the girl studied it, she brought her lancet to bear, and carefully began dissecting it. Screams of indescribable torment rose from the pages as she did so, and blood welled darkly and thickly upon the carpet. Yet the girl still bore an expression of innocence upon her face, a casual interest in the process that was unfolding beneath her scalpel.

Into Bolldhe's mind flashed an image, another message from outside: it was Scathur, at the top of the ziggurat, during the Siege. He was bent over something monstrous, too terrible to behold, and into this recumbent form he was pushing the flamberge, with the care and precision of a surgical instrument. Scathur looked up frantically at the approaching soldiers, but still did not cease in his work, pushing the sword in slowly, ever deeper—for Rawgr-slaying is no simple task. . . .

Bolldhe reeled. The corridor was gone, and he now stood on the roofed viewing platform of the tower, the soul-house's highest point. The stonework was splitting and exploding all around him, falling into the foggy oblivion that surrounded the crumbling edifice, and he knew just how little time there remained to him.

"A *decision*!" Yorda said to him from behind. "You must make one now!"

He stared down helplessly into the brown fog that still enveloped his soul-house. It was just as thick as before, except that this time he realized it was not fog, but a thick greasy smog, as though belching from a thurible. He glanced up at the shaking, riven ceiling, hoping in desperation that the rune Wodeman had spoken of with such consequence might still be there. But all he saw was a single eye staring back at him, even as it sank into the metal teeth of a meat grinder. . . .

("... *maybe the important point is your refusal to look at it* ..."
"*I'm a stubborn, arrogant sod* ...")

The gargoyles came skittering up the outside walls of the brass tower from their places above the gatehouse, squealing in fear as they dodged the chunks falling from the viewing platform. Finally gaining the top, they vaulted up onto the last remaining balustrade, and glared at Bolldhe. Three of them came in further, one perching upon his left shoulder, one on his right, and the third squatting before him with an expectant look on its stony face. As before, each bore the likeness of his quest-mates, though now injured and disfigured, spoiled almost to the point of ruination.

In the one that resembled Methuselech, all Bolldhe could see was a vision, an image of the soul of Mauglad Yrkeshta flitting about among the mounds of slain in the Chamber, trying desperately to find a new host to possess.

The hefty, blank-faced gargoyle was the Peladane. That stony plainness it possessed spoke clearer than any words. It said: *Hate Thine Enemy as He Hateth Thee.* Kill without mercy, without thought, for only an idiot stands still while under attack.

And behind him an entire host of souls exhorted: "Do as your leader tells you, Bolldhe. We made you what you are, and what you will always be: a Peladane!"

Even Paulus, that mercenary to the Peladanes, and Kuthy the ex-Peladane, joined in this chorus. But what were those two, Bolldhe wondered, other than future reflections of what he would be himself, one day?

His eyes flitted past the gargoyle of young Radnar, to land upon Finwald. The crumbled remains of this simulacrum, which now adorned Bolldhe's left shoulder, were little more than a heap of gravel, and yet it spoke. Though the words were no more enlightening than the crunching of old stone, they seemed to echo the same sentiment as the Peladane and his followers.

But you failed us, Finwald, Bolldhe thought. *You failed us all utterly— betrayed us even after dragging us all the way here. How much does* your *opinion count for?*

With one hand, Bolldhe brushed the pile of gravel off his shoulder and onto the ground.

Of them all, only Appa had ever rejected the sword outright. *"Nothing good can be achieved by it, Bolldhe,"* it now whispered into his ear from its position on his right shoulder. *"You of all people should know that. Just think what those Peladanes did to you back then, of the burden they loaded you with—one that you carry with you to this day."*

"But, downstairs, didn't your own god just tell me to use the sword? To take the flamberge and strike the Rawgr?"

The Appa-gargoyle hesitated a second, then shook its stony head. *"Forget what's in this crumbling ruin. Forget what you've seen in here. Your journey is not inside this place, but out there! Bring down those walls that enclose your courtyard and let people in. Live, Bolldhe, and love!"*

"Wonderful!" Bolldhe exclaimed. "But there's still the matter of the Rawgr and his horde. We're all about to be butchered! What d'you want me to do, go out and *love* them?"

Appa was struck dumb. Clueless as ever he had been on their journey.

In desperation, Bolldhe turned finally to the ragged little gargoyle that squatted before him. (The Gapp one still bounced up and down trying to be heard—but why would anyone want to listen to him?) The Wodeman-gargoyle, meanwhile, wore the hopeful yet slightly guileless expression of one who waits and, as usual, begged Bolldhe to look into himself.

"BUT I AM!" Bolldhe howled, and the roof of the tower was torn off and

borne away by the same gale that was demolishing the house, dragging its tatty clothesline along with it like the streamer of a kite. "I'm IN myself, and I *still* haven't got a clue!"

Then it struck him. He turned around and looked directly into the eyes of the one behind him. Yorda's eyes.

"YOU!" he cried above the increasing tempest. "You're me! So you tell me: what must I do?"

"YES!" squeaked the Appa-gargoyle, suddenly reanimated by hope. "Listen to her! She is the way! She is the path you should have taken so long ago! Behold your beloved; is she not fair beyond even your wildest dreams?"

Bolldhe paused and thought about this. His wildest dreams tended to involve situations like walking around a marketplace stark naked, and thus he had to concede that Yorda, though in truth a tad plain, was at least fairer than this prospect.

"So I kill Drauglir with love?" he asked incredulously.

A lull in the wind. A second's stilling of the quaking of the soul-house. Then Yorda fixed Bolldhe with a look forged of steel.

"No, Bolldhe," she replied coldly. "You stick him with your sword. It's the only way. You've known it all along."

Bolldhe was struck dumb. Throughout his journey with her, Yorda had not once proffered an opinion, had only ever asked him for his. But now that she had done so, Bolldhe found himself gaping in astonishment that she, of all of them, should be the one to say this.

"Decision! Decision!" the gargoyles shrieked. "Quickly! Now!"

"Quickly. Now," Yorda repeated softly, calmly. There was sympathy in her tone as well as strength. He began to quake in time with the shaking of his soul-house. Into his mind flashed images of his early travels, when at times he had wept with loneliness, and he had yearned to take that gentle hand that was offered him into his own. Yet, for all his desire to give in to her, still Bolldhe could not block out the faint smell of insincerity that lingered on her persuasive tongue. He had suffered so very much in his life, too much to allow anyone—even his soul-guide—to cash in on his miseries.

With a sickening lurch, Bolldhe felt the foundations of his soul-house give way. He was sick, so unbelievably sick of listening to others' opinions, so brainsore from being tugged this way and that, that he felt he might just go completely berserk. The tower, the entire house, was about to collapse, fall into the brown smog, and he along with it.

Then before him, the gargoyle that was Wodeman broke into a series of twittering chirps, and began cavorting in pain and alarm. It scrabbled madly at its face, until some of the stone flaked away, and Wodeman's face—Wodeman's real face—broke through.

Bolldhe!" he shouted. *"None of this matters! Just ask yourself what makes you so different!"*

Bolldhe stared at the cracking, splitting form of the gargoyle, and that vision he had experienced before entering Drauglir's vault came back to him.

Granite. That's what I am . . . Nothing to do with all this "metal" shit.

A scream went up from Yorda, and she lunged at the Wodeman-gargoyle. It tried to grab Bolldhe's ankle for support, but was too slow, too ponderous, and she kicked it full in the face, and sent it flying, howling, into the foggy oblivion.

She wheeled upon Bolldhe, and cold fire was in her eyes. "You think that Torca is any wiser than the others?" she screamed. "You believe him more than them? Let me show you just how honest he is! Let me show you where he *really* got that blood!"

She snapped her fingers and, for a brief few seconds, Bolldhe's eyes grew wide and hot and red as the sun. There before him was the scene from the storehouse out on the dock. There was the hedge-wizard, all crouched over and stinking; there was Yen, the Quiravian woman, pressed back against the wall in her fear; there were the malicious little rune tiles, openly laughing at Wodeman. And there, in the middle of it all, amid a widening pool of steaming blood, sagged the shuddering, leaking form of his only true friend in the world, his beloved Zhang.

". . . bastard . . ." was all he could manage.

Then the tower collapsed.

Down, down, through the cascade of falling masonry and shards of splintered brass they fell, through the freezing brown fog that tore the wind from their lungs, down toward an ocean-sized vortex of dark, seething gases and spinning fragments of soul-house. And as Bolldhe fell, so too did Yorda, with him.

Bolldhe!" she wailed. *"Save us! Save us all, for pity's sake!"*

Yorda, himself, his comrades—all dying at this moment. The old priests who had tried so hard and suffered so much just to help him . . . The funny little boy and his dog . . . Those crazy adventurers with their permanently pissed-off wyvern . . . And big, fat, laughing Wintus, he who might have been his friend . . . Now all lost in the melee of dead.

Bolldhe's mind reached out for them, even as he fell, struggled to call to mind a picture of them, of those he was defending, those he loved. But in spite of his efforts, there came nothing, save perhaps for the dim, skulking shadow of his own reflection.

"Strike the Rawgr, Bolldhe," Yorda called out to him, strangely calm. "Save those you love."

Still he fell.

"Strike the Rawgr!" she repeated, louder this time, and more insistent.

But still he would not. Still he fought his inner battle. The vortex reached out for him, expanded, howling louder than any sound he could ever imagine possible.

A pause. Then the voice of Yorda came, one final time, and the sound of it was harsh as dry twigs being snapped:

"Strike the fucking Rawgr, I said!"

The eyes of the Benne Nighe exploded before him, enveloped him, and into their crackling bonfire Bolldhe tumbled.

The tempest-roaring of worlds' collision, a world of souls screaming in torture all around, downward, ever downward, spiraling into the ripping and crushing mandibles of hell, and ever before him those hovering eyes, swelling in size as the hero dies, the eyes of Yorda—the Benne Nighe or whatever it was—pools of liquid fire, burning his heart out, an abomination of conflagration.

And *into* the Lake of Hell he plunged, every brain cell screaming in pain, stench of bubbling skin fouling the air, choke and gag on sulphur and smoke, searing gases blistering through nostrils and into collapsing lungs, great flames roaring around him, shriveling his flesh with unbelievable agony before his incredulous eyes that boiled, then burst from shattered sockets, skin charred to weeping blackness, bones splintered under the heat into fragments that suppurated with the marrow boiling up from within . . .

Bolldhe was in hell, and around him the company fell, chopped down, hacked into pieces, torn limb from limb, skin flayed from convulsing flesh, split by wire . . . and the eyes still laughed in victory before him.

In the last moment of most exigent need, all men cry out to their gods to deliver them from eternal damnation, some to their mothers, some to their sergeants, their comrades, their brothers . . .

. . . The ones they love.

But Bolldhe had no such bonds. No loyalties. No one. He was alone. A chip of granite tumbling all by itself through the void of space. It would not have occurred to him to ask for help, not even here on the point of his own total destruction. This he had to do alone, because for him there had never been any other way.

He had a flame of his own, a flame forged of steel, gripped fast in his hand. And those eyes—mocking, cruel, laughing at his torment, scorning his puniness, *gloating* over his failure—he had to plunge his sword into them, give release to his agony, his madness, his hatred, had to stab them, put them out, purge them with steel, hack, gouge and smite them with all the years of blackness in his heart behind each stroke, until they bled out their molten evil, and fled wailing into the abyss.

It was what *they* all wanted, what *they* all cried out for. Who would not have done the same? Who—unless it be a fragment of granite tumbling alone through the void of space?

But I am Bolldhe, he seethed, grinding his teeth in anguish. *I am Granite . . .*

". . . and I will not be directed!"

The words rolled like thunder from the summit of the ziggurat, and Bolldhe the Great, flamberge in both hands, swung the blade with all his insanity, away from the eyes, and straight down on to the altar stone by his feet.

At the first stroke of Flametongue upon the stone, the sword rang throughout the Chamber, but held. All movement within that place ground to a halt as each and every one there gaped in awe and held their breath; men, part-men, and parts of men, all stood stricken to the spot, waiting for whatever was to befall.

At the second stroke of Flametongue, still the sword held, but all movement beyond the Chamber, in and around the entirety of Vaagenfjord Maw, in every night-black hall and hellish crevice, was stilled; the bubbling magma, the gusts of snow, the waves upon the strand, even the crawling sea life that dwelt upon the ocean floor (that had never even heard of Drauglir, and would probably not have cared much even if they had, Rawgrs never having had much to do with fish in the first place).

Then Bolldhe, his soul-vision melting away around him, finally became aware of the sea of upturned faces, the audience below him, all around the zig-gurat and way beyond, that frozen congregation that had arranged themselves upon one side or another, and gathered here upon this day to witness the chance that would befall the world—and which still balanced upon a needle's point.

His vision focused upon Flametongue, that undulating serpent of metal that still shone with carnelian luster before his eyes, and yet held firm in his trembling grasp, intact, unblemished . . .

. . . As whole and flawless as when he had first held it in the silver mines.

They think it's all over, his stricken mind choked.

Then he brought it down a third and final time.

"It is now," he whispered, and Flametongue, the soul-jar that had con-tained the life force of Drauglir intact within its writhing case for five hundred years, exploded into a billion shards of violet and cobaltite brilliance.

The sarcophagus blew apart, Bolldhe was hurled backward through the air. And, amid the seething furor of coruscating light that broiled atop the ziggurat in a beacon of chrysoberyl, lapis lazuli and jacinth fire, the face of Yorda ap-peared. All coyness and cajolery were gone, replaced by a countenance of stunned incredulity and absolute incomprehension. Then, as the awful realiza-tion spread across those spectral features, the chimerical visage of Yorda dissi-pated, and transmogrified into its true form.

For one split second of inconceivable abomination too terrible for any of its beholders to suffer, the face of Drauglir finally appeared. It was the face of his uttermost undoing. His total despair. His last instant of existence.

Then, for a time in which no sound could endure, night became day, and an all consuming pulse of white light lanced through the eyeballs of all present, punched through the retina, and seared the brain beyond with its glaring in-tensity.

Cuna burst out into a shrieking, roaring thunderclap of unbelievable laugh-ter, and slapped his hands upon his celestial thighs in amazement.

Appa, blood-drenched and utterly spent, collapsed to the floor, his task, be-yond all hope, completed.

The ragged and battered Wodeman—in his gore-soaked wolfskin now re-sembling nothing more than fresh road-kill—fell upon his knees in blessed awe at his charge.

Gapp stared agog from beneath the sheltering arch of Schnorbitz's hind legs, believing (wrongly) that for the first time in his life, someone had actually *listened* to him.

And Mauglad Yrkeshta, with a tired but almost loving smile gracing his non-corporeal lips, blew out his candle, rolled over, and finally, gratefully, gave up the ghost.

The Breath of Life swept through the Chamber, a spring wind that carried blossoms' perfume across a winter landscape. It made no sound, it caused no sensation to the skin, and it carried no weight. But in its wake, the dead dropped, slumped to the floor without protest like string-cut marionettes. The Wire-Faces fled before it, howling in utter despair as they went. And the Chil-dren of the Keep, meeting it in their headlong stampede toward the Chamber, simply unraveled into a hundred slices of wriggling Rawgr meat.

Out of the Chamber of Drauglir it issued, and surged through every pas-sageway, every hall and every pit of Ymla-Myrrdhain, out through Smaulka-Degernerth, the Moghul, and into each and every last crevice of Vaagenfjord Maw, from the depths of Gapp's sea cave to the very pinnacle of Ravenscairn.

And, as it poured out over all the lands, the weight of it was ultimately felt by everyone, for in its momentum it turned the Scales of Good and Evil, and slewed the entire world around upon its axis.

17

Despair

So the last flickering gasps of Rawgr-fire sputtered, and died, and the reeking smog of the thuribles dissipated, both purged from the Chamber by the Breath of Life. But, in one corner high up among the corbels that adorned the upper walls, a new fire suddenly flared. It was the tiniest, most delicate flame of blue and yellow, one that sprang into life within a warm and fragrant bouquet of phosphorous smoke, and wavered daintily, uncertainly. In giant hands it was held, cupped protectively to shield it from the troubled currents of the astral wind. Carefully but without difficulty, these hands guided it toward the end of a white tube of aromatic, dried herbs, and held it there.

In the glow of the exquisitely swaying flame, Cuna's eyes were now the calm red of a westering sun. Pale now, their fire was diluted by the cool tide of approaching darkness, and within them the early stars sparkled clearly. He drew in a long, long drag of smoke, held it for a moment, then let it drift out of nose, mouth and ears in the most protracted and blissful exhalation of equanimity and contentment he had ever experienced.

"Oh . . . *man*, I needed that . . ." Cuna rasped in repletion, and, handing the roll-up languidly to the Syr at his side, flicked the forgotten match, with its tiny flame, down into the abyss of darkness below.

They were reclining at their ease on the smooth curve of cool marble that formed the snout of a giant idol of Drauglir, idly regarding the movements of little humans scurrying about upon the cold mounds of putrefying battle detritus below.

"Not many left, are there?" Time noted as he handed the roll-up back.

Cuna nodded, took another puff, and mouthed the word "No" while blowing a smoke ring. "Indeed, it's a terrible thing, war," he concurred.

"But you won't be losing too much sleep tonight, I'd guess."

Cuna put his hands behind his head and stretched out upon their marble perch. His smile was broad and carefree. "I have won the game, yes. I have triumphed over Olchor. But still I will not gloat. There will, after all, be other times, other battles, in which I may not be as . . . *staggeringly successful* as I am today." He chuckled nevertheless, and tapped ash onto the idol's nose.

Time nodded acknowledgment in what was almost a bow. "Enjoy your moment, Lord Cuna," the Skela replied without rancor. "You have earned it. I must admit that none of us believed your plan had any hope of success. Bolldhe is, after all, nothing more than an ordinary man."

"Don't be so quick to judge ordinary men. After all, some of the greatest deeds are achieved by their like. Just because a thing is cheap, coarse and plentiful doesn't mean it's of essentially low value. Bolldhe has qualities many men possess—"

"He's psychotic."

"—but never so much, and in such a unique combination. Only one such as he could have resisted the temptation to stab out those taunting eyes . . . He was in hell, yet *still* he refused to be manipulated. He remained Bolldhe right to the end."

"He is uniquely psychotic, then?"

Cuna hesitated. "Well, maybe. But it is still fortunate for me that he is the way he is. For without Bolldhe we would all be in a very bad place right now."

"And you foresaw all this in him right back then, before he had even reached Nordwas?"

"I cannot foresee *all*. Let's just say that I saw his potential. Don't forget, there was always the matter of his unreliability; yet that was one of the things that made him Bolldhe. This whole business could have swayed either way, at any time. But especially at the end."

"And that was your *best* plan?"

"That was my only plan."

"But you are a god?"

"Yes, but only an *ordinary* god."

"An ordinary god," Time echoed. "And how does this ordinary god estimate his servants on this day? Did they perform to his satisfaction?"

"Appa couldn't have done better," Cuna pronounced, "for one of his age. He wavered not once, and he has been true to me all along. I look forward to meeting that one in person."

"I doubt you'll have long to wait. Anyway, he did nothing. He was clueless right to the end."

"Yet still he endeavored to direct Bolldhe right to the end, and we all know how much Bolldhe resists being directed. And as for the renegade priest, well, I believe he got what he deserved."

"Yet he lives."

"If you can call that living. . . ."

Cuna grasped the string of eyeballs that hung from his staff, and the lantern atop it shone forth a beam of light from a different spectrum. Thus equipped, he projected his vision through the darkness and the great thicknesses of stone that lay between him and the tattered, ruined, retching figure that ran on and on and on through the endless labyrinth of Smaulka-Degernerth, wailing in damnation.

"I would rather be dead," Cuna shuddered. "And so would he. He knows he'll no more be able to leave this place than the ones who died here. But unlike them, Finwald will be aware of his ruin."

"Yet others in the past, who were guilty of a lesser apostasy than his, you have treated somewhat more harshly," Time pointed out.

Cuna shook his head. "Finwald was no apostate, for he never turned against me. Not really. He just lost the way, became a little deluded. He was never—still is not—evil."

"He essayed to revive the hell-hound."

Cuna shrugged. "He had his reasons. But, like I say, he was not evil. No, the only apostate here was that one down there." He waved a hand toward the lower-half remnant of Brother Number One, which had finally stopped kicking—if not twitching.

"Oswiu?"

"No, not Oswiu, damned blasphemer though he was. I'm sure he is now someplace where he should be."

"You mean Mauglad, then. Your Plan B?"

Cuna's red eyes half-lidded themselves, his mood all of a sudden not quite so comfortable. "Only a poor general goes into battle with no backup plan," he insisted. "And some words I may have used back there were said purely in the heat of the moment—"

"Really?"

"Yes, and they do not in any way reflect my satisfaction regarding the final outcome."

"Words like: 'Kill Bolldhe,' for example?"

But Cuna would not be drawn. He had won, and that was all that mattered.

"A neuropath, a non-communicant, a necromancer and a necrophile," Time reflected. "You really do pick them, don't you?"

Cuna laughed, before drawing the last smoke from his aromatic roll-up.

The Syr rose and made as if to depart. But, just before he did so, he turned back to the still reclining figure below him. "And Odf?" he asked, "what of him? Was he not proved the greatest of them all? The noblest of the noble? The only true hero of the quest?"

Cuna looked up blankly.

"Odf?" Time reminded him. "*Uglekort?*"

Still blank.

"Paulus!"

"Oh, him!" Cuna said finally. "Yes, I suppose you're right. Yes. Yes, indeed, he was. Absolutely. In fact, he proved to be so much more than the others, in the end. And, now I come to think about it, probably more than any who have ever done battle against Drauglir—even those champions of old."

Time cocked his head inquiringly.

"For *they* got what they wanted, those lionhearts. They knew their actions would buy them immortality, and among their own people their praises would be sung forever more. Ha! They were doing no more than was expected of them—toeing the military line. But Odf Ugle-thing, he knew he'd get no such reward. Yet still he did it, even knowing it meant him being misunderstood by all, and dying alone, forever reviled . . ."

As he trailed off, Time wondered if he could not perceive a rare star-gleam of pensiveness in Cuna's eyes.

"So, you'll embrace his soul, then?"

Cuna regarded the Syr curiously. "Not likely," he laughed. "He was never one of mine. Sod him."

And with that, he stubbed out the butt of his roll-up in Drauglir's marble eye and, together with the Syr, began to fade.

Just before they all disappeared entirely, Fate grudgingly slapped a small pouch of coins into the open, outstretched palm of Chance—who said naught, merely gloated, and vanished from sight.

"It was eerie, I can tell you . . . first . . . you started chopping that stone . . . just *exploded* into a thousand shards . . . then that complete silence . . ."

A growing, stabbing, throbbing pain—occupying every square inch of his back. On his front, a sensation of sandscraped rawness, almost as though from prolonged exposure to the sun or wind. Down his right arm, a numbness that had grown into pain also. Coating his chin, the cold slime of his own spittle.

And that smell, so potent that it had a presence almost physical, a weight of its own. It was like being smothered beneath the cold and damp embalming shrouds of the pestilential dead.

He felt he would never be able to awaken, to open his eyes, or even breathe properly, ever again. Too much pain, too much suffering, to recover from this time.

I'm dead, aren't I? he thought. *I must be.*

Somebody was pulling at him. Then trying to pull a weight off him. Trying to revive him. He attempted to find sleep again, or oblivion or, better still, death.

The voice went on, as familiar as it was irritating:

". . . you'd have expected something . . . well, I don't know . . . something a little more dramatic . . . But, no, he was just destroyed. *You* destroyed him . . . and then just that silence, that terrible, eerie silence . . . I say, are you listening to a word I'm saying?"

He managed to stir. He managed to prise open an eye. But the red glow, though dim, reminded him of blood, and he felt he would be violently sick.

"Oy, Bolldhe, d'you think you could shift yourself sometime? It's not that easy hauling your arse about, me having only one arm, you know!"

Bolldhe finally awoke. The light was poor, tenebrous, almost nonexistent. It seemed to come from more than one source, and it shifted about slowly. Above him swam the indistinct face of . . . *Elfswith?* . . . peering at him with a puzzled expression. There was indeed silence, a hushed stillness that rang hollowly in his ears after the insane clamor of the battle, yet underlain by muted and disembodied moans from the darkness.

His head lolled painfully to one side, but then something hard jabbed into his eye. He flinched back with a grunt, then peered closely at it, trying to identify it through the gloom.

It was a foot that protruded upward from the pile of dead, a bare foot with the texture of withered leather, hardened by death and time into something resembling a petrified tree branch. The nail of the big toe, long and twisted as a cracked and rusted bezel, had nearly punctured Bolldhe's eyeball.

He swung his head round to the other side in disgust, only to find Englarielle staring back at him.

Bolldhe did not flinch this time, but his eyes narrowed in curiosity. Though one of the Vetter's ears was plastered flat over much of his face like an oil-drenched rag, covering one eye, the other eye was wide open, and held Bolldhe in its fixed and strangely unfathomable gaze. Englarielle appeared like a child that sleeps open eyed, with a trace of confusion in its regard. But even in this light Bolldhe could discern how that same eye was clouded, opaque, and would never move again. And it was upside down. The head was upside down. And it finished at the neck.

Bolldhe remembered. At last he remembered. Remembered it all, every little bit: the killing, the horror, his engram, *his vision* . . . And his body, with mind and soul, convulsed, contracted in upon itself like a salted slug, in an agony of emptiness and despair that he knew could never end.

The pivots of the Scales need oiling if they are to move, and blood is such a plentiful lubricant. Bolldhe finally raised his eyes, looked past Elfswith, and beheld Gehenna—hell itself. The ziggurat now was a terraced hill, trickling with crimson that from multitudinous sources did spill, oozing down the marble steps in slow cascade. Over the grisly surface of this hecatomb, small flames hovered; not the gas-fed candles of dead men's souls, nor the lure of hungry will-o'-the wisps, but the dull, spitting flames of torches held high by the few who still breathed. Their smoke sputtered in oily reminiscence of the thuribles, their light casting a blood-corona over the black shades that bore them: corpse-mongers that drifted like salvage-hunters over worm-ridden refuse dumps.

Salvage-hunters: Bolldhe recalled the memory of them vividly. A city in the far east, a sprawling cesspool of a place with outskirts that reeked of destitution and disease; young mothers, tiny children, age-twisted crones, all roaming over the mounds of decay, searching for any mean thing that might prove of some value, however wretched; bent almost double, coughing and retching in the greasy smog that held back dawn's pale gleam.

Here now, too, the salvage-hunters wandered. Cold. Limp. Drenched. Numbed by so much death. Boots dragging through sucking mire. About the smoking hills of slain they went, scanning the corpses for movement, for old friends. The grinding of teeth; the occasional pop of escaping gas; the hushed voices of the soul-robbed, reluctant to be heard.

"Come on, Bolldhe, get up if you can. We're going soon . . ."

He heard the words of the half-Huldre, though they sounded muffled, as if he was hearing them from beneath a turf-piled coffin lid. Far-off—and irrelevant. They might take him with them, he knew, but what would be the point? Even if he could drag his old bones out into the open air, would that pallid excuse for a sun warm even the most meager flicker of life back into his soulless flesh?

". . . once we've found everybody."

Every. Body. Had he been able, Bolldhe would have laughed. They might have found his body, but his soul was dead, and would remain in this pit forever.

"Come *on,* Bolldhe!" Elfswith was losing patience. "We're *leaving!* You've won already. What are you waiting for?"

"Won?" What triumph was this? He was in hell! Broken flesh and crucified soul languishing still in the darkest bowels of this cursed earth. Sinking into the mounds of the slaughtered, embalmed in shrouds of dead skin and sarcophagus-oil, the flesh-eating acids of corrosion that from this hill of sacrifice did pour . . .

". . . This *what* that from the *what* did *what?*" Elfswith piped. "You useless prat! Get up now, or I'll stick you myself!"

Bolldhe's attention swung back to the little man above him. Elfswith's manner was fragile but light, and his coat the bleached-out white of a snow hare.

"Your arm . . . ?" Bolldhe managed, as a scrap of wonder penetrated a small way through his insensibility.

Elfswith did not follow Bolldhe's stare down to the newly frayed hem that Scathur had so impolitely tailored onto his coat.

"Don't worry about it," he said dismissively. "It'll grow back eventually. I'm just annoyed about losing the sleeve—there were some good little pockets on that one."

Bolldhe forced himself to sit up in a more or less vertical position. Parts of him still refused the order to stand, or move, as if they preferred the rigor of death to the vigor of breath. But eventually he coaxed himself upright, and, both supporting and supported by the half-Huldre, wandered, like the corpse-mongers, over the dead-mounds.

Bolldhe spotted the first survivors almost immediately. Elfswith tapped him on the arm, and pointed out the two bent and cloaked figures that scoured the wreckage near the ruins of the blasted crypt.

"Your religious friends," Elfswith murmured. "Shall I call them?"

As Appa and Wodeman combed through the layers of dead, torch in hand and their faces masked against the foulness, they appeared to Bolldhe like pall-bearers or grave robbers, he was not sure which. They had not noticed him yet, and, drawing Elfswith aside, Bolldhe headed off in the opposite direction. He had nothing at all to say to those two up there, and absolutely did not want them saying anything to him.

The next one he came upon was Eorcenwold. The thief-sergeant was still standing, but Bolldhe perceived in his slumped mien a measure of the despair he himself was suffering, and as he drew closer saw that those big eyes were coffin-lidded, and they turned away from him and Elfswith as they approached.

Though Chance had collected the coins of his wager with Fate, some of them had fallen through his fingers; not into the wish fountain, but rather carelessly upon the eyelids of those who would never leave here. Eorcenwold had lost over half his company, including all three of his siblings. He could find only scattered lumps of Cuthwulf, so far. And, though he could scarcely believe it, he definitely remembered seeing Klijjver kill Oswiu. Amid the clenching and shaking that manifested his bewildered shock, he cast the odd murderous glance towards the herd-giant he had once called friend. Even with the insanity prevailing back then, he could not fathom it: the Tusse had picked out his brother, lumbered over to him, and deliberately and repeatedly sledge-hammered his head into nonexistence.

But what was hardest for Eorcenwold to understand was why he himself had taken off the back of his dear sister Aelldryc's head with his morning star. Sightlessly, her sunken eyes gazed upward from where she lay, staring right through him, forever through him, and his mouth mumbled words too clotted for any to hear.

Eventually he would move. Eventually the black fog of his mind would thin just enough for him to depart this place, and leave behind not only those dearest to him, but his dream of riches too. And, when eventually he felt the fresh tang of salt air upon his face once more, he would think to honor those of his band who had emerged into daylight with him.

Especially Flekki, Grini, and Cerddu-Sungnir, for they, together with their leader, had succeeded in despatching the Darkangel Scathur. They were the Scathur-Slayer-Brotherhood, *Rawgr-slayers!* That, at least, had to count for something.

For the moment, however, those heroic three were still too preoccupied with picking through the fallen to feel much pride. For Cerddu-Sungnir this was only a half-hearted task; the half-Grell had sustained deep gashes to his torso, and was coughing blood. He could not manage to stand for long, and when he did, he was almost doubled over with pain. At length he gave up the search, and just stayed close to his leader, muttering.

Flekki was in a lighter mood. The River-Hauger had managed to stay out of the thick of the fighting, preferring instead to send her baneful little chakrams out into the enemy from a distance. More sprightly than most, she had returned to the fire pit, and had succeeded in dragging out the gibbering and spluttering wreck of Brecca. Staring gleefully into the wide and rheumy eyes of the Stone-Hauger (who still could not believe it was all over, and even less that he had survived) she sang:

"So, during the Great Vaagenfjord War, Daddy, what did you do?"
"Oh, I was busy cacking myself, hiding up the flue."

Grini, too, went off on his own. Needing no torch, the Boggart used his nose to sniff out those who had been closest to him. It did not therefore take him long to locate the still and leaking form of Khurghan, facedown in a pool of his own vomit, his back ripped open like a slashed bolster. The Boggart regarded his former leash-holder oddly, sniffed around him a little, and pawed at his broken form. After a while, he stopped whimpering: he had found the Polg's double dagger, the Haladie of Returning. With a casual expression, he slipped it into his hemp belt, cocked his hind leg over Khurghan's corpse, relieved himself, then hopped away to inspect his new treasure.

Of the remaining Tyvenborgers, Hlessi and Raedgifu would never be found. But there remained one thief that Bolldhe still desired to track down. So he trudged through the dead, the living, and those in-between, searching and sifting. For the moment, as for the others, there was nothing else better to do.

Two Vetters limped toward him, propping each other up. One, stockier than the norm, was gasping rather oddly, and the other—*Radkin?*—was dead silent. They passed Bolldhe without even noticing him, as if he were invisible, and went on their way, wherever that led.

So few, Bolldhe wondered. *So very few! Surely more than this survived?*

But they had not. Only five Vetters still lived. *Five!* Out of the forty-six that had entered the Chamber! And of the Cervulice there remained but seven. Eventually, these surviving twelve came together and gathered round the remains of their fallen leader. In a circle, they closed ranks, and were silent.

There was not enough of Engliarelle left to bear back to the high, green karsts of their beloved Cyne-Tregva, but they would take at least his helm, his gyag-axe and his war bola. Of the twelve, however, it appeared likely that a further three at least would not survive their injuries long enough to be dragged out of the Maw, never mind survive the harsh journey home.

Everywhere he looked, he saw death. Bolldhe was in a land of ghosts. In every new encounter, he would stare into the eyes of these lifeless husks whose eyes had not yet been closed. Did he expect to learn something from them, feel a sameness perhaps? See the shards of his broken soul reflected in their despair?

A voice intruded upon his wretched ruminations. Bolldhe looked up to see the silhouette of a man sitting atop a promontory of carcasses . . . and eating?

"You found him, then," the figure commented between mouthfuls.

"Just over there," Elfswith replied to his partner, and grinned up at Bolldhe.

Kuthy, at his repose, was watching Ceawlin down at the base of the ziggurat. The wyvern was limping around, covered in a lattice of gashes, and dragging her tail with its empty poison-sac behind her, but she was persistent in her search. Like a gigantic, red-beaked stork she waded through the morass of corpses, her head turning this way and that upon that serpentine neck as she sought to finish the task she had started on the Oghain.

Kuthy seemed happy to leave her to it. He did not look particularly interested in joining the search, preferring instead to rest his tired and aching body, and break open his rations. His terrible hair secret—had anyone even noticed it earlier?—was well covered up again, for he had succeeded in finding his hat earlier. It had lain quivering upon the floor amid a pile of the dead, its appendages wrapped over its crown like a frightened kitten covering its head against a storm.

Bolldhe glanced at Elfswith, and saw how he was regarding his friend Kuthy in a way that Bolldhe had not seen before. There was a light in the little man's yellow eyes that could almost have been affection.

"Normally he's such a shit," he said suddenly.

Bolldhe stopped. "What?" he asked.

"Callous, scornful, childish—the meanest, least praiseworthy of men. But sometimes, just sometimes, when you least expect it, he ups and does something so extraordinary, so dazzling, that you're once again reminded of who the Tivor is, and why he actually *is* so praiseworthy."

Cupping his hand over the cavity where his arm used to join, the bard, without a further word, strode away from Bolldhe and climbed up toward his partner.

Not at all sharing the half-Huldre's admiration, Bolldhe continued on his way. That man could trample over the battlefield like a god of death, breaking the heads of enemies and brothers alike, ears stone-deaf to their bleating, his veins flowing with limestone, his eyes like flint—*the sharpest eyes, the dullest soul*—and still, at the end of it all, blithely chew with relish upon skewered meats, sitting atop piles of men who cried out, likewise skewered. Perhaps, like Bolldhe, too much blood had tattooed crimson upon his eyes, so meant little anymore. Indeed, Bolldhe wondered whether he should pity him or envy him.

Other sights he saw that made him turn away, and sounds he heard that he would rather not have: Hwald, stricken mortally, lying in spasming dementia in the cradling arms of his mate, who could not hold back the tears; the low, quivering moan of Finan that reverberated around the Chamber like the sirens of war's ending; by the Parandus's side, Schnorbitz panting heavily and heaving on the foulness he had swallowed, but his forepaw laid comfortingly across Hwald's neck.

And there too, beyond all probability still among the living, was Gapp Radnar. One arm was slung around the shoulders of Finan, while his other hand gripped the forest hound's mane, as if the young fellow were holding onto life itself. At the approach of Bolldhe, he turned and looked up and, to Bolldhe's amazement, he smiled. His mask of dried blood cracked as he did so, and beauty of a kind flowered in his eyes.

Gapp opened his mouth to speak and, though the words were slurred and difficult to make out, Bolldhe's heart suddenly lurched to hear the humanity still in that voice, though sounding so ragged and coarse.

"Heard me, den? Heard wa' I zedd? Mm?"

Gapp broke into a fit of coughing, then continued. "Thort yu cou'nnt eer me, but yu god'm messidge, uh?"

Bolldhe did not have a clue what he was going on about. But for once, for the first occasion in all the time he had known this boy, he felt a touch of curiosity in what he was talking about. Something in the back of his mind warned him that the lad was about to divulge something of import. But, just as Bolldhe was about to ask, something flickered in the corner of his eye that distracted him.

It was a dull gleam, a meager reflection of the flames from a passing thief's torch, coming from somewhere out there in the dark morass of piled bodies beyond the ziggurat. It could have glinted from any piece of metal—a weapon, armor, even one of the discarded thuribles—but what tapped softly upon the shoulder of Bolldhe's inner awareness was the fact that this gleam held within it the faintest shade of *blue. . . .*

Oh no . . . please no . . .

Bolldhe did not think it possible for him to feel any more grief, but as he picked his way over the groaning mass to where that small piece of metal lay, a new sorrow opened in him. It was the sorrow of loneliness and, with it, the sharp pang of loss.

He carefully removed the gobbets of flesh from around the protruding tengriite vambrace that had caught his eye. He could see that these were not the Peladane's own flesh, but rather the pieces of his foe that Wintus had scattered about in his scything charge. And though he worked with the dispassionate deliberation of an abattoir hand, the curtain walls of his soul had been demolished and, for the first time since he could remember, Bolldhe openly cried out for that rarest of things in the world—a friend.

Gapp was by his side now, as together they hauled out the body of the fallen warrior. To their great astonishment, Nibulus, though slack and stinking, still lived. He was barely conscious and was covered in blood, either coughed up from his insides, or from the wounds on his outside, or from the countless others he had fought. But he was alive.

So their salvaging finished, and now there was nothing more to be done, no reason to tarry any longer, and they would be gone as swiftly as they might. For though the perpetual winter of Melhus awaited them outside, in here there was a far greater chill, and one that could not be thawed by any fire. All of them now yearned for the golden light of the early autumn that was unfolding without them in distant homelands, longed for the warmth of ember-glow in hearths that as yet lay cold, hearths where mice now played.

All those who had been pulled from the mound alive, they took with them. All those who lay dead, they simply left there. Of wounded Wire-Faces, there were but a few, for even after grossest injury those subhuman fanatics had fought on, and had had to be dispatched properly. The only ones the company ignored were either already dead or almost so. Though noticing here and there the moth wing's fluttering of eyelids, a twitch here, a sigh there, these they left behind, reluctant to deny them their last chance to savor the full knowledge of defeat and their slow, despairing dwindle into extinction.

Only one Ogha had strength enough to move. Bolldhe felt his cloak suddenly gripped by broken and trembling fingers, and looked down into the pleading face that stared up at him. Its face wires had been severed, and the spellbinding wrought by the Rawgr-captain appeared to be diminishing in its eyes. But Bolldhe merely shook his head, stood upon its throat, and then, after all trace of life had vanished, walked away.

There would be no mourning for the Wire-Faces.

As the company made their slow and painful way over the field of fallen, only one voice was raised.

[*"We brought hell to Hell!"*]

Wintus ranted, still battle-mazed and Gwyllch-glamored as he quoted from the book he clasped in his bloodied hands.

[*"We bedeviled the devils, struck them down before they could wonder, and we print now our signatures in boot-tread into their red, waxen foulness . . ."*]

Gapp gently led him out by the arm, and shook his head as the man continued his oration to heedless ears. Just words, quotations from a dead idiot, they meant nothing, did not apply. Only Bolldhe—though he himself still had little understanding of the how and the why—only *he* had destroyed Drauglir. Only to *him* did the words apply. Just as when he was eight years old, he alone of them understood that humans are the only ones who can teach Rawgrs what it is to be *evil*.

Appa and Wodeman finally tore off the makeshift masks they had wrapped about their mouths and noses, because they had at last caught sight of Bolldhe. But they did not approach him yet, because they could sense even from a distance just how loath he was to encounter them at that moment.

In any case, thought Wodeman, *it would not do for me to be seen like this.*

He had not only masked his face because of the stench of the dead, but also to hide a most bizarre blemish that had afflicted him. He could not fathom it, no matter how hard he tried. For not once during all the hammering received in battle could he remember getting kicked in the face. There had, however, been that soul-shaking blow to his head that had seemingly come out of absolutely nowhere, just seconds before Bolldhe had reemerged from the vault and brought down the flamberge. But, whatever had caused it, the shaman now sported a huge, smarting blister that covered the entire right side of his face. A footprint, it appeared, in the shape of a cloven hoof.

The Mark of Drauglir, he laughed nervously to himself, and he held his stony silence.

Wordlessly they departed the Chamber of Drauglir, and none would look upon his fellows as they went. They did not know why, but perhaps it was because, blood-masked, stained and ashamed, they all now secretly bore the Mark of Drauglir upon their faces.

As for the Slayer of Drauglir, he bore the most livid mark of all. His, however, was not caused by Drauglir alone, but also by the last of the Tyvenborgers that he had been trying so hard to find back there. For, moments before leaving, Bolldhe had finally come upon her body, where she had fallen—where he had planted her.

In the eyes of Dolen Catscaul, all he could see as he stared into their cold pools was the blackness of reproach, red-rimmed with her heart's deluge. A new, bright red mouth had he opened in her head, but her original, greyer lips kissed the stiff, cold hand of the dead man who had fallen across her. The six fingers of one hand stretched out before her as if reaching for a lover, though they intertwined with empty air only.

Then Bolldhe had wept. In a torrent of tears he had broken down, fallen to his knees, and sobbed so hard that he truly believed he would never stop. Long moments passed before he was able to stand again. But even now as he wandered after the others from the Chamber, his chest felt wounded from the ugly empty heaving that had continued long after his tears had run dry.

They trudged down the long, lofty passageway of tusk-buttressed ironrock, and left behind them forever the undercroft and its awful contents. The last susurrations of the dying reached out after them, still hoping in vain for some pity, some deliverance. But soon even these ghost-whisperings faded, and the only utterances to be heard were their own: the labored breathing, the whimpers of pain, the odd furtive disgorgement of vomit. These mean sounds were the only music to accompany the march of the triumphant from the Chamber of Drauglir.

Wordlessly the company continued down the passageways and stairwells of Ymla-Myrrdhain, echoing faintly still with the vestigial wailing of the fleeing Wire-Faces. Eventually they came out into the wider spaces preceding the tunnel of Lubang-Nagar, and here, were dismayed to see six shapes suddenly rear out of the shadows and move toward them. Too weary to even feel fear anymore, the survivors could only grip their weapons in readiness, and continue stumbling toward the newcomers.

But an uncertainty in the bearing of these six betrayed them for who they were, even before lamplight could reach them. It was the four Vetters and two Cervulice that had stayed behind after being wounded in the earlier skirmish with the Tyvenborgers.

Weapons were instantly lowered, heartbeats were stilled, and they finally embraced their kin. But it was not the sort of reunion any had expected, for they embraced oddly, stiffly, with a confusion of emotions in their eyes. Chief among these was the fear crouching darkly behind the brittle residue of their splintered courage. The six had waited for what had seemed like a purgatorial stretch of time in this limbo of darkness; hidden in terror as the army of hell had—mere yards from their hiding place—surged past them on their way to battle.

With this fear, also, came disbelief that so few had returned; dismay at their horrendous wounds; and a strange, numbing disorientation when it gradually sunk in that Englarielle would not be coming with them.

Bolldhe regarded them bitterly. He longed to hold them to him, to apologize for what had been done to them, to say something that might assuage the misery in their souls. But all that came to mind was: *Thanks for the help, lads, but we won't be needing you anymore.*

They had come to the end of Lubang-Nagar, and the start of that long and infernal trek through the Hall of Fire.

"Elfswith," Appa inquired with a hint of pleading in his voice, "how many can that bird of yours carry at one time?"

The bard's yellow eyes flicked over the sorry group of survivors as they huddled in the moving shadows of the tunnel. "None of those deer-beast types, that's for sure," he replied. "And those two," he added, indicating with his eyes the Vetters who had been severely wounded in the Chamber, "might as well give up here and now. They'll never leave this island, even if they do get out of the Maw."

The seethe of gases and the flow of magma could be heard as a dark rumor from outside. Inside, the words of the bard fell flat as molten lead.

"We can take four Vetters, as well as ourselves," Elfswith conceded finally. "All right, Ceawlin?"

The wyvern's head drooped almost to the ground, but she nodded wearily.

"Only up to the end of this fire cavern," Elfswith added firmly. "After that, they can walk. Ceawlin's hurt badly, and I'm not having her ferry the lot of you out of here."

"Better make it just two Vetters, in that case," Kuthy suggested. "That way Nibulus can hop on too, and guide them out from there onward. He knows the way . . . if he can keep his head together that long."

They appraised the silent Peladane. Like for a berserker after the battle frenzy has ebbed, Nibulus's wounds were finally sobering him up. Without a word, he nodded dully.

"You're not coming back, then?" Gapp gaped. "You're just going to bugger off and leave us to walk through this fire?"

Elfswith and Kuthy looked at each other inquiringly, then at Ceawlin. A moment later, Elfswith turned back to the company. "The Cervulice and Parandus will have to walk; but Ceawlin'll come back for one more load—possibly two, if she feels up to it. But not *those* lot." He nodded toward the thieves. "They can walk the whole way."

No one was in the mood to argue. A minute later, Ceawlin spread her wings and lifted off, bearing with difficulty her two friends, Nibulus, and a pair of clumsily splayed Vetters. Awkwardly she flew out of the cooler shade of Lubang-Nagar, and disappeared into the white glow of Smaulka-Degernerth.

The remaining fugitives stared after her, but said nothing.

After a short while, Gapp and some of the Tregvans stirred. "We're off," the boy informed Bolldhe and the others of his party. He indicated Schnorbitz, Finan, Ted and Radkin. Though Finan was sorely hurt, he reckoned he had strength enough in him to bear the two Vetters. The two Cervulice who had been shot in the pillar-hall and the seven that had survived the battle would plod after them. Even the Cervulus who was mortally wounded had decided to try to follow them; it would not save him, he knew, but he was determined to breathe free air once more before he died, rather than rot down here all alone. None of them, however, was in a fit state to bear riders; the Vetters would therefore remain here with the humans until such time as the wyvern might return.

Bolldhe gazed down at Gapp. The boy seemed to be just a mass of pain held together by cuts and bruises, appearing even smaller than usual. Nevertheless, he seemed to be bearing up, and clearly he and the ragtag remainder of the Cynen's army were sticking together. Bolldhe could tell by the look on his face that Gapp wanted to say something: something pertinent, something properly adult. Instead, he clung on to his Parandus with one hand, his dog with the other, his control with great difficulty, and all he could manage was:

". . . I'd just like to go home now, please."

Bolldhe shrugged. "Just follow the ledge. There's only one way. We can meet up at the end, where it's cooler, and guide you out."

So they left. Gapp on Schnorbitz, the Vetters upon Finan, all trying to get through their ordeal as quickly as possible. Without further delay, the Cervulice followed them out, though at a slower pace.

And after these went the six remaining thieves, keeping, as usual, a respectful distance.

With just the last remaining Vetters for company now, Bolldhe, Appa and Wodeman waited in the tunnel. They sat upon the floor, crouching below the worst of the fumes, and wedged themselves into the last shadow that the doorway afforded them before it opened out into the unshielded glare of the Hall of Fire. They were sitting, in fact, in precisely the same spot where Methuselech's body had exploded, and found themselves staring silently at the blackened and fizzing remnants of the Fyr-Draikke.

Even as they awaited the return of the wyvern, the two most grievously injured Vetters gave up and died within just two minutes of each other. Neither made a sound as they passed away, and neither did their kinsmen. The only thing that made the humans aware of their demise was that there was a sudden change in the air, an odd sense of emptiness.

Eventually, Bolldhe broke the silence. "D'you remember the dream?" His voice was soft, and disturbingly remote.

Wodeman, seated nearest the doorway, turned to him. In the poker-glow from the fire beyond, he could see that Bolldhe's face was already coated in a light mask of grey, pumice-like dust. He was staring fixedly at the fire-tunnel beyond, and Wodeman was not sure to whom he was talking.

"Dream?"

"Up on the ice field," Bolldhe murmured. "You know—the dream you gave me."

"Yes . . ." Wodeman admitted carefully, not sure where this conversation might lead.

"That Yorda I told you about," Bolldhe went on, still uncertain what his own thoughts were. "My soul-guide."

"The woman, yes," Wodeman replied. "The one from your past."

"Did you put her there?"

Wodeman shifted position. "I put nothing there," he reminded Bolldhe gently. "Everything you saw came from your own head. Yours alone, remember?"

Bolldhe nodded. "I know what you said. But she wasn't from my past. Or rather *she* was, but *he* wasn't."

". . . What the hell are you talking about, Bolldhe?" Wodeman sighed wearily.

"Yorda wasn't Yorda," Bolldhe explained. "She was Drauglir. Didn't you see her face when Flametongue exploded? And she turned into . . . *him*?"

"Ah, I was wondering who she was," Appa interjected.

Wodeman relaxed a little. "What you saw in your soul-journey up on the ice," he explained, "that was all from *you*. Like I said, your mind trying to sort itself out, sift through the troubled waters and layers of silt for the golden nugget hidden beneath. There was no Rawgr there. But whatever you saw when you went into Drauglir's vault . . . of that I have no idea. It might not have come from your head at all. A trick of the Rawgr, perhaps?"

"But it was the same place," Bolldhe insisted. "Two visions, one location: my soul-house. Only, the second time round, in reverse."

He then related to them all that he had seen in his latest vision, leaving out not one detail.

"A delusion," Appa assured him when Bolldhe had finished. "The Rawgr's deceit, an illusion to lead you astray."

"You reckon?"

"Indeed. I can't know for sure, but it would fit. Once you entered his tomb, you were in his world, and he could show you anything that might suit his purposes. Surely you've heard Drauglir referred to as the Father of Lies?"

"The Father of Lies? I've heard that, yes. And yet so many people worship him, dedicate themselves to him, and believe in his promises. You'd think with a title such as that . . ."

"Yes," Appa pondered, shaking his head at the innate stupidity of human beings. "They never learn, do they?"

Wodeman laid a hand firmly upon Bolldhe's shoulder. "The Rawgr read your memories, saw what he needed, and used it against you. I wouldn't believe anything you saw in your vision, if I were you."

Bolldhe did not react, nor say a thing. But something within him did seem to relax a little, as if some inner anxiety had finally been lifted.

Then he turned and looked Wodeman straight in the eye. "So you didn't sacrifice Zhang after all," he stated.

The furnace room air turned instantly to ice, and Wodeman was at the center of it. He turned his face away, and intently studied the blistered and popping mound of Fyr-Draikke lying outside, almost as if he saw movement there.

"Those Cervulice will never make it through to the other side," he muttered, almost to himself. "Or the thieves. Even *before* the battle, they wouldn't have."

"What?"

"Too hot for living things. We need a little something to help us . . ."

The heat began to increase, and it grew very, very stuffy.

"An augmentation . . ." Wodeman continued sickly, and beads of sweat the size and color of resin droplets exuded from his forehead ". . . a god-wind at our backs."

"Wodeman," Bolldhe said levelly, icily, "what did you do to my horse?" As he said it, a sweltering presence began to arise. It darkened his voice, choked out the light, till Wodeman found it difficult to breathe or even think properly.

"Bolldhe . . ." cautioned Appa from behind. The old fear had returned to his voice, and he pointed out into the hall beyond.

"Tell me now, Wodeman," Bolldhe said thickly, ignoring Appa, "exactly where did you get that blood for your strength-spell?" There were hot tears in his voice, and the dark presence continued to rise.

"*Bolldhe!*" Appa hissed.

"What is it, man?" Bolldhe snapped, and turned to glare straight into the wide and glistening eyes of the old priest. And then he noted that they were suddenly no longer glistening, for a black shadow had fallen across Appa's face.

They heard something large, something moist, shift itself out there in the hall. Beyond Appa, the Vetters were shrinking further back into the shadows of the tunnel. A heavy smell of blood sharpened the air. At their feet a puddle of dark, viscous liquid spread across the floor.

They turned, and looked up at the shape that was now blocking the light.

"You . . . were destroyed," Bolldhe whispered.

"Not quite," Scathur replied. "And what doesn't kill us only makes us stronger."

No weapon did he bear now, for no weapon did he need. Two seized-up, fossilized hands lashed into the faces of the couple nearest to him. Appa leapt back with a cry as the near senseless and bloodied forms of Bolldhe and Wodeman came crashing down at his feet. He was too weak to run, and could only stare up in horror at the nightmare vision of twisted profanity that bestrode him.

Scathur was diminished. Or at least, his body was—contracted somehow, shriveled, burnt out, but all the more repulsive for that. From stooped shoulders his habergeon hung like crumpled foil, those tortured faces within its scales long since released. The neck that protruded from it was no more than a leaking nub of gristle, like the rotten stump of a blasted tree sticking up from the poisoned earth.

Not very majestic at all.

Though they had definitely heard his words—those black expectorations of diseased effluvium—this lump of jelly-hung bone that was all that remained of his head did not look capable of speech. But then, neither did the rest of his body look capable of harboring life. Yet, unlike the army of dead that had ceased the instant Drauglir was destroyed, the Rawgr-captain still retained a few hate-fuelled pulses of life within him.

He did not have long left, nor did he need it. Appa was wasted, the Vetters had fled shrieking, and now both Bolldhe and Wodeman were almost gone, too. Granite-hard fingers had fastened around their throats, dug in hard, and began rhythmically beating the life out of their skulls upon the ground.

Bolldhe had always known that his past would catch up with him one day, and now he could *hear* it. Dimly at first but growing stronger with every crunch of his head against the crystalline rock, his past, like the wing beats of the Angel of Death, came racing toward him.

Something had already broken inside his head. This he knew. His brain felt as if it was being shaken apart, liquefying, leaking from every crack in his head. He felt his lips turn inside out and his eyes roll upward into his disintegrating skull. The wings of doom beat louder, drew closer.

"I—am—the—souleater. . . ."

There was still enough of his mind left to hear Scathur's words. One word with each impact on the ground, spoken like stone grinding on stone—like the lid of his sarcophagus sliding shut, eclipsing the light, sealing him in forever.

"And—you—will—never—EVER—leave . . . !"

Darkness howled toward him. His thoughts disappearing. Final sensations. Then a slight loosening of the hand at his throat . . . almost a hesitation. A sense of something vast that drove the air over him—a cyclone, a tidal wave, a shrieking, apocalyptic maelstrom that would suck all life down into its maw.

Then Bolldhe's head exploded, and he was free.

The hand of the strangler was ripped from his throat, and he could breathe once more. The weight of his tomb lid was thrown off him, and the darkness was rolled back in a rush and clamor of stench and thrashing limbs.

"Bolldhe!" Appa yelled, and he felt the priest's little hands fasten around his cloak and drag him away from the furor that raged above him. Bolldhe heaved foul air into his lungs, and for a time the world around him was all madness, as though the very walls and roof and floor of the tunnel had locked horns with each other and were tearing each other apart.

Then his eyes began to make sense of things and, still sprawled upon the floor in a heap along with Appa and Wodeman, he stared down the tunnel to the doorway which now framed the fiery image of the clash of monsters beyond.

Out there, in Smaulka-Degernerth, they fought. One, the torn and crumpled husk of a fallen Rawgr captain, whose obscene parody of a head spouted streamers of syrupy effluence in the madness of his struggle. The other, the angel-winged Wyvern of Deliverance.

Scathur, at last, had found himself assailed by something almost as vicious as himself. But, though debilitated by so many terrible wounds, still he was powered by his Darkangelic hatred. This fight could go either way.

Appa's face had turned ashen grey. "Bolldhe," he moaned, "we've got to go—*now*!"

Wodeman too was urging Bolldhe to stand up, tugging at him by his cloak, by his arms, even by his hair. "While they're fighting each other . . ." He seemed to be shouting above the roar of the titans. "Got to get past them . . . follow the others . . . make for the Trough . . ."

But Bolldhe simply could not move. There was no feeling below his waist, his head was spinning with a kaleidoscope of strange new colors, and the blood churned in his body in a way it had never done before.

Neither Appa nor Wodeman could see this, but they could see the vacancy in his eyes, the slackness of his jaw, and the drool exuding from his mouth. They finally ceased their efforts, in despair.

Already Scathur, locked in a death grapple with his massive opponent, was forcing Ceawlin back toward the lip of the ledge, and the river of fire roiling hungrily below it. Ceawlin was weakening, injured, and Scathur's hands still had strength in them to shatter those wings.

Wodeman glanced at Appa, weighing him up. *We could try,* he thought, *or we could die. . . .*

Then he looked down at Bolldhe's face, and up again at Appa's. And their eyes locked: the rheumy eyes of the little old man, and the green-brown wolf eyes of the wood-wight. An understanding passed between the two priests; they had brought him to this end and, for what it was worth, they would stay by Bolldhe's side right to the end. It was the least they could do.

The splintering of obsidian snapped their heads back up to the conflict, and they saw Scathur's feet poised right on the edge, as it crumbled beneath his weight and let loose a fall of sparkling emerald-jet scree into the churning current below. For an instant the Rawgr faltered, still grappling with his foe, teetering over the fiery channel, his boots fighting for purchase . . .

. . . Then he twisted around, lunged back, and managed to swing himself and his enemy back fully onto the ledge.

Appa's eyes dilated. Wodeman's closed. *Not long now,* they both thought.

Then, with a sudden scream, the wyvern's great beak gaped open, and clamped itself fully over the neck nub and shoulders of Scathur. Upper and lower mandibles sliced deeply into the flesh, there interlocked amid a havoc of meat and shattered bone, and held on limpet-like as Scathur's body bucked in grotesque spasms.

What happened next, neither of the watching priests could understand. For it appeared that the whole of the Rawgr's body somehow shrivelled instantly, as though some giant unseen hand were screwing it up like a damp canvas bag. There was a great sucking sound, and the wyvern's throat swelled up enormously. Then she ripped the headless, neckless and shoulderless remains of Scathur's body from her beak, and flung the bloody wreckage away.

Like an empty leather wineskin, Scathur's body tumbled through the air, then landed with a wet slap upon the rocks beside the remnants of the Fyr-Draikke. And Ceawlin, almost collapsing with nausea, promptly spewed the entire contents of her throat in a hose-like jet—gallons of blood, shredded viscera, and semi-liquefied bones—straight down the blazing chute of lava into the very foundations of the earth.

Despite himself, Appa had to smile. *Try getting stronger on that!* He grimaced silently.

Bolldhe woke up to a world of dazzling white light. Light so brilliant he was forced to shield his eyes and squint hard against its brightness. And for the first time since he could remember, he could feel no pain in his body.

None whatsoever? There was, in fact, no feeling in him at all. None, save perhaps an odd sensation of weightlessness, a kind of undulating buoyancy. But it was a strangely comfortable feeling, pleasurable, and in a way, bordering on the euphoric.

There was a cleanness here, an icy pristineness to the air that now filled him; familiar somehow, yet like nothing he had ever breathed before. *Like being transported from a dismal and benighted land . . . where people . . . drift coughing . . . through foggy streets like lost souls . . . to a world of sunshine and joyousness. . . .*

He was puzzled. *Eotunlandt?*

He could recall how it had felt when he and the company had staggered out of that hole in the ground to stand blinking in the daylight, swaying in the fresh air, giddy with the rush of colors, sounds, and smells assailing them from this dreamworld they had stumbled into. They had sprinted out into this land, afire with energy, laughing drunkenly with the air that breathed new life into them.

When? Today? Yesterday? Weeks ago?

And where, exactly?

No, this was not Eotunlandt again. This was altogether different. Because when they had entered *that* place, their numb, grey selves had been filled with color, life, and vibrancy. This time, though, it seemed more that all color and feeling had been drained from him.

A sharp gust of air, damp and frigid, slapped him around the face, and he felt a sudden lurch. The air that had previously felt icy and pristine now felt simply chilling and raw, and smelled of fish. The rolling buoyancy, too, was beginning to make him feel sick. Dull sounds came to him: a lonely wind, the desolate cry of seabirds, the plash of oily water against the wooden hull. The murmur of familiar voices . . .

A black pit opened up in Bolldhe's gut, and salt tears welled in his eyes. The dream rolled back from his mind, and those visions that had troubled his sleep, he now remembered, had not been visions at all.

The wyvern had come for them, saved them from the Rawgr, carried them from the Maw. Passing the other struggling evacuees that trudged along below through fire, then water, then shadow. Thus they had been the first to emerge into the light and the world of men once more. There was the harbor again, the same as when they had left it, unchanged, frozen in grey miasma just as it had been before Drauglir had been destroyed. There were the quays, the fortifications, the piles of debris; there were the limp folds of damp skin that hung from their skeletal masts; there was the little building where they had stored their provisions that still awaited them, and where they had stabled . . .

Bolldhe remembered turning his face away, unable to look upon that squat little hut where his best friend had been murdered, where he still lay now—just another lump of dead flesh frozen into this landscape.

No friendly faces had there been to greet them upon their deliverance, only the gaunt and detestable living skull of Yen. *Still alive?* She had approached them on the quayside, shuffling gingerly through the detritus toward them, but had remained as silent and expressionless as ever. She would not go anwhere near the Children's footprints that had melted the ice and blackened the rock beneath. Neither would she approach the ship that still squatted by the wharf, waiting for an army that would never return.

Over the next few hours the others had emerged gradually, some propped up or even carried by their fellows. All of them instantly collapsed, either on the wharf or where they emerged, in the shadow of the great gate. There had been a retching and a gasping, and also a death. A Cervulus, this time, if Bolldhe remembered right. The sorry creature had looked up to the sky, breathed in the air, then folded his great legs beneath him and died. Not a word was said by anyone.

As for the rest, as soon as everyone was accounted for, they had simply taken the provisions from the storehouse, boarded the ship Scathur had thoughtfully provided them with, and set sail. Thirty-two souls drifted out of the fjord that day, including Yen and the six Tyvenborgers whom they took with them. That meant just thirty-two out of the ten dozen and a half that had ventured to the Maw. And as the ship had glided up the silent channel, not one of them looked back.

It was a strange journey for Bolldhe, unnaturally hushed and seeming to last forever. The sea was dead, there came not a breath of wind to fill the sails, and the flat, pale sun hung over the western horizon for an age, unbudging, as though it were encased in the icy grip of that cold, colorless sky. None of the voyagers seemed to be doing much, either. Hunched over their own private pain, they merely sat there and let the ship take them wherever it would.

Of all of them, only the healers were moving about. There were so many hurts to be tended, and both Appa and Wodeman went from one to the next, wordlessly bringing succor to each person they came to. By the stern, to which the Tyvenborgers had been banished, the unpleasant smell of Flekki's salves mingled oddly with the salt in the air.

Even Schnorbitz did his part—though for the most part the healing properties of his extended tongue were graciously declined. Eventually he seemed to take the hint, and padded back to the prow where his *own* people—meaning Gapp, Finan, the Vetters and Cervulice—had positioned themselves. All just sat or lay there dumbly, vacantly, seemingly unaware of the ship's progress, or even the ocean around them. In their native woods they had never seen any body of water larger than the falls of Baeldicca the Great, and though they had encountered the sea just days earlier, had even traveled *beneath* it, that had been under the glamour of Jagt. But here and now was the first time they had planed across its vast surface, witnessed the enormity of it all. It should have been so fascinating to them, yet all they did was stare at the bottom-boards.

Bolldhe's eyes came to rest finally upon the thieves huddled together at the far end of the ship. They looked cowed and thoroughly miserable. Eorcenwold's haunted expression had not altered since Bolldhe had first encounterd him after the battle, and as for Klijjver, never before had Bolldhe seen anyone so big look so diminished. Caught in the withering glare of his own leader, his gaze remained fixed on some point out to sea, as far away from his current enforced company as possible.

Bolldhe shrugged, and turned over on his side. Or at least he tried to, but seemed unable to do that either. *What the . . . !* For some reason, his body was not responding to his wishes.

He caught sight of Elfswith. The half-Huldre looked a lot healthier than before and even now the pink stump of a new arm was beginning to bud into growth.

"Oh aye, the dead are rising again," he heard a quavering voice croak nearby—the first he had heard so far—and he swivelled his eyes to see who had uttered this rather tasteless remark.

At first he thought a stranger had joined them, possibly a barbarian herdsman, or even a whaler, for he did not recognize the figure that sat up on the gunwale at his side. It was a big man, bent over with age or infirmity, and clad from head to toe in tattered, red-stained rags and crude swaddling strips of animal hide. Then Bolldhe noticed that he also wore the shredded green remnants of an Ulleanh around his shoulders, and realized that this beaten-up old beggar from the wilds was in fact Nibulus, divested of his armor and bandaged all over with the torn-up remnants of his old bearskin cloak. The son of Artibulus now looked older than his father, and his voice was scarce more than a whisper.

As the two men regarded each other for a long moment, both could see their own feelings reflected in the eyes of the other. But there was something else besides all that memory of hurt, horror and death, something that parted the heavy drapes of grief just enough to let in a chink of light. It was something that almost amounted to pride, for they had *won*; they had triumphed over unbelievable odds, and had somehow emerged from the depths of hell alive. But, above all, it was pride because the pair of them had fought like *bastards!* A grim smile touched both their lips.

Somewhere off to one side, Elfswith had begun to play. The bard had fished out a small dulcimer and, with tiny hammers of silver, struck out the same sweet tune that he had played on his krummhorn just hours before they had entered the Chamber of Drauglir. Into this melody Nibulus began to chant, holding in his hands *The Chronicle of Gwyllch*. It was from this, the final entry in that revered tome, that he quoted:

> *"So we sette sayl, and bothe Heav'n and Hel we bore with us inne oure harts. Short wode be the voyage, but long the march. Yet even this wode be as a tern's dive next to that of our Blessed Fallen. Even now their blod we beheld, raining inne the skys to the West, to that far land where we were bounde. And in this we saw, for soothe: they had reach'd home ere we.*
>
> *Thus we griev'd no longer, but sang in voyces strong and true, oure prayse to Lord Pel-Adan, our psalm of blessing for the Everlasting Heroes, but most of alle, our song to ourselfs, to a brotherhod that will reign etyrnal."*

Words came with difficulty to Bolldhe. His tongue was swollen, feeling as thick and dry as an old leather glove, and he could hardly move his jaw. But he had to speak.

"Sh-sure I know tha' tune," he managed. "Elf's tune; erd i' when I wza kid . . . long time 'go. Fun'ral dirge, uh?"

Nibulus's face darkened in renewed sadness on hearing the stricken slur of Bolldhe's speech. But he nodded. "*The Pyre of Jubeigh III.* An old dirge from the west." Before he could stop himself, he added: "why? Would you like it played at your own funeral?"

This time Bolldhe had no trouble voicing his response, as articulate as it was cold: "No," he said. "At yours."

And with that he drifted off to sleep once again.

A strange voyage indeed. Outside the real world. Beyond time. Dreamlike. That pale sun refusing to move an inch . . .

Then, the next moment, Bolldhe saw that it was twilight. The sun, its uppermost rim now only just visible above the pencil-line of the lead-grey sea, had drifted far toward the north, like one of Gwyllch's terns slanting into the waves at the shallowest incline possible. Suspended in time, it seemed reluctant to go those final few inches that would take it down into the cold and lightless world below.

He must have slept for a long time. *Gods, it was so hard staying awake!* Waking this second time, his head felt woolly and insubstantial, and everything around him had fallen even quieter than before. The gentle lap of water, the steady rhythm of wooden creaking, a secret whispering of frosty air currents, and the occasional distant rumbling of fiery mountains far behind them; it was all so muffled, as if a heavy blanket were being drawn over the world.

There were voices too, hushed and reluctant to be heard.

". . . already done all I can . . ."

Some, at least, were talking now, though the words intruding on the stillness were not welcome. This one sounded like Appa's voice, but Bolldhe could not be sure; he had never heard the old man talk in such hollow tones, drained not only of the shrillness and irritability that Bolldhe had grown so used to, but also of any urgency.

"We all have," came another voice, just as subdued, and with a faint tinge of shame to it.

Wodeman! Bolldhe thought. *That bastard, well might he be ashamed.*

"So many hurts, so little healing left," came the first voice again, "and me so very old—so exhausted. Dried up, like an old prune."

Definitely Appa.

"But what actually happened to him?" came a third voice, probably Wintus's.

Why not just ask me? Bolldhe thought, a little annoyed at the way they were discussing him as if he were not there.

"He finally learned how to open himself to the truth," Wodeman replied. "To look into himself, and discover the treasures therein."

"He finally realized the truth of Cuna's message," Appa argued. "He finally accepted what I've been teaching him all along: *Reject the sword, or else reject life.*"

Nibulus snorted. "That's not what I meant! In any case, neither of you knows what went on inside his head up there on the ziggurat. Only he can know that."

Bolldhe smirked. *That Nibulus, of all of them, should get it right.*

"Does it really matter?" Kuthy butted in. "The important thing is, Bolldhe succeeded, and Finwald failed."

His voice was blunt, but with more than a hint of ambiguity. Was he genuinely satisfied with the outcome, or disappointed?

"Yes, he failed, thank Cuna," Appa breathed, and closed his eyes reverentially.

"Thank Erce," Wodeman corrected him, automatically.

"Cuna," Appa quietly insisted.

"Erce," Wodeman not so quietly reiterated.

The two priests regarded each other contemplatively, then experienced the odd sense that they were looking at each other not from the opposite sides of a narrow boat, but across a great chasm that stretched between them, wider than the ocean. Yet at the same time, neither felt any need to back away from that precipice. There was a mutual feeling that, on this occasion at least, their gods were reconciled, if not exactly united. And if one god had retreated or backed down a step or two, perhaps it was best not to know which one.

"No, what I meant was," the Peladane continued, "what happened to *him*, to his body? He looks as though he was trampled by a herd of baluchitheria."

"He was blown off his feet by an exploding sword, and landed on his arse," Kuthy replied. "That's what happened to him."

"Not the sword," Wodeman chipped in. "He got off lightly, there. No, it was the Rawgr captain that did that to him . . . *Euch,* did you see that thing? Just meat and slime, held together purely by hate and corruption. As damned as . . . Finwald."

"Him!" Appa spat. "Too bright for his own good, that one. I wish I'd never converted him back in Qaladmir."

"Bet he thinks so, too," Nibulus remarked sourly. "He'd be a lot better off than he is now—wherever he is."

A long time of silence ensued, till eventually it was broken by Appa. "It was his own fault," he said gloomily. "Finwald never really . . . got it. For all his youth and zeal, his brains, his study, all that, it still didn't sink in. None of it. He was a man of words, of learning—"

"A cunnan," Wodeman interjected.

"A cunnan, yes, but never a man of faith. Questioning, always questioning, yet so little real understanding. Cuna alone knows what books he dug up, what histories he studied. He dug too deeply—far too deeply—and yet the only soil he found for his faith was nightsoil."

"He got lost in the woods," Wodeman agreed, recalling Oswiu and the wayward Torca Saloth Alchwych.

"Yes indeed," Appa concurred. "Funny how people who stray from their religion always seem to end up with snake-bladed weapons."

The Peladane snorted. "What are you going on about?"

"Finwald's flamberge? Oswiu's kh'is?" Appa reminded him. "Remember?"

Bolldhe's mind instantly went back to Eotunlandt, and his eye ached again with the memory of the tip of the blade Oswiu had held against it.

"He claimed it sucked souls," Nibulus recalled. "I thought he was just being dramatic, but—"

"I wish I'd made the connection earlier," Kuthy cut in suddenly. "Things might have worked out rather *differently* if I had."

"What d'you mean?"

There was a slight pause before Kuthy gave his reply, but did Bolldhe detect also a certain slyness in his voice? "That sort of thing," Kuthy explained, "it's our business, our trade, if you like. It's what we do."

"And believe me," Elfswith added with less delicacy, "if we'd known what it was Bolldhe was carrying around all that time, well . . . who knows?"

"We'd often discussed it," Kuthy took over, "this legendary relic from a time before even Drauglir came down into the world. We knew there was something special about it, knew it had more to tell than any of the legends recalled. It had so many different names, so many intriguing and mysterious appellations, but—and this is the most irksome part—the one I'd forgotten right up until Bolldhe destroyed it, was 'Soul-Stealer.'"

"We often wondered what had become of it," Elfswith went on, "but neither of us ever guessed it had fallen into the hands of the Rawgr."

"So it was only when we saw Bolldhe destroy it—"

"—And what came out of it—"

"That we realized it'd fallen into the hands of Bolldhe, too. Ah well, such is life."

"Why?" Appa demanded. "What would you have done with it?"

Elfswith's coat turned sable-black, but he held his silence. Kuthy, on the other hand, began to lose his caginess.

"We certainly wouldn't have been so quick to just destroy it."

They noted the reproachful tone in his voice, and suddenly all eyes were upon him. The evening's last light was behind Kuthy, and in the shadow over his face the company could just make out the two pale glints of ice that were his eyes.

"To throw away such a fabulous treasure?" he continued, *"and* the soul of a Darkangel? D'you have any idea how much that would fetch on the open market?"

There was stunned silence from his audience.

"In fact," he went further, "why not do what Finwald was trying to do? Revive Drauglir—imagine that! Your very own Rawgr-Lord, at your beck and call!"

"You *wouldn't* have!" Nibulus gaped, scarcely able to believe what he was hearing. "You *couldn't* have!"

"Not even you!" Appa echoed.

"Why not?" Kuthy protested. "Is that so evil?"

They were flabbergasted. "Well, yes, of course it is!"

"If you could manage to control him, he'd be just a weapon; moreover, a very powerful weapon. And since when have any of us ever turned our noses up at weapons, eh, Peladane? I don't see why you should have to *destroy* him."

"He was a Rawgr, FOR PEL'S SAKE!"

"That's just *your* name for him." Kuthy shrugged, licking his lips. *"He* never called himself that."

"It doesn't matter, the bloody name!" Appa trilled almost hysterically. "He was still evil. That's what Rawgrs are!"

"Define evil," Elfswith demanded, recumbent now in the bow.

"They're stronger than us," Nibulus declared vehemently. "They kill us just for their sick sport—and consume us!"

"Oh, and that's it, is it?" Kuthy snorted. "That's your definition of evil? Even though *we're* stronger than the hart and the boar, which we also kill and consume?"

"For sport, too," Elfswith pointed out.

"For sport, too," Kuthy confirmed.

The company from the south just stared at the pair of northerners in disbelief. But there was nothing they could say to that. Nothing at all.

"Well, it's gone now," Kuthy concluded ruefully, "the power, the sword, the Rawgr; all gone forever. I don't suppose any of us'll ever know where it originated from, or what any of us would've done with the sword—or the Rawgr—if we'd had the chance. Well, maybe it's better this way. No point in crying over spilt milk."

"Or spilt blood," Wodeman said pointedly.

"That too, I suppose."

Suppose? Suppose! Bolldhe reflected, though he did not have the energy to say it.

"Suppose?" Appa said for him. "You two really are a couple of hard-hearted bastards, aren't you?"

"Anyway," Elfswith pointed out, changing tack somewhat, "it all depends on what you'd do with the Rawgr once you've got him under your control. D'you really believe we'd have used him for evil? Come to that, d'you believe Finwald would have either? Was he himself evil?"

It was a fair point, they had to concede, and all eyes turned to Appa. After a long and thoughtful silence, the mage-priest shook his head. "No," he admitted, "Finwald was not evil. Right up to the end, I perceived nothing of that in him. He may have been a complete fool, but he was not evil."

"He was no fool either," Kuthy corrected him. "He knew what he could achieve if he had the means to control Drauglir."

"Which he *got*, too," Elfswith added, "and in no small amount, either. In the end he had such power that even I was beginning to feel quite overwhelmed. I tell you, I could taste it in the air . . . though I still can't imagine how or where he acquired it."

"*They've* probably got a fair idea where," Nibulus said, indicating the remnants of the party from Tyvenborg that skulked at the far end of the ship.

"Yes," Appa agreed. "The Finwald I once knew wasn't the same Finwald that came out of that fire pit with those lot. Who can guess what they must've witnessed? What a story they could tell! Not that they ever would, even if we still had Bolldhe to translate for us. . . ."

You still do have him, you idiot!

"But I still say Finwald was a fool: the way he was, the way he always was. I should have seen it right at the beginning, years ago, even back in Qaladmir. The poor fool was bound to fail in the end. That constant pursuit of magic of his. With him, it was always about power, power for *himself.* He cared little for truth, no matter what he told himself."

He stopped when he realized he was beginning to preach as if he were back in his temple at Nordwas. But, to his surprise, he found Wodeman staring at him and nodding in agreement.

"Among my people," the Torca said, "the greatest attribute for anyone who seeks magic is patience. It's considered the highest virtue to dedicate your whole life to the search for answers, but I don't think that was the way with Finwald. He might have seemed patient in his studies, but he wanted it all too soon. And he wanted it *big.*"

"Yes," Appa agreed, "things do have a way of getting out of hand a bit, don't they? You start something, you set things in motion, one thing leads to another, and before you know it, they've started leading *you*."

"As they have *us*," a small voice suddenly piped up at the back. They looked around and, in the near-darkness, saw that Gapp had rejoined them.

"What d'you mean, Greyboots?" Wodeman asked.

"What I mean is, what exactly have we been doing all these months? What was it all for? You do realize you could've simply smashed that sword right back at the beginning, don't you? Right back in those mines when you first found it."

Bolldhe felt an extremely unpleasant iciness frost over his ailing flesh. *That,* he thought to himself, *was something I really didn't need to hear . . .* But he did not say a thing. Nobody else said anything, either, because nobody felt they could. The boy was absolutely right, and all they could do now was sit there frozen to their seats, as suddenly cold and motionless as Bolldhe.

Appa, of all of them, seemed particularly hushed. Indeed, petrified, even mortified. He appeared to be having some sort of problem with his hands. He kept clenching and unclenching them in a way that suggested some measure of anguish, and it was an anguish that was growing steadily worse.

Suddenly he lunged at Nibulus, knotted his bony little fingers in the big man's tattered Ulleanh, and yelled into his face: "The boy's right! It was all bloody USELESS, wasn't it! Your great quest was a total waste of time! We're not triumphal heroes, not one of us! We're nothing more than fools! The biggest idiots in the world!"

Everyone jumped in surprise. Even those at the far end of the ship stared in bewilderment at the spectacle before them. For though the Peladane towered above the little priest, for a moment Appa, his eyes blazing and his jaw jutting, was again every bit the mad old terrier he had been in the past.

Nibulus did not lift a finger to push him away. He just stared back at his assailant in surprise. As he did so, he too began to feel within him the rising energies of confusion and sickness that seemed to be emanating from the elderly priest before him. It was almost as if a great battle was going on inside him—as though he was struggling to understand the point of his very existence.

But in the end, all he could manage by way of reply was a weak: "Yes, I'm sure . . . you could be right. But, as I said before, I'm a Peladane. And the quest—well, that's just what we do."

Appa paused in his rage. Then the fire blew out in him and, cold and grey once more, he slumped back into his seat.

"I'm too sick to carry on," he announced to any who might have the energy to care. "Too sick, too weary, too old, too . . . everything. Just drop me at the next stop. I'll get off there."

"The next stop is Wrythe," Nibulus informed him with a note of sympathy in his voice. "Can't stop there, old chap."

"I don't care," Appa replied, almost sobbing. "I'm serious, Nibulus. I'm staying there. That journey damn near killed me. I only just managed it, and then only because the mission drove me. And now that's gone—in fact, never even *was*—what'll drive me this time? I tell you, I'd never make it back. Not now, not after . . . everything that's happened."

"Appa," Gapp said quietly, "there's nothing there but sickness and death."

"Perfect, then! Sounds like just the place for me."

"Well, let's see how you feel after we get there tomorrow," Nibulus said. "We're only stopping to rest and get some supplies before moving on. You'll feel better after a couple of days."

Gapp looked pained, and shivered to his very core. "I doubt we'll find much succor in Wrythe," he whispered, "even with Yggr and his devils gone. You lot don't know that place like I do."

"*We* do," Kuthy pointed out, reassuringly, "and they're not so bad really, those others, once you let them know who's boss. Once the Maj left, they just seemed to drift."

"And the bathhouse there is the finest anywhere in these parts," Elfswith joined in.

"I'm warning you . . ." Gapp muttered.

But Appa was not listening. His mind was made up. "I'm not going on any farther," he repeated tiredly, "no matter what you say. I'm stopping at Wrythe."

"Are you serious?" Nibulus asked. "You really aren't coming home? Not even to see old Marla?"

"I'm staying," replied the old man, in visible pain. "And I doubt I'll be the only one staying there, too."

"What, you mean Bolldhe?"

"Dead right. I can't see him getting any farther than Wrythe."

W-wait . . . What? Bolldhe exclaimed to himself, and struggled to move, though he found it still impossible.

"How is he now, anyway?" Nibulus asked. "He could hardly say a word earlier."

"No," Appa replied, even quieter than before. "He can't at all now, not any more. . . ."

I can't? Bolldhe thought in rising panic.

"And he'll never walk again."

I won't?

Then the last rim of the sun finally disappeared below the waves. A growing spume of redness slowly disgorged into the clouds above its final resting place, and against it, all Bolldhe could see in his fading sight was the silhouette of a little old man—the one who had brought him to this place—rapping his ring against the tombstone-shaped amulet that hung from its thong round his neck.

Strange northern skies! thought Bolldhe. *No stars—no moon. And this night!* Surely the blackest and stillest he had ever known.

Bolldhe's eyes were as wide as his sockets, and he stared about himself in silent wonder at this place they had drifted into. He had gone to sleep sometime during the night, he remembered. Just slipped away. When he had awoken, he found he was still aboard the ship, still lying where he had lain all along, but it was now all so empty, so hollow. Not a sound came to his ears, not even the slightest whisper of wind nor purl of water. It was as if they were sailing along the Trough of the Dead.

Almost in panic, he looked about himself for his companions. They were still there, he noted with relief, but for some reason that he found disturbing, none seemed particularly inclined to speak to him, or even look at him. It was as if they were avoiding him, somehow embarrassed.

Then he noticed that one was indeed looking at him, and he strained to see who it was. He realized it was Wodeman. The shaman was staring back at him, studying him long and deep. . . .

And then suddenly saw him, saw Bolldhe as he really was.

After a moment of frozen immobility, he suddenly said, *You still here?*

Still? Where am I supposed to be? Bolldhe replied, slightly nettled by this tactless and rather meaningless question.

Then he realized that the shaman had not moved his lips. In fact, neither had Bolldhe himself.

Panic rose in him afresh. He did not want to be here.

You have a long journey ahead of you, Bolldhe, the sorcerer declared. His voice, if that was what it was, sounded so thin, so insubstantial, and only Wodeman appeared to be animate now. The rest of the voyagers remained quite still, frozen in time; glints of ice in their ragged hair, crystalline moisture glistening upon petrified skin, hoarfrost-stiffened beards, and eyes glazed as if in death.

Others were there, too, Bolldhe now saw, sitting among them on the gunwales. But these newcomers were not frozen; they dripped freely with dark moisture that spread in pools about their feet. Some were human, others Vetter or Cervulus, but all were glaring at Bolldhe with gleaming black eyes.

Bolldhe's mind floated now on unstill waters. He could not remember who had survived the battle and who had not. Yet he was sure he recognized some of the dead among these. He looked along the line of staring faces, until he came to . . .

Paulus?

Odf Uglekort it was indeed. His body was the most torn up of all, and drenched with blood that stained the planking at his feet.

Even Finwald had joined this nocturnal visitation, though he was now little more than a shadow that flitted aimlessly about the darkened ship, jabbering and sobbing to himself without any idea of where he was.

Bolldhe found his own body was no longer broken, no longer shackled by crippling injury. Free now from his immobility, he shrank back into the stern, and pressed himself into a corner of it. There he remained, himself also now frozen, and could do nothing but stare back at them.

The living, those he was sure had survived, were now fading, thinning, vanishing. Then they were just spaces, gaps in the firmament, windows to the Beyond. Around them all was blackness, utterly black and solid; but *through* them he could see the stars, mocking stars that winked at him coldly.

Still frozen immobile, he began to shudder and his mind began to fragment. That subsonic, bestial breathing he had heard in the Moghul came back to haunt him, shivering through his frame. This time it was behind him, *right* behind him, breathing an icy fog with the smell of marsh mist upon his shoulder. There it settled like a wet glove, and began to spread.

He did not want to turn, and could not. He knew it was Zhang, nuzzling him as he had always done, but nuzzling him with a head of stretched, dead skin, lifeless eyes, and gaping throat.

I'm . . . so sorry, Bolldhe, Wodeman breathed, barely audible now.

Then he, too, was gone.

Bolldhe was alone on the ship. The others had all departed, left him. With a howl of protest, he lurched up, staggered about upon the slick bottom boards, then fled screaming down the length of the ship. Along sparkling, frosted planking he pounded, his footfalls thudding deadly. He was adrift. He was totally adrift, perhaps floating in this vessel upon a sea of clouds, moon-silvered and ghostly as they undulated about him. Or sailing off into the black spaces between the stars, the countless stars that now glinted in the sky like the shards of Flametongue.

Bolldhe had reached the prow, but he did not stop running. The horror of that which had breathed behind him propelled him on, and without hesitation he leapt straight off the ship.

Then, screaming loudly, he was floating, spiraling away through the coldness of space, drifting off amid the stars themselves, or else sinking into the sea, into that black realm of Jagt that somebody had once described to him, its tiny points of phosphorescent light winking like the galaxies above.

Up, down, water, air, space, time; it all meant so little now. All there was left to him was the din of his own wailing. Like a tiny creature of the woodland that screams at the world in impotent fury ere death, so Bolldhe departed, and the world did not care or even hear.

Along the star-beams Bolldhe found himself travelling now: through blackness; through the All-Void. It was cold here beyond anything he had experienced upon the ice field of Melhus, cold beyond comprehension, and it was utterly,

utterly silent. Glints of silver sparkled ahead, points of light against the black, and as he drew nearer, he saw them begin to take on shapes, though they did not move in any way. Shapes, symbols . . . constellations.

Constellations all around him.: the Torch, the Sword, the Angel, the Rawgr, Despair, Good Eye, the Death's-Head . . . He knew them all, of course; in his job, he had needed to, though he had never believed they really meant anything in truth. But the one he was hurtling toward, he could recognize now, was the Dolmen.

The constellation of the doorway, or meeting place.

Closer, closer he sped, the Dolmen growing larger and larger all the while, until it was a vast shape that stretched across the entire universe ahead, from end to end. But those points of light, the stars, were not stars at all, he realized now. For, as he came yet closer, he could see that they were menhirs, great standing stones hanging in space.

Nearer still, and the menhirs came together, drawing closer to each other in a rapidly tightening circle. He began to sense a lessening in the intensity of the coldness, and familiar sensations began to nudge in at the periphery of his awareness: smells of childhood, the sound of a lonely, chattering wind, a wintry tang in the air.

Then the briefest of flashes, so brief that he wondered if it had really happened or not, in which he had witnessed a vision. There was Light, a vast god of white robes and flying black hair, with eyes like red, exploding suns, and around this god were ranged the Skela, like black sunspots hovering in the corona of his celestial magnificence.

Then he was back in Moel-Bryn.

There was no doubt about it: Bolldhe was standing atop the high, rocky hill that looked down upon the town of his childhood. He looked about. There was that same old sky, a firmament of lead, a mass of roiling greyness, with perhaps the palest blush of scarlet already draining away into the grey. Between this and the horizon, there was a thin band of silvery light, diminishing as the lead curtain gradually lowered. And, stretching out toward this horizon, a bleak, frozen landscape that held the promise of nothing. There were the hills and heathlands of his youth, those grey remembered hills whose bases were mired in icy mist, those heathlands that were punctuated only by the occasional pinprick of light, the miniscule glinting of halls and homes.

It was late evening. About him were trees, leafless and black, broken and stunted; thorn bushes, web-hung and drear. In the last light he could also make out piles of copper leaves that were strewn about in damp piles like mounds of discarded and rusty armor. The ground beneath was frozen, mossy turf that appeared as dead as a lichen-grown tombstone. There were no beasts here, just maggots that poked through the rimed crust of earth to regard him hungrily; and no birds, just midges that cavorted in a dance macabre.

No people, either. Just the menhirs. Surrounding him. Looking at him.

Time, Fate, Chance, Law, Chaos, and the rest, they were all here: the Skela themselves staring down at him as impassively as the stone they were made of.

And him. He was also here, as he had to be. The broad-backed stranger in the yak hide kirtle, he with the lamp staff hung with glistening orbs, the satchel with its wet, lumpy contents, and the shimmering white coif. There he stood among his menhirs, regarding Bolldhe with those hot, red, knowing eyes.

"Who . . ." Bolldhe whispered, choosing his words with care, ". . . the shite are you?"

Cuna smiled. He was all smiles these days.

"I am Cuna," he announced. "Aren't you lucky?"

Bolldhe regarded the god thoughtfully. "Oh, so you do exist, then," he said, unimpressed.

"I may not have ever been *your* god, Bolldhe," he rumbled, "but . . . aren't you pleased to find that it is I who am the Answer?"

"Answer?"

"To that Question which all peoples of the world ask themselves: What is on the Other Side?"

Bolldhe looked about himself doubtfully, at the frozen land, the drear hills, and the standing stones that hemmed him in with this beggarly old crook. "I'd sort of hoped there'd be nothing at all," he replied. "None of that bedtime story stuff, anyway, which—"

At this, Cuna burst out into an uproarious fit of laughter. It rolled out of his mouth like thunder, echoed around the valleys like the report of cannonfire, and sent a reverberation through the earth that caused the ground to tremble. It was a laughter that could shake the very mountains to their roots. And even the Skela joined in this time.

"How *ridiculous!*" he guffawed, once he had regained control of himself.

Then he pointed vaguely over to a space between two of the Skela. "Look over there, my boy," he instructed in a voice that was as patient as the shifting of continents. Bolldhe looked, and now saw that there was a black shape hanging there. Just that: an oblong of black, about man-height, suspended in midair between two of the menhirs. As he stared at it, Bolldhe realized that he had seen it somewhere before: a small doorway, its barred gate open wide, and within it a darkness as black as the anti-light Bolldhe had witnessed in the Moghol.

"Know it?" Cuna inquired.

Bolldhe did. It was the final cell, the very last door in the dungeon passageway of his soul-house. Inside, the blackness of Nothing, of death without hope.

Oblivion.

The voice of the knowing god came as a swirl of breath vapor through the frigid air toward him: "It's there if you want it, Bolldhe. If that is what you truly desire."

Bolldhe turned his face away, and gazed back down the star-beam that had brought him here. There he saw, now only the tiniest atom of light, the ship that was carrying his companions away, itself like a star fading slowly from sight, winking out forever.

What would become of them? he wondered with an ache in his heart. How he would love to have been able to continue looking down upon them, to see how their journeys went, where they ended up, what the rest of their lives would be. Perhaps even sit by their bedsides now and then and whisper strange thoughts into their dreams. Would Nibulus remain a Peladane, either to take up the role of his father or die in some useless conflict under foreign skies, or would he have learned from his ordeal? Would Appa find some measure of peace during his last years, some reward for the torment he had put himself through? And Radnar, with all his life ahead of him, how would the boy use the experience he had gained upon this odyssey? What would he become: a soldier-of-fortune, a traveller, a writer?

Wodeman he absolutely did not care about, but what of the Tivor, and Elfswith? Would they ever find what it was they constantly sought? And as for the Tregvans? The thieves? Even Yen—could anything of her sanity, her life, be recovered at all?

The voice of Cuna sounded again. "Forget about them, Bolldhe. They don't concern you anymore."

Bolldhe turned back to the god that stood before him. Though still on the far side of despair, he could not help getting riled.

"Don't concern me?" he exclaimed, marvelling once again at the stupidity of gods.

But Cuna simply nodded. "They're still alive," he explained.

"What could you possibly know about it?" Bolldhe snarled. Then, without really knowing why he should even bother to explain, he added: "We went through *so much* together. . . ."

Cuna snorted. "What's that, Bolldhe? Surely not love? Don't you think you've left it a bit late for that?"

Bolldhe had no answer. The emptiness in him was all the reply Cuna needed.

"Don't feel so bad," he went on. "You did so well."

"Well?"

"Only you could have done it. You are unique, truly. Of all the people on Lindormyn, it was you I chose. I could easily have chosen one of my own followers. Bolldhe, you see this bag I carry?" Here he undid the clasp of his sodden knapsack, reached inside, and drew forth several of the round, pulpy objects that leaked their juices perpetually through the canvas. He extended them towards Bolldhe, till at last it could be seen they were heads. "One head for each race of people that worship me."

If he had expected Bolldhe to be impressed, he was due to be disappointed. Bolldhe stared back impassively, and said not a word.

"I see far, Bolldhe," Cuna went on, pointing to the chaplet on his brow, and then to the orb-strung lantern staff in his hand. "Not for nothing do I wear the Eyes of Urgnidh the Vulture upon my brow," he explained, "nor the Eyes of the Great Cat upon my staff. With Far-sight and Night-sight, there is nothing I cannot see in this world, no one I do not know, if I choose to look. I could have chosen a great champion, a wise mystic, a worker of miracles. But, no, I chose you, 'Bolldhe the Great,' for only Bolldhe could have done it."

If he had expected Bolldhe to be flattered, again he was to be disappointed. Bolldhe was struck more by the fact that one of the world's major deities was apparently in need of optical aids in order to see.

"Only I?" Bolldhe asked with a sneer. "You mean only I, or anyone else strong enough to smash a bloody sword. *Anyone* could have done that just as well."

"You sell yourself short, Bolldhe. Only *your* granite was hard enough. Only *your* loathing of manipulation strong enough. Since you were eight years old, you have resisted the schemes and machinations of those who would bend you to their will, and have resisted it still, *right to the end,* even when you were burning amid the fires of hell."

It was then, it was only then, that the full Truth of Cuna struck Bolldhe. It roared over him like a harbor wave, infiltrated every particle of his soul, carried him far away amid the unstoppable power of its deluge. Hardly able to speak through the ruination of his being, he wailed:

"So you used it! My . . . you used it! *You* were manipulating me all along!"

The blackest despair. The end of all things. The final, awful truth. The destruction of Bolldhe. For the one thing he had left to him, the only thing that had ever really mattered to him during his entire, rotten life, he now realized had been ripped from him as brutally as though it were his heart being torn from his shattered ribcage.

He had suffered so much. Not just during the battle, nor within his soul-house. For Bolldhe, it had been a whole lifetime of suffering: unloved, alone, a little scrap of nothing that would never be missed, a solitary insect crushed by a cartwheel on the side of the road. Now, here at the end of the universe, so it seemed, and seeing his friends wink out of his world, he was the loneliest atom on the farthest planet of the cosmos.

And to have that one precious thing ripped from him too . . .

It was too much, far too much. He looked up at Cuna, and shook his head. What did gods know about anything?

"So," intoned Time, "what of this one? Your greatest servant, even if such was never his intention, will you embrace him to yourself? Or will you grant him as little mercy as you did Uglekort?"

Cuna lit another roll-up, the final one in his packet. He slid it into his mouth, inhaled deeply, and breathed out. He was in no hurry.

"Do you think he likes me?" he asked Time.

"I think he hates you more than anything he has ever known, conceived, or dreamt about," Time stated.

"And so you ask me whether I should save him."

"You are Light. And Truth. And Goodness. And Honor."

"He thinks I'm an idiot. He hates me, he has never worshipped me, he—"

"Lord Cuna," Time interrupted.

"Yes?"

"He's gone."

They turned to look where Bolldhe had been standing, and Cuna saw that Bolldhe was, indeed, gone. Truly gone. Forever. For while Cuna had been arguing with the Syr, Bolldhe had simply walked through the black door, the last door, the final cell in the passageway of his soul-house. The gateway into oblivion.

"Oh."

"Oh, indeed."

Too much suffering. Far too much to ever be healed. And that final, cruellest blow, that final straw. Bolldhe had known that there was a chance he might have been granted a continuation of sorts by the god of Light, a life beyond Life; a place at Cuna's table, even. But even before the god's decision had been made, Bolldhe had chosen extinction rather than be directed. He would have no handouts from *him*. For at that point, when everything, even his pride, had been taken from him, the only thing left to him was the ability to *choose*. It was *he* that must make that choice, not they. It was the one, tiny thing left to him.

The only thing.

And he had used it.

Epilogue

Leading out from the straggle of huts and abandoned enclosures that formed the northern outskirts of Wrythe, a narrow track wound its way. Through the last of the trees it stole, uncertainly leaving the dark confines of that decayed settlement, and came out at last onto the wide open space of a headland that jutted into the ocean.

Here there was no refuge from the stark winds that raked the coastline, no dark sanctuary for pale creatures that prowled in shadows. It was a land of jagged rock, wind-chiselled into sharp, contorted forms, where tall grasses whipped about in shrill agitation, where scowling black clouds piloted their way across the sky, and where, far below, the vast, featureless, slate-grey mantle of the ocean was fringed white in a commotion of sea spume.

Down there, among the battle debris of shattered rock and decaying sea wrack, there came another flurry of white and grey, as a legion of gulls descended upon the sea life that had been thrown up onto the strand. Powerful beaks the color of fire and blood punched through carapace, ripped living flesh apart. Juices flowed; it was a battle that would go on as long as the world lasted.

But there was also a keen tang of salt that was pleasant to the palate, carried on an icy wind that was cleansing to the soul. And, over at the farthest extremity of the headland, was something altogether unexpected. What at first appeared to be a cluster of figures upon the promontory, huddled together in sinister converse, up close was revealed to be simply an assemblage of boulders, weathered and ancient, grey-green and shadowed, with just the occasional glint of sunlight to warm the life back into the virulent orange lichen that clung to their surface.

Set into the northeast side of these boulders, facing out over the wide expanse of water to the distant island of Melhus beyond, was an alcove. In here, among the clumps of moss and coarse grass that nestled between the rocks, was a torch. Or rather, *the* Torch, a Y-shaped frame of wood, roughly man-height, in the likeness of the symbol of Cuna the Lightbringer. Upon this frame was nailed the crudely fashioned effigy of a man. Of twisted sapling wood and twined creepers was it made, wrangled into shape by inexpert and ailing hands, and there was something about its style that did not sit well with its natural surroundings.

But, for all that, it had remained firm in this place for a very long time. For many years ago, Appa had set it here. Days after setting sail from Melhus, the ship of fugitives had finally reached land. The dank and grey tumor of Wrythe had opened like a corpse's sphincter to draw them into its clammy, stinking embrace. For those who had never been here before, there was much trepidation as to what they would find. But upon arriving, far from the morbid swelling that had been described to them by Gapp, Kuthy and Elfswith, the company found themselves entering a swept house, like a dried scab that had finally been suffered to heal now that the poison of Scathur had been drained from it. Wan Doll-Faces peered out at them listlessly from dark hovels as they entered the town, but eventually lodgings and board had been procured from the reluctant and slightly dazed denizens. Only then were the remaining bloodstains finally purged from the travelers' aching bodies, through the luxury of steaming water.

For sure, it was a dismal and dreary return to the world of men, and once rest, healing and provisions had been secured, little time was wasted lingering in that mournful place. The memory, if not the smell, of Scathur and his hideous harem still lingered in the air, and it would be a long time before it lifted—if it ever did.

The thieves were the first to leave. One morning the party awoke to find Eorcenwold and his band had simply disappeared, stealing off into the woods without a word. It was they who had been the first to disembark from the ship, the first to find shelter in the town, and once they had sufficiently recovered and taken fresh gear and supplies, they were the first and most eager to quit that place. They had left no messages behind them, no farewells, no apologies; just vanished like the last curls of smoke from a roll-up, and would never be heard of again.

Kuthy, Elfswith and Ceawlin had not tarried for much longer, either. Their secretive business with Wrythe, whatever it might have been, was done with the passing of the Majestic Head, and they had better things to do than hang around here for long. A few days after they had arrived, on a cold autumn evening as the company were returning from the bathhouse, they heard a whooping and a hollering from somewhere out in the shadows, and moments later the two adventurers came down the lane toward them. Each was riding piggyback upon a moaning Doll-Face, slapping their rumps and laughing harder than any had laughed during these months past.

Such was the level of amusement to be found in Wrythe these days.

Still laughing, they drew up in front of the four Southerners, slid down from their sullen mounts and, when they had finally recovered from their merriment, began to say their farewells.

" 'Bye then," Kuthy said, as Ceawlin alighted next to them.

None of the men from Nordwas was sure how to feel or what to say.

"Well, thanks for helping us out back there," Nibulus managed. "It was all quite an . . . eye-opener."

Kuthy gave him a sidelong look, and smiled unevenly. Neither he nor Elf-swith said another word, but (and this came as quite a surprise to the Peladane and his company) both adventurers hugged their comrades in a warm embrace, one by one. Then they simply mounted Ceawlin, waved one final time, and flew off. The four men watched them go, circling the rooftops once before the wyvern banked her wings and soared off into the west. The last they saw of them was a dwindling speck no larger than a fly, fading into the patch of fire-red that was spreading throughout the sky right above where the sun had gone down. Then they were gone.

For the Tivor himself, as he looked upon that rolling tide of fire clouds toward which he was being flown, there came to him a final vision of ragnarok. The same as he had experienced only days before, when they had first arrived at Wrythe. This time however, he knew there would be no World's Ending, and happily he had many more red skies to gaze upon still.

For those he left behind, still standing in the dirt lane of Wrythe staring skyward, there soon came a revelation of another kind. For it was only now that they realized just how much that last warm embrace had cost them all. Both Kuthy and Elfswith had ever been the light-fingered ones, and they did so love shiny trinkets.

But, as Appa magnanimously commented afterward, it was probably just their unique way of saying good-bye.

Then came the day that they too took their leave, and there was still one farewell to make.

"You're not going to change your mind, then?" asked Nibulus of the old priest as they faced each other on that cold and rainy morning. "It's still not too late, you realize."

"No mind to change," Appa replied, shaking his head. "I told you before: I have no choice in this matter. But I'm not staying out of despair, anymore; I'm not simply stopping here to die. You've seen how it is here; how lost these people are. I can *help* them. If there's one thing I can do in the world, it is to help."

"What sort of help?" Gapp demanded bitterly. "A mass cull?"

"A helping hand," Appa replied. "Something to get them back on their feet after Cuna knows how long under the influence of that evil bastard. Something to sort out the sickness in their heads. There's so much healing to be done, and they need me."

They recognized the truth of what he said. He should never have come along on this journey in the first place, and he certainly was not fit to continue any farther. Not this journey, nor any other journey now. And in fact, looking at the wretched Oghain wandering about in their state of bewilderment, it was difficult for them not to agree. Perhaps this wiry old terrier could do some good here after all.

But there was another reason for Appa's staying behind that his friends guessed at, though they would not speak of it. That reason was Bolldhe. The thought of abandoning him in these cold, black lands was too much for the old priest's heart to bear. So he stayed, and all that remained for him to do now was tie up one very last loose end.

To Gapp he handed a bunch of weba that he had found one day growing on the Jagt Coast, and it was only then that everyone knew beyond any doubt that Appa really was not coming any farther with them.

"For Marla," he explained, "so that she'll understand."

"Of course," muttered Gapp, though he was not sure that he did.

There was much work to be done in Wrythe. So much healing, so much teaching. It was a job Appa knew would not be finished in his lifetime, but at least he could start the boulder rolling. But before any of that came the matter of Bolldhe. He had died at sea, but none would suffer him to be buried there. So, in that alcove upon the promontory that faced Melhus Island he was buried, and upon his grave Appa had erected this memorial. An effigy of sapling wood and twined creepers, smoke dried and lacquered with preserving unguents from the locals' pickling stabbur, it was crude, culturally and theologically gauche, and incongruous within its setting. Bolldhe, without a doubt, would have hated it. But it was the best Appa could do, and by the time he had finished it, planted it in the rocks and blessed it, he was fed up to the back teeth and wished they had buried the old sod at sea after all.

As he had stormed off muttering down the pathway that led back to the town and his dreary little mission house, a break in the grey-black clouds had allowed a thin, silvery beam of late afternoon sun to slant down upon the headland. It had a pure light, a cleansing light, and had it shone just a few inches to the left, would have illumined the lacquered wood of Bolldhe's memorial in a burnished gloriole of the deepest brown. But it had not done so, and had fallen upon a creamy patch of guano instead.

Bolldhe was not to be forgotten by the Oghain. Appa saw to that. His memory did in fact, as the years went by, grow into a firm tradition locally, and many years later, despite the best efforts of the aging and worn-out Lightbearer, the figure of Bolldhe became the focus of a firmly established and depressingly religious cult. They would stand by his memorial, moan prayers, and throw flowers, votive oatmeal wafers and spinal columns into the sea just as the sun was rising over Melhus Island.

The Peladanes, now, they did things differently. Years later, if you had gone into any bazaar outside a temple of Pel-Adan, and headed past the stalls that dealt in more mundane merchandise, looking for the ones that stocked holier wares, you would soon have become aware of a new genre of religious artifacts. For, placed alongside the usual librams, icons and souvenirs of the faith, could now be found a whole range of goods concerning no less than the now-famous "Drauglir Quest."

There were books—some with the unwieldy, laughable and commercially suicidal title of *The Saga of Bolldhe the Great*, I kid you not—that purported to be faithful eyewitness accounts of the adventure from those who had taken part, many of which had been signed by the members of the company (even, in some cases, by the ones who had died). There was a series of woodcut prints, many tapestries, and a deck of cards, all depicting various scenes from the quest, some of which were even true. There were figurines, naturally, of all the characters and the monsters in a variety of sizes, materials, styles and colors, probably the most popular of which was a rather bizarrely abstract-looking toy Nibulus in gilt-edged tin that had moveable arms and an assortment of detachable weapons, all rendered down to the last, inaccurate detail. It was horrible.

There was even a role-playing game that utilized strangely shaped polyhedral dice, minute but overpriced models, and rulebooks the size of bibles. This was aimed at pale young men who mumbled self-consciously, washed infrequently, and never got picked for the stone-skimming team—and it was, frankly, a disappointment.

In all, the Drauglir Quest had achieved everything it had set out to, and great mirth and joyous laughter there was in the counting houses of the Peladanes for many an age to come. But various other types had also benefited. Kuw Dachs had been able to go private ever since sales of his Threshers had hit the roof; and anyone with red hair, an unkempt appearance and even the most meager scrap of wolfskin could charge eager young braves a hefty price simply for blowing herb smoke into their faces and disgorging a stream of metaphysical rhetoric on the subject of soul-journeys.

Yes, Bolldhe had made a big impression upon the Peladanes. Rather than just the marketplaces outside the temples, it was within the temples, and indeed within the Peladanes themselves, where the most profound changes had taken place. For a new breed of Peladane had arisen. Unlike his more traditional brutish counterpart, this new Peladane was more likely to affect an air of morose pondering or pained soul-searching than boastful swaggering or oafish debauchery. For him, too, the favored weapon was not the greatsword, but the flamberge.

None of them seemed to realize just how far they were from getting the point.

Ah, but what of the temples? The inner sanctum of the Church of Pel-Adan?

It was in here, more than any other place, that the greatest monument to Bolldhe could be seen. For in every temple throughout the north, could now be found a great statue, a tapestry, or at least a mural, of "The Deathbed of Bolldhe the Great."

In the temple of Nordwas, the Warlord Artibulus Wintus had commissioned the greatest statue of them all. In a quiet transept just off the main aisle, soft light through stained glass windows played upon rose-hued dressed stone, and shed its soft beauty over a tasteful array of wood relief pictures, depicting, among others, human-headed beasts, three Vetters hanging a hell-hound, and an especially inspired one of Bolldhe and Kuthy Tivor sticking bellows up Drauglir's arse.

But it was the central statue itself that drew the eye. For here could be seen, in full-scale, lifelike detail, the very last moments of Bolldhe the Great. Recumbent upon a bed of feathers brought to him by the gulls and terns, and surrounded by the weeping figures of his cohorts brave, Bolldhe was depicted accepting at last the Greatsword of Pel-Adan from the kneeling Nibulus, reverting to his old faith just ere death. Before him, all—including Vetter, Cervulus and Parandus (and even the hound, who was licking the Hero's fevered brow)—were bowed in reverence, in sorrow, and in thanksgiving. Even the thieves were present, prostrating themselves at his feet in penance and subjugation, repenting at last their ungodly ways.

When it came to the man himself, the artists had endeavored at first to honor the truth. They really had—at first. The stonecutters had originally shaped Bolldhe's eyes to be almost as bulbous as they had been in real life, his hair neither thick nor lustrous, and the face without the fair looks of a hero, but rather those of an ordinary man. The whole thing was, in effect, only a slightly ironed-out version of the truth.

In the end, however, under pressure from both the Peladanes and their accountants, they had given in, scrapped the entire image, and replaced it with a standard handsome hero who bore absolutely no resemblance whatsoever to the disagreeable, bug-eyed troll that Bolldhe had actually been.

Nor were the actions of those present at his death entirely truthful either, for rather than kneeling, weeping and paying reverence to the Great Man, as there represented in the statue, most had in fact been avoiding him, and were either smoking, bickering, or relieving themselves over the side of the ship.

Again, Bolldhe would have hated it.

Neither were the nature priests of Erce to be left out, though their memorial was somewhat less conspicuous, and decidedly less ostentatious.

In the woods outside Nordwas, in a part that lay deeper than any countryman might venture—but not too deep for the determined pilgrim—a rillet of clear water ran. From the darkness deep within the ancient stone it sprang, bubbling through cracks that tree root and frost had opened. Excitedly it ran

along an overhung sill of rock, illumined only by the barest glimmer of light
from outside, as pure and freezing as the crystals of late ice that still clung on to
the hanging moss in this gloomy place. Then with the reckless thrill of youth, it
emerged into the twilit world of a cool and verdant hollow, and fell in musical
rumor upon a green-bearded boulder below. Here the splash-drop haze was
kindled into a spray of rainbow-hued diamonds by a solitary sunbeam that filtered through the leafy canopy, before trickling through saturated cushions of
moss down into a silted bed, laughing at the toads that croaked around it.

Thence in a hubbub of sprightly chattering, the rill arrived into a secret
glade of hazel, where slow-worms slid through tendrils of ivy, a soft mist of rain
pattered upon leaf and stone, and the cool air trilled to the euphony of the song
thrush.

It was a sacred grove of Erce, the smallest of spaces amid a tangle of green
things striving to live and to grow.

Here, where the blackthorn buds were just beginning to bloom, upon a
bank of soft grass, among speedwell, wood sorrel and early bluebells, a single
lily grew. With petals of silvered cream immaculacy and fragrance of intoxicat-
ing honeyed sweetness, it was a lily of such ephemeral delicacy and evanescent
purity that the world, even this hidden glade of sylvan sanctity, seemed too
abominably crass a place to merit it.

Yet here it grew, planted by Wodeman many years ago, and tended to by
generation after generation of priests who came after him, those Torca to
whom he had entrusted the task, handing it down so that the memory of
Bolldhe the Earthfriend would never fail, and in the hearts of Torca would be
ever revered.

For the lily was their symbol of a cleansed soul, a prayer of hope for
Bolldhe, wherever he was, and also for the land that he had saved from that
Blackness from the North.

And behind it, delivered from the black places of the earth in which it had
lain forgotten, Bolldhe's axe was planted also. With haft set firmly into the
ground, surrounded by a maypole-dance of wood anemones, and anchored by
the writhing tendrils of blue-trumpeted bindweed, Bolldhe the man—king for
a day—was held, whether he liked it or not, in the sacred bosom of Erce, a
spirit he had not even known.

Yes, again, Bolldhe would have hated it. But it is probably safe to say that he
would, at least, have approved of the axe.

It was the middle of autumn by the time Finan had led the remaining travellers
through the tree-gate and into the lamp-lit haven of Cyne-Tregva. The days had
been gloomy and wet, and little of the color of autumn's changing could be
discerned in that darkest and most alien part of Fron-Wudu. It was dank and
bitterly cold, and for weeks all they had known was the ordeal of punishing,
numbing travel, stiffening wounds, maddening midges, danger that faced them

every day, and fear that robbed them of sleep every night. Now, after the never-ending trial that was sapping the exhausted company of any last reserve of spirit they might have possessed, Cyne-Tregva was like an impossible dream that had finally come true.

The Tregvans themselves had grown appreciably lighter of mood with each day that had passed, though it was true that their spirits were still held in check by what had happened. The shadow of memories would never be entirely lifted from their hearts. Nonetheless, they were coming *home,* returning from a nightmare that none of them could believe had really happened, and though they had left most of their company behind, these at least were alive, and for creatures of the great forest, that was all that really mattered.

For Nibulus and Wodeman, enticed along every step of the way by Gapp's stories of this magical place, there was also the added lure of discovery, and even a flickering of their old sense of adventure.

Yen, too, was with them still. She was thin and pale, had a haunted wideness to her eyes, and would rarely speak. But like the folk of Cyne-Tregva, she was alive, and for that she appeared to be beginning to feel grateful. Of wonder at Cyne-Tregva, though, there simply was not the capacity in her yet.

But for Gapp, despite the harshness of the journey, when the company finally reached the perimeter wall of massive trees and thorn-lashed logs, he hung back, and would not enter.

The last time he had been here, he had been a different person: young, intensely curious, and in the full flush of his newfound confidence. Also, more importantly, Englarielle had been alive. And over two score other Vetters, two score Cervulice, and poor Hwald. So too, though it seemed strange to think of it, had Methuselech Xilvafloese. In a way, at least.

So how could Gapp face this place now, knowing what he and his kind had inflicted upon its sons? How could he bear to meet the gaze—blank, silent and uncomprehending—of the Vetterym when they were told of what had befallen? How could he stand the guilt, heaped on in even greater measure by the forgiveness and hospitality meted out by those few that had survived?

In truth, he could not bear it. So when the company had passed within the safety of the tree-gate, Gapp simply remained where he was, his hound at his side.

Then the gloom darkened yet further, and the sounds that he had heard when first he had passed this way returned: beetles big enough to roar, ants that could carry off a man, invisible gliders that ghosted through the air. Gapp knew that not even Schnorbitz would be protection against the predators of this place.

Within minutes, he had rejoined his companions within the safety of Cyne-Tregva.

Rest was taken, wounds were treated, and strength was gradually restored. A week in the Vetter town, though the place was darkened and subdued by mourning, did much to heal and fortify the men from Nordwas. They wandered among the trees, the walkways, the many wonderful places that had been seen by no man but they and, despite their own hurts, could still marvel at it all.

But they, too, were homesick, and longed for an end to this whole episode. Bidding farewell to Radkin, Ted, the other Vetters, the Cervulice, and—with a terrible sadness—Finan, they were escorted by guides to the River Folcf-reawaru. Here they were ferried by coracles to the southern bank, and from there on left to the guidance of Schnorbitz. For here, in the Valley of Perchtamma-Uinfjoetli, they were just within the boundaries of the forest hound's ken and, come what may, it was up to him now to get them farther along on their journey.

Yulfric was pleased to see them. Sort of.

The Gyger was not sure exactly who these strangers from the woods were, but there was a shade of recollection as he looked upon Gapp, and he was in any case greatly relieved to see that Schnorbitz had returned at last. They stayed with him for a few days, helped around the house, and gratefully accepted the quirky hospitality of Heldered the invisible Nisse.

But it was an odd place, truly it was, and tempers began to unravel very early on. In addition to this, the three men were solemnly aware that they still had the rest of the forest to get through. And then the dismal Rainflats. And, worst of all, the Blue Mountains. All this, too, before winter set in. It was not a pleasant prospect.

On the day of their departure, it came as a surprise to no one when Schnorbitz came along with Gapp. It came as a surprise to no one, that is, except to Yulfric. He was so furious, he drove them all out of his home with loud bellows and harsh beatings. Even Heldered's disapproval was apparent by the eager swinging open of the stockade gates by unseen hands as they were all booted out. And how quickly the gates were shut behind them.

But it made little difference: Schnorbitz and Gapp had become a team, and nothing but death would separate them now.

The remainder of the journey was a lively one, though fortunately without a fraction of the troubles they had encountered the first time round.

Two days after being evicted from the forest giant's homestead, they arrived at Myst-Hakel. Coming from the relative shelter of the forest, the Rainflats were chill and drear, and the wind from the east cut through them mercilessly. Though it had never been a pleasant place through which to travel, this land was now particularly flat, grey and subdued. The only discernible living creatures at this time of year were the whimbrels, but even they were few, and kept out of the wind. Arriving at the town, too, the travelers were struck by how few people were out and about. Everyone seemed to be indoors, and there was none of the interest shown in them now that had been evident the first time round. Gapp did not know whether to be relieved at this, or slightly disappointed.

They stayed for two days only, just long enough to rest up and make a few purchases. Now that Zhang was dead they had no beast of burden at all, and none of the company relished the thought of that month or more of travelling that it would take them to get home, over marsh, mountain and wilderness, on foot.

In any case, all that time hiking in full armor had convinced Nibulus that, light as tengriite was, he was never going to repeat that experience. There was no option, therefore, but to sell his armor and use the proceeds to purchase some transport. This was done with no small amount of reluctance, but also with some surprise; the Peladane had truly never thought he would see the day when he would sell the most wonderful suit of armor in the north, but now that it came down to it, he was in a way rather relieved to get shut of it.

He did, however, make sure he got the best price possible. Though he knew he would never get even a fiftieth of its true value, he was fortunate that they arrived in town when they did. For at that time the Tusse blacksmith's cousin happened to be passing through Myst-Hakel, and he was a member of the mammoth caste of herd giants.

So, in exchange for the armor, Nibulus received a huge woolly mammoth, complete with a vast canvas and wood palanquin, two months' supplies of dried food, more winter pelts than they had seen on the entire journey and, as an extra, Nibulus asked the Tusse to throw in a bottle of gin "for the woman."

As a result of this exchange, he and his companions would be able to travel home in relative safety and comfort, and meanwhile the two herd giants would never have to herd or work iron again for the rest of their lives.

Only one other thing remained to be done at Myst-Hakel. Wodeman had still not recovered from the guilt of his betrayal, and here he felt he could do something to make amends. Alone, unarmed, and at the mercy of whatever there might be lurking down there now, he offered himself to Fate, and ventured back down the silver mine. All he took with him was the xienne lantern that Gapp had taken from Bolldhe after they had laid him to rest, and with this, he headed back down to where they had gone before in search of a very particular item of treasure.

It was still foul, and a memory of the Afanc leapt out of the darkness and into his mind with each footstep he took, each tap of the Knockers, each drip of water into icy puddles. Yet still he searched, for there was a duty here that he felt he must fulfill.

After a while, he finally found it: that treasure that meant more to the peace of his soul than anything else. Bolldhe's old broadaxe, rusty and wet, lay abandoned in a corner where Finwald had hidden it.

"It'll make a fine memorial," he said to himself, as he weighed it in his hands, and then left the mines forever.

High in the Blue Mountains, Gapp perched atop the mammoth, gazing thoughtfully at the immense views around him. Nibulus was sitting in the driver's seat, casually guiding the huge beast that rattled with pans, pots and barrels of provisions, while idly perusing his beloved *Chronicle of Gwyllch*. Wodeman had decided to join them up high, for once abandoning his customary place of proceeding at their side on foot, and Yen was up ahead walking the dog.

Suddenly, Gapp said: "Appa was right, you know."

"About?" asked Nibulus.

"What he said on the ship that night. It *was* all bloody useless, wasn't it? The quest, I mean. How's it going to look when we get back to Nordwas? What're you going to tell the people there, eh? Or your father, come to that? That the whole business could've been achieved by simply smashing Flametongue when we first got it, like I said back on the ship. Are you going to tell them that?"

"Of course not!" Nibulus snorted, chuckling at the boy's stupidity. "We're heroes! Why would we want to start telling the truth?"

"But we're not," the boy reminded him. "As Appa pointed out, we're the biggest idiots in the world. We—"

"Gapp Radnar," Nibulus cut in with an upraised hand, "listen to me. In a few weeks' time we're going to arrive home after having successfully completed a quest. That much is true, right?"

"Right."

"Also, we've *killed* things, we've picked up a good few *war wounds* to show off to the girls, we're going to make a *heroes' return* on this magnificent beast here . . . so who cares? As long as the plebes are left happy, don't bother thinking too hard about it. Just take the money, the fame and the women, and forget about irrelevancies like 'why?' We're heroes 'cause we've won, and that's all. Believe me, son, don't knock it. We've earned it."

The melancholy would not leave Gapp, however. But he did at least have to admit Nibulus was right. *We're just ordinary men,* he pondered, *doing what we do, what we can do, without ever really knowing or even caring why. People need heroes, and that's just what we're giving them.*

Cuna, had he been there, would have smiled.

Gapp tried to picture himself arriving back at Nordwas: the grand, triumphal parade, the mammoth—the girls, his friends, his family, all staring in amazement at *him*. He spent hours imagining this, feeding his fantasy, nurturing it, playing it over and over in his head. And then suddenly, a thought occurred to him.

"Nibulus, would you say I was handsome enough to be a hero?"

The Peladane laughed out loud. "Don't be a prat. Of course not! Why do you ask?"

"Because the heroes of legend are always handsome. That's the rule. Look at that book of yours, the way Gwyllch describes the heroes. They're always so perfect. Never a fester or even a grey tooth among 'em. Why is that, d'you think?"

"Maybe it's the deed that makes them beautiful," Wodeman commented. "Don't you think?"

"I don't know," Gapp replied thoughtfully. "I'm not sure what I feel at all. The thing is, I had a dream about it last night. . . ."

"Ah," said the shaman, leaning closer. "My speciality. Go on."

"Remember Paulus? Well, I was in this dark place, see, lost and alone. Then suddenly I heard a click, and when I looked up, I could see Paulus looking at me from behind this tiny shutter, or something. Then it seemed like the dark wasn't the dark of underground, but of night, and I was in a graveyard, and Paulus was in a tomb, looking out of it through this little shutter. Looking at *me*. He seemed to be trying to call out, to tell me something, maybe to say sorry, or to explain something, I'm not sure. Well, the whole place began to smell like the Maw, and I didn't want to hang around . . . but the thing that struck mc was that, even though he was in his grave, far from being even more rotten, he actually looked *better.* I could see his bad eye and bad skin were still there, unchanged, yet . . . it was still the most beautiful face I've ever seen. . . ."

Both Wodeman and Nibulus were silent for a long time. Eventually the Peladane shrugged, and said by way of reply: "Perhaps it just means the maggots left his face alone after he died. Even *they* have their limits."

Five weeks after leaving Myst-Hakel, the six of them—Nibulus, Gapp, Wodeman, Yen, Schnorbitz and the mammoth—finally reached Nordwas.

The *heroes'* return. This thought was what had, for most of the frigid days on the lonely road, kept them warm, kept them going.

But the closer they came to the town, the more perplexed they became. It was a freezing day that was hazed blue with icy fog, and hardly a soul was abroad, despite their having sent word on ahead at every village on the way. There were no other travelers upon their road, no farmers working in the frozen fields, and when they finally drew near to the smoky cluster of wattle and daub shacks crowding against the stockade wall, not one of the mean denizens that huddled within so much as poked his head out of the door hangings to see what these elephantine footfalls were that pounded the frozen earth outside their doors.

Nor even when they passed through those gates was there anyone to meet them. No cheering, waving crowds lining the streets to welcome the returning heroes, no one to marvel at the beast they rode; no one at all, save a pair of grubby children who began trying to sell them toffee apples.

"Home," said Nibulus, slightly numb.

"Home," repeated Gapp, equally numb.

Wodeman said nothing.

About the Author

David Bilsborough was born and raised in Malvern, England. Though he has lived in such far-flung lands as Eastern Europe and Asia, he regularly returns home to walk the Malvern Hills, the inspiration for much of his writing, and where possibly might live many of the original characters who feature so color-fully in his story. Author of *The Wanderer's Tale*, the first Annal of Lindormyn, he is busy creating further Annals.

F. Places

Baeldicca the Great—The waterfall that gushes out of the great cliff at the head of the valley of Perchtamma Uinfjoetli, source of the River Flocfreawaru.

Blue Mountains—Uninhabited range that separates Wyda-Aescaland from the "Wild North."

The Chase—Farmers' pub in Nordwas, famous for the ale known as SBA.

Cyne-Tregva—Vetter town in Fron-Wudu.

Dragon Coast—Sparsely inhabited northwest coastline. The "Edge of the World."

Eotunlandt—Fabled "Land of the Second Ones."

Fron-Wudu—Huge northern forest, entirely wild.

Ghouhlem—Northern land of the Dhracus.

Giant Mountains—Huge arctic mountain range entirely surrounding Eotunlandt.

Godtha—Southern land of the Dhracus.

Herdlands of the Tusse—Massive expanse of plain and scrubland, mainly inhabited by the herd giant nomads.

Jagt Straits—Arctic sea that separates Melhus from the mainland.

Last Shore—Northernmost coastline of continental Lindormyn.

Lindormyn—The World. A name meaning "Dragon."

Lubang-Nagar—The "Drake Tunnel" of Vaagenfjord Maw that connects the Hall of Fire to the Inner Keep.

Melhus Island—Large volcanic island, the most northerly in the world.

Moel-Bryn—Small town in western Pendonium; Bolldhc's birthplace.

The Moghol—The "Trough of the Dead," a deep subterranean chasm separating Vaagenfjord Maw's outer reaches from the inner.

Myst-Hakel—Small swamp town in the Rainflats. Its name means "Cloak of Mist."

Nordwas—Stockade town in northern Wyda-Aescaland.

Pendonium—Huge country in the extreme west; homeland of the Peladanes.

Qaladmir—Desert city, Finwald's birthplace.

Quiravia—Massive southern country, forested and temperate in the north, arid in the south; the much-vaunted "seat of learning and culture." Largely peaceful and prosperous, but with an undercurrent of corruption.

Ravenscairn—Cat's-tooth-shaped pinnacle above Vaagenfjord Maw.

Sluagh Valley—Largely unknown haunted cleft in the Blue Mountains.

Smaulka-Degernerth—Vaagenfjord Maw's "Hall of Fire," a huge tunnel that almost entirely encircles the Inner Keep of Ymla-Myrrdhain.

Trondaran—Tiny, isolated mountain country of Jyblitt, the Hauger King.

Tyvenborg—"Thieves' Fortress," on the western edge of Pendonium.

Vaagenfjord Maw—The fastness of Drauglir on Melhus Island.

Vregh-Nahov—Dark, forested country east of the Polgrim Hunting Grounds.

Wrythe—Most northerly town in the world; home to the Oghain.

Wyda-Aescaland—Mid-sized country south of the Blue Mountains. Originally home to the Torca, now predominantly inhabited by Aescals, but ruled by Peladanes.

G. Weapons, Warfare

Assegai—Short Polg spear with a leaf-shaped blade.

Bagh-Nakh—Spiked knuckle-dusters.

Bhuj—Meat cleaver.

Chakram—Small, Hauger-made metal discs, usually poison-coated.

Crow's Beak Staff—Short, hefty staff with a sharp "beak" at the business end.

Fasces—The old alliance between Peladanes, Oghain, and Nahovians that defeated Drauglir 500 years ago.

Flamberge—Ancient, heavy sword with an undulating blade.

Habergeon—Long coat of scalemail.

Haladie—Polg double-dagger.

Katar—Short, V-shaped punch-dagger designed to pierce heavy armor.

Kh'is—Mainly Olchorian sacrificial dagger with undulating blade.

Left-hander—Heavy, wide-bladed parrying dagger.

Manass-Uilloch—Company of 2,500 Peladanes—or 50 Oloch—under the command of a Thegne.

Maul—Very heavy, five-foot-long, two-handed mace.

Manople—Long blade attached to an iron gauntlet.

Misericorde—Long, thin, stiletto-like dagger designed to deliver the final blow to a fallen armored horseman.

Miter—Heavy mace-like club with a spiked ball as a head.

Moonspear—Huge flint-headed poleaxe, a Parandus speciality.

Oloch—Company of 50 Peladanes, under the command of a Sergeant.

Pata—A cross between a katar and a manople. The assassin's choice.

Swordbreaker—Hefty, notch-bladed knife used to parry, twist, and snap an opponent's sword.

Tengriite—Very strong but light metal used by Peladanes in armor- and weapon-making.

"The Thresher"—Barbed chain used to swing heavy swords around. Kuw Dach's invention, still at the prototype stage.

Toloch—Company of 50,000 Peladanes—or 20 Manass-Uilloch—under the command of a Warlord.

Tzerbuchjer—Primitive "sword," usually made of bone or stone, with a jagged edge composed of anything from predators' teeth to shards of pottery.

Ulleanh—The green cloak of the Peladane.

"Unferth"—The legendary greatsword of Pel-Adan himself. A name given to the greatswords of all Warlords.

Vambrace—Armor plating for the arm.

Voulge—Poleaxe with a spike extending at right angles from the main spear-tip.

Xienne—Yellow metal from Trondaran, used as fuel for lanterns.

Zibeline—Special leather monetary unit used in Peladane lands.

The first familiar face they came across was a valet of Wintus Hall, one of those big-fingered servants who had prised Nibulus and his cohorts from their warm, flatulent stalls on the morning of their departure. He looked uncertainly at the mammoth for a moment, then noticed who it was that sat atop it.

"Oh hello," he called out. "You're back."

"Yes."

"So, did you kill him, then?"

"Yes."

"Oh good. Well, see you later, then."

"Yes."

They continued down the same narrow lane, then turned into Pump Street. From one of the windows came the wonderful smell of bacon, eggs, black pudding and beef sausages, overlaid strongly with the heaven scent aroma of fresh coffee. It was late morning farmers' breakfast at The Chase, and it was at that moment, only at that moment, that the three knew for sure they were at last, truly, home.

Parking their beast outside, the three men, one woman and dog swung the doors open wide, and entered the steamy comfort of the inn. For a moment they just stood there, breathing in the warmth, the steam, the noise, and the smell, almost as though they were tundra-dwelling primitives who were experiencing its delights for the first time. It was quite overwhelming, and Gapp almost passed out from joy.

Yet, for all their dramatic entrance, only one or two heads looked up, and then only for a second or two before returning to the serious task at hand, namely that of seeing just how much breakfast they could squeeze down their gullets without rupturing their innards.

Nibulus, Gapp, Wodeman, Yen and Schnorbitz glanced at each other in turn. Then they shrugged, got themselves a table, and the Peladane politely shoved his way through the throng at the bar to order the biggest, hottest and greasiest breakfast his remaining zibelines could buy.

If the citizens of Nordwas are going to ignore us, he thought, *then that's exactly what we're going to do to them, too.*

By a strange coincidence, they found that the beef used in the sausages had actually come from Marla, slaughtered only seven days previously. Gapp, remembering something, put his hand into his pocket, and drew forth the sprig of weba that Appa had given him at their parting. He held it up for all to see, said a silent prayer, then crushed the dried leaves and ceremonially garnished the sausages with it.

"It's what he would have wanted," he explained, as the others looked on doubtfully.

"Oy, Radnar!" a voice suddenly called from one corner of the room. They turned to look past the ranks of intently gorging farmers, toward a small table at which sat four of Gapp's friends. The very same gang as had come to say farewell to him almost six months previously, in their gawky and uniquely teenage way.

"You back then?" one of them inquired of Gapp, coming over to join the party.

"Yes."

"You get it, then?"

"Get? It?"

"That gold. Or magic. Or whatever the fockin' 'ell you wen' off for," the youth elaborated, leaning rudely upon the Peladane's shoulder for support. "You know, that whatever you wen' off for in Quiravia. . . ."

"What? We haven't been to Quiravia, you diseased boy. We went *north.* To Melhus Island. You remember? To kill Drauglir."

"Oh yeah, that's right . . . So, was it all right?"

Here, right at the end, in his very home town, Gapp was probably more flummoxed by this than at any other moment in his entire journey. While Nibulus continued with his breakfast, seemingly unaware of the youth using his shoulder for support, while Wodeman curled his upper lip back to taste the SBA he had smeared on it, and while Yen slipped bits of weba-garnished Marla under the table to Schnorbitz lying beneath, Gapp simply stared at his friends.

"We . . . *slew a Rawgr,"* he tried to explain, not knowing quite where or how to start. "We fought with ogres, wolves, a Leucrota . . . we battled against swamp spirits, we were imprisoned by a Huldre, and—"

"You get that flat-skimmer Medraunt asked you to fetch 'im?" his friend suddenly interrupted. Gapp was struck dumb. Then he realized that the lad was not actually talking to him, but had switched his attention to one of the other boys.

"Brogi nicked the focker yesterday," the other replied, clearly relieved to be on more familiar ground now that the conversation had returned to extreme stone-skimming.

"Wanker," the first cussed, then rested his backside against the back of Nibulus's chair and continued their fascinating conversation, Gapp now already forgotten.

Gapp stared around himself, the fry-up only now beginning to make its weight felt upon his stomach.

"Well," he said, "I'm back."

Glossary

A. Races

1. DEMI-HUMANS

Boggart—Diminutive, downtrodden, and hairy, they are usually encountered scavenging on the edges of civilization, or used as slaves by Polgs. Certain strains of Boggarts do, however, possess shamanistic powers of an unknown nature.

Dhracus—Strange, isolated race of people that are rarely encountered, and then only ever singly. No towns or settlements are known to exist, even in their homelands. Superbly dexterous, highly intelligent, and said to possess psionic powers, the Dhracus are universally feared by other races.

Grell—A thug-like, brutish people of strikingly ugly appearance and demeanor. Found all over Lindormyn, either in their own stockade towns or living among other races.

Hauger—A short, slightly-built, flat-faced people that dwell in well-ordered communities. Highly civilized and inventive, they are excellent craftsmen and shrewd merchants.

> (1) **River Hauger**—More interactive with other races than their Stone cousins, due to their control over large stretches of Lindormyn's waterways. Noted for their expertise in herbalism and alchemy.
>
> (2) **Stone Hauger**—Plateau towns or upland escarpment villages are their favorite haunts. Lindormyn's most skilled engineers. Though quiet by nature, their kings retain sizeable armies of uniquely equipped soldiers.

Jordiske—A disgusting and animalistic race so far encountered only in Fron-Wudu. Arch-enemies of the Vetterym.

Marmennil—A largely unknown race of marine-folk.

Polg—Hunter-nomads of Lindormyn, short, lithe, and extremely tough. They are proud, fierce, and contemptuous of other races. Somewhat ostentatiously attired, they affect a permanent swagger.

Vetter—The short, almost rat-like Vetterym live only in the deepest reaches of Fron-Wudu. Though bestial in appearance, they have developed a unique and highly inventive culture. The only outside race they have had contact with is the Polgrim, and then only very sporadically.

2. GIANTS

Gyger (forest giant)—twelve feet tall but stick-thin, Gygers are nonetheless extremely strong and tough. Excellent hunters and trappers. They usually live in communities, but some prefer the solitary life.

Jutul (fire giant)—ten feet tall and extremely broad, the black-skinned Jutul are best-known for their skill with metal, especially the making of bizarre weapons, which they trade with other peoples for magic. Apart from this, they live out their strange, subterranean lives apart from the rest of the world.

Tusse (herd giant)—eight feet tall, the most common of all giants, the Tusse are closest to humans in appearance and culture. They roam the wide-lands as nomadic herders. Their society is divided into strict castes, with one type of herd-beast particular to each of these castes.

3. HULDRES

Abyssian—Shapechangers. They will take on the exact form of a person or animal, imprisoning the original within Huldre-Home, while they themselves wreak mischief in the world of their victim.

Afanc—Not a true Huldre, but the offspring of Huldre and non-Huldre. They are rare, and their exact nature depends on the particular combination of their parents; thus they can be of any size, any appearance, and possess any type or level of power. Frequently chaotic.

Benne Nighe—A spectral apparition that is very rarely encountered by non-Huldres. When seen, it is usually in the form of a cloaked and hooded figure washing bloodied clothes in a stream. (Female, naturally.) The onlooker may recognize the clothes as his own, and thus realize that his death is near.

Ellyldan—The Nahovian term for the Ganferd.

Ganferd—The most folorn and lamentable of all Huldres, found only in the most desolate places, this figure will entice travelers to follow it, trap them, and feed from their departing life-force.

Knockers—Fairy miners. Often heard, rarely seen; they have a reputation for spite and mockery.

Nisse—The smallest and most benign of household guardians. The Nisse appear as little old men, but then only rarely, as they prefer to remain invisible.

Succubus—Another Abyssian, but one that will only take on the form of a female human/demi-human. The principle reason why Afancs exist.

Urisk—One of the more benevolent, less chaotic manifestations of Afanc. In effect, an "outdoor Nisse."

B. Creatures

Adt T'man (slough horse)—A small, tough, agile horse that lives free on the Tabernacle Plains. Their eastern name means "friend horse," but westerners call them slough horse due to their molting.

Baluchitherium—Lindormyn's largest and strongest land mammal. A herd beast with exceptionally tough hide.

Cervulus (pl. Cervulice) / "Vettersteed"—Weird bipedal creature of Fron-Wudu, part-humanoid, part deer. Quarrelsome and aggressive, they fight with both horn and sword.

Forest hound—An ancient race of fierce pack-hunters, one of Lindormyn's largest land predators. The forest hound reaches three or four feet at the shoulder, and is eight to ten feet long. Larger varieties can be as tall as six feet, and up to sixteen feet long.

Fossegrim—The dreaded Sea-Wyrms of Aggedon, whose blood is the most poisonous substance in the world.

Parandus (pl. Paranduzes) / "Treegard"—One of Fron-Wudu's larger multi-part creatures, part deer and part Gyger.

Wyvern—Distantly related to dragons, though much smaller, Wyverns appear to combine features that are draconian, raptorial, grallatorial, orthopterous, and equine all at the same time.

C. Other-Dimensional Beings

Children of the Keep—Travelers to Wrythe usually assume these to be genuine Ogginda (the children of the Oghain of Wrythe)—to their cost. The Children of the Keep are, in fact, the most powerful of Scathur's servants; terrible rawgrs who, though lacking in intelligence, nevertheless surpass Scathur in many ways—most notably by their speed and their imperviousness to heat.

Fyr Draikkes—Dragon.

H'urvisg—Elemental earth spirits, contacted by Torca for augury puposes.

Rawgr (small "r")—Demons. The most ancient of all beings, older even than the gods. They existed in the chaos before the world's creation.

Sprites—Tiny imps made of smoke, originating from the elemental plane of fire.

Stained-Glass Demons—Entities that lurk in the dimension just beyond mirrors/glass.

True Giants (The "Second Ones")—After the rawgs, the 200-foot-tall Giants are the oldest of creatures, and the first born of Lindormyn. Extinct now, they can still, however, be summoned into corporeal existence by the "Spirit of Battle."

D. Races, Religions, and Titles

Aescals—Predominant inhabitants of Wyda-Aescaland.

Akynn—Bards. Storytellers. The keepers of history.

Asyphe—Desert-warrior people, living in the Asyphe Mountains south of Qaladmir.

Cynen—Polg title meaning king; also used by Vetters.

Lightbearers—Any follower of Cuna, including:

>   **Elder**—High priests of Cuna.
>   **Mage Priest**—Priests of Cuna.

Nahovians—People of Vregh-nahov.
Oghain—People of Wrythe, including:

> **Oga**—Women.
> **Ogginda**—Children.
> **Ogha**—Men.
> **Oghain-Yddiaw**—The fighting corps of the Oghain.

Olchorians—Any follower of Olchor, including:

> **Necromancer**—Priests of Olchor.

Peladanes—Followers of Pel-Adan, a racial religion, including:

> **High Warlord**—Supreme leader of all Peladanes on Lindormyn.
> **Warlord**—Leader of a Toloch.
> **Thegne**—Leader of a Manass-Uilloch.
> **Sergeant**—Leader of an Oloch.

Skalds—Bards.
Torca—Pagan people of the North.

E. Deities and Demi-Gods

Cuna—The god of Truth and Light, ostensibly.
D'Archangels—The three Arch-Rawgrs, most powerful servants of Olchor:
Drauglir (also known as Daemon, Fiend, Hell-Hound, Kelet the Devourerer of Whales, Night Stalker)—Most powerful of the Unholy Trinity of Rawgrs.
Gruddna—Second most powerful of the three, a Rawgr in the shape of a Fyr-Draikke.
Scathur—Third of the D'Archangels, a Rawgr in man-form.
Erce—The earth spirit.
Jugg—A fertility god.
Luttra—A Bard god.
Olchor—The dark god of Evil (according to his enemies).
Pel-Adan—War god of the Peladanes.
Shogg—A beast god.
Skela—The collective name for the Syr, the Keepers of Balance. According to Quiravian teaching, there are thirteen Syr in total, though some seers include another ten (lesser, non-neutral) powers in their number. In this story we see only Chance, Fate, and—head of the Skela—Time.